LARRY WOIWODE'S
EXTRAORDINARY
FAMILY CHRONICLE

"He can wring your heart. . . . This is a reflection of the true America that, in spite of scandal and bitterness, we still believe in."

Boston Globe

"Woiwode goes far beyond the obvious in his portrayal of infinitely subtle relationships . . . he has given us a work of enormous emotional intensity, where dreams and reality, the interior and the exterior, and the portrayal of a love that holds all in its power are illuminated with rare artistry."

Dallas Morning News

"A stunning and monumental achievement . . . haunting and powerful."

Cleveland Plain Dealer

(continued . . .)

BEYOND THE BEDROOM WALL

BEYOND THE BEDROOM WALL
LARRY WOIWODE

A Family Album

AVON
PUBLISHERS OF BARD, CAMELOT, DISCUS, EQUINOX AND FLARE BOOKS

FOR MY FATHER

AND FOR THE CHILDREN OF
MARIANNE AND LISLE EARLE,
LISA, JOHN, AND BILLY
God Bless

Fourteen chapters of this book first appeared in *The New Yorker,* most of them in substantially different forms. Other chapters first appeared in *The Atlantic, Audience, Mademoiselle, McCalls, New American Review,* and *Works in Progress,* also in different form.

AVON BOOKS
A division of
The Hearst Corporation
959 Eighth Avenue
New York, New York 10019

ISBN: 0-380-00684-7

First Avon Printing, October, 1976

AVON TRADEMARK REG. U.S. PAT. OFF. AND IN
OTHER COUNTRIES, MARCA REGISTRADA,
HECHO EN U.S.A.

Printed in the U.S.A.

CONTENTS

❧❧❧

THREE

FOUR

FIVE

L'ENVOI

"Reality," of course, is man's most powerful illusion;

but while he attends to this world, it must outbalance

the total enigma of being in it at all.

ERIK H. ERIKSON

Prelude

Sept. 6, 1800. *Near where we are camped [on the west bank of the Red River of the North, near the confluence of the Red and Park rivers] has been a great game crossing for many years. The ground on both sides is beaten as hard as a pavement and the numerous roads leading to the river, a foot deep, are surprising, and when I consider the hard sod through which these tracks are beaten, I am entirely at a loss and bewildered in attempting to form any idea of the numerous herds of buffalo which must have passed here.*

*

Sept. 11. *I climbed up a tall oak, which I had trimmed for that purpose, . . . from the top of which I had an extensive view of the country . . .*

The weather being perfectly serene, I could distinguish the Hair Hills on the W., though they were scarcely perceptible—nothing more than a blue stripe, running N. and S. The interval is a level meadow, with nothing to attract the eye.

*

1

Jan. 14, 1801. At daybreak I was awakened by the bellowing of buffaloes . . . The plains were black, and appeared as if in motion, S. to N. . . .

I had seen almost incredible numbers of buffalo in the fall, but nothing in comparison to what I now beheld. The ground was covered at every point of the compass, as far as the eye could reach, and every animal was in motion.

*

April 1, Wednesday. The river clear of ice, but the drowned buffalo continue to drift down by herds . . . It really is astonishing what vast quantities must have perished, as they formed one continual line in the middle of the river for two days and two nights.

*

From the manuscript journals of Alexander Henry, one of the first English-speaking explorers to enter North Dakota.

THE STREET

Every night when I'm not able to sleep, when scrolls of words and formulas unfurl in my mind and faces of those I love, both living and dead, rise from the dark, accusing me of apathy, ambition, self-indulgence, neglect—all of their accusations just—and there's no hope of rest, I try again to retrace the street. It's an unpaved street and it's the color of my hand. It's made up mostly of the clayey gumbo from the flat and tilting farmland all around this village so small it can be seen through from all sides, and its ungraded surface is generally overrun with ruts that are slippery and water-filled in spring, ironlike in summer, furred in fall with frost as phosphorescent as mountainy ridges on the moon's crust, and in winter buried beyond all thought except for any thought that clay or gravel or the booted feet of people crossing ice-covered snow above might have. It's the main street of Hyatt, North Dakota, and it's one block long. I lived in Hyatt from the time I was born until I was six and returned only once, at the age of eight, wearing a plaid jacket exactly like my brother's, too light for the weather, and ran up and down this street with changed friends, playing hide-and-seek between buildings that stand deserted, now that time has had its diminishing effects.

Every night I approach the street in the same way, from the east, along a long building that shields it from me until the last moment of unbelievability is banished by its being there. The building was once the machine shed of a John Deere implement dealer, so my father's told me, and is now the Town Hall and high-school gymnasium; this side is surfaced with sheets of tin die-pressed to simulate brick, and the shining gray sheets slant up and down, their seams mismatched, shifting in angle or height or

3

declination with every other step I take, and then I reach out, as I always do, and run my fingertips along the tin. Some nights I feel the entire building will collapse and be revealed as cardboard, and on other nights it's as firm to my touch as my wife's arm at this hour.

The Town Hall is the heart of Hyatt—the sports arena, the theater, the polling place, the movie house, the dance hall, and the band building, the social retreat, the inoculation center, the courthouse, the village palace with its changing set of kings, and every Thursday evening during the winter, when a man from Fessenden wheels a wooden crate mounted on skate rollers into the building and seats himself on a stool like the stools used by shoe salesmen, and straps on skates, the Town Hall is a noisy roller rink.

I come to the corner of the building and turn south on Main Street. At its far end I can see the raised roadbed and shining rails of the Soo Line, and, beyond the rails, flanking and towering high above the Western store fronts of the street, four grain elevators, one a faded barn-red with a green roof, and the other three, built together in a cluster, silver-gray. A quarter way down one of them, in black letters ten feet tall, I read N. J. LUDVIG & CO., and when the period after CO starts falling with sidewise swipes toward the ground, I know it's only a pigeon diving after spilled grain, a luncheon along individual lines, a new day for him, a new hour, a new time.

I start down the street, on a high-curbed sidewalk fractured and crumbling from severe freezes, and pass the front doors of the Town Hall, which are open, folded back in rectangles of knotty pine against the white siding, and hooked in place. There's a patriotic ceremony going on inside. My father is ready to give the reading he's been rehearsing at home for a week, and I sit in the audience, beside my mother, filled with a fathomless fear for her and my father. I wait until his voice makes its last swirl of lariatlike cadenzas in the air, and concludes with a whisper, and hear a spatter of applause, and am content, and then a rising wash of response like the sea. I walk on.

Next, a vacant lot overgrown with weeds, with a gray path winding through it to the end of memory, a lot that's flooded in the winter for skating and hockey, and then Friedrich's Meat Market, where stout H. P. Friedrich, wearing steel-rimmed spectacles and a white towel around his waist, mixes up in washtubs with his bare hands an incomparable brand of farm-style sausage, the spiciest the Northern palate can handle and still be pleased. And after Friedrich's comes—

I can't remember. I can't remember the building, the business carried on in it, or who it should be in its doorway, and this adds to my sleeplessness, is an ominous sign, so I turn in bed and try to work around to it along a less obvious line of tangentiality. Mr. Friedrich has powerful arms. He works with his sleeves rolled up, and the cords in his arms whiten and muscles bulge beneath his shirt. His face and cheeks are round and flushed and his steel-rimmed spectacles are often fogged. Tucked once along the trim of my father's roll-top desk was a photograph of Mr. Friedrich on the high-school steps, with 1913 on the lintel above him, wearing a cap with the earflaps folded down and a lined denim jacket buttoned tight at his throat; fuzzy gloves on his hands, the gold-colored ones that were worn then, by the looks of them; his even teeth bared in the smile of somebody unaccustomed to a camera. His first name is Herman. "I wonder if Herman will have the school warm this morning," I hear my father say, and see Mr. Friedrich in the boiler room in the basement of the school, a bulky silhouette against the glow of the open furnace he's stoking with coal. Besides being the butcher, he's the custodian and repairman at the public school, and on the mornings when the bell in the big and lofty, barnlike church a block away rings especially loud, summoning to weekday Mass the parochial-school children (a requirement), and nearly all the rest of the village, which is ninety-percent Catholic, I know that the usual bell ringer, Lowell Russell, a sickly man but the progenitor of twelve children, is ill in bed again, and the rope is being pulled by the powerful arms of Mr. Friedrich. His meat market is tan and its trim is chocolate brown, and next to—

I see a fluted lintel painted beige, a pair of plate-glass windows, but the rest is a blank, there's blankness behind the plate glass, and no matter how much I coax and prod, nothing further will appear, the place only turns more vaporous in resistance to me, so I move on to the Red Owl, which, for all the importance it has, might well be forgotten, since our family never shopped here, but nobody can control all the leaps and demands of his own memory.

Next is the alley, two-thirds of the way down the block instead of at its center, and then a vacant store, lime-colored, which was a barbershop at one time, and later a feed store smelling of flour; and then Eichelburger's Tavern, sheathed with white siding, stretches the rest of the way to the cross street of the block. Eichelburger's is so long there must be a dance hall inside, but it's impossible to know for sure, other than by entering—which I've never done, of course (never old enough)—because there are no doors along this side, and its front entrance and front windows, which look onto the tracks of the Soo Line, are covered with white curtains. The long, blank wall of the building is like the aura around the Eichelburgers themselves, who live just across the hedge from us and are accessible to me, but avoided by most everybody else in the village; they aren't Catholic, Mrs. Eichelburger smokes cigarettes, and their daughter, Susie, at the age of five, has begun to exhibit herself to boys. I was one of the first to see.

I feel a pressure behind and turn and there are the cottonwoods and willows at the far end of the street, along the edge of the lake, flying the maidenhair faces of their leaves into the wind, and beyond their crowns of trembling insubstantiality, across the lake dotted with cottonwood pollen, the blue and azure plain abuts against the horizon at infinity.

I turn to you in bed. You lie beside me, resting in an arcade of your dream, your closed eyes in motion behind your lids, your hair disarrayed over your arm on the pillow, your forehead marblelike and shining with sleep. At this hour, I feel alien to you, a creature you've never seen but call Tim, or Tinvalin, or my husband, or Dear, or more intimate names, none of which are me; nor am I Mr. or Professor or Sir, as my students call me, nor lector at the church, the principal's son, the plumber's son, *Deem*, or, as our children say, Dad. I'm so much the person I was in the past, I wonder how I can be given the number of names I have with so much conviction. My existence is a narrow line I tread between the person I'm expected to be and the person who hides behind his real self to keep the innermost antiquity of me intact. Will you wake if—I run my hand over your hair and you don't even stir. Housework and the children consume your energy and hours, and I know from my work at school how you must feel; the more commonplace the questions, the more bothersome the details of papers and giving out grades, the more my imagination is stunned. I look forward to sleep as an excursion from life, and fall into it like a stone. And then there are the nights, such as tonight, when I defy the principle and float. Cold hard bed.

Beneath your eyelids you follow the movement of the dream. Who peoples it? Can I enter it as a shade of color, a character, a melody, a landscape, and become a part of you? I feel my thoughts reach you when you sleep. Why else do you stir when one frightens me? You stir now. Tonight I went out on the steps, under a hooked moon holding part of a pale globe above it, and thought I saw a tent, or sleeping bags, or bodies under blankets at the front of the lawn. Who'd be sleeping out on our lawn in this suburban neighborhood, I thought almost aloud. I tiptoed over and realized that the way the light was falling must have formed a mirage. In the dimness I saw, instead, the tricycles of our oldest son and daughter, and the youngest one's baby stroller, parked all the way at the end of the drive, the edge of the lawn again, where I've told them never to leave them, as though all three lived out there in their reality. I left everything standing as it was, a stranger to their needs.

A girl in my biology class had brought some goldfish from the cattle tank on her farm, afraid they couldn't withstand the Wisconsin winter, and I'd brought them home in a jar; they were swimming in their substantial air above the countertop. You were at the table, leafing through the catalogue for an aquarium for the children, and I sat beside you and gave you feathery kisses over the dark brown covering your forearm. Did they make any connection between what happened before and the closeness of the moment then? Do you feel them now?

Three children within thirty-five months. Out of fear or possessiveness, or the beast in me, or what? My fear of death? Do I fear death? Do I fear it more than life? Should a scientist bring his science home? The oldest isn't five, so there's a continual battle for affection, or one brewing, and I feel streamers and beams running from them back to my brothers and sisters and me. The five of us were close in age. We were competitive and not always good company. We didn't have both our parents. We didn't live in a house like this, low and ranchlike and sprawled out on its lot, so brand-new and newlywedlike, underfurnished, that when Dad walked through it to see if there were any repairs to be made, I noticed his eyes unlimber and darken with pride, and then strain to the corners to add to the barrenness pieces burnished by the affection of years—real time to me. One dresser in one room. A chair and a bed in another. We're a wee bit poor about the eighteenth of every month. Tim'rous, wee, sleekit me.

Let's change lives. I'll be a fishing guide or an investment broker or a salesman or a poet, and you'll be a lover I met last night, exactly as you are, but I won't be blind to the qualities that made me marry you, and the others I've inhabited since, and won't handle you in any of my habitual manhandling ways; you'll be the same toward me, and we won't have any children. No, we will, but they'll be gone for a month. No, a weekend. I don't know. I envy your sleep and the dream you lie within. Do I move along its boundaries, as we moved down the Trimbelle creek that spring, when its banks on both sides were white with blossoming plum, and a hawk landed in the bare branches of a fire-scorched elm above and screamed down at us? When you wake in the morning to one of the children's crying, drugged with heaviness and not yourself for an hour, will it be from my influence on you? If this adjuration does indeed enter you or your dream, and if I tell you what I can't when you're awake, all through this darkness half the world shares, will you accept your morning disorientation, will you understand and forgive me, and will you listen again another night, or just remain here with me this morning?

I cross to the other side of the street.

On this corner is a brown building with its entrance at an angle to the curb. At one time it was the post office, among other enterprises, but the former postmaster, Bud McCoy, tall and thin, with thinning orange hair, is an incorrigible and blasphemous Republican, and when Roosevelt became President the post office moved up the street. Now Bud carries on the businesses that he ran concurrently in the building while it was a post office; he's the village barber (his competitor across the street lasted only a year) and the insurance agent. He and his wife live upstairs and Mrs. McCoy is a beautician, so it's not uncommon for a woman to be receiving a permanent in one barber chair while a man is shaved in the other; nor is it uncommon to smell dinner cooking in the midst of a haircut.

Next, going up this side of the street, is Ianaccona's Locker, where, behind a foot-thick door, a miniature of winter, smelling of ozone and stale ice, is preserved year round, and in warmer weather patrons are provided with an overcoat before entering that world, and are also given a pair of heavy gloves to keep their hands from adhering to the metal locker drawers. And next, an eyesore, a big storage shed with double rolling doors like barn doors—a weathered, graying, empty, unused building owned by N. J. Ludvig, the richest man in town. Here's where I hid on that day of hide-and-seek.

The alley again.

Sill's Cafe, a facade of counterfeit brick (orange shingle material) that's been lounged against so much the bricks are rubbed away in spots to reveal asphalt. Sill's is the only place to come when it's cold; there are marble-topped tables and metal ice-cream chairs, a counter with swivel stools, a row of comfortable booths along one wall, where I once watched Warren Lee Ennis hold lighted matches in his mouth, and a glass display case that contains everything from wristwatches to licorice to homemade cupcakes, cap guns, and jawbreakers. You can sit in Sill's all day without being disturbed and never spend a cent. Wooden-bladed fans, suspended from long pipes attached to the ceiling of stamped tin, spin above you all summer and activate streamers of paper intended to frighten away flies.

Next to Sill's, like a warning that you'll pay for overindulgence there, is a frame building less than seventeen feet wide which accommodates the chair, the cabinet of tools, a stiff waiting couch, and the drilling apparatus of K. W. Koenig, D.D.S., Iowa State, in a frame.

Beside his shed, and overshadowing it, the only building along this street that's made of real brick, and the only one that even hints at opulence. Flat stone pillars flank its entrance. Four wide steps of stone lead to a pair of doors so heavy they're hard to push open: beyond them, a heated foyer. Here I had my first glimpse of mortality; I remember a gray sack with "MAIL" on its side, wafers of snow melting on the floor, a crushed hat in a corner, too many men in one space, and somebody whispering to my father, "It was a stroke," a word I associate with luck, and then see, past the pairs of adult legs, a man on the floor with blue lips and a face the shade of newspaper. N. J. Ludvig. But that's all I'm permitted to see; my father hurries me on, and I walk through the foyer alone, empty now. The floor inside, made up of tiny white and green hexagonal tiles composed in a pattern that forms big white hexagons outlined in green, lifts, shiny with wax. There's a wainscoting of green-and-gray marble around the walls. Before the Depression, when the area was more prosperous, this was the Hyatt National Bank. Now it's the post office, and in the spring its plaster-and-marble walls echo with cheeping as baby chickens arrive in cardboard mailing cartons—thousands of them!—for outlying farmers who'll later sell chickens and eggs in town. The din of their peeping never alters the expression of the postmaster and his wife, Mr. and Mrs. Andrew De Fay, a prim-lipped, dignified couple in their late sixties who probably eat prunes or use Hadacol. Bud McCoy won't enter the building. His wife or bachelor son picks up the mail.

Beyond the post office, shadow that changes the day; an overhang supported by four round pillars that extends to the edge of the sidewalk. This is the portico in front of Schommer's Tavern. At the third pillar, a concrete platform projects from the curb out into the street and a tin-covered structure the size of a deep freeze sits on it. Near one end is a hand pump converted to power by a yoke and an eccentric, and on the third pillar of the portico, an electrical switch; every family in the village has to visit here at least once a week, even in the blizzards of winter that leave you so numb and astounded they affect only your eyes: Mary Liffert, the widow, arrives with a cylindrical pail equipped with a fitted cover; Dr. Koenig comes slipping down the ice street in a fur cap and fur coat, pulling a red wagon loaded with a five-gallon cream can; the Schonbeck boys, too poor to own a wagon or sled, pair up on a large open bucket, and there are slivers of ice in their drinking water by the time they reach home—the town well, the only place in the village to get potable water. The water tower above the cottonwoods and willows at the end of the block is for fire protection only. My brother once climbed it and peed from its top.

Between Schommer's and the next cicatrix, Tepke's Hardware, is a narrow alleyway that's excellent to go whooping down before returning home with the water pail, and in it a set of rickety steps leads to the roof of the portico, and from here snowballs can be dropped on people passing by. This leaves you to look out for Leo Rimsky, who makes up ice balls in winter and hoards them in a freezer in his father's store, and will bean you with a wallop to the back of your head in the middle of August, and those streamers of ice water down your neck then announce the entry of a winter-clinging film you once felt as a world.

Beyond Tepke's is Rimsky's store, where Leo's father, Leo Sr., a big-headed Russian with a peevish voice that's even more peevish when addressing one of his eleven children, takes the grocery list you've brought from home and checks off each item as he carries it to the counter, while you trail along behind and try to persuade him to give you another slice of halvah from the big brick he keeps cold in his produce case. Rimsky's is the last store on this side of the street. A vacant lot, where a traveling carnival once pitched its tents, stretches from Rimsky's to the end of the block.

There's a memory of mine, real or imaginary, that goes: walking in sawdust through a tent that smells oily and mildewed, and wishing I'd stayed at home; my mother holding my hand in a manner that makes me feel trapped, too much smoke and noise, and all of the stands and concessions bordered by three-foot canvas curtains I can't see over. Where are my brothers, Charles and Jerome? My mother stops so suddenly I feel a jolt in my arm, and then I look up to where she's looking and see a banner, painted in colors that are cracking away from the cloth, and am sure I haven't read right, but the gaudy drawing above confirms the words:

25¢ ! !   SEE THE TWO-HEADED BABY   25¢ ! !

"What?"

A smiling man, whom I can see only from the waist up,

comes over and puts his hands on the pipe that supports the curtains, and my eyes go into zigzags to take in all of the tattoos needled into his arms. "Just two bits, ma'm," he says.

"There's no such thing."

"Sure, ma'm. It's in that box where the curtain is."

"You're lying. An infant couldn't live in there."

"Oh, lady, a-heh-heh. It ain't *alive*."

"It's not?"

"Naw. Here. You want to see?"

I hear curtain rings singing across a rod, and then she grips my hand so tightly I want to cry out, but stop at her changed face.

"That's diabolical!" she cries.

"Ah, lady, it's just like your pickles at home."

"What if a child saw that?"

"There's many that have, ma'm, and kids, you know, it don't bother one bit. I've let you see now. You want him to?"

"You should be hanged," my mother says to him, and leads me out of the tent, and I know what it's like not to know when something important is up and exactly what it means to me. Or you. Do you see?

Across the way is the Town Hall.

A fluted lintel painted beige, a pair of plate-glass windows— Except for the blank building between the Red Owl and Friedrich's, there, the street is retraced, or at least as completely as it can be for now, and if that building were in place perhaps the right combination would come and cover me white with sleep. The building might have been a shoe-repair shop. I remember standing on that side of the street, watching a man pump a treadle that turned a long axle on which was mounted a series of buffers and grinding wheels—but wasn't there also a creamery there; cream cans moving on metal rollers through a spring-loaded trap door toward a cooling room, a centrifuge spinning two opposed test tubes in a tight circle close to my eyes?

A shoe-repair shop? He couldn't have been in town more than six months (I don't remember his name), and I'm sure he occupied the former barbershop–feed-store next to Eichelburger's Tavern. Or was the barbershop actually located in the blank building? There's a barber reflected in a mirror (Henry Mueller?), his scissors snipping around my ears and head, a leg pumping, the axle turning at a higher speed, the centrifuge widening into a toe of my shoe held into the bristles, and then as I turn in sleeplessness, or as my mind turns, the aspect of the street is changed. Cars are parked in the vacant lot next to Rimsky's store and several are flying miniature American flags from their aerial tips. The portico of the tavern is decorated with hunting, and lights have been strung from poles on its decklike roof, where a band is setting up to play the fox-trots and schottisches that will be danced tonight; every farmer in the area must be in town with his family, because the street is lined with people—a sight I've never seen. In all directions, firecrackers of every size and variety are stuttering and whamming non-stop.

It's the Fourth of July, 1950. I'm six. I was ill a few winters before with rheumatic fever, and had a relapse this spring; the children my age and ones even younger have grown taller and stronger, while I seem to have shrunk, and they're more graceful and well coordinated. Since the sickness I haven't been allowed to participate in sports, I'm short-winded and frail, my legs are bony, my ribs protrude, and as if to remind me of my condition, my mother has dressed me in shorts. I've been forbidden to compete in the Fourth of July foot-races.

I watch Dr. Koenig confer with two other men in the open doors of the Town Hall, where the patriotic ceremony has taken place, and then cup his hands to his mouth and shout out that the first race, for boys between the ages of five and nine, is ready to start. The message travels up and down the crowded sidewalk. Dr. Koenig draws a mark across the street with the heel of his shoe, and my brother's classmates and friends—Douglas Kuntz, the two Rimsky brothers, Buddy Schonbeck, Barry Kolb—begin lining up. I've worked free from my mother at the other end of the street, near Bud McCoy's, and now I pull off my shoes, take off my shirt, and trot out to the center of the line. I step next to Rudy Sill, whose teeth are gray-green nubbins from sweets from the cafe, and turn, hoping I'm somewhat hidden if my parents happen to be near, and see I've taken the wrong slot. My brother Charles is next to me. He's my superior by two and a half years, and he looks me over as a stranger might, and says, "What do you think you're doing?"

"Running."

"You better not. You know what—"

Dr. Koenig, with his characteristic flourishes and attempts at conviviality, is walking up and down the line, saying, "Get in your stances, now, boys—any stance you want. I see some of you have got yourselves holes dug and that's just fine. Hey there, young Rimsky, you want to take off your shoes? Oh, you got on *tennis* shoes. Well, Well, fine, then. O.K., now. Now all you guys know how I call it—'On your marks, get set, go,' and you're off. I'm rootin' for you all, I'm wishing every last one of you could win, but whichever comes in first gets five silver dollars, compliments of the merchants and this professional fellow here, too."

He walks to the side of the line, and somebody at the far end of the street waves a white handkerchief, then pockets it and with another man pays out a dazzlingly invisible string. A child is pulled up on the sidewalk.

My brother, who's down in his crouch, says, "I'd hate to be you when Mom finds out."

"On your marks!"

Somebody sets off a string of firecrackers and I'm so nervous I nearly bolt.

"Get set!"

Frightened, my fear and adrenaline building, I spring forward at the instant Dr. Koenig shouts "Go!"

A cheer rises from the crowded sidewalks.

I hear bare feet pounding on dirt and hard breathing, and see I'm staring at three backs instead of a dozen, and one belongs to Buddy Schonbeck, the tallest boy in the lower grades.

Past Tepke's.

Past the town pump, breath coming faster.

Dr. Koenig's, Sill's Cafe.

Then I hear my mother scream my name, and begin sprinting like a pursued beast, mad and half blind, imagining her at my back. There's a pain in my heart that blossoms through my chest, crowding the space of my lungs, and then the crown of my head detaches itself and wings upward over the crowd, light as a balloon, leaving the last living part of me, the soles of my feet, traveling over the earth.

Then the string.

A ribbon and five silver dollars are pressed into my hand like separate gasps or gaps of air I take to be free.

My brother and the Rimskys insist I be disqualified; I'm pigeon-toed, and they say that the sight of my churning legs, which are bowed, made them laugh so hard they could hardly run; and I ran cockeyed, they say, like a dog trying to throw his ass out of gear so he didn't crap all over the place as soon as he got going hard. But the race is mine, the ribbon and the prize money are mine, and I'm so lightheaded from the exertion and the triumph that when somebody grabs me by the hips, roughly and without warning, and hefts me high above the crowd, it seems that the street before me is also mine, a deserved possession, that the faces of Charles and Jerome and their friends, the cheers of—

But by now I'm asleep beside you in bed, and for right now, dear one, loved one, loved ones and friends, that's enough.

One

1

❦

BURIAL

He was awakened from sleep by his head slamming against glass. The train was going into a shuddering turn and his shoulder was crushed against steel. He pushed himself up in the seat, glimpsing his diminishing reflection in the dim glass, and the act of sitting and the sight of himself, gray and unrelated to who he thought he was, drained away his blood and struck him blind for a breath, and he had a hallucination of milkweed parachutes floating from a broken pod. Alcohol. The pain above his right eye was like a needle imbedded there and pressing upward. What was the form that had been so overarching, so vaulted and protective in his dream, as though he'd been sleeping in a cathedral? He pulled a pocket watch from his overalls; he couldn't have slept more than fifteen minutes. Where was the sun?

The faded velvet of the seat was impregnated with dust, dry and chalklike to his touch, and then his nostrils widened and his brain was blank numb fragments from the bang of a sneeze. He pulled out a handkerchief and wiped his mouth and the palm of his hand, trying to hold his head steady against the shock and sway of the car, and then took a telegram from his shirt pocket, ironed it smooth over his thigh, and stared at the yellowish strips of paper pasted askew on the telegraph blank.

MAHOMET NOR DAK
957 AM SEPT 24 1935

CHARLES NEUMILLER
COURTENAY NOR DAK

DAD PASSED AWAY THIS AM. NEED YOU FOR BURIAL. GOD
SPEED YOU.

AUGUSTINA

He pressed his fingers against his eyelids, as though the
message and the mounting pain it brought could be buried
in that internal blackness, where shining tangles of vision
shook and uncurled, and his cupped hand made him conscious of the alcohol on his breath. He'd been drunk three
times in his life: in 1913, when his first child, Martin, was
born; five years later, when the quartet in which he sang
bass received a standing ovation at the state S.P.E.B.S.Q.A.
convention (that drunkenness was an accident; it was the
first time he'd had sloe gin); and yesterday afternoon,
when he received the telegram. Except for the nap just
now, he hadn't slept since he'd received it. He looked up,
and the mural at the end of the empty car, bison outlined
against a background of tan, lifted toward him away from
the wall, as if to engage the tangle of vision within him,
and he shook his head to clear it, feeling a race of emotion he couldn't name.

At his feet was a faded carpetbag, made a decade ago
by his wife, that contained most of his valuable possessions
—his suit, a straight razor of German steel, and his portable carpentry tools. A newly set handsaw, wrapped in
newspaper, was tied to the carpetbag with twine. He
looked out the sooty window and watched the sun, which
was still hidden from him, form a hazy arc of light along
the horizon, and then light appeared across the plain as if
from the earth, from the plain itself, warming his face,
and fall colors became visible everywhere over the flat
land.

Familiar landmarks. In the distance, five elms with a
windmill beside them, and, beyond the trees, the silvery
gray outbuildings of an abandoned farm with an ocher-
painted outhouse slanting among them. He leaned his
cheek against the window, feeling the race of it again

overtake him—what?—as he followed a green line that wound through the gold stubble and dark-brown squares of summer fallow and then went faint at the horizon. Sand Grass Creek. On the other side of Mahomet, to the east, the creek formed a U around his father's farm. The train started slowing down.

A junk yard flashed past, a patch of sweet corn gone to pale stalks, a vacant lot where implements (hayrake, binder, mower with cutter bar lifted) were lined along a snow fence, one home, a grain elevator, and then, close to the tracks, a long wall of echoing stone—the rear of the old slaughterhouse. He put away the telegram and went onto the rocking platform between cars, a treadle above a cataract, and the shattering noise and cold air, coming in such a rush, sent a constriction around his stomach; he gagged up wine-flavored saliva, closed his eyes, gagged again. There was a shrieking of steel on steel, a smell of rusty steam, and then the train nearly came to a stop, and he started down the metal stairs and was thrown off balance as, with a clangor of couplings, it stopped for good.

He stepped onto a platform of railroad ties, down a distance from a yellow depot, and heard the bell on the engine banging and then a release of steam beside him as the train began to move. A sign hanging from the eave of the depot's porch read "MAHOMET," which was to him, Charles Neumiller, home. Two men were on a bench beside the open door, beneath the porch, and when they saw him they stood; one of them—Charles believed he recognized the son of the most recent manager of the co-op elevator; he could hardly concentrate for the noise of the train—turned away and took off on a trot. The other stood as though waiting, and then moved in his direction. It was Clarence Popp, tall and shambling and bent-shouldered, with a flat, mask-like face and a long lantern jaw perpetually covered with copper-colored stubble. Clarence had once worked as a hired man for the Neumillers and was Charles's age but was closer to Charles's father. How did Clarence continue to survive, Charles wondered. He was sacristan and unretired altar boy at the church, but hadn't had regular work for several years and lived by himself at the edge of town in a wrecked caboose he'd patched up and somehow made habitable; yet he always appeared healthy, and always had liquor on hand.

"Chuck," Clarence said, and took his hand, and Charles realized that Clarence was perhaps the only one in the world who would call him, Charles, such a taciturn, solemn-countenanced, and decorous man, "Chuck" and not consider the irony in it. Clarence frowned. One of his eyes was smaller than the other, and it gave him a curiously discerning but defenseless look, as though an orphan of five were peering out from within him. "Or I guess I should call you Charles now," Clarence said. "I heard about the telegram going out and thought you might be on this train. There's not much a person can say at these times except you have my sympathy. You have. I'm terribly sorry. I thought a lot of your dad."

"Yes."

"Was the end difficult, do you know?"

"I haven't talked to Augustina."

"I haven't seen Augustina myself in a while."

"Who brought the telegram in?"

"I hear she walked in herself. A crime, a real crime, and now her out there all alone, by dammit, the poor woman. I hadn't seen your dad, either, in—I don't know—three weeks at the least, I guess. He was poorly, and Augustina and I had the agreement that when he was poorly I wouldn't come out—you know, the drinking. Your dad, of course, he wouldn't come to town. He hasn't set foot in this place in a year, and I don't blame him. The way he was being talked about, well, it'd burn your ears off."

"Then I'd rather you let mine be."

"People talking behind his back, blaming him for things he couldn't have had a hand in, and the worst going on like he was responsible for even the dust storms! Jesus! Pardon," Clarence added, and blushed under his stubble; he knew how Charles was about profanity. Then, in a wondering tone, "Lord, how long has it been since I've seen you, Chuck?"

Charles shrugged, aware that his hair had grayed in the last year and a half and that his face, as deeply lined as his father's, was hollow-cheeked and colorless from alcohol.

"I was out to Dad's this summer but didn't see anybody in town."

"It must be four years."

"It must."

"Will Marie or any of the kids be coming in?"

"No."

"No? Why not?"

"Martin, Elaine, and Vince are away at college, and it would be too hard on Marie to bring all the little ones. She might be with child again."

"Huh. That will make—how many then—eight"

"Nine."

"That's quite a family, Charles."

"It is."

Clarence raised the brim of his engineer's cap and shifted his heavy shoes. His yellow braces, both of which held N.R.A. buttons, were faded and frayed, and his trousers were split over the thighs, showing skin. "Who'll be saying the funeral Mass, I wonder. We haven't had a priest in town for three years now, you know."

"I'm sure the missionary from Hankinson will come over."

"He's away to Fargo on a conference, starting today, and won't be back till the end of this week."

"Then a priest from Lidgerwood."

"Charles, they're all gone off to Fargo, too, I'm afraid."

"Then maybe I'll have to bury him without a priest," Charles said, and knew it was wrong to mention an idea so heretical to Clarence, who was a prude himself and a worse gossip than any number of women.

Clarence's face took on the blankness of a seasoned magistrate's, and then he winked his small eye and said, "Why not, Charles? And say, will you need help?"

"If you want, you can come out Thursday afternoon. I should be ready then."

"But that's tomorrow! That's a day and a half!"

"If I could do it today, I would."

"But what about the people that—"

A gray-and-tan nanny goat, a fixture in town for fifteen years, came around the corner of the depot and walked into the shade of the porch, its tapered hoofs tapping over the heavy planking ties. Then the goat drew up and regarded Charles with a coin-like, pragmatic eye, while its tiny jaws moved in a tidy munch. Charles turned and walked beyond its working beard, toward a road that crossed the rails at the other end of the station, and felt his intestines expand and slide over themselves inside him.

"You're not walking?" Clarence called to him.

"Yes."

"Surely somebody will give you a ride out!"

Charles walked on. The road, a dirt road that angled away from the edge of town, was dry and unshaded and soon he was in open countryside. The sun was rising, driving off the morning chill, and now and then a spout of wind would pick up dust from the road or a field bordering it and spin itself into oblivion in a few seconds. Otherwise, the day was still. Bird song, rising from the earth and different levels of the air, swayed and teetered on either side as though from a fixed point at the center of his hearing, a feeling he'd had before this, he felt. The road began to follow Sand Grass Creek, which was lined with low willows and cattails and dry saxifrage. The cattail heads were swollen and splitting, their silky seeds spilling from them, and in front of him, keeping a fixed distance, a red-winged blackbird went dipping from head to head as though stringing between them shining beads of its quicksilvery, reiterated song. The road turned. He stopped and shifted the carpetbag to his left hand. He could see, a mile and a half ahead, the stand of trees that marked his father's farm.

Otto Neumiller emigrated from Germany in 1881. "I was twenty-four then. The wind was so big the masts rocked down to the waves even full-trimmed." He bought a wagon and a team of oxen in Minneapolis and headed west. Even in the Old Country he'd heard of the virgin Dakota plain, as limitless as the sea to look upon— "And Otto knows the sea"—and with resources perhaps as infinite. "At first I didn't think there was such a place, seeing so much timber in Minnesota, but once I came across the Red River, I could feel the current of its waves." He entered a homesteading claim in the Dakota Territory in the spring, and sold the wagon and one of the oxen to buy a plow and supplies. Trees were so scarce there was no lumber for building, and what sometimes looked like trees in the distance were the last remnants of the buffalo herds moving off toward the Missouri. "Red deer and antelope were crisscrossing everywhere out there, too. I drove on out. The buffalo looked so big I was afraid to shoot the buggers. I hardly saw a one after that." He built his homesteading shack of sod. The first fall, his garden and twenty acres of wheat, which he planted by hand, went up in a prairie fire. His ox and his implements were lost. His shack would have burned, too, if he hadn't situated it in the curve of Sand Grass Creek, where it was all but encircled by water. "And the next year the hoppers came. The sky was so dark with them we had to light the lamps at midday. It was crops they got."

He was penniless, there were no neighbors, and he didn't trust himself to withstand the winter alone, so he went to family friends in Chicago and found a job as a drayman. At a neighborhood church he met Mary Reisling, an immigrant girl. "She was down there from Winona to work the winter, too." He married her in the spring and took her back to his homestead, and that year the crops bore, though battered by a bad hail, and he bought a milch cow and improved the shack so it was more livable. The following spring his first daughter, Lucy, was born. He planted poplars and maples and elms along Sand Grass Creek to serve as a windbreak. "When those trees began to grow, they were the only ones you could see for twenty-five miles, sir."

The railroad extended its line beyond Wahpeton, and it was possible to buy lumber from the East. He built a twelve-stanchion barn and began work on a house. The crops that season were the best they'd been in a decade—a windfall, a bounty, and he opened his first bank account in America. Another daughter, Augustina, was born. He took on a hired man and broke up twice as much acreage, and again there was a windfall. He finished the house, two stories with four bedrooms, and bought a dozen head of Hereford and a hundred sheep. "That year North Dakota entered the Union and I became a citizen of the U.S. of A." He began to acquire bordering farms that had been abandoned, and by the time his son was born, in 1891, he was the most prosperous landowner in the area.

"If I had a son, I always said I'd name him Charles after his Grandpa Neumiller, and John after his grandpa on Ma's side. But he came on Christmas Day, so I added on Christopher. I walked to Wahpeton to get the doctor and the snow was so deep the doc had to drive his buggy down the tracks, opened by the train, and wouldn't trust his old mare to get us both there, so I walked all the way back, too, and the boy was born when I got here."

He was a shrewd but simple man, embarrassed by his German accent, he cared so much for this country, and what he mostly wanted to do was please; he was of the generation old enough to see, from the knife point of 1900, equally well into either century, and see at a look what might last.

Against the advice of everybody he knew, he put in two hundred acres of corn, a crop that hadn't ever been raised in the state, except by the Mandan Indians, and it was a success. He bought another section of land. Mahomet was going up at the junction of the Great Northern and the Minneapolis, St. Paul & Sault Sainte Marie lines, and he made some sound investments in the first businesses there. "Then Lucy married below herself, to a cattle buyer, and they went to live near Fergus Falls." When contributions were being solicited to build a Catholic church, he donated fifteen hundred dollars to the fund. On Charles's twenty-first birthday, he took Charles aside, handed him a bankbook, and said, "This is one quarter yours." There was ninety thousand dollars in the account. "The Neumillers have always been took, my dad used to say to me, but this is one that ain't going to be, Charles."

In 1915, he built a large house in town, said he was retiring, and gave his farm to Charles. In town he was elected county commissioner and appointed to the school board, and when a group of farmers started a co-op elevator, he invested in it, and persuaded business friends to do the same. The farmers were uneducated and suspicious of strangers, and naïve about financial matters, and the man they hired to manage the co-op, being one of them, was mistrustful of Easterners and got taken in by some buyers from St. Paul, who bought from him below market price, promising bonuses to the co-op at the end of the year for volume, and then reneged. After which the manager became so cautious he failed to sell when he should have, and then had to sell at a loss. The elevator went heavily into debt. Otto Neumiller was elected to the board of directors in 1927, and two years later the Crash came.

He lost thousands in the grain market, but was the only member of the board of directors who remained solvent, and when this was discovered bill collectors came to him. "I felt responsible for the man we had there and the losses my friends took." He raised enough cash to keep the co-op from closing, but in doing so had to sell his house in town and all the land except the eighty acres he'd originally homesteaded, and would have sold this, too, but the property was in both his and his wife's name, and she refused to sign the papers. "We argued about it all through the night, and when I woke the next day the papers was gone." Co-ops were closing all over the state, but as long as the one in Mahomet stayed open he never doubted he'd be repaid. "I figured if we could keep this one open we'd make acres of money." When it closed, he and his wife moved back to the home place, and Charles moved his family to a farm forty miles away, near Courtenay-Wimbledon.

Everybody in Mahomet knew that Otto Neumiller's farm wasn't under mortgage, as theirs were, and imagined he had money hidden away while their children went hungry and in rags. "And I did walk around with a shovel for a while, looking for those papers that had been hid." He raised a little grain each year and kept himself and his family in food, and not much more. There was no way of explaining that this was the way things were. People had stopped visiting him and inviting him over, and in town they crossed the street to avoid him, and even moved out of the vestibule of the church when he stepped in. He felt guilty about the wealth he'd once had and went to closing auctions and bought articles he didn't need and let them stand on the grounds for others to take.

His wife died. He became dazed and slovenly about his health, and began drinking too much. His wife had signed her share of the farm over to Augustina, who'd never married, and Augustina stayed on and tried to care for him. He'd go for days without eating, and reverted to speaking German. He and Clarence brewed beer in the basement and sat up at night drinking and playing cards. He was old, his heart was bad, he'd always been a heavy drinker, and the daily drinking added to his general decline. He let his fields go to pasture, to weeds and pocket gophers, and kept only the garden. And now he was dead. And for Charles it was merely a matter of time.

He stopped at the mailbox. There was nothing in it. "Bills are the ones with windows in them," his father often said. *Otto Neumiller* was painted across the box in an ornate Old World script, in bright orange paint. "If you're going to do a job, do it right" sounded in Charles's ears, as though his father had spoken at his side this time. His father loved work brought to completion well, to the point of perfection, if possible; the care he lavished on the simplest tasks and his exuberance as he worked, small and elflike, smiling, wide-eyed, winking and asking you to come and see, as innocent of his pride as a child. Every spring he retraced his name on the mailbox with new paint. His hand was still steady.

Charles stepped back. The pole of the mailbox had been struck and knocked aslant by a piece of pulled machinery or a passing car. He put his carpetbag down and shoved and tugged at the box, trying to loosen it, then went down on one knee and drove his shoulder against the pole. It hardly budged. He threw his weight against the pole again and again as he pivoted around it, driving packed earth away from its base in a widening ring, and at last, shaking and lifting at the same time, pulled it free. He was flushed and fighting for breath. He held it at the top, close to the box, picked up his carpetbag, went down the lane to the house, and propped the mailbox against the chimney, near the porch.

Augustina opened the screen door and came onto the porch. Her gray eyes, magnified by glasses, were fearful and apologetic, and she was twisting a handkerchief at her waist. She raised a hand as if to speak, and then clamped her lips tight and her eyelids closed. Her forehead was higher than his, and her eyebrows thick and mannish. The handkerchief looked ragged, her dark dress was worn and dingy, and her hair, once a reddish aureole around her face was tan-gray and drawn into a frizzy bun. He was hurt by how she'd aged, and by her lack of concern about her appearance. He stepped onto the porch and took her in his arms.

"Charles. Thank God."

Her body beneath the dress was surprisingly feminine, frail yet full, her breasts large and firm against him, and he realized how easily she could have married. Had she remained single out of fear—since adolescence she'd been high-strung and terrified of strangers and subject to "spells" —or was it simple devotion to their father? For her devotion to him was always overabundant and colored with a childlike awe.

"I thought I wouldn't be able to bear waiting or keep myself sane," she said. "I haven't slept since he died."

"How was the end?"

"It was as if— He'd been feeling all right and I brought him— Come inside. Please."

They went into the parlor, bare except for a faded carpet, a long oak table, and a horsehair sofa, and before Charles could adjust to the room her arms were around his neck and he felt through his shirt the dampness and heat of her tears. He eased the carpetbag to the floor and pressed her head to his shoulder. "Here," he said. "Here now."

"I feel so sick and ashamed!" she cried.

"Why?"

"I helped the doctor lay him out and haven't gone near the room since."

"Why should you?"

"I feel he's still alive."

"That's foolishness."

"I can't help it, I feel it! I can't sleep, I can't eat, I feel sinful and sick and that I'll never be the same from not seeing if he needed me."

"What could you do?"

"Talk to him?"

"Ach!" Spiritualism irritated him more than anything he could think of, and he was surprised that Augustina had let herself be taken in by it. "What did the doctor say?"

"What did he say?"

"What was the cause?"

"His heart, he thinks."

"He wasn't sure'"

"No. He's so restless!"

"Old Doc Jonas?"

"Dad!"

"Augustina, please. Be *rea*sonable. He's at peace now."

"I can't even pray."

"You will."

"I hate too much."

"Hate?"

"How can I help it? They've already been out. They heard he died and they've been carting off machinery and grain, and Frank Kubitz even took the team of bays. His only—" She swayed as though off balance and held him tighter.

"That'll stop."

"They tell me it's owed to them and I tell them to wait, at least till you're here, but they won't listen! They just walk off with what they want."

"Everybody thinks they're owed something when they're poor."

"We're poor. *He* was."

"I know, I know, but they don't."

"Make them understand!"

"I will."

She drew away and wiped her cheeks with the handkerchief, wiped under her glasses, and then across her high forehead. "I'm sorry," she murmured. Her eyes were depthless with a feeling he couldn't define. "I've never been alone before. I'm so thankful you're here. How are Marie and the children?"

"Fine."

"And you?"

"As well as can be."

"I understand," she said.

"How was the end?"

"I brought him breakfast and he seemed in good spirits, he talked and laughed, and when I looked in to see how he was doing, he had a piece of toast in his hand and was staring straight ahead—thinking about something, I thought—so I let him be. He's been reliving so much of his past life since spring. But when I went back a while later, he was in the same attitude. He died that way."

Charles went across the parlor and opened a door. The curtains of the room were drawn, the air dim and gold-colored, and on the high bed with its carved-oak headboard he saw the outline of his father's body beneath a sheet. He stepped inside and closed the door behind him. He dipped his fingers into a font of holy water fastened to the molding of the jamb and made a sign of the cross, and then turned back the sheet to his father's shoulders; thick silver hair rayed upward over the pillow, giving his face an unprotected look, lips dark and parted, and the white scar across the bridge of his nose violet. A scar from a fight. When had it happened? Why? The lid of his left eye was halfway open, and a clouded iris showed. Charles closed the lid with his thumb, but it slowly retracted, and was once more open on him.

In the top drawer of his father's bureau he found a leather change purse, took two silver dollars from it, pressed the eyelid down, and placed the coins over it. He snapped the purse shut and held it, trembling. His father's beard, shorter and thinner than he remembered, flared up from his lifted chin like a silken brush. With his fingers Charles stroked the beard smooth, the way he'd seen his father stroke it from the time he could remember.

God rest you, Father.

He drew the sheet back over his father's face as he'd found it, crossed himself again, left the room, and sat at the oak table in the parlor. He pressed his fingers against his eyelids, which were stiff and felt thickened and numb, and the pain in his head suddenly brightened and went spiraling deeper until he wanted to cry out. He said, "Did Dad receive extreme unction?"

"Several times."

"Has a priest been out recently?"

"Two days before he passed on."

"Did Dad receive it then?"

"Yes. He asked to."

He uncovered his eyes and looked up. "There might not be a priest to say a Requiem."

"I know. There's a conference in Fargo."

"Does it bother you if there isn't a Requiem?"

"I haven't felt we've had a priest in town since Father Meyer left," Augustina said. "And neither did Dad."

Charles took his suit and white shirt from the carpetbag and went to the foot of the stairs, where coat hangers hung from wooden dowels.

"I suppose we'll have to sell out," Augustina said, and he turned. Her eyes were plaintive and tearful, and she was twisting the handkerchief again. "And what will I do then? Could I come live with you and Marie? I could help with the children. I can still do chores."

Charles finished hanging up his clothes. "We'll talk about it later," he said. "I have to rest. You should rest, too."

He went over to the horsehair sofa and, before he was aware of striking its leather cushion, was asleep.

In his dream the German word *best* had a new significance: now it was a homonym of "beast" and a synonym of it, too, and it applied to him, because he'd been deformed. He was lying on his back in a meadow smaller than his body when a horse mower came toward the *best* (beast) part of the meadow and mowed his hands off as cleanly as hay.

He sat up on the sofa. He'd held his hands, crossed at the wrists, so tight over his chest they were asleep. He rubbed the inside of his wrists with his thumbs, then took out his pocket watch; he'd slept less than an hour. There was a smell of coffee, real or imaginary, in the room.

He went into the kitchen and Augustina, who was at the stove with her back to him, swung around and put a hand to her throat. "Oh," she said. "I didn't know you were up."

She'd set a place for him at the table, a china plate with the silver next to it resting on a white napkin, and he sat with his back to the window, as he'd sat in this kitchen for most of his life. Augustina had put out on the table sliced roast beef, a plate of homemade bread, a dish of honey, hard-boiled eggs, corn relish, cottage cheese, sour cream, and sliced turnips; there was a butter dish with a butter knife beside it. She took a long-handled spoon and fished an eggshell out of the coffeepot, and poured Charles a cup, then herself, and sat down across from him.

He took a swallow of coffee, lukewarm, as he liked it, and said, "I think you should ask Lucy and her husband to come live with you."

"Oh?"

"He's been laid off by the railroad, and they're having trouble keeping up their rent. They don't have children and they'd be good company."

"Oh." Augustina looked reflective and less anxious. Charles knew that children made her nervous. "But I thought Marie might like help with the kids."

"It would be nice. But unless things change for the better, we'll be moving on from here soon."

"Where to?"

"Illinois."

"To Chicago?"

"Further south."

"If you need money, Charles, sell the place here. It's actually yours, I've always thought of it so; Dad gave it to you."

"No, the place is free and clear, and it's best now to keep whatever you have."

"Why Illinois?"

"J. D. Prell is there. He used to be with the Hankinson Bank, and I brought him out once to try and talk sense to Dad about that co-op. Now Prell is working for a land bank around Havana, Illinois, that's buying up farm properties."

"And you'd do that?"

"It wouldn't be to my taste. A lot of the farms are bought by paying off a mortgage or back taxes. Prell says that the barns and outbuildings on most of the places have been let go and the land bank, or Prell's development company, or whatever, wants them repaired before they sell. He's asked me to come down and start a carpentry crew. I'd work for him but more or less be my own boss to hire and fire and fix things up as I saw fit."

"It seems a good opportunity."

"It does."

"Could the boys work with you?"

"The oldest ones, I suppose, if they want."

The fall sunlight coming through the window lay in a broad band across his back and around his sides, embracing him with its warmth. He thought of his sons and of how unreservedly he loved them, and realized he no longer had a father. He lifted up a spoon of honey and tipped it and let the honey spill in a thick strand into the dish. "Do we still have bees?" he asked.

"One hive. Dad kept them up until spring, and then Clarence took over."

"How is the garden?"

"In good shape."

"Are the strawberry plants covered with straw?"

"Clarence did that."

"Clarence will be out tomorrow to help me out."

"Poor man, I don't know what he'll do without Dad."

"Yes, they were very close. Clarence doesn't have any real friends."

"That, too, but Dad's kept Clarence in money for the last couple of years, you know."

"I should have," Charles said. "Well, you could take Clarence on as a tenant farmer. He certainly knows the land, and then you'd have a little income."

"Oh!" she said, and looked down.

Charles sighed. "I won't move from where I am unless I have to. I love this country, and a farm is the only place to raise kids."

He felt sententious and as though he'd spoken more in the past five minutes than in any previous year of his life. "I have to be busy," he said.

"But you haven't eaten."

"I'm not hungry."

He got his carpetbag in the parlor, went outside and got the mailbox, and walked down to the barn. He un-latched the side door, a Dutch door whose halves were hooked together, and proppped it open with the mailbox. The barn had stood idle for years and smelled of musty hay and old oats going bad in their bins. His vision hadn't adjusted enough to see them, but he could hear the scrabbling and the thumps of rats as they scrambled for cover, and there was a flapping of wings in the loft overhead as a large bird left by some exit. A tiger-striped cat bolted toward a dark corner where some harness hung. Lumber was stored on brackets suspended from the joists above him. In a closed stall were two wood-burning stoves, two washing machines, a half dozen horse collars and some hames, fence posts, a dynamite crate filled with a tangle of fence staples and nails, and stacks of old catalogues. There was a pair of sawhorses. He pulled them out and sat on one and sketched a coffin, with measurements, on the back of the telegram.

He stood on the horse and sorted through the lumber and located several long pieces of one-by-eight shiplap and pulled them down. He took out his steel tape and found that they made up enough board feet. In the crowd-ed stall he picked up a scrap of hardwood, sawed two scraps of pine to its length, a foot and a half, and nailed the pieces of pine to the hardwood in a channel shape. He took out his protractor and in the bottom of the channel drew a pair of opposed forty-five-degree angles, and then sawed edgeways through the pine boards to his pencil marks, and had a miter box. He glanced toward the house and the sunlight, so brilliant from the interior of the barn it revived his headache, made the trees and grass of the barnyard look bleached.

He began to saw the boards for the base of the coffin to

length. The sound of the saw—the *rarp!* tssss, *rarp!* tssss —echoed in the empty barn in a rhythm as regular as his breath and matched the pattern of sunlight and shadow on the floor, where sawdust was snowing down. The smell of pine pitch cleared his mind of death, and the air of the barn seemed to brighten around him. Drops of sweat started falling from his face onto the boards and were soaked up in a second, the wood was so dry. He slipped his overall suspenders off his shoulders, removed his shirt, hung it on a harness peg, and slipped the suspenders onto his shoulders again. His bare back was sensitive to the building's dimness.

He cut three cleats to go across the boards of the coffin's base, beveled their edges with a block plane, nailed them in place—moistening the nails with saliva to prevent the dry wood from splitting—and then turned the base over and clinched the nail ends that were pointing through the boards and polished bright. He turned it back again and nailed pieces of one-by-three hardwood over the two end cleats, letting the hardwood project six inches on either side, and had handles for carrying the spacers so the ropes used to lower the coffin could be pulled free. He began to miter one-by-eights for the coffin's sides and ends, and felt eyes on him. He turned.

"Charles." A figure was silhouetted in the doorway.

"Clarence?" Charles couldn't make out features, and the voice reverberated beyond recognition in the barn.

"Yes, Clarence." He shambled up to Charles as though gliding, his face a dim mask. "I noticed the door open and heard the saw. I got to thinking after you left. I thought you might like a hand today, you know, with—" Clarence gestured with his jutting jaw toward the coffin base.

"It's really a job for just one man. Thank you."

"Well, then, I thought you might like some of this." Clarence pulled a partly full pint of whiskey from his hip pocket. Charles removed the cap, poured a dash of whiskey in it, and tossed the whiskey down. "Thank you," he said, and handed the bottle back to Clarence.

"I know you don't drink, Charles, but, goodness, you can sure have more than that and not get stumbly."

"That's just enough to remind me of yesterday, which was enough for the rest of my life, I believe."

"Oh-ho," Clarence said. "Yeah, I thought there was a sort of cloud hanging about you. Well, here's to the good days that are gone."

Clarence put the bottle to his lips, tipped it, and the whiskey appeared to percolate as his gullet swelled and throbbed several times. He recapped the bottle and became contemplative. "Well, I was also wondering if you didn't want me to get started in at town, at the cemetery, you know, on the grave there. I'm the one usually does that." The whiskey was working in him; creases appeared in his stubbled cheeks with his smile of pride, and his eyes turned lustrous.

"I'm going to bury him here," Charles said.

"What do you mean?"

"I'm going to bury him on the farm here."

"Here?"

"That's what I said."

"But your mother's buried in the cemetery at church! The gravestone there has your dad's name on it!"

"I'm aware of that."

"This isn't consecrated ground!"

"It was to him."

"What will the priest say?"

"I have no idea."

"Charles!"

"I believe a priest can bless the area of a gravesite, if he'd like."

"But this is against all your beliefs!"

"If it was, I wouldn't do it."

"What will people say? You know, your mother buried where she is, in the cemetery there, and then your dad way out here?"

"People always say what they want, no matter what. I've decided."

"It's heathen," Clarence said. He uncapped the bottle and sat on a sawhorse. He shook his head, as though to shake free from it a daze of disbelief, and finished the whiskey. "Well, Charles, if that's your decision, then how about me starting the grave out here?"

"It would make things easier, but I'd best do it myself."

"You don't have to pay me."

"I'd rather, because I would. I want you to help tomorrow, though, as I said, and I can pay you four dollars."

"I don't want money, Charles. You have a wife and kids, you—"

"I can pay you four dollars."

"Whatever you say."

"I want to bury him at noon. I'd like you here an hour earlier."

"I will. Absolutely."

"It was thoughtful of you to come out. I think you should stay for lunch"—Charles pulled out his pocket watch—"and I think Augustina would like you to stay, too. We have something to ask of you. And it's lunchtime right now."

Charles got his shirt from the harness peg, and Clarence brushed off his clothes, lifted his cap and smoothed back his hair, tucked his shirt tighter into his pants, and dropped the whiskey bottle inside one of the wood-burning stoves. When they were both at the open door, Charles turned to him and said, "But after lunch, Clarence, I have to be alone."

*

Charles finished the coffin at two o'clock. He sealed the cracks and seams in it with wood putty. He found a binder canvas with most of the slats missing or removed and cut it in lengths to fit the sides and base of the coffin, then painted the interior of the coffin with tar, and pressed the lengths of canvas into place. The lid was identical to the base, but with a flat, one-by-three strip around its edges he hoped would help make it seal, and the cleats on it faced inward. He painted the top of the lid with tar, laid canvas over it, nailed over the canvas another thickness of one-by-eights, rasped their outer edges round, and sanded them smooth.

He wanted to trim the base of the coffin to match the lid but there was no more one-by-three material. He began ripping a one-by-eight in strips. The rasp and sob of the crosscut saw going with the grain. A sharper smell of pine pitch rising as the saw blade heated, a sensation of rising with it, incorporeal as aroma and omniscient, observing thick, nicotine-stained fingers and calloused hands perform work in a world below, where light and shadow clashed. He cut his thumb and blood soaked into the board in a spreading stain. He raised up and spatters of blood appeared over the board as though springing through its surface from beneath. There was no pain. He pinched the thumb at its base, and then took out his handkerchief, tore a strip from it, wrapped it around his thumb, and pulled the knot tight with his teeth. He finished ripping the board and trimmed the coffin's base.

He brought the mailbox into the barn and removed it from its pole. He cut into the domed top with a hacksaw, the parted metal shrieking against the metal blade, and sawed off the side of the box that held his father's name. He drew marks radiating from the center of the name, used them as a guide to draw an oval around it, and cut the oval out with tin snips. He placed the oval on a piece of wood beam and, with a nail set as a stylus, hammered into the orange paint of each letter, countersinking permanently into the metal "Otto Neumiller," as his father had printed it. He punched holes through the sides of the oval and nailed it at the head of the coffin lid. Darkness spread over his back, and the barn door slammed.

He picked up an iron bar leaning against a feedbox and propped open the door with it. He'd brought the crucifix from his father's room out after lunch, and now he fastened it to the center of the coffin lid. He tarred the inner edge of the lid, tarred the top edge of the coffin walls, and then started nails at two-inch intervals along the lid for securing it down. From the stall he took a fence post, nailed the channel-shaped miter box to one end, filled the saw cuts in its pine sides with putty, fitted a block into one end, and then roofed the box with a wider board. He put the post over his shoulder, grabbed the iron bar propping the door, and went out to the road. He set the post in the old mailbox hole and tamped rocks and dirt around it. He stepped back; it was standing true. There, Augustina, he thought. There, Augustina, or whoever else lives here.

He went behind the house, past the woodshed and the garden, to the flat where Sand Grass Creek formed a U, and searched around in the weeds until he found a shallow depression, which was nearly square, and had a ridge around it that was formed when the walls of his father's homesteading shack deteriorated and sank back to the ground. One of Charles's memories was of his father pointing out the place and saying, in German, "You see that, Charles. That's where my real home is." And later, when Charles was older, he was walking through it behind his father and his father said, "Dis is where da stove was. Here da table. Food in a wall here. Here we slept." As his father grew older, every time he passed the area he'd say, "There's where I want to be buried, Charles."

The last time Charles came to see him, his father said from his sickbed, "Where do I want to be buried?"

"You shouldn't be thinking such things. You're a strong man. You have years ahead of you."

"Naw, I'm done. I feel done. I'm past the Bible age. I want to be buried." He winked. "Why not? Everybody has to. I'm tired of the days, the days, the days. I want to be happy. I want to die and sleep forever. Now. Where do I—"

"Dad, this sort of attitude—"

"*Ach!* Attitude! Do you hear what I'm saying, boy? Now. Where do I want to be buried?"

"You used to say where your shack was."

"Good! You're right! I do. And if you got anything to say about it, Charles, you'll see it's there, *ja?*"

"Mother's not buried there."

"Ah, well, your ma wanted better tings, she always did, God bless her. I don't. I want what I want. If there's a heaven, I'll meet her in heaven, and if not—" He threw up his hands. "Our bones ain't going to do anything in the ground together, especially locked up in steel boxes." He winked again.

Charles was about to say these weren't light matters.

"Shush!" his father commanded, and lay back and closed his eyes and said in a weak voice, "I've spoke my piece."

Charles had started out of the room, when his father said, "And I don't want to be buried in no steel box! I want a wood one!"

From the low ground of the homesteading shack, looking across the creek to the north and the east, the plain stretched off in golds and grays and blues to the line of the horizon; to the west, he could see the buildings of Mahomet and the road to the farm. A prairie willow grew a ways downstream, and standing closer was an oak his father had planted, nearly bare now, with large mismatched limbs bent by prevailing winds, and a brown-gold layer of leaves around its base.

Charles walked into the depression, to the place where his father had said, "Here we slept," and lifted the iron bar with one hand and drove it into the ground.

God forgive me if I'm doing the wrong thing, he thought.

He went to the barn, picked up an armful of feed sacks, his metal tape, a tiling spade and a shovel, and came back to the gravesite. Using the bar as a center point, he measured the grave's dimensions, cut its outline into the sod with the tiling spade, moved the bar, which he'd need for rocks, and spread feed sacks over the weeds to hold the spaded earth. He began to dig. When he reached a depth of three feet, the sun started to set. There was the aroma of a storm in the air, and the temperature had dropped ten degrees. He could see the gray vapor of his breath as he worked. He looked up at the sky—greenish blue, banded with yellow ribs of cirro-cumulus that were tinged pink and were bending toward the horizon as though being bent by the sun—and thought, Surely it will snow tomorrow.

He stepped the spade into the bottom of the grave and got up on ground level, went to the creek, lay in the grass at its edge, leaned and drank his fill, then removed his cap and plunged his head in up to his shoulders, blowing air out his nose, came up for a breath, plunged his head in again, and shook it and scratched at his scalp to get it clean.

He came up and pressed the water out of his hair and wiped his face with the scrap of handkerchief, and just as he stood there, with his shirt soaked to below his shoulder blades, the atmosphere around him changed. The air darkened and a strong wind tore most of the remaining leaves from the oak and carried them across the creek, and a sheet of blowing dust filmed his eyes. He turned his back to the wind and blinked his eyes clear.

Why did he care for this godforsaken country so much? He turned again, and though he felt like running as he had when he was a boy, he walked up to the house at his usual pace, jumped onto the porch, and was in the parlor's warmth.

Supper was cooking. It was mutton stew—one of the dinners his mother made with such regularity when he was a boy he could tell a mile from the house what day it was.

"Charles?" Augustina's voice came from the kitchen.

"Me."

She walked into the parlor, her face flushed from the stove, and he saw that she'd tidied her hair and changed into a different dress.

"Will there be a storm?" she asked.

"It feels it."

"A freeze?"

"Perhaps."

"You aren't sweating in this weather."

"I washed."

"Your eyes look bad."

"The dust."

"You're worn out. Why don't you rest before supper? I've made up the bed in your room."

"I believe I will rest," he said, and started up the stairs. "Oh. I'll need a lot of clean rags, a sponge if we have one, some clean sheets, towels, the rose water, and a needle and thread, probably. Why don't you just leave out your sewing basket. Also, lay out Dad's best suit."

She nodded, and then bowed her head, as if she'd forgotten why he was here.

His room was nearly bare. There was a bed, a dresser, and a straight-backed chair shoved against the wall beside the bed. A picture of the Sacred Heart (with palm leaves plaited into the shape of pine cones dangling over its frame) hung from an eightpenny nail above the bed. He went to the window and listened. A pane was loose, and the high, shifting wind was making it hum in nearly perfect fourths: F#, B, F#, B, baaaa, beee, baaaa, beee, it kept repeating an octave above C, in the tenor range. He hummed a low D and held it while the pane passed through its pair of notes several times. How he'd love to be able to afford a good pipe organ for the church in Mahomet!

It was nearly dark, but when he lifted the curtain he could see the gravesite, the mound of dirt, the upright iron bar, the blue of the grass and the outbuildings, the blue-black of Sand Grass Creek. This room had been his father's favorite, and when Charles was young his father used any excuse to come upstairs and talk to him here; and from the day Charles's mother died until just a few months ago, when his father's final illness confined him downstairs, he'd slept here. Charles let the curtain fall.

He went to the closet, opened the door, and was surrounded by a smell of cedar and camphor balls. Who'd put the camphor in a cedar-lined closet? The smell of it and the needlessness of it here gave him a wash of the nausea he'd felt on the treadle of the train. When he was a child, he used to sit in the closet with the door closed, and pretend he was on needle-blanketed ground with heavy boughs above him, in the green center of a forest, or a forest as he imagined one; he'd never seen a real forest in his life, not to this day. And sitting in the closet, he visualized the walls of his bedroom around him, and around his bedroom the house, and around that the farmyard, the shape of the creek around the fields, the shape of the county around the creek, and around that the rectangle of North Dakota, at the center of North America, and felt enclosed in layers of protection, invulnerable—marginalia of a boyhood now gone from him beyond regret.

Why was it that he so seldom thought of his past?

He never thought of it. And why, when he thought of himself in this room as a child or a young man, could he picture himself only from the chest down, as though he'd had no face? Because there was never a mirror in the room? He sometimes fell asleep in the closet and slept through the night, and it was here he'd first committed the boyhood sin he was so ashamed of, God forgive. "Jackup," a classmate in the third or fourth grade had misnamed it, and he'd had an image of the big steel screw jacks under the granary, and then he'd received from the classmate, in the school pony stable, a demonstration.

Clothes covers made of chintz, like old cloaks, were draped over groups of garments hung from the closet rod. He opened one out. There were dresses inside—his mother's, from the dark colors and cut of them—and behind the dresses he saw the shoulders of a man's coat. He unhooked the hanger, pulled the coat out, and lifted it open by a lapel. There were trousers with it. The label over the breast pocket read "L. J. Frantz, Fargo."

It was his high-school graduation suit. His father had

taken him on the train to Fargo to buy it, had made an occasion of the day, had embarrassed Charles by telling the clerks and old man Frantz that his son was a high-school graduate, and had picked out the suit himself. It was black, of a heavy hopsack weave, and its cut, Charles had thought then, was old-mannish and European, and he'd hated it. Had he worn it a dozen times? A half dozen, maybe. How decent disrespect seemed to him then.

He removed the jacket from the hanger and tried it on. It fit so perfectly it could have been tailored for him. He took it off, hung it over the chair back, took off his overalls, and pulled on the pants. They fit nearly as well, but were big at the waist. The suit he'd brought, his only suit, was tan-colored and baggy on him, and he decided to wear this for the burial. He lifted the upper mattress, held it aloft with his head, smoothed the trousers over the bottom mattress, and lowered the upper mattress down on them. He went across the room in his undershorts and closed the closet door.

He pulled open the top drawer of the dresser. Inside were mismatched stockings heavily darned, a bronze bust of the Virgin, a white statuette of an elephant that tasted, he knew, like alum; arrowheads, a sachet, a slide rule, a screwdriver, and a clump of tangled rosaries. He took out a wallet-sized notebook with a cover of stiff brown paperboard and thumbed through it. Poems, mostly of the self-improvement sort, were copied in the book in Augustina's correct and girlish hand—"The Psalm of Life," "Aim High," "Daughter, Don't Let Mother Do It!"—along with inspirational quotes from Abraham Lincoln.

Following the quotes and poems were several pages, which must have been dictated, entitled "Edicot."

Stopping to look in shop windows is against the rule of street edicot.

To eat anything on the street is a sign of bad breeding.

A lady must recognize a gentleman by bowing before he can acknowledge any acquaintance with her.

And farther on:

*In entering a carriage be careful that your back is toward
the seat you are to occupy.*

*If there be a step for entering the carriage land on it
with your left foot, or there are two steps put right
foot on the first and left foot on the next in order that
you may enter the carriage with right foot.*

*Sink easily into the seat and if you are to sit on the
other side reverse the action.*

*The seat facing the horses is the seat of honor and
should be given to the eldest lady.*

What was this from?

Charles flipped the pages backward and saw, on the inside of the front cover, Augustina's signature, and after it
an address in Chicago. Their father sent her to an academy
and finishing school when she was sixteen, but Charles
couldn't remember, now, a time when Augustina was away
from the farm. He did remember stories about her and
her difficulties in the city; how she was terrified of the
crowds, the forward men, the trolley cars and the noise,
and especially the lake—the big lake she couldn't see the
other side of. She kept to her room, and took sick often,
and didn't finish out the year.

He dropped the notebook into the drawer and closed
it. What was he doing while Augustina was away? If she
was sixteen, he would be what? Eleven? Twelve? All he
could really remember from most of his boyhood was
working here in the fields, and the changes of season—as
though his past were composed of only four memories:
the work in the spring, the work in the summer, the work
in the fall, and in the winter little work, except tending
to the stock and digging out after blizzards. Details were
heaped within the walls of those divisions, and he'd
never bothered to look back on the details again.

He realized he couldn't remember when Augustina
was away because he was also away then. His father had
sent him to a Benedictine abbey west of Bismarck for the
seventh and eighth grades; he wanted him to have a better education than the country school could provide before he entered high school—for he was determined that

Charles finish high school—and also hoped that the life of
the abbey would appeal to Charles enough to interest him
in the priesthood. Was his father hurt that he'd asked to
leave the abbey after his second year? Of course. The mind
could see better backward than what was at hand.

He'd learned his Latin fairly well. All of the teachers
were Benedictine priests and his Latin teacher, the only
teacher he liked or really remembered, a flashy Irishman
who knew seven languages, referred to him as *Der Alte*,
because he was so formal and solemn-faced even then. It
wasn't that he disliked the abbey; he simply knew from
the beginning that he'd never become a priest.

He went to the bed and lay on top of the covers, drew
the comforter at the footboard up to his chin, willed himself to be awake in one hour, and fell asleep.

*

When he woke he rolled in bed and reached for his wife
and realized where he was. He took his pocket watch from
his overalls on the chair; it was eight o'clock. He dressed
and went downstairs, and saw that Augustina had laid out
the articles he'd asked for on the oak table.

After supper he said to her, "You'd best go to your room
now."

She took up a kerosene lamp and went to the foot of
the stairs. "I'm going to write Lucy and her husband," she
said. "I think they might like living here."

"I'm sure they would."

"And it was good of you to think of Clarence. I won't
worry about him now. I won't worry about the farm. I
feel I've been delivered from worry."

"I'm glad."

"God bless you, Charles. I'm so grateful to you, I—" She
turned away and went up the stairs. He followed her
footsteps after she was out of sight and realized, as she
passed his room, that he could hear, from where he stood,
the two notes of the windowpane, and wondered if she'd
marry Clarence. He turned up the lamp on the table, went
into the kitchen to the sink pump, pumped a basinful
of water, and brought the basin in to the table. He pushed

everything aside and laid down a thickness of sheets, went to his father's room, and put his hand on the knob. He'd never prepared a corpse.

He opened the door. The room had a warm, rank, sweetish-foul gastric smell, and he waited inside the doorway until he became acclimated to it, then drew the sheet away and was startled to see the silver dollars. As he moved around the bed, the floorboards groaning under him, he pulled the lower sheet from the mattress, folded it over the sheet already covering his father's body, and worked his arms under his father's back and thighs. He lifted and went backward, off-balance, the silver dollars crashing to the floor, and struck the bureau with his rear end and made its legs grate. A silver dollar circling on its rim chattered to a stop. He'd braced himself for a hundred and fifty pounds, his father's weight, but at this moment he couldn't weigh more than eighty. His body was as stony, dehumanized, and rigid as bone. Charles carried him to the table and laid him on the thickness of sheets there.

He sloshed a bar of soap in the basin of water and washed his father's hair and beard with the sponge. He held a cloth over his index finger, dampened it, and wiped the features of his father's face, where light from the lamp lay yellow-gold and remembered him saying, "I'm not pretty, but it's me, so I guess I've got to like it, and I do." Charles went to the stairs, took the straight razor from the breast pocket of his suit coat, hearing F#, B, F#, B, and placed his foot on the second tread of the stairs and stropped the razor across his overall thigh.

He rubbed his fingers over the cake of soap and moved them ahead of the razor as he shaved the stubble grown in around his father's beard. Sweat was falling from his face in gray splashes on the sheet, and his intestines trembled and gave out a groan. He was grateful for the notes of the windowpane and concentrated on them until he became abstracted from his work.

Clarence carrying o'clock twelve.

He emptied the washbasin in the kitchen and refilled it, then drew the sheet away from his father's chest. He drew the sheet down farther, below his stomach, which was swollen and discolored, and washed it to the line of metallic-gray pubic hair. The yellow-gold on his father's face trembled and faded, his features went brown, then orange, and then the wick recovered and the lamp burned evenly again over a face no longer a face, but a skin of chrysoprase about a skull. Charles laid a towel across his chest and stomach to absorb the moisture of washing, and removed the sheet completely. It was the first time he'd seen his father's genitals.

He washed his arms and hands, his legs and feet, then cleaned his nails with a pocketknife. He rubbed rose water over his body, and then folded a clean towel, placed it beside his head, his mind moving F# to B and D, and turned him face down. The backs of his arms and thighs, his shoulders and his buttocks, were flattened and plum-colored, and his rectum was plugged with a cloth. Charles washed his back and rubbed it with rose water and turned him again.

He got the clothes Augustina had laid out and worked the trousers up his father's legs to his waist and then put on his stockings and shoes. His father's arms, bony and blue, were so rigid against his sides Charles knew that, without help, he couldn't put on the shirt and coat. It might be possible to pull them up his arms, but his skin, which was parchmentlike to the touch, slid so easily over his flesh Charles was afraid it would tear. He took a pair of scissors from Augustina's sewing basket and cut off the sleeves of the shirt, cut through the back of the collar and along the side and shoulder seams, and removed the back panel. He tied the tie around his own neck, loosened the knot and removed it, and then laid the shirt front over his father's chest and slipped the tie underneath his head, around his head, and down to his throat, tucked the tie under the shirt collar, and used it to draw the collar tight.

Then he took the coat and began to rip it up the back, at the center seam, but the sound was so amplified in the silent house he murmured a prayer and used the scissors to cut the seam up to the collar. He stopped there. From the center seam, at shoulder-blade level, he cut across the back of the coat to the right sleeve and down the seam of the sleeve through the cuff; he did the same to the other sleeve and opened the coat out. He slipped the collar under his father's head and buttoned the front of the coat. He had to remove, at the side seams, the two panels of the back, which made too much material to work with. He tucked the sleeve edges between his father's arms and sides, tucked the top of the coat under his shoulders, folded the towel beside his head so that a clean side was out, and turned him face down again. He drew the sleeve edges and coat sides through, up to each armpit, laid the panels he'd removed in place, and then took needle and thread and sewed up the coat.

He turned him once more, unbuttoned the coat, sewed the sides of the shirt to its lining, and buttoned it up again. He put the razor back in his suit, removed a comb from the breast pocket, and combed his father's hair and beard. He took the best sheet Augustina had left out and went into the bedroom and spread it over the bed. He lifted the window shade. The woodshed and the weeds beyond were silver-blue, the weeds swaying with the wind in the moonlight, and from the window he could see, far off to the left, the mound of dirt and the upright bar. He drew the shade. He carried his father into the room, laid him down, and folded the clean sheet over him. He found the silver dollars—one beside a chair leg, one under the bed—and put them in the change purse in the bureau. He crossed himself at the front and closed the door.

He washed the table, gathered the sheets and towels up, took them into the kitchen and washed them in the sink, and went into a utility porch off the kitchen and hung them on clotheslines, then returned to the parlor, turned the lamp low, and took it with him up the stairs. There was a line of light under Augustina's door, and he remembered that she read at night, sometimes all through the night, until exhaustion overtook her. Inside his own room, something was wrong; the bedcovers had been straightened, and the jacket was missing from the chair. He opened the closet door. Augustina had hung it up. He set the lamp down on the dresser, glanced behind him, and then drew open the dresser drawer and took out Augustina's notebook. What was there about this that unsettled him so?

Never open your napkin entirely but let it lay on your lap partway folded.

To blow soup to cool it or pouring out tea or coffee

for same purpose shows ill-breeding and is never seen in society.

Many of the entries were not in Augustina's usual hand, were ragged or wholly illegible, as though she'd been forced to take dictation too fast, or was under mental strain, and he wondered what all she'd gone through during that year. He felt eyes on him from the doorway and turned. Nobody was there. Augustina must have seen him with the notebook and stepped back in the hall, out of sight, to keep from embarrassing him. He dropped the notebook into the drawer, closed it, and cleared his throat. He could feel a presence just outside the door and turned, waiting for Augustina.

Then the presence moved into the room.

He stepped back and struck the dresser, and lamplight rocked in wobbling lines over the walls. The atmosphere of the room had changed as suddenly as the weather; it was cooler and less claustrophobic. The presence moved past him to the window; he'd summoned his boyhood self to this room by remembering, earlier, so much of his past here, that was it. The presence was so tangible he could even gauge its height at the window, just above the second mullion, and it wasn't his height as a young man. It was the height of his father. It turned a more powerful side in his direction.

"Ah!" he cried. He grabbed the lamp and hurried into the hall and saw Augustina in a nightgown, silhouetted in the door to her room, her hair undone and down to her waist.

"Charles?"

He couldn't speak.

"Charles?"

"Water," he said, and felt as if not he but somebody else, a fugitive inside him with a hand at his throat, had spoken.

"What is it, Charles? I heard you talking."

"Need some water."

"Are you all right?"

"Yes."

"You're sure?"

"Yes."

He started down the stairs, and her door closed. At the foot of the stairs he stopped, realizing how he'd react if any of his children came to him in the night and told him they'd felt something similar; he'd say it was foolishness, their imagination, and tell them to go back to bed. He climbed the stairs, entered his room, and went to the window. The air was as mellow and cleansed as summer air after a rain. It was the alcohol, the sleeplessness, his nerves, and handling his father's body that had affected his mind to such a point. How many times had he traced its shape while he washed and rubbed him with rose water? He hummed the D to harmonize with the pane, nearly noiselessly this time, slipped a suspender off his shoulder, and turned to the chair.

The presence was now prone on his bed. He went to the bed and held the lamp high. There was no indentation in the covers. He passed his hand over the mattress and felt nothing but bedcovers and mattress, but when he drew back he could sense somebody there. He'd heard that the spirits of certain people, troubled or restless people, sometimes wandered searching until the detail troubling them was taken care of, or their restlessness met with affection and prayer. Was it right to bury his father so far from his mother? Should he wait for a priest?

He took a rosary from the dresser drawer and went down the stairs to his father's room. He put the lamp on the bureau, closed the door, and went over and opened the window wide. The out-buildings and the weeds beyond were the same shade of blue, but it was colder now, and he could feel dew falling through the night air. He set a chair beside the bed, turned to blow out the lamp, and saw his father's missal on the bureau. He picked it up and a square of paper adhering to its back dropped onto the bureau top. The paper was folded several times and had been handled so much it was oil-saturated and had the feel of old cloth. Charles unfolded it with care, seeing that most of the creases were worn through and parting, and opened it to the dim light. It was dated three years ago and was written in German, in laboriously formed old-fashioned script, and Charles saw that it was from his son.

Greetings, Dearest Grandfather!
I send you this on the occasion of your seventy-fifth birthday to let you know you have my admiration and fondest wishes. A seventy-fifth birthday is a great

*event and needs a grand celebration. Please enjoy
the day! You are many times in my thoughts here
at the university, where I'm working my hardest to
get as fine an education as I can, and I hope this
letter will let you see that I've learned more than
a little! God bless you, dearest Grandfather, and I
send you once again my greetings, my love, and
all my warm thoughts to you.*

> *Your Grandson,*
> *Martin*

Charles slipped the letter into the missal. He felt chastened by Martin, and was ashamed that he himself had never been as open and affectionate to his father. He blew out the lamp. He sat in the chair and pulled it closer to the bed and, when his eyes became accustomed to the darkness, realized he could see, visible through the sheet against the moonlight, the dark shape of his father's body, and thought, *Have I displeased you, Dad? Should I have shown more filial love? Am I wrong to bury you here? Would you like a priest and a Requiem? Is there a way you can let me know what you want? Should I pray now or just sit beside you? Do you want me to sit with you here until morning?*

He tried to say the Rosary but couldn't and put it aside. He began his boyhood bedtime prayers, which he hadn't said since he left this house and which once had a soporific effect on him equal to ether, and before he was halfway through them woke to see sunlight shining in the open window.

There was a sound of metal wheels spanging over gravel and a horizontal pole passed outside, and then the implement to which the pole was attached, a hayrake, rolled into view. Charles got up and ran out on the porch. Blue-gray mist rose from the weeds and grass like smoke from an extinguished fire, and a man in gray coveralls, Sy Rolfe, a young fellow Martin's age, the son of the neighboring farmer, was pulling the hayrake through the yard by hand. Charles ran out and took hold of a wheel. Sy pulled hard on the pole, swayed it from side to side, jerked it, and then said, "Now what the—" and turned. His eyes were the luminous, unsuspecting blue of youth.

He said, "Oh. Mr. Neumiller. I wasn't sure you'd got in. Hi. I'm sorry about your dad."

"What are you doing?"

"Pa told me to come and get this."

"Is it yours?"

"No."

"Then, why?"

"Pa said your pa owes us for seed oats from five years back that Clarence got, or something. Pa figured they was worth about this much, er—" Sy raised and lowered the pole of the rake as though measuring its weight in money.

"Take it back where you got it," Charles said.

"But Pa said I was to come home with it."

"Tell your father he can make claims on the estate, if he has any, through the lawyer in town when the estate's being settled. There'll be no more of this. Now, take it back."

Charles released his grip on the wheel and Sy rolled the rake backward, close to the tool shed, let its pole drop, and went up the lane toward the road, glancing around at Charles as though his back got more vulnerable with each step. The mist lay in coiling banks that came to his elbows, and for long stretches his legs couldn't be seen; he'd walk a ways and then appear to glide to the next break in the mist, then walk on ground again. On the highway he moved above a gray-blue sea. Charles went out to Sand Grass Creek, where weeds were silvered with dew and dripping, and began digging again.

He finished the grave at nine o'clock. The mist was gone. He brought ropes and the coffin lid from the barn, laid the lid over feed sacks on top of the mound of dirt, concealed the ropes under it, and then got the coffin (the smell of tar was hardly noticeable in it) and carried it to the front porch. He went to the river beside the oak, pulled off his shirt and washed himself, and then removed his shoes and let his feet soak in the cold water as he took out a sack of tobacco and a package of papers, and had a cigarette for the first time in two days. He went to the house and washed again at the kitchen sink, a more thorough washing with soap, and then shaved, told Augustina he wouldn't have breakfast, and went upstairs and changed into the black suit. He knelt at the bed and prayed for the peace and repose of his father's soul, and asked forgiveness for himself if he'd done anything amiss.

*

Clarence arrived from town at ten-thirty, wearing a jacket and bow tie with his worn trousers, and he and Charles carried the coffin into the parlor and placed it on the table. Charles went into his father's room and folded back the sheet and saw that both of his father's eyes were open and bulging in their sockets. Clarence came into the room and stared down at the body, wide-eyed, shaking his head as though about to turn and leave, and then he sighed and his smaller eye wobbled with emotion. He looked at Charles, glanced over his shoulder to the parlor, where Augustina was waiting, and eased the door shut with his hip. "Charles," he said, and pulled a pint of unopened whiskey from his pocket. "Do you mind?" He gestured toward the body with his chin. "You know, if I sort of give him this?"

"No."

Clarence slipped the bottle into a pocket of the sewn-together suit coat, folded the flap closed, and patted the pocket. "Who knows, Charles?" he said. "Who really knows? The Indians used to do it."

"It might have pleased him."

Clarence opened the door, Charles rolled the sheet into a tight roll on one side of his father, Clarence rolled it into a tight roll on the other, and then they lifted. "He's so light!" Clarence whispered. And Charles was astonished to see that his father's limbs were now as limp and slack as if he were sleeping. They carried the body to the parlor and lowered it into the coffin, and Charles unrolled the sheet, drawing it into gathers, and arranged the gathers along the base of the coffin and around his father's sides and head. He'd built the coffin small, only two feet wide by five feet eight inches long, and still his father looked dwarfed by it, so diminished and childlike that Charles had the feeling he was retreating from the three of them in front of their eyes.

Charles went into the bedroom, took the missal from

the bureau, and gave it to Augustina. Her face was ashen, with blotches of red, and she'd removed her thick glasses to dry her eyes, or to keep from seeing too clearly this representation, this husk of their father.

"Clarence," Charles said, and went to the head of the coffin, facing down its length, and nodded for Clarence to go to the foot.

"Didn't you tell me it was to be at noon?"

"We're ready. I'd rather it was done." They were both whispering.

"Whatever you say."

Clarence took the foot of the coffin by the hardwood handles, Charles the head; they lifted; Augustina opened the screen door, and their heavy shoes scraped over the boards of the porch as the weight of the coffin swayed between them. Clarence held the foot higher as Charles came down the steps, and Charles saw a wet line running down his shaved cheek. Clarence took another hold and turned, facing forward, and they went around the house, past the woodshed and the garden, and walked through thick weeds; and the brush and lateral sweep of the weeds across the coffin filled Charles with a sudden hope, the nameless emotion he'd felt on the train, and then he looked down at his father's face.

They set the coffin beside the open grave. Charles took the missal from Augustina, unable to look at her, and read the last rites at the grave in Latin. He sang *"Requiem aeternam dona ei, Domine"* and Augustina and Clarence gave the responses. He placed the missal beside his father's right hand and saw that his forehead and nose and beard were dusted with pollen. The shadow of Charles's head across his body looked deformed, and he reached up and discovered he was wearing a cap. He removed it and was amazed; had he actually been wearing this striped work cap with his suit? And the shredded strip of handkerchief was still around his thumb.

He stood, his thigh and chest muscles trembling, and began to sing, from the Benediction after Mass, *"Tantum ergo Sacramentum."* His voice found its natural placement and opened in deep tones, his breath appearing in columns of different lengths in front of his lips, and after *"Tantum ergo"* he started with hardly a pause his favorite song from Benediction, the slower, more sedate, more minor *"O*

salutaris Hostia, Quae coeli pandis ostium." And he could
see the censer at Benediction swinging from its chains,
myrrh burning on charcoal, the ciborium beside the tabernacle, beside that the sunburst of the monstrance, which
suddenly sent its rays through the walls and ceiling as his
voice rose, and then there were arched windows letting
in light, then arches of pure light, and he was lifted into
the center of his voice, bodiless, and went gliding down
the arches and emerged over a field of ripe wheat, limitlessly gold under the sun, and the sun became an entrance
his voice passed through.

"Amen."

Charles stared at the coffin lid, at the crucifix, the oval
with his father's name countersunk into it, at the nails along
the lid, each with its black shadow, at the hammer beside
the lid, and felt such an uncharacteristic and malevolent
bitterness that he had to lock his knees to feel his legs
beneath him. He wanted to see lightning across the entire
sky, a violent storm, falling snow, or a dove burst from
his father's breast and fly off from the coffin—some sign
that his father's life and good deeds had not gone un-
noticed on earth, not for his father's sake or his own sake,
but so his sons and daughters would always feel he believed in a just and reasonable God. He replaced his cap,
got the lid and laid it over the coffin, picked the hammer
up, and went down on one knee and drove the first nail
home with a single blow. Augustina touched his shoulder,
and Clarence said, "Wait." Charles looked up, and then to
where Clarence and Augustina were looking, and saw, in
the direction of the farms to the north and the east, and
in a ragged procession along the road from town, dark
shapes, mourners in black clothes, grownups and children
moving over the plain, coming to pay their last respects
to his father.

2

❦

NEW YEAR

He'd dreamed he'd been sleeping in the catacombs, those cold and nitrous tombs he'd heard of only out of history books and from nuns' lips. The shuffling of a pair of slippers traced a tangle of paths and passageways through his sleep, the sound of an object being dropped struck deep into a dream and turned up as a spatula, and somebody in the kitchen (who?), whispering to Dinah in a banjo tune, mingled with the hiss of a kettle making steam, had washed out a great cave, the echoing hollow where he now lay. There was a cold crown around his ears and forehead and a frosty network stiffening his nostrils, and he felt, at the outline of himself, a heavy and constricting, wrinkled skin. And then he remembered that he hadn't undressed.

There was a rumble of a cookstove grate as coals were shaken down, and he saw a pattern of cracks, as intricate as in shattered ice, across the leather back of the horsehair sofa, and January 1, 1936, rose above a horizon in his mind. It could mark the beginning of a new life with the new year. Oh, let it, he thought, and was seized by a trembling sigh and half yawn. He covered his head with the quilt. Until Alpha came downstairs, the world wouldn't know he was awake. He'd be a mole if her brother or parents appeared, hibernating under silver webbing in a niche of the cave. He'd be— Last night, here in the Jones house, he'd asked Alpha to be his wife.

This mole is smiling in his burrow with a star-shaped nose of gold, Martin Neumiller his name. He started out yesterday, the sky violet-blue against the white of the plain, the air so still and brilliant that trees and buildings seemed sculptured out of its iciness, and then on his way to Wim-

56

bledon to get Alpha a gift, a box of chocolates, snowflakes started drifting out of the violet, and then a wind hit, rocking the car on its springs, and by the time he pulled into their yard, a distance of three and a half miles, the white stuff was up to the axle hubs of the Model A.

The blizzard swirled away the drifted surface of the countryside and wrapped the house in blackness, while the clock on the piano chimed and showed twelve noon and the windmill in the barnyard spun in the rising wind like a corrective gear. Nobody dared to go out and shut it off. A woman on the other side of Wimbledon, a Mrs. Lundby, left for her barn last year in a similar storm and lost her way and was found twenty paces from her back door, frozen to death. So the windmill clattered and shrieked in the distance, its lifter banging like a mallet on tin, and Ed Jones cursed it, and murmured, "That barnyard will be a skating rink the rest of the winter, folks, you can bet your ass on that."

The kerosene lamps were lit, split railroad ties brought in from the back porch—along with two lumps of coal, precious coal—the potbellied stove in the front room was fired up, and blankets and rugs were draped over the doors and windows, where the wind hit and billowed them.

"We're in a tent," Alpha's little brother, Lionell, cried. "We're living in a tent!"

"Thank your lucky stars we're not," Mrs. Jones said. She opened the door of the potbellied stove and pulled up a rocker and sat staring in at the flames.

Alpha chorded a slow hymn on the piano and then swiveled around and wrung her fingers. *So cold!*

"We've got a few dozen storm windows under a porch somewhere," Ed Jones said. And then he unblocked the fireplace, and in a few minutes a shuddering blaze rose above his hard-bitten profile with its big hooked nose. He sat on a couch in front of the fire with his legs apart, rubbing his hands and saying, "Ah! Ah, God! Ah!" And once when he and Martin were alone in the room, he leaned over and whispered, "Say, boy, doesn't that warm up your balls?"

He stared at Martin as though he expected a direct reply. His sea-green eyes, sunk in deep sockets, overhung by heavy eyebrows that flared up at the ends, as gleaming and fierce as a bird of prey's, were filled with a fulminating look Martin could never fathom: anger? deviltry? anguish?

Jones had a square jaw of the English sort and lips so thin all you noticed of them were the two peaks of red at their center. It was his eyes; they seemed brimming with an incendiary knowledge that had no outlet, and with the same fulminating look in them, he could say, "Martin, God love you, you're one of the finest young fellows hereabouts." Or, about a milch cow that bedeviled his wife when he wasn't in the barn to supervise. "Someday I'm going to take that muley bitch by the tail and pull her tits out her eardrums."

Now Jones went from the fire to his bedroom and emerged in a suit and tie and highly polished shoes, trailing a smoky and medicinal smell of whiskey, and sat in his chair as if in state. He was five feet six, or less, and Martin, who was studying history in college, couldn't help thinking of him as Napoleonic. His piercing stare and the emanations that came from him and kept Martin silent gave Jones a power over people he seemed afraid of. He kept retreating into the bedroom for surreptitious nips, growing more glassy-eyed, aromatic, and withdrawn, and spent the afternoon telling God, in variations of His name, what He was doing to the livestock and wildlife with His storm. While Martin, a wordless subject in this court, stared at the fireplace, then at the horsehair sofa where Lionell lay with glazed eyes sucking his thumb, and thought, How will I get home? How will I get to church tomorrow? It's a feast day. It's a holy day of obligation, dear Lord.

After one of Jones's trips to the bedroom, he pulled a silver hip flask out and held it in his lap. "The wife and daughter got me this," he said. "Although neither of them wants me to drink. What do you think of that?"

Martin shrugged.

"I think it was an act of trickery on their part. Or else trust. I once had a flask exactly like this, but I gave it away, or loaned it to a friend, or threw it in a hole in the ground—however you care to look at it. Tergiversationatory irrationable man." Jones winked at Martin. "So the two gals got me this." He revolved the flask in his hands, and his hands and reflections of his hands, joined at the fingertips, slid around its silver curves with his face framed between. He tipped the flask toward Martin. "Some virtues of the earth, boy?"

Martin shook his head.

"Oh, come on. It'll make you feel smart."

"I'd rather not."

"Sprinkle some on your breath. Have a whiff of it."

Martin managed a smile.

"Oh, so you're going to try to kiss and woo the daughter again, huh?"

Martin blushed.

Jones was usually attentive to Martin's moods, but when there was no letup in the blizzard, it was Mrs. Jones who finaly spoke: "It's no use trying to drive in this weather, Martin. The couch will be yours tonight." She was at the cookstove fixing supper and kept her back to him as she said it, and Alpha, who was in the kitchen helping, turned and winked at him.

Then the evening meal, a traditional Scandinavian holiday feast, with meatballs and boiled potatoes, creamed corn, fruit soup and *lefse,* and for dessert, *fløte grøt,* sweet cream cooked with a little rice and a little sugar until the cream formed liquid butter on its top; and there were sugar cookies and *julekake* and rosettes and *krumkake* and *fattigmann,* plus a main course of *lutefisk,* which Martin wouldn't touch; the fish was soaked in lye until it turned translucent and rubbery, and he'd heard that wholesalers in the city stacked slabs of it like kindling outside their shops and then dogs came along and yellowed it. After the dishes were done and Lionell was in bed, the adults sat around the table and talked, and Mrs. Jones permitted herself to play a few hands of euchre and hearts, since it was a holiday and money wasn't involved, and then it was twelve o'clock.

They shook hands around and wished one another a happy New Year.

Mr. and Mrs. Jones went off to bed.

Then the fire. In front of it on the braided rug, their faces fevered with its heat. Popcorn and divinity in bowls between them. Their fingertips touching. The intonations, the animal-like tones, the lamentation of the blizzard outside, as though the plain were mourning until the human race was no more. The two of them, privileged beings, spared and set down on a warmed island below the wide-wasting malignancy of it. Alone. On the oval of the braided rug, the O of love with them in its center.

Sinking through echoing silence toward the light of the world, and then the question, alive in him for two years, rising of its own accord.

"If you ever asked," Alpha said, "I knew it would be tonight."

"How?"

"I just did."

"You mean you've—" Martin swallowed and his necktie climbed his swollen gorge.

Alpha put her fingers to his class ring, which she wore, wound with yarn, on her right hand, and turned its insignia straight.

"I'm really afraid," Martin said.

"I know. I've been afraid, too."

"What of?"

"Me. You. The way everybody's been." Alpha glanced toward her parents' bedroom. "What makes a man afraid?"

"Everything. What you?"

"I'm not, really, now that you asked."

"Then, will—" It was impossible for him to repeat it. The wind rose and the flames swayed toward the left.

"Yes," she whispered.

Or did he imagine it? Mrs. Jones walked into the room just then, wearing a nightgown and a robe, and a dark shawl over her shoulders. "Alpha," she whispered. "It's past time you were in bed." And then she held a quilt toward Martin. "Here," she said. "This is yours."

Alpha's footsteps went retreating up the stairs.

Mrs. Jones stood at the fireplace, chafing her upper arms and murmuring to the flames, and pulled her shawl closer around her; she was tall and frail and had a yellowish tinge to her skin, and was often ill, or lying down to rest in order to keep from becoming ill, or to recover from a recent illness. Martin wasn't sure of the nature of her complaint, since it was referred to in such vague terms, but assumed it was feminine. Even her voice was weak, high and adenoidal, with a gasping asthmatic whine to it, but she radiated such righteousness and strength of moral character he always forgot her physical frailties and felt she was about to strike him for all the shameful things he'd done.

She began laying more logs on the fire, ignoring his offers to help, and saying, "Shoo! Shoo!" to him in a tone that was almost playful and, for some reason, made him blush. Then she stood with her back to the flames, facing him, and opened her palms at her sides to catch the heat.

He couldn't see, from the sofa, the expression on her face, and it was impossible to know if she'd heard.

"I sleep light," she said, and left the room.

The floorboards above him groaned and creaked and gave out cracking sounds in the cold, and he tried to visualize Alpha above him, and when he did, so vividly, tried not to. He said three Hail Marys. His boyhood prayers, so familiar they no longer seemed constructed of language, went flying through his thoughts with the speed of an express. He discovered that there were five buttons on his shirt and ran his fingers down them, gripping each as he said a Hail Mary, and then ran his fingers up them—a decade of the Rosary—and touched his Adam's apple for an Our Father.

What did Alpha do, moving around up there for such an eternal length of time, before she even got under the covers? Then there was a sound of springs as she settled into bed and that was worse. Her legs quicksilvery as moonlight entangled with sheets. He lost track of the times he'd touched his Adam's apple and rolled on his side and said an Act of Contrition so complicated with fleshy imagery it wouldn't have got him beyond the walls. The fire in the potbellied stove was burned down and its bulging sides no longer gave off a glow; the fireplace wasn't intended to heat the house in this sort of weather (indeed, it seemed to be sucking up what warmth there was), and with the sudden absence of human sounds and movements, a deeper chill spread through the house.

Had Alpha said yes, or was it the wind and the fire? Her hand said yes, her fingertips touching his ring; the angle of her head, bowed so that her dark hair concealed her features, showing only her high brow bronzed by the fire; the fold of her legs below her dress, her bare feet, her tipped shoes lying beside them—all this said *Yes, yes,* but did she? Alpha and Martin Neumiller. The names sounded indivisible on his tongue, but if she said yes, if they were to be married and not merely speculate in a romantic way about a future married state, as they had, then it would be difficult for them both from now on. Their mothers never spoke and didn't get along, which was a common enough predicament among married couples, perhaps, but in this landlocked state of so few people it was almost unheard of for neighbors not to talk, no matter the quirks of personality or grievances from the past, and their mothers were openly at odds.

Nearly five years ago, in the spring of '31, after his high-school commencement, his mother went out to get the mail and saw a stranger walking down the tracks at the end of their lane toward town. She came into the house and said, "He was so little, I thought it was a child at first —also because he wasn't wearing a hat, not even a cap, mind you, in this weather. Then I saw that his hair was half gray. It was mussed up like a madman's and flying in the wind. He saw me and stopped, and I shook in my boots. His eyes are as mean as an old billy goat's, and they were looking right through me. He made a sort of bow in my direction and then kept on in a beeline toward town. He walks with a limp."

And she wondered if he could be a freight bum, or another of those Okies, or somebody she should know about.

"Oh, that's old Ed Jones," his father said. "He just moved in at the Chet Hollingsworth place. I believe he comes from around Hannaford or Dazey."

That night the Neumiller household woke to the sound of somebody singing and shouting obscene songs, and looked out to see a dim figure weaving down the tracks in the moonlight: Ed Jones on his way home. His mother felt her children's ears had been scalded, and was convinced that Jones was trying to pervert their innocence. She couldn't bear the least bit of obscenity (the worst words Martin heard his father use were gol-dammit and *Scheiss*, and those were in the barn) and couldn't tolerate anybody who drank; a drinker was dissolute and bound for hell, and his family, to permit such a condition to exist, had to be as dissolute as the drinker, or at least tending in his direction, to continue to live on with him.

His mother had very little patience with non-Catholics in the first place, with people who couldn't see, when it was right there in front of them, that the Catholic religion was the one true faith, since it had been founded by St. Peter and went way back to the time of the early Romans. She was an Old World woman, proud of her religion and her family, the Krulls, who came from Berlin

and had produced a cardinal and a scholar of ecclesiastical
law; proud of the fruitfulness of her womb, of God's
beneficence in permitting her to have six sons and two
daughters, thus far; proud of the devoutness she'd instilled
in her children; proud of her cousin, Selmer Krull, who'd
become a priest and headed the parish in Courtenay; of
her husband's family, named in state record books as
homesteaders, and of the money the Neumillers once had.
Her largesse to the world was her children, and her only
duty, other than to God, was to them, and now she
wanted somebody to do something about this dirty-
mouthed Ed Jones.

"Ach, *Marie,*" his father said.

"Well, if you don't, I will. I'll go out and tell him to use
the road like everybody else. I'll give him the what for!"

She was never equivocal with words and was at least
one half of the force of the family to be dealt with, so
one day his father walked down the lane to intercept Ed
Jones on his way to town, with Martin and his two oldest
brothers, Vince and Fred, trailing along behind him, and
after introductions and a few pleasantries, their father, who
was absent of guile and by no means an artful conversationalist, said, "I wonder why you walk the tracks so
much."

"I don't have a car," Jones said. "And I'll be goddamned if I'll waste the wear and tear on a good team just to
go into town and get soused, and that's where I'm bound.
These tracks are the straightest shot I know from those two
sections of quack grass back there, which some piker
pawned off on me as a farm, to the closest gin mill. And
after scratching in quack grass for a week straight, I don't
mind admitting I like a shot of juice and a few pinches
of snoose, or vicey-versa. What do you folks do about
quack grass? I've never seen it grow so like unto an ungodly sonofabitch. I cultivate it with the machine, I beat
it with a hoe, I keep the wife and daughter and the boy
after it, I pull it up by hand—roots, runners, and all—and
I even burn the crap. That's right, you laugh; you boys,
but I do, by Christ, I burn a hayrack of it a day, and next
week it's up as thick as ever, choking my crops."

It was his tongue and way of talking the boys laughed
at, not his problems or him.

Their father said that the Hollingsworth place was one

of the last pieces of land in the area to see the plow; the sod was turned under barely ten years ago, and only a few crops were put in before the Crash.

"So that's it. It'll take me years, then, or my life, before all that buried stuff comes up where I can give it the ax. Jesus. Well, I'm a hard-working old fart if there ever was one—it's true, you boys—and I'll keep at it till I win. It's partly my fault I got took on the land. I left my old place for this Hollingsworthless brute because of the barn. Have you ever been inside of it? It's a beauty! It's built better than a brick—Well, I've been in a lot of barns in my life and it's the best I've seen, and I've always maintained that if a man can't sleep in his own barn, then it isn't a fit place to keep his livestock. We burden the poor beasts with our work and whims their whole lives, we beat them —I do—we make money on them when the market's right, we don't let them run wild the way they did, so the least we can do in return is say 'No, goddamnit!' when it comes to locking them inside some drafty, stinking, jerry-built shack that's never warm and you can't keep clean, isn't it?"

Everybody nodded.

They talked for a long time, or rather Jones talked while the Neumillers, taciturn by nature, listened, blinking, overcome by the outpour and gasconade. At last old Jones said he had to get on with it, said he expected to see them all soon, and then headed down the tracks. They went in for supper and their mother said, "Well?"

"He seems all right to me," their father said. "Let him walk where he wants."

"*What?*"

"Anybody who uses God's name as often as Jones has God's praise in his heart, or at least His fear." To his children he said, "When you hear somebody take God's name in vain, you can change the words, in your own mind, into a silent Ejaculation. Every man worships in his own way, and we're not here to judge one another."

"But he's an atheist!"

"Marie."

"He's a drunkard, that's for sure."

"He's troubled."

"Insane would hit it closer. He'll be back again tonight with his insane performance."

"He needs somebody to talk to. I'll try to make a point of it."

"Is that right?"

"What do you mean?"

"You always say, 'You are judged not by who you are or what you are, but by the company you keep.'"

"For goodness' sake, Marie, I'm not in at Shella's drinking with Jones!" Shella's was a Prohibition haunt. "I'm here with my family."

"Jones is your neighbor."

"Marie! Be *rea*sonable."

This admonition from their father to their mother meant that a topic was closed. And, for the time being, Jones stopped walking the tracks; it was cutting season and he was busy on the weekends, along with everybody else in the area, running his binder. Their mother hardly mentioned him again, but didn't seem appeased about him; and she was also suspicious of Jones's wife, who was so much younger than he was, at least twenty years, that she looked like a niece or a housekeeper instead of a spouse. Was there something that a proper person wouldn't suspect of normal people going on there?

A detached eighty of Neumiller's land lay across the road from the Jones farm, which sat bare and unprotected on the plain, without even a windbreak of poplars around it; Hollingsworth had no practical head, as everybody knew. Martin and his father were cutting barley on the eighty one day in the late summer of cloudless infinite blue. They'd had a series of breakdowns due to the rough going and glacial rock, plus third-hand equipment to begin with, and quit early in the day, before the first sign of darkening, and drove over to the Joneses' in the car and asked if they could leave their tractor in the Joneses' farmyard instead of the field; there'd been trouble lately with migrants stealing parts and gasoline.

"Sure, sure," Jones said. "What the hell, you should've just driven it right on over. Jesus, what are neighbors for?" He threw open the door of a tilting machine shed. "Park her right in here. It's empty anyway. Come and have a drink first. Today's been a bitch."

Jones, who was walking with a cane he carried when he was on his property, and was sauntering and gesturing with the jerky torso movements of a short man, led them down to a circular water tank made of cedar staves and worked the handle of a shrieking pump until water spouted out. There was a tin can to drink from. Jones was talking about horses, and the contrast between horsepower and mechanized farming—"all those machines are going to gas up the land, whereas horse apples are good for it"—but Martin hardly heard; his mind closed like a door on the mouth of this man, and he let his father bear the brunt and burden of listening to him.

The day was dead calm, the temperature in the nineties, and Martin was shrouded in an apathy as heavy as the blue-dazed vault of heat-thick air around him. All those break-downs and this place. The house was gray and unpainted and so weathered the grain in the wood siding shone out in relief; chickens were scratching at the last patches of green in the yard, a starved-looking dog was snapping at a swarm of gnats, and some old molting Muscovy ducks, whose heads were entirely red wattles, came scuffling around the water tank and started poking their bills into his cuffs to get at some grain in them.

Why even speculate about farming, he wondered as he emptied the cuffs out, when it was so clear that farming was no way to get ahead, or even make a living. He scooped water from the tank, where feelers of spongy moss grew from the staves, and rubbed it over his face and the back of his neck, and then patted water on the insides of his wrists. He felt eyes on him and took a quick look toward the house. A face disappeared from a window.

"How many kids, altogether, did you say you have?" Jones asked. "Or did you? I've seen quite a number at your place."

"Eight," Martin's father said.

Jones whistled. "Say, you folks aren't Catholic, are you?"

"Yes."

"I should have realized. You don't seem like a fool, like me. I've got seven." Jones sat on the edge of the tank. "How do you do it?"

"What?" Martin's father asked.

"Keep them all in food and clothes?"

"I do repair work and carpentry in town. I might take a job as the janitor of the grade school this fall."

"Yes, I don't think anybody can make it strictly on the land any more, not in this territory. We haven't got a goddamn nothin'. We're so hard up I had to farm out my oldest boys, Conrad and Elling, and then I've got two little girls, Bernice and Kristine, who've lived with a pair of maiden aunts for so long I hardly consider them mine any more. No, nobody has to worry about keeping up with *these* Joneses. Elling, who's my oldest, is with the wife's sister and husband in Wisconsin, on a dairy farm outside the Twin Cities. The couple hasn't ever had any kids, not by choice, I don't think, but biology, so I imagine Elling gets his share of attention. He's a hard worker and pretty bright, too, but I must say—and I say this without compunction—I don't miss his tongue; he's a smartass like me. You can't tell him a thing and he's at the worst age now, eighteen."

Martin glanced at Jones, but this didn't seem a reference to him; and how would Jones know his age? Jones's attention centered on one subject, Ed Jones & Co., and Martin felt a twinge of distaste for this tiny man always puffing away to keep himself inflated and get you interested in his everyday affairs in a womanish, preening way, when, my goodness, if you thought about it, he was old enough to be Martin's *grandfather*.

Jones laughed. "Lately, I've been getting letters from Elling, long detailed sons-a-bitches telling me how to start a proper dairy setup here. Ha! As if this was Wisconsin, or I could afford another cow, much less the equipment, although I've certainly got the barn for it. I need every spare acre I've got for grain, I say, where I can work it in among my test plots of quack! Quack-quack!" He poked at the Muscovys with his cane. "Ah, but there's good in the boy's heart, too, God bless him. If he makes any money, any hard cash, he sends it home to Ma. He's out running and hustling one month and the next won't do horse piss for nothin'. Pardon that tongue. I imagine you folks are religious, so I'll try to watch it around you."

Jones changed the angle of his polished shoes on the ground, as though positioning them for a portrait photographer, and leaned on his cane. "When Conrad writes home, which is seldom, it's like getting a letter from a nine-year-old. Conrad's seventeen. He's with my bachelor brother in Crosby, Minnesota. Hit a wasp across the border and you've got the place. Do you know it?"

"No, I've never been out of this state in my life," Mar-

tin's father said, and there was such pride in his voice
that Martin bristled with filial sympathy.

"Two of one is eight to another," Jones said. "There's
fair-to-middling land around Crosby, and if this place
doesn't work out we'll probably move there or closer that
way. Not too close to my brother, Cal, though. He's a
preacher and has a finger in his Bible most of the time.
He also raises Aberdeen Angus breeding stock, and is he a
sanctimonious soul, when you figure he preaches one day
of the week and sets his bulls to it the other six. He once
called me 'sinner-man.' Oh, Lord Christ, Cal! *Sinner-man.*"
Jones wiped a long sudden tear from his big hooked nose.
"Well, Conrad seems not to rub him wrong, being the
quiet type. Conrad's a tall fellow, taller than you, Martin.
What are you? Six one?"

"Six foot exactly."

"You look taller than you are. He's six two. I can't understand where he gets his height, unless it's from the
wife. He's slow-moving and a bit slow-witted, too, but not
dumb. No, I've got no illusions about either of the boys,
but I miss them. Also, on the practical side, I could use
their help. Jerome's the finest sort; obedient, bright—
wheels within wheels always whirling and seesawing in
his head—but he's only ten and doesn't like farming. It
appears he'll grow up to be the artist type."

The door at the back of the house opened and a girl
came down the porch steps, and for Martin the air around
her seemed to lighten with each stride, as though she
were walking from a more rarefied season into theirs. Jones
was still speaking of Jerome in adulatory tones and didn't
notice her. She stared at him as if to draw his attention
with her stare, her eyes the poetical blue of deep afflic-
tion, and then seemed impatient, or embarrassed that he
was still talking, and turned and went up the stairs and inside again. Jones said that it was time to examine the
barn, which he knew they'd find extraordinary, while Martin's father wondered if perhaps they shouldn't get the
tractor first, and Martin, who had some of his mother's
fastidiousness about language and the way it was used, said
that *he'd* go get it. He walked over to the eighty in the
heat, trying to preserve the image of the girl as he'd seen
her, and take on as his own whatever it was that gave such
depth to her eyes.

He parked the tractor in the shed among torn harnesses, scrap iron, and a forge and anvil, and came out and closed the door, looking for his father and old Jones, and saw the girl beside the Model A. Her hands were clasped and her head bowed. "Mama's not feeling well and needs something from town and your dad said it would be all right if you drove me in to get it. My name is Alpha." She said this as if she'd rehearsed it, in a low voice, her head still bowed, and then raised her eyes to his and turned milk-colored under her tan, and then flushed and looked furious. All the way in to town she sat on the edge of the seat, bolt upright, gazing through the windscreen with such fixity it seemed she was guiding the car.

"Haven't you ridden in an automobile much?" he asked.

"Of course. We used to have two. You drive with half your mind."

"Oh."

She held her left hand in a fist in her lap, her fingers whitening, and now and then gave it a nervous glance, and then returned her eyes to the road. He felt a tendency to swerve when she glanced down, for his attention, as she'd sensed, wasn't really on his driving. She was short and dark like her father, but her face was oval and finely boned, her eyes spaced far apart and frail-lidded, her upper lip curved like a crossbow, the lower so full and suggestive it looked engorged with blood. She must have been working in the heat before she was asked to run this errand; she wasn't wearing a brassiere.

"Are you through with high school?" he asked.

"I'll be a junior next year."

"You're sixteen?"

"Not quite fifteen." She lifted her straight legs toward the dash and touched its bottom with her shins.

"Do you like his part of the country?"

"No."

He parked on the main street of Courtenay, in the central block, and she first opened her fist, glanced into it, and then jumped out of the car and ran off. The object she'd been gripping so tightly, he saw, was a silver dollar. It was one of the few times in his poor provincial life he'd seen one ("It was a novelty to me," he later said to her) and he realized it must be the only cash the Jones family had. Whatever Alpha purchased with it was in a green paper bag. He took her home and over the days that followed couldn't remove her image, or afterimage, from his mind, and thought of driving over to the Jones place and asking her to the county fair, but then thought better of it; she was too young.

Two weeks later Mrs. Jones gave birth to Lionell, who was so undersized and sickly that he and his mother had to be hospitalized for a week, and this could only have added to the Joneses' financial woes; and sometime during the same summer, Elling, in Wisconsin, rolled his aunt and uncle's car, while drinking, it was said, and escaped without a scratch, but the car caught fire and burned to a bare hulk, and now he was wondering if maybe his dad couldn't help him pay for it.

That fall Martin went off to Grand Forks and began his first year of college at the State University. He'd been promised a baseball scholarship by one of the university's roving scouts. He was a pitcher. He'd pitched a string of no-hitters in high school, and in the summers, while still in school, pitched for the Courtenay men's team. But when he got to the university, he learned that none of the coaches had heard of him, and that the scout, who was caught recruiting for Minnesota colleges on the side, had been removed from the university's payroll. There was no scholarship. After the first semester his money ran out and he came back home.

Alpha had befriended his sister, Elaine, a senior, and came to the house often to visit and study and stay overnight. His oldest brother, Vince was about Alpha's age, but a year behind her in school, and began driving her home after her visits, and then, when the weather turned nicer, walking her there, and he took longer and longer to return from these walks, so Martin put her out of his mind altogether. He attached a bucket to a wall of the barn and pitched at it for control; he'd become so fast over the year that none of his brothers, not even Fred, would catch him any more.

The Wimbledon businessmen offered him fifteen dollars to pitch for their team that summer, a step upward, since Wimbledon was four times the size of Courtenay, and this was a paying job; he accepted, and one hot Sunday traveled with the team to Bismarck to play the inmates of the State Penitentiary. Some of the prisoners had been in the farm leagues, others were from big cities in the East, and they practiced every day and were out for the only sort of blood they could shed now; notorious for spiking, hitting catchers with a backswing of the bat, tripping and elbowing base runners, flashing mirrors into outfielders' eyes—they knew every inch of the courtyard they played in—and because of this had an unbeaten record.

The game went into extra innings and Wimbledon didn't have a relief pitcher. Martin grew tired and frustrated and let the prisoners who comprised the cheering section (behind wire mesh, nevertheless unfettered in their use of language) get on his nerves, and when they realized the effect they were having, their language got so foul he felt they could be locked up just for it. He started throwing harder than he ever had. His control stayed, surprisingly enough, and he fanned two batters with six pitches, but then something slippery and excruciating (was there a doctor in the prison?) happened inside his elbow. His fastball was gone. The only pitches he could manage were a floating roundhouse curve and a knuckler that didn't travel much faster than it appeared to; and after each pitch his elbow straightened less. The prisoners started hitting him as if it were batting practice and the cheering section went wild. Wimbledon lost the game, of course, and his pitching career, if indeed there'd been the possibility of one, was ended; he hadn't been able to throw a fastball since.

Jones commiserated with him the next time he saw him. Jones said that he, during his youthful peregrinations, had been a baseball player himself, a professional, actually, and he could imagine how Martin must feel, but that was no need not to buck up. No, Jones hadn't been a pitcher; he'd left that up to the big, muscle-bound fellows. Jones held up a hand. His short fingers were enlarged and square-shaped at each knuckle.

"Breaks," he said. "Every one of them's been broken at least once, and I've played a whole game with a break or two. I caught." Jones cut quite a figure in the uniform, if he might say so himself, and could have made a career in the league—there was only one professional league then, of course—if he hadn't had such a love for horses and this unholy need to be a jockey. So he'd jocked for a few years,

imagining it was the romantic life, and had got this broken
nose out of it and some occasional tail. Also, there was
trouble with his first wife—he'd been married once before,
you know—and he'd had to run from her and hide himself
out West for a while, and there wasn't any real baseball,
paying baseball, that is, here in the West in those days, as
Martin surely knew, didn't he?

Could this man be believed?

He yammered on in his mad and effusive manner, mentioning dead and retired players he claimed as friends,
and citing statistics that dated back to the 1900's, and his
face suddenly took on the wild and crusty look of Casey
Stengel; he could be Casey's twin. His fierce eyes were
flashing and his big jaw moving so fast Martin couldn't
keep his eyes off it, and then he realized that Jones must
have sensed his disbelief, and felt he had to vindicate himself: he replayed several games from the past, running
through the batting order in particular innings, mentioning
which hitters were weak and why, and which men he threw
out, before he let Martin go. The next time Martin was in
Jamestown, he went into the library and got out a baseball
record book and found, in a column of old players such as
Hughie Jennings and Wee Willie Keeler, EDWARD
JONES, *b. Galena, Ill., Oct. 31, 1871.* Jones was listed as
a rookie catcher who had the highest batting average of any
rookie up until 1923. Jones hadn't mentioned his hitting.
Martin closed the record book, and with its dull, declamatory thump, felt that something unalterable had happened
between him and Ed Jones.

He went back to school, at last, in the fall of 1933, not
to the university, which he was soured on for good, but
to the state teachers college in Valley City, about fifty
miles from Courtenay-Wimbledon. Alpha was also on campus. Her brother Elling was paying her tuition and room
and board. Elling and Mrs. Jones wanted one of the children to finish college, and it was assumed that Conrad
wouldn't attempt school; there would always be time, later,
for Jerome and Lionell and the young girls, and Elling
himself had been expelled from Concordia in St. Paul
when he was discovered in a closet in the women's dormitory with a flask of gin on him, and refused to give the
name of the girl if there was a particular girl, with whom
he'd planned his rendezvous. He had two pairs of blue

bloomers in his coat pocket, too. He was now a salesman of heavy machinery in Minneapolis–St. Paul.,

Martin occasionally saw Alpha at school and once in a while they rode the same train home. They were merely polite. It was as though they were shamming at education, being farmers by birth, and could expose each other's duplicity. The possibility of this seemed to shame Alpha more than he would have thought, considering her father. At times she seemed too vulnerable to exist. For years he'd carried her image, suffused with the blue-dazed warmth, the *heat* of that day he'd driven her to town, and in all that time no woman had displaced it. Oh, there'd been the usual interest and flirtations; he'd dated the Carlson girl down the road a few times, and for a while at school had been attracted to a pretty blonde, Norma Egstrom, the daughter of the depot agent in Wimbledon; he hadn't paid her court or much attention, while she was in town. She was too young. They met at the college radio station, KOVC, where they were performing in a Christmas pageant; she was a soloist for the musical interlude, he was playing the part of Joseph.

She was beguiled, as she put it (and he was, too, to tell the truth), by the theater and dramatics and the idea of entertaining in general, although in her case the interest lay almost exclusively in singing, an unfortunate choice on her part, he thought, since she was such a natural actress and her singing grated sexually on him (then again, he was tone-deaf), and the two of them appeared together in other radio programs, including one based on the works of Edgar Allen Poe, and in several theatrical productions at the campus auditorium. He considered himself a dependably entertaining character actor on the order of Edward Everett Horton, but played mostly leading men. They made a handsome couple, people said. She was attractive in every aspect of her hearty, big-boned Scandinavian healthiness, a little overweight at times perhaps, with a wide mouth set in a soft pout at its center, and could be cold-eyed and immovable when she knew she was right. She fell in love with her voice coach, it was rumored, and Martin felt less rebuffed than a victim of her contradictory whims. He'd heard that sometime since, within the last year or less, she'd gone off to Fargo or St. Paul or somewhere, determined to become a professional singer, and had changed her name to Peggy Lee.

He started dating Alpha then, in 1934, in the late spring when the Juneberry trees came into bloom, the grass greened and darkened with its health assured, and the sound of tractors plowing nearby fields could be heard across the campus.

"Don't you want to be out in the fields?" Alpha said to him.

"No. I want to be here." She was kneeling beneath a low-crowned blossoming Juneberry.

"Would you always like to be?" she asked.

"What do you mean?" *Beside you here on the grass, the full moon on the blossoms making them glow like stars around your shadow-darkened hair?*

"Here in Valley City," she said.

"Sure, I guess."

"I would. It's the most beautiful city I've seen. Whenever I'm ready to settle down, if I ever am, it'll be here for sure, you can bet your shirts on that, boys."

Her *if I ever am* opened another new wound in him. The school year was over in a week. They returned home and the next day he drove over and asked Alpha to a movie. Mrs. Jones wouldn't let her go. Mrs. Jones, he learned, was a Missouri Synod Lutheran of the strictest sort, and didn't approve of motion pictures, popular songs, dating in automobiles, tobacco, alcohol ("Just a snort, Ma," Jones would say when he was juiced. "It'll put starch in your drawers"), profanity, cards, and gambling; and she had a hardly mentionable low opinion, like most Lutherans of her mold, of Roman Catholics. It seemed unsavory to her, just to begin with, the way they bred so much.

Well, Martin did have a lot of brothers and sisters, so many he couldn't keep track of their ages and birthdays himself; none of them had asked to be born, of course—nor did other children, as far as he knew—but each arrived with such a naturally formed, individual nature and abided by it in ways nobody could predict, as though moving to an inner melody, it seemed they'd asked. And now that they were a part of this world and his memory, it was impossible to imagine himself existing without their related lives.

Alpha's mother couldn't be called unkind, couldn't be

faulted in any of the ways that might suggest sin, but she'd remained standoffish toward him, a cold uncoiling barrier, and he caught himself thinking, now and then, that maybe it had as much to do with the Joneses' finances as his faith. Mrs. Jones and Alpha often talked about the former places they'd lived in, the large farmhouses and big rooms, the furniture they'd had, the pure-bred livestock, the machinery and conveniences and cars. The fireplace in their present home made the place endurable for them, they said, because it was one of the few to be found in a country home in Stutsman County, N.D. One of the possessions that Mrs. Jones had clung to, through all of the moves and family upheavals, was her upright piano, certainly the most unwieldy, but one that bore value and status; an anniversary clock on its top, enclosed in a glass bell, spun golden balls in a ring-around of time's spin. The guiding words and light of her life seemed to be "getting ahead."

It made him uncomfortable just to drive into their yard, knowing they had no automobile; and he didn't run many more errands for Mrs. Jones—the better she got to know him, the less she seemed able to ask favors—and this Christmas, hardly a week ago, he'd brought a package over and placed it on their kitchen table, and said, "Mom sent these over for all of you," and then opened the box to show them; it was filled with brownies, divinity, and pfeffernuesse packed in layers of tissue.

"Boy, are these delicious," he said, and picked up a pfeffernuss and popped it into his mouth.

And Mrs. Jones said, "I can remember when your little brothers and sisters were so hungry they used to walk over to our house here, poor, bony things, and come to the back door and ask would I please give them a peanut-butter sandwich, would *beg* for food. I can remember—" Her frail voice had gone into high and girlish modulations, and then it broke, and Martin, who still had pfeffernuss on his tongue, was astonished to see tears curve around her mouth. She stalked out of the kitchen into her bedroom and slammed its door with a bang.

And so, that first summer home from school, after they'd started dating, it was a strain on Alpha and him, and on their families, for the two of them to be alone together too much. Jones himself was friendly, at least at first; he'd come out with his cane when the Model A appeared, so garrulous and exclamatory he was a welcoming party in one, and clap Martin on the back, *Ha!* and call him "boy" and "son" and speak to him as an old-timer about Roosevelt, "the ass-kissing oaf," draft horses and thoroughbreds, the repeal of Prohibition, and their common interest, baseball. It was impossible for Martin to look Jones in the eye when the subject was brought up, and Jones sensed this and finally dropped mention of it altogether, which was even worse. Who was it in Martin who'd opened that book in the library—an academician, or something unformed?

And then, out of nowhere, Jones started teaching Jerome to pitch. "Well, well, we've got to have one in the family, eh, boy?" Jones said to Martin, who'd pull into the yard and see the two of them working away out there, as though they'd seen his car coming and said, "Let's go," Jones down in a crouch with a farmer's cap he never usually wore turned backward on his head, snapping the ball to Jerome and keeping up a natural chatter, Jerome going into the pump and windup and working on the stretch and form and control, so absorbed that Jones would only glance at Martin between pitches, with a look that was businesslike, and then get on with it. Or talk to Jerome so personally you wanted to leave them alone as father and son. Was Jones purposely trying to antagonize him?

Alpha couldn't say. She couldn't categorize her father's behavior or character—"I don't know if he's cruel; I don't know if he's kind"—and spoke of him as though he were an enigma to respect and beware of. She knew little about his past; she understood that, besides playing baseball somewhere and riding horses, he'd traveled as a supporting lead with an itinerant Shakespearean company and had worked for a while as a ballroom-dancing instructor. That made her laugh. This was before he'd hurt his leg, which was shattered at the knee by the kick of a horse. He'd traveled through most of the East and Midwest, moving in many strata of society, and was, as he said, part Welsh, part Scotch-Irish, part Norsky ("Norsky" to irritate her mother, a full-blooded Norwegian), and part sonofabitch.

He married Alpha's mother when she was nineteen and he in his forties. Nobody knew his exact age, not even his wife; he sometimes claimed he was born in 1869, and then swore it was 1879, and he'd also mentioned every year within that decade, saying his memory slipped. He was more than vain, considering he was a farmer, and wore, in spite of the family poverty, shirts and suits that were obviously hand-tailored and looked brand-new. But Alpha said, "He's worn the same clothes as long as I can remember. It's the way he takes care of them, I guess." He was courtly yet flirtatious with every female he met, combining in himself flattery, deference, intricate courtesies from another century, smooth talk, and winks. He felt he'd been plagued most of his life by missed opportunities, that his sense of timing was out of tune with the world's, that his closest friends had betrayed him the worst, for they'd all betrayed him, and that a curse had been placed on his life by a hostile and unremitting God. He was an alcoholic, of course.

Once when Martin came for Alpha, her face was parched-looking and discolored from tears, and she said she had an "awful truth" to confess.

Had Jones beaten her? Had she taken a lover at one time? Had it been Vince? Martin felt arteries from his groin to his temples dilate and strum, and couldn't get his breath. "Well?" he said. "What is it?"

"Daddy's been married before this. Mama's not his first wife. He's been divorced. Mama just told me. You might as well take me home. Oh, eeee!"

Martin had to smile, partly at her way of referring to her parents in the diminutive, when their personalities, to him, were so large and intimidating. "But, Alpha, I was aware of that."

"You *were?* Well, how, for God's sake!"

"I assumed it was common knowledge. I believe your father even mentioned it to me once."

"He *did?*"

"Yes."

"When?"

"A couple of years ago, I think."

"Then why didn't you say something about it to *me,* you lame-brain? Just how do you suppose this makes *me* feel?" Her eyes were as furious and fulminating as her father's.

"But, Alpha, I hardly knew you then. I—"

"You know me now, dammit to hell!"

"Well, yes, of course, but I always assumed that you'd be the first to learn about anything like——"

"Oh, shut up," she said, and started crying again. They went in to a baseball game, as they'd planned, but she refused to leave the car for fear somebody she knew would see her face. The pitcher was mediocre and Wimbledon lost, five to two, which made Martin whistle off-key with well-being as he drove back, and then Alpha asked him to stop the noise of the car so they could talk. He pulled off the side of the road, into some weeds, and killed the engine. "Yes?" he said.

She leaned her head on his chest and didn't say a word.

"I want you to know that what you've told me doesn't bother me one bit," he said.

"What about your parents?"

"Ach."

"Your mother, then?"

"Oh, well. She has enough of her own to worry about."

She kissed him through his shirt. He slid down in the seat and put his arm around her above her waist. It was starting to get dark and a dove was mourning in the distance with a sound as circular and pure as the beginning of time's first dot appearing out of infinity. There was a ghost of a full moon in the sky and the three notes of the dove's song, the first two proclaiming the two of them together and alone, *You* and *You*, and the last long *Oooo* as stretched out and desolate as the plain. Heart, heart, does it have to end here? Holy Mary, Sanctuary of—— He put his fingertips to her chin and lifted her face, pupils large and dark, and kissed her on the mouth and let his hand fall, not purposefully, but as it would, to her lap, and felt the springy and textured bulge of pubic hair beneath her skirt.

Something struck the windscreen and they jumped. Fifty feet away, above them on the railway embankment, was old Ed Jones, who flung aside some pebbles in a silent spray. His eyes were on Alpha and his jaw was moving in a below-the-breath monologue that seemed tinged with the obscene. Then he turned to Martin, jerked his thumb over his shoulder, and yelled, "Get that girl of mine home this instant, boy, before I take you and your car apart!" And then continued down the tracks toward town.

Alpha held to Martin's arm all the way to her place and made him promise to stop over the next day.

"Has he ever beaten you?"

"Yes."

He knew it! He pulled into their yard in the morning, pale and afraid, and realized immediately, from the look on Alpha's face, that her father hadn't said a word to her mother yet. Martin went inside. Jones was in a rocker, looking haggard and hung-over, reading with a dark scowl, through wire-rimmed bifocals, a worn and dog-eared copy of Shakespeare's sonnets. He glanced up at Martin and seemed to look over his head, and then winked, and whispered, "You sure made tracks last night, boy." And turned back to his sonnets with hardly a pause.

The rest of the summer he was busy in the barn whenever Martin showed up.

He and Alpha went back to Valley City in the fall, and the separation from their families and their nearness to one another at school, where they were partaking of learning, an experience that none of their parents had had, must have made their relationship appear, to their parents, natural and perhaps preordained. His mother had Alpha over for dinner when they were home; Mrs. Jones said more than hello to him. Ed Jones became friendlier than he'd ever been, more vocal and revelatory, and often broke into moments of what might be termed paternal advice: "Never lamp a dog, boy. Never look one straight in the eye. It shortens his life and scares the hell out of him. He thinks you've come down to his level, and what he needs is a master, a real seeing or overseeing eye. A dog *needs* one. And never ever stare at a person when he's asleep. It'll mix up his thoughts." And Jones and Martin were able to talk baseball again. "Has-beens is what we are, both of us," Jones said, and laughed at him.

It was the most rewarding year of school for Alpha and Martin; they were together as often as they wanted, and were more involved in the theater, the forensic society, the debate team, and their separate church groups, and their grades were better for a change. Elaine and Vince were on the campus, too, and the four of them got together once or twice a week, and had such lighthearted, memorable times that Alpha said she was beginning to feel what it was like to be one of the family without the wor-

ries that go with it. And then the Juneberry trees pronounced the end of the term, and Alpha received her
Standard Certificate, which qualified her to teach in the
lower grades, and said she was going to get a job right
away; she wanted to help out at home and also put aside
enough money to send Jerome through school.

During the summer that followed, the summer of '35,
Martin and his father were employed by the county to
work on a road gang, and tallied up twelve- or fourteen-
hour days (not for the extra pay or overtime, neither of
which they got, but so their jobs weren't given to other
men who might work more), and one afternoon were a
mile and a half from the home place, scything weeds along
the right of way, and piling up the rocks they dulled
their scythes on, when there was an explosion that
reverberated in the air so much they seemed to hear it
several times. They looked at one another, attentive as animals, and his father said, "It's probably Carlson." The
neighboring farmer had been using dynamite to blast out
a hole for a pond he intended to stock with carp. Martin
and his father kept at their work, and about twenty minutes later Vince came galloping down the road on the riding horse. His face was blackened and most of his hair
burned away.

"Terrible accident at home," he said. "Emil— We were
—" He slid off the horse and handed the reins to his father.
"Dad, you better go."

Their father leaped on the horse, wheeled her, and set
her in a hard run toward home, and Vince and Martin took
off over the fields. Martin didn't learn any details until
later in the day.

Vince and Fred and two of the younger boys, Jay and
Emil, were weeding a seven-acre potato patch and picking
potato bugs from the plants. They filled a gallon can with
the bugs and then poured fuel oil over them and dropped
a match in; the oil wouldn't burn well, and eventually
appeared to go out, so Vince and Fred went over to a
fifty-gallon drum to add gasoline to the mixture, and
when Vince pressed on the spout of the drum, unaware
that it was empty and filled with fumes and that the oil
was still burning, the drum exploded. Its circular end
blew loose as if an opener had been applied, and went off
in a tumbling flight. Vince and Fred and Jay, who were

standing beside it, were mostly scared and shaken—they said they hardly heard it going, and then were picking themselves up off the ground—but Emil, the youngest, who was on his way to the house, turned at the noise and the drum's sailing end hit him below the knees. Both bones in his right leg were shattered, a length of tibia torn away, and the leg was held together by shredded tendons, blue muscle, and skin.

He was put in traction with the hope that, as the tibia knit, it would bridge the gap of missing bone, and was in traction for six months. He was ten. Mrs. Carlson had been a registered nurse before she married, and she walked over to the house every day to dress the wound. The long period in traction had been a success, it seemed. Emil was now hopping around on crutches with his leg in a cast, but hadn't yet put any weight on it, and Vince, who felt responsible, had become more moody and unpredictable than ever.

And then it was . . .

Jerome was precocious, an avid reader and a recluse who went for long walks over the plain, sometimes as far as Verendrye Creek, where he'd sit for hours and— Who knows why he went there and sat? He didn't like to fish. He didn't believe in blood sports of any kind. He didn't like violence. He was the only one who could calm Ed Jones when he was drunken, or unhinged, or "out on a wren's perch with a wild hair up my ass," as Jones put it to drinking friends. Jerome knew the native plants and wildlife and was always the first in the area to find the season's first wildflower. He showed it to Alpha and then gave it to his mother. He was four years younger than Alpha and with Mrs. Jones ill so often Alpha had partly raised him, and was maternal toward him, but also spoke to him and of him in a straight-forward and womanly, wifelike way. He wasn't physically attractive. He had big lips and his father's nose, and was skinny—stringy-thin, like Mrs. Jones—and the back of his head bulged out in such a big way you could see what was meant by the word "occiput." He had an unnerving habit of staring off in the distance while he wound and unwound his hair around a finger. "What's beyond those mountains?" his mother would ask.

He tried to get the town of Courtenay to start an Audobon Club, a Wildlife Club, an Izaak Walton League, or even something local, but there was no interest. He was often talking, in the phrase of the time, of "conservation of the land," and when his family had any sort of fruit, which was hard to get this far north, even in the summer, he gathered up the seeds and planted them in different types of soil in different locations. Would they grow here, he wanted to know. Had it ever been tried in North Dakota? He broke into an abandoned farmhouse because he'd heard there was money in its basement, and confessed to the act the day after, before the break-in was discovered; and when his mother, hysterical at the lawlessness of it, asked him why he'd do anything so irresponsible and foolish, he said, "I wanted Dad to be rich."

Jones said he had a strong pitching arm for his age and was developing a breaking curve, and planned to try out for the high-school team in the fall. Then there was a steamy scandal at school when Jerome, who was at the head of his eighth-grade class, was discovered in the furnace room with Eunice Winandy, lying on the janitor's cot. Martin's father was the janitor; he slept on the cot during the worst of the winter nights in order to keep the furnace stoked with lignite. Jerome was allowed, after a suspension and deliberation among the teachers and school board and community leaders, to graduate as valedictorian. Martin's father might have had a hand in the decision; the superintendent kept coming to him and he kept assuring the superintendent that, yes, Jerome's knickers *were* buttoned when he walked in on them.

Jerome's commencement address also caused a stir. He didn't keep to his written text, as he'd been instructed to, and in his extempore speech insinuated that the community was hypocritical; the natural beauty left in the area, the real plains grassland, he said, would soon be lost, along with people's false pride in it, if all that governed their lives was progress, plowing up more land, and money. Alpha stood and applauded when he was finished; she'd bought him a copy of Theodore Roosevelt's essays as a graduation gift. "Dammit, girl," Ed Jones whispered, and jerked on her skirt. "Sit! They think we're crazy the way it is, the bastards."

Jerome said he wasn't going to the class picnic. He felt he'd changed. He wanted to stay home and help his father;

there was fieldwork to be done, cattle to fix, the sheep were lambing, and he knew he'd neglected his duties on the farm up until now. But Mrs. Jones told him there would only be one such picnic as this, and one afternoon out of this new life wasn't too much to ask, and besides, what would people say if the valedictorian wasn't there? She gave him a two-quart jar of pickles to take.

"He wasn't content to just carry the jar under his arm," she said. "No, he braided twine around the neck, made all sorts of loops and knots, and braided a handle that would have looked proud on a picnic basket. 'I bet this would hold fifty pounds,' he said to me. He went off down the road and when I looked out the window, when he probably figured he was out of sight, I saw him swinging that jar of pickles around his head in big circles, and I thought, 'Sure as the Lord lives, he'll break that before he gets it there.'"

It arrived intact. It rode between Jerome and Eunice Winandy on the drive to Spiritwood Lake. A close watch was kept on the two the entire day; the superintendent wasn't about to trust a pair who'd demonstrated how brazenly they'd comport themselves if given a chance. After the picnic, Jerome and Eunice, and two of Jerome's friends and their girls, got into a boat and poled a ways out from shore. Jerome stripped down while people from the shore looked on aghast, and then they saw that he was wearing bathing trunks. "I bet I can make it to the diving float," he said to his friends, and leaped overboard and went under as though weighted. His friends and the observers on shore thought he was playing a trick when he didn't at first appear, and then they knew it was serious. A lifeguard was on duty, but it wasn't until twenty minutes later that Jerome was pulled into a boat, releasing streams of water into the lake. The lifeguard labored over him for a half hour, saying, "Jerome, Jerome," as though Jerome were his brother, and then in a desperate voice. Jerome lay at last on his back on the ground, still and water-blanched and composed, his open eyes staring out beyond the faces of his classmates as at the dim-visioned dreams along a creekbank now dead within him.

The superintendent and the lifeguard brought his body back in the superintendent's car, but stopped first at the Neumillers and got Martin to help them face the Joneses with this. Mrs. Jones got into the car and uncovered his body and held him and talked to him as if he were alive and listening to her, while he lay in her arms with his head thrown back, his blue mouth open to her kisses, a milky substance forming over his eyes, and no one, not even Alpha, dared to part her from him.

Martin and the lifeguard walked out to where Jones was cultivating corn with the horses. Jones pulled up the reins, threw them loose over the cultivator seat, and came trotting up to them.

"What is it?" he asked. His face was drawn back against its bones and he was breathless from the run.

"Mr. Jones," the lifeguard said. "I'm terribly sorry. Well, er—"

"What is it?"

"It's Jerome."

"He's drowned," Jones said.

"Yes, he—"

"I knew it, by Jesus. I knew it, I did." Jones pulled the bandana from around his neck and threw it to the ground. "You sonofabitch!" he cried up. "You dirty double-dealing sonofabitch! I'm never going to be sober again in my life! I'm going to shoot all the livestock! I'm going to throttle the wife and that frigging prissy-ass daughter of hers! I—! I—!" His knees gave out and he fell on the ground and said in a voice broken by hiccups and a sob, "Wake me when the world gets off, dear Jesus."

*

Martin opened his eyes. He uncovered one ear and listened for Alpha's footsteps, but didn't even hear noises from the kitchen now. Had the Joneses gone out to milk? And then he felt he was asleep and still dreaming. A fly, a large fly from the bumbling buzz of it, hovered near the sofa where he lay, moved off and hovered near again, and then went into widening sweeps of flight, weaving all over the blizzard-locked room the aura and essence of summer, laughter on wing.

He did all he could to comfort Alpha after the drowning; took her for drives nearly every night, consoled her and held her, got her to talk about Jerome as much as she could, and gave him his class ring. And whenever Alpha asked him, he'd drive into town and fetch Jones home from the tavern. The bad bouts of his were even worse now. Alpha was slow to recover and perhaps never would, nor would her parents, both of whom blamed themselves. Later, in the fall, Martin came to take Alpha shopping and drove up to a house that looked deserted; it had been more barren since the drowning, but tonight it seemed the family had packed up and moved off.

He went to the porch and knocked on the door. When there was no answer, he pulled it open and found Jones on his back in front of him, his graying hair haloed out over the worn floor-boards. He was snoring and held a bottle of gin over his chest like a child a doll. Martin went out to the water tank and sat, staring up at Alpha's window. Was no one else at home? The Muscovys had left leaflike prints in the mud at his feet. The moss in the tank was now in long strings. There was a tapping sound and he saw Alpha at her window, pale and distraught, her face cleaved across its center by a reflection; she gave a sign that she'd soon be down and tried to signal something else, then disappeared from the window.

The back door opened out. Jones came from behind it with one hand above an eye and the other hanging on to the doorknob for balance. He stood on the top step, swaying and keeping his grip on the knob, unbuttoned his fly, and let go a splattering stream, groaning and erupting with gas as he did, and then noticed Martin, blinked as though to blink back into oblivion a bad dream, and once again turned his attention to the matter at hand, playing it around with such fervor and attentiveness it seemed he was signing his name. He shook himself dry, buttoned up, and turned to Martin, who could understand now why his mother once described Jones's eyes as resembling a billy goat's; they were depthless and blank, jellylike extensions of a mind not entirely human.

"You screwed her yet?" Jones asked in a slushy voice.

Martin blushed and stared at his shoes.

"I say, you *screw* her yet?" Jones asked even louder. Should Martin simply leave?

"Tan't ya cock? Pardon," Jones said, and spat a tobacco-browned stream to one side. "Cat got your tongue? I hear all you Catholics like to do is dive for the beaver. Whoo- who*oooo*! Is that right? What I heard, I mean?"

Martin went to the Model A and got in behind the wheel. Jones stood wavering, as though deliberating something worse, and then shook his head once, in contempt or disbelief, and stepped inside and closed the door. Martin was about to crank up the car and drive off when Alpha came out. She said this drunkenness was driving her insane, and destroying the life of her little brother, Lionell, and all she could do about it was apologize.

"Did you hear what he said to me?" Martin asked.

"What?"

"Oh— It was sort of jumbled up. I could hardly make it out."

"What was it about?"

"Nothing, really."

"Well, he better not bother you," Alpha said. "If he starts that, I'll leave home on the bobtailed drunken old liquor fiend."

One evening Martin came to take Alpha to a movie (movies were no longer *verboten*), and heard Jones talking with a neighbor and drinking crony, Len Melstrom, in the front room, so he waited in the kitchen, where Mrs. Jones was at the table leafing through a Sears, Roebuck catalogue. She licked her fingers every time she went to turn a page, and Martin, who had the same habit, wondered why Alpha was always after him about it, then heard, in Melstrom's voice, he was sure, something about "mackerel-snappers." He cleared his throat in a loud and rattling way to let the men know he was in the house.

Jones said, "Show me a Catholic, and I'll show you a hypocrite! They're the most sanctimonious band of—"

Were they drunk? He coughed and cleared his throat again, and kicked his toes against the floor as if they were freezing. There was a rise of volume in Jones's voice. "They'll trample or maim a man and call it divine, because they're the chosen and doing what's right. They've got a direct line to the Almighty, you see, and we don't, and I'll tell you why; it's because of the *beads!*"

Mrs. Jones got up from the table and said, "Excuse me." She paused with her hand on the door and turned on him the vague and glazed eyes of a convalescent. "Excuse him," she said, and went as though to put a stop to this, he thought, but her footsteps carried on beyond the men to her bedroom, and then bang.

"The daughter here is going with one, you know," Jones said, and now his tone was conspiratorial. "Oh, he's all right by me, he's a fine boy, upstanding, upright —polite, too!—but someday, if she doesn't watch it, I say"—more volume and a change in tone, as though he'd lifted his face toward her bedroom—"I say, 'Alpha! One of these days you're going to have a dozen kids in the same room with you, all of them swinging those rosaries like lassos, and yelling, *Yippee! Whoopee, Ma! Let's go to church!*' "

On trembling legs Martin made it out the door, out the back porch, and down to the water tank. He pumped water over his head and wiped the back of his neck and the insides of his wrists with a wet handkerchief, and then got into the Model A. Alpha came out at last, flushed and tearful, and said, "I just gave him hell. He's never said any such foolishness to me in my life, although now I've heard it, of course. I'm leaving home no later than a week from now."

"Oh, Alpha!"

She slumped in the seat, her face pale and empty of expression, and stared at a kerchief she kept wadding and squeezing in her lap. As they got close to town, he wished he would have said to the men, "If either of you pip-squeaks in there has anything you really want to say to me, then why don't you say it out here, where I can see if you really intend to make a joke of it." He felt the weakness and trembling in him solidify and become his mother's moral outrage and all-inclusive indignation, but when he tried to speak of it to Alpha, she said, "No. Please. Don't. He's been even worse to Mama about her religion, especially recently. It's because of Jerome. Also because your mother never comes to talk. Yesterday he said—" She stopped as though a hand were at her throat.

"What?"

"He said, 'If there was a God, I'd wring His neck, the bastard.' "

There was a sound of logs rumbling down a wooden runway, or else another part of his dream was rising through this one. He slipped out of half sleep into a skin cold and oily from sleeping in his clothes. He opened an eye to the darkness under the quilt. Where was he now? There was whispering in the kitchen, and now it was real, unattached to the luxurious tangle he could weave of it in dreams, and then the back door banged, utensils were moved, a liquid was poured, and the wet bottom of a kettle started stuttering on the stove top. He strained to hear overhead, but the floorboards were silent, and then the back door opened and closed, and footsteps came across the kitchen, snow creaking under them against the cold linoleum.

"Where are you going?" Mrs. Jones asked in a whisper.

"Right here," the voice of Lionell said.

"In the middle of the room? Look what you're tracking in."

There were creaking sounds around a small area. "It stuck to my boots. It always does."

"Why do you think I ask you to sweep them off?"

"It's on them the next day, too."

"Ouf! *You*."

The creaking sounds came closer and Mrs. Jones whispered, "Don't you dare go in there!"

"Is he asleep?"

"Yes."

"Still asleep?"

"That's what I said."

"How come?"

"I imagine he's tired."

"Why?"

"He stayed up late."

"I didn't stay up late, did I?"

"No, son."

"Are you ever tired, Mom?"

"Of course."

"You don't sleep like him, do you?"

"I go to bed earlier."

"Because he's a man and you're a woman."

"That has nothing to do with it. Here, have this to nibble on."

There was a long silence, and then Lionel said in a changed voice, "Did you stay awake and see the New Year, Mama?"

"Yes."

"Was he wearing diapers like I did once?"

"That's from those foolish picture magazines!"

"But I'm getting bigger and bigger. I'm bigger now to-day."

"I guess."

"My hands are bigger. See?"

"They look about the same to me. Did you wash them last night?"

"For forty-fifty minutes."

"Oh, go on with you! What's Daddy doing?"

"Lots of stuff."

"What?"

"He broke his ax, and he spilled some milk out there, and he still can't get that car to work, so he called it bad names."

"I mean—"

The back door opened, admitting more chill, and heavier steps came creaking across the kitchen.

"Ed!" Mrs. Jones whispered and her whisper could pierce tin.

"Yes yes yes, sweet love."

"What are you *doing?*"

"What does it look like? I'm taking this in there."

"No, you aren't."

"You mean this stuff?" Jones said, and there was an altered angle to his whisper. "What the hell. It's clean snow."

"You'll wake him."

"He's got to get up and get out of here, by Jesus!"

"But that's so rude!"

The footsteps came into the room, bringing along an aroma of the outdoor cold on foreign clothes, and then kindling tumbled into a woodbox so close Martin felt it had fallen on his head, and had a flash of termites in the woodbox. *Termites?* There was a hissing of clothes, the crack of a stiff joint, newspaper being ripped and wadded, and then some pieces of wood clunked into the stove. He lay in suspension, expecting a fire to rise, and started to drift asleep again.

"Hey, boy, aren't you awake yet?"

There was no recourse; he uncovered his head. "Yes. Good morning." He could see his own breath out in their world.

"Good morning, hell!" Jones frowned in the dimness of the blanket-draped room. A fur cap was pulled down to his flaring eyebrows and a horsehair coat nearly touched the toes of his gray-felt boots. He kept frowning, with eyes that touched the cold in Martin's bones, and didn't turn to the stove. Alpha must be waiting upstairs for a fire, too, and meanwhile freezing.

"Well, I finally got that windmill shut off before it rattled its goddamn brains out," Jones said. "The wind quit at four and I ran out then. I don't suppose I woke you."

"No."

"I figured not. It's a good thing you're going into education, is what I say. You don't have what it takes to make a dirt grubber, boy. What time do you teachers have to get up? It's nine o'clock now."

"Oh."

"You're damn tootin'! And it's thirty below out."

"Oh."

"Oh, oh. Didn't you hear what I said?"

"Yes. I mean, what that you said?"

"I said it was nine o'clock, boy."

Of what importance was time on this particular morning, on the new day of the New Year, snowed in by the blizzard, when he was looking forward to helping Jones with the chores, and having leftovers from last night, and more quiet card games and genial talk; and was hoping for the chance, after another tête-à-tête with Alpha (if she'd said yes and would agree), to announce their marriage to her parents first, on the occasion of this day.

Jones moved closer, his black eyelashes fringed with big beads of ice that were beginning to melt and run down beside his nose, and screwed up his face in a scowl. "Hey, boy, what the hell is it with you?"

"The cattle," Martin said, and shoved off the quilt and sat.

"Cattle, hell. They've been taken care of hours ago."

Martin slipped his stockinged feet into the cold sheaths of his shoes and bent to lace them and, Oooo, his bladder was as big as a pumpkin. Ooooo, *two* shoes!

"I tried cranking your Model A for a quarter hour and couldn't even make it go poot. How do you adjust your spark?"

"All the way down."

There was a ringing laugh from the kitchen, and Mrs. Jones said, "That's what I suggested to the old fool all along!"

Martin started trembling and not from the cold. They were turning him out on purpose before Alpha was up. They'd worked up this plot together, for some reason, and were delirious with the way it was moving ahead of him. Jones acted drunk. He scoured his leather mittens together and gave them a clap close to Martin's head, showed his teeth in a fake smile, or so it seemed, and strode into the kitchen like a martinet.

He followed, and saw Lionell at the table in a yellow snowsuit, red-cheeked and round-eyed, with a pile of pastry crumbs on a plate beside him. Mrs. Jones was at the cookstove stirring a steaming pot. She turned and gave him the merriest smile he'd ever seen from her, and said, "Good morning, at last. Sorry you can't have breakfast."

She'd heard him propose.

She pulled his coat from the cookstove shelf, shook it out, and held it for him by the shoulders, and he turned, his lips beginning to tremble, and saw Lionell taking this moment in with the all-seeing eyes of a four-and-a-half-year-old, and felt his coat, heated from the stove, slip up his arms.

I'll be reasonable, he thought.

"Jesus, boy, you look like the soup's been sucked out of your bones," Jones said.

The coat held warm comfort around him and he turned to thank Mrs. Jones but hardly got it out before she plopped his cap on his head, and said, "There's no need for thanks. Goodbye, Martin. My best to you."

Jones grabbed his elbow, opened the kitchen door, pulled him onto the back porch, and kicked the door shut. The windows of the porch were covered with tar paper and it was so dark he felt he'd stepped into night again. "My overboots," he said.

"Right beside the separator there."

They were stiff from the cold, difficult to get on, and felt like ice water around his ankles. His fingertip froze to a buckle. He jerked it loose, leaving a wedge of skin, pulled out his gloves and yanked them on. How could he be so naïve as to miss the point of all this?

Jones clucked his tongue and said, "You're so bass-

ackwards and slow and sheepish this morning, boy, I'd say
it was because you haven't taken your leak yet."

He straightened, standing tall above Jones, and decided now was the moment to have his say about this,
but Jones hit the outside door and two shafts of pain,
like flying icicles, were driven home above his eyes. When
he finished blinking and his vision cleared and became
grayly chromatic, he saw the Model A stranded in a drift
up above its running board. A team of black Percherons,
stomping and nodding against the traces and blowing
blossomy plumes from their frost-ringed nostrils, stood at
the front of the car, hitched to its bumper with logging
chains and eveners, their heads stamped upon the morning with a permanence that made them shine.

The white day was still as death. Jones took his arm
and started dragging him through drifts, through deep
trails left by the horses' big hooves. "I know it looks pretty
bad, but I walked out to the main road and it's already
been traveled, so there won't be any trouble once we get
that far, or if there is I'll pull you all the way on into
town. And there, by Jesus, is the team that can do it."
Jones turned to him with a smile of pride, but it changed
into consternation. "I'll be go to hell," he said. "A tie."

"A tie?" Martin said.

Jones dipped back and his sea-green eyes, more striking in the sunlight, narrowed down on him. "Aren't you
well, boy, or didn't you sleep last night either, or what?
I'm not up on all your rigamarole, but I know today is a
holy day of consecration, or whatever, and you've got to
get to church. Now, do you want to borrow a tie from
me?"

"Oh, no. I have one in my pocket. I—" He started to
pull it out.

"My first wife was a Catholic, you know, so I'm up on
a few of the ins and outs of your Church. That first marriage was so unfortunate, I can't begin to tell you how.
We had to get married, knocked up. I've got another
daughter roaming the world somewhere, though nobody
knows about it but Ma—not even Alpha, and Alpha better not hear about it until I'm ready to tell her, or I'll
know where it came from. I didn't even tell Ma herself
until a few years back—I was afraid she wouldn't have
me if she knew that—and then when I finally did, to ex-

plain why this girl kept writing me, she got so out of hand I had to say, 'Well, dammit, Ma, the girl was a Catholic! What did you expect?'

"And now it seems imprudent of me to have said that. It rankled Ma more than ever about that marriage, and sure as hell didn't do *you* any good. Ma was a regular churchgoer once, too, you know, so she understands how important this is for you, and she's been after me all morning to get you to town by ten, when your Mass is. There at the first, when you first showed an interest in Alpha, I suppose Ma figured you were just out to give her the dong and then run off, and I must admit, because of my experience"—Jones looked up at him from under the flaring eyebrows—"I thought the same thing. But I knew you were serious about her from the way you took her in hand after Jerome— When— After that, I didn't think I could keep myself together if she went off and left us too, but of course I can. I'm going to stop trying to scare you off now. That's my New Year's resolution. Well, it's one of them."

Jones winked an ice-fringed eye at him.

"I must say, though, I do feel a lot better, now that you've gone and proposed. Easy, now. I know all about it, and I'll always be able to say I was one of the first to know. The old lady— Oh, Jesus, why do we call them that when we never think of them that way, especially in bed. The wife, Mrs. Jones, overheard you and Alpha talking last night. She wasn't snooping. She's not a snooper. She just happened to hear, and when she came in to bed she told me. Didn't you hear us? We were up half the night. Can you imagine me a *grandfather?* Jesus!

"And then Alpha couldn't sleep with the excitement of it, so she came down around five, after I got the gag on that windmill, and told me to my face, and I had to pretend it was the first I'd heard of it, and go through the hugging and kissing and try to shed a tear.

"It's too bad you sleep so late and we're so rushed, because the wife and I wanted you to know how much we wish you well." Jones grabbed Martin's hand and gripped it through mitten and glove. "Do you want to know something else, boy?"

Martin nodded, which was all he could do.

"Well, with all the churchgoing and whatnot the wife

has had, it really pleased me that I was the one, not her, who knew about this holy day and how you had to be to church on it—which I wouldn't have known, by heaven, if I hadn't been married to a Catholic once, and, Jesus! doesn't it amaze you the way the world goes round?"

                              *

Less than a half hour later, Martin was kneeling in the furnace-heated warmth of St. Boniface Church in Wimbledon, asking God if Alpha could be his wife.

3

JOB APPLICATION

THE QUALIFICATIONS OF
MARTIN NEUMILLER

PERSONAL DATA . . . I am twenty-three years of age,
six feet tall, and weigh 185 pounds. My physical
condition is excellent. I am a Catholic, but have lived
all my life in a Protestant community, and so I can
be at ease among Protestants as well as Catholics. In
1931 I was graduated from Courtenay High School.
I attended the State University at Grand Forks for one
semester in the school year of 1931–32, and in
1933 enrolled at Valley City. From the State Teachers
College I have received my Standard Certificate
and will receive my degree in May, thus completing
my work on the Secondary Degree Curriculum.
SCHOLASTIC RECORD . . . The titles of the courses
of interest I have had in college are: Literature,
Drama, Grammar, Rhetoric, Dramatics, Forensic,
Speech, Shakespeare, Poetry, Language Methods,
German, Political Parties, English History, European
Governments, Economics, Vocational Guidance, Child
Psychology, Adolescent Psychology, Educational
Psychology, Physics, Botany, Crop Botany, Journalism,
General Science, Music Appreciation, Educational
Sociology, Introduction to Education, Education
in the United States, Social Problems, Baseball and
Track, Principles of Secondary Education, Community
Life, Algebra, Observation, Teaching, Literature,

and Hygiene. My major is English, and my minors are German and History.

EXPERIENCE . . . My teaching experience consists of nine months' work in the Training School of the Valley City State Teachers College under excellent supervision. My teaching here was in History and Speech.

FORENSIC EXPERIENCE .. . . In high school I participated in dramatics, readings, and oratory. In my junior and senior years I was fortunate in being a member of the one-act play cast that took county honors. In my senior year I had the good fortune to be selected as the best actor in Stutsman County. At this same time I won first place in dramatic readings and also in oratory. At college I continued my work in these fields, and have also had one year's work in debate. In dramatics I have been in the eight major productions given at the college since I enrolled. In addition to this, I have helped put on programs at various churches, club meetings, and gatherings, in and about Valley City, whenever called upon. Last year I won the college oratorical contest. Broadcasts over KOVC have also given me valuable experience.

ATHLETIC EXPERIENCE . . . I participated in both basketball and baseball in high school. I pitched two fairly successful seasons for the Courtenay High School in the years 1930–31. Last summer I coached a Junior League baseball team at Courtenay. In college I participated in inter-society basketball. In the spring of 1935 I had charge of the state Kiwanis tennis tournament in Valley City. The fact that I was working my way through school limited my participations in athletics.

CAMPUS AFFILIATIONS . . . While at college I was a member of the Student Union, International Relations Club, Viking Yearbook Staff, Budget Staff, Tau Lambda Sigma, Newman Club, Dramatic Club, and the Alpha Phi division of the Alpha Psi Omega, a national dramatic fraternity. I have held various offices in these organizations during my enrollment here.

PREFERRED SUBJECTS . . . I prefer to teach English, History, German, and General Science, but am willing and feel qualified to teach, in addition, Physics, Psychology, Algebra, and Botany.

RECOMMENDATIONS . . . If interested in my application, you may secure my references by writing the College Placement Bureau here at Valley City.

Martin's roommate, Phil Rynerson, an older, married man who had returned to school to pick up some education courses, put down the two, single-spaced typed pages, and turned to Martin. "Well, it certainly is complete," he said. "I can say that."

"That's what I want."

"I was wondering, though, why you put this in, in the first paragraph here, this about Catholics and Protestants?"

"Because I figure I might as well lay it right on the line," Martin said.

4

❦

GIRL OF THE PLAINS

1936

NOV 9 *I've skipped back here to write (I actually got you, Five Year Diary, on the 14th) because this is my birthday and you were my gift from Martin, who couldn't be here for the event, on a weekday, of course, because of school. And now that I've got you I'm going to record my life as it is for Martin to read in five years. I was 20 years old on this date. Twenty! Lord. I feel like my life is just getting started or already half done.* [The diarist is Alpha Jones. All the entries in her diary, a six-by-five-inch volume covered with back-padded calfskin, and with a clasp lock on it, are in ink pen, unless otherwise noted. There is an entry for every day of the five-year period. The quirks of the entries are reproduced here as they stand. Each page of the diary has a date at its top and five red-lined spaces below with blue lines inside. There is about as much room for each daily entry as on four lines of a child's writing tablet, and in some instances, if the diarist anticipates a long entry, it begins down the page minutely, to the bottom blue line for that day of the year, touches the red, and then sentences ascend the first sentences in a ladderlike fashion, the writing even more minute, to the top again, and, if there's still more to say, once more descend. Some of the entries spill over onto the space for the next year. Margins of the diary are used.—ED.]

NOV 10 *I might as well write on in this space too. It's fun! I'm working, but not too hard, teaching 11 kids in a country school out beyond the outskirts of Leal.*

*That's in North Dakota, folks. Not where the Black
Hills or the Badlands are. They're mostly in South
Dakota, and nice, so I hear. I get $60 a month but
run the show as much as I want. The trouble is I'm
responsible, as my contract puts it, for "all janitor
duties." That means the usual janitor's cleaning, and it's
also up to me to start up oh*

NOV 11 *(I'm continuing on in this space) start up
the potbellied stove on cold mornings and lug that damn
coal bucket with freezing hands. Last Friday,
splitting kindling, I wanted to chop off my big toe. I
live with the Domans, a farm couple in their late
sixties with a farm and a half. They're a mile from
school, so I have to get up early to get there—the
downpours, the rain around me, those hours, ugh! I'm in
their daughter's room and have everything I need—
two windows, my books, and more time than I know
what to do with, plus Alpha Jones. And now this
nice diary.*

NOV 15 *Was Home. Domans fetched me in their
car, and on the drive to their place, in the back seat,
I read E. Guest's poems. So-so. They'll be all right
for my school kids to recite for Playday in April,
if they want. I must get to bed. It's after 10 and I
promised Martin, No more staying up late. Never later
than midnight, ever, I hope. Oops.*

NOV 19 *I got the letter from Martin I've wanted
all week and it's made the time since more bright.
November sky. Two parents visited at school, just about
my enrollment for the six grades, and they both
complained. Figure my batting average from that,
Daddy. There was such a heavy snow I'd hardly stepped
outside before I was "changed from a civilian into a
captain," as Jerome used to say—snow on my shoulders.
I felt Jerome in my eyes and spirits as I walked
down the bright road.*

NOV 21 *I went to a couple (3 to be truthful) dentists
in Valley City today, until I decided on young
Fagerland for me. Then I spent from 3 to 5 and 7 to 9 in
his old green chair. I would have screamed with
that drill inside my mouth and whizzing, if I hadn't
thought to think, "Martin will pick me up soon, now,
soon. Martin will pick me up . . ." On the way home*

*we stopped the car and had a tussle the likes of
which I can't remember since I was six and Elling tried
to roll me in the hay and had my pants off. Mama's
the only one who sympathizes with me and my bad
teeth.*

DEC 3   *I forgot my gloves at school tonight and froze
my hands on the walk home—oh, they were shrunken
and numb—and saw when I got here that I didn't
have on Martin's class ring. His ring that he's entrusted me
with! It was dark out, and darker with snow, so all I
could do was wail until my throat gave out.*

DEC 4   *Found Martin's ring in the gloves I left at
school, in the cloakroom it was, and was so happy I
could have sung! Doman chauffeured me home
where I found Mama sick in bed* [Mrs. Jones's illnesses
seem largely psychosomatic.—ED.] *and heard about
Martin's new brother, who's going to be christened
Davey and was born on Dec. 1st. That's their ninth.
I've been planning my Xmas program to keep from
hearing Mama's smart remarks. Lutherans don't
do that. They embroider their kids. It's 12:15, time for
bed. With the upset about the ring, it was 3 am last
night. Oh, Lord, pray for me.*

DEC 5   *Worked at home all day. Mama still ill.
Walked to the Neumillers at night to see Mrs. N and the
baby, Davey, who looks like Martin except for no
teeth. Mrs. N claimed their house was so cold the day
he arrived, she had Mr. N build her a big fire in the
cookstove and then sat in front of the oven and
had Davey there. Sat? That's what she said. I saw
Davey before Martin, ha, and Mrs. N even let me hold him
for a while, and you'd never know how proud it made
me. Vince drove me home.* [The names and ages of
the Neumiller children, at this juncture of the diary, in the
order of their ages, are: Martin, 23; Elaine, 21;
Vince, 19; Fred, 17; Jay, 15; Emil, 12; Rose Marie, 9;
Tom, 6; Davey, newborn.—ED.]

DEC 14   *Practiced for the Xmas Program in school
and was told by my conscience to do so all week. Heard
Martin in a radio broadcast over KOVC this evening.
He was the lead in a Xmas story, a tasteful one,
about some shepherds on the night of Christ's birth.
Most of the parts were well portrayed and I enjoyed*

*the program, but the sound of his voice made me so
lonesome, I was ready to start off walking for Valley City,
Oh, my love!*

DEC 19 *Day Of My Program. Woke last night and
heard the wind blowing a gale. Went to school but
so dark nobody could see to read, so sent the kids
home at 11. The wind died down later and there was a
crowd at my program after all, though I won't say
the number. Martin brought Mama and Lionell but
had to hurry on to Valley for who knows what? Domans
took Mama and Lionell and me home and all evening
I've been swallowing tears because Martin didn't see
my program.*

DEC 23 *Cleaned house all day, then helped cursing
red-faced father lay two new rugs, put up curtains,
painted woodwork and a dresser, baked, and put
the Xmas cutouts the school kids did for me up in all our
frosted windows. Mama is always saying about Mrs.
N, "I can't understand how she has so many and
still has her health—much less keeps sane." I heard
Mama say once, "Lionell is the last straw."*

DEC 24 *Christmas Eve. I delivered two of our fat
turkeys today—one to the Neumillers, the other to the
Carlsons, and then stopped at the cemetery on the
crossroads back and stood at Jerome's grave and tried
to pray, wondering how he was resting, and it started
to snow. I thought of him as a naked boy drowned
in dirt.*

DEC 25 *I woke many times last night thinking about
Martin, my perfect man, and then dreamed I was
at the cemetery, as I had been, except I was off a ways
watching when Jerome said, "Snow on your soldiers,
snow on your soldiers," as if he couldn't say shoulders,
like the Armbrust boy in the third grade. Xmas
wasn't a holiday for us without him. Mama had to
leave for her room and lie down, and then Daddy went
to the barn and stayed there half the night. He's
drunk now.*

1937

JAN 5 *Tuesday. 22° below. The music of a real N. Dak
blizzard is celebrating outside our walls. No school*

*or mail or letter from Martin. I went to bed at nine
with wide eyes, afraid of Doman, a drunk who doesn't
keep to himself as Daddy does. I'm so lucky Martin
would never allow himself to be found in such a
state. I took a bundle of his letters to bed and read them
over and over until his voice put me to sleep, or I
thought it did, and then saw I was writing this. How
old and butter-pink are Time's eyes.*

JAN 22   *Temperance Day. I talked for an hour on the
subject at school, too long, since even the kids at Leal
know I'm the daughter of Ed Jones. It's now 4 am.
I've been listening to the Flood Relief program over
WLS and can't sleep and keep worrying about the victims
in the Ohio Valley. Will I ever see Ohio or the honey-hive
of the East?*

JAN 29   *The fifth month of school done. Time
passes, after all, even if it doesn't for me. As I stepped
out the schoolhouse door, I saw a stray, wolfish dog
sniffing around the swings for a place to pee, and yelled,
"Get out of here, you pest!" just as the Lutheran
preacher, Rev. Grigson, came walking past. My cold
breath on the air was like a blowtorch!*

FEB 23   *It's blizzarding as badly as it's blizzarded all
year. We couldn't see the barns until 2:00, when it
let up a little, and then I walked to school facing it. It
wasn't cold but the wind was so strong the walk
wore me out and my forehead froze and slowed my
mind. Greeted in the schoolhouse by a snowdrift up
around the potbellied stove. No pupils. Shoveled snow for
forty minutes and am still creaky from it. No letter
from Martin again. I'm in a shining desert, but ice-cold.*

MAR 1   *Handsome Axel Anderson just a ways down
the road got his handsome Pontiac out of hibernation for
the spring and took me for a ride this afternoon
and, Oh, what a ride! We knocked down a fence post!
He wanted to paw and paw, is all, Ma, and then
invited me to a dance. I declined, kind sir.*

APR 13   *Danny, one of my calmest, brought news to
school today of seeing a pair of horned larks. They're
being more observant, what with my prodding and
my talks about Jerome. I worked out with the 11 on
speeches for the Declamation Contest this week,
and then wrote an application for a position in the town*

*school at Leal. And've felt a traitor ever since. No
mail again. A fly's been crawling on my face all
evening with eyesight.*

APR 19   *If you didn't have a lock on you, this wouldn't
go down. I keep you in my purse, anyway, just to be
safe, Martin. We were dress-rehearsing the declamation
speeches when Ruth, my brightest and best, said
something swell-headed to me—I don't even remember
what, now—and I took her by the shoulders and
started shaking her and couldn't stop. She was crying
and I must have looked a ghost. I let school out early
and lay in the cloakroom and wailed for us both
for an hour. Then my hand was where it shouldn't
be and waves went up my mind till I blacked out. Who
can I explain this to if not you, Martin, God?*

APR 24   *Awake all night. The wind was fierce and
trembling. I left for Valley, for Playday, with the
winners in Declamation from my school, three of them,
and barely made the train. I fidgeted for my kids but
Ruth and Danny received a first, and how happy they
are! When Mama heard about the first places, she said she
was proud of me. Proud. It wasn't what I wanted
to hear, but it was so good to hear that much, I lay my
head in her lap and cried for all the times I've deceived
her since I realized I could—broken, braked just
like a little girl.*

MAY 2   *Walked to school in the rain, which ruined my
disposition after hearing Daddy had bought a car and
was coming by later to pick me up. He got to Domans
at 5 and we cranked the old-new Model T from
then on until 7 and after. My hands blistered out
early so I wasn't much help. "Even machines are against
me," he said. He leads the life of Lorenzo Jones.*

MAY 20   *LAST DAY OF SCHOOL. I made out
final reports, my first, and learned what a nuisance
they'll be from now on. I worked on them through the
night till 7:30, and then picked wildflowers all the way
home. The sunlight was so clear it lay like weight
on the ground.*

MAY 28   *I went to Valley with Mrs. N and Jay and Elaine
and Davey (cuddled in Elaine's lap) to watch
Martin receive his degree, and thought he looked so*

*handsome all in black. But how I envied him! I've
decided I might go to summer school and intend to tell
him tomorrow right off.*

JUNE 7 *Jerome's birthday. We left for Valley in
the N's busy car and Elaine rode along. I talked her into
attending this session of school with me and we're
still both laughing and holding our sides! We found a
basement apartment, really rather nice, that will cost us
only $10 a month apiece, girls, fancy that! I got
my very first permanent wave, which took from 6 to
10:40 and was administered by Elaine, and look queenly
in the·mirror tonight. I hope I will tomorrow. Vince
is here for summer school too.*

JUNE 9 *I was so afraid in History Class, the instructor
looked so mean, I tried to be invisible and resolved
to study all my lessons from now on just to appease
him. Elaine and I cook such family meals we can
hardly finish them ourselves. The week is going fast, to
my mind; Elaine, however, thinks the opposite. That's
our life! Tonight we had our first entertainment, a
marshmallow roast over the gas ring and, believe me,
we're in love!*

JUNE 13 *Went to church this a.m. with Elaine—
the first time I've been at a Catholic Mass. I couldn't
understand the Dope's Lingo, as Daddy calls it, or why
they were sitting and standing and sitting and
kneeling all the time, so I just sat. They didn't sing
any hymns. I read most of this p.m. and then Elaine and
I played cards and had strawberry shortcake and
both sat there and burned.*

JUNE 15 *Put in a sleepy morning at my classes
except for History, where I didn't know my lesson
and shook so much my bones hurt. I'll be kinder to
my pupils, or else worse, after this. Saw the Coffer-Miller
plays in the forenoon and evening, and thought them
dreary, except for the one about Henry the VIII's
philandering and trouble with his wives. It made me
wonder about Daddy's past again and if he was a lover
like that slick old king.*

JUNE 23 *What a day for heat! In the high nineties.
Nevertheless, Elaine made candy and baked a cake.
We use the kitchen upstairs, and while she was busy in her
little hell, I slipped down to the apartment, where*

*it's cool, and worked like a student on my studies—
even Elaine so thought. Vince came over later and
said when he was leaving, "Don't you still care
for me a lot?" I said, "Sure" but shouldn't have. He took
my hand and stared at me as if I'd said much more.
No letters from Martin yet. I'm a warm and furry
creature tonight. Twelve holes.*

JULY 2   *The forenoon passed and found Elaine and me
happily on our way homeward, to quote a muse.
I was so glad to see Martin I would have danced
around him, but was too bashful to lift my eyes. Fr.
Krull was visiting and embarrassed me the most I've
ever been by saying, in front of Mrs. N and all the rest,
that I was "Mrs. Neumiller-to-be." Martin drove me
home and tried to make me.*

JULY 10   *Back at school in the smelly basement. No
mail from Martin again, when I was sure I'd hear!
I washed clothes, ironed, sent postcards to my school kids,
and then cleaned a suit and ruined my arms in the
cleaning fluid. They're turkey-red up to the elbows
now. Later, Elaine and I picked Juneberries on the hill by
the water tower, and came back and had berries and
sour cream on waffles, and now I'm a bloated sow
in heat. Suey!*

JULY 15   *Went to have studio pictures taken by
a pro today and weighed myself in at the drugstore.
121. Then spent my last nickel on licorice and ate and ate*

*till it was gone. I saw my fat shadow on the wall
here a while ago and got so angry I took a swat at it.
Miss Pig.*

JULY 17   *Woke early and washed clothes and my
head. Elaine waved my hair and I studied a while and
after supper was out on the porch, doing a maidenly
turn on the swing, when Martin and Jay drove up.
I knew there was a reason I'd got all gussied up, and
almost tripped over myself getting to the car. We
left within the hour for home and I loved the evening (the
morning?) with Martin, and the rain all over our
nakedness.*

JULY 27   *I picked up my pictures at the photographer's
and one is less awful than the rest. The schools I
apply to will imagine, maybe, they're getting a nice,*

*fat, jolly old wallowing—Oh, hell, I'm at the border of
no hard surfaces at all.*

JULY 30 *The last of school, for this time around.
B+ in Lang. Methods, B in Psychology, and History
there's no reason to write down. Back here at home I
washed, ironed, baked bread, helped in the garden,
and then walked overland to the Neumillers', where I
made a spectacle of myself by storming out when
Mrs. N said, "I think you and Martin are too serious
for just kids."*

AUG 3 *I began my hired-man role by riding the binder
for Daddy all day. Martin took me to Fr Krull's
in the evening, where we played cards and talked as
if we were educated for the first time this year. Then
Martin and I had an argument on the way home,
about religion again, and started fighting, really hitting
one another, and then—I don't know what happened—
we were making love like wildcats. I was so afraid
afterward I couldn't walk to our porch alone and
Martin held me there until I was my mother's daughter
and my starlit self again.*

AUG 21 *I shocked barley from 9 till after 2 and
came home with a brain-breaking headache from the
heat. My eyes couldn't let another bit of sunlight in.
Martin drove over in the evening and brought the good
news—he has a job teaching at the H.S. in Rogers.
I'll be teaching at the town school in Leal. We
went to the N's for a celebration and cards, and a belated
birthday party for Martin (it was the 7th) and later
M and I walked along the tracks and then sat down in
silent guiltiness. He said he'd see me again in a week but
I wish he'd come whenever he wants me.*

SEPT 7 *Leal. The second day of school. I wish it
were the second to the last. I'm not nervous this year, but
bewildered as to which books and materials to use
—I'm teaching seventh grade boys—and put out
by the living arrangements. Single teachers have to
room in a boarding house next to the school run
by Sarton, the principal, and his wife. There are some
rowdies to put up with and Martin will never be able
to sleep overnight here. I walked many miles after
supper, to be alone, and got back to school at
8 and worked until 10, then wrote my letter to Martin.*

*I wish I could see his room and know how it's
arranged, and where everything is in his office at the high
school in Rogers, even the papers in his desk, so I
could hold him for good when I get afraid about myself
and what I'll do in the state I'm in.*

SEPT 21 *Payday. With my first check I bought a
Shetland pony for Lionell. I haven't been a good sister to
him. He's too sensitive to Mama's moods. Martin
and I have been having foggy talks about religion.
Today, though, for no particular reason, the atmosphere
seems settled, and I'm in love as I look into Martin's
eyes in the frame on my dresser top. Where has my
bonny life gone hiding?*

OCT 8 *Last day of a thankless week. Discipline
problems. I've never encountered boys so mean. Because
they're bigger, they think they can get away with
throwing shelled corn, pestering girls, making farting
noises when I'm trying to talk—everything! I hate
them. I made three of the uglies stay after school to write
a 500-word piece on "How To Behave During Class
Hours" but cut it short when I saw Martin pull
up outside. What's that going to teach them? Lordy, Lord!*

OCT 23 *I was waiting for the Courtenay train when
Martin surprised me and drove up. We talked non-stop
until noon. My throat's still raw. In Wimbledon
after supper I got my hair waved and then Martin
and I went to the show "Sing, Baby, Sing," the worst sort
of trash I've endured for two bits. Later, Martin played
Romeo to me and talked about setting a date for
the summer and had me on my knees. I hinted at our
plans to Mama and she said, "I always thought you wanted
to do something decent with your life."*

DEC 31 *Daddy must have thought his Xmas meager
this year, until his real gift arrived in today's mail.
Mama had ordered him a pocket watch like the one he
lost the summer Jerome drowned. It took Mama's
egg money for the year and most of my last paycheck.
"Send the SOB back!" he said. "I need a corn
planter! I need a new drill!" And then he went out to
the barn and spent the day there and he's been cranky
and confused and afraid to look at us ever since.
Why can't some people accept as much as they give?*

1938

JAN 5   *Rushed around getting ready for the rotten*
job awaiting me in Leal, and then the Model T
wouldn't start, so Daddy, Mama, and I started off in the
lumber wagon but only got a mile out on the white
highway when Carlson came by in his car. Daddy
tied the team to a telephone pole and in we went.
Back here, warmed by two stoves and my hate for this
place, I wrote cards and letters, corrected papers
(left from before Xmas) and pasted photographs in
the new album Mother gave me. Then I hymned all
evening. The only way I can feel alive in the world
is by hymning. Brobdingnagian. Huge as all this stretch
of sod.
JAN 6   *I've dreaded this day, the first of school after*
vacation, and it was worse than I'd pictured in my
dread. The kids, those three boys, mostly, raised so
much hell I was ready to hamstring them all, and shook
up two until their back teeth clattered and clacked.
Went to Sarton after 4 and told him I was going to quit.
Today. He said he'd try to change some assignments.
I was crying so little-girlishly the front of my dress
was wet.
JAN 10   *The 7th grade boys went up the stairs, the*
8th grade girls came down to me, and it was like a
vision of heaven in Leal Public School. But when night
came and I went to my new assignment, coaching
girls' basketball (basketball is played with a basketball
and baskets), woe unto me! I struggled through but
but now I'm so fatigued and shaky I'm bumping
into my shadow. I planned to spend the evening cutting
out poems for my scrapbook but I'm going to fall into
bed instead and turn out the light. The one inside me.
FEB 27   *Here in Rogers at the Rynersons', Phil and*
Lou's. Phil is Martin's old roomate and the principal at
Rogers now, and the Rynersons' might become my
home away from eyes. Mar came over before anybody
was out of bed, and then took me to breakfast at
the Belmont Hotel. In the afternoon we listened to our
favorite radio programs with Phil and Lou, who like
the same, played bridge, and then the Rynersons

nicely went to bed at 9:00. Martin was here until three in the morning. Why?

MAR 1 *A day comparable to April 1st. I went around to every room at Sarton's, trying to find somebody to play—cards or sock-and-wrestle—just to play, but no luck. So I went for a walk in the unplowed fields, thinking about Martin and our future freedom, and then back here shoveled snow from under the clothesline. My contribution to real life. Then I washed all the school windows, or at least smeared dirty rainbows around on them, and sat on the steps as the sun set and watched birds scratching at the crumbs and grain they've come to expect me to put out for them. How happy I am.*

MAR 9 *Had my hair newly cut and waved and had to sleep on my nose all night, and then no Martin. Damn! School went okay, when I could be heard between coughing sieges. The flu is raging. I say school went well, but I seem to remember doing a lot of caterwauling. My throat's still sore from it. I finished the embroidery on my "Sunday" (I hate "quotes") towel set tonight, and now I have those, an everyday set, and the tablecloths I've done. There are only a few more pieces to do for the hope chest Dad Neumiller built for me.*

MAR 21 *The first day of spring was disappointing—a messy dust storm. No Mail. I must be suffering from spring fever, I'm so worn out and loggy-legged. Or else I'm pregnant.*

MAR 26 *No mail again. Are my friends deserting me? Do I have any? Sarton came into my room after school and said I'd been rehired by the school board, then said, "But I'd advise you to look for a different job, such as teaching primary grades." Primary grades. I said, "Goodbye to you. I won't be teaching your scoundrels again!" I'm so livid I can hardly see through it to keep awake. And unsettled! What if I can't find another job? And what if Martin's and my promises about the summer have been vows into the wind again?*

APR 15 *Met Mar on train but too bashful to*

greet him as wanted. Spent whole day dying to get decent mark.

APR 16 *Sick all morning. Mar came to bring me to Fargo in a few minutes. I kept some here. $89. Stayed overnight at N's. Almost asleep when a voice says, "How'd you like to get inside your mother's skin like it was long underwear?"*

APR 17 *Ran home from 6:30 till 7:05. Not greeted royally. Walked to church and back again without any help. Let Mrs. N know I've got a church.*

APR 18 *They'll have to be up with us with* [A wavering line is drawn across the page here.—ED.] *an affair he'd give up the river. Almost asleep, a voice again. No words.*

APR 19 *Wrote the four preceding entries in my sleep or when I was crazy with no sleep. Besides everything else I said and shouldn't have said and should have done and didn't. In my sleep. I can't eat or talk or make sense of the simplest word. I feel I'm crawling with the Lord.*

APR 21 *Another terribly dusty day. The farms are flying over our heads.*

MAY 6 *The mystery in the air at the N's has been given a name. Illinois. Mr. N wants to go and look at property there—Mr. N, who's always lived in the state and done so well for himself. Martin said he might drive down too, and since I didn't hear from him or see him tonight, I know he has. I'm bereaved knowing he's so far from me, and with this cold my nose is running off my face.*

MAY 10 *Was I surprised when somebody knocked at the door and I found Elaine back from Ill already. She brought a gift from Martin, a blue swan made of real china, and said all of them liked Ill. They might move there soon. Mar came over later, sheepish and indefinite, so I know we won't be married this summer as we planned. I live on air and lies.*

MAY 27 *School Year Is Over. A beautiful day for our picnic, and I romped and frolicked in the sun with the children until my arms were burned bright red. Graduation exercises in the eve. I had to sit on the stage, a fogy, and be stared at, and then Martin came afterwards and waited while Betty Sarton bathed*

*my arms in tea and made them mine again. Hands
directly from her heart. M helped bring back home my
junk and me, and said his Dad is moving the family
to Illinois as soon as possible. So there. My cockpit
of falling freedom gone.*

MAY 30   *I walked to Carlsons' to plan a farewell
party for the N's and found out plans were already
made and finished. I'm sorely disappointed in them,
however; a summer-on-the-farm buffet. I felt I'd dissolve
into air all the way to the N's, where Martin dug
up irises and tulips from their flower beds, and then
planted them around Jerome's grave for me. Martin's
father has left for Ill already, before the closing
sale, and Martin said, "He can't stand that everything we
own is being sold. He'd worry about the stock if he
knew who had it." Then why sell out? Why give
monikers to plants and cattle and poultry and machines
of work?*

JUNE 2   *Walked to the N's for the Homemaker's
party for Elaine and Mrs. N but spent the whole day
outside with Martin in that blizzard of silence that
comes when one of us is being deceitful. I met
Adele, Vince's girl from Ypsilanti, and she has her
claws into him like a cat on a rock. Back home, I
cleaned out the cellar, took off storm windows, washed
crystal and wanted to throw the watch away, though
it's the most meaningful gift I've got from Martin,
not to mention the cost.*

JUNE 4   *I got my hair cut short, just below the ears, and
waved it the way I used to, with curlers on the lamp
chimney, and went to the Neumillers' sale. Vince
and Martin did most of the handling of it. I sat in a
car with Adele. She wanted to talk about Vincent
when he was young and I wanted the car to drive away
with just me inside. I walked home and hardly got
here when Vince and Adele came after me but
wouldn't say why. At the N's, Martin told me he'd changed
his mind. He's not staying. He was leaving for Ill right
then. I helped pack some final pieces in spite of my
eyes, and then watched Martin go off, riding on a
truckload of furniture with Fred, because the cab of it
and the car were full, Davey was suspended in a blanket
sling from the ceiling of the Model A. I lay in a*

*grain bin in their barn and wailed until it was dark
outside. Then I walked home alone, or I'd be alone for
good.*

JUNE 18   *Got a card and letter, via air mail, from
Martin, but no news. Cleaned house for the seventh time
this week to drive away memories thick as my hair,
then read the 55 letters I received from Mar from
Sept. through May. I can't sleep and haven't taken a
leak in two days.*

JULY 28   *I'm a harvest hand again, riding binder and
shocking grain, and so weak I can hardly walk.
There were breakdowns every round and after one
Daddy yelled, "You're a piss-poor man on the binder!"
I started crying and wanted to confess how unhappy
I am. "Quit it," he said. "Don't be so God—sensitive!"
A letter from Martin. He says he'd like to go to
school in Ill and maybe even teach there. My face
will be white for a week.*

JULY 29   *Today we thought we'd finish the barley,
but no. I went into Courtenay with Daddy from work, in
dirty shirt and bib overalls, and was escorted into
the tavern, where he bought me my first drink—a
glass of wine. It was terrible, melted tin, but I
finished it and had a few more, and us field hands made
it home just fine, folks, singing through the night.*

JULY 30   *We didn't finish the barley till after 4, as
a result of canvas trouble and wine. See above. I went
into Wimbledon and found out I'm hired for next
year at Uxbridge—lovely Uxbridge school that I
looked at all last year during every trip back home
from Leal the way a calf looks at an udder. Ooooo!*

AUG 15   *A restful day. No fieldwork due to last
night's rain. I practiced the piano all afternoon and then
went into Wimbledon, hoping to find excitement,
but no. Rode home in the big box of Tony Mendelson's
truck and was almost blown overboard. Tony said
he saw it all and gave a wink. There was a letter
from Martin, three pages which hardly said a word I
wanted to hear, and then at the end that he was
lonely. Lonely! Lord, isn't this body where he belongs?*

AUG 22   *After today's letter from Martin, I helped
Mama put up the rhubarb, 35 quarts of it, and canned*

*17 of corn myself, and then chopped up a whole
RR tie. And wrung a chicken's neck, <u>gladly</u>, for our
meal tonight. Went into the tavern and had another
type of drink, rum and Coke, and it wasn't so bad. Rode
home on Tony Mendelson's lap and could have
had myself. I'm single again.*

SEPT 3   *I woke at 5 in the morning to a car horn
and knew it was Martin, and it was! My first kiss from
him in three months, and just in my pajamas! Mama was
shocked. Martin's definitely at Rogers for the term,
at <u>least</u>, he says, and seems much more happy and free
with himself away from his mother. Three months
evaporated with his lips on mine.*

SEPT 13   *School in Uxbridge isn't bad—thirteen kids
in the first four grades (isn't that <u>primary</u>, Mr. S?)
—except it's difficult to find something for the
different classes to do all the time. I have my own
room, a big one, in the teacherage run by the janitor and
his wife, Dick and Irma Reese. Just Cissel, the
principal, and me and two other teachers live here.
There's a phone. Martin came and said Vince was in
Ypsilanti to see Adele, so we drove down after supper to
visit them. They plan to get married in two weeks.*

SEPT 24   *Wedding day. I intended to get up at 5
but couldn't. Mar came at 6 and we were witnesses at
the marriage, in the front room of Fr Krull's.
Vince was gray but looked strong and he laughed
once. His laughter comes out of him with as much
pleasure as there is in his eyes and always makes me
laugh. There was no music, or real ceremony, and
what there was was over before it got going. Mrs.
Donnegan, Fr's big housekeeper, stood with her
stockings around her ankles, shaking with tears. It could
have been me marrying Vince, I realized again and
again, and Adele isn't a Catholic, either.*

OCT 9   *Mama's ill. I went to Mass with Martin and
then came home and got the last of the carrots
from the garden, and cooked them up with a chicken for
stew. Martin took me to Fr Krull's in the afternoon,
for a trial in instructions. It wasn't agonizing, as I'd
thought, but Martin left Uxbridge right away for
Rogers, when I wanted to talk about the lesson,*

*and I'm worried Mama will be worse if she hears where
I've been. I looked at the catechism and then lay
on the bed, dozing and waking in fits of surprise, and
wondered, Has my role as a wife already begun?*

5

ABOUT FATHER KRULL

Alpha's mother, Electa Jones ("No wonder we've got such weird names," Elling once said to Alpha), was vocal and aphoristic about her likes and aversions, a compendium of arcane beliefs and outright prejudices. "Men with dark hair have minds dark as water," she said, and Alpha's father's hair, except for the silver on the sides, was nearly black; Martin's hair was as black as a Sioux's. "Grown men who chew on a chaw of chewing gum deserve no respect; it looks like their mouths haven't grown up yet and makes you wonder if their minds, which are mighty close, have either." And, "If you don't eat in little bites, if you bolt your food or chomp it with your mouth open wide, or slurp soup like that, people will think we feed you from a trough." The use of tobacco, of cigars and cigarettes, especially, was one of the filthiest acts permitted to take place in public, to her mind, and she often said, "People who put their cigarettes out on plates should have to eat their meals out of ashtrays."

And Alpha'd heard her say that the biggest bane on the entire human race, other than cigarettes and alcohol, was the Roman Catholic Church; that Catholics were just interested in liquor and getting you to go to bed with them, and not much else; that their rule of eating fish on Fridays was just another way of making themselves look like superior folk (she'd heard it was supporting European fisheries), and anybody who heeded such a rule was a sheep who let his life be dictated by the Pope, a man who lived in Italy, in Europe, you see, and wore women's skirts and little beanies!

"Ma," Ed Jones said, "I wore some pretty funny-looking clothes myself when I did Shakespeare, you know."

115

"Sure. To play make-believe roles up on a stage some place."

"I made it up to Buffalo!" he cried, and then scowled hard. "Well, what the hell do you think the Pope's doing, for Christ's sake, if not playing a role!"

"But Catholics all over *heed* what he says."

"If they did, Ma, how could they be up to all the things you say they are?"

Ed Jones went to church for weddings and funerals— "One in the same; I can't keep 'em apart"—and maintained that every religion, "Well, every one of them just makes holes here in your head." When the family was on the farm near Hannaford, he dressed up once in his best black suit for the funeral of a neighbor and friend, but when they got to the church, said, "We'll see you afterward," and went out into the grass-covered cemetery plot that lay to the back and side of the church. It was hot August, the windows were open wide, and the congregation kept craning their heads to get a look at him. He stood under a single elm in the cemetery, a tree that rose like a showering and entangled fountain above the plain, one foot planted on the mound of newly dug earth, holding his coat and tie back, his mouth moving as if in argument, as he leaned and addressed the empty grave, and now and then extricated a silver hip flask from his breast pocket and took a long Adam's-apple-pulsing pull on it. He started away and then came back and flipped the flask into the grave, and walked down the gravel road toward home until he was out of sight against the plain.

*

Alpha's mother seldom went to church from then on, even after they'd moved from Hannaford to Courtenay, as if she couldn't rid herself of the ignominy of that day. She read the Bible and hummed and sang hymns while she worked, and on Sundays, with Alpha singing alto to her voice and playing along on their old and tinnily untuned upright piano. The concordance to her Bible was a book called *The Perfect Woman*. Alpha hadn't been to Lutheran catechism or to Bible school (she'd always had to work), and had never really been instructed by her mother in the faith, other than to believe. Martin often made Alpha think of her mother's prejudices; and the circuitous way in which the closed minds of parents come around again left Alpha fighting an affection for the Catholic Church.

Martin partly helped change her mother's predisposition against Catholics. He was a non-smoker, he and his father were teetotalers to a tee and seemed honest, and had proved honest, so far, and Mr. Neumiller did so well by the family he might be a Serb; Martin gave off an aura as brawny and brainy and wholesome as fresh-baked bread, and her mother remarked to her about him, more than once, "He's one of the most innocent young men I've ever met, dear!" and, well, it was just too much for the two of them, plain rural women, as they thought of themselves, to take down and digest at one time. But then gossip had it that Mrs. Neumiller had let it be known, when she found out that Martin and Alpha were about to be married, that in the first place Alpha would have to convert to the Church.

"Well, that's it!" her mother cried now. "That's the limit! No child of mine is becoming a Catholic while I'm alive. I'll die first! Isn't she satisfied that her boy is taking—is taking—" Her voice was rising into its high and girlish modulations and she couldn't go on.

"I don't intend to be a Catholic, but if I'm going to marry one, mightn't I as well have a few instructions about them for free?"

"Who said?"

"Martin."

"When was this? What's he up to?"

"It's a requirement of the Church."

"What makes those people think they have the right to hold a control over the lives of others, is what I'd like to know! What gives them the *gall?*"

"Oh, Mama. All I have to do is read a catechism and talk to some priest once or twice."

"Where'd you learn this? From a priest?"

Alpha bowed her head and fiddled in the lap of her dress for a while. "Martin," she said.

"So his mother already has the poor calf bawling after you about it, huh?"

"No."

"They'll make you convert! They always do! They'll ruin your natural wonderment and belief in the Lord. You'll see! You'll end up like *Daddy*." It was a turkey gobbler's gargled gorge the notes of the name came out of now!

"Mama. My goodness. It's Father Krull, you know."

"So much the worse! He's not just a priest, he's her *cousin!*"

"But he's so—"

"Don't ever claim I didn't warn you, when I have again and again," her mother said, and went tripping noisily into her room as she did whenever Jerome was brought up, and flung herself down on the bed and lay unmoving for the afternoon, her arms covered by the undone mass of her golden, hip-length hair.

*

Even before Father Krull was ordained a priest, he was looked on as bishop material, perhaps even the stuff of which cardinals are made. He was a little overweight, but not really. He was a logician and as well versed in canonical law as some of his instructors. And funny, too! He loved old books, footnotes, knowledge, the smell of dusty pages, and his superiors and fellow seminarians sensed that his was a helpless love above his head. Oh, well. He earned one of the best academic records at St. Bede's, in St. Paul, but it was understood that this was merely another outgrowth of his love and not a goal. Or was it at that? His first appointment, then, was to St., ah, Whatyoumay-callit's in Wahpeton, and there he soon advanced to the position of assistant pastor and everybody's friend. He was about to be made a monsignor and be transferred again to the cathedral in Fargo, St. Mary's, and be a part of the gang of boys in the bishop's office there, at St. Mary's, when he asked to serve, instead, as pastor of the church in Courtenay, another St. Mary's, a tiny church, a mission, actually, being served by the priest out of St. Boniface in Wimbledon, Father Stahl; Courtenay was Father Krull's home town, his birthplace, and his request so out of line his superiors suspected that perhaps he had, indeed, learned too much too easily—how could they know his mind?—and advanced too fast, and might need to humble himself for a time. His request was honored, of course. He was sent to Courtenay. Within the year it became obvious why he'd asked to be sent there. He was going blind. He wanted to go blind on home ground.

He began to walk with an uncharacteristic, taut-limbed, trembling, jittery unsteadiness when more than a block from his house or the church, and made fewer house calls than before. He'd been gregarious at first and that's how he'd been remembered as a boy. Now another boy, a constantly shifting and changing one in altar boy's clothes, guided him by the elbow for processions and graveside rites. He'd taken care of his own house until now, but a cleaning lady started to come twice a week and then three or four times. She caught him moving his hand in front of his eyes. His books and newspapers had to be read to him. The top of his head turned bald. A length of clothesline wire ran from the back corner of his house to the outhouse. Wires were strung around the lawn, and a strand led to the church and another to the front door. His face went round and gray and his remaining hair fell out in patches. He had to give the parish back to Father Stahl. He stopped wearing his rabat and collar, and his grayish or black clothes were usually soiled and smelled of a male. He had his cousin's husband, Charles Neumiller, build a platform and an altar and tabernacle along one wall of his living room, and said daily Mass there, performing the ritual entirely by touch, his altar boy usually Bernice Donnegan, his live-in housekeeper now, a broad-shouldered, curly-haired, affable-lipped and mannishly loud but lightspirited, two-hundred-and-fifty-pound Irishwoman, her cotton stockings almost always down around her ankles because they were such a bother with the shots of insulin she had to give herself.

"At first I could distinguish between daylight and the dark," he said, "but I can't now. Not with my eyes, that is. I feel the change on my skin now, especially here." He touched his cheek beneath the eye. "The day is filled with less activity than the dark—just the opposite of what I'd always thought and been taught to believe. Or maybe we don't really listen during the day. I don't believe in demonology, of course, the presence of spirits or any of that sort of nonsense, except in the respect that there might be saints in some form, but the dark has a personal-

ity, is my word. It's benign. I study it as I might a poem,
discovering resonances in it I've never heard, or seeing a
portion of it appear in another dimension or plane beneath the page. I can feel when somebody in the neighborhood is sleepless, you see. And if anybody is in pain,
it comes to me in streaks that are red with silver beams in
them. Cats must feel the same way at times. During the
day they sometimes move in harmony with the dark.
That's why we watch them. I should have one, I suppose.
A *black* one! Hah! Every night has its distinctive color,
or layers of colors, like the layers of colors in a lake, and
every one appears in a different form from the one before it. Last night, for instance, when the sun was all
through with his display, I felt a current of molecular
change around my head area here like an electrical charge,
and saw a moment of light. Off, on. And I felt if this
could happen, why then God, through his son, Jesus, could
certainly change water into wine for a wedding ceremony.
And most of my life I'd inwardly scoffed at that as 'the
Cana magician's trick.' That ruffed grouse has been drumming in the same corner of that field for four nights now.
I know if a particular wren is nesting here, as one did
this spring, or which dove that was. Each has a voice as
individual as yours, my dear."

He raised his eyes, grainy-gray and protuberant, and
stared out of their opaqueness with such inner illumination
it seemed he was studying you with approval, and then
he bowed his head and his fatty lids covered his pupils
halfway. "Is there anything in this lesson that bothers you?"

"The Trinity," Alpha said. "Those three-Gods-in-one."

"There's a tale, probably apocryphal, about one of the
saints—Thomas or Peter, I believe. He was walking a
beach, sand with rocks around, determined to prove his
worth and solve the riddle of the Trinity, when he saw a
golden-haired boy filling a sea shell with water and pouring
it out on the beach. 'What are you doing?' the saint is said
to have asked. 'I'm emptying the sea, sir,' the boy told
him. 'Even if you kept at it without a rest, you could never
do such a thing in your entire lifetime, my boy,' the saint
said. 'Nor will you, in your lifetime, sir, understand the
Trinity,' the boy said, and disappeared."

"Why didn't the saint offer to help?"

"Oh, ho, *you!*" Father Krull said.

"I don't know if I'm angry at the Trinity itself—I mean, not the people in it—or just so prejudiced against the Church I figure everything it teaches is purposely misleading me."

"If it were either of those, I don't think you'd be here."

"Don't I have to be, sir?"

"Ha! Yes, but you could sit there, like the others I counsel, and keep saying, 'Uh huh, uh huh,' so I could say 'Fine!' and you could get married. It's not necessary to understand all of this, much less believe in it. This is merely to help you understand how Martin's mind works on certain matters out of reflex. If you know some of the reasons, you can be closer to him in your marriage, or so I've always assumed."

"I figure if there are three Gods, then why not five or six, huh? Or a dozen of them. And then there are all the saints, who could include just about practically anybody, the way it seems in your Church. That sounds like paganism to me."

"I know you've acted in high school, and at the college, I hear, and I'm sure you can portray more roles than the Lucy you did for us, can't you? Your voice was so singing."

"Of course I can."

"Couldn't you use that to help you see the Trinity, thinking of it as different guises God could assume?"

"I guess I could."

"It's easier to have a feeling for it if you've grown up with the religion, as Martin has, and it has to be felt to be believed. Religion is visceral." He drew back in his chair. "Your hour is up. Martin's pacing the sidewalk again. He doesn't realize you're really interested in the faith and not just wrangling."

"I am?"

There was a silence between them, interwound with the scrape and crush of Martin's shoes on the sidewalk, *creer chee, creaca chee, creesh shee,* and then Father Krull said, "Ask him to come in and have a cup of coffee with us."

"All right."

"Unless there's something more?"

"It doesn't have to do with this lesson. It's the paper I have to sign, where I promise to bring my children up in the Catholic Church, the one Adele signed. Well, it makes me *sick* to think that people who aren't even born yet are going to be bound by a promise of mine."

"That document's primitive and absurd, and in violation of even your civil rights. There's no justification for it, and someday it'll be thrown out of the Church altogether. When you come to signing it, if you do, cross your fingers."

"What!"

They both laughed.

"But don't tell any of the Neumillers I said that. Now let's have some of that coffee. Bernice! Coffee for three, or four, if you care to join us. It's Alpha and Martin."

Martin came in. He brought her to these sessions and left right away and went shopping or on errands, or drove out of town and over the gently tilting farmlands all around until Alpha's hour was up. She always stayed longer. She talked to Martin about what she and Father Krull had talked about, which he wasn't sure you should do, and her persistence and breeziness made him uneasy with himself and her. He didn't look forward to the time, near the end of her instructions, when they'd have to counsel together—such a sharp tongue! Just the idea of arguing with a priest made sweat come out along his hairline. This afternoon, after coffee and sympathetic small talk, Father Krull said he wanted to speak to him alone. What was up? Alpha went out and down the steps, sashaying with her purse toward the car, and Father Krull came to the screen door where Martin gripped a trembling hat, and stared beyond him, as if following Alpha's walk, and said, "Isn't she a fine girl?"

"Yes, she is," Martin said.

"I don't give personal advice, but since you and I are related, I will to you. When you're married, and I expect you will be soon, live as far as you can from your mother. Give her time to accept Alpha as your wife."

"Certainly."

"And you'll have to be very attentive to your husbandly duties. Alpha is one of the most passionate women I've met."

Martin blushed; he'd never expected a priest to make such a confession to him, he who usually confessed to Father here, but had started dropping anonymously into confessionals in Wimbledon or Rogers or Jamestown lately, so Father wouldn't hear how much he already knew of that part of her.

"One thing more," Father said. His lids lifted, exposing his eyes, and he shook a finger so close to Martin's chest it seemed for an instant he could see, and Martin felt from him the sudden emanations of his intuition and moral authority. "This: Don't you ever, ever, even if your life depends on it, try to persuade that girl to become a Catholic, do you hear?"

6

IN LOVE WITH MYSELF

NOV 24 *Martin took me to Thanksgiving dinner in the Belmont Hotel and proposed a late December date for our wedding. I approved. So toward the 22nd we go, hearts clean as razors, and I'm praying all the way*
NOV 26 *At Home. Ironed clothes, seven dress shirts for Daddy, and did other Saturday chores, trying to work up courage to tell Mama about our wedding date, and did, finally, down on my knees with floor wax. To my great surprise she took it with calm. Daddy just laughed and made eyes like a wolf. Woof! Mama planned and talked and gave me simple womanly advice, and I was so happy I wanted to hug her and say, "I love you, Mama! I'll miss you a lot!"*
DEC 7 *As we were sitting down to supper in the teacherage, Martin walked in, took my hand and led me up to the front of the room, and put a ring, a half-carat diamond, on the finger that will hold the matching band, and I felt my heart would leave if I breathed out, the diamond's so huge! "Yes," I said, holding the ring on show and being an actress. "I'll be married soon. you know." And then I realized how terrified I was and felt I wouldn't be peeing again for a while.*
DEC 11 *We went to Fr Krull's and had supper with Fr and Vince and Adele, who'll be standing up for us, tit for tat. After supper, while those three visited, I had my last session with Fr. I was wondering to him earlier if I hadn't got interested in religion because of Jerome, and wanted to say some kind word to him now, and then he said, "Why don't we just spend these last few minutes together in silence." I listened and*

124

*heard the Lord in currents of wind through wheat
or flax! I'm alive at last or have died.*
DEC 22 [The entries for the rest of the year are
in pencil and the handwriting is rapid and minute.—ED.]
*My heart's so full I feel it's been carrying me around
smiling instead of me it. I cried so much at noon I was
afraid to go back to school and when I finally did Cissel
said I looked so bad I better leave. I took a shower
and worked up so much lather I gagged on it, afraid
Martin would come in with my hair all soaped, and
was dressed and ready, for once in my life, when HE
showed up. I got my face straightened, tried to make
it smile, and walked out the doorway toward the end of
my life. Vince and Adele were at Fr's. We were married
at 5 p.m. I was numb from below the waist and
saw the legs of Martin's trousers jiggling with the shakes.
We were a fright. We went home royalty to Mama,
at last, legal, at least, who had a wedding supper ready,
but could stay only an hour, a disappointment to her
—forgive us, Mama, I'm in such a rush!—because we had
to get back to our places at Uxbridge and Rogers and,
pack by 9 for the train to Ill. Then at Rogers we
learned the train was an hour late, so wouldn't have had
to have hurried so much, Ma, dear, and had time to
address our Xmas cards "Martin & Alpha N" We're here,
I thought. Then Vince and Adele, my new husband,
and I all got on the steaming train for Ill with Mr.
Bujalski, the stationmaster, showering us with rice.
Vince's touch. I cried so much at his thoughtfulness and
the day that Martin got mad at me. I'm just a girl of
the plains, I guess, and I'm riding the Soo Line.*
DEC 23 *We rode the Soo until 7 and then got on
the Burlington Zephyr, which is elegant. Porters are
your friends. We took the Rock Island from Chicago
and got into Peoria at 9. Fred met us at the station
and drove us all out in silver starlight to the small
farm where the N's are renting, about 3 miles from
Forest Creek. None of the family but Vince and Adele
knew we were married, and when Mrs. N saw
me along with Vince and Adele and started wondering
where I could sleep, Martin said, "She'll sleep with me,
Mother." Oh, Lord, the look on her face would
have won a prize in trying not to show what you really*

feel. Martin said, "She's my wife, Mother. We were
married yesterday." She smiled and said she was glad
of that. Who ever knows what she's up to?
DEC 24 *We went into Bloomington in the afternoon to
get Jay and Mr. N, who've been working on some
kind of building there. When Mr. N heard about our
marriage, he cried out and threw his arms around
me and beat me on the back and then gave me a big
kiss! I love him better than Martin, I lie. In Bloomington
we had our wedding picture taken and did some
last-minute Xmas shopping together as man and wife.
On the way back, Mar felt queasy and feverish, and
his lips were on fire but not for me. We went to
Midnight Mass in Havana, a high one, and I sat
through the whole mournful bore of it watching sweat
pour off his face until the side of it was glazed gray.*
DEC 25 *What an awful Xmas and honeymoon! Mar was
like an oven beside me all night, but with real fever!
I think neither of us slept, nor did we do more.
He sweat until he and the bed were soaking. My new
negligee got wet! He has a raw sore throat along with
the fever and I'm so helpless I'm in tears most of the
time and want to change myself. There's so little time
in this nightgown, I love him so much, I'm so
glad to be married, and now if only he were well and
in good voice!*

DEC 28 *A cold wave has moved down and settled here.
Martin is feeling better from the warm cloths I
held over his throat, but now he's insulted by himself
for getting sick at such a time, and that makes me feel
worse, of course, because I want it, oh boy, do I,
oh boy, yes! Our wedding pictures (the proofs,
actually) came today and all are surprisingly good. Do
I really look that young and pleased and will my
children always see me so?*

1939

JAN 7 *Home. Mama not well. We got here before
anybody was up and I washed clothes all day for Mama
and my husband, while he chopped kindling for the
fire for it. The water for it. Oh, hell. Tonight is the last*

*of our 17 day honeymoon and after the day's work,
when we finally drug ourselves clunking up to
my room, Daddy had put thumbtacks and dried
chicken manure and everything else imaginable in
our bed, including a patched-up old inner tube.
"Horse condom," he said, when I threw it down the
stairs at him. "You better make sure he knows how to
use it."*

JAN 9 *I was so tired my first day back at school I
couldn't even enjoy being called Mrs. Neumiller.
Or maybe it's because I'm in Uxbridge, the same old
place, Martin is in Rogers, and the days go on the same
as before we were married. Our wedding pictures
came in the mail and I was disappointed after all, at
least with my face, which looks like the fox that
got the grapes.*

JAN 14 *I didn't sleep all night nor all morning and
began looking out the window as soon as it was light.
Mar showed up at 10, walking fast and carrying
a heavy suitcase that hit my toe when we embraced.
He'd walked from the station at Leal, all those miles
against the beginnings of this blizzard that now howls,
and his back ached all day from the strain of it. I
washed his clothes and hung them out but shouldn't
have; they frosted and dried so slowly they're streaked.
After hours of love, we wrapped our wedding pictures
and sent them out and began reading Anthony Adverse
aloud to one another and the cold air.*

FEB 25 *I was disgusted with Cissel because he had a
hangover (shades of home) and wouldn't drive me to
Rogers until noon, and I'd expected to be at Martin's
making love. We did, all the rest of the afternoon,
and in the evening I went with Martin to the Ladies
Aid Supper. After the meal he read them one of my
favorite pieces he does, Laska, and moved some
of the women so much I was jealous, damn. He's so
good all around!*

APR 17 *After my last class, I came upstairs and
wandered into Cissel's room and started reading one
of his off-color magazines, and suddenly got so tired I
lay down on his bed and fell asleep. I must have
slept for hours. It was dark when I woke and I felt*

*somebody's eyes on me. I turned to the window and
saw Jerome's face outside, not really glowing but
with a particular light, just his face, and wasn't
frightened a bit. We stared at one another and were
both calm. He seemed to be saying my worries would
work out. Definite word has come today. I'm pregnant.*

MAY 24   *Don't feel well. I'd worked all night on my
final reports and was surprised, or shocked, when
Mother N and Jay walked into the schoolhouse at bright
dawning. They're here to take Mar and me back to
Ill, and I thought it was still undecided whether or not
we were to go. I had to finish my reports, so they
went on to Rogers without me. Did Martin write and
tell her we'd both be done with school today? I feel
deceived.*

MAY 27   *At Home. Martin drove up in a nearly
brand-new Chevrolet, a pretty shade of blue, which I
thought he'd just made a deal on. It turns out it's
his mother's. They have two cars now. We're going back
to Ill in the blue one. Martin plans to teach there.
I washed our clothes out and did most of the packing
while he drove around the countryside saying
goodbyes. Then I went to the cemetery in the late
afternoon, to fix up Jerome's grave before we left, and
it was so peaceful there I lay down on the grass above him
and slept for hours under this sky I love.*

MAY 31   *Mama was very ill all night, so it was not
easy to go this morning, but we did, at six, with Daddy
waving goodbye till we were out of sight, poor love.
We stopped at Fr Krull's to join up with Jay and Mrs.
N and they followed us to Ypsilanti, where we
picked up Vince and Adele. They're also moving to
Illinois. We drove through a terrible gale of dust and
dirt and stayed overnight with Mr. N's sister,
Augustina, in Mahomet. She's so fragile she looks held
together with piano wire. A man called Clarence kept
hovering off in the shadows. I like the way the blue
car rides.*

JUNE 2   *In Illinois. We stopped at a car ferry not far
from here—I forget where—and couldn't cross on it
because Adele got hysterical about floating over water.
We arrived home two hours after Jay and Mrs. N as
a result, which disgusted Martin. After greeting*

*everybody, we drove down to Spear's, a half mile down
the road from the N's, where Mother N thought we'd
like to rent—three nice upstairs rooms in a tenant
farmer's house. Nobody lives downstairs but somebody
might later in the season, they said. We carried our
sacks and boxes and books up the stairs to the place.
I wasn't feeling a bit well, so I made up the bed and
fell into it with a bang and was out for a while. It's
now 3 o'clock, a.m., of course.*

JUNE 3   *I woke at 5 with pains and went downstairs
to the outhouse. There was a steady stream from
somewhere deep inside me and it wasn't urine, my
whole body knew. I ran back upstairs. It got so
unbearable I started screaming and had to throw
myself around on the bed as if I could break my way
out. I knew it was a miscarriage going on. Mar called the
doctor, who came after the pains quit, making me feel
a fool, and gave me two kinds of pills to take. I had
more pain later today but not nearly as sharp. I've
made it through.*

JUNE 4   *Already I felt well enough to get up and
start unpacking and get settled in here. Mar was
going to work in the fields but stayed home all day and
helped me, and Mrs. N came over later and helped out
too. (Later) About five I felt such a deep burning
hole inside me I had to go downstairs. I felt myself
pass—I can't see to write it. And then Mrs. N went
down and, Oh God, found it, and they took it to*

*the doctor, who— Who knows what? A three-month
fetus, "well-formed," they said—a life to me. I thought
about Mama and all she's been through and felt blessed.
It was a boy, they said.*

JUNE 6   *When Martin went out in the morning to
help Spear unload and uncrate a corn picker, I got out
of bed and sat up for a while, but was weak and the
world went black on me. Martin planned to be in in
an hour but wasn't here until late afternoon. I didn't
mind being alone. He's been the greatest husband
through this—washing and cooking and dusting and
carrying me up and down the stairs on my dirt chute
runs, oh me. Elaine and Davey were here in the
evening and Davey brought me a bouquet from Mrs.
N's flower bed, and then later Fred came over with*

two quarts of ice cream, so the five of us had a feast. I love being part of a family. I haven't peed for a week.
JUNE 7   I was furious when the doctor said I had to stay in bed for four more days! I crawled around an hour this morning straightening up the bedroom, then started scrubbing the kitchen floor but gave out. Cried most of the evening because Martin wants me to stay at the N's the next few days, and I don't want to and won out, finally, thanks to his understanding and my tears, and wanted to eat him. Elaine came over later with lemonade and sponged me off and gave me a few laughs, plus spatters of ice water over my back, and then I wrote to Mama and told her about my own small tragedy. Please answer, Mama, and tell me what to do.
JUNE 8   It rained all day so Martin stayed home with me and worked hard, scrubbing floors, dusting, and cleaning up in general, which he does well. Then he varnished the hope chest Dad Neumiller made for me, painted four chairs bright red, and hung pictures in our bedroom. So we're almost settled in here, at last. When he left for confession in Havana, I sneaked out of bed and downstairs and went for a long walk over the countryside. It's what I needed to clear myself of death.
JUNE 14   I'm getting stronger every day. I rode with Martin and Davey and Dad N to a place near Mason City, where Dad is to work now, building a corncrib, I think it is. We stopped at Vince and Adele's little apartment in Forest Creek in the eve, and later Vince and Adele came out to our place and said they were going back to N. Dak, which nearly knocked us off our feet. They'd planned to settle here and find work like us, we thought. The confusions of being similar, but not.
JUNE 15   Walked over to Mrs. N's the first thing in the morning to see what Mother N thought of Vince and Adele's plans. She said, "I think they're crazy to go back there, and so does anybody else with any sense." "Oh, I don't know," I said, and then laughed too hard at Jay's sign in their bathroom, "WET PAINT. USE BARN."
JULY 12   A pleasant surprise today. A telegram for

Martin arrived from North Dakota and I carried it out
to the field where he's helping thresh wheat. It was
from Phil Rynerson, his principal at Rogers; Phil's
the superintendent at Hyatt now, a little town 50
miles north and west of Courtenay, and he said in the
telegram that Martin was hired as History and Math
teacher, and head coach of the six-man football team, if
he wants the job. I'm not going to say a word to
affect his decision and I'll have to stop smiling like
this. Oh, Lord, the joy of it.

JULY 16   Martin signed the Hyatt contract and I
walked out to the mailbox in the dark after he was asleep
to mail it, when he dreamed he was sleeping with me.

AUG 19   M worked at Spear's in the morning while I
began to pack, and then he and Fred came and
helped in the afternoon, and we finally got everything
loaded. Fred is with us to bring the car back. Then
Fred and Scott, Elaine's new beau from Havana, went
out and stole so many watermelons for us we couldn't
fit them all in the car. Big buggers. M and I had
a bath together—can't ever fit well to make it nice—
and then supper at the N's—roast chicken followed
by three gallons of ice cream. Oofda, boing! We pulled
out at 9 for N.D., leaving everybody in tears, especially
Elaine, and then just out of the lane M said, "I can't
see! Tell me if I'm on the road! Tell me if I'm driving
in a straight line!" He and Elaine are twins to me.

AUG 22   At Home. Mama rose from her sickbed like
Lazarus when we drove up and it was as good
to see her as it's ever been. Elling is here, too, so it
was a grand reunion for all, and after our trip I'm
filled with family love. Martin, Mama, Fred, Elling, and
I went into Hyatt to look at a house that's up for sale
—small and cozy but not in top shape. They want
$300 for it and the lot. "Buy it, Martin," Elling
said. "Buy it. You'll never do better in your
life." I could have wrung his fat neck. We had dinner
at the Rynersons' and then had to drive like disaster
60 mph, to get Elling to Valley City in time for his
Twin Cities train.

AUG 24   At Home. I went to the bank the first thing
in the morning and withdrew my money ($150)

*from last year, now common property, then signed
my postal savings receipt as Alpha Jones* [This
name is crossed out several times.—ED.] *Neumiller.
I stopped in at Montgomery Wards's to look at
furniture and saw a burgundy-colored studio couch I
really liked. Then we heard from the owners of the
house in Hyatt. They've turned down our offer of
$260. What now, Elling?*

AUG 27   *They're threshing here, so Martin shoveled
grain for Daddy all day. Fred took Mama and Lionell
to Carlsons' in the morning, and while Mama was away
I gathered my things together and made a pile of
them in the living room. Fred came back and
helped me load and reload, and finally Daddy walked
over and said, "You'll never make it, kids," and
hitched up a trailer behind the car. We filled it and the
car to overflowing—bookshelves sticking out one
window—and got into Hyatt a little after six. We
unloaded on the Rynersons' front porch and are to
spend the night here with Fred and the two of us in
one bed. I hope it doesn't rain over the weekend.
And that Fred doesn't roll, ahem, or kick.*

AUG 28   *Back Home again. We looked for a house
in Hyatt all morning. The parish owns two places in
town and I guess we'll rent the littler of the two,
next to Fr Schimmelpfennig's, until we find our own.
We had dinner at the Rynersons' and then drove to
Jamestown and argued about furniture within earshot
of Fred, who laughed and laughed until he was in
tears. We finally decided on a couch at Mont-Ward's,
like the one I saw in Wimbledon, and also a mattress
for the old bed frame Daddy gave us. We drove
up to the home place late, after 11, all of us worn out
and hating one another, and in the house here it
felt like home, for once, for good, maybe forever. Love.*

AUG 31   *We took the train from Courtenay to
McCallister and got off and bought out the dime store
—all the knickknacks and gadgets you need to get a
house going, plus plates and spoons and forks and
other shiny stuff, and got into Hyatt about noon, on a
slow train, and a Mr. Russell hauled our things from
the Rynersons' over to the parish house on a little
wheelbarrow truck. I don't care for the place one bit.*

*It's filthy and stinks. No stove, so no coffee, and all
we had today were rolls and grapes—the first dry,
the second withered—from the local Red Owl, along
with cold cups of cold water. The kitchen sink has a
faucet that actually works. Our studio couch had
arrived and was waiting at the depot, but was so badly
ripped across the seat we didn't bother unpacking it
completely. The mattress sleeps okay. Zzzzzz.
Goodnight, boys.*

SEPT 1   *I don't know what to do in this house, it's
such a dirty hole. I scrubbed out one closet and it
took me the whole morning to do the damn thing
well. Most of the day I just cursed and found I've
got as fancy a tongue as Daddy's. I put two big window
shades up on Fr Schimmelpfennig's side before
evening and don't feel peeped on now. It's his
housekeeper, Wilhomena; he's beyond the state of
seeing bodies, this priest. Mar started washing kitchen
walls, a futile job, and then simply painted them white,
so they'll at least look clean. I scooped some mouse
turds out of the cabinet drawers and washed a few
layers of fly poop off a ceiling.*

SEPT 3   *Sunday. But not like Sunday here. Mar
painted all day and I kept shoveling manure. Phil
Rynerson stopped over toward evening and helped
nail up a cupboard. He said he'd heard this house was
up for sale and about that moment a troupe of people
came parading through, who might buy it, scrape,
scrape, they said, and I imagine they will, clomp,
shuffle, now that they've all been through it and seen
at least that it's clean.*

SEPT 4   *Mar went over to see Fr about our house being
sold but Fr said he'd have to wait until he heard
something definite from the other end. You'd think
he would have told us; we're these bodies that
keep getting in his way. M was at school for nine
hours, although it was just Teachers' Orientation Day.
His load is much lighter this year and it's a pleasure
for him to be working with Phil again. If he stays on
he could become principal, Phil said. I was on my
hands and knees with my head in another closet when
Fr walked in and said the house had been sold. Good
for the old boy.*

SEPT 6   *I painted quarter-round in the kitchen,
even though we have to be out of here by the 15th
and there's no reason to, and then went for a long
walk around the lake at the edge of town. Martin
came home with the news that maybe we could
get rooms across the street, at a Mrs. Glick's, so over we
went and made arrangements for 3 of her front rooms
for $8 a week. Her place smells of potatoes and old
clothes. A certain Mrs. Liffert keeps staring at me as
if I'm unbuttoned somewhere, and has me feeling I'm
Martin's mistress, not wife.*

SEPT 7   *All morning until after nine I watched the
kids on their way to school and felt old and as though
I had typhus or impetigo and was being left behind.
What will I do with time? I went to the depot to
see about our damaged couch but the building was
empty. Weighed myself on the scale there. 117.
Not bad. The Fortune Dial said, "You can make your
life more happy." What a terrible thing to see. Oh,
pride, pomp of thy purple plume on me!*

SEPT 8   *Martin came home early and scraped and
sanded and varnished my old bookshelves, while I read
to him from The Grapes of Wrath. The story is
becoming a part of our lives but I could do without
some of the language. Too close to home. Martin says
it leaves a brown taste—sticky roast beef?—in his mouth.
He painted Daddy's rusted bed frame with aluminum
paint and then we carried our mattress over to Mrs.
Glick's and found out she's not quite ready for us to move
in yet. There's some rats she's got to git. So we
came back and made a bed on our unboxed couch
and I kept rolling off it all night. Once when I hit the
floor face down I felt Martin was underneath me.*

SEPT 11   *At Mrs. Glick's. I washed clothes with Mrs.
Glick a new, goofy way—putting them in pails and
squishing them with a kind of plumber's friend, a
cone-shaped piece of tin on the end of a broomstick—
and she lent me her scrubboard to scrub all my
pieces that needed it, plus a lot of her old linen thangs.*

*Oh, well. I was too ill to eat all day, with morning
sickness, I'm in fear and trembling.*

SEPT 14   *I went uptown before nine to mail a letter*

to Mama and found myself off on a long walk similar
to the one the other day. The lake here is lovely,
especially at this time of year with the trees all in brown
and gold along it, and the town looks so peaceful
from its far side. I got home at noon and didn't have
Martin's dinner ready on time again. Is this becoming a
habit? I was ill at dinner and unable to eat, and even
more ill at supper, so Martin mixed up and fried his
own pancakes and just the smell of them sent me
outside gagging. We went to Fessenden with Phil and
Lou after supper, to see about some new furniture,
and I slept in the back seat of their warm car all the way.
It rained during the night—hard and thundery,
trembling the leaves of Mrs. Glick's lilac trees, and
now this morning the air's still misty. I'm sure I
must be pregnant again. Dear Lord, I hope for a boy.

SEPT 15   Two weeks of school are over already. What
happens to time? I went uptown after the mail in
the forenoon, and we got a letter from Illinois at last,
from Elaine. It came air mail and contained not
one scrap of news except about Scott, along with a
picture of him holding up—by their necks—two
Canada honkers. When Martin got back from school, we
went together to the depot to see if the replacement
for our damaged couch had arrived, but no. We walked
around the lake and I showed him the spot where
I like to sit, near the little dam, and then we had a
late, late supper because I felt ill, as usual, at our usual
suppertime. Then I lay in his arms for an hour in
the semi-darkness of our porch-dining room and was
at ease inside for the first time since when? I'm in love
with myself and him and the condition I'm in. And
I'm ready to begin at last at the beginning of my life.
[Here end the selections from the Five Year Diary
of Alpha Jones, now Alpha Neumiller. At this juncture
in her writing, she is twenty-two and Martin
twenty-six. The diary continues on, with an entry for
each day of the year, until late in 1940.
Love & Peace.—THE EDITOR.]

Two

and the new principal's wife, Mrs. Martin Neumiller, had a 7 lb 10 oz baby boy on Sunday, May 21st, at the McCallister hospital. The Neumillers have given their baby the different but pretty name of Jerome.

We Process All Yo

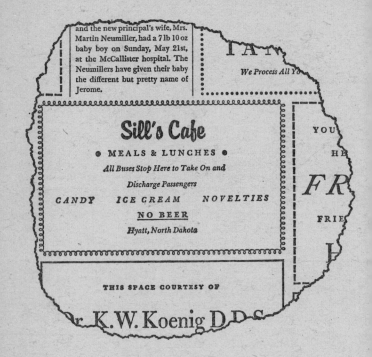

Sill's Cafe

● MEALS & LUNCHES ●

All Buses Stop Here to Take On and

Discharge Passengers

CANDY   ICE CREAM   NOVELTIES

<u>NO BEER</u>

Hyatt, North Dakota

YOU

HE

FR

FRIE

THIS SPACE COURTESY OF

Dr. K. W. Koenig D.D.S.

7

⌘

THE LAKE

What I remember most from that time, before I was six, when no demands were made of me and all I did was lean on my parents' love, is the lake at the center of the town. It was a creek, really, damned up a mile east on the open plain, and when it backed around toward town, filling in the sloughs and flatlands that bordered it, it spread to a breadth of three hundred feet in places, and there were deep holes where only older boys could dive down and touch bottom. Its townside bank, over thirty feet high, cut a curve along the center of Hyatt, and houses here followed the curve for a few blocks and then gave out on the plain. A gravel road ran along this bank. Looking across the lake from this road to what seemed an island (but was a peninsula, actually), you could see the town park, where five or six shade trees stood, with picnic tables and swings and a merry-go-round beneath them, and bathhouses and outhouses for each sex, and beyond them a swimming area with a floating dock.

On those summer afternoons before dog days set in, when clouds lay along the plain in formations so motionless they seemed hollowed out of the sky, my mother would take my brothers and me to the park. My sisters weren't born yet, and my two brothers were too young to be a threat to my mother and me. I'll be honest. I'd take the hand of one and she'd hold mine and the hand of another, and we'd walk along the lake through heat that rose from the gravel in silver shimmers, past the water tower, to a jetty of land overgrown with willows, and at the tip of this was a wooden footbridge fifty feet long. The bridge led across a neck of the lake to the park. Four or five high-school boys once trapped a girl on the bridge and stood hacking and spitting up "oysters," as they called them, to the girl's distress, and the word always reminded me of fetuslike clots floating over still water. "Grow up," my mother said to them.

Below the guardrails of the bridge were crisscrossed one-by-eights painted white, which gave it a primary and self-suspended look from a distance, as though children with no sense of mechanics had built it. It was supported at its center by a pier of railroad ties. I always stopped at the pier and hoisted myself up on my stomach and leaned over the rail, seeing moss and long weeds sway away from the sunken ties beside my reflection, and watched for bullheads and carp, my face rippling with a greenish patina until I was the water, or so it seemed (and once I saw a goldfish as long as my arm), I'd resolve to bring my rod and go fishing the next day, but never did. It would have taken away from the time I had with her.

"Jerome. Help me, please."

She took out the blanket she'd brought and I helped her hold it square and floating down to the grass, in the shade of a tree. Then I went into the men's bathhouse, where a latticework of light lay on the floor from the cracks in the walls and roof, and undressed in the cool air and unrolled my towel and pulled on my swim suit, and then went to the corner, where a crack had been widened with a knife, and stared toward the women's place. There was never anything to see, but if everybody who looked from here had an intent as powerful as mine, then I'm sure it's the reason the bathhouse leaned in that direction. And the women's bathhouse leaned toward the men's.

I'd tie my shoelaces together, and fold my clothes and roll them up in the towel, and go outside, where sunlight on the water and the whitened pea gravel made my eye sockets and back teeth ache. The pea gravel was spread over the swimming area to keep back bloodsuckers (or leeches: some form of fresh-water *Annelida;* we called them bloodsuckers there) and I once saw a boy who waded beyond the gravel walk out of the water with bloodsuckers fringing his ankles like leaves.

I'd go to the blanket, blinking against the loss of color, and lie beside my mother, who was sitting or kneeling and undressing my brothers in public, and watch her hands move over their bodies and imagine their bodies were mine. This observance of affection, without receiving any, seemed to me the burden of being an older brother, and still does. If I could somehow recapture the sound of her voice as she talked then, merely to talk to us and soothe in her musical way, I don't believe it'd be so necessary, now, for me to work so hard at every task, as though I could attain within myself some measure of perfection, or to comfort others and attempt to strengthen and repair their bodies and minds. I'm an M.D.

A wooden catwalk projected twelve feet into the water, with its trembling reflection beginning ten feet below, and at the end of the catwalk was the high-dive board. Alan Pflager, the lifeguard, was usually stretched out on his back on the board in the broad sun. I don't think he ever had to assist a swimmer in trouble, and the one summer somebody nearly drowned—Brian Rimsky, falling from the high dive when he was four—he was pulled from the water by Pat Ianaccona; it was the summer Alan Pflager had shingles so badly he felt he was being blinded.

"All right, Jerome," my mother said.

I'd lead my brothers to the edge of the lake and leave them, and wade out alone, always frightened, and dog paddle to the floating dock and pull myself onto it panting. And after I'd rested, I'd have to dive off and paddle back to shore. Neither my mother nor my father could swim, and my mother's brother, my namesake, drowned when he was a boy. I'd leave my brothers splashing and throwing gravel, and go to the blanket and lie down beside her. I could have a sandwich now, or a piece of pie, or an orange or an apple, which she always brought along in a covered basket. She usually had a book or two with her, also, and after I'd eaten I'd try to read over her shoulder, but she'd close the book with a sigh and lay her head on her arms. I'd turn on my back, or turn on my side and pretend to be asleep, and she'd say, "Oh, this heat tires me," and then she'd glance in my direction, and I'd see her closed eyes part to study me. Then she'd become restless and roll on her back, one arm flung out on the grass, and murmur, "You'd better go get your brothers. We better get going. Your dad'll be home soon." In the summer my father worked in the fields as a farmer, and for some reason the idea of this, and her bare arm lying on the grass, filled me with fear and an unnamable sympathy.

And now I'll have to tell it. One afternoon I got angry at her for the way she was being, however that was, and went downshore from the swimming area, where a set of rotting steps led down into a deep hole near the foot of the bridge, and sat on a step in water up to my throat and wondered how it would feel to slip under and start gulping and sending up the bubbles of the drowned. It would be the sort of family story, because of the names, that would be repeated for generations to come, I was sure. My mother kept calling and, when I didn't answer or appear, sent Alan Pflager, who led me up the steps and into the bathhouse. "Time to go," he said, and I told him to mind his own business and get out, and he did. I pulled down my swim suit and had to clear my eyes before I realized what I was seeing. A big bloodsucker was attached to the top of my thigh, close to my penis, and a tangle of babies were swirling in a clot of blood beside it. I screamed and started up and my swim suit around my ankles brought me down. My mother and Alan ran in, and she held me while he took a forbidden cigarette from his trousers on the wall, lit it, and touched it to the bloodsucker's back. He ground it into a stain in the boards when it fell free, and went bowing out.

"Hush," my mother said. "People will think something awful has happened." She wiped my thigh with her handkerchief and tried to put an arm around me, but I pushed her away.

"What are you *doing* in here?" I said. "You're not supposed to *be* in here."

"All right," she said. "Get dressed, then, and come out and help with your brothers." She disappeared through the rectangular blaze of sunlight and left me to me.

If I'd been able to think then, or had any thoughts, or been more mature or had foresight, I probably would have thought, This is how it is. This is the way it will be.

⊷₴₴⊷

8

THE OLD HALVORSON PLACE

A family of fourteen had lived in the house for ten years. Their name was Russell. Mr. Lowell Russell was the sexton at St. Mary Margaret's Catholic Church and the janitor of the parochial school, a frail and ailing man, and of his seven sons and five daughters, ranging in age from eleven to thirty-three, one son had thus far been ordained a priest and three daughters had become nuns. Another daughter was said to be an accomplished musician, and yet another had literary leanings, and these two composed the words and music of the school song still sung in Hyatt to this day; it begins

We'll raise a lofty, mighty cheer for you,
Straight from the hearts of students fond and true . . .

and concludes

Deep as the ocean, our love and devotion
For the Hy—! Hy—! Hyatt High School!

Martin Neumiller was now principal of the high school and had been annoyed for years by the stilted and solemn phrasing of the old song (sung to the tune of "On, Wisconsin!"), and persuaded the Russell girls to write this new one. The parish owned the Russell house and everybody in the parish expected the Russells to live out their lives in it, a monument to the faith. But one day old Mr. Russell went to Father Schimmelpfennig and said he was giving up his job and moving out of town.
What?

He was grateful for all the parish had done, he said, but felt there were better opportunities in South Dakota for him and the children still at home.

Father offered him the house rent-free.

He couldn't accept charity, he said. No, Hyatt wasn't growing and wouldn't ever grow, he was afraid, and he wanted to get in on the boom down there around Rapid City, maybe go into business for himself, and he wanted his children to attend the better schools.

Two months later the Russells were gone. They were a self-confident, cloistered, close-knit family, nearly monastic in their devotion to the faith, and, other than the song, they left little trace of themselves behind when they moved.

Father let their house stand vacant for a year, as if unable to admit they were gone. He didn't accept defeat gracefully, and was known by his fellow seminarians as the donkey, or the jackass, whichever way you cared to take the German word, because of his resistance to the Third Reich, whose leaders he called thugs and idiots from the start, openly. Then he went to Rome to be ordained, in violation of one of Hitler's edicts, and came back an enemy of the Reich and a marked man. He often talked in a cheerful manner about a winter manhunt for him conducted by the SS boys in black leather with their big black dogs. "After all, dey were chust ordinary louts up against me. And dere were plenty of people in and out of da church willing to help a priest. I made it to Switzerland. I ended up at Fargo Diocese. Dey said dat all dey had was Hyatt, and I said, 'Gif it to me!' And den when da people dey were so agreeable, I knew dis was da place for me. I can't ask more from life."

He had a painful-looking crease in his neck from his clerical collar, and came toward you with a light stride for the bulk of him, the gold in his front teeth gleaming, his jowls so heavy they made his forehead look small, and, close up, triangular folds of skin beside each eye disappearing into his hairline, his smile was such a wholehearted and consistent part of him; a wide mouth with purplish lips stained tan in one corner from his panatelas and cigars; water-blue eyes behind round gold rims. He loved children and knew every girl and boy in the parish by name, and never got names or siblings mixed up, and

gave them all a quarter or a half or silver dollar on their
birthdays, depending on how well they were doing in
school, since he was the figurehead of the parochial school
and acting superintendent of it—and thus had been further
hurt by Russell—and also kept track of all their grades.
Not even the most retreating child in the village was afraid
of him.

In the big rectory there were potted plants on steps
and sills, two walls lined with books, large mirrors, a tree
in a tub, a marble-topped desk and a grandfather clock in
his study, a dining room with French windows, an open
maple stairway to the second story, and cases of foreign
beer and wine in the basement. He had a housekeeper
from Germany. The rectory was next to the church and
next to it was the three-story parochial school of buff-and-
clay-colored brick with its white cupola and white cross
on top—all his domain. He'd entered the seminary expecting to be a monk, and see how this tiny place had
brought out the aristocrat and bohemian in him! *Ahem!*
Once a week he had a card party that filled the rectory
with tobacco smoke, while beer bottles went popping and
cash passed hands. Was he leading the men in town, most
of them prominent ones, down to the Devil? No, no,
they all understood it was just a way of having fun between the boys and getting away from the wives for a
night. The wives needed time off, too. What was there to
do in a town this size? There were unlimited opportunities
and freedom here! But he should probably try to be a bit
more priestly and businesslike in some matters, if he
could. Now about this Russell place. He'd heard the Neumillers were looking for a new house again. Well, let
them have it! And at a reasonable price, too. Who needed
money? The parish would have their new church within
a few years, a brick one to replace the barnlike wood-
frame one they had now (although he liked the old one;
his voice echoed in it as in a cathedral), and that was all
the parish asked of him, other than absolution, of course.

Martin was a devotee of his family and ambitious for
them, but without guile—Biblical, as Father thought of
him, because his purity and strength of character came out
of unclouded ingenuousness. Over the years, Martin had
become his best friend and confidant, his confessor, practically, and Martin had three intelligent, promising young

sons. You could never tell where priest material might spring from!

*

The Neumillers' luck with houses in Hyatt hadn't been good; Mrs. Glick promised to make herself "so scarce you won't know I'm here" but never did; in another place the furnace never worked properly and a smell that originated inside a kitchen wall was amazing, and since they didn't feel right about breaking into the wall of a house that didn't belong to them, and were afraid to complain because they'd let it go so long, they kept wondering, What could it be? and were never informed. In the last, the basement flooded to the floor joists in the spring (bringing up buried salamanders that went floating out into the yard), and eroded the foundation so badly that walls began to part from the ceiling. And each place had its noisy population of mice and rats, driven indoors by the prolonged, windswept, blizzard-flayed winters, and not one of them was large enough. This was in 1945, and the Neumillers' three sons—Jerome, Charles, and Timothy— were still sharing the same room for sleep and play; and although Jerome, the oldest, was only five, Alpha was pregnant again.

The Russell house had three bedrooms plus a big walk-in attic on the second story, and two more bedrooms downstairs. There was a living room with a bay window, a kitchen with a pantry as big as most kitchens, a basement with vegetable bins and shelves for canned food; an indoor bathroom (rare in Hyatt—there was no municipal water system) with all of the fixtures; a front porch, with turned posts and gingerbread trim; an enclosed porch on the south side; and, attached to the rear of the house, a lean-to which had once been used to stable a pony and was now a workshop and utility room and coal shed. The rent was twenty-five dollars a month.

Alpha knew that a house wasn't any better than the lives that went on in it—some were wrecks after ten years, others stood fresh as morning after several hundred—and there was a feeling about this one that it would endure.

She went pirouetting through the empty rooms, saying, "The space! The space! The space!" And less than a month later was leaning against a wall with her arms folded and a smile on her face, watching a dozen birthday guests (Charles was four) play Red Rover in her living room—her *parlor,* you might call it; she saw herself as the heroine of a nineteenth-century novel filled with the moors, glamour, and more glamour. The room was so large that her upright piano, which had always been in the way in their other places, seemed to have shrunk three sizes. Her piano! She sat down and started playing "Clair de Lune," and the children stopped their game and stared at her as she played.

Martin could understand how she felt. There were articles close to her heart, family samplers and other heirlooms, and wedding presents that hadn't been unpacked since the day they were married, and some of their furniture—a dining-room set with inlays of bird's-eye maple, a handmade gate-leg table—had never been used. And around town and at the Friday-night pinochle games at Father's, Martin was heard to say, "She loves the place, sure, how could she help it? But it's always been like this. The happiest times of her life have been when we've moved."

*

Martin's father had started his own carpentry business in Illinois, but was visiting relatives and friends around Mahomet, so he drove up to Hyatt to help them move, and somehow got stuck with bringing in the basement junk, and toward the end of the day stopped in front of Alpha with a solemn face, and said, "I've carried nine hundred and ninety empty fruit jars down these stairs, I want you to know." He made minor repairs around the house, and persuaded Martin to pour a concrete slab that began at the outside wall of the lean-to, went in a wide-swinging arc around the corner of the house, beyond the steps of the enclosed porch, and abutted against the bay window. It took five men a day to do it, and Martin's father finished troweling it by the light of a floor lamp

Martin held above him, then leaned back on his haunches, his trowel turned up with gray bubbles streaking its face, and said. "There. Now the boys have a place to ride their tricycles, Martin."

Martin took Jerome and Charles upstairs into a room overlooking the street corner, where an enormous rolltop desk stood against one wall. "Look," he said, and turned to them as though offering a gift that would soon appear in his hands. They glanced at one another, and Jerome shrugged.

"Well, don't you see what's happened?" he asked.

They didn't see.

"First of all, you can tell by looking it never could have come up the stairs. They're too narrow. The door to this room is even narrower, and the windows are narrower yet."

He squatted at the desk and rapped on it with a knuckle. "That's solid oak, you hear? The corners have been dovetailed and then trimmed over. You can feel the dovetailing here in the back. Right here. Now, nobody could take this apart, once it was built, without damaging the wood somewhere, especially the dovetails, and they certainly would have left a mark on it. But the finish is practically perfect—the original, I'd guess. It's hand-rubbed. Isn't it lovely?"

They nodded, eager to get their hands behind the desk and onto that dovelike, cooing, feathery or whatever surface he was talking about.

"There's only one conclusion!" he said. "When this place was built, an old cabinetmaker came into the house here, carried his hand tools and materials up to this room, and built the desk on the spot where we're standing right now! But why would anybody want to build a desk like this way up here?"

Mysteries, for Martin were a source of delight. There was nothing unnatural about them at all; they were an ingredient of life to be explored and marveled at, but never feared, and seldom explained. Where others saw no mystery, he could find it, and kept himself in a constant state of childlike wonder, exuberance, and joy.

His father stepped into the room, and said, "Why would anybody want a desk up here? Why, Martin, to enjoy it!"

Alpha was surprised that the inside of the house wasn't

more beat up. Fourteen people had lived in it for more than a decade, after all, and from the outside it seemed that it would be; paint was flaking from the north side, the roof of the lean-to sagged, and the hedge that bordered it on three sides had grown up to the windows of the second story. But it was structurally sound, Martin's father said, surprisingly so, and the hardwood floors didn't need refinishing; the baseboards were battered, but otherwise the old oak woodwork, the sliding doors of oak to the master bedroom, the turned posts of the oak banister leading upstairs, the bookshelves around the bottom of the bay window, were hardly scratched, and their gold-and-black grain stood out as though new-minted and burnished to its highest sheen. There were no stains or adolescent carvings on the roll-top desk upstairs.

The Russells had left with the desk a matching chair that looked brand-new, and Alpha couldn't understand why, unless it'd been there when they moved in, and they were that honest. There was no other clue to their life in the house, no old receipts or letters, no stray socks in any closet, not even a drawing or set of initials on the walls, or, as she put it, "not a speck of themselves or their dirt."

The attic, however, was filled full of valuables, none of them the Russells', and they were so layered with dust it looked as if the Russells had never touched them; these belonged to the Halvorsons, the family who'd built the house and lived in it in its first state; their name was on daguerreotypes and photographs, on the flyleaves of books, underneath chair seats, and even written, along with a set of measurements, across the bosom of an old raggedy dress form.

In the attic Martin found a large, decaying, leather-bound volume, *A Century-End History and Biography of North Dakota,* and in it an engraving of a daguerreotype of Mr. Halvorson, a twin to a picture of him in a shoe box, along with this:

ALVARD J. HALVORSON. This gentleman, of whom a portrait will be found on the opposite page, occupies a prominent position as a real-estate dealer in Hyatt, Stusrud County. To his influence is due much of the solid prosperity of Stusrud and Ecklund Counties.

Our subject was born in Hamlin Township, Michigan, Aug. 1, 1839, and was the only son of William and Dora (Waldorf) Halvorson, the former of Scandinavian and the latter of German descent. Mr. Halvorson was raised on his father's farm and attended country schools and at the age of nineteen went to Indianapolis, Indiana, in company with his father and later was engaged in business and also in farming with his father in Indiana for about twenty years.

Our subject moved to Valley City, North Dakota, in the fall of 1879 and became interested in Stusrud County lands in 1881, since which time A. J. HALVORSON CO. has added as much as perhaps any other firm in the development of the possibilities of the agricultural and stock-raising interests of North Dakota, and he now conducts an extensive real-estate business in Hyatt, where the family located in 1895, two years after the founding of Hyatt.

Our subject was married at Indianapolis, Indiana, in 1865, to Miss Catherine Maxwell, who is of Scottish descent. Mr. and Mrs. Halvorson are the parents of three children who bear the following names: Olivia C., Alice N., and Lydia. The two older children were born in Indiana and the last named in North Dakota. Politically, Mr. Halvorson is a Republican and has taken a highly active part in affairs pertaining to local government.

Nobody living in Hyatt at the present time could remember the Halvorsons, much less say why they'd moved and left so much behind, or where they'd gone from here. Martin drove to McCallister and did research in the county record books and didn't find many allusions to Mr. Halvorson, but learned how it was possible for him and his family to be forgotten the way they were; the area had changed that much. The U.S. Cavalry, while routing out the last of the Sioux in the area, used to bivouac near the village site, on a prominence now called Hawk's Nest, and the village itself was plotted in 1892 by Richard Hyatt, an English lord, and began as a settlement of wealthy and cultivated Englishmen and Scots (one of whom constructed the artificial lake and a nine-hole golf course at the edge of town), and then turned into a trading center for the German and Scandinavian and Irish immigrants who homesteaded in the area, and for a while was the county seat; and then after being missed by the main line of the railroad, and suffering the effects of the Crash and the Great Depression, and having the county hall hauled away to Fessenden in the dead of the night, it became what it was now, a poor village, mostly German and Roman Catholic, with only the lake remaining as a reminder of its past. "It seems old Hyatt knew his Longfellow well enough to name the lake Hiawatha," Martin said. "And had the taste not to name it Gitche Gumee." Hyatt's population was two hundred and thirty-two, a figure Martin knew before he began his research; he'd taken the 1940 census.

Families other than the Russells must have lived in the house since the Halvorsons, but it looked as though nobody had bothered their effects in the attic, as though to tamper with them or remove them were to tamper with the heart of the house. Could that be? Or maybe they'd had so many possessions (wasn't the desk theirs?) that people had merely taken what they wanted without much diminishing a large, original store. Martin, for instance, as he walked around the attic, said that when they left, if they ever did, he was going to take those candlesticks, that teapot, the horse collar there, and a wheelbarrow full of these books.

Alpha said that just to stand in the place made her temperature drop ten degrees, and she'd rather he left everything the way it was.

"But what about these?" He held up a set of copper bowls with pewter medallions on their handles. "These are collector's items for sure."

"I have more bowls than I know what to do with already."

"What about a book? Wouldn't you like to read a few of these books?"

"I would if I'd bought them." She picked up Timmy, who was dropping fluffs of dust into a china commode, and started out the door.

"Let's have an auction," Jerome said. "Let's sell all of this stuff and make a bunch of money." He and Charles were sorting through a dusty stack of phonograph records.

"Leave those alone," Alpha said. "They aren't yours. I

don't want the two of you playing in this attic—ever, you understand. I want the hook at the top of the door to stay hooked, the way the Russells had it when they were here. You don't belong in this place."

They turned to their father, who was rummaging through a round-topped trunk bound with leather straps, and Jerome asked if they could move this—he rapped on an old Victrola with a knuckle—and all these records into the room next to the attic; the door was plenty big, he pointed out. Martin's eyes were bright and abstracted, and, unaware that Alpha had spoken, he said, "Sure, why not? Let's get it in there and see if it works."

*

The Victrola sat in a corner of the upstairs room that became their playroom, near the door that led to the attic. It was such a tall machine they had to stand on a stool to put records on its turntable, and inside its lifted cover, beveled like a coffin lid, "Lydia" had been scratched into the wood with something sharp, and the name, foreign to them, seemed strangely appropriate there; no needles survived with the machine, so their father fashioned one anew from the end of a nipped-off safety pin. They found only a single record they liked among those in the attic, and the rest, thick Edison records with hymns on them, they sailed out a second-story window toward Brian and Leo Rimsky and Douglas Kuntz and other of their friends, who stomped on the ones that went rolling, and caught some they tried to sail back.

They played that same record over and over, in spite of the scratches on it—years of them, layers of them—that made the metallic tenor sound as though it came out of the center of a gale, and never tired of hearing the voice tell about Sal, a maiden fair, singing Polly Wolly Doodle all the day, with her curly eyes and her laughing hair . . .

They stood on the stool and worked the crank, staring at the name scratched into the lid. "Fare thee well! Fare thee well! Fare thee well, my fairy fay!" The voice was adenoidal and no matter how many times it brought up, frail and tinny from the ancient grooves, the image of a grasshopper sitting on a railroad track (singing Polly Wolly Doodle all the day), they always had to get down, laughing, and roll around and slap the floor to get themselves sane again.

They had their own library in the playroom, and they had clay, blocks, marbles, and mallets, dominoes, Lincoln Logs, an electric train; and a handmade alphabet with wooden characters five inches high, which they'd found in the attic and kept in dull-green ammunition boxes their Uncle Jay had brought back from the war. But none of their toys captured their interest like the Victrola, and when they weren't playing it, they spent hours at the roll-top desk.

Their father had appropriated the desk. "Boys," he said. "Here is where I'm going to sit when I write that book of mine," a project he talked about often, especially after an unusual or moving experience, or after he'd told a story out of his past. He referred to the book, simply as "the book of my life." When he'd been up to the room for an evening, Jerome and Charles would go to the desk the next day, slide its slatted cover up, and search through the drawers and cubbyholes for evidence of the book, in which they hoped to be included, pulling the wonderful pranks they pulled. Usually there was a neat pile of paper in the center of a green blotter, with a pen beside it, presumably full of ink. A bottle of ink and one of eradicator stood ready, as did the large, leather-bound volume from the attic, appropriated now, too. There was also a portable Underwood typewriter that their father let them bang away on when they wanted to work on those wonderful stories of theirs.

Digging through the pigeonholes of the desk, they found old letters, scripts of dramatic and patriotic readings their father had performed in high school and college, a rubber stamp that reproduced his tall, tilted signature, a watch fob braided of his mother's hair (a lighter shade then), a broken pocket watch, some rocks from the Badlands, and a tiny tube they could look into and see a pyramidical pile of fieldstone and the inscription, *Geographical Center of North America, Rugby, North Dakota.* In a drawer was a half-filled box of flaky cigars with "It's a Boy!" on their cellophanes, and in another a metal file that contained insurance policies, birth certificates (their own and their parents', too, which was unsettling), government savings bonds in their names, and their father's baby book. In the center drawer were pens and pencils and a ream of that same white paper, which never seemed to diminish.

Once, there was this on the top sheet:

CHAPTER ONE
—My father's influence on my life
(Mom's too)

CHAPTER TWO
—The Depression Years

CHAPTER THREE
—I meet Alpha, my wife-to-be

CHAPTER FOUR
?

Other than some notes to himself and a Christmas-card list, they never found anything else their father had written.

*

They couldn't resist the temptation of the attic, although their mother was upset by this. She disliked the place, disliked even more the idea of anybody's being in it (she never entered it herself), and was so fervent and humorless in her dislike that their father started calling North Dakota "That cold-storage box way up at the top. The *attic* of the United States!"

They'd put a record on the Victrola, move a stool to the attic door, unlatch the hook, ease the door open wide, and sunlight coming through a window in the far well fell over them with a warmth sunlight had nowhere else. Cobwebs powdered with dust, and shining filaments recently strung in place, sparkled in a shifting radiance inside the golden air. The dress form, a brass bedstead, the boxes and trunks of memorabilia, a wooden wardrobe with a dress sword and sash hanging from its top, chairs books, an oval mirror that held their tilting reflections, stood around them in solid eloquence.

Charles tiptoed over to a settee, upholstered in red velvet damaged by moths and mice, and sat down. He bounced his weight on its springs. Who'd sat here? What had they talked about? Had anybody cried on it, as he had on their couch? Or done a flip on it? He looked at Jerome, who hadn't moved since they'd stepped inside; the Halvorsons' effects were as real and awesome as a roomful of strangers, and part of a world removed from them by time —by half a century, their father said—and by convention and law: the world of adults. But here they could handle and examine that world in detail, in its many manifestations (and only through touch would it give up its mystery), as they couldn't examine the world of their parents in the rooms below.

Only a few moments after they'd unhooked the door, they'd hear, "Are you two into that attic again?" from the foot of the stairs.

"No!" Both at the same time; a dead giveaway.

"You stay out of there when your father's not around! You hear?"

"We aren't in here," Charles said.

"Don't lie to your mother!"

They looked at one another—Jerome pushing out in a curl his big upper lip—and then Jerome went over and began to examine an object of more interest than Charles's numskull knavery, as Charles picked up a wooden doll with most of its limbs missing, while the dented and damaged dress form, made of varnished strips of paper lifting up in crisp translucent curves, stood above them, unmoving and silent, like a second, more permissive mother. Jerome studied a wooden box with wires and disclike electrodes dangling from it; its lid swung open like a little door, and from what he could make out of the instructions, which were pasted inside, it was a device for giving shocks to the head and feet.

"Look at this," Charles said. He took a lace dress from a trunk and held it in front of him. "This is what they wore then. What would you think if you saw somebody wearing this? What would you think if I was a girl?" He wrinkled up his nose and giggled like one.

"Quit it," Jerome said. "Put it back." He was more like

his mother; a dress was too personal to disturb. He picked up a candlestick and was removed to their living room in a different setting, at night, with candle flames lighting the faces around the table, a sound of silver scraping on plates, a rustle of skirts, and then a man's voice, gentle as candlelight, rising from the shadows: "What I'm going—"

"Hey, look at this," Charles said. He'd slipped on the rusty jacket of an old black suit of tails many sizes too big for him.

"Take it off. Put it back."

"Okay. But I get to keep this." It was a book, *Children of the Garden,* that personified the common domestic flowers, giving them human features and appendages, and names such as Betsy Bluebell. "We'll keep it in the playroom."

"Oh, all right. But don't leave it where Mom'll see it." Jerome went to a box of daguerreotypes and fading tea-colored photographs and found pictures of rural families lined up in front of farmhouses; the farmer, bearded or with sidewhiskers, sitting in a kitchen chair; beside him his wife, her sun- or gray-streaked hair pulled back tight, wearing a long black-sleeved dress, seemingly old enough to be the children's grandmother; and the children, all of them, even the babies, were big-headed and looked mature.

There were pictures of houses they recognized, of Main Street as it had been at one time, with a horse and carriage in front of Schommer's Tavern, and several views of their own home. Jerome motioned to Charles and showed him a rear view of their house, and then put his fingertip on the attic window.

"Look at this," he said then, and wiped his forearm across another picture: a plump man in muttonchop whiskers stared up at them with the fallow and sparkling eyes of an old roué. Jerome frowned. "It's Mr. Halvorson." He flipped past the photographs of him and his wife, who was broad and square-jawed and looked enough like her husband to be his brother. Two of the daughters looked like her. In a portrait of the third girl, however, Jerome saw what he was looking for in the others. She was sitting at one end of the settee, an open book in her lap, a finger along her cheek, staring out with sober eyes on the world beyond; her long hair, coiled on the settee, covering one thigh and part of the book, a white bow at her crown.

"See," Jerome said, and touched the lace dress she was wearing. "That was hers."

"So?"

"You shouldn't be playing with it."

"Why?"

"If it was hers— You just shouldn't. Look how pretty she is."

"Not any more."

"What do you mean?"

"She's old and ugly by now, or else dead."

Jerome turned the picture over, and read, "Lydia, at the age of thirteen, in the year of our Lord, 1904."

"See," Charles said. "That's even before Dad was born, and look how old he is."

Jerome wasn't listening. He saw the girl running through the downstairs hall on a day as sunlit as this one, coming up the steps, her hair a shaking tangle in the sunlight, and into the playroom to the Victrola. He turned. His mother was in the doorway, flushed and out of breath from climbing the steps in her condition.

"What did I tell you two? Get out of here! Get out, get out, get out!"

*

In August, Alpha gave birth to a daughter, whom she named Marie, after Martin's mother, in an effort to say that that part of the past was forgotten for her. Jerome and Charles were envious of all the attention the girl got, and embarrassed by her. But Tim, who was always left out of their projects and play, would stand at her bassinet with his hands clasping and unclasping behind him, sometimes for an hour, as though she were his only hope. Martin was proud of her in the way that only the father of a daughter can be proud, and while Alpha was in the hospital he painted their bedroom pink and white and bought an expensive camera he shouldn't have. Alpha had always wanted a girl and was happier than she'd been in years.

The house was becoming hers. Over the first winter,

she'd closed off the whole upstairs, to save on heat and cut down on cleaning chores, but now it was open and a major piece of framework in the home she was building within the house; she put a sleeping cot, white organdy curtains, and glassed-in bookshelves she'd got at an auction for a couple of dollars and thought she'd never use, in the room the roll-top desk would never leave, and called it "Martin's office and that desk's of his." In a battered box of junk, she unearthed the shell of a turtle Martin had found, empty, along the county right-of-way when he worked on the road gang with his father the summer Emil was injured and Jerome drowned. He'd had his father and other county employees sign it on the dome, leaving the colored whorls of its plastron clear as paint, and then filled it with cement and varnished its outside and used it as a paperweight. It was a misplaced, much-missed talisman, and she put it on the pile of papers on his desk. She sat in the chair. Could she write here? She was flooded by a fluttery grayness that made her get up and go to her own upstairs room, a sewing room with an easy chair and a lamp for reading, when she wanted to relax and be away from the boys, if they weren't up here. The closets of the room held all their winter clothes out of the way and there was so much space she was able to leave her curtain stretchers permanently set up. It was more than she'd expected to have, in Hyatt or anywhere.

She painted the cupboards in the pantry and kitchen with white enamel, and Martin put down new lineoleum in every room. He trimmed the hedge around the house, all of it, down to four feet, and got blisters and sores and then hands as hard as horn from the job, which took him two weeks to complete. And then there was still a huge mountain of branches at the back of the yard. He installed an oil heater in the living room, so they could keep the chill out of the downstairs on fall days without starting the furnace, and when school dismissed for the summer, he hired a neighbor, William Runyon, as a helper, and they scraped and wire-brushed and repainted the outside of the house. It was the color Alpha had always wanted her house to be—warm yellow, with white trim.

She had a place for everything from the rocker she'd begged from her mother to her open-toed summer shoes, and every piece of their furniture was being put to use;

and then Martin, bless him, went out and bought a bed-room set of solid maple she'd dreamed of owning for seven years ("$210," she dashed down on an address page of her diary, to always remember. "But who cares?"), which had a tall dresser for him, and a vanity with a mirror high and wide enough to satisfy even her. And still the house looked underfurnished. Which suited her fine, a sort of perfection she'd hoped to achieve, where nothing or nobody was ever underfoot.

She helped Martin lay out a vegetable garden beyond the lilacs at the south of the house, and they kept the rows as straight as the planting strings, and well weeded. She canned and preserved from the middle of summer into the fall, and the shelves in the basement began to fill up. The potato bin was full. There were parsnips, kohlrabi, turnips, and rutabagas, all dipped in paraffin to preserve them, in other bins, and carrots buried under sand. She brought out the winter clothes and began to mend them.

*

One afternoon in October she was sitting in her rocker in the alcove made by the bay window, absorbing the last of the warm sunlight before winter, and knitting a heavy cardigan for Marie, when she thought she heard a knock at the front door. Nobody in town ever came to that door. She put her work in the seat of the chair and looked ino the boy's room and found all three playing there, up to no mischief. She went through the living room, down the hall to the door, and opened it. A young priest she'd never seen before stood rocking his weight in a kind of feint on the porch.

"Hello. I'm James Russell. Just call me Father Jim."

"Oh. Hello."

"You must be Mrs. Neumiller."

"Yes, I am."

"I used to live here."

"Well, come in. Please, sir."

He stepped inside and his eyes traveled in rolling waves over every area of the entry and stairs as though follow-

ing a familiar course, and stopped; the boys had trailed
after her and were at the end of the hall. "Ah," he said,
"I see you have three fine sons."

He strode past her, his billowy cassock smelling of
cologne and cigarettes, and went to them and tousled
their hair. "Your father's a fine gentleman," he said. "He
taught two of my brothers and two of my sisters, and they
have nothing but praise for him. You should be proud.
Have either of you older fellows made your First Communion yet?"

"Me," Jeróme said.

"What do we mean when we say that God is all
present?"

"When we say that God is all-present we mean that He
is everywhere."

"If God is everywhere, why do we not see Him?"

"Although God is everywhere, we do not see Him because He is a spirit and cannot be seen with our eyes."

"Is God all-wise, all-holy, all-merciful, and all-just?"

"Yes, God is all-wise, all-holy, all-merciful, and all-just."

"Good, good. You've learned your catechism well." He
turned to Alpha. "Do you have others?"

"A daughter, two and a half months."

"Is she asleep?"

"Yes."

"Ah, that's too bad. I'd like to bless the little darling. Is
your husband here?"

"No."

"Will he be back soon?"

"Later today. He's gone to McCallister."

"I'm afraid I won't even get a chance to see him, then,
I'm so awfully rushed. That's disappointing. I haven't
been in town since I was transferred to St. Paul, which is
three years now. I'm with the Jesuits there. I believe they
thought it best if I didn't visit the family for a while. We
were all very close." He rubbed and wrung his hands as
if washing them and looked toward the door. "But the
family, God bless them, is gone now, so I don't feel guilty
I stopped. There's a conference in Bismarck the Monsignor couldn't attend—one that might be important to the
laity, by the way; it deals with sacramentals—so he dele-
gated me to go and loaned me his car (I left it running;
I'm already late), and since I was so close, I couldn't re-

sist. I had to stop and see the old place. Isn't it a lovely house?"

—He stepped into the living room and strode around, displacing the air as none of them did, his eyes moving with such speed and restlessness he kept changing direction, turning to look behind, looking up, turning again. "You've done very well by the old place. It's decorated with real taste and is as neat as I can remember. The outside looks stunning, too—I mean the new paint job and the hedge, which I think Father let go the last years. I can't understand why he felt compelled to go to South Dakota. The hardware store hasn't worked out as he expected, not in that place, and he just suffered a second stroke. Well, God works His will, and sometimes His ways seem strange to those of us who merely stand by and watch. Edward and Jackie have left home, of course, but Dennis is still there to help. Dennis is a good lad. Enid has decided to take her vows—a surprise to us all, she seemed so involved in the arts—and Margaret graduated valedictorian this year. That makes five in the family so far." He stopped at the bay window.

What did he mean?

"I always liked to stand here and admire this view. Mother loved it so. She'd look out and pray the Rosary here at night, when the children were off in bed, and before her fingers had gone a decade, you could hear a pin drop. I used to believe she put us to sleep that way. Ah, childhood! The lilacs, the garden beyond, that oak down the road next to the Runyons'—somehow the arrangement is so pleasing and serene. I hope nobody ever builds on the lots to the corner. It would ruin this view. You can see past the highway all the way to Hawk's Nest and beyond. There were supposed to have been some Indian battles there. For many years the Indians used it as a lookout point and fortress, or so I've heard, and then the Army surrounded it and starved them out. In all the years we lived here, I never once got out to see it. Isn't that a shame? It stands nearly in the next county, you know, yet from here you can see the creases and valleys in it, especially when it's clear like this, and those big trees at its base—see? They look like pines, and surely must have been planted. Those always intrigued me. Here's where I decided to become a priest."

He removed a handkerchief from the sleeve of his cassock, blew his nose hard, and then refolded the handkerchief, still staring out the window, and restuffed it up his sleeve. Then he started to pace again, peeking into the kitchen, the boys' room, and through a gap in the sliding doors to the master bedroom.

"I'm sorry I'm in such a terrible rush. I'd like to sit down and visit, or have dinner with you, and I wanted so much to see Martin." He stopped. "I'd love to run up and look at my old room. But I'm afraid that would really be imposing."

Alpha started to answer, but he held up a hand. "Also, I don't know if I could face it now. Patrick and I used to share the room, and we lost him in the war." He crossed himself in a hurried way that looked involuntary. "Well, boys, remember to always honor your father and mother, don't forget your morning prayers, and keep yourself pure, for there's nothing more honorable in the eyes of God than purity. Now, come now, kneel down, and I'll give you my blessing."

Jerome and Charles knelt in front of him with their hands clasped and eyes lowered, and Tim, copying them, did the same. He sketched crosses in the air above their heads and spoke the Latin three times without hurrying the familiar words, and then thanked Alpha for her hospitality, again apologized for his rush, reminded her to greet Martin, and went ahead of her to the front door.

The boys watched her accept his blessing, and then he jumped from the porch and ran across the lawn, out of sight, and they heard the sound of his car engine echo off a building and grow faint.

Alpha leaned her shoulder against the door, thinking of priests and nuns, converts, herself and Father Schimmelpfennig, the size of Catholic families, and the way the religion could be youthful and vigorous, as shown by Father Jim, and didn't involve rosaries, religious pictures, statues, crucifixes, Sacred Hearts, or any of the visual trappings she could feel on the walls and shelves behind her—shadows and undusted squares, as though the Russells had just moved—and had come to think were a part of every Catholic's need to believe with fidelity in the "true" faith. She wondered about his relationship with Patrick, and if it had had any of the qualities of hers with Jerome, and then saw, as if on shards of pink-tinged glass, Jerome, her son, crying as he had in the bathhouse, because he couldn't go swimming every day of the summer and felt he should, out of duty to her; Charles on a bed with pieces of the glass beside a leg, blood on the sheets; Tim's skin blistered and Indian-red while slugs the size of fists moved beneath it; Marie trying to kick her way out of a closet, her face blue; and whole seasons and aspects of all of her children, and other children, who'd rise and grow up without her touch or praise or her acknowledgment that their lives as a whole were lived within such short and brightly illuminated early years.

She turned to the boys, six open eyes she couldn't deceive, and felt they'd had a glimpse of what she'd felt, and felt also, now, over and above that, that the Russells, as well as the Halvorsons, would always occupy a part of their house. And she was sure, too, that no matter how much she might resist it, it would only be a matter of time before they moved.

9

THE TWO AT HIS DESK

"What is it?"

Jerome, who was seven hardly a week before this particular afternoon, narrows his pale-blue eyes and evaluates the sheet of paper. "This is a house," he says, and places his finger at the bottom of the paper, where there's nothing. "These are the people living in it." His squint, critical and fierce, makes wrinkles appear beneath his blond eyebrows, and Charles copies the look, hoping it will endow him with the superior vision his brother apparently has.

"I can't see anything."

"Naturally. It's invisible."

Which reminds Jerome of a detail. He takes up the pen, dips it into the ink eradicator, and holds it poised above the sheet of paper, kneeling in the oak chair at the roll-top desk, in a shaft of afternoon sunlight that bleaches his blond hair white and makes his angular features look even more like an old man's, and before he lowers the pen he does a sort of waddle on the seat of the chair, settling his weight down to serious business.

Charles locks his hands behind his head and rests his elbows on the writing area of the desk. He looks at Jerome's eyes, darkened now with concentration, at the shadow of his lashes below, at the downward curve of his thick, heavy lips, and then at a leaf of reflected sunlight resting in the hollow of his cheek. When Jerome's absorbed in this way, when he practices the piano, when they play duets, or when he has to rehearse for a reading, he turns pinch-faced and pale, as if a part of him were bleeding into each task. They've been initiated early into

164

the theater by their parents (not that they wanted to be), and are called upon to perform at club meetings and card parties and other feminine functions in Hyatt, where they're looked upon, with smiling benevolence, as future fruits or freaks.

Some of their readings, from poets such as Poe, Longfellow, Kipling, and Eugene Field, are easy to memorize, because of the hobbyhorse metrics and the cymbals of rhyme, but there are the long monologues in prose, by obscure or anonymous writers, that are harder to cope with: the lyrical piece about the child whose father, so his mother has told him, is away on a business trip with the angels; the one about the "real boy" whose freedom has recently been encroached upon ("Aw, shucks, I been keepin' my turtle in that ole crib." Nasal twang) by a baby sister; or, with the rattling added difficulty of dialect, the piece about the Swede who's just seen his first baseball game, nah, ja, *shure*.

Charles emphasizes ripe words, highlights phrases for effect, plans pauses for breathing, and subdues the piece until he has it sounding the way he wants it to sound, but Jerome gallops through both tragedy and farce with the same hurt look in his eyes, as if any attempt to enact what he felt could only destroy the purity of his feeling.

Now he's drawing this. Charles sinks to the floor, detaching himself from the concentration, and smells a fragrance of old raw oak that the open desk breathes into the room, so dense and enwrapping it seems to him he's leaning against it. He closes his eyes and can distinguish other smells, more delicate and elusive, mingled with the heavily resinous smell, and they arrange themselves in layers that he attempts to see as he separates a sweetness of glue, a bitter yellow perfume he knows his mother never uses, a tang of ink, a hint of oily age similar to the smell that slips from the riffled pages of a big dictionary or old book. He opens his eyes and the sunlit room drops ceiling and walls around him. He looks at Jerome, whose lips are compressed in a tight line as he draws, and realizes that the purpose of the picture is somewhat beyond him. He studies the bottom drawer of the desk.

From the swirling oak grain he isolates the shape of an archway, a swallow in flight, a rising flame, an old man's face, an eye; he thinks of these as dovetailing. Then a cloud crosses the sun and the grain moves to a greater depth, the silvery highlights shift, and colors alter; from coppery brown, rose, bronze, and gold, the grain changes to dark umber, dark brown, and black. He stands at Jerome's side, twisting his forefinger in the hair above his ear. "Why don't you use a color crayon?" he asks.

"Nnnn?" Hardly a response, Jerome is so absorbed.

"So I could see it."

"It wouldn't be any good then."

"How come?"

"Because then you could see it."

"Oh."

Charles isn't sure whether to concede to this logic, and needs information that's more precise. He moves so close he can see curved shadows, like faint pencil marks, lying beneath each blond hair on the bulge of Jerome's free forearm, and watches Jerome move the pen in rapid pinches of his fingers while the hand and arm lie absolutely still, and finds himself, though detached from the act, participating in it in such a physical sense that a cloak of sensation covers his shoulders and then, as he moves to speak, shudders down his back.

"How do you know it's good?"

"I'm doing it."

"But you can't see what you're doing."

Jerome looks up, distracted from his task, a veil of creation clouding his eyes, and being as patient as he can be with somebody so young, not even six, says, "Nobody can see it. It's invisible."

"That's what I mean!"

"I know."

A reply to stun most any literal mind into silence. Now he studies the drawing and sees that it's complete. He prints his name (*is* it his name?) at the bottom, puts the cap back on the bottle of ink eradicator, puts it in a pigeonhole of the desk, puts the pen away, and puts the blank sheet on the pile from which he took it.

"What are you *doing?*" Charles cries.

"I'm finished."

"Don't put it there! Dad'll use it in the book."

"That's all right. I know what it is."

"He'll write a letter and send it away!"

"So? They won't see it."

"Well, make it so they can!"

"Then he wouldn't send it away."

"Make it so *I* can see it."

"If you could, it wouldn't be invisible."

"Why do you want it invisible?"

"Because it's mine."

They'll be necessary to each other the rest of their lives; the one with his passionate need to know and be told what everything means, the other already serene in his knowledge, and living among elements that are invisible and his own.

10

❧⑤❧

SOME OF HIS STORIES

"When I was a young man and we were living on the farm near Courtenay, there were hard times. One summer it was a plague of jackrabbits, I remember. There were jackrabbits every direction you looked, hightailing it over the fields and pastures and eating up every green shoot the second it appeared. To us, they were eating up our providence, so we went after them with rifle and shotgun. I carried a twelve-gauge on the back of the tractor so much there was a groove worn in its stock where it rested on the toolbox. I learned to shoot the thing one-handed and drive the tractor with the other, although your grandpa warned me not to, and I made a little money that year; there was a bounty of twenty-five cents on jackrabbits and if you had ten dollars in those days you were rich. I remember at the co-op elevator in Courtenay, where they paid the bounty, the carcasses were piled up one winter in a mound as high as a haystack.

"This was when the Depression was coming on. There was a drought. The crops dried up and the blowing dust blackened the air so badly it was dark sometimes at midday. We put rugs under the doors and stuffed rags around the windows but the dust came right through the walls. It was topsoil. You couldn't keep clean no matter how often you washed, and even the sugar got gray. We didn't have money to buy seed for new crops and there was very little to eat. Many days, I remember, your grandma made up a big pan of johnnycake and it lasted us the three meals. There were eight of us then and your granddad did all it was possible for a man in his position to do. He kept us alive.

"We had a neighbor in those days by the name of Iver Seim."

He smiles and Jerome and Charles nudge one another. When he tells his stories, he's so transformed in the telling they're nearly as much affected by the transformation as by his words. His oval face broadens at the mouth and looks round, and his eyes, bright blue and nearly circular, become enormous behind his gold-wire glasses; he punishes his hair until curly locks of it cover his forehead; tugs at his watch chain, at the green suspenders under his vest, and becomes so nervous he can hardly sit.

"Iver was one of the most brilliant and interesting men I've met and he fancied himself a poet and had a good wife, but he ruined it all with drink. His motto was, 'There must be an easier way.' I'm not saying he was a lazy man; that wouldn't be true. He farmed two sections of land and there wasn't anybody able to keep up with him when he wanted to work, and in his spare time and at nights he was also always working away at his poetry, but he drank. He was skin and bones from worry and hard work. We never saw the lights in his house go off before 3 A.M. He was writing a book-long piece of verse he called *A Medley of the Plain*. He recited stanzas of it for us now and then, but I was too young to really remember much. There was a line that went, 'There must be a Creator or my life wouldn't be going up in flames every day.' Or something of that sort, better said. His language and ideas were generally above me then.

"He had plenty of ideas, it seems, but was never able to get them off on the right foot. Or maybe he depended too much on that motto of his. I remember one time he decided to reshingle his barn. We all wondered why, since it was his house that leaked and was in such sad shape. Dad—your grandpa—offered to help him with the job, but Iver just winked and said, 'Wait till you see what I've got up my sleeve, Mr. N.'

"He built a mechanical rig to lift the shingles onto the roof. It looked like an oil derrick to me. Iver said he'd use it later to lift engines out of his tractors and cars. Who knows where he got the materials to build it or those shingles he had? He lived on a fertile farm in a good lo-

cation and got regular checks from some place else—
some said it was a rich uncle, others said it was his father-
in-law—but never seemed to have a cent. He often tried
to borrow from Dad and was always bartering with neighbors up and down the line for food.

"His shingle-lifting boom was built out of logs and
pipework and ran off the power take-off of his tractor,
and must have taken him weeks to build. On the second
load it tipped over—'Geet out!' he cried—and tore an
eave off his barn. Oh, Lord! Those shingles sat beside
that barn in stacks, with moss growing on them, for as
long as I can remember. I suppose it seemed an easier
way at the time to him.

"He got tired of shoveling manure and decided he
needed a mechanical barn cleaner, was what he needed
now. He bought up feed chains from broken-down
threshing machines, cut the cleats in lengths to fit his gutter, and linked the chains in a series that revolved. He
had to burrow the length of his barn beneath the gutter
to do it, but got it going at last. This contraption also ran
off the power take-off of his Case. It worked well for a
while and farmers were coming from around to admire
it, and the officer of an implement company in Duluth
even showed up one day to check out the possibilities of
mass production of it. Iver sat on his tractor taking nips
from his jug and got the cleaner going like crazy, but apparently hadn't put the proper sort of bracing in his burrow; part of the barn floor collapsed. The tractor reared
up and tipped on its back and pinned him by his coveralls
and the cleaner kept going long enough to drag the tractor
and him into the barn with a crash. 'Holy balls!' he cried,
and I thought those would be his last words, but he was
hardly scratched. The luck of that man!

"Your grandpa patched up the wall and the one eave
above it. That barn certainly took its knocks. 'He isn't one
to ask favors,' your grandpa used to say. 'But you wish
he would, before he's in so deep you can't help, because
he always ends up needing one.'

"He bought a dozen Shropshire sheep to keep the yard
around his place looking mowed and tidy. 'It's a bit of old
England I've got here now, isn't it?' he said in an accent.
But he'd neglected to fence off his garden and the sheep
leveled it in a day. His wife liked that. We helped them

out with vegetables that winter and got a lot of mutton in return. I still can't stand the stuff. Iver showed me this." Martin raises his left hand and pops his cuff. "If you wear your watch on the hand you don't favor, on the inside of your wrist, like this, it's less likely to get damaged, and the crystal doesn't scratch up so much.

"Around the Depression there were a lot of closing auctions going on. Iver was attracted to them in a way you wished he hadn't been. He'd go to one and start bidding and couldn't stop. It seemed he wasn't so interested in the items as in coming out on top. Again, I don't know where he got the means. He'd come over all liquored up and say he'd *just* sold a poem, but I didn't ever see anything of his in a book or magazine or even scratched on a pad of paper, as far as that goes. I took him at his word. He drove an old Dodge truck and he'd leave each auction loaded with so much furniture and junk you'd wonder where he'd put it all, and unload it at his back door as if he had gold. Unless he was too drunk, and then it'd sit out and get rained on a few times. He had two or three of just about everything you can think of in just about every room of his house. When he had company, there was hardly a place to stand. There was five or six beds, as I recall it, and he and his wife didn't have any kids. She kept every piece of furniture and knickknack he brought home as clean as the day it was made. She was a hard-working, solid Scandinavian, that girl, and I never once heard her complain.

"He also bought tractors. He had several makes you don't even hear about now. They were parked all around his farmyard and he had about a dozen hidden away in an old horse barn. He claimed those were special breeds, and priceless, but I think he was actually embarrassed at the number he had. None of them would run when he needed one, of course, or if he got one going, it didn't last long. He was his own mechanic, you see. When one gave out he'd leave it sit where it was until it occurred to him what to do about it next, and there were a few he'd plowed around so many times they were a part of the landscape.

"Oh, what I could tell you about starting those old tractors of his! The Waterloo Boy was cranked something like a Hart Parr, along the side instead of up at the front.

And then there was the Rumley Oil Pull. It was cooled by oil, not water, like most, and had a flywheel on the order of a John Deere. You had to grab that flywheel and give it a spin with all your might, and when it finally took hold, it shot clouds of blue smoke out of a big stack under its square front and the flywheel sent you flying!

"He had an old Flour City, which was made in and named after Minneapolis, and stood on big steel wheels, six foot high or so. It had a platform at the back where you stood to drive it. You also cranked it from there, at the back, by the platform, and the cranking spindle revolved all the while the engine was going once you got it going for good. That spindle scared me; I figured sooner or later it was going to catch me in my crotch. Iver had fun kidding me about that and then the spindle caught him there. Not a word. The Flour City moved into the horse barn with his special breeds.

"He had three or four cars he had trouble keeping on the road. There was a particular Model T he rolled three times in the course of a year. He spent his time in between tinkering on it. He had an idea on how the steering could be improved. He drove too fast, of course, and the inside of the car was always tinkling with empty liquor jars. It seemed he never went anywhere unless he was juiced. He wasn't ever hurt in any of the accidents, and neither was the mandolin he always had with him. He loved to play the mandolin and sing, although he couldn't do either, really, not well at all, and, my Lord, that infuriated him! He was jealous of your grandpa because he could carry a tune! Dad called him a misguided perfectionist. He said that Iver was probably the kind who couldn't let a— Well, you know how you toot when you eat beans; that he couldn't do that without taking time to stop and get a good whiff of it.

"One day he came running into our yard and yelled, 'One of my cars is on fire!' 'Where?' we asked. 'Just down the road here! Hurry up!' We all took off, about six of us, counting kids, and, sure enough, there was fire coming out of the raised hood of an old Pontiac of his. He'd thrown his shirt over the engine and the shirt was all burned up. He started scooping dirt up in his hands and throwing that on the fire. 'Help me!' he yelled to us. Most of us obliged and started throwing dirt, although we figured pretty soon this whole car would be blowing up. He pulled off his trousers in front of us kids and started whacking at the fire with those. Dad meanwhile had turned back when he saw the smoke, and now came running up with a weed sprayer filled with water and put the fire out.

" 'How can I ever thank you?' Iver said.

" 'How did it happen?' Dad asked.

" 'Well, I cleaned the block and rocker-arm covers with gasoline this afternoon,' Iver said. 'I really shined her up. I used all the gasoline I had. I was coming over to ask if I could borrow some from you, so I could turn that hay of mine that got wet last week, when the car here ran out. Then I remembered I always carry a five-gallon can in the back here, because the gauge in this doesn't work, so I poured that into the tank but it wouldn't start, so then I siphoned some of it back out—I also carry a siphon hose—and I took off the air cleaner and poured some in the carburetor, and I guess it got slapped around. When the engine finally took hold, flames shot up. How can I ever thank you, for goodness' sake?'

" 'Before you thank me,' Dad said, 'I think you better check that engine there. Your spark-plug wires will have to be replaced, at the least, and that fan belt. You got a pile of dirt all over the top of your carburetor somehow, and now this water has just made it mud.'

" 'Do you think it'll start?' Iver asked.

"A few weeks later I went by his house and most of the windows were broken out and his furniture lay in the yard in a circle around it. He'd gone on a bender and cleaned house. For the next few weeks he was repairing furniture like a penitent. And then his wife disappeared. Run off to her father, some said; off with another Swede, according to others. I imagine Iver had bad luck with that poem of his, too.

"His belongings and his farm were eventually auctioned off. All of us in the family felt too bad to go. They say that Iver ran alongside the auctioneer, trying to convince the bidders of every item's worth, and scared people off. I saw Iver once after that. The folks and the kids were away at church and I was doing the chores alone. I was sixteen. I was walking toward the house in the dark with a bucket of milk in each hand when I heard something big in the grass. I took off for the porch spilling milk all the way, and then through the grass came this— Well, it was Iver all ragged and dirtied up and wearing a cowboy hat. He was crawling along on his belly. He crawled up to the porch and cocked a bloodshot eye at me. It was the first time I'd seen an adult act like this, and I was deathly afraid.

" 'Am I headed right?' he asked in a tiny voice.

" 'What?'

" 'Headed right. I've been traveling this state by the stars since I struck the river's mouth.'

" 'What do you mean?'

" 'An ash can,' he said. He had his hands like paws on the ground.

" 'An *ash* can?'

" 'Yes, Martin. Even an ash can tell a Norse from a souse.'

"Well, I had to laugh. Who knows how many times he'd pulled that one? But here he was, out a wife and farm and on his knees, on his belly, literally, and still trying to be his same old self, or whatever he was, and I thought, Here's a man I'd like to help. So I put down the milk and locked my knees and lifted him up, and he slapped my back and cried in a funny voice, 'Thanks a lot, Martin. I'll write that *Medley* yet.' And then he ran off down the road laughing in a way I'd never heard any-body laugh before, and hope not to hear again.

"He'd come to our house once before, on a Halloween, in that same cowboy hat and a pair of long winter un-derwear. He had a tractor chain around his waist with an alarm clock wired to it, and when Dad opened the door he pointed a keyhole saw at him and said, 'I'm the Bony Granger, and I've about had it. Put 'em up.' Oh, Lord, Iver! He had a pinto riding horse he called Bone-head. I keep looking for a book entitled *A Medley of the Plain,* or any book by Iver Seim, but I've yet to see one to this day. In his own fashion he had a knowledge of the world in order to act the way he did at times, and it's a knowledge I'm just coming onto."

He's moved to the edge of the chair and placed his hands on its arms, elbows turned out, as if to rise. Jerome and Charles move back and can feel from be-hind, from the couch where their mother sits embroidering on a dish towel, a current of empathy and protectiveness. Their father clears his throat and settles his weight into the chair again. If he's relaxed, his stories rise of their own volition from an untroubled, indemnified, and inexhaustible source.

"When I graduated from high school, in 1931, there wasn't money to send me through college. No money? My Lord! Our farm was mortgaged to the hilt, we'd sold most of the stock, we kept a Model A going on the road with binder twine and coat hangers, and your mother and your Grandma Jones looked on us as rich. Ha! I'd heard so much about the money my Grandad Neumiller had I *felt* we should be rich, but that's another story for another time. When your Grandma Neumiller needed flour or sugar from town, I'd ride in after it on a little old bicycle with hard rubber tires that had once been Dad's, to save on gasoline. He'd built a cart with steel wheels that hitched behind the bike, which was an antique that once belonged to him, as I said, and he'd bequeathed it to me and it had since passed down the line of kids, I'd graduated to a car and now I was back on that, pulling a hundred pounds of flour behind in the steel-wheeled cart. Oh! my knees stuck out on both sides, like this, the steel wheels squealed and creaked, and I knew everybody in the whole countryside was watching me! Every time I got demoted to that—*thing!*—I'd take the long way around from town, so your mother wouldn't see me in my shame."

He removes his glasses and with the back of his hand wipes a wet streak of laughter from his cheek, composing himself into the person he shows outside the house: solemn; the decorous high-school principal, the parishioner who attends Mass every day, the conscientious paterfamilias with a garden in his yard and a clipped hedge around a newly painted house, which townspeople and neighbors like to look at now.

"I knew it was important to your grandad that we kids get a college degree, and I figured I had to try to set an example, since I was the oldest, even if I went for only a year. There was confusion about a baseball scholarship that I don't want to talk about right now, and then I applied to Valley City State Teachers College and was accepted. I found a job that summer pitching bundles.

You went out with a hayrack and team and loaded up the bundles of grain that had been stacked into shocks to dry, then drove to the threshing machine and pitched the bundles from the rack into its rattling feeder teeth. It was a chaffy, dirty inferno around that machine at the tail end of August, I'll say, and the pay was twenty-five cents an hour, for man and hayrack and team, and I was grateful to get it. I missed Iver. He always worked hardest at threshing time. I gave your grandpa a dime on every quarter I earned for the use of the wagon and team. He wasn't going to accept it but I insisted, by George; it was *his* team and wagon and I made that stick. I put in two hundred hours, fifty dollars' worth, and even taking into account your granddad's cut, I remember going off to school that fall with the feel of a lot of money in my purse. I had one of those leather purses with a clasp lock at the top then.

"I joined the National Guard because they gave you a uniform and I needed pants to wear. For most of my meals I had breakfast food with water on it. Milk was too expensive. I used to walk to the other side of town because I found a bakery that sold day-old bread for three cents a loaf. The following quarter I got a job at a sorority, waiting table and washing dishes and floors, and had my meals there. At first I could hardly hold it down, the food was so rich."

His eyes blink and scintillate and he stares beyond them with a fixity of focus that makes them feel the past is so close he's staring at a particular face in it.

"When I was eleven and we were on the home place outside Mahomet, your grandpa bought a Golden Guernsey heifer calf. She was one of the few Golden Guernseys for miles around. She was registered. We had the papers on her. We had to transport her a hundred miles to have her serviced by a registered bull, and it took several trips to get her with calf, but it finally happened at last, and we could feel a better future ahead, or at least I could. The calf would bring a good price and when we got back on our feet financially Dad was going to start a herd of Golden Guernseys.

"One day I went out to fetch the cows for the evening milking. It was one of the first nice days that spring and I could see the buildings of Mahomet and the windmills of neighbors who lived miles off. The cattle had been barned up all winter, so the pasture was heaven to them, and they'd found a growth of grass in a swale along the creek and wouldn't leave it for love of God nor me. I hollered and slapped their rear ends, but they'd just switch their tails and step to one side. I got so mad I picked up a rock the size of a baseball and threw it into the bunch of them. The Guernsey dropped like she'd been shot. Instantly killed. It probably couldn't happen three times in this world.

"The rest of them smelled death and ran for the barn, and I sat in the pasture beside her and started bawling and couldn't stop; this beautiful creature that held our hopes now gone because of me, her sides big with calf. It got darker and darker and then I saw your grandpa coming toward me over the fields—"

"I bet he spanked you."

"Wait, now. I want you to hear what kind of person he is. I saw him coming and wanted to run and hide, but knew I couldn't hide forever, so I sat there like the stone I sat beside. 'Even if she's dead, it can't be that important,' he said. 'Yes, it could be,' I said to him, and told him what I'd done. 'You should never lose your temper,' he said. 'I've told you that, I've warned you about it, and now you see what you reap.'

"You're right. I expected a licking to last me the rest of my life, but instead Dad lifted me to my feet and said, 'Come home and eat now. You've suffered enough.'"

He removes his glasses and lays them in his lap, where reflections on them geometrically shine.

"Oh, there are so many good stories. At the time they seemed terribly sad, or troubling, or made me wonder about the justice on this earth, and there were a few I didn't think I'd live through, such as the Guernsey, but I did, and now when I look back on them it seems that they happened in a way that was almost ordained. No matter how many times I think them over, or try to write them down, they always have a quality about them that language won't quite explain for me. When I write the book of my life, when I get around to it, that's the way I'm going to make them.

"Goodness!" he exclaims, and presses his fingers on his

thighs and throws his head against the chair back, then grabs his glasses by an earpeice as they slip down a trouser leg away from him. "I'm beginning to sound just about as bad as Iver Seim!"

11

۰ई۵۰

PENNIES

Jerome opens out the bottom doors of the linen closet in
their bedroom, steps up on a bottom shelf, opens the top
doors with a swaying-out boost and lift from Charles,
and hands down from a high shelf the quart jar and one-
pound coffee tins that contain their collection of pennies.
He and Charles bear the jars and cans to their double
bed, while Tim, small for his age, sits in silence on his
cot at the side of the room, his eyes hanging on tendrils,
and watches them empty the containers until the bedspread is covered with coppery sunshine. Jerome and
Charles look at the dates on the coins. They examine
Abraham Lincoln. They look for dimes tossed in mis-
takenly by their father. They look for quarters and
nickels and half dollars, too. Their hands begin to smell
metallic and bright green. Tim groans from his cot.
Where's he been?

Jerome and Charles start dividing the pennies by hundreds into two equal shares, and grow tired of it; there
are too many to do. They pour the pennies from jars to
cans to hear the coppery-brown roar of them. They dump
them out on the bedspread and lie down and make swimming motions with their arms over the layers there. They
try to dive beneath them and hurt their foreheads. They
decide to count them and arrive at three thousand, licking saliva from their lips as though there's a run on it in
this exchange, and then Jerome tosses a handful heaven-
ward and it spatters down on the layers of pennies
spread out on the bed around them.

"There are just too many!"

He starts shoveling pennies with both hands and covers Charles's stomach the way the people at the seashore do in their father's large green cartoon book. A big fat man here in the middle.

"They're really heavy, Jay!"

Medallions and sunlit triplicates of coins float and hover and rock on the ceiling above them. The air in the room is brown-golden, and these children, for the first and only time in their lives, are as rich as princes or kings, or Father Schimmelpfennig, who buys a new Chevrolet every fall, and sometimes sells their father his old one; it's O.K. by their father, and not that expensive, either, he's told them.

"Then why not just buy a new one?" Jerome asks now.

"I have no idea," Tim says.

They all laugh at the imitation of their father. Jerome and Charles throw coins at Tim for speaking so boldly, and then quickly retrieve them.

"Get out of here," Jerome says to Tim, who's examining a silvery-gray circular piece, all dull and tarnished, which is, believe it or not, a real penny.

"Go wipe yourself," Charles says. He does a raspberry and lets pennies clatter from the hand pinching his nose into a can.

"Go crawl in Marie's crib and diddle around with yourself, like last month," Jerome says, and lays a compact and eruptive childlike fart in a jar, and then sticks the mouth of it toward Charles as they lie back on the layers of their pennies laughing. It's real money! and grinds and pulses under their backs like the music of planets circumscribing arcs around musical spheres. Now stars are on the ceiling and the air bright-blue and tingling; its extraterrestrial! Jerome finds a dime. Well, at this moment, take it from me, these children are richer than anybody anywhere in the world will ever possibly be, except for Tim, of course, who's turned to lie face down on his cot and is probably weeping—poor Tim, who isn't bossy or aggressive and wants only to please, and doesn't have a penny among him.

12

❧

TIM'S DAY

Tim hears a loud cry of *Deem! Deem!* He lowers his eyes and stirs his cereal with his spoon. His mother has bathed Marie and put her in her crib for her nap and now she's in the pantry across the room from him, finishing up the breakfast dishes. All but his. She lets him sleep late and eat late, as he overheard her telling his father, because the day is so long for him. His father leaves for work before he's awake, and his brothers are both in school. He isn't old enough to go yet. He's only four. His birthday is May eighth.

Deem! The cry is louder and sounds closer, too, as if it originates inside the wall behind and travels over his shoulder in purple shafts. Is that possible, probably or not? He looks up and finds her studying eyes set on him in a frown.

"Are you done with your breakfast already?"

"Yes."

"Do you want to go out today?"

"Yes, I do."

"Let's get you dressed, then, and out, before he decides you're not going to show."

He walks to the wall behind the stove, where outdoor clothes are hung on hooks, and stands as though for inspection, while she opens the door, and says, "Just a minute, Donny. He'll be right out." There's a cry of recognition and other noises she closes the door on, and then slips Tim's wool-tweed topcoat, once Jerome's, up Tim's arms, turns him to face her, and starts buttoning it up. She's worried about him. Almost everybody in town calls him "the principal's son," and his brothers "the Neumiller

181

boys." How sad for him without his knowing it, or does
he? He hasn't made any friends as Jerome and Charles
did at his age—they collected them—and doesn't seem inclined to. The only child he really likes is Susie, the Eichelburger girl across the hedge and alleyway and white barn,
who's high-strung and secretive, and every bit as friendless
as he is. They drive shingles into the ground to make pens
for Susie's dolls, or count out bottle caps her father has
brought back from the tavern uptown, and bury them in
treasure boxes, as they call them, small tins from the ash
piles up and down the alley, and are so feverish and
hushed in all they do that— Well, about a week ago the
two were caught in the Eichelburgers' barn with all their
clothes off. So Tim certainly is precocious, I'd say. And
Susie must be lonelier than even her mother has imagined.

"Should we give them both a whipping?" Mary Eichelburger, who'd caught them, asked.

"No, I don't think so," I said.

"Thanks. Neither do I. I'm afraid Susie would just get
to enjoying the goddamnable abuse of it."

"Goodness, you sound mad—or angry at me."

"Well, how would you feel if a holy terror of a two-bit
Catholic town like this had screwed up one of your kids?"

She flipped away her cigarette and strode up the back
steps and into her house, a heronlike waddle to her high
waist, and then the door swung to with a bang, while I
thought, so there's one who feels even more outcast than I.
She's handsome, exotic, and time-attuned, and hates working for her husband at the tavern when he takes his half
days off—beauty putting up with smart remarks—and
there must be an even more fertile secret curl inside that
"abuse of it," huh?

Tim watched every second and aspect of it when I was
breast-feeding Marie, and would say sometimes, "Mom, do
all girl babies have eyes that big?" Oh, the innocence and
the duplicity in it! He'll come up when I'm busy with
housework, his eyes enlarged and dark as far as I can see
into them, and say, "Remember the day you brought Marie
home here from the hospital and laid her down on her back
right on the kitchen table?" And even though that's what
I did, he was only two and a half at the time and it's inconceivable to me, even though I'm his mother, that he
could remember the moment so well. When I asked him

about it he said, "Oh, maybe Charluss" —his name for Charles—"told me that. I don't know."

"Mom, when will Marie walk?" he'd ask, and then when she began to walk, "When will she talk to me?" And lately he's been wondering if brothers and sisters could become close enough to be friends. He never speaks directly to Marie, yet never treats her like an infant or a child, or, thank the Lord, a plaything, but more like an adult he's waiting for to wake from sleep. He seems so mature in ways of intuition usually considered a part of the feminine mind.

Should I encourage him to befriend Jimmy Ianaccona, the neighbor boy across the front, who appears outside his house in short pants and mittens, or in mother-made cowboy suits (and once in a skirt of hers), looking lost and dazed inside the outdoor world shining down on him, who cries if he gets dirt on his clothes, or gets too cold, or wet, or hot, or bored, or stultified, and if he should wander a ways from the house—God forfend and protect us in life! —she'll come onto the porch, a brown shawl about her narrow self, and scream, "Jiimmy! Jiiiimmy!" in such a desperate voice it stiffens your neck cords no matter how many times you've heard it, or how many walls it's come through. Her *Jiiiimmy* has been more than once the swimming bees of serenity's death.

When Jerome and Charles let Tim in on their roughhousing and games, he becomes so rowdy they can't contain him. Once they tied up his hands and feet with a jump rope and locked him inside the room with that old Victrola they keep insisting is theirs. I heard him calling out and kicking on the floor and asked Jerome what was up, before I went and *saw,* and he said, "Oh, nothing really. Tim just doesn't belong to us."

"You be good to Donny," I say to him.

"Yes, I will."

"You're his protector."

"I guess so."

Donny Ennis, the youngest of seven boys and a girl, is six feet tall, with a pair of matched shoulders from my personal heaven of men, hands larger than Martin's, and thighs and calves that pop his pants; he holds his hands, limp, in front of his waist or chest as he walks, half flexed and tentative, as if to search out feeling in the air to guide him, and jerks his feet with high steps out of tangles nobody can see. He's thirteen and can't speak, but can understand well enough what you're up to, if spoken to as even pets and plants are spoken to, but he, being neither so tame nor unanimal, seldom is.

Mrs. Ennis ushers him out of the house in the morning, or perhaps of his own volition he goes, and he wanders the streets, usually pulling an empty wagon behind him, until time for recess at the parochial school, and then stands across from the playground, in our yard, watching at a distance and working his jaws; he knows the nuns don't want him near; his fly is left undone and he'll pull it out wherever the need overtakes him, and, oh, is it *huge;* little girls shouldn't have to endure that, not yet, and on that the nuns and I are in accord, but I've seen the barnyard habits of a lot of men, and of the animals in the barnyard, too, and know it's natural for him to follow his instincts, but there was still the size of it, and the idea that the girls might get, terrifying or later candid, ah, that men were all that big. It came splattering out of it and foamed with rising steam, moonlight and ice and a pale leg seen.

He cheers the children if there's a game, and, when they go inside, crosses the street and tries to imitate their play; he can't make the swings work, is afraid of the ladder of the slide, and bangs the teeter-totters so hard, wooden *whonks,* that the janitor or the principal, Sister Celestina, has to tell him to stop. School-boys sneak behind and slap his back and make him swing around, and then another slaps him from a different direction, until he's spinning so fast he falls. They switch him with sticks and he can't move quite quick enough to catch one. His gums show when he laughs, so he tries not to laugh hard, but likes to, and is patsy for the simplest and most harebrained jokes of theirs, because they know if they can get him to show his gums they've got him going non-stop, a captive laugher.

The Ianaccona kid found a car-flattened snake and wouldn't touch it, or course, but carried it around on the end of a stick for a day, and when Donny saw what it was, he went stumbling backward and hit a tree and stood there, fixed, his face a craven, unvoiced cry, as though the snake were a representation of an evil bred into all of us that still resided inside in some way, while Ianaccona brought the thing closer to his eyes, and then I stepped out the door and yelled, 'Jimmy! Your mother wants you home!"

Last winter Donny came pulling a sled down the street and stopped and stared at our pantry window, where I usually am. Tim looked out, too, and then I dressed him up and he went out and sat on the sled, no word spoken anywhere, and Donny pulled him around the streets until he asked to be taken home. Donny came with his sled the next day, and then the next, and then winter passed or capsized into spring, and he began to appear with his wagon. If Tim isn't here when I want him, or if I get anxious about him out of any of my personal fears, I'll call him, not in Mrs. Ianaccona's pitch, but maybe in one that bothers her, for all I know, and in a few minutes he'll appear, drawn up to the back door by Donny, who'll be grinning like a dog who's just chased and nipped his first deer. And then about a week ago when he came with the wagon, he cried, *"Deem! Deem!"* So there were possibilities of speech in him.

"O.K.," I say to Tim.

He goes out the door and down the steps with me in his wake and when we appear Donny cries aloud and claps his large hands as though we're in a movie he's seeing that captivates. His black hair is a tousled haystack that needs rearranging and some shears, his nose is running in bubbly gluten over his lips onto his chin, and his green jacket, held at its center with a safety pin, is so small that his big veined wrists spring out of the sleeves of it. Its front is covered with mucus and drool.

"Come here once," I say, and lift Tim into the wagon, take the handkerchief from my apron and wipe Donny's nose, his upper lip, his big chin. He's beginning to get a beard.

"Now you take good care of Tim."

He smiles and shows broken and many-shaped gray-green teeth, which must cause him terrible pain, and cries, "Yeh! Ahyatata, Nin Neunhaour!" Then he turns away and begins to pull, and I think again what a pity it is to put him to such a task, but what is there that he'd like more, or more like to do, in a place and time such as this?

*

Tim gripped the wagon and looked from the left to the right as they rolled along. He bent and looked over the side. It was spring and the sun made a squat shadow of the wagon and the two of them. The big snowbanks had sunk beneath the ground and the grass was green in spots, circled by black-brindled crusty ice patches backed by thinning brown snow. Puddles in the road had oily rainbows spiraling over them and he was about to tell Donny to stop, thinking he saw the fat nose of a frog in the center of a rainbow, but it was a rock that stood still, or else a toad. A bird like a duck it landed so fast, a robin, hopped across the Eichelburgers' lawn after it came down past them.

He liked Donny's smell. It was like his dad's sweat and pee and old bread all mixed up together. And then Donny made a turn that meant he was taking the long trip around the lake, where blue ice would be floating in big blocks that banged and bobbed. Good. Winter made Tim weary of the indoors, and he liked the nice rattly feel of the wagon under his rump, *titabum*. They passed the Congregational Church on the corner, with moss growing on its concrete steps. Nobody ever went there. Why didn't they take it down or give it to somebody who could use it for whatever they needed it for? Could you live in a church?

The next house was Mrs. Liffert's, and it would take Donny fifty-eight steps or so to reach it. If he got home early today, he'd build a fort with his brothers' Lincoln Logs, unless they'd hidden them again, or figure out how their Victrola worked, or learn to shoot marbles by flipping a thumb, thuk, the way they did. Then he could go behind the lilacs, where nobody would see, and practice throwing a ball from the croquet set. He didn't know where they kept their baseballs or softballs, and they said he threw like a girl.

Mary Liffert, the widow whose three sons have entered the Marines instead of the priesthood, where she'd prayed all three would find their vocation, the gray-haired lady who can be seen each spring spading her garden up in fishing waders, watches from her window as Tim and Donny pass, and makes a sign of the cross. Lord have mercy on that Alpha Neumiller's soul, she thinks. Any mother who'd let her kid out with an animal

like that should have her head looked at. And maybe
the kid could use it, too. He sure was a strange one, that
one, him and his May eighth. And then Jerome and
Charles came into her yard when she was away just last
spring, while Wilhomena was watching, and slashed
down her flowers, every last one, with swords they'd
made of wood lath. She could feature Charles doing it,
but Jerome was the perfect model of an altar boy, who
made you wonder after all if there was such a bugaboo
as original sin. Their mother had made them come and
apologize, but that didn't make her feel any better about
the woman, or bring back her flowers—Father was always so complimentary about her side-altar arrangements
—and as they left the yard, she heard Jerome say, "I
might, if she bothered Mom again." What? Level her
flowers with their laths? What had she done to her in
the first place, other than give her the cold eye or
shoulder, perhaps, for being such an obvious Lutheran?

Where was that Ennis taking him now? What did they
do on these tours? She couldn't follow the two, and the
women in town thought of her as so devoted to her de-
votions to the Blessed Virgin, she couldn't ask. She'd
have to get Tim and his brothers over to her house somehow (date bread? hearts?—potato pancakes, like Mrs.
Glick?) and see that they had their catechism down pat.
Just being around a non-Catholic like her could absorb
it right out of their heads.

Why didn't any children ever visit her in her house?

Watching from the rectory across the street, the
housekeeper and cook for Father Schimmelpfening,
Wilhomena Noedler, sighs and makes the sign of the
cross, and whispers, in German, Bless them both, poor
Donny, poor Tim; Tim who came to the rectory last
spring and knocked on the door so politely she didn't
hear at first, and when she did, and opened it, expecting
a note from his mother, as was often the case, he
marched up into the porch next to her, and cried, "My
birthday's May eighth! My birthday's May eighth!" And
then went over to Mrs. Liffert's, on to the Pete
Schommers', and on and on to every house on this side
of town until his mother caught up with him and dragged
him home by the collar of his coat.

When Father heard about it, he gave her a silver dollar to send to Tim on his day; and during her vacation, and on visits to other rectories, she told the story every chance she had, she found it so amusing. She didn't get to gossip or talk much here in Hyatt, because everybody was convinced she repeated everything to Father, who compared it to what he'd heard in the confessional and seen in the collection box. She told the story so many times it became a recital, and then she thought of Tim walking from house to house, where some of the people were strangers to him, or people he'd seen only in church or on the street, and announcing his birthday as though it were important to them as it was to him, and never told the story again.

Bless them both. They are strangers to us, the two of them, Tim as much as Donny, though both are familiar to us, and the worst of it is that Donny, for as long as he's lived as one, doesn't know that he is, and that Tim, at his age, already does, and is living as one. I bow my head. Teach me poverty of spirit and let me learn to love those of yours not so obviously blessed as Father. Help me to accept my life as a nun in everyday clothes.

There's a flash of another building front, an outhouse, the sprouting shimmer of lilacs along Mrs. Glick's light side of the street, the water tower, weeds crushing under Donny's shoes, and Tim's eyes keep step with each step Donny takes, until Tim believes that he's Donny and making Donny walk and the wagon move the way they do, while Donny imagines Tim's sweet and soapy skin and sees all the fresh-washed clothes Tim wears, as though Tim had the entire bundle trunk of them on his back at one time, a fat bug with shining wrappings around him, a lightning bug in his hand. *Deem.* The wagon moves and the two strangers travel over sunlight on the storehouse of the earth that cushions theirs and everybody else's cloud-capped, many-lamented fears and furtive, futile fantasies of being alive at times in the spiraled intertwinings of time and place, in this all-alive time of life we live inside, today, today chimes, like a hand-wrought old mantelshelf clock: *ching.*

❦

13

THE BASEMENT

It was impossible for them to reconcile their mother's feelings about the attic. She didn't mind the basement one bit. There was no floor in the basement, Mother. It was just bare dirt with planks put down over the dirt to form paths. A single bulb, filmed with coal dust, exuded a light that made the blackness around the planks appear bottomless, and the shadows it cast along the wall concealed, if looked at in the right way, those un-animal-like creatures with outlines of neon that followed us through the nights of all the days of all our childhood dreams; pools of water gleamed from the bulb and white plants grew around them and were reflected on them, and beneath their surface—now and then breaking through a reflection, revealed when the pools dried— were salamanders, newts, and tangled clumps of angle-worms. One of the paths of plank led to the furnace and the pile of clinkers in the corner (plus that old coal bucket we lugged paired-up), and another to the potato bin, where my brothers and I were sent twice a week to sort through the smelly potatoes, picking out the best for meals, tossing aside the ones that gave way in our hands and sent smell through our skin to the center of smell, trying to forget about those, and taking pains not to touch the sprouts that grew out of the eyes of some and wove a network of white tubers over the succulent pile. Another led to a set of shelves lined with jars of vege-tables, meats, jellies, and fruits; and the dusty jars, with their contents looking out of them (some spoiling, ring-ing the lids with crystals, or forming snowstorms of mold behind *Mason* on their insides), reminded Jerome of a

Horror Comics story in which a woman chopped up and canned her husband and was finally caught, but just barely, when somebody went into her basement to fix a leak and noticed an eyeball in some fruit. He and Charles and Tim go down twice a week from the afternoon sunlight of the large and airy uptown house, down to these shelves lined with jars by their mother, with their mother, and are administered cod-liver oil in or out or on our honor in our mouth. And when the spoon cut the corners and tasted of August lakes, arched darkness, vaulted space, and foam over the ribs at the back of the throat, and I saw the shining insides of a fish's belly spilling in a flash the way her insides must have spilled on the day I was born or the day that I spied, I ran up the basement stairs, their shoes just behind me, before I was, as I feared that I'd be—*blee*-blee-blee-blee-!—be devoured: Bea devoured this ole crystal pistol's BBs, beeee bee, wee tea pea, *bditt!* (pee peculiar, mister?) right down to the root, the root-beer bottle rage of Ginger (grease your palm, sister?), be Bea, be miss priss or do the knees-up spinning twist this minute ("Later"), be my woman, woman ("Uh-oh." "Oh-oh"), Oohooo-wooo, be my bride!

And this place our mother didn't mind one bit, or so it seems now, or was then, once, or is so forever in our present-day eyes.

14

❧

IN A FRAGILE, METALLIC GRIP

Alpha's spirit was crippled by the injustice of it. Charles had turned six and was dying. After a winter of illnesses, he'd developed double pneumonia, and when he was rushed by car to the McCallister hospital, a doctor told Martin that he had about a fifty-fifty chance of pulling through. His condition had worsened.

It was nearly impossible to get pencillin, the new antibiotic they were trying on him, in this underpopulated part of this underpopulated state, and if there was another blizzard like the one last week, the shipments wouldn't get through. Already the roads to McCallister were all but impassable—the plowed banks piled higher than a car top most of the way, with only a single lane opened in the worst places—and there was no working airport at McCallister, which was the only town in the three-county area with a hospital. The hospital's oxygen tent, its only one, had to be shared with other patients. Charles had received the last rites of the Church.

The probability of his death had invaded her, weighted her, moved into the marrow of her bones until she was so heavy with it she hated the details of each day, beginning with the sun; she didn't want to get out of bed, or fix meals, or take care of the other children, and couldn't eat. The sound of Marie cooing or crying, or the sound of the children's voices when the parochial school recessed, infuriated her so much that tears would sting and kindle at her eyes' rim. All she wanted to do was stand at the bay window, as now, and stare out at the snow; it was mounded four feet high in the tangle of lilac stems; the wind had eroded a corrugated bank of it along the foundation; streamers of it were traveling at an angle across the yard, up and down drifts, and filling in a cave Jerome and Tim had dug. She wanted to go there and hide.

He'd been the easiest to raise, and the most difficult. He seemed hardier and less vulnerable than Tim or Jerome, and there was an incident, two days after his second birthday, that was so typical of him she recorded it in his baby book; Jerome was crying about some internal loss, or something eternally lost to him, when Charles said in his most convincing tone, "Jerome, I got an id*ee!*" And when Jerome didn't respond to this, he came to her and said, "I never cry, do I, Mama?"

He seldom cried and wasn't prone to tantrums, though if one overtook him it was a day before he recovered. He was fearless and driven to frightening acts; he climbed the water tower when he was five, a hundred feet to its top, and then walked around the catwalk on a dare from below, leaping the open trap door as he did. He preferred to assess a subject on his own, to observe and listen and read rather than bother you with questions. And his face was more mature than other children's, the future person that would emerge already evident around his lips and in his eyes. His eyes. Each day deepening with their own secrets. So bright blue.

There were times when he seemed to be considering everything and everybody about him while merely going through the motions of play, the quality she watched the closest, and respected the most, and the one she feared the most, too. Was it like her? What was he thinking then? Could he have known this was coming? Impossible. An impossible, horrible thought. Hers.

All she'd been able to do when he was home was feed him orange juice and ice cream and aspirin mashed up in honey, change his bedclothes when they were damp with sweat, give him alchohol rubs, or help with the bedpan. Jerome and Tim were as silent around him as if a stranger had appeared in his bed. What did they sense? She'd been so distant and abrupt with them lately they stayed upstairs, relearning one another's limits and likes, or moved around the house with hesitance, guilty and apologetic, as if they'd done her great harm. She had no words to comfort them. All her energies were centered on Charles, and to expend them on anybody else, even Martin, seemed to diminish his strength.

She was able to visit him only once a day, if that often; the hospital was fifteen miles, she didn't drive still, and there was seldom a sitter available for the three separate sets of visiting hours that divided and measured her day. If the Rynersons were still in town, Lou would come with her children and sit (it seemed everybody available had children), with no fears of them getting what Charles had, but the Rynersons had moved on to a better job near Minot in the fall. Old friends gone, too. Martin made it for all the visiting hours—as principal of the high school, he could come and go as he pleased, especially in this situation—and she resented his freedom and the position that assured him he'd be free. She resented his maleness, his patience, his faith, everything that made him who he was, and could hardly bear to talk to him. Unless they were speaking about Charles— painful, dragged-out phrases that made them both afraid to look at one another—their conversations were fencing and monosyllabic, and never moved out of time.

"Eggs?"

"Two."

Or, "How was your day?"

"Fine. Yours?"

"Fine."

"The kids?"

"Fine."

Or, "Good night."

"Good night."

He'll take her hand and stare at her in silence, his large eyes widening—with commiseration? helplessness? guilt? what?—until he looks so pitiful that, even though a moment before she felt like unburdening herself to him, she'll have to turn and walk out of the room. I need something physical, she wanted to tell him, not sympathy.

When she went to the hospital and saw where they'd put Charles, in an oversized metal-slatted crib covered with a plastic tent, he looked so reduced, bluish, and dehumanized through the crinkled and tinted plastic, she had to leave the room until she got control of herself. Did he know that? In a recurring dream she sees him in his own crib, the one he grew out of three years ago, as an infant, and while she stands above and watches, he grows smaller and smaller, and at the final gray line, just before he disappears into death, she feels him return inside her and wakes tense on the bed with the cold dark room around her, afraid that if she moves she'll kill them both.

One day when he was home he became incoherent, distant and feverish, his eyes brimming over with an inner vision, and began babbling along in a naked way about nuns scrubbing him in a wooden washtub, silver wires above in the air, and stickmen made of colored tubes chasing him with a shadowy ark—while she swabbed at his face with a washcloth, wanting to shake him or slap him until he talked sense, or hold him so tight he couldn't speak, or put on her coat and walk out and never return. Then Martin came from school and she told him the boy was ill beyond her powers to nurse or comfort him, and if this kept up she'd go insane.

Martin went into the boys' room, sat on the edge of his bed, and took his hand. "Charlie," he said. "It's Dad. Are you awake?"

"Uh-huh."

"How do you feel?"

"Pretty good."

"Do you want to go to the hospital?"

"Oh, no. No, I don't need to. I feel better now."

"You're sure?"

"Oh, yes."

But about twelve o'clock that night they heard him calling, "Dad, Dad," and ran to his room.

"I'm here," Martin said. "What is it?"

"I think I was wrong."

"What do you mean?"

"You better take me to the hospital."

She went to him and placed her mouth on his forehead to test his temperature and his fever against her lips was like a sun. Martin went out and warmed up the car—he'd have to go alone; she couldn't wake the other children or risk Marie in the car in this cold—and then they wrapped Charles in quilts and rugs, and as she was tucking him into the front seat with the exhaust and cold air fuming around her, she said, "Now, hurry up and get well, so you can come home quick, do you hear?"

"Am I coming home?" he asked.

"Of course you are!"

But the way he asked the question would be imprinted on her mind forever in a roseate glow; straightforward, without fear or self-pity, as if he simply wanted to know the truth. And what could she say to him but "Of course, of course, of course"—it was all she could say.

His condition got so critical the doctor called Father Schimmelpfennig, the only person in town besides Dr. Koenig with a phone, and he picked up Martin at school and then came to the house in his black car and drove them on in to McCallister. Charles's skin was bluish-ivory and he was passing in and out of consciousness as they watched. They tried to talk to him, and then Father sighed, removed his black overcoat, took out a purple stole, kissed the gold cross embroidered at its center, put it on, and stood over the crib.

"Charles? Charles?" he kept repeating in his heavy German accent, which made it sound nearly like "chalice." "Charles?"

"Yes." Finally. A dry whisper like the rustle of weeds.

"Have you been a good boy, Charles?"

"What?"

"Have you been a good boy? Have you done any bad tings, committed any bad sins?"

There was an unintelligible reply.

"Do you have anyting you'd like to tell me, confess? Like in the confessional?"

"Hnn?"

"Do you have anyting you'd like to tell me?"

"Uh-huh."

He put his ear close to Charles. "You can say it. Nobody will hear you."

"I'm never happy any more."

Father paled, glanced at them to see if they'd heard, and then took out a prayer book and a leather kit with a pyx in it, and bent over Charles and began murmuring in Latin and applying the oil of extreme unction, and she walked out to the hall, half blinded by a chrism of tears, blundered into a rest room, the wrong one, and vomited up her stomach into a urinal where hair and paper matches lay curled.

If she could believe in the Catholic Church, which defined the character of God and gave Him substance, perhaps she could, like Martin believe in God Himself and be united with him in a further way, and bear all this with more equanimity and self-control. He carried his rosary everywhere, even to school in his suit pocket, and there were nights when she'd seen him take it to bed. The Neumillers, for such a large family, were closely attuned to one another's needs and had grown up to feel protected, not only because of their size, or the protective mantle of Martin's father, but because of the religion they shared and could talk openly about.

When she was younger and went to church, it was sometimes alone, or else with the neighbors; her mother hardly ever attended a service, and the only time her father referred to a deity of any sort was during a natural disaster, a personal setback, or in a moment of terrible anger or pain, when he cursed God as though He were a hired man, a dimwitted, hairy, incompetent one, sitting in the same room with him. Which was as reasonable a tack to take as any, by God. God. Ha! You clumsy, ignorant, unfair sonofabitch!

There.

Her tears opened paths and open beams to the grief in her.

When she was a child, she used to sit in the door of the haymow and watch as it began to get dark, while below her, in the barn she could hear the calves baaing almost like sheep, cows lowing to them, the clash of a bucket, footsteps, and the muffled voice of her father as he did the chores. The chicken coop was below her, across the lane from the barn and suddenly, at a certain stage of darkness, chickens, white blurs, would appear from the brush, from the wheat field, from the pasture on the other side of the road, and begin moving toward the coop as though drawn to a magnet, some of them running, catching up to others and frightening them into a run, some moving slower through the darkness, alone. Watching them, listening to her father murmuring to the animals below, she was filled with peace and, for some reason, a sadness that displaced the peace. Then the windows of the house lit, her mother stepped out and called, "Alpha! Supper! Ed! Elling! Conrad! Come and eat now!" There was such calm and simplicity in it, yet such an urgency, too, and she ran toward the house as though pursued. Then the yellowish light from the kerosene lamps, a light with the added dimension of smell, the serenity of her mother as she moved about the room, testing the food on the cookstove, setting plates and silverware at their places at the table, and dipping and bending and stepping back as though in relation to them all and this moment, which would come soon, in Hannaford or Dazey or Cooperstown or Wallum or Casselton, or even in that shaky little place of theirs outside Courtenay, and the fitting together of the sterilized pieces of the separator, so it would be ready when Daddy and Elling came with the milk. The steaminess of the cookstove at that hour.

Why don't I, my mother's daughter, have a soothing effect on my children? On Charles? If Mama were here, she'd uphold all of us here now, just as her will within the walls of a house kept those houses from collapsing down around us, it felt. It's inconceivable to me that I'm a mother. Even more inconceivable that one of my children could die.

Could he?

Here at the window in this empty-seeming house, on its sill a skin of dust. What are the reasons for death, its cause? Can its course be altered? All those graceful clouds shaped like fish, like leaping deer and flying geese, get drawn down with the sun as if to slaughter. On the sill the skin of dust. Of my already dead son? My grandfather? My brother? Oh, Jerome, remember the relationship we had. Where are the bonds that bound us together, now that you're earth? Who in the face of death can hold himself tethered?

Do the dead forget we sometimes didn't love them, as we forget? In our lives going on ahead at moving speed? The least death should bring is a mindless kind of limbo, as the Church calls it, where there'd be no consciousness of want or pain. On the window an array of my breath. I've hated enough to make a ghost of myself, but still live and make steam; it's time I decided my disposition toward me and other lives and the ties that reach out and return and unite us, but how can I be who I am with my face gone and part of the winds again? Because I'm alive, I'm my life, I thought, and it was a lie.

Lord, where are the ends of this life of yours? My sight

extends to the edge of Hawk's Nest and stops. What's on the other side, where I've never been, bear over the mountain again, either, sir? A perpetual field? A golden green tree? A fledgling weaned from flint, a feather of faith? My hate at all the lessons I haven't learned and the places I'll never see empties my heart. And what's *it*? A piece of my anatomy? Who gave names to pieces of me, as Mama gave to the unprotected frame around it all, the chrysalis of Alpha for eternity? Only Christ could fill me, a ciborium overbrimming with praise, at this late, long-awaited hour, and if I had Him, I'd give up my life and be this dust, I'd die for Charles, if it were in my power.

Beyond the bay window, the yard came into focus, growing dark, the wind risen now, the snow swirling higher into the air in streaking wings. There was a gray shape beyond the lilac stems. It moved toward her, growing larger and more dense at the edge of the window, and then she looked up, her eyes adjusted, and she was staring into a reflection of Martin's face.

"Alpha?" he said tentatively.

"It's time I made supper."

He watched her walk on rigid legs into the kitchen, and then stepped up to the window, which faced east, in the direction of McCallister, and was frosted at the level of his chest from her breath. He couldn't blame her for avoiding him. His thoughts were base and vile. He was horny. He'd never been this horny in his life. All through their marriage, he'd hardly looked at other women, not so much an indication of his moral character as a sign of his love; he was so immersed in her and making her happy he had no time to look. But lately, at school, he'd begun to notice the development of his female students, the delicacy of their hands and fingers, the shape and size of their breasts, the breadth of their hips, their bare legs, and the curve of their buttocks against their skirts, and once when he was at the blackboard, mechanically writing out an algebraic equation while most of his mind hovered over an image of Alpha, of her at home alone, nursing the boy, trying at the same time to care for the other children and keep up with her everyday chores, he found himself in the center of a dead silence, the entire class staring at him while he stared between the parted legs of Carol Hahn, a red-head whose skirt had slipped above her knees. Her face was crimson and shamed. He feigned illness (and after catching himself at that, he felt ill) and dismissed the class for the day.

The graver Charles's condition became, the more his own needs narrowed to sex, it seemed, as if there were a balance to be achieved in this disparity, and Alpha apparently sensed it; there were times when she looked like she wanted to talk, but the second he came close she'd turn and walk away, out of the room, as if in disgust. He'd tried everything he could to keep his mind off those areas of her—novel-reading, prayer, meditation on the Blessed Virgin and the Trinity, cold showers, chopping wood, no pepper on his food—everything. Good Lord, he'd even started carrying a rosary to bed with him!

The night he got home from taking Charles to the hospital, after he'd told Alpha what the doctor had said, and after they'd talked and tried to reassure one another, they got into bed and lay on opposite sides—"I don't really want to be touched now," she whispered—sleepless, tossing in anxiety under the covers, and then their legs touched, she turned, and he fell on her like an animal and couldn't use the whole of it it was so hard. Since then, it seemed to shame her to have him close. This morning before the children were up, when they were at the breakfast table, he was picking at a grapefruit, trying to decide whether to mention to her what had happened at the hospital the day before, when she said, "The crisis should come today, shouldn't it?"

"Or tomorrow, he said."

"He'll call and let us know?"

"He'll call Father."

"And we'll leave right away?"

"Of course, dear."

And with those words, he knew he could never tell her, no matter what. She was staring into her coffee cup, and it was as if he were seeing her anonymously, across from him in a train or a bus, and he realized again how divided her face was, and how that enhanced her beauty of delicate lines. Charles had her cheekbones, her nose, her lips, sharply outlined, the upper curved like a crossbow, the lower full and sensual— The throb of an erection tightened his pants, and in a moment of revelation—her eyes were cast down, showing violet lids, and her face pale—he saw her as the corpse of Charles.

"Alpha!" he cried. "You've got to eat!"

She got up and left the table.

Her grief was dynamic, even when expressed in anger, and she was always busy, angrily busy, working to ease her grief. His sat in him like a stone. He hated to speak, to eat, to perform the simplest task in her presence, because he knew his actions would expose his hidden feelings, as hers did, and reveal his guilt, lack of hope, horniness, and something worse he'd discovered in himself and was trying to cover up by carrying a rosary everywhere—his growing conviction that there was no God, beneficent or otherwise, by Lord—and because he knew it agonized her and made her even more angry, now that Charles was near death, to see unimpeded life in anybody else. Since he'd carried Charles into the hospital and left him there, he felt responsible for the way she was acting, and this, in the entrapping logic of emotions, made him feel responsible for the illness to begin with.

And what if Charles died?

He chewed on his upper lip, which was cracked from the heat of the house, and pushed his glasses up to grip the bridge of his nose; he hadn't known you couldn't enter a child's helplessness with all the skills of adulthood, and make him whole, but had to stand off with the knowledge adulthood brings, helpless, and watch the child suffer and hope that your hopes for him touched another source and returned to him as strength from the Lord. Or perhaps he wasn't a good parent. He thought he heard the baby crying. He listened for her voice, for Alpha's footsteps going into her bedroom, but had imagined the sound. He massaged the bridge of his nose until the wailing waves were gone, and then let his glasses fall back in place.

Whenever anybody asked him who his favorite was among the children, he said, "Whichever one is sick or in trouble, that's my favorite; that's the one that needs me the most." But he was in such fear for Charles's life he could hardly bear to bring him to mind, much less lend him emotional support, and the minute he walked out of the hospital he couldn't even picture the boy's face. Sometimes he'd see for an instant, as if stopped in an eruptive exposure of lighted surprise, a vivid detail that made his breath catch; a nose with a plastic tube in one nostril, enlarged; a white profile with its eye rolled back in death (imbued with an imaginary smell of hospital alcohol and ether); a buttock honeycombed and bleeding from needles; a broken bony forearm on the velvet of a coffin; an ivory head levitated against black. That was how he saw his son.

And once in a moment of extreme stress, when the tension threatened to deprive him of the power to reason, he found himself calculating how much more money they'd have if Charles died.

He looked at the white oval of his face on the window, looked into its eyes, beyond them to the outside, and felt a chill branch in patterns of lines over his back; loose snow was rising in columns and pillars that swayed and bent in every direction, collapsed, rose in another place, and went whirling toward the southwest out of sight, a blizzard warning. If one of those hits this window, he thought, Chuck will die, and then a tall enlivened sheet, taller than the electrical wires, with lacy streamers coiling along its outer edge, came speeding toward the house, and as soon as he readjusted his thought to, No, it means he *won't!* it swept past the lilacs and hit the window with such force the house rocked. He clung to the rosary in his pocket.

What was he *doing?*

He saw a sheet being pulled over a face, a mound of dirt on snow, a yellowish tonic, fear, an oval at the bottom of the grave, and heard voices, his and Charles's, laughing in a closed space. Yesterday Charles was more lucid, and talked about the other boys, the recent snow, the sled they got for Christmas, a long one that could hold three, about school and some of his friends, and then said in a quavery voice, "Dad, what do I have that's so bad?"

"Pneumonia."

"What's that?"

"Oh, sort of like bronchitis, only deeper in the lungs. More fluid, I guess."

"How do you spell it?"

"P-n-e—"

"Not an N?"

"No, a P."

"Why a P?"

"It's Greek, I believe."

"Hard to learn?"

"P-n-e-u-m-o-n-i-a."

"Oh!" Charles said.

"Is it pretty?"

"Pretty pretty. Why the P?"

"I guess it's Greek, I said."

"It's Greek to me."

"Oh, you!"

"Greek, GREEK, *greek,* Greek," Charles was grunting and creaking, as though mesmerized by the word and acting out its meaning in the air.

"Where's the P?" he asked.

"What do you mean?"

"Where did it go?"

"At the front of the word?"

"No, where did it *go,* Dad?"

"It went in hiding!"

"It did?"

"It went *pee*-moniaing!"

"Dad, stop!'

"Pneumoniaing?"

"I'll have to cough!"

"Does it hurt?"

"Whenever I breathe in or out or have to cough."

"Up pneumonia?"

"Or have to cough."

"Can you hang on?"

"Yes, I guess I will."

"Good boy!"

"Where's the P?" he asked again.

"The P in pneumonia or the P in hiding or the P in me?"

"The P in me!"

"That's the fluid.

"That's what I *thought!*"

"I'll cough for you. Blark! Hrgh! Krouf!"

"It keeps killing my breath."

"Hecka, hoofth!"

"My pee *in* me, too!"

They laughed and Martin bared his teeth and did a clutching grab at his belly with both hands and shook it up and down like a jiggly Santa Claus. Charles laughed harder and then started to cough and the cough wouldn't stop; it went on until he was choking and fighting for breath so badly Martin had to run for a nurse, and when the two hurried back into the room, Charles's face was blue and he was unconscious, having convulsions.

If Charles died, it would be his fault.

He heard pattery footsteps behind him—Alpha's when she was determined or in a fury—and turned; she stopped, her face tense and her eyes feverish-looking (was she also getting sick?) and empty of expression. "Father Schimmelpfennig is here," she said. "They say it's time."

*

When he thinks of his parents, which is seldom now, he thinks of them as the monarchs of a kingdom he once visited in a dream; his mother wears a full-length dress, flaming red (though when he sees her back from a distance it's a brown tweedlike coat), whose color increases the humming in his ears, and never shows more than her profile, like the queen on a playing card. His father has on a fur cap with fur earflaps turned up like half-moons, and carries a broom or a crozier in one hand. His bass voice has lost its usual timbre and sounds like (Charles observes this with interest but without puzzlement or surprise) the squeaking of a rubber mouse. What is it he's trying to say, Charles wonders, and sees himself older, with his father's face, at a table, extricating needles from his head of hair with pain. When his real father, looming moonlike over the bed, speaks to him from his real face, it's as difficult to understand; his ears seem sealed with cellophane that vibrates with every outside sound.

"Herzz verritzz swowoza bee."

"Brrrodja deezzz."

His own voice is a dampened hum at the center of his head, and his lips, split by fever, taste like coins turning green. His bones are ice and the ice is wrapped with layers of flesh that burn but have no effect. His brain is a fluid that exerts pressure at the base of his nose and occasionally leaks from it, or runs rawly down his throat, and puts pressure behind his eyes, which are dry as paper. The band of pain constricting his chest strangles the

air he breathes, and the shallow breaths he takes beneath
the pain are becoming more shallow and rapid each hour.

He has no center. When he opens an eye, he might be
looking up from his stomach or out a knee. Sometimes
he's the size of a thimble, and at other times so enormous,
a toe of his could cover a city. One day his arms, which
are either too heavy or too light, were gone from him for
a while. Where? His illness is a sea and others are on
land, unreachable. They materialize beside him at a great
height and he stares up at them from beneath rocking
water while their images sway with the movement of the
water he sees them through (as their mouths move) and
his body rocks beneath, as if bows saw on strings that
flow through him from the firmament. The nurse arrives
with a hypodermic the size of a pine tree, turns him on
his stomach (wasn't he on it?), and as she drives it
through his back the white-haired man across the hall
screams again. Or was the hypodermic a spinal for him?
Charles turns, or imagines he turns, and it's night once
more.

His father appears, his mother appears; they float and
rock outside the bright, burning layers of fever that enwrap him like tinfoil, in a fragile, metallic grip, and a
cold wet hand spans his forehead. Yes? Yes? They disappear into a brightness like the sun, and he sees a player
piano, shining, crystalline, made of ice or glass. Jingle
ping tink-tink. Jingle *ping*. There's a pain above his left
eye like an embedded ax. His parents appear again and
confront him with a phenomenon that makes no sense:
there are, after all, other people in the world besides
him, real people, and they're alive. They're his mother
and father. Why are they so happy, then?

They smile and talk, showing their teeth, and now
they're high above him, elongated, blurred and haloed in
yellow, and smaller, as if seen through a tube. Their
voices buzz and vibrate in his ears and then go away. A
blue numeral two bends and unbends where they were.
They appear again, smiling and talking, jingle *ping*. Yes?
Yes? To reach their sanctuary, he has to lift himself upward, rising on an elevator of his will, and hold his body
on the sea's surface with all his strength. He grips the
bedclothes and turns his parched corneas on them. Only
his father is there. It's as if Charles has entered a house

in the night, one he's never seen before, has found his way to the living room and in a brilliance fed by outside whirs and hums has fulfilled fate's appointment (Dad! Dad!) with the right man. What's he *doing* here, he wonders, and feels his strength leave as he descends beneath the sea of sickness again, deeper than before. *Dad! Dad!* he tries to cry out in his real voice, and lifts himself once more, for the last time, it seems, and holds himself on the surface until his father says something that makes him laugh; the laughter turns to a cough that splits his chest, breaks the ice of his bones, and drives splinters into his flesh until blackness comes. He'd rather be alone.

Above his left eye (the other stays closed), a bright disc, which might be a ceiling light, pulses and burns. It seems the last power he has to contend with. He pleads with it to move—it won't—or go out. Even when he closes his eye, it clings to his lid, expanding and contracting, changing colors, to a profile, a queen, a circle of icy piano keys. If he could deal with the light or the profile (now a numeral he's seen perform in this same way), he'd be at peace, because this isn't an ordinary day for him, he knows. He can feel a heaviness, like honey and salt water, rising in him, and though it hurts him to breathe it more than any other phase of his illness has hurt him, he breathes it deeply and evenly, trying to drown.

Then he's chewing bubble gum. His jaws move from side to side in a soft, erotic, cowlike mastication. He's home again, in bed, asleep, yet not asleep; his eyelids are transparent gems. He sees there's nothing beyond the bedroom curtains, no yard or hedge or houses or countryside, only a shading of light blue, like sky, and as his jaws move he hears a sound between his ears like the shuddering roar of a waterfall heard from a distance, rising in volume each time his mouth opens wide. He chews the bedclothes. The curtains blow in and cover the bed. He chews them. The jaws move farther apart each time; the cascading roar increases, closer, while the jaws work at the curtains, becoming more rubbery and speeded up and voracious, chewing everything within reach—a dresser, a nightstand (which turn elastic like the bedclothes and curtains), a closet, a wall; and when the sunlight, blue in color, pours into the room, they begin chewing it.

Then they move off and change, become otherworldly, impersonal, but still remain a part of him and continue to chew with ceaseless and increasing violence, rising as high as the house, slamming down hard, higher, *hard,* and then they turn, turn again as if seeking direction, turn and start toward him. He tries to get out of bed but the curtains cover his legs, and now are as heavy as sand on him. The jaws, flying apart in bits so wide they disappear awhile, reach the edge of the mattress and get a bite of it. Hot breath. He makes an effort to move, a final one, using the last of his remaining strength, the ration he's held in reserve, and breaks free into an icy brightness, borne on a current of chilling blue air, and sees a mirror image of his body, tiny as a doll, heading toward a black hole in the shining universe, a blue baby blue in the night as he spins out past constellations of echoing stars and comes back on a separate trajectory into his own silence again.

*

The doctor drew away from the crib and straightened, and Charles's reflection slipped off the round mirror strapped to his forehead.

"His fever's broken," the doctor said. "He's going to be all right."

15

◆﹖◆

THE BLACK FOREST

When I completed my second year of parochial school, I was eligible, as Jerome had often told me, to become a member of the club that met in secret in the Black Forest, or so the members called it, a name picked up from some adult conversation most likely, most likely by Douglas Kuntz; it was a quarter block of swampy lowland that had been left to itself over the years and now held the heaviest concentration of shade trees and brush to be found in any place in Hyatt. One of the playing fields of the parochial school, with a stone wall a foot high around it, bordered so close on the Black Forest that lilacs dropped their blossoms onto the end of the wall my classmates and I passed every day. We never entered the Forest, though; it was forbidden by the Sisters, and once when I was caught there by one, merely to have a look and not testing my limits, I received a whipping with a switch torn from a tree ("Don't ever let me know what's happened to you at school, expecting sympathy," my father often told us, "because from my experience you probably deserved what you got, and then some, and just might get more from me"). The Sisters knew what could happen behind bushes, of course, but claimed the Black Forest was off-limits because it belonged to Orville Sanderson, a bachelor who drank too much, had a foul tongue, and hated children—perhaps from all those years of hearing recess—Catholic ones especially (although he himself was a Catholic), and had been known to chase them for blocks if he found them on his property.

I followed Jerome out our drive, across the street, and down the alley, carrying an "offering" for each of the club officers, as I'd been told to. We passed the end of Wheaton's garden, where seed packages were tacked to laths and straight rows of green were lining up above the loam behind the laths and paths crossed, passed the goal line of the parochial school's football-softball field, and entered the Black Forest. I could see to my left, through breaks in its leafage, the rotten posts and sagging squares of the wire fence that restrained its advance on the alley; the brick back of the school, the back of the church, the back of the rectory; and to my right, the boulders of the low wall. A membranous network of leaf shadow slid over Jerome's hair and down his back as he knocked aside the filaments that spiders strung up tirelessly across the trail every day, in spite of our efforts to dissuade them, and then the shadow stilled in place. We were at a clearing's edge, a small dirt-packed one, and on the other side, the trunk of a dead tree, barkless, its surface smooth as skin and silvery-gray, glowed in the shadowy foliage.

"Chockowah," my brother said.

A password? Beyond the dead tree was a long laticework trellis, eight feet tall, overgrown with morning-glories, grapevines, ivy, and rambling rose, and I knew from my foray into the Forest that a catwalk was attached to the other side of the trellis and ran from the alley to Orville Sanderson's back door.

"Chockakeewah," a voice off to the left said. "Enter brave scribe and guest you've got."

We stepped into the clearing and people began to appear from beneath the catwalk and out of the brush around us —Buddy Schonbeck, Douglas Kuntz, and the Rimsky brothers, Leo and Brian—and in the silence I felt I was being appraised, and wondered, What's Brian doing here? He was my age and was so mistreated by his older brother, Leo, he'd become the object of everybody's abuse. He was small for his age, but had a head bigger than most adults', and shaped like a light bulb, with a petite pointed chin and the wizened thin-lipped smile of an old woman's mouth, and seemed angry most of the time, sullen and righteously pugnacious, and was always being sent to the library, a narrow room with roll-down maps and statues of saints everywhere, in punishment for his sins of misconduct, disobedience, and disrespect. He had a sack in his hands now and looked as apprehensive as I felt.

Douglas Kuntz came over and stared me down. Then he said, "Where's your offering, *k*-new one?"

I took the cigars I'd found in my father's desk from under my shirt front, three of them, and handed them to Kuntz, who was, as my brother told me, The Ruler. Leo Rimsky was Ruler Number Two and Jerome was the secretary. Kuntz examined the crackling cigars, and then at last gave one to Leo and one to my brother with a solemnity unusual for him; he was usually laughing, showing horsy yellow teeth, at a practical joke he'd devised, or a name he'd made up, such as the one for his sister's cat, a dog-sized beast with dugs that all but rubbed the ground: Tittyole-buzzard.

"Are you a Catholic?" he asked me.

"Yes."

"Have you made your First Communion yet?"

"Yes."

"Are your parents Catholic?"

"No."

"What do you mean by that?"

These questions seemed unnecessary and foolish, since Kuntz had sat in the same schoolroom with me, and I wasn't sure he wasn't having me on.

"Why aren't they?"

"Oh, come on, you—"

"Why?" Kuntz said. He was soberingly serious now. "Just answer the questions I ask."

"My mother hasn't converted yet."

"How come?"

"I don't know."

"Will she?"

"Yes, probably."

"When?"

"Maybe this summer yet."

"Good. Do you know any Latin?"

"Yes."

"You better say some then."

"Confiteor Deo omnipotenti, Beatae Mariae, semper Virgini, Beato—"

"O.K., that's enough."

Kuntz began to interrogate Brian in the same way, his

voice low and nasal and accompanied by a buzzing murmur from the center of his nose, which was so long it gave
his small eyes a look of constant cunning. There was a
scar across the center of the bridge of it where it had been
broken, by Kuntz's father, everybody said; his father was
older than our parents, worked for the railroad and was
seldom at home, and seemed to have moral reasons for
keeping himself so obscure. Kuntz had an older brother in
the Navy and a sister in high school—they all lived
in a yellow-painted railroad car pulled from a siding out
to the far edge of town—and was tough and self-reliant,
but not a bully, as he could have been. He listened a lot to
the radio and was as in love with the Lone Ranger as a
boy his age could be and still be a boy. During the summer when he spent his time outside, or in the fall, practicing football with the rest of us (tackle, without equipment,
to toughen us up for the school team), he carried an alarm
clock along with him and when it went off, at a few minutes before six, he ran over and held it above his head, the
alarm still going, and cried, "Hi-ho, Silver! Away-y-y!"
and then took off for home in that lumbering, one-
leg-ahead-of-the-other hobble that does as a horse's gallop
among children, or did then, slapping his ass with his
free hand as if to get it to catch up with the rest of the galloping parts of him.

Now when Kuntz instructed Brian to say Latin, Brian
said, in his pugnacious way, "Oh, Gobbledegook, you
dumb-ass. You know I—"

Leo slapped the back of Brian's head. "Watch what
you call our Ruler, or you won't be in," he said. He spoke
through clenched teeth, hardly moving his lips, in the peevish voice of his father, but always with amusement in his
eyes, as if mocking his father's manner of speaking, or
the idea that he had a voice like his father's, and the
amusement shone brightest when he was beating up on or
bettering Brian.

"Oh, come on," Brian said, and turned to him. "You
know he's as dumb as—"

This time the slap came from Kuntz. Kuntz seemed intelligent enough, but the Sisters flunked him in the second
grade, twice, and considered him a bad influence and a
fool—flicking girls' butts as he did, and referring often to
his sister's "buzzooms," which were that big—and when

one Sister once asked him what he expected to make of his life with this attitude he always had, Kuntz said, in the deep voice he did so well, "Go into the Black Hills of South Dakota and ride Silver, Sister Mary Michael Theresa, by golly, yessir!"

"And I haven't seen your offering yet," he said to Brian now.

Brian unrolled his paper sack, took a jar out, and handed it to Kuntz.

"Hey!" Kuntz said, and his big teeth appeared in the horsy smile. "Hey, look at this." He showed around a jar that looked painted from the inside with white opaque paint. "It's marshmallow cream, you guys. It's one of my favorites!"

"That's what Leo told me," Brian said. He looked close to tears.

"All right," Kuntz said. "Give them the old initiation treatment! How-wah! A-Huggah! Rhee-hee-hee-*him!*"

I saw arms grab Brian and then other arms brought me down, and there was the stench of the ground, rank and sewery, leaf mold and decay, bodies covering mine, hands gripping me, and a succession of knuckle rubs ran vibrating over the top of my head until one eye ached and my skull swelled into a lopsided element blooming beyond my hair at some balloonlike areas rubbed thin. I could hear Brian cursing and crying out and then a set of knuckles was gentler on me—my brother? Kuntz?—and I realized that Brian was getting the worst of it; his nickname was Little Fititzer and he was always getting a "fititz," a quick skidding knuckle up the back of his head, his head was such a temptation to scrub on or rub or desecrate, or simply touch, it was so big.

"O.K.," Kuntz said. "That's enough. Let 'em up now."

"Damn you!" It was Brian. He was on his feet and swinging at Leo with whirlwind fists. Leo grabbed his arms at the wrists, tripped him so he hit hard on his butt, and sat across his stomach where his shirt was pulled up. "Get off!" Brian cried. "Let me up!"

"Stop punching first."

"I'm not, now!"

"Your hands are trying to, Little Fititzer, I can *feel*."

Brian stopped arching his back and a tear streaked from

one eye into an ear. "I bet none of the rest of you guys got this crap!" he cried.

"I bet we did," Leo said to him.

"Oh, yeah? Well, who gave it to Kuntz?"

Leo, still astride him, turned to everybody with his amused look, and them smiled with clenched teeth. "We all gave it to him," he said, and nodded at Kuntz. "Not?"

"Right," Kuntz said. "That's right. O.K., let him up, Pajinsky Bear." Kuntz began to pace like a teacher who's just about ready to have something to say. Pajinsky Bear was his name for Leo, derived from Leo's smile, which reminded us of Theodore Roosevelt, a hero whose boyhood we had to study, even in lower grades, since he was the only President of the United States who ever lived or had a home in North Dakota, or cared to come close, it seemed. Kuntz also named Jerome "Paws" and me "Lids" and Buddy Schonbeck he merely called Buddy, which is what Buddy's parents called him, and had named him, in fact. He was skinny and thick-lipped, with a gangling elusiveness that marked him as a halfback or end for the high-school six-man football team, and wasn't friendly to anybody, much less a buddy to them; he spoke only to be contentious, even with the Sisters and Father Schimmelpfennig ("Yeah, well, that's not the way my dad said it went"—about the Crucifixion), about any topic, to the point of absurdity, and he'd even switch sides to keep the argument going. He insisted the Sisters wore rubber bags under their skirts, because nobody had ever seen them go pee, etc. I could understand Jerome's nickname—he held his fingers apart and his hands somewhat away from his sides when he walked, a little like a gunslinger stalking a street—but I was bothered by my own, and once when I asked Kuntz what he meant by naming me that, Lids, he said, "Because you're thin as a pencil lead." *Lid*, Kuntz?

Now Kuntz went to the dead tree, rolled out a sawed-off section of log from it, and sat down. "All right, you and you"—to me and Brian—"sit here on the ground in front of me. Suey!"

We sat down.

"Cross your legs."

We crossed our legs.

"O.K., now here's the deal. This is your initiation time,

you see. It lasts for a week. You get the head treatment every day and—"

"Oh, come *on*," Brian said.

"You get the head treatment every day." Kuntz held up a hand to stop Leo from whapping Brian. "And besides that, you've got to learn our ceremonies—or else you're out. You have to learn them exactly, too, like that lousy Minuet we did last winter, puck, puck, pa-*cock!*"

Everybody snorted, chuckled, or guffawed.

"And besides that, you each have a duty you have to do. Everybody's got to have a duty to do. We'll decide on yours a while later, here. Now, after a week we take a vote on both of youse, and if more than two are against you, you're out."

"Yeah," Leo said, and his laughter shadowed the leaf-shaded clearing with the dark intent of the intonations in it.

"Should we show them our hiding place, Number Two and scribe?" Kuntz asked.

"Sure," Leo said. "Then if we don't let them join in, or just one does, and somebody breaks into it, we'll know who it is and go get him so he'll never forget, Pajunkety Camelhump, old Toaderspies!"

The nose, the *nose*, I thought, and could feel Leo's smile behind me.

Kuntz took us behind the dead tree, where there was a round depression into which his log, or stool, or throne, or whatever, must sit, and brushed away some leaves and dirt at the bottom of the depression, revealing a board recessed into the ground. He lifted this up, took a wooden box out from beneath it, and opened the box on votive candles, clean white handkerchiefs, a glass jar filled with farmer's matches, silver needles, and an oval tin of Cavaliers.

"Hey!" Brain cried. "I know where you got those cigarettes! Dad just put a display on them up in our damn store!"

There was a smacking report close to my ear as Leo, of course, got Brain again. Leo wasn't amused now. "Of course they're from the store, *dummkopf!* How many places in town do you think have got them in? If Dad sees any missing, I'll know why, you hear, you slimy little puke of a morfadike!"

Brian bowed his big head. "O.K., Leo," he said.

"Schonbeck! Paws! You know your duties," Kuntz said. "Get at it!"

Buddy took some cigarettes out of the tin, broke each in two, three halved, took out matches and placed them beside the cigarette pieces, on top of Kuntz's wooden seat, and then took the tin and the jar of matches behind the tree again, presumably to hide them. Jerome came over to the dead tree. It had been snapped in two by lightning about eleven feet up, and its upper half, still attached by a splintery hinge of graying wood, had fallen close to its trunk, forming an inverted V; shrubbery and vines grew in a profusion inside this natural arch, and Jerome pushed some of these out of his way and then reached deep in them and began pulling out branches of cut lilac and laying them on the ground, and as more and more came out, I could see, resting on a limb level with my eyes, an apple crate or an orange box covered with a green cloth.

Leo went to Jerome and they each took opposite corners of the cloth, turned toward Kuntz in unison, as if serving at Mass, said *Domine, non sum dignus,* and drew the veil. The crate was lined with rich, red, velvetlike material, as rich as the best vestments Father wore, and standing inside was a plaster statuette of the Blessed Virgin, in blue and white gowns trimmed with gold, her head bowed, her palms turned out and held below her waist in patient supplication.

"Is that neat," Brian said, and the two of us moved closer. "Where'd you get it, guys?"

"You can't call us that yet," Leo said.

"Father or somebody threw it out," Kuntz told him. "Over there."

I looked where he was pointing and saw through the leaves to the ash pile behind the Catholic church, like the large blue-gray, glass-glittering one behind Eichelburger's Tavern, which we picked through sometimes to find cigarette butts; drunkards put them out long. Then I noticed that the base the Virgin was standing on—the upper half of a blue hemisphere overlaid with different-sized silver-colored stars—was broken off, and the front part of her feet and the head of the snake she was standing on were gone. On either side of her were vigil glasses, a nubbly yellow one with a chip out of its rim, and one blue. "Where'd you get the vigil glasses?" I asked.

"Those aren't what you think they are," Kuntz said. "Those are our cruets."

"No, sir," I said. "Cruets are—" But stopped at the look from Jerome.

"Pajinsky Bear and I snuck those cruets out of school in our lunch sacks," Kuntz said.

"Oh." One of the duties of the third grade was to clean out the vigil glasses that had been used for so many offerings they were filling with wicks and unburned wax and those tinnily thin silver plates from the base of each vanished candle; the Sisters brought the glasses over to school from the church and supplied the class with table knives for the task.

"We never burn candles in our cruets," Kuntz said. "You got that? You never do or else"—he made a motion across his throat as though he had one of the knives now—"grick! They're where we keep our relics. Here."

He reached and stopped, a startled look in his eyes, and then whirled his forefinger close to one ear in a blur, and everybody separated and stepped noiselessly into neighboring brush, Brian led by Leo, who had a hand over his mouth, and me by Jerome, and then I heard the heavy stride of somebody on the catwalk, Sanderson, and saw the blooms on the trellis tremble like the musculature below my heart. After a while everybody came back into the clearing, and Kuntz said, "Yeah, I should have told you about that." He whirled his forefinger in the same way. "Anybody, even you new guys, can do that if you think you hear him coming or on the prowl. He's a *Scheisspot*. O.K., the relics."

He took down the yellow cruet and held it out to Brian and me and I saw miraculous medals, a square scapular of brown feltlike cloth, newly minted pennies, and several small, circular glass reflectors—red, yellow, orange, and blue—that had been pried loose, by the looks of it, from the big-buckled, broad cowboy belt Kuntz had on now. He put back his cruet and took down the blue one, which was filled with shredded and spicy-smelling herbs or weeds or—

"It's just dead leaves," Brian said.

"Spearmint," Kuntz said. "It's good for chewing after we smoke."

"I chew bubble gum," Brian said. "It kills the smell the best."

"O.K.," Kuntz said. "That'll be your duty. You keep us supplied in bubble gum all summer."

"O.K.," Brian said.

"No, no, wait," Leo said. "I've got a better one."

"What?"

"Bring us a jar of marshmallow cream every week, *ha!*"

"Yeah, well, hey now, that *is* a pretty good one," Kuntz said.

"Oh, come on, Leo! Dad knows hów much there is there, he counts the damn jars, you know that. He knows *you* like it. What if he catches me stealing some?"

"Tough titty, if you want to be in this club."

Brian turned on me. "What's his duty, then?"

"I got one," Kuntz said, and laughed his nasal laugh with its accompanying buzzing murmur, then the long teeth. "He can beg Hershey bars from Wilhomena. She'll give you one if you go to the back door and beg like you're starving and a fool for food. Grrrompf! *'Du Deibel, du!'* she'll squeak at you. He can beg a Hershey bar every day for two weeks from her. Haw!"

Kuntz and Leo kept laughing at this and Brian said, "Oh, boy, tough duty." And then to Leo, "What's yours, I'd like to know?"

"I got to cut new branches when these get dry, the lilacs, to keep the shrine here covered up."

"Oh, boy."

"Plus the cigarettes. So you also got to do the bubble gum, guy!"

"What's yours, Kuntz?"

"I lead you on raids into the neighborhood country-side on my mighty steed, Silver!"

"I quit," Brian said.

"Good," Leo said.

Brian bowed his big head again, his wizened mouth constricted tight. "No," he murmured. "I don't quit, you guys. Please."

"Don't *call* us that yet!" Leo cried.

"O.K., here's the next thing," Kuntz said, and went to

the shrine, reached to the back of the cloth-lined box, and brought out another glass, much larger than the other two, and scarlet-colored, with an image of the Sacred Heart, crossed with thorns and bleeding, embossed on it. "This is our sanctuary lamp. We burn our candles in here. Never in the cruets. You got that separated yet? Allus in this." He held the glass close to Brians's nose. "You know where I got this? Out of the church. Right out of the sacristy when Father was there, serving Saturday Mass one time. And the candles we burn in it? I swipe them off the church's offertory racks when I'm out on my raids."

"Yeah," Buddy Schonbeck said. "You got anything to say about that?"

"No," Brian said.

"You?" he said to me.

"No." It seemed wrong to steal from the church; just the idea of it made my watery knees feel they might have to take a leak, too.

"Maybe you'll have to help me," Kuntz said. "If we let you join in." He put the sanctuary lamp back, directly in front of the statue now.

"Start them in on the ceremonies, Ruler Number One," Leo said.

"Yessir, yessir," Kuntz said. "O.K., now you guys watch everything we do, and if you can't learn to do it in a week, you're out, sorry, boys, that's it, but you are, boo-hoo." He passed around the cigarette halves. "Turn the raggaly end out," he said, as if aware I'd been wondering. He lit the sanctuary lamp and then lit his cigarette from it, genuflected, and then Leo came up and lit his, genuflected, and then Jerome . . .

"Do we have to smoke these?" I said.

"Do you want to eat it?" Kuntz asked.

"I haven't ever smoked much and sometimes——" My vision popped out of focus and flooded with blue along its edges, while a warm sensation, like a sprawling bee sting, rose and spread over the back of my skull, and then I could see again.

"This is part of the ceremony now!" Leo said. "Don't ruin it!"

"Right," Kuntz said. "If you don't learn to smoke and inhale, boys, you're also really out. Ka-choom!"

"Inhale?"

"My big brother showed me. Watch." Kuntz sucked down a thin puff, his chest heaving with a cough, coughed hard once, bit it back, his face going violet, and said in a wheezy voice, "Like that. You have to do that in a week. Aghh! Only sissies and old ladies don't. They couldn't take what it does to you. Gough! Gough! *Hee*-haw, utta ka-CHOO!"

Brian and I went and lit our cigarettes, genuflected, and started hacking up smoke, and I saw as from a distance my perceptions narrow to this white column in my hand, the talisman to master before I could enter this club, and all of the possibilities it evoked.

"After three drags, we put them out like this," Kuntz said. "He spat in his palm and rolled the sputtering cigarette end around in it. "Bleck! And then we put them back down here on top of my gospel chair."

Kuntz and Leo knelt down, side by side, in front of the shrine, Jerome and Buddy knelt in a pair behind them, and Kuntz told Brian and me to kneel behind those two and leave plenty of space in between. "Also," Kuntz said, "you got to keep your eyes closed during this. It works the best." Into the dizzying darkness, where echoing sparks and spheres colliding in brown and blue and beige outbursts threatened to pull me off balance, Kuntz's quavering voice came and said, "Well, I guess you'll have to keep them open for a while until you see how we do this, guys. Pardon me. What a dummo! A goof! Gorp, yawlk!

"Allah!" he cried in his commanding voice, and everybody lifted their arms above their heads and then lowered them, outstretched, to the ground, bowing as the turbaned men bowed in the Sabu movies shown in serial form every weekend at the Town Hall, and then everybody rose and did a thumping and a mea-culpaing of their chests, which Brian and I joined in on on our private drums, and then we lifted our arms up to the outcry of "Allah," and prostrated ourselves again. We continued this for eleven times, as I counted it, and I kept parting my lashes to peek and see if any variations were being added (none were) and confronting the soles of the shoes and above them the close big bent butts of Buddy and Jerome, bowing, bobbing down, and once when I glanced over at Brian, to see how he was doing, his eyes were open also, and he stuck out his tongue.

We were done with that, then, apparently, and Kuntz once more handed around the cigarettes (was this mine, I wondered, staring at the damp-ended butt), which were lit as before from the sanctuary lamp. "O.K.," Kuntz said. "Now you kneel there and smoke the whole thing down as far as you can, and inhale it three times while you stare at Our Lady of the Black Forest. Now, you can't look at anybody when they're smoking and mess up what they're thinking about, and you also gotta sorta examine your conscience real hard. This is serious."

"Examine my conscience," Brian said. "What the hell for?"

"Confession," Leo said. "You've got to think of things so awful you did, you wouldn't even tell them to Father. Go to it, guys!"

I tried to smoke and stared at the statue, which took motion under my stare or from the smoke crossing between. My eyes burned, my throat was so swollen it was hard to swallow, and my skull was pulsing as if receiving directly the rhythms, currents, and contents of my heart, burgeoning, so displaced I kept having to shift my knees to remain upright, while the scarlet-colored sanctuary lamp cast streaks of red and yellow across the statue, which changed color and location and shape with the changing flame, a wide red one quavering up and down as it contracted, lenslike, blue-white along its edges, and then disappeared and was replaced by a yellowish band wobbling lopsidedly at a lower level, then the red reappearing in a lighter shade, pink-crimson, salmon, rose, rising as high as the Virgin's neck and tilting back and forth there, and then flowing down the folds of her gown and tilting at a lower level, until I was filled with the fears and fantasies that had troubled me since I'd seen, through a split panel in the door between my room and the closet off our bathroom, my mother with raised dress and sagging pants put inside a white harness a big wide cottony bandage up between her thighs: legs in front of pink curtains, turning to catch the light; legs with flowery tops on their stockings, sheathed or unsheathed; the way certain women's breasts were right for you no matter

what age; the red-blond or coppery-black spiky fur fringing the outer edges of the inner band of their swimming
suits, and more in a more blossoming and a more me-
lodious way that—

"Yesterday I saw my sister's buzzooms," Kuntz said.
"It was right after she washed them off and, boy, did I
want to diddle around with them! *Ma*ma!"

"I went upstairs when my mother was dressing and
caught her in her pants and tittycups," Leo said. "A
mama mia, too!"

"I put my head down on the ground right in the grass
underneath Susie Eichelburger so I could watch the piss
come out of that little hole she's got up in there," Buddy
said. "You know, right?"

"I pretended to fall against the bathroom door when
my dad was in there and got a look at his dingus," Jerome said. "It's like the sausage of a horse!"

"Did you want to diddle around with it?" Kuntz asked.

"Oh, come on, Kuntz, that's enough!"

"I stold mash— Crap. I stold marshmallow cream
from my dad's store," Brian said.

"No good," Leo said. "It doesn't count! Tell him why,
Kuntz."

"Well, I wouldn't ever say that to Father in the confessional!" Brian cried.

"Think of something else," Kuntz said. "You got to
have something new every time we meet, hot diggity, a
rarf! rarf!"

"The other day I wanted to pick up a rotten knife and
stab Leo in the back with it!" Brian cried.

"That's good," Leo said. "That's a good one, Fititzer."

"I saw Susie Eichelburger with her pants off," I said.

"No go," Leo said. "Schonbeck already used her."

"I saw Susie's mother with her pants off," I said. This
was a lie, but I'd seen enough of my mother to say it; the
white of her thighs naked in the darkness.

"You saw Susie's *mother* with her pants off?" Kuntz
said.

"Yes."

"Was there fuzz on it? Did it look like a beaver?"

"Yes."

"Did your peterdink get stiff?"

"Yes."

"Real long?"

"Well."

"Did you want to jump out there and diddle around with it?"

"Sure."

"Oh, wow!"

It seemed Kuntz's eyes wouldn't be small again, and also that this part of the ceremony was at an end for now. Buddy gathered up the cigarette butts and dropped them down a hole in the top of a fence post. Kuntz leaned against the dead tree, yawned, and said, "O.K., now you can just relax and enjoy the club, guys." I stretched out on my back on the ground, copying other members, and slipped my hands under my head. There was only the sound of the leaves in the trees above us. Kuntz mentioned the prank he'd played on Mary Liffert last Halloween; defecated in a paper bag, put it on her porch, set it afire, and then banged on the door. "And she came out with her jiggly legs going all over, kicking around and hopping and dancing, screaming, 'Fire! Fire!' and then started stomping up and down on the bag like she was going to give it the kibosh, and I wanted to say I was sorry it was such a wet one. Wawk!"

There was a quiet wave of laughter in the clearing, beyond civilization now.

"Did you hear what old man Ianaccona did last Halloween?" Leo said. "The high-school guys were always tipping his crapper, so early Halloween night he moves it ahead a little, and when the guys run up to give it the push, whoosh, they all fall in the hole, ha! Imagine both your legs all the way to the top in that mob of dead guts. Phew!"

There was a lighter scattering of laughter among the leaves.

Jerome said, "When we were living at our old place, once when Dad was out in the can there, dumping, he heard voices and then the can started to go, so he yelled, 'Hey-ey, at least wait till I'm *done* in here!' It must have been some of the kids he taught, and then it got around school, because nobody ever bothered that can again."

"Wasn't that the one that was wired down?" Leo asked.

"The owner of the place, Peter Schommer, did that."

"It just makes the guys want to tip it over all the more," Leo said.

"I know," Jerome said. "That's the way it seems sometimes."

Again their was only the sound of the leaves. I was still dizzy, vertiginous, displaced, and felt I was being rocked by the branches above me, cradled and rocked, and wondered what it was like before, once, when there was ground beneath. The subdued conversation moved to the topic of parents and older people, and all the mistakes they made, and we agreed that when we grew up our lives would be different from theirs; we'd never get married or have children, or worry, or go to church all the time, or have a job you had to go to every morning and always complained about, but actually liked because it got you away from the house, or have headaches, or have to lie down and rest, or drive a car that was always breaking down either where there were no other cars close to help or else out where everybody could see, or go to parties because you were expected to and people might gossip if you didn't show up (and the leaves above us swayed with the wind and clashed together, saying, *Yes, you will live like this, yes, yes, you will, yes*), or do any work to merely do work and please others, but instead spend our energies on ourselves, moving from place to place in search of pleasure and others like us, and our parents would be surprised, and then envious, because we'd be living lives that they'd only dreamed about, if they'd gone that far, and ours would be the happiest lives that had ever been lived—the trees and brush taking on the density of a real forest, with branches stilled and back-turning a webwork of limbs within the core of memory, shielding us from the village and its inhabitants, who'd never understand us and all of these sinful desires we had.

And again there was a long silence. The afternoon light was leaving in the lifting way it leaves the plain, as though tilting over in the air toward the sun, which then draws it on forward and out, and we all felt hungry in the numbing one-minded way in which boys that age get hungry at that hour, while the village smells of mingled cooking drew around us. This was no Black Forest to us now. We got up, replaced and hid the shrine, said goodbye to one another in a solemn manner, and then all of us, once out of sight of one another—Jerome and I were no different from the rest—took off on a dead run toward home.

*

A week later Brian and I became members of the club that met in secret in the Black Forest, but Brian barely so; Leo voted against him and got Buddy Schonbeck to do the same, but Jerome and Kuntz wouldn't listen or be moved by him. The rituals went on for a week without change and I sensed everybody becoming like I was: listless and defiant of rules and orders, of Kuntz and Leo, and more violent in their fantasies; most of the women in the village had been seen naked or in some form of undress, and Father Schimmelpfennig was discovered in the dark of his back yard, "taking a tinkle like a lady because priests they aren't allowed to have a pecker, you think, right? Ah, hee, hee."

It was during this time of unquiet, boredom, and barefaced lies, on an afternoon as I lay under the enveloping leaves, that I knew for sure, as I'd always sensed, that somebody watched every detail of everything we did. I'd see a pale patch above the stone wall. Or a form would go in a running retreat down the alley at times. Or there'd be a flash or a shimmer of light. I thought it was a scout from another club, one formed by the public-schoolers in town, a minority, a group that didn't mix much with the Catholic kids, and wasn't welcome to.

I mentioned the possible scout.

"Oh," Kuntz said. "That's only Ribs. He's allus hanging around."

"Oh."

Everett Ritter, or Everribber, or Ribs, as he was called, due to his physique, had big brimming dark-brown eyes and blue-black hair, and a delicately modeled brunette woman's face—caves, bone, and shadows of rest and prayer. A few years ago his father had been found dead on the road with the pickup he'd been driving crashed a hundred yards ahead of him, and it was never known for sure whether he'd accidentally leaned on the door handle and fallen, or thrown himself out. Ribs lived with his mother and sisters at the edge of town in an unpainted house with shells of abandoned automobiles around it. His father had been a mechanic and Ribs spent most of his time in one or another of the cars, his hands on its wheel as if driving— Where? His mother did washing and ironing to support them, and Ribs wore worn and patched hand-me-downs from nearly every family in town, so you'd sometimes find somebody else—"Oh, *Ribs,* excuse me"—inside the shirt of an old friend. He never spoke on his own and when he was spoken to, when he was delivering clothes, or picking up groceries from the Red Owl, he answered with a single word or a shrug, or just lowered his eyes and walked on.

"Hey, listen," Kuntz said. "What should we do about him?"

"Make him a member," Brian said. "And then give him the old initiation treatment!"

"How so?" Leo said. "He ain't Catholic."

"He could learn the stuff," Brian said. "I did. It's easy as pie. Look at me."

"You haven't even learned half of what you think you have," Leo said. "And you still look like a goddamn pumpkin on legs."

"We could use him as a spy," Jerome said.

"Hey, that's good," Kuntz said. "We could find out if anybody else in town has a club and raid the buggers, *clop, clop,* hocka pa-tchew!"

"Right," Leo said. "Wreck the place!"

"Let's fake like we want him in with us," Brian said, "and then everybody pile in on him."

"What a stupid idea," Buddy said. "I've never heard such a stupid idea! Fititzer, you're so *stupid!*"

"What's your bright idea, limp lips?"

"Watch out who you're calling what or you'll be out!" Buddy cried. "How do you think you got into this club in the first place?"

"Not by no help from you. You voted me out."

"I did not!"

"Leo told me."

"I did not! I voted you in!" Buddy's face was red and thrust so far forward on his neck the cords of it bulged, and there was spittle on his big lips.

"So where's your bright idea?" Brian said.

"I'll run him down and throw him a flying tackle, by golly!"

"Oh, boy," Brian said. "Oh, boy-oh-boy."

"You're too big, Schonbeck,' Jerome said. "You'd hurt the kid."

"Let's just take him down and give him a knuckle rub and turn him loose," Brian said. "Or else pull off his pants and run them up the flagpole for the rest of the afternoon. Somebody be a sport, guys!"

"Shush," Leo said. "He's back. Over there by the playing field."

It seemed a network of darkness darker than the leaves had settled down on us. I saw a shock of blue-black hair and part of a face among the boulders of the gray-black wall.

Kuntz went to the edge of the clearing. "Hey, Ribs!" he called. "We see you. Come on out! We want to talk to you."

Ribs sprang back into the open in a crouch, ready to run.

"Take it easy," Kuntz said. "We won't hurt you, Ribs. We want to talk to you about joining in with us."

Rib's face paled more as he shook his head.

"Is it all right if I come over there?" Kuntz asked.

Ribs shook his head.

"See!" Buddy whispered.

"I'll make a treaty with you," Kuntz said. "I'll leave all these jerks right here and just me come over and talk. I'll stay on this side of the wall and won't come close to you. I'll hold my hands behind my back."

Ribs glanced over his shoulder, as if the trap suggested by all this was behind him.

"It's O.K.," Kuntz said. "I give you my word of honor, ah-*rooo*-ha, bright steed, Chuckaluck, ah, whoooo-up there! Really." And then he walked over with his hands behind him, in his pockets, and stopped a few feet from the wall. "Hey, we don't want to hurt you. We'd like you to join in with us."

Ribs stared at him with his wide and tremulous eyes.

"Wouldn't you like to?"

It seemed no response would come.

"It's simple. You could learn the stuff in a day."

"Oh, yeah!" Buddy yelled, and Ribs tensed, about to bolt.

"Shut up!" Kuntz shouted at him, and then turned back to Ribs. "Really. It's simple. Here's part of it: Are you a Catholic?"

Ribs shook his head.

"Was your mother ever a Catholic?"

Ribs shook his head, his chin tucked in, and his eyes widened in anticipation of the next, logical question, but Kuntz said, "You believe in God, though, right?"

"No."

Everybody was on their feet and after Ribs, Buddy out front, passing Kuntz, leaping the stone wall when Ribs was halfway down the field, and then catching him before he reached the far end, where there were shrubs along the wall, and throwing that flying tackle he'd talked about. Ribs went sailing with his legs in a hug and his head hit the wall. The sound was like a football punted, stone hitting stone, a watermelon dropped, and we all stopped as though it had happened to us, and then Kuntz, who'd stood where he was, came pushing his way through us and punched Buddy on the shoulder. "I gave my word of honor, dumb-ass! What'd you do that for?"

"It's what you told me to!" Buddy said.

"It was not."

"Well, did you hear what he *said?*"

Kuntz punched Buddy again, in the chest, and Buddy went stumbling backward until gravity caught him and seated him with a shock, for good, it seemed the way he was splayed out. Kuntz took Ribs by the shoulders and turned him; whites of his eyes wiggling, lips parted and grayish, his tongue out and bleeding, head jerking with the torturous energy of an uncontained epileptic. Kuntz kneeled and said, "Hey, hey, hey," as he held Ribs head in his hands and massaged his cheeks with his thumbs. Ribs woke. "I knew you'd do that," he said. "I knew you were all a pack of lies." A blue-white swelling was forming a dome on his forehead and he started to cry without covering his face, as though tears weren't a shame among boys who'd reached our age and got by.

"It was a mistake," Kuntz said.

"No, it wasn't," Ribs cried. "You all meant it, all of you!"

"Here, here." Kuntz helped him to his feet and smoothed the dirt off his face and out of his hair, and then brushed off his clothes. "It was that screwball Schonbeck did it," Kuntz said. "Do you want me to walk you home?"

Ribs nodded that he did.

"I'll tell your mother it wasn't a fight," Kuntz said. "But sort of, we were, well, er—" They were through the hedge and off together down the block with one of Kuntz's arms around Ribs's neck. The rest of us returned to the clearing, repentant and uneasy, if others were like me, and lay down around the shrine, where the sanctuary lamp still burned.

"I told you you'd hurt him," Jerome said.

"No, you didn't! Kuntz said that!"

"I was conked out once," Brian said. "You don't even feel it." Everybody looked at Brian's big head. "Except after you wake up."

There was only the occasional sound of the leaves. I felt chastened, reflective, and bothered by dark doubts; Kuntz had asked a question he wouldn't have if Ribs hadn't been so different from us, or Kuntz able to sense the difference in him, and it frightened me the way we'd got up on our feet and gone after him at the same time. Would I have tackled him? Perhaps. I looked around at the others, at Leo and Brian lying next to one another near the trellis, at Buddy digging in the ground with a Popsicle stick, tears dropping off his chin, at Jerome in front of the shrine on his stomach, and they all seemed absorbed in the same question, or a question of a similar kind. I looked at the sanctuary lamp casting its colored light across the Virgin's gown, and heard again, *Do you believe in God?* The final word came out of a whorl winding down from a great height, our parents, the authority of the Sisters, and Father Schimmelpfennig himself; *God*, a word I took for granted the way I took my heart for granted—although I couldn't see it or watch the way it worked, I never doubted its being there. I believe in God, of *course* I do, I thought, but then as I listened all I could hear inside myself was silence. Didn't I? Had I returned from the ragged jaws of pneumonia only to live inside silence and emptiness? Wasn't that a sin? What was it I believed in, then? There was some force that guided me from day to day and act to act and assured renewal and integration to all that I did, roughly as I might do it at times, and assured my good nature, too, and its stability within the progression of time, wasn't there? I listened. Wasn't there? Then the wind sprang up and the light on the Virgin swayed to one side and fluttered above her neck, higher than I'd seen it go, and stained her face scarlet, and *Yes,* the voices of the leaves whispered above me in a chorus—made by a mother who was made of earth—*Yesssss, Yessss.* It seemed a dream or a miracle to me at the time then, and even more so today, now, still, as once in New York after my wife had had a miscarriage, I woke from sleep and saw over her body to the curtains of our bedroom windows, white-silvery, lit by the street lamp outside and imprinted with frondlike patterns of leaves, and silhouetted against their curves saw the shadow of a head, and before I had time to resort to reason or detachment, knew that the shadow was the shadow of our dead child, and that he was looking in on us, watching us with a patience so infinite it was no part of my experience and made it obvious that we were observing one another from opposite sides of a transparent mystery. *Yes.*

*

She'd studied under Father Schimmelpfennig for five years in a dilatory way, and was brilliant, prideful, witty, well read, limited, uncompromising, hyperbolic and extreme, open-minded, too critical both ways, serene, conservative, saintly, down to earth, yet a romantic who could feed on the food of illusion, and Father's fingers began trembling now, in the way they'd trembled only once, when he was ordained, as he took from the gold-lined ciborium a consecrated host and placed it on the curved bridge of Alpha Neumiller's wet, extended, orange-pink tongue.

16

◈

AMATEUR HOUR

Held at arm's length, he watches her eyes travel over his body and fill with unabashed pride. She's been to her storeroom and worked with awl, needle, and thread, and now, at last, he feels properly dressed. Covering his blue jeans are the chaps ("shaps," she told him, is the correct pronunciation) that her father wore when he rode horseback over the unbroken plain farther west, a young man at the time. The leather legs of the chaps, rolled up and sewn to fit him, are faced with goat hide that she's brushed until its silver-colored strands of hair glisten like her brushed hair below his nose, fragrant with her scent. The holster below his hip holds a heavy pistol. Then the plaid shirt and blue bandanna. Their eyes meet and there's a smile of complicity between them.

"Here," she says, and rises and takes a hat off a hook on the wall behind him.

Charles says, "But it's Dad's."

"His old one. Come here once." She kneels on one knee, and again her face is at his level.

"But it's too big!"

"With that head, I wouldn't be surprised if it fit."

Her tone of voice exposes him as he's exposed when she checks to make sure he's had a thorough bath. She sets the hat on his head, steps back a step, crosses her arms, and then crosses one leg over the other at the ankle.

"Well," she says. "Not quite!"

If she weren't his mother, he'd know that noise is giggling, which he detests, but the truth doesn't register: his ideal of her blinds him to her spontaneity.

229

"I'm anxious to go over it now that you're in costume. Aren't you?"

He nods, the hat brim hits his nose, and there's more laughter from her.

He lifts it. "See, I can't wear this big old thing."

"Stop whining. You sound like a *girl*. We'll put some tissue in the crown before tonight. Where's the script? Where did I put the script?"

"On the table. Like always."

"I'm so nervous I can't think," she says, and her changing voice contains less nervousness than delight, as she goes to the table and sits down. She's been rehearsing this monologue with him for two weeks, two hours each day, and it was her idea to coach him, although his father has had more training in speech and dramatics and the theater; his father defers to her in such decisions.

She folds back the blue cover of the script, smooths it flat on the table, and inclines her head over it, chin in one hand. To him, her profile against the brilliant window is a silhouette, dark and featureless, and when she turns to him he bends back the brim of the hat and squints to see her clear.

"You look like a fool!" she cries, and now there's no doubt that she's laughing.

He throws the hat on the floor.

"No, no," she says. "Don't. You don't look so bad, looking a fool."

Charles thinks that perhaps his father is right when he says to her, "You know, sometimes you act like a kid," which makes her turn white-faced and walk off. But his father is just as bad, or worse; he works jigsaw puzzles and plays games with an exuberance that irritates the boy, who's dead serious about everything he does. His father doesn't smoke or drink or swear, like others do, but sits home and reads books, and sometimes even cries over them—a burning shame. And he's as easily affected by dramas on the radio. "Nonsense, I don't believe you!" she'll say to the radio speaker. Or, "How did she get a job as a professional? Listen to that shoddy articulation. Listen to that twang!" But in the end she usually succumbs in the same way as his father, and then stalks into the kitchen and busies herself there until she has her feelings under control.

A few nights ago, when she was shopping in Mc-
Callister, his father took him through a rehearsal. "Start
off," he said, and his large eyes swept and swam along
the lines of the script as Charles went from the beginning
of the monologue to its end without being stopped once.
He was wary; he didn't think he was doing well, and his
mother usually interrupted him the moment he went off-key
and helped him find his way again. He waited, shaky and
anxious, for the criticisms of his phrasing, his timing,
and his comic sense, and wondered if his father would be
as severe a perfectionist as his mother and make him repeat the lines again and again until it was right according
to his father's ideal. His father raised his eyes, which were
liquid with emotion, and said, "I don't know what to say
to you. I really don't know what to say. You've got this
whole thing memorized word for word."

"Ready?" his mother asks now. "Hat and all?"

"Oh, be quiet."

"Oh, all right. Let's both be more businesslike. This
might well be your last rehearsal before tonight."

"Tonight" settles below his lungs and sends out appendages that cut off his breath, enjamb his self-control,
and threaten to destroy all the techniques he's mastered in
the last two weeks. He wishes he'd said, like Jerome, when
he was asked to perform, "No. I'm not in the mood to
talk in front of people any more."

He's a weakling, he's sure of it, but knows it better not
be seen by her, and begins:

> *"I'm a buckaroo from the Wild West,*
> *I rope and I ride and all the rest . . ."*

The words aren't words any more. Repetition has removed from them any meaning, and they affect only his
vocal mechanism, which vibrates around their shapes,
subdues them, and fashions them into images he can see
as he speaks. They won't meld together at first, and come
out as separate geometrics—an oblong, an oval, a triangle
—and fall to the floor in a multicolored jumble he
can practically see but wouldn't care to look at. Then, as
he grows confident, they begin to link and flow toward his
listener, forming a current of feeling between them; that
sentence, painted in primary colors, strings together the

apples, bushel baskets, marbles, and coins from his first-grade arithmetic book; that pause before the last, fat, rhymed word of the line, is a beheading. In these phrases a locomotive takes shape, cars link behind, a caboose is there and it all starts down the polished tracks, its wheels settling into a regular clacking, the metallic singsong of a train, the S-curved sound of its whistle retreating into silence, and then the roadbend explodes and its scattering fragments are flushed quail roaring toward the cover of trees.

He tries to affect her with his voice, sending her his version of what she's taught him, watching for her response, and when she has to shield one side of her face to hide her pleasure, or when her laughter draws her head toward the script and her dark hair swings over her cheeks, shining in the sunlight, he feels in himself the size and grandeur of an adult, filling with adult sensations, which, for some reason, in spite of their vastness and desirability, aren't quite satisfying.

"No, no, no, no, *no!* You brandish the pistol in the air. You *bran-dish* it." She laughs at her exaggeration of the word. "You don't click the trigger, son." The tone of her voice and her stare—uncompromising, deep blue, a blue he can see and feel even though her features are in shadow—make him shrink back into the constricting limits of his years, seven, to be exact.

"It's distracting. If you do that, nobody's going to pay any attention to the line, understand? All right, then go on from there. You were doing fine with the speech itself, it was just that pistol." She turns to her script, and says, "The next thing I know, you'll be wanting caps for the damn thing."

"Can I?"

All it takes this time is the stare. He lowers the pistol into the holster, dwelling on the act as though he hopes it will last forever. He focuses on the linoleum, through the geometry there, and goes on, feeling each word ring thin and hollowly in the air, convinced he's disappointing her. He reaches the end.

"Now let's have a look at that hat," she says, in a voice that's strangely social and nonchalant. There's been no praise or encouragement, not even the usual criticism; he's failed her and might as well go back to the boys. In her silence and her concern for the hat (she puts on a version of one of her scowls as she studies its inside), she's withholding the truth out of kindness, he's sure, aware it would upset him so badly he couldn't perform "tonight." But her silence is as destructive. He wants to run and hide, be like backward footprints vanishing up over sand, so he'd never have to face her again. He doesn't even care about the Amateur Hour, although his goal for two weeks has been to win first place, his gift to her.

He's more than surprised, then, and more troubled than ever about his mother, when she tosses the hat into the air with a cry of "Yippee!" and gives him, most rare and consummate of her rewards, a kiss on the lips.

*

People are appearing on Main Street and moving around the Town Hall, the building covered with tin that looks like stone. A few feet above the foundation the tin is polished silver from children running their hands over it to create a miniature thunder as they walk past, which Charles does now. The slanting sheets are burnished by the orange sun and the building looks changed and portentous. Instead of housing the usual friendly social gathering, the Town Hall will be the setting tonight for what feels to him like a war. He steps into the entry, carrying a cloth laundry bag with his costume in it, and stares at the ticket booth (knotty pine, the same as the walls), where a half-moon is removed from the bottom of the window, and on another half-moon—the wooden tray for counting out change—a white hand is resting. Because of a reflection, the hand is all he can see, and the anxiety he's been holding down, now that the hand is there as a focus, swells in him and makes him weak inside, and his eyes bulge.

"Don't just stand there and gape," she says. "They know we're on the program. We don't have to pay. Tonight we're not hoi polloi, boy. Ha! I didn't mean that to sound that way! Sorry about that."

They go toward double doors that open onto the auditorium and the reflection slides to one side, revealing the heavily made up face and bejeweled breast of Mrs. June Koenig, the dentist's wife. "What's the matter with him?" she cries, her high voice made indistinct and flat-sounding by the enclosure she's in. "Is he ascared already?"

"No, he's not," his mother says, and takes him through the double doors. He's surrounded by a smell of old varnish, damp crepe paper, mildew, and human sweat—a smell that's meant recreation and friends in the past, but doesn't tonight. He sniffs the air as an animal would, testing it; tonight it will be carrying the sound of his voice. The basketball backboard at the end of the auditorium has been hoisted against the ceiling, the curtains drawn across the stage, and the smell seems responsible for the curtains' particular shade of purple, for the way the folds in them fall, the way shadows curve between the folds out of sight, and then feet patter across the stage, the curtain billows out along its chain-weighted bottom, and somebody is saying, "Children's Division is first, and that's of course the one he'll be in."

Dr. Koenig, possessor of the biggest hands and broadest fingers he's ever seen (a judgment that has nothing to do with seeing them close up when the doctor works on his teeth), is the master of ceremonies; he's got through the preliminaries with Charles's mother, just inside the double doors, and now turns to Charles. "Got the jitters, boy?" he asks.

"Not half as bad as I have," she says.

"Well, you can't blame a kid for a case of the nerves. I've got them myself, just knowing I've got that introducing to do."

"He'll be all right. So will you."

"I'm glad to hear it!" the doctor cries, in the same tone he'd say, bringing a tooth up in front of Charles's eyes, *I got it, boy!* "And I hope you get that prize of ten silver dollars right off! Your first year! I bet you haven't had that much in your hand at one time, have you, Chuck?"

"Yes, he has," she says. "And anyhow, Doc, the money's not the important thing."

They both laugh.

"Where's your brothers and that baby sister of yours?" the doctor asks.

"At home," Charles says to him.

"With your dad?"

"Yes."

"I bet he has his hands full, the poor guy."

"Jerome is good with Tim," she says.

"How is that baby sister of yours growing?"

"Fine," Charles says.

"Just like a weed, huh?"

"Like a girl," he says to him. "They'll be here."

His mother puts her hands on his shoulders and turns him toward the stage.

"Just a second," the doctor says.

They all study one another in quick and searching sudden looks.

"There's this." The doctor holds up a jar filled with scraps of paper, and shakes it until his bluish jowls also shake. He offers the jar to Charles. "We have to find out when you come up in here. On the program, I mean, of course."

"Don't get your hand stuck in there," she warns him.

Charles unfolds the paper, looks at her, then at the doctor's round eyes with tan-colored circles haloing them, then at her, and says, "Five."

The doctor sets the jar on a wooden folding chair, takes a piece of paper from his shirt pocket, takes a pencil from behind his ear (each movement resplendent with the precision and ominousness Charles finds so frightening in the dental chair), traps the paper against the wall with one hand, and says as he writes, "Number 5, Children's Division, Chuckie Neumiller. You'll go on right after Nick Schonbeck sings us a song. The boys and their mothers are using the dressing room to the left of the stage, so that's of course the one you all'll have. The girls are in the other. Oh, does your play-act have a name?"

" 'Bronco Boy,' " she says.

The doctor tilts back his chin and releases his rusty but resonant laugh, which, as always, ends abruptly, with bewilderment in his eyes, as though laughter were an enigma to him. " 'Bronco Boy'! Sounds like a good one to me, all right!"

"I didn't title it," she says, and takes Charles by the hand, gives a jerk to get him started, and leads him down the side aisle toward the dressing room. There aren't any people in the rows of folding chairs on the auditorium floor, and the stage spots haven't been turned on, but the blue twilight shining down on him from the high windows at the side of the building gives the place a theatrical glow, and the chairs themselves are like the audience, cold and folded in containment, waiting for the first mistake, or least betrayal of fear. He looks away and sees, on the walls and the ceiling, dangling from thumbtacks, scraps and strips of crepe paper of every color—some of it faded, some stained, some looking new—and recalls that at the carnival last winter he was allowed for the first time to stay up until the children were told they could tear the decorations down, but didn't enjoy it; his mother wasn't there. She'd sat alone at a side table most of the evening, fiddling with a trinket he'd won at the Fish Pond, ignored by most of the women her age and older, and finally said she was tired and put on her coat, pulled its collar around her throat, and went home, leaving him and Jerome with their father.

From the dressing room he can hear excited voices that flow over him with more force when his mother opens the door; he takes in the female legs above (the dressing room is up a few steps), the smoke and lights, the smell of burnt cork and makeup. Faces turn toward them, there's a catch in the noise, and then it picks up again at a lower level. She leads him down the dressing room, narrow as a corridor, past women putting rouge on their sons' pale cheeks, wiping away streaks of dirt with saliva-moistened handkerchiefs, going over the *do re mi*, and, in one instance, taking Scotch tape off a wave of hair taped to a forehead. Nobody greets them.

Near the back, a woman is telling her son, who's slumped on a bench and crying, to grow up and act like a man, because he's going to get out there and sing whether he likes it or not. Nick Schonbeck.

Charles's mother stops and releases his hand. "What's wrong?" she says to Nick.

"Oh, don't ask me!" Mrs. Schonbeck cries, and blows air out of her lower lip, lifting a wisp of hair from her forehead. "I've been after him for weeks about tonight, and a couple of days ago he seemed all for it. He said he'd love to do it, sure he would, of course, and now at the last minute he wants to up and quit on me."

"He decided just two days ago?"

"That's right."

"Well, when has he had the time to rehearse?"

"Well, he's been singing in school all along, and so much at home it gets on the husband's nerves. So all we had to do was find a piece he liked that I could play on the piano."

Charles's mother kneels in front of Nick and takes his hand in hers. "Are you scared?"

He nods at her, his jaw trembles, and his tears, having wet paths prepared for them, slide down his cheeks.

"What grade do you get in singing at school?"

Nick opens his mouth wide and bawls, "AAAAAA's, Ma, don't I!"

"Charles gets C's. I tell him a C means he can sing like a canary, but it's a lie and he knows it, too. Have you ever heard him sing, Nick?"

Nick snuffles and studies her with a mixture of skepticism and shame.

"What does he sound like instead? Think of an animal with a name that starts with a C."

Nick wipes the tears from his cheeks with the back of his hand and looks at Charles. Then he grins with all his teeth. "A cow! He sounds like a cow to me!"

"Exactly. Now, knowing there are people who sound like that, and how you do, and what a wonderful gift it is to have a voice like yours, don't you ever wonder if it isn't a little strange for you to be afraid? Aren't you even a little ashamed of it, as good as you are?"

Nick lowers his head and, after a moment, nods it twice to her.

"That means you're sorry for being this way, causing your mother such worry, which means you'll sing twice as well—see if I'm not right!—to make up for it."

She pats him on the knee, rises, and takes Charles to the back of the room, where she sits him on a wooden bench, and, as she begins to undress him, says, "Don't be jealous. If you'd like, you can be angry. I didn't appreciate the way he said that either, about the cow. But you're a pro. And you're grownup enough to understand why I said what I did or I wouldn't have. Here, now! Stand up straight!"

Then, as she helps him on with his costume, which feels chilly and stiff after his street clothes, she generates a silence that shields him from the disorganization and tumult of the room, and he leaves the hubbub about

them, conscious only of her, of her hands moving up
the buttons of his shirt, her eyes traveling over his face
and clothes, examining them quickly but with care to
each detail, her breath passing over the side of his neck,
pausing, passing over it again, and once again he senses
that he's an adult, and thinks, This will last forever.

From the gentleness of her touch he understands more
what she meant about Nick than her words could say,
and realizes that this gentleness, present no matter
how straightforward or unpredictable she might be, was
communicated to Nick when she took his hand. And
then he's jealous, and his face burns as with the fever of
pneumonia.

She rechecks the tissue in the hat, the bandanna, the
belt of the holster ("Whatever you do, don't click that
thing!"), and the broad, bow-curved, tooled-leather belt
of the chaps, and says, "Just do what you've learned,"
and leaves him.

He goes out the side of the dressing room and stands
in a darkened wing of the stage, filled with her serenity,
her gift to him, and walks to a traveling drape gathered
near the cyclorama, takes the drape in one hand and
turns several slow circles, wrapping himself up in its
folds, and remains there until he's heard applause for
the first performer, and then unwinds himself, and sees
light, and feels a detached, trancelike pall over his
emotions. Why is he here, now, tonight?

Mary Beth Friewirth, in the opposite wing, makes a
hurried sign of the cross and walks into the spotlights in
a white dress, her First Communion dress minus the veil,
and sings "Dear Hearts and Gentle People." Applause.
Edward Hyerdahl, dressed as Uncle Sam, does a tap
dance to "I'm a Yankee Doodle Dandy." The clash and
rattle of his metal taps on a Masonite square. Applause.
Nick Schonbeck, with blackface covering whatever remnants of fear his face might betray, stands with his back
to the audience, polishing imaginary shoes, and sings
"Chattanoogie Shoe Shine Boy" to the jangling and
thrum of his mother's piano and at one point a cry of
"Go to it, boy!" Applause. Then Dr. Koenig's penetrating bass voice, "Doing a thing called 'Bronco Boy'!"

A sensation that's only skirted him before, brushing
him when he imagines performing, making him aware of

the complexity of his insides, falls over him with its full weight, and his intestines sway to one side as if to make room for greater fear. His tongue is hard and dry; there's a rope around his throat as he walks into the brilliant light, blinking against it, and though the outer elements exert so much pressure it seems he's growing smaller with each step, his composure keeps them outside; but they have an exhilarating effect, bearing down on his senses, and he feels he's taken his first steps onto the broad swath of the world. He notices details he wouldn't under normal conditions—the shade of his thumbnail (why is it so purple?); a strand of hair on the chaps, longer than the others, that's discolored (what from?); the grain in the boards of the stage; the specks of dust, brightly lighted, that seem to have been arranged over the grain with an eye for symmetry; a piece of blue thread stuck to the sole of his boot, and the shadow of the thread, also blue—and takes them in in a matter of steps.

The houselights are off, but he can see rows of faces and identify separate people. He finds his mother and, closer up front, Tim and Jerome, and sees that the contestants who've finished are sitting on the floor below the stage (Nick Schonbeck appears) along with some of the Rimsky boys, Kuntz, who cries "Wowk! Wowk!" and Ribs, off to one side, alone, and realizes that he's not only made it to the apron and executed his bow but is smiling and ready to begin, preapred for anything but the giggling all around, and not just at Kuntz. Then the white arms of some girls in the front row point at him. They're laughing at the chaps! His Grandpa Jones would thrash them all if he knew they were mocking anything of his, and his mother has worked over the chaps for hours to assure a perfect fit, so where's the reason to laugh? Are they laughing at her? Who? In the many-layered level of impressions, through anger and hints he's received of her attitude, he thinks, Those people out there are dumb farts. Hicks. He hates them. And once emotion has broken through, the details fall away and he sees only white. Blue-white. Blue, and then races at a rattling speed through the speech without a thought to the phrasing and imagery he's worked on with her, each line emerging with a spattering flay of fierceness it's never had, and at the climax, "Yippeee!" to close off the fools, he grabs the hat and pulls it down over his eyes. The big hand of Dr. Koenig settles across the width of his back and propels him in the proper direction, off-stage into the wing.

He pulls the hat free, and the tissue lining its crown drops to the floor. What will she say about this? He tries to recall if he clicked the trigger and can't. He can't even say if he finished the speech. Was the cap pistol there? And that isn't all. The audience is still making a sea of noise that supports the loudest cries, and above it all he hears Dr. Koenig wheedling, saying something about wool and eyes, and finally, after another swell, there's absolute silence out there. He bends down, trembling, and picks the tissue off the floor, as if it's essential to salvage every part of this he *does* have, and goes into the dressing room. His mother is there, alone, waiting for him, and before he can say he's sorry, she grabs him by the scruff of the neck—a button pops off his shirt— drags him to the rear of the room, and slams him down on the bench so hard that a warm pain sends out tentacles of numbness from the base of his tailbone.

"Why did you pull that hat down?" she says in a fierce whisper, shaking his shoulders. "What kind of a second-rate performer are you, anyway?"

A wave of emotion smothers his words, hoarse empty voice.

"I've never been so mortified in my life! Do you think I took you through two weeks of rehearsal to see you ruin it at the last minute with a piece of cheap slapstick like that? What's the matter with you?"

She begins to undress him, and his shirt rips under the armpit. Only children feel with such acuteness what's communicated through hands, and these are the hands of his mother. He feels desecrated all the way through. The gentleness, the tremor of understanding usually there even when she spanks him, isn't, and when she tugs wrath-fully at one leg of the chaps without unbuckling the belt first, the tears that have been building beneath his eyes gather on his lashes, send around turning tines of light, sidewheeling rays, and then burn with an acidity from holding them back.

"After a stunt like that, you don't deserve to win a dime."

"I don't want to!"

"You've performed and you'll be judged. Except for that slapstick, it's the best you've done the speech. I thought they'd never stop applauding! Oh!"

"I did it because they made fun!"

"When you're performing, you have a duty to yourself and your audience, and can't lose control—you were so good!—and when you're onstage you might well expect to be laughed at. Isn't that one of the reasons you're out there? You're not there to vent your temper, you know. There's more than enough opportunity for that in everyday life. And if you don't learn to control your temper there, too, in everyday life, I mean—your temper and that terrible pride of yours—life's going to give you an awful lot of trouble, believe me! I know!"

She kneels in front of him, picks up the tissue he's dropped, puts it in his hand, and closes his fingers around it. "Here," she says. "Dry your eyes now. Pretty soon they'll be announcing the winner. You."

A few minutes later he walks onto the stage to receive, as she's predicted, the first prize of ten silver dollars. The houselights are on, illuminating the auditorium, but he sees the audience only vaguely, and the faces of his friends and their applause have little effect on him. He accepts the prize money from Dr. Koenig, thanks him, and as he turns away is grabbed up under the arms, above the head of the doctor, who waltzes him around the stage in big dips a few times to the cries and amusement of the audience, singing something under his sweet-smelling breath that seems to have the streets of Detroit or of old New York, or both of them, mixed up in it, and then Charles comes down near the edge of the traveling curtain, walks into the wing and places the money in the hands of his mother, his real, his unequivocal, and, as the slow unfolding of years will come to prove, his only competitor, his only stumbling block, and his only real friend for life, or so it seems at times, here in the present, as he looks up to find himself alone in a room.

17

❧

PLUMBER'S SON

Now I'm known as the plumber's son (or I was then, after I graduated from being called the principal's son for so long it gave me a sense of character and pride), and it gives me such pleasure to walk in the wake of my father with a coil of copper tubing slung over my shoulder, along with some pipe fittings laced on a wire, I couldn't care less what anybody says about either of us. He's given up his principalship at the high school, and since the summer has been known in town as the man with two jobs. Actually, he has four; he sells life insurance the year round, he works on a book of memoirs that nobody knows about but Charles and Jerome and me, he drives tractor on a farm in the spring and fall, and, fourth, in his spare time, he and I do any plumbing in the area that needs to be done. If we didn't, they'd have to hire a union man from McCallister, and they'd be surprised at the prices they'd have to pay these days. Everybody in Hyatt is putting in plumbing, now that the new mains are in, so there's always work for us to do over the weekends, or on the days when Dad isn't driving across the countryside and state, to Grand Forks, or Minot, or Devil's Lake, or Bismarck, to sell insurance.

We buy our materials at Pflager's, which faces the tracks and the depot, and is down the street from Eichelburger's, beyond Bill Faber's blacksmith shop. The Pflagers are the only family in town with two cars, and they also have a pickup at the hardware store for making deliveries. They live in a big, gold-colored house, kitty-corner from the front of ours, their yard surrounded by a fence made of iron bars with big spearheads on their tips. Mrs. Pflager is known as Penny, although her real name is Margaret, because of her red-gold hair. She grows marigolds along her fence and garden and a copper-colored spaniel—purebred, they say—exercises in the yard behind the fence, its metal tags clanking like car chains in the night when you want to sleep but a car is on a prowl of town.

Penny has a set of twins, Chris and Heidi, with hair like hers and her complexion; and though the twins are likable, and both my age, naturally both, I hardly ever play with them, and neither do many other kids. The twins spend their time in their yard and seem to speak a language of their own, and are so intent upon one another it feels embarrassing to intrude on them. The Pflagers' porch is crowded with cages of tropical birds and plants from all over the world, one of which eats bugs; I make sure it stays away from me. The Pflagers say the area is growing and prospering (optimists, my father calls them) and that someday Hyatt will be built up as big as McCallister, or bigger, and I hope that happens. It'll give us more plumbing to do.

Mr. Pflager speaks to me as if I'm an equal and not a little fellow who'll come up with a laughable statement if a grownup makes enough faces or acts as grownups never do, but Penny is my favorite; she used to be a registered nurse and when I was ill with rheumatic fever came to our house every day, at twelve noon, and took my temperature and blood pressure, and did, as my mother said, all that it was possible to do. I love the touch of her padded hand across my forehead as much as my mother's, her smile that puts cushioned dimples in her cheeks, which are always flushed, and makes creases at the tail ends of her eyebrows. Her eyes are violet-blue and study you from behind glasses with round gold rims.

"You're worse, you know," she'd say when I was worse, but this doesn't hide her kindness, which comes from her, like most of the feeling around the Pflagers, with a warmth that's golden in hue and curve. I've heard my mother say she often wished Penny didn't have to work —Penny handles the dry-goods section of the store, Mr. Pflager the building and hardware supplies—because she feels she and Penny could become close friends; and I've also heard her say, "Penny's one of the few people in this town I can talk religion with."

My father and I go into Pflager's. The wood floor is worn and warped and oil-darkened; the air smells of linoleum and denim jackets and new boards.

"Martin!" Mr. Pflager cries. "How you be?"

"Fine," my father says.

I've never known my father to say anything but "fine" when he's asked how he is, and I guess he always is fine; he hasn't been ill in his life, as far as I know, except for strep throat, and that was only once, and he didn't stay home from school for more than a day or two.

"What today?" Mr. Pflager asks.

"Your company, first, Eldon," my father says, and leans his elbows on the countertop, as Mr. Pflager leans across from him, and they begin to talk. My father loves to talk and I've often felt his real profession is making friends, and *that's* why he sells insurance now. I haven't moved since we came in the door. I never do. Just inside, at this end of the counter, is a square display case, with glass sides, that swivels on a pedestal of wood. Inside the case, on velvet-covered shelves, are wristwatches, pocket watches, clocks, and jackknives. I turn the case until my watch comes around. It lies on a middle shelf and I have to look up to it. It's a wristwatch with a black band that I've wanted since I could see in the case. Mickey Mouse stands in the center of it in red shorts, with one gold-gloved hand, its forefinger extended, pointing to the minutes, the other the hours. I've never wanted anything so much in my life. If there weren't a padlock on the case, I'd have stolen it by now, though I've never stolen before, not even cantaloupes or gooseberries or pear tomatoes from a neighbor's garden, as most of the kids do.

I know it's a sin to want an object so much, even if I don't steal it, and I know this though I've never taken catechism or been instructed by the Sisters. I *feel* it's a sin. The Sisters will have me in first grade soon enough (although I'll have to admit that since my father quit teaching, I can't help feeling I'll never have to go to school; and as it turns out, they *won't* have me). I used to be afraid of them and ran whenever they came outside; those white faces looking out from all that black, and gliding toward you as though there were nothing below the black but old curled birds' claws, rumors of heaven, beads that clashed, and beaks of crows. I dream of faces without arms or legs or anything beneath except black holes and big beads that pop and propel them, and I'd probably still be afraid but once I was letting Donny Ennis chase me around the playground, and checking over my shoulder to see how far behind he was, when I crashed into the skirts of one of them, and she said, "Oh, little boy, you've hurt my knee!"

My mother has become a Catholic. After living in this town for ten years without being one, she's become a Catholic, and I'm the cause. There's a story I've heard my father tell his best friends in hushed tones from the time I was three, that goes, "When Tim was born and Alpha came home from the hospital, one of the first things she did was call me in to her bed and say, 'Martin, I've decided. I want to take instructions in the faith. I want to become a Catholic.' And I was stunned. Because here after all these years—how many now?—without me saying a word, here it came out of the blue. 'Alpha,' I said. 'Are you sure? Are you sure this is what you want?' 'Yes,' she said. 'I'd like to start seeing Father Schimmelpfennig right away.' So she's been seeing Father ever since, although few people but Wilhomena know about it: for *three years*"—this has grown to *four years,* and then *five years*—"she's been seeing him! And she absolutely will not convert until she's resolved every doubt about the faith in her mind. Father says she's practically a saint. I've had no hand in any of this, by the way."

Every time my father reaches this point in his story, which is its end, I see my mother with her hands clasped and a halo around her, like a picture on a holy card, rising through the ceiling, through the upstairs and the roof of the house, and disappearing into the sky, and I wonder, How did I manage to cause this? What kind of power do I have? I hardly talk to anybody for fear something worse will happen. And how did this? She made her First Communion when I was on a vacation to my Grandma and Grandpa Jones's farm, but I can tell you what she wore: her navy high-heeled shoes, the blue dress with white polka dots and wide red belt, and a piece of lace over her hair. She wrote to Grandma Jones about it and told what I have and more. "Why do I want to know all this?"

Grandma asked, angry, as she read the letter, and I saw moisture behind her glasses, and then she said, in a changed voice, "Well, I imagine your dad is finally satisfied, ha?"

Penny comes from her part of the store, the dry-goods side, and says, "Oh, Martin, hello! How are you?"

"Fine."

"Where's Tim?"

"Here."

She comes over and stares down and I feel the violet-blue eyes envelop me with a warmth like flame. Then she sees where I've been staring—I've even glanced away from her; I can't keep my eyes off it—and says, "Why don't you have your dad pay you a wage so you can buy yourself that watch?"

Like my father in his story, I am stunned; this has never occurred to me; I had no idea—

"Where are you working today?"

"At Schommer's."

"Inside the *tavern?*" Penny is shocked!

"Down the basement."

"Oh."

"Putting in soil pipe for a new drain."

"How long will it take?"

"Just today, probably. We were there last week."

"Well, when you get on a house, on a big job, go on strike for a quarter an hour!"

"Maybe I'll try."

"Try nothing. Do it, you hear!"

My father comes over with a string of five-pound ingots of lead and a roll of oakum. "O.K., helper," he says. "Let's go."

We walk to Schommer's, down the echoing alleyway beween Schommer's and the hardware to the back door of the tavern, and go down the steps into darkness. He pulls a chain and the basement appears around us as if called. He kneels at the portable white-gas furnace that holds the ladle for melting lead, and pumps the plunger at its base before he lights it: when we're done, I'll give the screw top of the plunger a twist and let the leftover air escape in a *whish;* it's dangerous to leave the pressure built up, he's said. He starts the furnace and its high-pitched whine against the stone walls surrounds us. He

tears a five-pound ingot from the strip of five and drops
it into the ladle now. He lays a long piece of black soil
pipe in the trench he's dug, lays a level on it, makes a
rumbling sound of approval low in his throat, and I bring
over the cold chisels—one straight, one with a crook below the handle—and the ball-peen hammer, and hand
them to him.

He tears off a length of oakum and begins tamping it
into the joint of the soil pipe, all the way around, and
when I hear a solid chink of the chisel, I tear off some
more oakum and place it in his hand as he reaches behind to me. He takes his cap off by the bill and wipes the
sleeve of his work shirt over his forehead, where beads
of sweat are beginning to form, and moves the unlit cigar
he's chewing to the opposite corner of his mouth. He fin-
ishes filling and tamping the joint and I bring over the
asbestos rope he'll fasten around the fitting to hold the
lead in place when he pours it around the pipe.

He sets a Y on the floor, fits a piece of cut pipe into
one branch of it, and I hold it in place for him. He unwinds the oakum from the roll and presses it into the fitting, the black flange turned back. I like the oakum's
tarry, auburn smell; the salty, steamy smell that rises
from him, a metallic smell made more so by the smell of
his cigar; the way he sucks in air at the side of his mouth
to keep the cigar clenched tight in his teeth; being close
to his work shirt; the rainbow-colored whorls forming on
the molten lead in the ladle; the way the furnace doesn't
send up smoke but makes the dark air above it shimmy;
how the bulb above him makes his head and shoulders
look haloed and ablaze.

I know I'll never ask him for a wage. I don't want one
and don't want him to give me one, or our relationship
would change, and, anyway, since he's quit teaching, I've
been hearing around our house, more and more, the word
"afford." I know he couldn't afford one, and I know, too,
how much he loves to work with his hands—to build and
farm and garden and plumb—but I wonder what it was
that made him quit teaching; he was the principal, the
next to the highest, and then just quit. Even my mother
can't say. Was I the cause of this, too? Doesn't he think
I'd understand if he explained it to me? I hear the sound
of the furnace, the chink of the chisel, his sucks of air,

and watch sweat darken his shirt over his chest and run down his face and drop onto the dirt floor in beads as firm and circular as the beads of molten lead that spill from a fitting and roll in slithering colors over the powdery dirt, and I remember my grandmother reading my mother's letter to me, and wonder, *Is* he satisfied?

18

❦

PHEASANTS

Alpha went to the window in the pantry at the back of the kitchen, lifted the curtain, and looked down over the hedge toward Main Street; there was still no sign of him. The moonlight on the leaves and on the deserted walks wet with rain came with fall coldness through the glass to her face, feverish with anxiety and impatience, and she put her cheek against the pane. Two blocks down, a street lamp went on, lighting the side of the Town Hall, and a prowling cat made a blur as it bolted for cover in brown grass. Late with them again tonight. It was after nine and the children were in bed.

Delbert Faber came from the shack under the high blue-gray water tower, where he'd thrown the switch for the lights, and went along Main Street through the cone of the lamp, trailing illuminated vapors of spent breath, his head bowed, his hands in his pockets, and then did a sudden jogging side step. Drunk again. She'd hear about it from Mrs. Faber at the next card party, and what could she say to her? She couldn't sympathize with women who complained about their husband's drinking; she'd been through the fruitless world of that with her parents and herself. The only way a man stopped drinking was by taking a look outside himself at the world of his family and this real world (his interior, as he knew himself, was a hell), and if his wife was prattling on about his problem, or scolding or annoyed, or even concerned for his sake when he did look out, then she might as well be off in another century, or be another shot.

In the space between pane and sash, on a card there, was a picture of Joseph, Mary, and Jesus—the Infant

standing on the Virgin's knee with arms out like a balanced statue's—and on the other side, the side facing out,
were instructions for an act of perfect contrition, followed
by a list of life-insurance policies and their average yearly
rates, and, at the bottom, in the blunt type of a hand
stamp:

HOLY FAMILY LIFE INSURANCE
Martin Neumiller, Agent
P.O. Box 3 C
Hyatt, North Dakota
"Honest as my policies"

Surely one of the boys, not Martin, put the card there,
she thought, and blushed for him, and then felt exposed
to the whole village; when he told her he was going to
start selling insurance, she said, "You're the perfect one
to be selling it; nobody has a better life."

She let the curtain fall. She'd defend him against anybody who'd be charitable about the job. The home office
was so pleased with his sales they'd offered him the area
around Fargo-Moorhead, but he turned it down; he
wanted his children to grow up in the country, he said,
as he had and his father before him, and so on. They
sent him on a paid vacation to Custer and the Black Hills
with several other agents, but he wouldn't be moved. He
didn't have to be selling insurance in the first place. The
president of the board came to the house again this fall
and tried to persuade him to take back his teaching job,
even hinted that he might be in line for promotion to
superintendent, but Martin waves away his words. He
wouldn't teach again until he'd succeeded or failed at
selling insurance, he said, which might take years, and
whenever she tried to imagine that future she felt her
personality, or inner self, or good sense, or whatever, was
loosening at its roots and leaving her and could be swatted
like a fly.

Martin was one of the dozen men in the county with a
college degree, and he had a gift for inspiring the young;
they saw in his eyes that they could mature and still retain the purity of their beliefs; adulthood didn't mean,
necessarily, deception and double-standards and world-

weariness and guile. There was a dignity to his innocence, and it brought out trust and fearlessness in others, especially the young, who wouldn't stand for cant or sham; but last spring, at the end of the school year, he came to her and said, "I'm never going to make a decent wage teaching school, and you deserve a better life than this. I'm going to find a job that makes real money."

"No, no!" she wanted to cry out, but held herself silent. Fear burns all dreaming. She'd never interfered with his decisions and never would: "Wives, submit yourselves unto your own husbands, as unto the Lord." That had the rough-tumbling thunder and lightning of Paul in it, and was him, for sure, but wasn't even a remote part of her guiding source from above. Martin felt confined by the school and longed to get into the country and drive for miles over the plain again, meet new people, live outside his wife, be free of the invariable workday; and when she was a girl, when her family was about to leave another farm, she'd heard each time an argument as old as time itself:

"Why do we have to leave?" Her mother.

"Because we have to!" Her dad.

"Why?"

"Because I'm not getting ahead."

"Why can't you be satisfied for once with what you have?"

"Because I'm not getting ahead!"

There was no reason that could be used with a man in that condition; it was more a matter of whether you wanted to be married to him or not. And when she decided to marry Martin, she vowed she wouldn't sustain the argument any further, for the sake of her sons, if she had sons. Her mother and father had moved again, with Lionell, across the border into Minnesota, because her father believed the opportunities for him and the family were better there. Daddy, Daddy, she wanted to say to him, *Stop.* Mama would be satisfied with a sod shack, if you'd slow down enough to take root in the present, where she's waiting, as she always has, for a few minutes each day of the straightforward love you met and courted her with. You take yourself so seriously, Daddy, you're made of air!

She went into the kitchen and held her hand over the

oven vent at the back of the stove. Warmth was still rising from it. What was real in real life? She smoothed the tablecloth, which was already smooth, and straightened the silverware beside Martin's plate, and then felt emptied of energy, her current drained down the floor, and sank in a chair and put her face in her hands. She'd gone over and over the reasons she'd converted to the Church. It tied her to a past more ordered than hers. She felt her life lengthen backward, watching rituals she knew had been performed in the same way over the world for hundreds of years happen again; her mind had new strength and new freedom to roam now; old fears were given names, others disappeared, and doubts were discarded to gain a new end. The prayers held her within a written framework with her feet on the ground. The Church's scholarship and its mysteries were beyond the comprehension of any one man and wife, and she felt an infinity of thought and brotherhood about her. Also, it was easy to follow rules set up by somebody else. She'd balked at the idea of the infallibility of the Pope, and then Father said, "Think of him as far, far off, which he is, and transparent—a window you can look through and see the saints. Theirs are the lives to emulate, darling."

But none of this was enough to win her over, by and in itself. She'd converted because of the feeling of light, a light she sensed but couldn't quite see. The more she studied the Bible and the catechism, the stronger the light became, until she felt it just above her the way she could feel the sun on her back when she went down into their root cellar on the farm outside Dazey. Since her First Communion, the light had stayed.

But now she was pregnant again.

At this rate she'd catch up with the Russells. She'd become accustomed in their house to luxury of a kind, and when Martin bought the new bedroom set, she started to think how nice it would be to have the clothes she'd never had, a new stove, an electric sewing machine, and of how she never could if they kept having children. She was willing to try birth control, other than by rhythm, at least once, to see how she felt about it, but Martin wouldn't agree. When you were born a Catholic, it was in your bones and blood, while she could believe in a way that

Martin wasn't able to; entirely with her mind. Was that pride, plumed pride, again, or a worse sin?

Maybe her thoughts, through her touch, had been communicated to him and transformed in him into this ambition of late. Or maybe her conversion affected him more than he could comprehend; he seemed to need to be near his family much more, and they went to Illinois nearly every summer vacation, those three months, and to her parents only over holidays or for a weekend, usually. Martin sometimes adopted an all-inclusive indignant whine that was his mother all over again. He said he didn't want to hear any more of her ideas about religion; he just wanted to believe. His serpent? And why had she had the thoughts? There was such a rush and array of detail to daily life (to say nothing of the eternity of detail inside your mind), when your life was divided among husband and children and housework and keeping peace and social obligations and relatives and friends and the community, that there seemed no time or room left for the form there was in her mother's day. The particular mind. That she'd once kept a diary now seemed a vain and luxurious excursion into self-idolatry.

She went out of the kitchen and through the living room, where the oil heater cast an orange oval onto the linoleum, through the sliding doors into their bedroom, and sat on the bed. Across the room, in the vanity mirror, she could make out her reflection in the near dark, dim and featureless, a bluish form, and it was as if she were seeing through her face to another time. There was a grass-covered plain with nothing on it but a dark shape off in the distance, breaking the line of the horizon high up and thin. The grass was thick and lush green and was swaying and windswept by currents of the universe or a world of different times than this, and then it moved off and was a globe covered with the same grasses, hairlike, current disturbed—the earth as it had always been. Her breath caught. No, the view from one of the houses they'd lived in when she was a child. She couldn't remember which. Which house. They'd moved so much then. Oh, houses, help!

"Wasn't that pretty?" she said to her dark reflection, and felt her words inside swell up. Martin was too considerate to be a good salesman. He made sure a farmer understood a policy completely before he sold it to him. He'd spend an afternoon in a kitchen or farmyard, clarifying and advising, and then the prospect would decide he wanted more time to think about it, or say he didn't need a policy at all. So Martin was making less money than when he was teaching. He took part-time jobs to keep them in food and clothes, without having to draw on their savings, and since the spring had been working full time as a farm hand for Evan Savitsky; during the planting season they plowed until three in the morning, using the tractor headlights to see by, and for two weeks Martin slept over at the Savitskys'; these days, Mrs. Savitsky picked him up at six in the morning and then Evan brought him into town at night, drove straight to Main Street, and went into the tavern—Eichelburger's one night, Schommer's the next, so as not to show favoritism—and Martin, who didn't drink and never set foot in either place, had to walk home.

She asked him if Evan couldn't practice a little restraint and drop him off at home first, and Martin said, "A man should be grateful for what he gets and not expect to get one thing more."

The worst part to her was that he was working with his hands. The country here was so identical from mile to mile, it was the same as the sky above it; bleached bleak infinity. It was for the buffalo, for grazing creatures and tumbleweed that moved over it like cloud shadow made corporeal by a stroke of the Lord. When men uprooted it and fought it and tried to subdue it to their needs, it became a part of their outlook on life, was in whatever task they took up, was the direction they moved in, and they were never free of the bleakness or the dirt of it; or if they managed to transcend its encompassing futility and find success, it came in a way that was too unlimited to handle, with so few people to talk to and balance them off, and they saw others only as objects to be used, or not used—simply discarded—as if success had rendered them all powerful as the land. Rough clods. Servants of the earth. A hard taskmaster makes the worst sort of slave.

You could mold an outlook unattached to it with knowledge from other frames, and now Martin moved down highways or section roads, or through wheat fields or time, with individual grace and with "Martin" written all over him. His father would always be a farmer, no matter his present occupation, and her father, for all his travel and boastfulness and womanly bickering and affectations and worldly mind, carried the soul of the land inside him.

Sometimes she ached for more college education, even a simple stint of summer school again.

She lay back on the bed with a hand over her eyes. She was holding herself more at a distance from Martin. Many days she felt relieved when he left the house, even, but the children, and especially Tim, for some reason, filled her with a loneliness that had no limits, no bottom to touch or height to rise above, and then she couldn't wait for him to get home. She needed him now. This morning she'd been thinking about her mother as she looked when she was young, working at the cookstove, hoisting the cold butter crock up from the well, turning down bedclothes, and saw how these simple acts were given dignity and significance by her maternal hand; and then she remembered her mother's favorite photograph of her, taken when she was five or six, which her mother had had enlarged and gave as a wedding gift when she married Martin.

She's on the plain in a pair of baggy jumpers that fasten around her upper arms and just above her knee. Her limbs are plump and dimpled. She has on a sunbonnet that's too big for her, which must be her mother's, and part of her mother's affection for the picture. Its ties are hanging loose over her shoulders and throat. She's smiling into the camera's eye and holding out a child's bouquet of black-eyed Susans and blossoming grasses. The sky and the plain are nearly the same shade of gray, and are the only elements in the picture besides her, except for an irregular grayish puff or tuft just above her shoulder, as though rising from the bonnet, which must be a tree.

The more she thought of her mother, the more real the picture became, as if the sun were appearing from behind a cloud, and just when it seemed that all of the details were as lifelike as on the day the picture was snapped, she, the girl in jumpers, turned and walked out of sight. All that was left was the plain and the dark shape against the sky. A cottonwood tree.

She sensed the nearness of Martin and was up out of

the bed; she listened a second, and then started toward the other end of the house, and was passing the oval of the oil heater, when somebody started rapping at the back door. Who? When Martin got home, he came into the side porch, where he left his work clothes, and into the kitchen that way, never through the back door. She lifted the curtain and looked; the porch was empty, bare. A broom stood. The back door, like the others, was unlocked. Then the rapping came again, and was so close and loud it startled her. Only a neighbor, she thought, but as she went toward the door her knees weakened and sent tremors up inside her inner thighs. She opened the door enough to see out.

"Boo," Martin said. He was below her at the bottom of the steps, a smile on his dust-colored, sweat-streaked face. She opened the door wider on him.

"What on earth are you doing back here?" she asked, and was surprised at the alarm in her voice.

"This," he said, and lifted his arm and held out a brace of pheasants. Their green heads and shimmering breast feathers gleamed in the dim light, and the shifting eye rings were like poppies to her.

"Where did you get those?"

"Hunting! Where do you think?"

"You've been hunting?"

"Evan took me. Aren't they beauties, hon?"

His deep bass voice made a dense sound within the confines of the lean-to porch. He went to the edge of the swath of light from the kitchen, reached up, located a strand of wire on the low roof, and wrapped the wire around the pheasants' legs. They swung noiselessly from side to side, and then one wing outstretched and sliced into the light.

"I'll leave them there," he said. "I can clean them in the morning I guess."

"You should do it now."

"No, they'll be all right. It's plenty cold out. Well, maybe I should bleed them. No, no, it's too late for that. Oh, they'll be all right here. We'll have some for supper tomorrow night, and I'll take the rest to the locker, if there are any rest left."

He came up the steps and she went to embrace him, but he held up his hand. "You'd better wait for that till I wash first. I'm filthy." He tossed his cap onto the counter beside the sink. "How have you been?"

"The same."

"And the kids?"

"Fine."

"It's too bad I hardly get a chance to see them any more."

"Yes."

He dipped water from the pail into the basin in the sink and she saw his broad back as it swung from vessel to vessel (the municipal water was still too dirty to wash with), and was disturbed that he'd been hunting; it was the first time in five years. Five seasons ago, his closest friend other than Father, Ivan Savitsky, Evan's older brother, went pheasant hunting with his hired man, a full-blooded Sioux, and they got more than their limit and stopped in a roadside bar to celebrate and boast, and bought two cases of beer, and on their way home, on the curve outside Bowdon, went off the road in the car and rolled several times and were thrown from it and killed. Martin drove out when he heard and came home diminished and shaken, and said, "I'll never hunt again. Every time I lift a shotgun, I'll see that ditch. There were beer bottles and shotgun shells and blood and pheasant feathers everywhere. And them." Sometime later, when they went around the same curve in their car, she saw a pair of diamond-shaped signs with black X's on them, and they reminded her of her brothers, Conrad and Elling, who were killed in a similar accident, at one time, in the same car, too much for her now.

Martin looked over his shoulder. "Are you all right?" he asked. "Is everything all right, dear?"

"Yes."

"Are you sure?"

"Yes."

"What a day!" He put his glasses on the counter and plunged his hands into the basin and rubbed his face until his skin squeaked.

She took the food out of the oven, put it on the table, and sat in a chair facing his. The inadequacies of the mind, or else its omniscience. What was it trying to tell us in times of confusion? Was it a friend?

"Just after lunch, when Evan and I were getting the tractors ready, Evan's neighbor, Frank Crimmins, drove up. I figured something was brewing. Crimmins doesn't usually get out of bed until noon, and then he loafs around the house while his wife does most of the chores. He's only got a half section of land and hasn't even got his hay in yet!

"Well, he drove up and said that the pheasants were thick as grass down around Pingree. He said the three of us deserved the day off—that was some way of putting it, when you consider Evan has six sections to get in before the freeze, and that I have no say in it, and that Crimmins is perpetually off—he said we deserved the day off and should take it off, by Lord, and go get some pheasants for ourselves before the sportsmen came up from all over and took them from us. Oh, he can talk a stream.

"Evan asked me if I'd like to go, which surprised me. I know he's afraid of falling behind this year, even with me on as a hand, and then Ivan—But there's a split in that man!"

Martin turned his glistening face to her, looking blind without his glasses. "As conscientious as he is about work, it takes second place to him if there's an opportunity for some sport. Crimmins saw that, too, and started fast-talking again. I told Evan I didn't have a license and, anyway, had sold my gun since— He said I didn't need a license and could use his old 20-gauge. He was already convinced."

Martin slipped his glasses on and leaned against the washstand and crossed his arms. "But he wouldn't leave that easily, either, not Evan. No, we were out by the gas tank, greasing up the tractors, as I said, and he pointed out a chicken by the garden, about thirty feet off, and whispered, 'See that? Watch. I'll check with the powers that be and see if my aim's on. If it's on, we go. If it's not, to hell with it.'

"He held up the gun and gave it a hard pump, and the chicken took off squawking, flapping its wings, with a big glob of grease on it. Oh, oh, ya ha! It just goes to show you the *luck* that man has! So we got out the guns, took off in separate cars, and went down to Pingree, and within an hour we all had our limit, all three of us, and that's not all. I got some work done on my own, too."

He came up and kissed her along the forehead. "But, you. What about you? How was your day?"

"Fine."

"You didn't get overtired again?"

"No."

"You're sure you're not?"

"Yes, I'm sure."

He passed his hand over her hair, and she glanced up and saw him staring beyond her at the wall clock.

"Is it that late?" He sat and helped himself to the peas and potatoes and canned-salmon loaf. "I'd better get moving, then. I'll be late the way it is."

"What for?"

His fork hesitated in the air and his large eyes, nearly circular in their intensity, studied her in disbelief. "What *for?* It's Friday night!"

"Oh. I forgot."

"You made salmon loaf!"

"The other, I mean." On Fridays he played pinochle with Dr. Koenig, Eldon Pflager, William Runyon, and a dozen other parishioners, at Father Schimmelpfennig's.

"You should know by now I'm as regular as clock-work," he said, and clucked his tongue. "I mentioned getting some other work done. Evan dropped me off at the Stahls' and Hyerdahls'. I've told you about them." His voice suddenly drew away and became more guarded with her. "They're both on the line for new policies, and I talked with them while Evan waited the car for me. Then we tried to finish up an eighty with the pony drills. Then the rain came. I'm sorry I'm late. I'm not sure about Stahl, but I'm positive Hyerdahl will buy, and that'll be the third policy this month. Won't that be nice?"

"It will."

"Weell," he said, prolonging the word in the local farmers' way, so it sounded nearly like "wheel," which irritated her, and then pushed his plate aside. "I'd better get going now."

He went back to the bedroom to put on a suit. She cleared the table and dumped the oily, grayish water out of the washbasin, and then took down an aluminum pan and started the dishes in the sink. Hands, strong and warm, smelling of after-shave, gripped her shoulders hard. She turned, startled and annoyed, and the annoyance stayed as she studied him, sharpening her perception of his necktied chest and face and lips, and then she was angry at herself for being aroused.

"Are you sure you're all right?" he asked.

"Yes. You frightened me."

Their eyes met and held. He narrowed his, and then leaned and lifted her and she turned her face, grazing his close stubble with her chin, and fitted her mouth to the familiar shape of his. Then her feet touched and she stepped back and couldn't look at him.

"Alpha, it's the only time I ever go out in this town."

"I know."

"I have two cigars, and most nights win a couple dollars, especially with Father as my partner, and those dollars help."

"I know that. Go on."

"I'll stay if you insist."

"No, go your way."

He went to the door and snapped its lock for a change. "Why don't you wait up for me?" He backed down the steps looking uncomfortable and ashamed and closed the door.

She breathed out and leaned against the sink to ease the moist swelling in her and a nimbus formed around the light bulb above the table, and then trembled and sent out shafts of incipient tears. These stories of his were his way of avoiding whatever he was afraid of. What if she'd taken the time to tell him about the picture, and how she'd felt about it? She probably never would now. She wiped her cheek with the heel of her hand and straightened her dress. She wouldn't be weak like every other woman she knew, all of whom she hated.

She grabbed up an oleomargarine package and broke the pellet of dye at its center and squeezed and kneaded the package until the lard-colored margarine turned a uniform gold, then threw the package on the counter, went into the living room, switched on her lamp, sat in her rocker, and took *The Ordeal of Richard Feverel* off the table and opened it at her marker, a scrap of dress material; Adrian, the wise, fat, self-anointed philosopher, was giving another blowhard's lecture to young Richard. She closed the book with a bang.

On the wall across the room was a set of corner shelves

Martin's father had built and sent to her. In the box along with them he'd enclosed a white statuette of an elephant, which tasted, she discovered, like alum, or worse. The boys wanted it for their playroom, but she put it up on the shelves when Martin installed them. They were such a clutter now she couldn't see the thing. She moved her tongue over a canker sore to a molar at the back of her mouth that was so hollowed out she could fit the tip of her tongue into its sharp-edged crater. She hoped none of her children inherited her teeth. The worst sins of avarice and ambition and greed rose out of poverty, somebody said. "For the *love* of money is the root of all evil." Paul again.

There was a knock again at the back door. Martin. He'd decided not to play cards. Home with her. She ran into the kitchen and unlocked the door and pulled it wide.

A tall man with a hooked nose and a shock of curly hair showing in front of the raised bill of his baseball cap stood on the top step, only inches from her—the young man who'd bought the lot across from their garden, dug a basement with a tiling spade, built a little house, and moved into it in the spring with his new wife. She was so sure it would be Martin she might as well have embraced the kid. Man.

He raised the bill of his cap. "Hi."

"Hello."

"Is your husband in?"

"No."

"Oh. Well, I was out hunting today and got my limit of pheasants, and it's too much for just my wife and I, so we were wondering if you folks might like a couple of them."

"We would, usually, any other time—" She looked up and saw that his brown eyes, moist in the light, were studying her with a calculating, interested stare. One eye was slightly crossed in a handsome way. She made a gesture over his shoulder and he turned. "Martin was out and got his limit, too."

He slid his hands into his back pockets, his elbows turned out, and began swinging them back and forth. "You won't need any more from me then, I guess."

"No, I'm sure not."

"My wife, she said I should come and ask, so here I am, asking." He made an amused gurgle at the back of his throat.

"Thank you."

"You're welcome."

She stared at the floor, conscious of his eyes traveling over her hair, her face, the front of her dress, and felt like saying, with her father's fire, Are you the sort who'd take on a mother of four who's got another in the oven?

"Maybe I'll go see old Runyon," he said. "I doubt if he hunts, and they might like some of these there then." He held up his hand. Another bouquet. He must have had them lying behind him.

"He'll be away at Father's. You could ask his wife."

"I will ask her."

"Well, thank you."

"You're welcome again."

She closed the door, her heart beating hard inside her dress, went to the rocker and took her sewing basket and threaded a needle with trembling fingers, and then worked a light bulb down into the toe of a stocking lying in her lap, which looked big as a floor. The stocking was one of Martin's that dated from Tim, and if it were worn any thinner she'd be darning air.

"Mom?"

The voice came from the boys' bedroom. She waited to make sure that whoever of them had called was awake. Boys' dreams. The frittering they should let be done.

"Mom?"

It was Charles, awake, so she moved her thighs to move the basket, stood, put it in her rocking rocker and went heavily over and set the door of their room ajar. "Yes? What is it?" Still the alarm in her voice.

"Is Dad home yet?"

"No. Now, go back to sleep."

"I thought I heard him talking."

"You couldn't have. He's not here."

"Where is he then?"

"Oh . . ."

"Was somebody else here?"

"No, nobody. Go to sleep now. Good night."

"Turn on the light. I can't see your face. I want to *see* it."

"It'll wake your brothers, you fool."

"I'm awake." The voice of Jerome beside her. "Why don't you tell us a story, and maybe Dad'll be back by then."

Why did she lie to them? Why did Jerome always have an idea of what to do?"

"We'd wake Tim," she said.

"*Tim?*" Jerome said. "I doubt it. Tim sleeps like the dead."

Where had he picked up such an expression? But it was true, perhaps, metaphorically at least, and, in any case, she didn't care whether Tim woke; she needed the company of them all. She found the pin-up lamp inside the door and twisted its switch and light fell over the foot of Jerome and Charles's double bed; gray clipper ships sailing out over silver blue. She went to the cot along the wall in semi-darkness, where Tim lay, and covered him better, and then sat on the edge of the older boys' bed. "Now, then. What is it here?"

"Just a story," Jerome said.

"Where's Dad?" Charles asked.

"At Father Schimmelpfennig's."

"What's the matter?" Charles asked.

"Nothing."

"Is something the matter with Dad?"

"No, nothing's the matter with him."

"Well, if he's at Father's, wasn't he home first to change?"

"Of course. You're right. That's right. He was."

"Was he in and out so fast you almost forgot?" Jerome asked.

"Just about." She bowed her head. Now What?

"Tell us about Grandpa Jones and the billy goat," Jerome said, and grinned at the story, which he knew by heart.

"No," Charles said, forgetting everything to rise above Jerome and see her more fully. "Tell about yourself, when you went to town on the pony you bought for Lionell, and it was snowing."

"I'll tell them both."

They struggled around in a noisy uproar of covers until

they were sitting with their backs against the headboard. Jerome brushed his hair aside and she saw that the youthful blond was going from it, and that they both needed haircuts again. Their eyes were as luminious as their father's and fixed on her with his intensity for the sign that meant she'd begin, but a current of feeling scattered the order in her and she took them in her arms and held them against her. "Oh, God!" she cried.

"What?"

"Mom! What's the matter?"

She saw the pheasants' plumage catching the light from the kitchen as they swung from the wire, and that other light, the light she sensed above her, dimmed and for a moment was gone, and she felt that a shadow of harm would fall from her over Martin and the children and be lifted away, when it was lifted, by hands other than hers. How could hands other than hers, which had helped shape them, hold them from harm?

There was a rustle from the cot across the room, and Tim sat up, his eyes startled and wide, and cried, "Mom! Hey, Mom, what are you *doing* with those two guys?"

19

✿

OSAGE

The Neumillers are on the road to the farm the Joneses have moved to, near Osage, Minnesota. Their car, a '47 Chevrolet bought second-hand from Father Schimmelpfennig, is arranged as it usually is for trips of more than a hundred miles, with a steamer trunk wedged in the well between front and back seats and covered with blankets, so the boys can lie down and sleep if they wish, and pillows piled everywhere. Marie alternates between the front and the back, depending upon her whims, and Alpha, six months pregnant, sits in the passenger seat and orchestrates the moods of the children and the moodiness that comes over Martin when he has to drive with all six of them in the car.

Outside Valley City, out of the violet sky, snowflakes appear in a tentative stir, and beyond Moorhead come down in a flurry and form a shifting screen around them as the wind picks up and begins to wail across the flatlands of the Red River Valley. Snow goes slithering over the road in snaking sheets and makes the slow-moving car appear to be traveling sidewise. In bordering fields billows of it rise like many-headed, amorphous ghosts and turn into a wind-carried curtain over fifty feet high, with edges that can't be seen and whirlpools and cloud fragments coiling inside, that comes sweeping over drifts where cornstalks show, past a telephone pole, a snow fence, and hits the side of the car. It yaws and shudders on bad shock absorbers. They adjust their winter coats.

Most other cars have left the road, but an occasional semi comes barreling past in the opposite lane, dragging behind it a long concussion of sound that for a moment knocks the snow aside. Jerome and Charles kneel, their elbows on the front seat, and cheer the trucks, and call out the names of towns—Dilworth! Glyndon! Hawley!— until Martin tells them to sit back and be quiet so he can concentrate on the road. He leans toward the wheel, as if the inclination can bring them to their destination quicker, and wipes at the icing windshield with the backs of his bare fingers. He scratches at it with his nails. Dorsals of snow begin to rise from the road like spines and fins of creatures rising from below, and thud under the tires.

St. Michael and the dragon, Alpha thinks. Er, *George.*

Tim lies down on the trunk. There's a heater fan be-low the driver's seat, which he's often inspected by laying his face on the fibery bristles of the floor mat, and he can hear its whir and tinny blades tinging against candy wrappers and cigar cellophanes. He feels the warm draft of it above the trunk. In half sleep he remembers waking like this with the sound of water sloshing. It lay in the floor well and spotted the dun fuzz of the seats. He rose and saw a gray plain of it as high as the car bumper in every direction, blended with a dim sky by a bright mist. "Where are we, Dad?"

"West Fargo, I think."

A man in fishing waders and a black slicker came floundering out of the mist, splashed over a guardrail, and leaned slipping on the driver's side. His eyes were wandering and hard. Tim's father cranked the window down past him.

"What is it?" he asked.

"Pardon?" The man's eyes wouldn't focus anywhere. "What's this?"

"A flood. A flood. Go back. Sandbags gone." He slipped and almost fell, and shook his head to clear it.

"My Lord, man," Tim's father said. "How long have you been up?"

"Three days," the man said, and slipped again with a splash.

Tim falls asleep.

Charles, angered because he can't see the countryside, lies down on a pile of pillows and falls asleep.

Jerome feels like a sentinel guiding the car and keeps his eyes on the road until his father says, "Ah, thank God, here's the turnoff, isn't it?"

"Yes."

His father heaves a tremulous sigh and Marie cries out, as if to share his release, and throws her arms around him. The road swings away, fence posts, the clutch pedal making a wallop, evergreens across the window in spiky patches, and with muffled thunks and a slam that sends Jerome flying, the car goes backward into the ditch. Its nose points toward flake-streaked blue, the Minnesota sky, and it's balanced so precariously it rocks from wheel to wheel as his father grabs for the keys to shut it off. Marie is screaming.

"My stars," Alpha says. "Is anybody hurt in here?"

Nobody says they're hurt.

"Is everybody sure they're all right?" she says. "Move around a little. But don't jump up and down! We're on a seesaw here."

Marie screams and the boys say, Yes, Yes, Yes, sure, of course they're all right.

"Well, I'm not, not yet," Marie says. "Let me sit a minute till I stop shaking. I was sure we'd roll."

"We're lucky," Alpha says, and laughs.

"Oh?" he says. "I'll have to walk to the folks now, I suppose, and have Dad or Lionell come out with the tractor to get us out of this. What is it to their place from here? A mile, would you say?"

"More like two, dear," she says, and laughs again.

"I better get going, then, before this storm gets worse."

She pulls out extra blankets and dispenses them. He eases out, letting in flakes that melt where they settle on the seat and dash, stops the car's seesawing, and slams the door. He waves, and then takes off in a trot down the road, and soon is engulfed as if by smoke. Alpha turns in her seat.

"You back there, all three of you, I want you to thank your guardian angles right now that none of you were hurt."

Guardian angel? Jerome thinks. Goodness, I haven't believed in a guardian angel since I was seven.

Three

20

THE NEW HOUSE

One winter later, Martin's only consolation until the end of January was a line he'd learned in college when he took the role of Claudius in a classroom scene from *Hamlet:* "When sorrows come, they come not single spies, but in battalions." And after January there was no consolation. The sorrows began even before they moved from North Dakota.

One morning he read a letter at the breakfast table with all of them present including Susan, the baby, who was learning to sit up and behave in her high chair. The letter was from his father, who'd incorporated his business and moved to Forest Creek, and was building a new house there; only the basement of it was completed, he said, so they'd set up temporary housekeeping in it, which was rough, what with Tom and Davey, though twenty and fourteen, at one another so much it made it seem the whole family was there; but the main reason he wrote was to say that Forest Creek had formed a consolidated school here with Pettibone, and now the school board was looking for a new principal. Alan Spear, that fellow they'd rented the tenant house from in '39 and '40, was president of the board and had said that Martin's qualifications sounded perfect. Would he apply?

He folded the letter and turned to her. Well?

Well? Since he'd gone back to teaching, wasn't he satisfied with the job he had? Oh, of course, but there wasn't much chance of getting ahead in North Dakota, especially in a village this size. Wasn't he the superintendent of the high school now? Yes, that was true. And didn't he make enough to keep them happy? More than enough. Then

271

would it be wise to give up the job he had, and give up the house, and move to Illinois, where it was so hot and humid, when a job hadn't actually been promised him yet?

Didn't she like Illinois? Not especially. Well, they'd only been there in the summer and he imagined that was why. At first his father hadn't liked it either, but now he called it God's country, or had once. Then why did he come back to North Dakota so often? Well, North Dakota was his home state. And wasn't it theirs? Yes, sure, but his father had done so well for himself down there, and maybe they could, too. Wouldn't she like a nicer house? This was the house she'd always wanted; how could there be a better one? Well, his only reason for considering the idea at all was that his father was getting older and wanted the family reunited; she knew that, didn't she? Yes, she said. And anyway, he'd always felt they'd moved to Illinois themselves, back in '38 when the family moved, and they'd be in Illinois right now if she hadn't come walking across that wheat field with the telegram from Rynerson here at Hyatt. She knew that, didn't she?

Yes, she said.

He took her hand in his. Wouldn't she like it if they were in a bigger town where he could make more money and she could have more friends?

She bowed her head the way she did only when she was unhappy or very ashamed, as if she'd heard the news she'd waited for until this moment in her life. She said the one situation she wouldn't tolerate was living for any length of time with his parents.

Oh, of course not! She'd heard what his father had said about Tom and Davey and the new house, hadn't she? The situation in that basement wouldn't be fit for another footstool, much less them.

She couldn't impose four children and an infant on his parents, now that they were growing older and their own children, or at least most of them, had moved out and were living away from home; his parents were ready to return to the state that couples can share only twice in their lives—before any children are born, and after all of the children are gone.

"You'll take this job, I'm sure of it, so the first thing I want you to do after that is find us a place to live."

"I will, Alpha. Goodness gophers!"

He went to Illinois and interviewed with Spear and Spear said the job was as good as his. There were few houses to be found—nobody seemed to move in or out of the area much—but he finally came across a six-room, semi-furnished bungalow in Pettibone, with a yard of box hedge and flower-bordered paths (a quaint touch), which would be comfortable enough until he was established in the job; the rent was fifty-five dollars a month, and the owners of the house, an elderly and reserved but decent country couple, promised to sell any pieces of furniture Alpha might want for a matter of dollars. They were moving back to their farm outside Forest Creek and had all the furniture they wanted in the farmhouse there, they said.

While he was in Illinois, he also found a mover, a trucker, actually, who did commercial hauling and had worked for his father on and off over a period of years, and the man offered to move him for such a reasonable price he couldn't refuse. He went back to North Dakota with good news for Alpha and the family, and a new house.

The trucker arrived ten days late. He was hauling lime for corn and couldn't leave Illinois when he wanted, he said, and during the time they waited they lived out of boxes that had already been packed, and slept on mattresses from the dismantled beds—an adventure for the boys, but for Alpha barely endurable. She was pregnant again. Father offered a room in his house to her and the girls, but Alpha said no; she wanted to be with the children; she wanted all of them together for now.

Then the trucker finally did pull into the drive, and Martin saw he'd been a fool to attempt to save money by hiring the fellow; his two trucks weren't moving vans but open farm trucks fitted with cattle racks.

"Well, I hope it doesn't rain between here and Illinois," Alpha said.

The trucker and his driver were tired from the trip and slept on the floor overnight and shaved the next morning in a bathroom bare except for fixtures, while Charles and Tim stared at them as though they'd never seen a man shave. Hadn't they ever watched *him*, Martin wondered. He helped the truckers load the big pieces first.

"Take good care of my piano!" Alpha cried.

Father came over in the afternoon and supervised, and then Dr. Koenig and his wife showed up, then the Pflagers and the Runyons and the Ianacconas, and Wilhomena and Mrs. Liffert—then the Savitskys with baskets of chicken and potato salad for a picnic, and by the time the trucks pulled out for Illinois, there were a few dozen townspeople, and at least as many children, in their hedge-bordered yard; the adults kept up a cheerful-seeming chatter, but the children—the Rimskys, the Schonbecks, Everett Ritter, Susie Eichelburger, Douglas Kuntz—stood off at a distance, silent and grave, as though Jerome and Charles and Tim were strangers who'd survived some sort of accident and were still touched by their brush with death, and were meant to be merely observed. And then Jake Ennis, Donny's father, drove up in the county road grader, hopped down from its high yellow cab, and came over and said thank you and then goodbye to Alpha and Tim.

Father had held a farewell party for Alpha and Martin two weeks before and most of these people had been there, and seeing them now was too difficult and complicated to be borne by somebody who could say goodbye only once, if then, like Martin. He looked over their heads toward Alpha. She was giving the baby to Mrs. Pflager, and then she went over and took Jerome and Charles by the hands and turned away, and he realized that she wanted to walk through the house one last time with them, which he saw as the perfect way to help bring this part of their boyhood to an end, and then somebody took hold of his hand and started shaking it again.

He got them into the car, at last, in a daze, and drove away from the house with their friends standing in the yard waving hands and handkerchiefs and crying, "Good luck! Good luck!" They were out of town and onto the straight-edge of the highway, and had passed the trucks burdened with their belongings and covered with tarps, when he said, to ease the silence among them, "Well, did you see anything in the house that we missed or left behind?"

"No," Alpha said.

"Yes, sir," Jerome answered. "There was a *Fargo Forum* right in the middle of the living-room floor."

"Hunh!" Martin said, and for some reason couldn't remove from his mind the image of that newspaper lying alone in the big empty house.

It was crowded with them all in the car, along with their luggage, plus the necessities to care for a one-and-a-half-year-old; the boys wouldn't sleep, or behave, and he swung wildly at them once in the back seat with one hand on the wheel, something he'd vowed never to revert to. Susan was wailing most of the way and was so restless it was a torture for Alpha, who was four months along, to have to hold her in her lap. And Marie wanted to be there also, since that's where Susan was, not knowing yet how to compete with a girl, and a younger one at that. They drove straight through and arrived in Illinois at 3 A.M., too unreasonable an hour to stop at his parents', and went to the house he'd rented in Pettibone.

"I'll open it up and get the lights on," he said. "Then we'll take some of this in and make it a little comfortable. It doesn't look as bad inside. They know we want to buy at least two of their beds, so that many will be here."

He went onto the porch and dug in the letter box, where the key was to be left, and found his nails scraping tin. Then he heard voices inside. He stepped to a window, cupped his hands, and was looking into eyes that widened and went retreating from him. Whose? The porch light came on. Hinges creaked, and an elderly man, the owner, stood behind the screen door in undershorts. What's happened to him, Martin wondered; he'd gained at least thirty pounds, his face shining fat, and there was such unyielding defiance in his eyes his pupils appeared red. "This is some hour to show up," the man said.

"What do you mean? Here *you* are and we agr—"

"The wife's had a change of heart."

"But it's July twenty-fifth!" Martin said, as though the date could make the man's pounds disappear until he vanished. "You've had two weeks to be out! My wife, my kids—" He turned toward the car, to indicate the misery entrapped there, and saw Alpha's pale face, like a pale constellation, shining out from behind the car window on him.

"The wife's decided we're staying here in town, and that's that."

"Why didn't you at least let me know, for God's sake?"

"I lost that card of yours."

"Why didn't you tell my father?"

"Who's he?"

"But surely you can't—I mean, my Lord! I've paid the first months's rent and the deposit!"

"Take it easy." The man shifted back and was invisible in the darkness. A light deeper in the house went on, it went off, and then the screen door creaked out and the man handed him a sheaf of bills, and Martin knew without counting that it was his one hundred and ten dollars. The screen door quickly closed and was locked fast.

"Just what the *hell* do you think you're doing?" Martin said.

"Watch it, this is our house."

"I mean—" Martin stared into his eyes and had an impulse to put out the light in them, blast at them through the screen and do the man the violence of the bloodiest of his dreams, but this was *his* fault; he'd done business as he always had, on his word and a handshake, which he'd never do again.

He turned away and went down the porch and out the walk toward the celestial geometry of the children around Alpha's waiting face.

*

There was no recourse. They went to his parents' to spend the night; they stayed on. They stored their furniture in an unfinished garage attached to the half-finished house and covered it with tar paper, blankets, and rugs that they unpacked. There was nothing for rent in the area that wasn't too small or frailly falling apart, or priced beyond their means, so he decided to find a place to buy instead, on the basis of his job, and started searching in a widening area, then a wider one yet, and gradually felt the search become halfhearted, helpless, without hope, conducted mostly for Alpha's sake, as he walked through tumbledown farmhouses and lemons and white elephants, thinking that when he wrote that book of his, this chapter would have to be headed "The Way Things Happen to Me Now."

And while he looked, his parents and Tom and Davey and Alpha and himself and the children—eleven in all— slept and cohabited and tried to sort out themselves and their lives in the basement. Only one room of it was partitioned off, the room his parents slept in, and hanging up blankets for privacy was a joke, and then not a joke, and then abandoned. The meals were picnics outdoors, unless it was raining, and then they ate off card tables or the maze of their many-sized beds. A plastic curtain was strung across one corner where there was a floor drain, forming a makeshift shower that was used by everybody except the little girls, who had their baths in a laundry sink of slate. Shower times were assigned each night by Martin's father.

A blight of box-elder bugs moved in from the State Forest at the edge of town, and Alpha, who'd never seen the insect, was appalled by its roachlike appearance. Trunks of trees appeared to pulse and waver from the black-and-orange-shaded masses of bugs in motion on them; they dropped from branches onto the picnic tables, into hair and food, and traveled so much on the sidewalks you couldn't step anywhere without crushing some, and covered one sun-warmed side of the house in a trembling epithelium. They got inside and down to the basement, which was perpetually damp and smelled of lime and cement paint and the overworked sump hole, and that week Alpha and the baby went to bed with bad colds.

The boys dug a foxhole in one corner of the yard, camouflaged it with branches, and slept in it on the nights when it wasn't raining. One day they'd enlarged it to twice its size and were digging tunnels off its sides and adding on more foxholes. "Should you be doing that?" Martin asked. "You're ruining Grandma and Grandpa's yard."

"Grandpa said it's O.K. This hasn't been landscaped yet."

They were picking up a technical jargon from his father, who let them trail after him while he worked and answered their questions with thoroughness and absolute patience. Martin felt he gave only commands and that they were wearying of him as a father.

"But why make it bigger? Somebody could fall in and get hurt. Why can't you leave it the way it was?"

"We're building a house."

They'd go crawling through the caves and labyrinths formed by the furniture in the garage, and spend hours searching for a particular piece they remembered and missed, and then emerge dazed in the sunlight, sullen and bewildered, as if they'd been tricked into believing their lives were intact.

Davey built a tree house in the branches of an old oak, and there *he* sometimes slept. He'd attached a homemade machine gun to the tree that clacked and rattled as he turned a crank; he had war-surplus materials and souvenirs that Fred and Jay (whom Davey called "Dingle") had brought back from overseas, and he and Jerome and Charles were always dressed up in Army equipment and shooting at one another. Would Jerome and Charles, born during a war and aware of the newly awakened force that had ended it, be marked by that in any way, Martin wondered. Oh, probably not, but merely to have to speculate about its effects on them added to his guilt and sense of failure as a father. Did they think him unmanly because he hadn't served in the war? He was the last male school administrator left in a three-county area at the time of the Battle of the Bulge, and was expecting at any moment to be called up, when the president of the school board came to him and said there was a movement underway to get him a deferment. He said he didn't want one, or to be made a special case of, and would have no hand in it, but the board seemed determined and must have gone ahead with its plans; he was never called up.

When he wasn't looking for a house, he worked part-time for his father or for Jay, who was a plastering contractor, and once spent fourteen hours tiling a church basement; being on his knees for so long seemed to exacerbate an old injury: when he was twelve, he'd been thrown from a hayrake and hit a rock with his right knee. It hadn't bothered him for twenty-five years—indeed, he'd forgotten it; it was his father who reminded him—but now he felt heated cinders were being pressed against his kneecap whenever he put weight on the leg, and his knee became so inflamed it wouldn't flex.

A doctor from Pettibone, the only doctor around, a watery-eyed, evasive man who seemed so rich with ideas of treatment it was a trial for him to decide on one, put heat packs on the knee, then ice packs and Denver mud,

and then tried pills and a series of injections; then decided
the knee would have to be lanced, so he lanced it in the
basement, without anesthetic, and then lanced it again,
and lanced it yet a third time in still another spot. The
swelling stayed. Martin had to walk with a cane and be
helped up and down stairs, and began to feel like an old
man near the end of his life. Ed Jones without the vinegar
in him. He'd wake in the middle of the night, groaning
with pain, and realize from the tenseness around that he'd
waked everybody in the basement.

And then his mother caught Jerome and Charles smoking in the foxhole, and brought them to him, pulling each
by an ear, and said it was a disgrace for children their
age to be smoking cigarettes. Martin agreed as she shoved
the boys down in front of him and went off. He'd caused
such uncertainty and confusion in their lives, he'd have
to remedy it soon, he thought, but now shook his head at
them, prodded the floor with his cane, and said, "Please,
boys, please don't smoke till you're older. Especially
around Grandma, promise?"

One night as he lay awake in the basement, empty of
the desires that had kept him awake as a young man (for
he no longer felt young), he recalled, with a clarity that
made him wipe away the recollection, that some of the
happiest times in Alpha's life had been when they moved.

*

He found a house at last, or, rather, his father found one,
in Pettibone; a long, plain, unhandsome place at an angle
across one corner of a block, facing a busy intersection.
A concrete drive abutted against its front foundation and
fanned out to the streets on either side. In the thirties or
forties the place had been somebody's grandiose notion of
a service station; there was a large central part, a small
house in itself, with a second story and a basement, where
the station attendant and his family had lived, with matching wings extending from either side of it—wings which
were oversized double garages, thirty feet deep and more
than twenty feet across, with large windows around them,
and the wing on the left hand had been closed up and
partitioned off and made a part of the house; "the other
side of the house," as Alpha immediately called it.

The walls inside were finished with stucco of a Spanish sort, textured into high, pointed nibs, a technique he'd thought was used exclusively on exteriors, and when Alpha saw it, she said, "If one of the kids fell against that, they could cut themselves or put out an eye."

"Yes, Alpha, they could."

With Susan in her arms, she looked back over her shoulder and cried, "And fix this screen! If there's one thing I can't stand, it's a bunch of those big-ass blue-and-black barnyard flies buzzing around all of my holes."

The front yard was merely enough to make a few passes over with the mower, and there was a chevron of stunted hedge at the streetside corner of it. The house stood on a pair of lots, nearly a quarter of a block, so there was a back yard with plenty of room for the children to play, and directly in front of the house, where a third street Y'd away from the busy intersection, was a triangular park with a shuffleboard court, a flagpole, and a seven-foot slab of gray granite that held a plaque commemorating the men who'd served in the Great War. All the streets around the park and leading away from it were overarched with magnificent elms.

They moved in. Their furniture and belongings stood around in disarray until the gravitational lines of this new life became established and drew everything into place, and meanwhile became covered with plaster and years-old accumulated dust from inside the walls as the remodeling began. Alpha wanted to spade up a corner of the back yard for a garden, or at least start a few flower beds, but they found that old crankcase oil and a cinderlike compound used to absorb oil and grease had been scattered over the entire back yard, and the soil wouldn't support anything but weeds and the hardy variety of grass that grew there in browning patches. Beside the alley was an incinerator, made of four sidewalk grates set on end and wired together, and Alpha put in hollyhocks around it.

Alan Spear showed up at the house one morning when Martin was working in the kitchen, and stared around with what seemed embarrassment at the torn-up room. Martin apologized for it. Spear waved his words away and asked about the remodeling, to be polite and to have questions to ask, it seemed, and then said that he was new at the job of heading up a school board; there were the other members to contend with, and he hadn't realized that the superintendent had so much say in hiring teachers, especially the principal, who was the one he had to work the closest with over the year, or more, if he was staying on, of course.

Martin sat at the table and laid his hammer on it. "What you're trying to say, Alan, is my job has been given to somebody else."

"I'm afraid so. Yes, it has, Martin."

Martin turned the hammer over. "All right, I'll teach English or Math or P.E. I'll even take a job in the junior high school."

"We wouldn't want somebody of your caliber and experience to take just any job, Martin. And it's so late on in the year now, I don't know; I'm afraid maybe most of your real good openings might be filled up. I want you to know that I take full responsibility for this."

Martin stared at him and Spear's eyes moved away. "Are they, Alan?"

"What?"

"Are all the openings in the district filled?"

"I'm afraid they are, Martin."

Every other school in the county had filled its openings, too. Martin started working for Jay as a mixer and hod carrier on a plastering crew. He'd been passed over for the job because of his religion, he believed, but wouldn't think of mentioning that to anyone, especially Alpha; the Neumillers and a few rural families, plus some elderly women, were the only regular parishioners of the Pettibone Catholic church. Everybody in town was Methodist. The superintendent was, and the superintendent and Spear and most of the members of the school board belonged to the Masonic Lodge. Those rings they wore. And Martin's father often said that his only difficulty when he moved here and began his business was getting people in the area to realize they could trust a Catholic.

Alpha never really recovered from the summer cold she'd caught in that basement and, with every new arrival of bad fortune and reversal, drew deeper into her illness, as behind a screen from which she looked out in dimness on the six of them. None of the furniture was moved except to get it out of the way of the remodeling. She sat for hours with her head bowed. The Pettibone doctor said she probably had some mild form of jaundice, prescribed iron pills and eating a lot of liver, and said not to worry, but seemed irritated with her for continuing to be ill.

She fell behind in her housework and fatigued so easily she couldn't even shop. One night she said she'd sent Tim to the store to get some canned soup and he'd come back close to tears, because the lady clerk had said to him, "I bet this soup is for your lunch. I bet your mother doesn't have anything else ready yet, does she?"

"Did you?"

"No. And I'm still stinging that anybody would think that of me. Haven't I always been sort of organized?"

"Of course you have!"

"I sometimes wonder, now."

It was December twenty-third and they still hadn't bought any Christmas gifts for the children. She gave him a list and he ran uptown and got what he could in the local stores, trying to bolster its meagerness with bags of candy, and bought one of the last Christmas trees in Pettibone. They couldn't find where they'd packed their lights and decorations, and perhaps it was as well; the tree was so small they had to put it on a table to have it above the children's heads, and its branches, which were sprayed with some sort of silver-metallic paint that made them appear artificial, didn't seem they could support much more than themselves.

On the day after the New Year, he woke with rolling waves of chills that racked him so badly through the night and into the next morning, he didn't feel well enough to work, and spent two days lying on the couch in his bathrobe, staring up at a ceiling he'd soon have to finish, listening for the least sound of her voice. Anger or suffering? Not a sign from her, not a word. Every time he slipped into sleep he dreamed about the basement.

21

❧

BLUE CHINA

At the age of eight I wasn't afraid of the dark. When I ran down a deserted street at night, I knew the chilling pursuer I felt at my back was put there by my act of running and would disappear, like any creature of the imagination when put to a test, the second I slowed to a walk. The gray hands that reached for me as I lay in bed were of my own creation, too, and once I'd proved and reported my power to summon them up, I could let them retreat back into darkness again.

When the change came, it came in a moment, but I think I was being prepared for it; I think it began when we moved to Illinois. Pettibone was on the highway between Havana and Pekin and was known mostly for its export of peat. The kids wore their hair in heinies or burr cuts, as they called them, played basketball instead of football, and had bicycles gaudied up with saddlebags or BB-gun holsters, or streamers on the handgrips, or rear carriers with car aerials on them. Everybody talked in an accent and called Forest Creek "Forrus Crick."

My father started remodeling a duplex that was once a gasoline station. He ripped out twelve-inch baseboards and tore stucco and wood lath off the walls, knocked down a six-by-six enclosure in one corner of the living room (what it was, no one knew), sawed a long hole along a kitchen wall and put a partition up on this side of it, dropped a new stairway from there down to the basement, and converted the concrete island that had once held the gasoline pumps, a car's breadth from the front door, into a flower planter with seats, a place for recreation. Jerome and I were inspired and learned to tote and swing hammers and swung them at the awful place, too.

The bedroom that my brothers and I were— Oh, yes, I'm Charles. Our bedroom had no window. It was an upstairs room with a ceiling that took its sharp slant from the pitch of the roof—an attic, really, or less than that. There wasn't a floor laid down in the rest of the second story, so the room was surrounded by wide-open ceiling joists (and more than one foot went through), and was as islandlike and desolate as we were in this gasoline station we'd moved to. No window to let in light, no smell but the smell of dust and car oil and old lumber (it had been a storeroom), and no communication with nature or the colors of the earth; the seasons outside were merely changes in temperature.

When our father first took us through the room, he said he'd install a dormer there, pointing, and fill the room with daylight after he finished the downstairs more, but for the time being, all he did was move in a double bed for Tim and Jerome (I was at an age when I couldn't stand to be touched, much less sleep with anybody), and set a narrow cot up against one wall for me.

I'd lie awake at night and listen for sounds in the wind or otherwise to bring good news or keep me company, Black Forest leaves above and friends below. A wooden catwalk with no rails ran from the door of the room to the steps downstairs, and I'd get out of bed and go along the catwalk and down the stairs toward a house deep asleep, and enter its warmth as though stepping down steps deeper underwater. A low hallway (I could hear it) led from the stairs to the left, past the bathroom, and opened on the long living room. I never snapped the wall switch in the living room, because windows would blink, rugs snap flat, chair backs straighten and make ready for you to sit in them. At the far corner of the room, near the front entrance, the door of my parents' bedroom guarded their sleep as their sleep guarded me from bad dreams, or so I thought then. Another arch led to the kitchen-dining room—a higher star-lightened arch that was like a door on the night. Pans sitting out, and the faceted-glass knobs on the kitchen cabinets, picking up bits of starlight, were like the eyes of creatures gathered beneath this sea.

Back in bed, hearing the whole house creak and sigh in its heavy sleep, I thought of my family asleep inside it, and prayed that I might be, too, soon, but the dark air was alive with excitement; a passing train, a car, the lashing of a tree, a cat scaling the tree, and other disturbances that made no noise, sent currents of feeling over my skin. My mother's sleeplessness came to me in cold waves. When the sun rose, the air grew thick and agitated and harder to breathe, and some nights, for a reason I could never understand, it thickened and pressed against me.

There was misunderstanding, or ill will, among the board members of the new consolidated school, or somebody made a promise he shouldn't have, or there was a mix-up in the hiring (none of this was explained to us children), and our father started working in one of Jay's plastering crews. The remodeling of the house slowed to a stop; gray rock lath rose to shoulder height and above it the bare studs, black with dirt and age, stood exposed. Our father wasn't one to break a promise, or leave a job undone, but the dormer to our room never appeared.,

My mother didn't like the new house and was upset that my father wasn't teaching again, and this time not of his own free will. And I was old enough to know that she was pregnant again. "Well, we've got enough to make a basketball team, and now we'll have enough for a six-man football squad," my father would say, trying to lighten her mood, but there was never any sign that she heard him. He watched her from the time he came home until he went to bed. How was she feeling today? Fine. Was there anything he could do? No. When her answers turned from single words to shrugs, and his smile and time-honored burlesque of the schottische, with a broom for a partner, failed to cheer her up, he became silent, too.

*

One afternoon I was at the top of a stepladder in the kitchen, nailing rock lath to the partition my father had built. She sat beside the kitchen table below me, ignoring the noise I made, and embroidered in the middle of a silver-colored hoop. I missed a nail completely, and the stud, too, and a moon-shaped hole appeared in the lath where the head of my hammer had hit home. I cursed and she didn't look up. She usually washed my mouth out with soap when she heard me curse. My father never swore around her or anybody else and now she was letting me get away with it. I felt manly and arrogant and made even more noise.

And then I realized how much she must have changed, to be able to ignore what once angered her so, and I studied her from the top of the stepladder. Her face was dry and chapped and there was a color to it I'd never seen. Her hair, which had almost always hung loose, was now pinned behind her ears as if to hide its stringiness and oily sheen. At her temples I could see the bones of her skull. She paused in her sewing and looked at her hand, first the palm, then the back, then the palm again.

"Mom? Are you O.K.?"

"Yes," she said, but she picked up her sewing in such a quick way it was as if I'd caught her at something.

"Don't worry about me. Just do your job."

Her tone of voice frightened me. I came down the stepladder, marked a piece of lath, and cut it with a razor knife, shakily curving off in the wrong direction two or three times. I snapped the lath across my knee, snapped off the hinged endpiece, and started up the ladder. An emotion rose from her and pressed on me like a hand. I stopped and stared at the grooves of a step and tried to figure out what she was feeling, and then turned to her and the grooves seemed to lift with my eyes, reach through the air, and link us. She lifted her eyes to me. At any other time she would have smiled, or told me, with a blush, to stop staring, but now she held me with her eyes until I was the one who blushed, and so badly I had to start hammering again.

"Don't," she said.

"Don't what?"

She was running her fingertips over her embroidery.

"Don't work any more."

"The noise bothers you?"

"I don't want you to work."

"Why?"

"Go and play."

"Who with?" I took a nail out of my mouth and pounded it in place. "Dad told me to finish this wall."

"You're too young to work."

"I am not."

"Don't argue. Go outside."

I couldn't see her face and with her face hidden her voice didn't seem a part of her. I came down the stepladder, angry, ready to force her to look at me, and saw that the length and breadth of her cheeks were wet with tears.

"You're never to work with your hands," she said. "Do you hear? Never!"

I went out of the kitchen and sat on the back concrete steps. It wasn't right for her to go against my father, and she never had, and now she was even going against herself: *Just do your job.* She wouldn't talk to you, and when she did she wouldn't look at you, and then she cried. If something was wrong and she didn't want me to know what it was, then I wished she'd leave me alone. Whatever was bothering her was affecting the rest of us, and that wasn't fair of her and I wanted it to stop.

Then I remembered the long unguarded look she'd held me with and felt ashamed.

One January night I woke and felt that the dark air had thickened. It was denser than it was when the sun rose, and a sound was fluttering up through its denseness to where I lay. I strained hard to hear, my eyes aching from their search of the dark, and caught a breathy creak like a beating pigeon's wings, a sound that came from below and traveled toward me and almost touched, then fell to an ebb. I rolled over and my shoulder struck the wall.

Light switches clicked, there were footsteps downstairs, the telephone bell jingled as it was cranked to get Central, and I felt the heavy throb of my father's bass voice. There were a number of throbs, punctuated by silences that were like humming question marks in the dark air, and then the receiver snapped into its holder, my father's footsteps crossed the kitchen, and another switch clicked; a white rectangle, opened in equal wings on the wall and the floor, unhinged—the light in the hall at the foot of the stairs. He made hurried trips from the bathroom to their bedroom and back again.

"Jerome?" I said. There was no answer.

I went out the catwalk and looked down the stairwell.
A flowing shadow fluttered over the bottom steps.

"Dad?"

There was a long silence, and then my father's face
appeared around the corner, his features holding darkness
from above him. "What are you doing up?"

"Nothing."

"Then get back to bed."

"Who were you calling?"

"You heard me on the phone?"

"Yes."

"What did you hear?"

"Talking. Who was it?"

"The doctor. Do you realize it's three o'clock?"

"Is somebody sick?"

He stared up at me, and then said in a whisper, "Get
to bed! Please!"

I did, but I couldn't sleep; the birdlike sounds rose up
again, his footsteps crossed the house, in long strides this
time, and the jingling of the telephone was prolonged. I
got out of bed and went to the bottom of the stairs before
I could hear. "—realize it's practically a half hour since
I called? You can't be more than two blocks away and
if— *What?* How can a man *read* at a time like this?
Well, I don't give a damn about your *damn* family doctor's book!"

The profanity, so wrong on my father's tongue, frightened me, and his voice was usually under control; I'd
never heard it like this. "No, you listen to *me* now. You
be here in five minutes or I'll come and get you!"

He dropped the receiver into its cradle, leaned against
the wall, and said, "Oh, Lord, help me, please." He drew
up to his full height and when he turned his face to me
it wasn't my father's face. It was so pale it seemed his
day-old beard had caved it in, and his features still held
shadow from the upstairs.

"What are you doing?"

"Are you sick?"

"What are you *doing* down here?"

"I have to go to the toilet."

He gripped the bridge of his nose and moaned as
though dangerously ill. "Go," he said.

"What's wrong?"

"Do as you're told."

I went to the bathroom and stood at the stool. On the hamper beside it was a pile of sheets that looked thrown down in haste; one hung on the floor. The stool was still from the days of the gasoline station; its bowl leaked and the boards of the floor were damp around it; it was to be replaced. Boxes of floor tile stood under its perspiring tank.

"What are you doing in there?" I heard from outside and my stream went over the toilet seat and onto the floor.

"What do you think?"

"Come out here!"

I cleaned up and lifted the sheet from the floor and saw that the other was covered with blood. I ran out and found him blocking the hall.

"Hurry," he said. "I'll turn out the light."

"I want to see Mom."

"No. Not now."

"Why?"

"She isn't feeling well."

"I want to *see* her!"

"In the morning. Go now."

"She's sick?"

He nodded his head. I couldn't ask him anything more, or disobey and run past him to their bedroom, but as I climbed the stairs I felt I'd done something wrong and couldn't think what it was; and then I realized, more from the silence than from what he'd said, that my mother was ill, not him, and began to shake as though with the fever of pneumonia, but with chills inside this time. I got under the covers, the winged rectangle on the floor went, and darkness lay on me with a weight it had never had before. It took all my imagination and strength, and closed eyes, to keep it away, and then I heard unfamiliar voices, several of them, it seemed, and gave up to the dark.

I dreamed I was walking with my mother through a large department store. The walls and ceiling were white and the floor was of white marble. There were low display casts set at great distances from one another. My mother had my hand in hers. She wanted to go upstairs and I wanted to stay where we were, on ground level, and look in the display cases. I pulled away from her and ran to one. *Don't! Don't look!* she cried, and her voice echoed through the empty store.

The case was filled with blue china figurines. There was a blue swan, like the one in our kitchen, with a hole in its back, so it could be used as a flowerpot, there were blue angels, and small blue busts of young children. My mother put her hand on my shoulder and said, *Come with me.* I turned to tell her no, and couldn't breathe. She stood high above me, taller than she'd ever been, her face made of blue china, her eyes alive and staring at me as they had in the kitchen. She pulled her coat close up around her throat and walked away. I tried to run after her but my feet wouldn't move in the sand of deathly dreams.

I woke to darkness, twisted in the blankets, my heart beating hard against the mattress. I had to see my mother right away. I started out of bed and struck the wall. The wall was on the other side of the cot. I tried again, and again I struck it. There wasn't a wall on that side of the cot, and not all the logic in the world, or the wall itself, could convince me otherwise. Being reversed in bed never occurred to me. I tried again and again. I called for Jerome and there was no word. Was I *outside* the room? Finally I fell back on the cot, exhausted, and my left arm stretched out into blank space. If there was a wall where I knew there was none, then what lay in this emptiness where the wall should be? I pulled my arm onto the safety of the cot and held it over my chest, afraid to move, afraid of the dark.

*

In the morning, without having to be told, I knew my mother was gone. My father, who'd had no sleep, gathered Tim and Jerome and me on a cot he'd set up in the kitchen, close to the telephone, and said, "Last night your mother had to be taken to the hospital. I want you all to pray that she'll be all right. This is a time when we have to keep close together, boys." Without being able to confide in him, or in anybody else (once the sun has risen, the dark seems partly imagination), I knew I'd never see my mother again, and started preparing and blaming myself for her death before she even died.

22

SNOWFALL ALONG THE ILLINOIS

Martin hadn't ever had a telephone in the house, and disliked the instrument and its way of invading his private life. One night it rang at 1 A.M. He got on his glasses and grabbed up the receiver before the thing rang itself out; it was the doctor on the other end. He'd been looking through his family doctor book, he said, and thought perhaps Alpha might have an acute form of hepatitis and should maybe see an internist in Peoria or somewhere. He went into a lengthy explanation of hepatitis, of the relationship between the patient and his disease, explaining that this information came from the book lying open in front of him, and soon his speech became rambling and convoluted and took sudden shifts that had no relation to logic, yet made sense to Martin as he listened in. There was a sound of lengthy sighing and then a long pause.

"Well, I don't know why you're telling me all this at such an ungodly hour," Martin said, and hung up.

That morning he called an internist in Pekin to see about an appointment; the internist asked who Alpha was presently seeing and Martin told him.

"Oh, goodness."

"Why? What's that about?"

"I'm afraid the poor fellow's about to lose his license. There have been a lot of complaints about him and we're about to get a full-scale investigation under way on him. We're pretty sure he's been using opium."

An appointment with the internist was scheduled for two days later, and the next night Martin woke to an unnatural coldness that seemed to emanate from beside the bed. Raw-throated sounds, powerful yet constrained, were coming from the direction of the coldness, as if Alpha were crying and attempting to stifle it, but he'd never heard her cry in such a voice. She wouldn't answer, and then her fist hit his face; it was tensed and beating at him with a fury he couldn't fathom. He threw back the covers and turned on the lamp; Alpha was unconscious, having convulsions, and bleeding into the bed.

He ran and called the Pettibone doctor, who came on at once and was levelheaded and concerned and told him to make sure her tongue was forward in her mouth, to cover her and keep her warm, if it would ease his mind, but mostly to keep back and not hurt her by trying to help her; he'd be right over. Martin went back to the bedroom and the convulsions had stopped; she was breathing through her mouth as if asleep. Her tongue was as it should be.

He pulled the damp and stained sheets off the bed and covered her well, piled the sheets in the bathroom, and then sat on the edge of their bed. He took her hand and thought, Must I go through this?—feeling he'd been through it before. Her eyelids trembled and opened on him with a tentative stir; she took a long time to focus. "You're so pale," she said.

"You look better."

"Why do I feel so light? Have I lost the baby?"

"No, no. Don't worry now. The doctor's on his way."

"The doctor?"

"You've been ill."

"How long?"

"Just a while."

"I feel I've been under a spell a hundred years. Is this the hospital?"

"No, we're at home now."

"Where's the big window that looks out on the front porch?"

"Here in Illinois."

"Oh, I'm really confused then, or else I've been dreaming. So it's true that I'll lose the baby."

"No, no, no. The baby's just fine."

"No, I'll lose it. It'll be as much sorrow to you as losing me, and you'll think of us together."

"What do you mean?"

"It's a girl." She turned to the wall and tears went over her nose and dropped in rapid spots over the ticking.

"Alpha, I want you to know——"

Her fingernails cut in and her face was transfigured as her spine arched and beat with the force of another convulsion. He grabbed her and held her while the raw-throated sounds went and came as if she were falling down past him from a building and trying to cry out some final message or name. Then stopped. Then with a gasping intake of breath went up again and again came flying by with the important syllables missing. until he was afraid he'd do her harm if this didn't stop. Then she lay still on the bed beneath him. There was bloody foam on her lips. Her tongue was cut.

He ran and called the doctor and was ready to hang up on empty ringing, relieved at least that the fellow was on his way, when the receiver lifted and a calm voice came on talking in a rambling and convoluted manner about the nature of illness and this book of his. Martin shouted something and slammed the receiver down; he was going to call Central and have them get through to the internist in Pekin, when he felt somebody and turned.

Charles stood in the room, staring at him with Alpha's deep-blue, afflicted eyes. Martin couldn't speak and felt faint for fear the boy had seen her, but he hadn't, and Martin hurried him off to bed as quick as he could, and then got on the phone to the internist, who told him to have an ambulance bring Alpha to the hospital in Pekin right away; he'd be in the emergency room. Then Martin called his mother to come and stay with the children, and she arrived just as the ambulance attendants were wheeling Alpha's blanket-covered body out the front door.

She was operated on in the morning and a full-term, nine-and-a-half-pound girl was removed from her womb, dead. When a doctor brought him the news, Martin remembered her saying "You'll think of us together" and sat in a chair he felt he'd never rise from.

Then the doctor said, "I'm afraid I also have to tell you that your wife has uremia."

"Uremia?"

"Yes, sir."

"Is that serious?"

"Very. I'm afraid the child has overtaxed her system."

"What do you mean?"

"Her condition is critical."

For the next five days Martin hardly slept. Since he'd known her, he'd begged her to see a doctor, any doctor, about the way she could go for days without peeing, usually during a deep despondency, but she never would. Uremia. The word lay like a mold in his mind and mingled with the name Alpha had picked for the baby: Dacey. It seemed a pitiable name to him. Was he in mourning? He could feel globular cells like the saclike bubbles attached to water weeds multiplying over the base of his brain. Soon his mind would go. He woke one night from sleep and felt that a growth of pimples as long as his hair, and filled with clear fluid, was swaying from his forehead.

Alpha's condition grew worse, and he decided that the oldest, Jerome and Charles, should be allowed to see her, at least once, for a while, in case the worst should happen and started out for the hospital one night with them beside him in the car. The radiator hose broke along the way and he had to pull into a farmyard The farmer who came out had boils over his face and the back of his neck. He and Martin worked on the car under a yard light, while a collie dashed around their legs, and threw itself on them, keeping up such an endless yapping they could hardly talk. But together they got the hose patched, finally, with friction tape and wire. Martin slammed down the hood and saw Jerome and Charles staring out at him from behind the windshield, and wondered if maybe it wouldn't be better if they didn't see her in her present condition. He got into the car and drove home.

The next day Alpha was transferred to a hospital in Peoria, which had an intensive-care unit and more specialists on call.

All along, the doctors had assumed that she'd soon be improving, that there were more positive signs of recovery on the way, but Martin no longer trusted them. There was a detachment in her he'd never felt before, and she'd ask him not to look at her, or to leave the hospital before he was ready to go. One night she took his hand and said, "I'm going to show you how I pray the Hail Mary." She said this in a fury, and began the prayer with an emotion close to fury, but then she looked away, her expression cleared, and it seemed she was staring at a face in front of her, and he felt through her hand the current and aura that aroused him, but instead of resting inside and spreading in him in its usual way, it passed through him with pulsing surges that grew in strength, and then a radiance appeared around her lips. Or was it his mind again?

"Amen," she said, and turned to him with eyes so distant she didn't appear to recognize him.

As he was leaving, a young, unfamiliar doctor came up and introduced himself, and said he'd started a different regimen of treatment that Alpha seemed to be responding to; there were a few signs of improvement. Martin stared into his eyes, for any trace of ambitiousness or self-deception, and saw only that the doctor believed in himself. He drove home forty miles an hour, hoping the children would be in bed by the time he got there, and when he walked into the house heard the phone start its ringing again. He picked it up.

"Mr. Neumiller, this is Dr. Morrow, the physician who spoke to you this evening?"

"Yes?"

"I'm afraid I have some very bad news for you. We're not sure of the reasons yet, but your wife's gone into a coma. Can you come right in?"

Martin nodded his head and hung up.

*

He was working with Jay in a subdivision in Delavan, trying his hand at troweling rough-coat in a closet, when he heard a car come racing toward the house, and went to a window and saw it squall outside, its hood nodding toward asphalt, and then the silvery-haired subdivision developer, the man Jay was contracting under, came toward the house in a middle-aged man's run. Martin put aside his hawk and trowel and sat on the scaffold, seeing himself do this a multitude of times, as the man came trotting into the room, out of breath, and said, "A doctor just got in touch with me through your dad! You're supposed to get to the hospital right away! It's about your wife, he said."

Martin nodded to the man and bowed his head. He wouldn't want to be the one to tell Ed Jones that Alpha had died, and yet he sensed the old man was the only one of the Joneses who wouldn't hold him responsible for her death. He shifted his weight and shook his head once, as Jones might, and found he could stand.

The developer was still in the room staring at him.

He went down a hall and through rooms damp and brown-gray from rough-coat, and felt that brown-gray rooms led off them into infinity, and half fell into the room where Jay was skimming on finish.

"The doctor called," he said. "Alpha. It's an emergency."

Jay jumped from the scaffold and took him outside by an arm, and Martin blinked at the bright air, and then drew back and gestured toward his Chevrolet, parked under a tree on a mound of plaster-splashed clay, a perforated fringe of rust around his frame. "We better take—" he said. "I can handle—"

The car looked changed, stranded on its tires, a part of the past that wouldn't carry him through time or over the broad swath of the world any more.

"The hell," Jay said. "You aren't even going to drive."

Jay got him into his station wagon and within a while they were doing a hundred. Martin was sorry the working of circumstance had put Jay at the wheel; he was a perfectionist, high-keyed and self-critical, and if anything went wrong, a flat tire or any other minor mishap, anything more, then Jay might blame himself for it with his flaying conscience. There was a sound of a siren and a reflected red light appeared in flashing sweeps across the windshield. Jay pulled onto the shoulder, ran back to the police and reappeared in a moment, and then the squad car swayed out around them, leaving rubber, red light pulsing, siren on high, and Jay, close behind, was soon doing a hundred again.

Martin covered his face, and then removed his glasses and pulled his cap over his eyes; he didn't want to see any more of the outside world, not in its least manifestation, and with his eyes covered he was back inside the morning he'd lain under the quilt on the horsehair sofa, waiting for Alpha to wake, so he could find out if she'd said yes to his proposal, and how for a moment he'd mistrusted the Joneses' motives (did that have any effect on this, now? the book closing with its declamatory thump?), and then outside the house how the white world left by the blizzard lay spread out around him as limitlessly as his hope, a hope that grew as Jones talked, the horses plumed and stomping; and then five weeks ago, on their twelfth anniversary, he brought home a dozen long-stemmed roses, red roses, one for each year, and she'd said, "Just as sentimental as ever, aren't you?" And then studied the roses and smelled and arranged them, and said, "I love them. Thank you, Martin. These are exactly what I needed."

He'd wept so much in the past few weeks he felt emptied of tears, but the cap kept dripping them on him.

"Martin?"

The emergency entrance of a hospital materialized around them. Jay got him inside and there was a note for them to wait at a downstairs desk. They went into a glass-walled waiting room and took off their caps and sat on a couch and stared at separate corners. Martin's hands were chapped and ivory-colored from lime, and as he clenched and unclenched his fist, his knuckle lines opened on flesh; the wrist above read 4:43. It grew darker outside and then through the glass he saw snow start to come down.

The internist started up a corridor in their direction and Martin stood as the corridor blurred and tilted to one side, while his ears echoed with a sound like the sea, and the doctor, who looked an infinity away, kept marking time or walking backward down the corridor away from him, and then everything straightened and moved true to life and the doctor stepped up in front of him.

"Mr. Neumiller—" His eyes went to Jay and then he tugged at the gauze mask around his throat. "We've used all of our medical knowledge, the new drugs, and the most sophisticated equipment that's available to us, and it's just not enough. Your wife died about an hour ago. We tried to get in touch with you earlier, but couldn't. I'm terribly sorry, sir."

Streamers of light, comets or falling stars he'd read about or seen, sped down the hall and entered his shoulders from the front and behind and held him on his feet. The doctor took his hand, then wavered and bent as though underwater, and said, "Would you like to see her?"

He nodded and his upper lip started fluttering toward

his eyes. The doctor led them down a different hall and around a corner, and set a door ajar. "We've brought her down here," he said. "You can go in alone, sir."

Martin closed the door behind him. She lay on a high, wheeled stretcher beyond an empty bed, her face uncovered in the dim light, free of the tubes and masks that had sustained her, her hair, curled since she'd gone into the coma, the massy tangle it was when she was a girl. Her hands arranging the roses in a vase. Her critical and artistic eye.

A glass shattered down the hall.

"Oh, God," he said, meaning she was only thirty-four.

Dark-brown bruises around her eyes and in her cheeks and along her throat. Her skin dry and chafed and a darker color from the disease. Stiff lips that tasted of crystalline gall. He knew it was wrong to keep kissing her as he was, but couldn't stop—intolerable that she was lying dead to his touch and that he still loved her with a love as undiminished as on the day they'd first mingled their flesh and half become one another and he'd felt their soft parting as a seizure of loss he might not be able to live with again without her. Her face, a mask of flesh, was turned to one side and rocked with the arm he rubbed. Her hairline was wet. Loose eyelashes lay on her cheek and her lids were parted and would soon tremble with a tentative stir and open on him.

"Alpha," he began, and his being closed around the name, the last of her he could physically hold. "Alpha, if you're anywhere close, if you can hear me, forgive me. Forgive, for—"

He turned invisible below his eyes and struck across his back on the bed behind him. He rolled and tore at the covers to find the entry or exit to this, and then felt hands at his shoulders, drawing him away from his voice, and then was in a corridor with Jay's and the doctor's arms around him.

"Will you see about any arrangements?" he said to Jay. Jay said he would.

"Make sure they call Mom and Dad right away?"

"Yes."

"I have to be alone awhile."

"Where?"

"Outside here."

The doctor and Jay were whispering as he went out the emergency entrance, drawn tight against the top of his spine, his only unerring support, his limbs swinging loose in another realm. He got into Jay's station wagon and drove off. Outside Peoria, beyond Bartonville, the snow started coming down in broken sheets, and he realized he was on a road at night, in a strange car, his heart sending out powerful shocks against his ribs, and then the headlights blossomed and widened until he was covering the entire road. He pulled onto the shoulder. Large lacelike flakes were floating down in the darkness and disappearing over the hood as if passing through it. *Where was the wind of the world if there was one?* The snow suddenly stopped.

He drove through Pekin, past Powerton, the bad railroad crossing there, over the roads he'd driven past weeks to visit Alpha, and on out into the countryside, until he came to the big steel bridge spanning the Mackinaw. He got out and stood at the guardrail. The river was frozen along its edges and a channel of lime-colored moonlight lay in corrugations over the open water. To the west he knew was the dark-blue shape of the levee, and beyond the levee the broad expanse of blue-black where the Mackinaw emptied into the Illinois— A glimpse of himself striking the lime-colored channel with a surge of exhilaration, and every detail of his life, every shade of gesture and speech and emotion, every nuance of time, a preparation for it, and was this why he'd never in his life learned to swim?

There was a full moon in the bright and rolling-clouded silver sky. Escape trails. A streak of her? Answer, oh, answer, oh, he'd given as much as he could to her and still survive and now there was no more. Nor her. How, when he'd lived his life as he had so he could live it the way he wanted when they were out of their thirties? Eeeeuunnnnoe! Blark hallers, holy tree of her, dying furnacework, down in Midvale, a tonic of yellowish sun on the street, the way the simplest skills or a prayer to some people seem magical, the board of no return, laughter and the horse laugh, too, in life; and now night.

He turned and a dim ghost of a man once himself stared at him from a car window. There was something hard and icy at his back and he slid down it to this pile of stones. Or was it beaded water? Was this his afterlife as well? There was a stern and dark-browed teacher who didn't belong in Christendom. The snow, each flake flying out of the straight sky down the air at him, descended past the base of the cone he was rising through, and then the flakes began to whorl and sway with him, incorporeal and air-dependent, rocking and shifting and tilting in sudden side sweeps with the movement of a new wind in the night. He was aware of a cold crown over his forehead, a numbness in his fingertips, and then ice melting through his clothes.

Headlights were approaching from the direction of Pekin. He got to his feet; it was Jay, of course, Jay and the police, and the police were after him for everything he'd done or hadn't done in his life, or for having such unreasonable thoughts as he'd had. He took off in the car and watched the lights diminish to silver dots in his mirror, and then saw that he was doing ninety, heard the rush of speed, and thought, Now all I have to do is jerk the door handle; tumble hard down toward it on dark asphalt, fractured and crumbling from severe freezes in a mound as high as a haystack, boy, before I take you and your car apart! And Dinah in her nitrous and banjo tomb he'd heard of only out of *That cold storage box way up at the top! The attic of—*

The space, the space, the space!

A block and a half ahead was the triangular park, the house. He shut off the headlights and then the ignition, and coasted onto the concrete drive behind his father's car. He got out and started toward the house and heard the faint and musically pitched voices of Susan and Marie mingled in crying, and knew they already knew. He got back in the station wagon and rested his head on the steering wheel. What about Jay? The phone, of course.

Headlight beams swung over his shoulders and he looked up and watched the car go slishing past. A curtain in the living room parted and the face of his father, pale and stricken, appeared behind the glass, and across the room he could see his mother on the couch with the baby in her arms and the other children lined up beside her, their shoulders crushed together, trying to comfort one another. The curtain fell.

He got out of the station wagon and slammed the door.

There was one task that remained for him and it was a task he couldn't fail at; he had to keep himself and the children together as a family with all that was left of him and his life. Less than one half, he thought, as he wiped the melting snow from his face and then walked through the end of January toward the front door of the house.

23

MERCY

Telegrams and long-distance calls to relatives and friends; trying to comfort the children and give reasonable explanations for the death, a lifetime of this. Walking down a corridor to the rear of a funeral home, where caskets stand open on display along the walls; the price of the funeral based on a casket's cost. Clothes hangers shrieking across a closet rod of pipe. His hard breathing, the heavy blows of his heart as if it demanded release. The children away at his mother's for the night, tonight only, so he can remove the traces of her that remain here in her clothes. Her pajamas and underthings and shoes already in the incinerator, and now her dresses, all of these dresses that once held her, many still dense with her smell.

He threw an armload into a cardboard box and hangers clashed and dress materials slid over one another like many-colored liquids pooling. Two more armloads, emptying her half of the closet, and then he picked up the box to go to the incinerator, but it was waste of a sort that Alpha would fly out at; he'd give these to his sister Rose Marie; she and Alpha were of a size and exchanged clothes. He tried to straighten the dresses but they slipped through his fingers with a fountaining of memories of her in him. He stood and swayed off-balance from the weight of images displacing one another.

This dress, the one she wore when she received First Communion, he couldn't give away—dark blue with large white polka dots, which echoed now with eloquence. He tossed it onto her vanity. And this, the navy suit she wore the day they were married, he couldn't allow anybody to have, or bear to see again; nor this, the cotton maternity

302

dress she had on during the long drive from North Dakota when they moved, Oh, Lord, have mercy on me.

He jerked open vanity drawers. Hats and nylons and handkerchiefs and scarves and more blossoming undergarments; the middle drawer filled with makeup containers, hair combs, barrettes, perfume, a crucifix, and a rubber-band-bound stack of birthday and anniversary cards he'd given her; the card he'd enclosed with the roses on top. Into another box, the two dresses and the suit, a knitted tam she'd worn only once because he laughed when he saw her in it, a hat she was trying to decide on in McCallister while he waited outside with the boys so she wouldn't be bothered, and then she came out to the street and called him in and pointed to two choices on a dressing table, and said, "Which do you like?" Both looked equally attractive, but he said, "The brown."

"Then I'll take the green," she said.

Green, green, august grass aglow and wind-shaken in his hand. He pulled out other vanity drawers and dumped them, one by one, into the same box. And the middle drawer? He took out the crucifix and placed it on the vanity top. And the cards and notes? Yes, that was over; he wanted no reminders of himself, either, as he was then, and emptied it all into the box. Face powder fumed up, coating his nostrils, and he saw Alpha dressed up and ready for an evening out.

In the box still smoky with powder was the Five Year Diary. From her? He lifted it out and wiped it on his shirt. He might have read it a dozen times, but always wanted her to hand it to him on her own, twenty or thirty years from now, so he could relive that part of their lives through her. Now he never would. He riffled through its pages to see her handwriting and see it move, and stopped at the final entry, in 1940, when they were in Spear's house; in a hurried hand, a single sentence: *I'm counting the hours till we leave for Dakota.*

He closed the diary and put it at the back of the middle drawer, and then sat on the bench of the vanity and covered his face, and when he looked up again, it was dark in the room.

He turned on lights all through the house, and then thought of dinner, but saw her dishes and utensils and couldn't eat. He put on water for coffee and sat at the table where he and Elaine had had an argument last night; she wanted to adopt Susan and Marie and he agreed with some of her points (what *would* he do when they were teenagers?) and knew she was making the proposal out of concern and responsibility, and was the woman closest to Alpha besides her mother, but said no to her from the start, definitely not, and finally had to strike the table to make his point; then he asked her to leave, because she was so upset he was afraid the children might hear what she was saying, and what would they think?

And then his mother got upset with him and Elaine; this was a house of mourning, she said, *please;* and wanted to stay the night, in case any of the children woke, but he asked her to leave, too. He'd have to learn to deal with their most precarious feelings from the start, and on his own, if they were to remain together. And yet he didn't know how he'd survive the coming week without somebody to talk to who was close to him and Alpha, yet unattached to their families, somebody who could counsel him and give him advice—any sort, just so there was a course to follow that would free him from making everyday decisions, which were like Badlands landscape flowing backward over him.

There was a corrosive odor of fouled electrical wiring, and he jumped to the stove and found the water boiled away, burned his fingers on the handle of the pot, and then took a towel and carried it to the sink and turned on water. The black handle shattered over the sink. He tried to clean it up but his fingers knocked the pieces around so much they seemed to be in motion. On the wall at eye level was a plaque in the shape of a maple leaf, with a cup shelf on it, that Jerome had built at school and given to her for Christmas, and he remembered her staring at the plaque, and saying, "Jerome's one I'll never worry about."

"What do you mean?"

"In case something should happen to me."

"What a way to talk! Why should it?"

"If it did, I'd never worry about Jerome. Isn't that strange? He's the one I always thought I'd worry about."

He went to the other side of the house and put the box for Rose Marie at the back of the closet there, carried the other box out the back door to the incinerator and dropped it inside. He'd brought out gasoline earlier, and now he soaked the box and clothes with it and then stepped back and threw a match. There was a rush of air and then a concussive thud like a thick rug snapped and blazing flame flinging stuttering tips toward the telephone wire, while the snow around him turned rose and orange and yellow-crimson and the shifting unnamable shades of color of the stars overhead.

He realized he was standing outdoors in his shirtsleeves and snow was melting into his shoes. Lights went on in the Ebbinger place across the alley, and he looked and saw it was ten. He ran across the dimming snow to the back door and stepped inside and stamped his feet, breathing hard, and then hiccups jarred the colunn of air in his chest, and sent pain through his heart with their powerful unpredictableness.

He sat in his easy chair and stared across the room. He'd buy a television set; that thought-numbing novelty his parents had, he'd get, to bridge the night from one day to the next, and use as a sitter for the children. Where would the girls stay when he was at work and the boys in school? It would be too complicated with Elaine. Rose Marie had three children already and was pregnant again. Mom?

He felt pressure against him, as if in an accelerating car, and found himself at the table in Hyatt with the family around him, reading the letter from his father, and tilting it from side to side because of the sunlight, and then Alpha, in maternity clothes, bowing her head as if ashamed. What? And then he heard the moving trucks pull into the drive, and ran out and said, "You might as well turn around and head back! We've decided not to move!" Then went inside and found the kitchen bare, the family gone, the furniture cleared away, the house empty except for a *Fargo Forum* on the living-room floor, and heard the rackety sound of the moving trucks starting up and pulling off, and wanted to run after them, but was on the spread-out newspaper, or on a cutout of the state, and if he stepped off it, would step off the edge into Alpha's world.

Or was he there? Where was this? His hands moved, his arms moved, his wristwatch ticked and showed 3 A.M., and there was a steady knocking at the door. He ignored it; for days he'd heard Susan crying when she was asleep, Alpha calling him from other rooms, and underneath all this, as though a record were playing inside his ear, a children's choir singing, "At the cross her station keeping, stood the mournful mother weeping. . . ."

A white face was staring in at him from the frosted front window. The face was familiar, out of dreams or the distant past, and he thought, with an eroding sense of ease at his center, that he'd lost his mind, at last, and couldn't be held responsible for himself from now on.

Then a gloved hand rose beside the face and rapped on the pane.

He went over and opened the door and saw Father Schimmelpfennig's black homburg and the shoulders of his black overcoat whitened with snow. "Martin, are you all right?" he said. "I saw you sitting so—"

"Father. It *is* you!"

"I brought some tings for the kids, but it's so late now." Martin stepped into the falling snow and embraced him.

"We've been having one of the worst blizzards of the year up north, otherwise I wouldn't be alone, Martin. The Koenigs and the Pflagers and the Savitskys and Wilhomena and Mrs. Jake Ennis—well, three other cars altogether—started out with me, but the weather got so bad they had to turn back."

"How long have you been on the road?"

"Twenty-two hours."

"Have you slept?"

"No."

"The funeral's this morning, Father."

"I know, Martin. I've come to give her eulogy."

24

ᴗᶟᶟᴥ

PHOTOS OF TIM AND CHARLES

That spring there was one of the worst floods that could be remembered by anybody in Pettibone. The Neumillers were affected by it. Their house sat in one of the lowest areas of town, and in the triangular park across the street was the central reservoir of Pettibone's antiquated municipal drainage system—bare pipe guardrails (good for swinging from your knees from in better weather) around a concrete-capped, grate-covered drain; it plugged with leaves with the first of the spring rains, and the rains lasted for seventeen days.

A concrete viaduct three feet high and a foot and a half wide ran underneath the edges of the front yard, the quickly mowed wedge, and one day Tim and Charles, against the warnings of their father, went floating through this viaduct over and over with the force of the rising water pushing them outward toward the open ditch the viaduct flared into; they'd start by lying in the water in the ditch in shirt and blue jeans, supported on their hands, the chill of twilight above them, getting well aimed, and then push with a submerging splash into the viaduct, whose cement walls, pitch-dark and echoey, hardly wider than their shoulders, slid gleaming along the sides of their eyes as they floated, touching the sand-muddied bottom with a hand now and then to keep their balance, their legs spread to catch as much of the current as they could but not so they scraped the sides of the viaduct and slowed themselves, about six or eight inches of air space to breathe in, although there were higher rushes, their hair scraping the cobwebby slab above, and then at the juncture of the busy intersection the viaduct elled off

307

to the left at an angle of ninety degrees, and every time they made the contortions necessary to accomplish this turn, and shoved off in that direction, moving faster toward the colors of the brightening ditch, the rectangle of light ahead sent them gasping for the world that spun out away far beyond Pettibone.

The next day the viaduct filled to the top. The ditches beyond were small streams circumscribing the block. They went swimming in them in undershorts, with long-sleeved shirts above to fend off the cold.

The day after that the basement started filling up. Their father and Uncle Fred ran out and bought two centrifugal pumps that worked off garden hoses, and came back and stood in the basement with water cascading in lateral sheets from the windows they'd opened around them to run the hoses out, and realized they'd have to pump the yard dry, which would pump dry a whole lot of Pettibone, before they could pump dry the basement. Tim and Charles sat a quarter way up the steps and watched as the two men stood in wet pants on soaking chairs and nailed the windows shut, and then asked one another what they'd do if the panes in them started breaking; that night they woke to the sound of a series of miniature waterfalls in their basement.

The level of the water moved up the concrete drive and touched the front step. Would it come inside and run over the floor, Tim wondered, hoping it would, in a way. No matter which direction he and Charles went from the house, they had to walk a block and a half on the raised center of the street, shuffling along in overshoes that wanted to float and more often than not overflowed, or *in*flowed, along their tops, before they reached dry ground.

The old Opera House on its quarter block of elms, across from the back of their house, was reflected in water around it the shade of gray it was painted, but spikes of grass rose in shattering patches through its placid reflection.

The mud sometimes sucked loose their overshoes, the sound and mechanics of which would have been a joke at any other time, without all this water around, and the outdoors became less pleasant for them than they'd ever thought it could be. They went to bed with bad colds, and were sniffing and hacking up brown-green clots in the toilet bowl. Except for their wades to school, they stayed in the house for two weeks and tried to re-teach one another the knitting their grandmother had taught them while "she" was in the hospital, to no avail, and were so hushed and feverish about it, and so sealed off from the rest of the family, Martin felt at the threshold of death again.

*

There are some photos of Tim and Charles taken a few weeks later, by Jerome, most likely, at the front of the house. In the first, Tim stands at the entry, the white beams flanking it showing at the picture's sides, his truncated feet apparently on the concrete drive below. He wears a cap with GOLD BOND printed across its crown. His face looks puffy and strained and his smile is cleft by a half-moon-shaped shadow cast by his nose. His head is ensconced in the furry collar of their father's sheepskin coat. He holds his right arm up in a wave but his hand can't be seen. The coat's that big. The dark-colored bulk of him covers every crossbar of the screen and his head reaches to the base of the outdoor lights on the beams, the height of their father when he stands here. Tim's grown. The coat is buttoned down its front and has an elbowish bulge at its waistline. Grandpa Jones's goatskin chaps jut below its bottom hem into the picture's white border to

MAR   •   51

In the second picture, Tim demonstrates modified duck lips, and has shrunk. His head is below the first mullion of the window in the entry, at the level of the screen-door handle. His arms are at his sides and the ends of the coat sleeves touch the concrete step. The coat overflows into the picture's border, as though Tim's deflating or melting or

MAR   •   51

In the third picture, Charles stands in a dark parka with ragged cuffs. His legs are bowed out arch-comic-cowboyically, covered by the goatskin chaps. Beside him a white cat of Susan's with tortoise-shell crests around its eyes, and a tortoise-shell saddle, holds its mouth open in an arrested miaow, its tail blurred and the tip of it arched toward Charles: later, that summer, Susan and Marie put the cat in a traveling makeup case of their mother's— its mirror broken and its blue-silken interior in tatters— so they could pull it around in the wagon without its always leaping out, and then left it all standing in the sun, and as Charles was burying the cat in the back yard by the incinerator in the makeup case it was found in, to their protests and tears and wondering why, he said, "Well, you see, it just sort of drowned on its own carbon dioxide."

A grimy right hand of Charles's is raised in the picture, in a rancherlike manner, and a pushed-out lower lip glistens above his depressed and wrinkled chin. His eyelids are lowered in an "It's all O.K. now, folks" gesture, and his straight hair touches his eyebrows and the top of his broad nose.

What's Jerome thinking at this moment out of this series of

MAR • 51

Charles's eyes are closed in the last picture, I notice again, and then, shuffling back, can't see Tim's eyes for the black shadow cast by the bill of the cloth cap in the second one; and in the first, the same shadow makes Tim's eyes resemble the depthless phosphorescent reflectors they become when headlights shine straight inside to the backs of them (and Charles, of course, is underneath the sheepskin coat in this one)—as though both are attempting to hide from observers the look that should beam out and reveal all that's happened within less than a year of their lives, but the two are children still, by legacy and for good reason, and in their dim faces can be seen the force of the water that rose and overflowed most of Pettibone, now their new home town, with only a father left to cling to for life, at play here restlessly and at rest in a source outside their primitive designs at last, entrapped in time, caught in these few photographs. Click.

25

THE WAY YOU DO HER

She lifts the earthenware cream crock from the dishpan in the sink, shakes shining beads of water down its oatmeal-colored sides, and sets it, upside down, on the drainboard. Her gestures as she lifts and shakes and sets it are both dignified and precise; when she walks, she holds her body erect and along a straight line, as though her soul were liquid and could spill with ease. The boy beside her smiles. Her youth and grace make him forget she's not his mother, who doesn't seeem to have died, but his mother's mother, and her gestures firm the air around him in such a familiar way that when he breathes deeply, as he breathes now, he breathes comfort and strength.

He stares at her, a dish towel draped over his open hand like a magician's silk, and feels himself retreat in a waver to the day in Hyatt when he stood in the kitchen under his mother's blue stare and looked down the legs of the chaps to his father's hat fallen on the floor. His grandmother's hair is auburn-blond and plaited into big braids coiled round and round her delicate skull. Her face is angular and colored now by sunlight, coppery-gold in the golden air, and could be a figurehead on a Viking prow, and then the copper breaks into movement, and he's both startled and pleased and shivers cold.

"Quit gaping," she says. "And close your mouth or it'll fill up with flies, sure as I live, ha!"

"It's not open."

"It most certainly is, dear sir."

"You can't tell. You aren't even looking this way."

"I can tell about you, boy."

She's sensitive to her beauty that's been altered, not

by age in any radical way, but by a set of dentures an older male relative persuaded her to be fitted with when she was twenty, and as part of his persuasion promised to pay the bill, and then sent her to a cut-rate dentist; the mold of her lips and the area around her mouth have never been the same. She hasn't allowed a photograph to be taken of her since then, her twenties, and when she combs out her hip-length hair at night, or when he combs it out for her, chasing blond and pink highlights down the ripples raised by the braids, she sits on the edge of the bed, facing away from him, away from the mirror, the tentlike shape of her frail head bowed.

She reaches in the dishpan and lifts out a bundle of forks with sunlit beads dripping from their tines, gives them a shake, and holds them out for him to dry, and as he takes them, he touches her skin. It's smoother than the silver and so transparent her lilac veins and amber freckles glow in it. She smiles and he stares down at his bare feet and curled toes on the linoleum; even more than watching her, her touch gives him strength.

"Lordy, Lordy, you're so bashful!" she says, almost sings, in a voice that awes him because it's like a girl's, gravelly yet girlish, younger than his mother's, with a whispery nasalized sound over sibilants, and full of a teasing bravado so thin and pure it seems it could crack, like fine china. "Nobody knows you're bashful but me! They think you're quiet or just plain dumb. Or maybe you're not even bashful, maybe you don't want anybody to know what really goes on inside that head of yours, ha? What would they think if they knew that, ha?"

"They" refers to the Neumillers. She's stolen him from them over Easter vacation and for the summer—as she'll continue to steal him for every vacation she can for the rest of her life—and the idea of stealing him, which she often mentions, makes her proud; when she and he are reunited, as they want to be, she routs out any affection he might have built up for "them" over the months and examines it with cold decisiveness; and then with a scandalous air of indiscretion lets him know that love, which she feels for him (in contrast to the guardianship they take for granted), is more observant and refined. But if she senses she's been unfair, or wronged them, or colored his emotion too much, she changes from criticism to breathtaking asides of over-painted praise: "Your Grandma Neumiller is one of the most unaffected women I know. Your dad's a saint."

"I'm not bashful," he says, and feels a baby again, and hopes he can sustain this state of suspension for days with her.

"You're not? You're not, ha?" She puts her damp fingertips to his chin and tilts up his face, which he still holds immobile in mourning. "Then why are you blushing, ha?"

He pulls away, turning to put the forks in the chimney cupboard and her *Ha?*, which she repeats and relishes repeating, rises into high laughter she doesn't seem to be able to control, and so settles into with more relish. She's trapped him within the net of a general female truth.

"Grandpa doesn't talk either," he says. "He just grunts."

His grandfather is the painful area and Charles knows it. He's close to eighty and affects dress pants and pinstriped shirts with sleeves that blossom foppishly above bright arm garters, whether he's in the living room listening to baseall on the radio, or in the barnyard with his favorite team, Colonel and Queenie, feeding them cookies. If Charles were his grandfather, he wouldn't feed sweets to the horses, he'd shoot them; last winter, when his grandfather was gathering hay with the team, they bolted, and he was pitched backward off the hayrack and broke his spine.

The accident has diminished him. He was always small but the top of his head doesn't reach his wife's shoulder now. She keeps the cookies in the same place on purpose, so he knows where they are and can get at them easily, but he believes he steals them without her knowledge, and laughs under his breath so much at his foxiness, he seems diminished in other, worse, ways. All that remains of his former passion is the temper that once compelled him to kick a milch cow so hard its rear legs collapsed and it sat down in its stanchion—that temper—and she scolds him for it with a temper of her own that's just as bad. She talks down to him more than to Charles, and begins arguments that lead to him cursing her to her face and her in tears. She claims he isn't more grateful for the times she's nursed him because he's self-centered, thankless, and as hard as nails. She says, "Maybe your grandpa doesn't talk much now, but there was never a smidgen of bashfulness in that man in his life. He's a miserable, miserable, spiteful old crow!"

These last words were so harsh Charles has looked up. Beneath her cheekbones, color appears and spreads in a rose wash down her jaw. If he hadn't seen her rock his grandfather in her arms, singing, "So, so; so, saso; so so . . ." on the nights when he wakes from his often-repeated dream of being locked up forever in a hospital, he'd think she hates him.

She empties the dishwater into the sink and from the sink it runs splashing into the bucket of slops that sits beneath, and then she takes a dipper of hot water from the reservoir at the side of the stove, swirls it in the pan, and sloshes it over the wooden paddles of a butter churn she's washed. Her anger has evaporated and she's humming in her high and girlish voice a Lutheran hymn, taking different harmony lines as she hums, and her serenity and detachment make him jealous.

He says, "Why don't you have drains, or hot and cold running water, like Grandpa and Grandma Neumiller do?"

"Because we're in the sticks. And plumbing out here comes too high." This is said in the voice she uses in her bedroom, faraway and elegant, as if she's murmuring to herself in an empty palace room. She begins to dry the pieces of crockery and he sees *Red Wing Pottery* stamped into their bottoms, and feels trapped again.

She says, "When you get to be a big man like your dad, you can build me a nice new house in town somewhere, with plumbing and the other contraptions everybody else seems to have now."

"No, I can't. You'll be dead by then."

"What!"

"You'll be dead by then."

"Charles! What sort of thing is that to say to your grandma?"

She tilts up his face once more. Wherever in him these words have come from, he's now himself again, a responsible nine. In her eyes he sees hurt and stern anger, and then disbelief, and then she laughs and says, "If that doesn't take the cake! So I'll be dead by then, you say. Is that what you really think?"

"I just said that. I don't want you to be."

"Oh, of course not. I know you don't. I know, I know," she says, and takes him in her arms. "So, so, I know you didn't mean it. I know you don't want me to be. I know you didn't want your mother to be, either. Even so, won't you still think of me a lot, the way you do her?"

26

ᦂᦎᦎ

KICKING AROUND

"'Ed!" she calls.

She's hoarse and in a foul mood, her face yellow-tinged with fatigue, and now she slumps on one hip and lays her face along the frame of the living-room door.

"Ed! Come and eat!"

He's in a square-backed rocking chair in the corner by his radio, leaning toward the left, his dainty feet dancing a few inches off the floor, his right ear, his good ear, held close to the radio's circular, perforated speaker of brass, through which a baseball game emerges at full volume. He holds a cane in a two-fisted grip, and now its hooked handle turns; somebody's struck out. His face is gray and unshaven, his lips pressed in a white line, and his eyes, hooded by prominent bone that's emerged more over the years, as gleaming and fierce as an eagle's, flash back and forth, tracing a mental record of this baseball game for the sake of future arguments with imaginary friends.

"Ed! Do you hear?"

He doesn't. And it's not so much a question of his hearing, which has failed, as it is him. He doesn't care to hear. He can't bear for her to keep intruding on him and his baseball, as if she's jealous of even that. It's vicarious now, the last of his final pleasures, and elevates him out of the present, where he's become old, nearly eighty, been proclaimed a cripple by the medical profession, and had to hand the reins of this virginal and promising farm, which has the potential to vindicate those decades of grubbing in bad soil, over to his wife and son, goddamnit.

What more does she want? Her wish about the grand-kid, Charles, is fulfilled; the boy's spending his summer here. Everywhere this cane carries him, he sees the kid running all over hell and damnation, chousing the heat-afflicted cattle, kicking at chickens, making this clinker of an old man feel worse. Oh, it isn't the kid's tearing around that really bothers him, though it bothers him enough, being a gimp, but that the boy reminds him so of his dear dead daughter it's enough to make him, the terror of her life, the noisy drunkard who never once told her he loved her—it's enough to make him cry out at the sky. Hardly more than a girl and already gone from them to the grave, gone at the age he was when he met the girl's mother. Dear God! Outlived by him, just as he's outlived three of his sons—all in accidents, as though the curse he claimed was on his life, if there was one, had passed through him to them and they'd suffered it in his stead.

What for? All his life he's felt as tangled and stranded within himself as nails in a keg. The only way to freedom was to pull a tangle loose and hammer them into a new day. But he hadn't done that since he was forty. He held back for the kids. They were his hope. They were a way home. And now they were gone, all of the boys except Lionell, *she* was gone, and this husk of a man who was once Ed Jones was paying out endless dues to the demands of the past. He wasn't even well enough to attend the funeral, or so the doctor and wife told him, to give her a final grace, a father's goodbye, his final word: forgive. When they talked before she left for Illinois, she took his hand in a sudden clasp and covered her eyes as if to say it was the last time there'd be this current of touch between them. And he thought, Well, it's my turn now, I'm a goner soon, and she knows it, and won't say. But it was her time. And he might have realized it if he hadn't been so afraid for his own skin. Too afraid to enter and help ease the tragedy she ended up living out alone.

Martin, my penance, as you'd call it, and my duty is to help you if I can. Those days when she was a baby, wasn't even walking yet, you missed, boy. We'd sit on the floor and roll empty thread spools back and forth, spools of Ma's I'd painted every sort of color in a mad and drunken scramble for her Christmas that year, and I could hold up the purple spool and say "Purrr-ple" and make her laugh so hard she turned purple and red. She wasn't a year old yet and nobody else could make her laugh that way, and it was a word that did it. I miss those days so much my insides are rising out my back teeth, and the chunks of fillings there sing and taste of sin and silver. Oh, the times we had when she was young and I wasn't afraid of her because of the hallucinatory effects of booze. She was so intelligent and changeable she felt alien, a threat to my stiff mind, an angel with the energy of a sun, and it radiated from her eyes if you could look there.

"Ed!"

I felt unworthy of her and poured down even more of the stuff. I had to stay clear of her and her eyes for my sanity's sake. It made her wary and as afraid of everyday life as I was. I'd ask her a question. She'd look at her mother. Then she'd turn back to me. Or does a girl always hesitate that way for her father? Do your daughters do it, boy? I was so old compared to other fathers I must have looked to her a walking ghost. And yet I'm alive and she's not, and I sit here stranded in strife. Oh, sweet Jesus, please forgive me my sins. I'm afraid of burning in hell now. A dirty cringing frigging chicken coward still. Why don't any of the kids send a message about the other side?

The worst of it is I want a drink this minute.

I was afraid all along about the way she'd go, and knew how she would, and should have been a man and told you, Martin; all her married life, and even before she married you, I kept saying to her over and over, "Alpha, don't have too many kids. Please. Don't ever have too many kids. You'll hurt yourself." I knew it from the time she was four and lived with it since in this silence. She was too delicate, too pliable, too possessed and clinging to her mother then, and her palms were such damp and blue-veined wells. And I knew it was a hard and dangerous world out here. Oh, what energy was expended on that energetic child! Either she was the real reason for reality, or else there's no proof. I'd give half my years if she could have another year on earth and knew over that year she was dying, for her and her kids' sakes. Now there's that creaking and rush in my ears that must be the sound of the end. Oh, ho, ho, Lord, these old bones will shed themselves and soon be pools for bugs to drink at. Give Martin and his kids a long life. Forgive, Alpha, for—

"What's the matter?" his wife asks. "Are they losing again?"

His blurred fingers, swollen broadly at each knuckle, remind him of the youngster who caught for the best pitchers around, when there was one major league and pay was unpredictable, equipment poorly made, and the fast ball the most frequent pitch. There's an unexpected crack of a bat and the fingers flex with pain.

"Ed?"

She walks up and jerks a week-old copy of *The Fargo Forum* from between his back and the back of the chair, where he's draped it to absorb his sweat. He doesn't respond. She shakes him by the shoulder and says, "Ed, for God's sake, come and eat!"

He turns his fulminating face full on her. She's become his barber and guardian, his nurse and hired man. Whatever she says he can't do, he can't now. Her Christliness has him in chains. She does the chores he can only in his mind, which is the way he occupies himself when he isn't busy with baseball. If she loved him, she wouldn't tackle all the tasks he cares about—the shame of it!—and is too crippled up to do now; she'd let Lionell handle them. If she loved him, she'd leave him to his baseball and himself. She'd let him die.

"Do I have to lift you out of that chair?"

"You do—" The tobacco in his mouth, which he's forgotten about and now tastes, has drawn up so much saliva there's no room for his tongue to move. He swallows it down, and says, "You do, and I'll crack you with this goddamn cane."

She seems less frightened than disenchanted, and her interested eyes retreat from his. "You're a mean old fool," she says. "And you get meaner every day."

"And it'll get worse before it gets better, you can bet your ass on that, milady."

"Stop!"

"When you stop your yipping."

"As soon as you come and eat."

"After this inning."

"This inning nothing! After this inning it'll be the next inning, and after that the next game, and then it'll be night. Lord, you infuriate me! Right now! The food's getting cold."

"Pee on the food."

"Ed!" The tremolo in her voice climbs close to tears.

"I'll turn it up so I can listen in there."

"Up? *Up?* It's been going full blast all day! I have a headache from it! *Damn!*"

"You're not going on low yourself."

She reaches over and revolves the knob three times (his illuminated master-scene dimming as she does this) until there's a click that recedes into a ticklish spot in his brain. She touches his shoulder. "Please. Chuckie's at the table, waiting."

Chuckie, my best horse's ass, he wants to say, and does get out "horse's" as he pulls himself to his feet with the aid of the cane; he gets his balance and goes toward the kitchen, limping hard on his left leg, his free elbow swinging backward with that uneven stride. His suit pants are belted at the bottom of his chest, a yellow-and-black package protrudes from his hip pocket, and with each belabored step toward his place at the head of the table, a concession to his former authority here, the package rises higher until *F. F. Adams & Co.* and then *Peerless* can be read. The package doesn't fall.

"Ed," she says. "Wash your hands first."

"What's that?"

"Wash your hands first."

"What for?"

"You're going to eat."

"So? I washed them this morning. A man can't get dirty sitting on his ass all day."

"It's my food you're eating and you'll wash before you do."

"Bull—"

"Watch that tongue! There's a child here!"

"Child, hell. He's got a hammer on him just like me, hasn't he?"

"Wash!"

"By Christ, I don't know what it is with you! I can't understand it! Why can't you leave a man alone? I haven't got a goddamn nothin' but my balls and you keep kicking them around the kitchen! *What is it?* Say what you want and I'll crawl up your bung to do it. Stop this picky shit!"

"I said *wash!*"

He shakes with exasperation, and then executes a turn, gets the tripod of him going noisily to the washstand, and dips his hands into the basin of water she's poured. He hangs his cane over a wrist, picks up a bar of her honey-colored, homemade soap, and it slips in a shot through his fingers. He kicks out and gets it with a toe before it hits the floor. She hurried over and places it in the basin, avoiding his fierce eyes, and blushing to her forehead.

To hell with soap for today, then.

He wipes his hands on the roller towel, runs his thumb along his gums to remove the matted tobacco, drops it into the slop bucket, and goes to the table and eases himself into his chair. Charles is across from him with his hands in his lap, staring at the flowers on his plate, and the sight of the boy like this fills him with regret. He'll end up like Lionell.

"Where's Lionell?" he asks.

"Out cultivating," Charles murmurs.

"Good for him!" He also wants to say, For Christ's sake, Charles, buck up. I'm here to help you out, for God's sake.

He turns and hangs his cane on the chair back, sensing the ball game drawing to its conclusion, and this fills him with unrest and a different sort of sadness. He looks up and discovers her eyes on him, and they stir him with their warmth, their interest in him, and their lack of pity. He picks up his fork, fumbling, and begins to eat.

He remembers when he courted her. He was in his thirties, closer to forty, had just left his first wife, and was working as a swipe and jockey for a stable in Fargo, but with pasturing and paddocks spread out across the state; he'd been to Pennsylvania and Ohio and New York, where he'd picked up a wardrobe of tailor-made clothes, and was looked upon as a dandy, even among the jocks. There was one wizened little juicer with a face that reminded him, now, of Lionell's, who referred to him as "Every woman's dream of having a baby who's also hung." Eduardo Jonas, he sometimes called himself, since he was dark-skinned enough to pass for a Mex and the ladies went for that then. He had a reputation as a ladies' man, which he was, and which he was able to be with extraordinary ease, because he didn't give a damn about ladies. All he cared about were horses and baseball, and real baseball, professional baseball, hadn't yet made its way West.

Then he met her, a country girl with gold hair piled high on her head, high breasts and slim hips ("The closer the bone, the sweeter the meat"), skin as cool-looking as ivory, and a profile—high brow, straight nose, full parted lips—both sensual and strong. She was seventeen, shy and untouched, and refined in a way that Eastern women were bruited to be but weren't; they were just jaded and cold, the ones he'd known, while she was as graceful and spirited as the fine thoroughbreds he worked with. And she was tall, tall and elegant, a head taller than he was.

Immediately, he was ill at ease, which had never happened to him when he was with a woman, no matter who or what the woman was or how she was built. He hated himself for being so short. He hated the fancy clothes that called attention to his size. He hated her for making him feel as he did, and after that first meeting vowed never to see her again. But he came to her house the next night and every night after, and sat in the drawing room, silent and in pain, and watched her fingers travel over her needlework as she told pleasant and intelligent stories about school and the children she taught there. She never talked about herself. After months of this, he finally said in a fury, "By Jesus, Electa, you better marry me!" She flushed at the tone of his voice and, with eyes still lowered to her sewing, told him that she knew he was unhappy, that she'd loved him since he walked through the door, and wanted to live with him for the rest of her life, however he decided it.

He was terrified she was trying to do him in. He went back East, hoping to rid himself of her and the torment she stirred in him, but couldn't stand being apart from her and not knowing how she'd spent her day, even if it was with those damn kids, and so, with a store of contempt for himself at having run off like a coward, he ran back and married her. He cursed her and browbeat and berated her and brought up all the women he could think of, plus a few he invented, who had the power to make her hurt; he told her she put on airs like an assy-pants, and wouldn't let her go visiting down the road, go to church, wear flattering clothes, have women friends, and went on drinking bouts that lasted for weeks. Then one morning, waking in the web of her hair, he realized he wasn't caught, wasn't in torment, hadn't broken her spirit, and that he loved her.

He looks at her eyes, which are turned down; at her profile, her face demure and vulnerable-looking now while she eats; at her hands, delicate in spite of the work she does, and flushes with pride and arrogance. She still has her beauty; she's still the same. It would take some doing to win her over again, to make her quail at the tone of his voice, or surrender, and he makes plans on how he'll storm out to the barn, harness up the team, hitch them to the mower, and start to mow the yard while she watches, and then she'll come out to tell him to quit, and he'll rise from the seat, balancing on the axle, and cry, "Get away before you get hurt! Get back in the kitchen where you belong!" And then drive to the hay field on the forty back in the woods and mow all of it, and get drunk on a bottle out in the horse barn and come in late at night, covered with pollen and filth, stinking of horses and booze and armpits, his lights and vitals healthily afire inside him, and crawl into bed like that.

He breaks out with scattering cries of pleasure and delight. Maybe he'll have to try that. Maybe tomorrow. Their eyes meet, hers tentative and questioning, still like a girl's, his shining with slyness, and by Jesus, he decides, he *will* try it. Soon too. As soon as he can see through the present to the dust that he is and be alive again.

27

AT HEIGHT OF LAND LAKE
WITH FATHER

Charles stepped up from darkness into the frame of the door to the horse barn as a black Chevrolet pulled into the farmyard and stopped near the house, a hundred yards off, and even at that distance he could see that it blazoned a North Dakota license plate, and then the door on the driver's side winged outward and Father Schimmelpfennig rose up from behind it, his balding head bare and glazed by the sun, and turned in a circle as he surveyed the farm. Charles took off on a run, his heart flinging seizures around the column of air in his throat, and then slowed to a walk when Father saw him and waved, but soon his legs betrayed him and he came up to the car as out of breath as if he'd run the mile and a half to the mailbox and back. "Father!" he said. "What are you *doing* here?"

Father smiled down at him, his gold-capped tooth gleaming in the summer light, and reached out and ruffled his hair. "Well, well, well, and how is my Charles today, ay?"

It was like a return to the comfort of the past to have his name pronounced in Father's accent, like "chalice."

"Have you been a good boy, Charles?"

Charles flooded with color and looked down; Father had heard in the confessional about his problem with bad actions, as Charles called it, and the problem had become worse.

"Ach! I didn't mean mo*rrr*ally," Father said, rolling the *r* with his rich foreignness. "I meant, have you been a good companion to your grandparents?"

"I guess."

"And your Uncle Lionell?"

"Yes."

"This is a nice place they have here," Father said, and looked around once more, shorter and older than Charles remembered him, with violet-veined cheeks and deep-set wrinkles at the corners of his eyes; and his stomach, plumper than before, parted his double-breasted jacket with a blacker space, his dainty feet shod in hook-and-eye shoes, like Charles's grandfather's, the high polish on them holding reflections of Charles and the car and—

"Do you always stare down when you meet people you know?" Father asked him. "Aren't you as happy as I on this bright and sunshiny day?"

"Yes," Charles said. He'd spent most of the summer walking from one fence line of the farm to another with his eyes on the ground, wondering if the dead ever really come back to life.

"What's that?" Father asked. He pointed toward some rough-cut lumber, stacked to cure, as children stack matchsticks, into interlocking houselike squares.

"Green fir," Charles said.

"No, no, no. That ma*chine*."

Lionell's car was parked between two squares, to protect it from the weather, he said. He'd just finished high school and a current local fad was to have an outlandish car; one of his friends drove an antiquated hearse with kitchen curtains in its windows, and Lionell had told Charles that he and the friend had had girls behind the pulled curtains on the main street of Park Rapids. Lionell had repainted his own car, a '36 Plymouth sedan, with white house paint, and over the white had painted red and blue polka dots the size of dinner plates; had, indeed, used one of his mother's plates as a template.

"That's Lionell's bug," Charles said; and then it occurred to him: "How'd you know where I *was*?"

"Well, your dad wrote and said you were here over vacation, so I wrote back and said, 'Where is this farm in Minnesota? Are there any good lakes close?' Because even in the Old Country we heard that the fishing in Minnesota was the best. And then I was thinking of my vacation coming up. Priests must take vacations, too, you know!"

"But how'd you find it?"

"Your dad drew a map and your grandma's friends are friendly to priests. Have you been fishing often yet?"

"Not too."

"I thought when people lived in Minnesota they went every day."

"Lionell's been pretty busy." Lionell had taken over a lot of the work of the farm since Charles's grandfather was injured, but he'd also been hanging out with his high-school friends more, and dating, and said he'd outgrown the sport of catching fish.

"Is he in the fields now?"

"I don't know." When Charles last saw him, he was on his back in the middle of the living-room floor, asleep, in spite of the radio going at full volume; he'd been drunk the night before.

"Well, here's what I was thinking," Father said. "Why don't Charles and Lionell and I go fishing today!"

Charles was off on a run toward the house.

"And maybe your grandma, too! Wilhomena is with me." Wilhomena, dark-haired and plump, with fleshy filled-out features, leaned out of a reflection partly obscuring her and twinkled her fingers at him from behind the windshield.

Charles ran up the steps onto the porch and opened the screen door, then let it close; the house inside was spare and well swept, with all but the kitchen shades drawn against the sun, cool and dark even at midday, parts of it sparkling from the pinholes of light let in by the shades, its air so dense with mourning and unspoken memories you weren't sure whether you were touching somebody's arm or a piece of furniture, and had to stare to make sure. Charles knew that the aspect of him that his grandmother and Lionell liked the least, for differing reasons, was that he was a Catholic, and didn't feel Father would be welcome here; he turned and said, "If they don't want to go, will you still take me?"

"One of the reasons I came so far, Charles, was to see you fish!"

He went through two doors into the kitchen, where his grandmother was at the cookstove, stirring an iron kettle with a wooden spoon stained violet.

"Grandma—"

"I know, I saw," she said, and held up the steaming

spoon and touched her tongue to it; she'd met Father once, in January, when he preached the eulogy for Charles's mother, and now as Father stepped into the kitchen Charles felt afraid for him. His grandmother nodded, and said, "Good morning, sir."

"Good morning, Mrs. Jones, good morning, my dear!"

He took her hand and patted it, and Charles, seeing the impassiveness of his grandmother's face, was aware once again of Father's accent. "Eet's so goot to zsee you agane, ant in yorrr own 'ome dis dtyum. You haf a lufly bplace herrre."

"It does for us."

"Eet's a bparrradice, Meesusz Chones!"

They regarded one another as courtiers must have, with sympathetic separate selves but across a vast and frosty tract of silence where neither had yet trod, each able at any instant to issue a challenge, and then she grasped her apron and looked down. "I've never had the chance, and I've wanted to thank you for the kind words you said about our girl, sir. You buried her as well as we could have asked."

The tremolo in her voice contained a sadness Charles had heard only in song.

"You know, Mrs. Jones, if I could have had my choice, I would have rather it was I who had died."

"That showed in your sermon, sir. I liked it that you said she was a saint."

"It was no exaggeration!"

"She would have liked that."

There was an exclamation from the living room and Charles saw his grandfather, in his rocker by the radio, staring in a startled way at Father; he gave his head a hard shake, as if to shake it from dream, grappled with his cane as though it were a weapon he'd use, and then pushed himself up and went stumping past Lionell's outflung arm into the back bedroom, leaving the radio playing on high to his empty chair that continued to rock.

Father hadn't seen him. He said, "Charles and I have been talking about an outing, a fishing trip, and we decided you'd all like to go. My housekeepr is with me, and you ladies could keep one another company while we men fish."

"Daddy couldn't go," she said with sudden force. "He's too crippled up."

"Then you and Lionell," Father said.

"I just got this batch of blueberries going."

"Will they take long?"

"Two hours." Was this exaggeration?

"That's fine, then! We have to go to town anyway, to get some tings and see about accommodations. We'll want to fish all afternoon, ay, Charles?" He winked. "So we'll need a place for the night. Is there a hotel in Park Rapids?"

"Yes."

"Good! They outshine motels in my business, Mrs. Jones. We'll get ourselves some rooms, then, and come by after lunch to pick you up."

"Well, I—"

Father's forefinger came up. "Ah-ah, Mrs. Jones, you can't say no to me. I'm a priest!"

She gave a girlish cry and then bit her lip and looked away.

Lionell came in from the living room, barefoot, the crown of his flattop smashed, his eyes swollen and mean-looking from sleep, and scowled and clenched his fists; he was short-tempered and combative and returned sometimes from his nights out with a black eye or a cut on his face. "What's this?" he asked.

"Lionell," Father said, and took one of his big fists in both hands and gave it a shake. "We're going fishing!"

Lionell glanced at his mother as if for a sign of the attitude he should adopt.

"We're all waiting for you to tell us the best place," Father said.

"Oh?" Lionell said. "Well, I wonder who's going to cultivate my corn when all this is coming off."

"Ouf!" she cried. "You never work anyway, you fool!"

Her handling of Lionell made Charles uneasy, and she'd been angry at her youngest son over the summer in a way that made their relationship worse; he slept late, came home with liquor on his breath, and a week ago, doing the wash, she came across a prophylactic in a pocket of his pants and ran upstairs, where he lay asleep, naked under the sheets, and started slapping him with a flyswatter and crying shame until her voice gave out.

"Well," Lionell said, and shook his head once, like his father. "You better talk to Ma. She's the boss around here."

"Oh, you oaf, you," she cried. "Shut your mouth before I hit you over the head with this spoon!"

"Eek!" Lionell said. "With a *priest* here, Ma? What manners have we not?" He laughed in a high *hee hee hee* he'd picked up from a friend, and then winked at Father to indicate this was a joke between them.

Father winked back.

"Which is the lake, Lionell?"

"They're all pretty good around here, Reverend."

"But which is the best?"

"I've been hearing some pretty wild tales about Height of Land lately, but that's thirty miles off."

"Thirty miles is nothing!" Father said. "It's Height of Land for us!" Out of his sleeve he popped a wristwatch up. "At one-thirty, then, we'll come for you. That will give you time for your blueberries, Mrs. Jones, and for Wilhomena to pack some tings for a picnic for us."

"I have some cold chicken I can bring," she said.

Lionell gave her a dry and crusty look and she turned from him to the window. "It'd be nice to get out in the open and away from this stove."

"Good!" Father said, and was out of the kitchen with Lionell and Charles behind, to his car, where he introduced Lionell, through the rolled-down window—Father had whirled his finger at her—to Wilhomena; she was effusive about the scenery, the woods and fields and cattle they'd seen, and her blissful innocence, as enveloping as her perfume, made Charles wish he could protect her; she spoke in an accent exactly like Father's and her fluty adenoidal voice, with its liquid whine of monotone, always reminded Charles of a back-timber mosquito droning close to his ear. Lionell, he was sure, perceived it and her plump translucence in more picturesque terms.

"I believe we'll take this," Father said, and laid his hand on the hood of his car. "Charles has introduced me to yours, Lionell."

"What did you think when you first saw it? Tell me the truth now."

"I thought it was absolutely exquisite for you. But if I were to ride in it, Lionell, well—" He held his hand

-horizontal, fingers outspread, and teeter-tottered it back and forth. "People might wonder if the Second Coming wasn't on them."

"Yeah, well, I've been having trouble getting it started lately, anyway," Lionell said. "I think the gas pump's shot."

Father got in the car and put on a black homburg and the bluish window lowered past his face as Wilhomena's went up. "Is there anything in town I can pick up, Lionell? Tackle? Groceries? Night crawlers?"

"*Angle*worms?" Lionell said.

"Aren't they good on trout?"

"Yeah, well, you won't find many trout around here. We'll be going after line-busting muskies and pike, with maybe a walleye or two thrown in. Only Indians use angleworms."

Charles was surprised at Lionell's tone; his girlfriend for a year was an Indian from the settlement over near Nevis, and during his and Charles's former fishing days, he'd put a fish head in each hill of sweet corn, as the Indians did, and say, "That way the corn can see where it's growing." There was the ratchety sound of a Chevrolet starting motor, and then Father held up a hand and nodded and smiled, the gold in his mouth giving off a flash, and guided the black car around the turnabout and out the drive. Lionell and Charles went back to the house, where Lionell high-stepped past his mother with sneaking strides, and in the center of the room gave off an air-tearing whistle and jumped up and slapped the ceiling with both hands. "Whooopee!" he cried. "A hotel in Park Rapids! Do you think they'll get separate rooms, Ma?"

"Of course!"

"Adjoining ones?"

"Hush, you."

"Because I thought the old boy looked like he could use a little *ahem!* before da beeg feeshing treep."

"Lionell, stop!"

"Well, she's got mighty big knockers on her for the housekeeper of a priest, Ma, did you catch that? Oh, them ole boobavoobadoobies"—he was fluttering his lips with a finger and making a kazoolike booby-beleaguered blubbering buzz as though it sputtered up and came from the end of his thumb—"a blub blub blub blah-blah-blah, Ma!"

She unslung the dish towel from her shoulder and threw it, a zigzag in the air at him, and he leaped off to one side, catching it where he'd been, and tied it over his head like a babushka, and sang: " 'Vilhomena! Youf gawd aual tda boisss vacky en dah nauggin' "—he crossed his eyes and rapped on his head—" 'eeeein Koooopenhaugin'!'"

"Stop it," she said. "You stop that right now!"

But Charles could see creases of inconsistency appear around her mouth, and then she turned to the stove, blushing, and tried to conceal a smile. Lionell kept up the song and broke into a clumsy clog step in his bare feet, which he made seem snowshoe-sized, and she glanced over her shoulder with eyes that flashed surrender and devotion and feelings deeper than maternal love.

Charles went outdoors, past the lilacs, where chickens scratched and sat ruffled and blinking in oval bowls of dust, past the tool shed, weathered gray, and pressed down on the lowest strand of barbed wire and started toward the grayish-green hill of pines that separated the barnyard from the pasture, walking in the winding path the milch cows continually took, cut like a trench into the sod of the cattle lane, and entered the strip of pines, old trees, forty and fifty feet tall, their striated trunks the girth of his chest, their lower limbs swaying only inches above his head with a sound of expired breath, the earth coppery-orange with enmeshed needles that gave under his feet and glowed with pools and ladderlike rivulets of sun. With a trunk at his back, ass down, legs spread over the cushiony ground, he looked up through the needles above and wondered if anybody had ever really seen a wood tick fall or drop from a branch onto anybody, and when. The blue of the sky rippled above with its summer intensity.

In Hyatt, under the doorbell of Father's house, on a lettered name card fixed beneath glass, following Father's first initials and his name, were D.D. and Ph.D. Charles's father explained what the initials meant and compared them to the B.A. he had, in terms of school attended, plus a thesis and special reading, and said that Father and earned both of the degrees from the University of Heidelberg, where Hamlet went. In Father's basement, in a brick-lined cave with a white-mortared brick arch above

covered with fusty and nitrous old cobwebs, were honeycombed racks that held bottles of wine, plus cases of beer
with foreign printing on them stacked to the ceiling. Two
or three times a year Charles's family went to the rectory
for dinner, and there were so many plates and glasses and
pieces of silverware, he didn't know where to begin, and
could hardly see the food anyway, because only candles
were going, tidbits of light; and as if hidden from them by
the shadows cast, Charles's father, who never usually
drank, drank then, drank wine, and kept up the general
spirits with amusing stories from his past. The dishes were
vast affairs arranged by contour, or subtlety of color in the
special light, and were unlike any Charles had tasted before, and his mother, who was at the least particular, once
said that eating at Father's, where the mood of the meal
and the people gathered about it were more important
than the food, was eating in style, a word that won es-
teem with her, while her least word to Charles added
her dimension to his simplest event, and when she enjoyed herself as she did at Father's, he felt he could step
off his chair and float. Straight as a star. After they'd
moved to Illinois and she'd died, he was digging through
a box that was still unpacked and came across his baby
book, and saw, in her hand: "Charles' baptism. Nov. 26.
He wore the full-length embroidered gown with the under-
slip that his dad wore when *he* was baptized. Wilhomena
held him, proxy, because his godparents, Gram and
Grandpa N, couldn't be here. Every time Fr touched him,
he opened his eyes and smiled."

*

They pulled up to a gray-black weathered bait shop covered with soft-drink advertisements made of tin; one of
them held a huge thermometer; it was close to ninety degrees. Fifty yards ahead lay Height of Land Lake, and the
air around, stained blue-gray from the expanse of it,
smelled of pine pitch and fish scales and some sort of
subterranean mold. Father sidled through a stand of bean-
pole birches, their webwork of light sliding over his clothes,
and stopped at the water's edge, planted a foot, placed his
fist at his belt, throwing back a flap of his jacket, and
gripped his cigar tighter in his teeth, and Charles remem-

bered his father looking up from a book, and saying, "I'd like to see Father portray one of Shakespeare's kings on-stage sometime; he has the right face for it, his manner is so courtly and European, and he has the presence of a king," and Charles's mother had smiled in her way that meant this was meaningful, and said, "He'd make a perfect Henry VIII."

Lionell and Charles went out on spongy grass beside him, the unruffled blue of the lake reflecting the cloudless sky, as though blue were being distilled over the surface in front of them. A band of pine and fir encircled the blue with green. It was a Wednesday and there was only one boat, a single-manned rowboat, on the whole of the large lake. "Lovely," Father said. "I'm sure there are fish here, but it's nearly enough just seeing it, Lionell. I feel something's in store for us. Thank you for thinking of here. Now"—he clapped his hands and rubbed and wrung them —"we'll need a boat."

"They rent them at the bait shop, Reverend."

"You pick one out for us, then, and I'll go take care of it, and we'll be off!"

Charles followed Lionell onto a narrow dock, where green-painted rental boats were tied up and rocking on either side of them, and Lionell stepped down into one, sending it off in a lazy glide, and started checking its oarlocks. Charles went out to the end of the dock and saw a cage of wire mesh fastened to a post of the pier there. A big bluegill was finning from corner to corner in quick flits, in a continual and abstracted restlessness, rootless here, and Charles saw himself walking the boundaries of the farm, and felt the constriction and smallness of all he did and the meagerness of its effect within his known world. Lionell was hard on him, to make a man of him, Lionell said, and expected him to be at his side whenever he worked, and, lately, when he went to bed; there he made Charles masturbate him until he came spattering off, flopped over on his side, folded into himself, and fell asleep, and what was Charles to do with his tingling bat-swinger alone in the black dark? More often than not, to keep from waking Lionell by going whacking away to work at it, he wanted to cut it off where it got a good start. "Yours is too little to get a hold of," Lionell said to him.

Lionell borrowed a wide-wheeled Farmall Cub from a dirt-poor, skinnily T-shirted, electric-eyed Fundamentalist, Leon Flisher, to use for cultivating corn, and since there was no room for Charles on the hitch or near the seat with the cultivator attached, Lionell had him sit at the front of the tractor, on the support and tie bar that ran out to the right wheel: "This way, if you fall off, I'll see you before you get cultivated under," he said. Charles sat rigidly balanced, his feet skimming only inches above ground and ticking down some of the flappily flowing and unfolding corn crop, hill by hill, afraid to show fear, the bucking tractor jolting him closer to the hypnotizing tire, and then on one sharp turnaround at the end of the rows, as he grabbed out to keep from falling or hitting the barbed-wire fence that came in three spraddling springs through the green-tinted air toward him, his thumb got crushed in a steering knuckle. Before he could pull it out or get Lionell stopped by his scream ("Hell, I thought you were just jacking around up there," Lionell said), it was torn open down its length to bluish-white bone with blood-spotted cords parted over it. Lionell took him on his shoulders on a run back home, and they showed the wound to Charles's grandmother, who was in the garden in her broad-brimmed summer hat, and asked what she thought. "Soak it in Lysol," she said. "Then see how it looks."

Lionell soaked it in Lysol, and then took out a pair of sewing scissors—"Does that hurt?" he'd ask with smiling irony—and trimmed off all the ragged pieces of skin and flesh he could find, shaming Charles for behaving like a child. Which reminded him of lying underneath this floor at nearly the same spot, at a screened-in foundation vent, with La Verne Flisher, who had his father's eyes and a baldish sort of head with hair pulled out in spiky patches, and while they studied one another and whispered probing talk, smoking one of the rare long butts from Lionell's fairly well concealed (enough to satisfy his mother) cigarette habit, Charles asked the kid, at least a couple years younger, why he pulled out his hair that way, and Flisher said, "My ma says it's because I'm not one of the Chosen." Just that afternoon his mother had come into the house with a collation of dates and of the numbers in Revelations which proved, she said, that eternity would come during this year, perhaps in a matter of hours. "But she just says that when she's mad at me. I think she really thinks I'm some kind of new savior or something. Just when I nail her with a thought, she blinks. One time I went out and hid in the woods and got cut up bad and she bawled about it for days. I pull it out because I can't keep up with the hours, or something. You know. Or else there's electricity coming out of my ears. Or something in there is itching to get loose. I don't know. I've thought about it a lot, for hours."

Now the purplish-white scar along the inside of Charles's thumb stirred with sympathetic currents at the memory, and he rubbed it and began humming a song with uneasiness, out of tune, he supposed, as Lionell would soon tell him. One of his chores was to let the cows out of the barn after each milking, kicking at those that wanted to stay behind and hump up to leave a good dribbly mess; he was too short to reach the lock at the top of the stanchions, so he stood on the edge of the manger to manage the task. There was a sulky Brown Swiss with big curved horns, Yokie, a hater of children, and one evening when he released her—she was always the last he let go —she lunged out and hooked him with a horn near the heart, and sent him flying into the manger. For a while his wind was gone and his voice wouldn't work; a coil of flesh ached along his left side and seemed to swirl up into the air. He started crying for help and kept crying out until it turned dark. He stumbled through frames and currents of a daze up to a white house and lay down on a porch. The cream separator was slowing down in that deeper and loosening wobble that touches around on all the edges of equilibrium, about to settle on a center so like an infinity. Lionell came out the screen door in yellow light and asked what was wrong, so Charles told him, Yokie, and said he thought at least two ribs were broken and he better be taken to the hospital, and Lionell said, "For God's sake," and carried him in in so much pain they might have been broken, and laid him on the couch; and later, when Charles was half asleep in the honeyed parlor of semiconscious pain, he heard Lionell say to her, "He's a sissy, for Jesus' sake, a baby-face! He stubs his toe and it's 'I want to see a doctor! I want to go to the hospital!' You'd think he grew up in one."

"Yes, I know," she said, and gave a great sigh of weary disillusionment. "I think his mother coddled him too much. Yup." With her tongue she gave two clucks.

The bluegill tacked and finned in spurts from corner to corner, and Charles thought that the only time he'd received any special attention from his mother, if ever, was when he'd had pneumonia, and at that moment felt a presence behind him.

"You making friends with the fish?" Lionell said in a squeaky voice. "You think it'll help you? If you fish the way you talk, it'll be like a man with a paper ass and cardboard teeth."

A screen door slammed and Father came out of the bait shop with a big smile, holding a cane pole upright in each hand.

"Oh, for holy Jesus' sake," Lionell cried under his breath. "Don't tell me he expects to niggerfish!"

"Ladies! Ladies!" Father called. "I have the perfect solution for you for when you get bored. These!" He handed them each a pole and gave Wilhomena a paper cup which contained, Charles was sure, angleworms, and gestured to Lionell; they went back into the birches, where white wooden lawn chairs were sitting like wide-open wings, and dragged two of them down to the water's edge. "There," Father said. "Now you even have *thrrrrones* to sit and fish from! All we're missing now is the motor."

"Motor?" Lionell said; he'd often mentioned they should have a motor, so they could cover more of a lake, and troll, but wasn't ever able to afford one.

"I've rented us a motor," Father said. "I thought we'd need it to move around more, and troll. If you'd get it, Lionell, I'd be grateful. I started to, but—" He indicated his suit with a downsweep of his hands and wrinkled his nose. "They're *oily*, Lionell."

Father led Charles to his car, unlocked its trunk, handed out Lionell's tackle box and their two rods, and then leaned into the dark cavity, pulled aside some burlap bags, and brought out a tall, tinnily shining tackle box of aluminum, opened a top compartment, took out a belt-wide elasticized band dotted with the feathery tufts of fishing flies, and slipped it on over his homburg, then shook translucent shafts, sections of a fly rod, out of a

cylindrical case, and started fitting the lengths of them together.

Lionell came up and leaned the motor against a tree.
"Uh," he said. "I don't think you'll need all that fancy
stuff."

"Oh?"

"Naw. We just use a rod and reel with a spoon. Maybe
a jig or two if you've got one. 'Tarred ob libin' and
feeeeerd a-dyin'!' "

"You're the boss," Father said. He put away the elasticized band, pulled out a bottom drawer of the tackle
box, which was self-contained and had a handle on its
top, and unsheathed a springy bluish spinning rod from a
velveteen case.

"You're a real fisherman, huh?" Lionell said.

"Ach! I've hardly had time to go since I've been in the
States, and I haven't been in Minnesota once. Otherwise,
I'd be boss." He looked out with his appraising eyes over
the top of his bifocal-indented lenses. "Do you like beer,
Lionell?"

Lionell glanced in the direction of his mother, and then
stepped up to Father and said from behind his hand, as if
to confide. "To tell you the truth, Reverend, I'm a swine
for the stuff."

"Would you be unhappy if it was warm?"

"Any old way is fine with me, gluck gluck!"

"Good." From the trunk Father pulled out a carton
that contained six bright-green bottles not quite full to
their tops and beaded inside with fine foam. "We'll take
this much out in the boat, then," he said, and clinked the
carton against a cooler in the trunk. "All the rest of this
that's on ice, well, we'll save that for later, until after
we've all got our limits, right, boys? *Ahem!*"

*

They'd been on the lake for nearly an hour and not one
of them had even had a strike. The day was dead calm
and the temperature kept climbing higher into the nineties.
Four of the beers were gone. They'd fished several areas
where Lionell and Father both felt the terrain and atmosphere were right, and now sat lightly rocking in a high-
banked cover where reflected firs formed a shadowy-green

sawtooth around them. Lionell opened the fifth beer and the *hiss* of its bubbles was audible in the miniature-seeming stillness. "Well, should we pull out?" he said, generally, and Charles heard a noise that vied with finger-nails on slate; his ratchet was on; he punched at it with his thumb, not sure whether it should be on or off, but startled by the sound, and then his line swayed way off to the left and appeared to speed backward over the water toward him as it was drawn under in a dive.

"Don't worry about that lock!" Lionell cried. "Let him take it out if he wants! Don't give him any slack! Set your hook!"

Charles was in the bow and felt he couldn't turn fast enough to keep up with the sidewise, weighted, and erratic course of the line as it crossed and recrossed toward the boat's opposite side, so he lay back on the gunnel, letting the rod pass over his face in a lateral exchange, and as he sat again had to release one hand to get his balance straight. The tip of the rod went underwater in a bulge.

"Oh, for God's sake!" Lionell cried.

Charles stood and reeled in, leaving the rod where it was in a sorrow-beyond-any-amenities pose, and saw, just behind him flashing spoon, a fish that looked the length of his leg, a northern pike trailing a rusty streak of blood from its sharp-pointed undershot jaw. "I've got something," he said, trying not to tear off a scream, and, with the rod underwater, led the fish, which seemed tame and at-tentive to him, past Father in the center seat, to the stern, where Lionell reached under, grabbed it by the gills, and lifted its water-flinging length onto the seat beside him. He got loose the treble hook with some shedding of scales. "Well, it's not quite according to Hoyle, but would you look at that?" he said, and held the fish up for Father. "It must be about four pounds."

"It's a beauty, Charles," Father said. "My congratula-tions to you." He cast in a wide backhand to where Charles had hooked up. "And now I'll get one as big. Watch."

They sat for another half hour and Charles got a medium-sized bass—"Enough to make my day," Father said—and Lionell a sucker over a foot and a half long; he stomped on its head and threw it overboard, and murmured, "Rough fish. They'll ruin a lake before you know where they got off. Or in it. Yup."

Father removed, first, his double-breasted jacket, revealing that the black shirt beneath was actually a dickey held around his waist with an elastic band. "Hoooo!" Lionell cried. "This heat, hunh?" Father took off his homburg and mopped his head, then took off the dickey and his white collar, too; against his skin was a sleeveless garment with a scooped neck, made of a coarse-looking, granite-colored cloth. He broke open the last beer and fanned his face with his hat, and Charles was surprised to see knotty muscles bunching in his upper arms. "I'm ready to start p*rrr*aying," he said, and handed the beer across to Lionell.

Lionell threw the stringer of fish forward to Charles, and cried, "Tie these up there, so they don't get chopped into mincemeat by this eggbeater of a boat-loader of a motor, boy! Heigh! We're going to troll!" He was getting juiced. The back of the boat swung out to one side, turning Charles toward the open lake, like a sea to his eyes, and he felt ready for a long, fast ride.

"Whoop! Whoop!" Father cried. "It's my turn now!" His rod was arched toward the water and its end plunged down in sudden dips as he reeled in. He drew back on it, reeled, drew back again, and the boat began to slip in his direction. "Ach," he said. "A snag."

Lionell lifted loose an oar and rowed over while Father reeled in until his line went straight down, and then pulled up so hard his rod bent into a trembling omega, and weaved it from side to side, making the line sing, but still his hook held. "Ach," he said, and took out a gold-colored cigar clipper and snipped the line. "One must expect losses, too, if there is to be a gain today, don't you agree, Lionell?"

"All I know is that now we're going to troll," Lionell said, and got the motor going a speed higher and guided the boat toward a pine-studded peninsula where long-legged birds ran on a ray of sand like a wisp of sun, and then Charles cried, "Wait! Hey, you guys, hey, Lionell, *wait up!*"

Lionell looked over his shoulder and cut the motor with a slap. "For God's sake, why didn't you pull in till we were clear of this place? You're hooked up in the same spot he was, goofball."

There was a feathery flurry of water at the spot, flying spray and ripples that shattered surrounding reflections, and then Charles's line went fleeing off his reel in a flight he tried to slow with his thumb, but it began to burn without having any effect and the mechanism shook in his hands. He looked for the button of the lock but couldn't get at it for the tugging upheaval in his hands, and then stood and pulled back to set his hook, and the line took a slack arc and floated over water.

"Do one thing at a time!" Lionell cried. "If he's hooked up and wants to take it out, let him, *play* him, goddamnit!" His head dropped and he glanced up at Father from penitentially lowered lids. "Pardon me, sir."

"We're all men out here, Lionell, not convent sisters, and we're after these fish. Is he gone, Charles?"

"Yes, I guess."

"What do you mean, you *guess?*" Lionell said. "Of course he is. You know that. You're too damn impatient, is what's the matter with you. You make too much noise! You've got to learn to play him and tire him and let him go his own way at times. You can't expect to land him the minute you get a hook into the sonofabitch! Damnit, Reverend, you'll have to forgive me! I've spent so much of my life around a gutter, my mind is always in one, among the cow flop and——"

"This isn't the confessional, Lionell."

Charles felt he'd done well with his second fish and hadn't, in his handling of it, received any of Lionell's usual sour critical disdain, and was reeling in with sadness over the loss of this one, perhaps a big fish, when there was such a muscular surge at the end of his line he jolted the boat to get his leg braced; the boat dipped and yawed in that direction and in a few seconds his line was far out beyond where he'd hooked up. The reel crank was knocking against his knuckles and he could see the gleam of the spindle begin to appear below the unraveling, criss-crossing rolls of line. Lionell started the motor and eased the bow of the boat around in the direction the fish had taken, heading toward open water in a zigzag course close to the surface—a fin would sometimes trail willowy streamers—and then it swung to the left and dove hard.

Lionell cut the motor and Charles cranked wildly to catch up, his line soaked and beaded and water flying back at him, until his blurred reel below was almost full, but there was no more tension on the line. He reeled in slower.

"Well, now you've gone and lost him for good!" Lionell said. "If you're going to be that slow and clumsy and womanish and lackadaisical about it, then I don't know what the Sam Hill you're doing out here!"

And then Charles saw, over Lionell's shoulder, about ten feet out, homing in toward him with a spoon in its maw, the largest northern he'd ever seen on a line, and before he could say anything the fish finned up and started tearing up the water around the boat.

"Holy Jesus!" Lionell cried, and came in rocking strides toward the bow. He grabbed Charles's line and pulled it in hand over hand, and just as he jerked the fish up out into shining reality, it came unhooked, and Charles had to duck his flying spoon, which splashed with a jingle on the other side, but he felt something foreign strike the boat itself and saw the fish back in the stern, beating against the bottom as though it would break it.

Lionell stunned it with his heel and held it up lengthwise, laughing, and said, "Holy Jesus! It's got to be a five-pounder, at the least!"

"Charles, I won't congratulate you this time," Father said. "That was to be my fish. I was there before you."

"What kind of a spoon are you using now?" Lionell asked.

It was the same spoon Charles had used all day, a Daredevel, and now Father and Lionell had Daredevels attached to their leaders as they trolled around the peninsula and a ways up a muddy shore beyond, where shadows were forming, and then stopped in a shallow bay and cast along a stand of cattails; and then along a stand of high, greenish-beige water weeds with a blue channel winding deep into the mass of them. The next time Charles hooked up he kept tension on the line and played the fish, as Lionell had told him to, but when he got it close to the boat and was about to land it with the net Lionell handed him—where did *this* come from?—it took such a sudden plunge he was pulled off-balance and might have gone overboard if Father hadn't grabbed hold of his belt from behind. Lionell said that that's for God's sake why you sat down in a boat, was that clear now?

With the tip of his rod underwater, where the northern had pulled it—it was another northern, about the size of the first—Charles reeled in until his spoon struck the end guide and again led the fish back to Lionell, who landed it and went forward and put it on the stringer before Charles had a chance to really look at it, and threw the stringer overboard with a clattering splash.

"Is that a new trick of yours?" Lionell asked.

"What?"

"Holding the end of your rod underwater, for God's sake, and leading the damn fish around like it was a dog!"

"They don't seem so scared that way," Charles said.

"Are you? Could you handle one if it was? Can you walk straight?"

Charles went back to the bow and as he sat, with Father shielding him, he started to laugh, and though he knew he might be bringing on bodily harm by doing it, the harder he tried to stop, the worse it got. They trolled up and down the lake until after five o'clock, and then Father suggested they try their original spot, where Charles had got the three. "Reel in, then," Lionell said, and raced off across the lake at bolt-shuddering, shattering speed, the foamy spume fountaining high behind and widening into the white-edged furrow of their darker-colored tapering wake, and then they sat pitching on their ripples the shore returned to them, casting into different areas of the cove. Charles went at it halfheartedly, afraid he'd catch another one.

"Would you quit that goddamn cackling up there?" Lionell said. "You'll scare away every other fish you haven't already pulled out of this place! What's the matter with you? Do you need change for two-bits in your pipsqueak life? Do you want to be locked up in a *zoo?*"

Father reeled in and rested his rod across his knees. "Lionell, I don't usually do this, but I'm going to give up skunked. It's not our day. Are you?"

"No, it's not, or I'm not, or it's godawfuled hot, or a screw's loose, or it's not loose, and the worst news is that we're both screwed, or piss in the pot." He threw his rod in the bottom of the boat and jerked on the starting rope.

"Just a second," Charles said.

"Oh, holy Jesus, another *hot*-damned moldy dick again!"

"No," Charles said, and his stomach was seized with pain and anti-relationships to the comedy of this he tried to control. "It's just a—! It's still that same *snag!*" He angled his rod down, took hold of the line and tugged on it, and fifty feet away a shimmery-jacketed fish came catapulting up out of the water, arching its head toward its tail in an unencumbered shimmy through the air, whipping his line into swirls of language, and skipped once on its side before it dove down.

"It's a trout!" Lionell cried. "It's a *brown trout!*" He stood and stared in a rocking step toward Charles. "Here, let—" And then his control came over him and he sat. Charles was grappling with the rod to keep it from going overboard, and when he finally got the handle in his hands the line went out with a snap and backlashed across his reel. He pulled at the snarled loops of it, freeing or drawing tight the worst of them, and reeled in beyond their fluttery whorls until he felt a tautness, which he tested with a slight tug, and the trout came breaking up above the surface again, flinging spatters over the water as though shedding its inner life, and sent a font of spray splashing as it fluttered along the surface refusing to dive.

"Whoopeee!" Father cried.

"Give him the business!" Lionell yelled, as the fish went down. It was a big fish and a fighter from the feel of it, the fish of the day, perhaps, and the first trout Charles had ever had on his line, and he didn't feel he deserved it. The boat rocked as though over a precarious world he'd summoned out of himself that could soon dissolve.

"Aw, Charles, do it!" Father cried. "This time, too! You've caught them all because you're so pu*rrr*e in heart!"

Charles fought the fish for what seemed forever, a few minutes more than he felt he'd be able to, and then had to swing the line over Lionell's ducking form, to keep contact with the shuddering tenseness that thrummed up the line and through the rod in a way he'd never felt before. "Lionell," he said. "Do you want to take him?"

"Nope." Lionell was staring out over the lake.

"I'm sort of tired."

"You hooked him. You bring him in."

It took some time before it was close enough to land, and then Lionell skimmed it out with a flick of the net. "About three and a half pounds, I'd guess," he told them. "And I'd say it lost about a pound in fright." He took the fish from the net and laid it out on the bottom of the boat and stared at it awhile, then reached down and ran his fingertips over the gloss of its spotted side. He looked up at Charles in the bow with a sober face. "Chuck, it's a beautiful fish," he said. "I don't give a damn which of us got it, you hear?"

Then they went back at the same bolt-shuddering speed to the other shore, where the ladies were waiting in the lawn chairs with their cane poles leaning into the branches of a birch bloodied by the low sun. After their wash went, and they'd tied up, Wilhomena said in her whining, fluty voice, "I got tree sunfish and Missus Jones here, she's better wit the waroms, she got five sunfish and tree crappie, I tink. Hee hee." She smiled with a catlike pull to the corners of her curved-up mouth, her broad arms on the arms of the chair like a sphinx's, as if too content with herself to move.

"How'd you guys do?" Charles's grandmother asked.

"A big fish apiece for the five of us," Father said, and turned to Lionell, who held the stringer up with a fisherman's pride.

"Who got what?" she asked.

"Well, the boy got them all," Father said.

"Really!" she cried.

"Well, I at least got a great big old long granddaddy of a *th*ucker," Lionell said. "I've never been so under mortified in my life. Sheesh!"

"Where is it?" she asked him.

"With Davy Jones, Ma."

"Auf, Lionell, don't joke like that! They're not bad eating, you know."

"Ya, ya, *shure*, if you got a day or tuuu, like ole Unca Einard says, to sit there and pick out all of them diddly-poop, goddang bones, a hoo hoo!"

"Oofda, *you!* With two ladies, a priest, and a child here, Lionell? Shame on you!"

"We've already settled our score about that, Ma. Outta strikes tonight!"

"He got them all?" she said. "That big one, too?"

"Yup!" Lionell said, and his voice echoed across the lake and came back through the trees again.

She started to laugh in the tone Charles had been laughing in, and it seemed that she, too, couldn't help herself or stop, slapping her thighs with fast hands as her false gums showed. "Yuck it up!" Lionell cried, and grabbed the motor and brought it in banging steps toward the bait shop, while Father went to the trunk of his car. Wilhomena took up a blanket draped over the back of her chair, and she and Charles's grandmother spread it in a fluttery sinking square down out on the grass, orange-pink over the green, and began to unpack the picnic dinner together. Charles wasn't sure whether it was better to be with the women or the men, since both had their separate pleasures, and saw his grandmother's sunbonnet, inverted beside her chair, filled with blueberries she must have picked from the woods, which were now spilled over the hat's brim and down onto the ground in a dark and miniature galaxy. Father and Lionell came from the car carrying the cooler in concord between them, and set it beside the birch supporting the two cane poles, and then Lionell dragged another lawn chair down for himself, drew it next to his mother's, and sat back, and Father started breaking open beers. "Come, come on, everybody," he said. "We have to drink a toast to our fisherman. Hurrah!"

"None for me," Charles's grandmother said.

"Ah, Mrs. Jones, you must, for today, as I predicted, has been a special one!" He poured a few teaspoonfuls of foam into a paper cup and handed it to her. "I take all the sins this brings on you onto my own head. Now let's drink to Charles, our boy!"

"If she does, it'll be the first time in her life," Lionell said.

"Oh, you!" she cried. "What do you know about me or anything of the sort to begin with?"

"You mean you've been deceiving me, Ma?"

"I mean I've maybe been holding back a lot more than you might know about, or that you and another might not be old enough to hear, and to by-jing with the rest of it!"

"Oh, yeah?"

"Yeah."

"This, Charles, is for you," Father said, and handed

over the nearly full bottle he'd given his grandmother a taste from.

"Should he have that much?" she asked.

"Oh, of course. He's a grown boy, Mrs. Jones, and he's also our he*rrr*o right now." Father raised his bottle. "I propose a toast to Charles, the fisherman of the day, maybe the summer, even, and a nice boy, too."

Everybody murmured and their heads went back and Charles blinked at a blur, moved, and was surprised to see Wilhomena drinking out of the bottle. He tipped up his own and tasted the gaseous-smelling liquid, with its hint of bread dough and acetic fruit, and knew at the taste that this would be involved in his life in some way, and was alcohol.

"Without further ado," Father said, and tucked a towel into his collar, sat on the ground at the edge of the blanket, and began to eat. Charles sat beside him and the others brought food on paper plates back to their chairs; besides the cold chicken, there was liverwurst, summer sausage, corned beef, pumpernickel and rye, sliced onions and tomato wedges, lettuce and mustard and mayonnaise and pickles, sauerkraut, chunks of three different kinds of cheese, baked beans, potato salad, a watermelon kept cold in the cooler, fresh apples and pears—Wilhomena had also brought along a thermos of coffee and one of tea—and Charles had an intimation of the quiet meals at Father's house. The day was so calm even the birch leaves were silent.

The filamentlike vessels below Father's cheekbones turned darker as he ate and drank, and it seemed to Charles that he and Lionell were related in some way. Father finished a drumstick and sighed, and then nibbled and licked and sucked his fingers clean, and there was a familiar convulsion inside Charles that came out in the laughter from the lake.

"Oh, for God's sake," Lionell said. "Not that again."

"It's the beer," his grandmother said.

Charles's bottle, giving out conelike beams from its top and bright edges, lay empty beside him.

"Ach, it's good for him," Father said, and gripped Charles's shoulder and gave it a shake, and then said in a different voice, "Before I forget, before the light goes, we must have a picture of this day, for us and for Grandpa to see, too." He tossed his towel down on the blanket, strode away to his car, and came back carrying a camera with a big protruding lens, pushed back his hat, lifted a lid on the camera's top and looked down, aiming it in their direction, and then retreated toward the lake and made some quick screwing adjustments of some kind.

"Be happy!" he cried.

There was a clash of the camera's internal mechanism.

"And now our hero alone. You must take your fish and go out on the dock. I want to show the lake, too."

Charles stood and the rare-colored blanket rose and trembled and heaved up as he stood and then fell with a sigh. The grass was an unnatural green to him. He headed toward the lake, where Lionell had left the fish, and discovered that his left leg was longer than the other, so he adjusted to compensate for the difference and then his right leg grew longer. The ground gave way and collapsed under every other step he took.

"He's drunk!" his grandmother cired.

"Naw, he's just feeling his oats, Ma!" Lionell said, and laughed in his high *hee hee hee.*

Charles felt himself part at the beltline and hig legs go rambling ahead on their own, clad, for some reason, in his grandfather's goatskin chaps, but with no jeans beneath, dark hanging down, and the ground rose above his waist, as if viewed through his grandfather's bifocals, and enfolded within itself and flowed back from his ears in drumming surges that rose in pitch and kept gaining in ominousness of tone. And the strangely colored green of the grass was wavering tales underneath and in front of him: You are Father's hero, You've caught five fish, They were guided to your line, A feast has been spread because of you, Your close and only friends have shared in it, They've toasted you, They're laughing at the pleasure you've given them, Lionell respects you now. These are your fish.

He saw the rainy array of their scaly sides on the underwater side of his reflection, the beads of their eyes, the metal spike holding the stringer in place, and leaned for them and nearly fell, and at that heard his grandmother's girlish laugh go off soaring with the laughter of the rest of them, and realized she'd allowed her photograph to be taken without protest for the first time he was aware of (because of *him?*), and then walked onto the dock dragging his catch, twenty or so pounds, over the rough-cut slabs of board behind, and heard their slap and clatter like ungainly footsteps catching up to him, and turned. And had to jam one foot to the side to hold the dock in place.

"Lift the fish high now!" Father cried. "And look proud!"

He was too weak to lift them above his waist. He looked up again. The camera was aiming in at him. Bulking behind it was Father Schimmelpfennig, who embodied all that was pleasurable about his days in Hyatt. He'd always wanted to be a hero to somebody, and especially Father if he had his choice, and now was, by Father's word, and Father had also called him pure, which was what he'd needed to hear, for some reason, since the night his mother died; and through the mist caused by his laughter and the beer, his grandmother was his mother back again, free of the grave, Lionell was his father beside her, white wings wide, one of those women laughing was his grandmother from both or either of the family's sides, his grandfather hovered near Father's bulking form, rocking back, too huge to retain now, North Dakota unfurled in the distance behind them, his past was intact, he was healed and whole once more, and he'd never again be alone in his life, he was convinced of that.

"High, Charles!"

Charles lifted stiffened arms and there was a clash: *Charles is caught in the upper right-hand corner of the gray-and-black photograph, on a dock shown all the way to its end, where a kerosene smudge pot sits, a dark boat hanging in back of him, while he stands wearing a T-shirt and blue jeans that are rolled up in the style his Uncle Lionell favored that year, one of his shoes turned on its edge and his hips swung out in a big curve, as if to brace himself against the weight of the fish, which draw the whitened line stretched between his hands into a deep downward bow, and reach from his chin to his groin. The smile on his face, unself-conscious and transfiguring, can be found in most of the photographs dating from his childhood, and will never again appear in any photograph of him after this point in his life. Above him is the sky. Behind, of the same gray as the sky and stretching off for as far as the camera can see, is the infinite stillness of the lake.*

*

"Becky, come see the fish I got," Charles says, and his four-year-old daughter, scrambling up over his farmer's overalls, a somewhat costume, is in his lap as quick as his cat, called "Dad's cat" to distinguish it from her Siamese, would be.

"Uh-huh. You holded them nice, Dad."

"I was a boy then," he says, and rubs his palm up over the bristly stubble on his chin.

"I know, I see," she says, and her voice is Susan's in his mind again. She puts a fingertip into the cleft of his chin. "Did I know you when you was a little boy, Dad?"

"No, hon, I'm afraid not."

She drops her finger and grabs his hand and measures and touches it with hers as if weaving a charm or a prayer over its safety in their known world.

"But you're here now, and so am I," he says. "I'm with you. I'm here."

"I'm getting *big*," she says, but not with her usual conviction, in a voice that sounds tellingly close to the emotion that comes over her when there's something she can't understand.

"Oh, I know. I know, little Becky, sweet one," he says, and presses her head to his chest and rocks her from side to side, and feels they'd plummet out the bottom into the vitals of the earth in an instant, if he weren't so stubborn and turtlelike and didn't have her and her mother, and if her fingers didn't grip him so hard.

"You'll grow up soon enough, and have a husband, and a house, and maybe a horse, if you want, and even some kids maybe, like Mom and I have you."

"Will you be there with me, Daddy?"

"Probably not."

"Why, Dad?"

"Well, where were we? Let me see now. Your husband wouldn't want me there to begin with, and—"

"Why not?"

"That's the way it goes. Freedom and age and propriety. A right sort of life at times. And he'll want you for himself, of course. We all have our lives to lead."

"Daddy, do you love me?"

"Well, yes, of course I do!"

"Then why won't you be there, Dad?"

"I'll have to let you go."

"How come?"

"I'll have to, that's all. And you'll want to, too. Nature has to run its course."

"But why, Dad?"

"Because I love you," he cries under his breath, and has no need to wonder why these unaccountable tears of his keep showering over the cloudlike, daffodil-glowing, sun-lightened heaven of her honey-gold hair.

28

❧

A FAMILY ALBUM

Its black cover has a pebbly texture and the edges of it are ashen-colored, worn through, crumbling and clothlike to the touch, and its pages of heavy black paper have been leafed through over so many silent evenings by so many hands that several of them have come loose. A black cord with silken tassels at each end is laced through a pair of metal eyes along its left side, and the cord is tied in a bow that's been pressed into the same shape for ten years. On the heavy pages are rows of photographs, held in place by black corner mounts, and a careful hand has written a caption underneath each in white ink. Piled into its front and back, and interleaved among its pages, are postcards of vacation spots the family has visited, an envelope holding a lock of the oldest son's first hair, their father's report card from the eighth grade, a folded purple felt pennant from the college both parents attended, a birthday card signed "Much love, young one, Grandma" with a rabbit on it holding up a white number two, an immunization chart for one of the children with only the first series of shots filled in, a recipe for orange cake, a letter written by a seven-year-old on his first vacation away from home, a mournful face repeated over and over on strips of school pictures which weren't traded away by a son who had trouble making friends, a pressed corsage from a prom one daughter attended, somebody's ribbon, pink, a threaded needle, a smell of frailty and age that seems to rise only from this heavy black paper, as though the past itself were composed of elements as permanent-seeming yet frail, and dozens and dozens of photographs that there was no time to mount.

◦§§◦

29

THE PTA

They'd hardly settled down to the meal when his father whispered, "Where's the script? Do you have the script, Jerome?" He'd been asking the same question in different variations all evening, and Jerome answered, once again, "Yes."

"You'd better give it to me, then. I think I'll use it after all. God, all this noise!"

Jerome gave the frayed and finger-stained script to him and he tucked it under his plate and stared toward the stage, and then around on all sides, where folding chairs and tables were set up in rows on the floor of the Forest Creek gymnasium and four hundred people were eating beneath a noisy sea of conversation and silverware clashing, and screwed up his lips; he was here at Elaine's behest. She was chairman of the entertainment committee of the Pettibone–Forest Creek PTA, and she'd asked him to perform at this celebratory spring banquet, the first held by the consolidated schools, and said she wouldn't allow him to say no: "You've been a fool to sit around the way you have. It's unhealthy, you know. You've got to get outside and get out in public more, and if you don't start right now, Martin, you never will, knowing you as I do."

"All right," he said. "I'll read one poem and I know which one I'll do." It was "Laska" by Frank Desprez. Jerome helped him rehearse for a week, even though he was so familiar with the piece he had it by heart nearly the first run-through, and on some evenings was thrown off-guard when his father dropped lines as if to catch him asleep, and then he'd look up to see him confused. Jerome liked the piece well enough for what it was, but felt his father should do something more topical or light-hearted; he was adamant, however; no, he said, this was one of Alpha's (he'd just started using her name to Jerome) favorites, and in a way he was doing it for her. And then paled.

It was a monologue in rhymed verse, about a hundred lines long, that began:

> *I want free life and I want fresh air;*
> *And I sigh for the canter after the cattle,*
> *The crack of whips like shots in battle . . .*
> *The green beneath and the blue above,*
> *And dash and danger, and life and love.*
>
> *And Laska!*

Laska is described as bold, wild, passionate, self-sacrificing, and dangerously jealous (she once stabbed the narrator, nearly fatally, in a fury), and she rides beside him on a "mouse-gray mustang." One night a herd of cattle stampedes and she throws herself over the narrator to protect him and is killed. He digs a shallow grave and buries her.

> *And there she is lying, and no one knows,*
> *And the summer shines and the winter snows;*
> *For many a day the flowers have spread*
> *A pall of petals over her head.*

And ends thinking:

> *And I wonder why I do not care*
> *For the things that are like the things that were.*

His father unpursed his lips and looked across at the stage again, where PTA officials and school administrators were sitting with the dignity a stage bestows, sucked air through his teeth, and tapped the script with his fingertips held in a row, as he tapped when he was playing pinochle, but kept it up in a way that distracted Jerome, and was somehow out of time. His hands were whitish-gray from the effects of lime, as bloodless-looking as a corpse's, and his fingernails were black-rimmed even tonight. When the meal was over, he went up to the stage and sat, and Jerome saw that he'd left the script underneath his plate after all, an oily drop on it. There was a business meeting, a woodwind trio played a Sousa march and "Greensleeves," and then the stage was turned over to him. He came up to the podium, gave a few surprisingly witty introductory remarks, considering they were as off-the-cuff as Jerome knew them to be, gave the title, and with the first word of the poem something was wrong. His voice was too high and had a faulty tone to it, as if it were caroming around at the top of his throat, and didn't carry. *His* voice? People leaned forward to hear. He cleared his throat with a vehemence that must have startled some, pardoned himself, and began the poem again, and then Jerome saw, as if they'd sprung intact from his face, a shining trail of tears down each cheek. A phrase broke in his throat, he shook his head as if flinging it clear, started the phrase again, and suddenly his hands went high in the air, gestured, gestured and fell, and then he walked off the stage into the locker room, and the noise of the audience rose as though with a governed purr and soon was at its original level again.

30

TRACK MEET

From the way the children, all five tonight, gathered around him at the dinner table, he knew there'd be troubles and remorse. He put his fork beside his plate, leaving untouched the "toofla" he'd prepared and heaped there, and leaned his forehead on clasped hands as if to say grace. He was reaching his limit. Behind his closed eyelids, inflamed by lime burns and bits of sand, he saw glistening trailways, as though his vessels were of neon, and then the strength of his limbs pressed upward, pulsing, and he felt out of touch with his body, imprisoned within the sphere of his eye. The size of his world now.

He'd quit work late, drive from wherever in the three-county area his plastering business had taken him that day, back to Forest Creek, and pick up the little ones, the girls, at his parents', and then drive back home and cook supper and call the boys in to the table—now that it was spring, they spent most of their time outside—only to see that they were trying to conceal they'd misbehaved. And then another circuit, familiar as the first, began. He'd have to travel through their day, forcing his way into it, find the troubling incident, find the troublemaker, and then set him right, or, if there'd been fighting, punish him. He hated it. It was hard for him to judge the children and even harder for him to see them hurt. Alpha had always handled the discipline.

She was at the periphery of every thought of his, closing around his mind and conscience like a second self. His ideas, before he could speak them, were observed by her and he gave them up. His intuition, before he could act on it, sent off warning signals because of what had happened with her, and he held still. The sheen of her hair was in the hair of Marie, who was seven now, and to run his hand over it was excruciating and as close as he came to a sin. She was in his voice when he started arguing with Jay on the job over details he'd never have noticed without her eyes. Jay suggested that he bid on patching and specialty jobs, which were profitable, and which he could do as he wanted, working as hard as he liked, on his own time. Jay said that he himself would rather get into commercial work and leave the fussy jobs, as he put it, to a man with patience and a knack for dealing with people. So Martin traded the old Chevrolet in on a used International pickup (*M. Neumiller & Sons, Plastering,* he hand-lettered on its doors and tail gate), Jay paid the balance on it, and now he had what could be called a business of his own. The hours were longer but he was making twice as much as he had a year ago. Still he never got ahead and had no idea where his money went, or why, or when the last had gone. Alpha had always handled that. He went to her every payday and handed her his monthly or weekly check, and even during their poorest times, as when he farmed with Evan, they'd always had money ahead, plus untouchable savings and an emergency fund, plus health and life insurance ("You're the perfect one to be selling it; nobody has a better life"), and now he was in debt for the house, in debt to his father for two thousand dollars, and even deeper in debt to Jay. How had this come about, he'd ask as plaster purled across a wall under his trowel, and where was the remedy? He never really knew whether Alpha believed he'd received such a strong promise of a teaching job, or whether she thought he'd moved to Illinois merely to be closer to his mother, and now he never would. He knew she was hurt that he'd turned from teaching again, but now there was no reason to turn back. He'd quit carpentering for his father because it displeased her so, and when he started working for Jay she was too ill for him to tell how she felt from what she showed. The torment was more than grief; it grew, linking one memory to another, linking networks of them together, and the nets and webwork wouldn't let her go.

"Dad? Are you all right?"

He let his arms drop beside his plate. "Yes. Just tired."

All they had for transportation was the pickup. In winter and when it was raining hard, the six of them rode in the cab, the boys holding the girls on their laps, a smell of a bad electrical circuit and gasoline enwrapping them. The girls sang at the tops of their lungs and could harmonize already, and the boys' bodies beneath jolted with the blows they gave one another in silent anger in the dark. Bags of plaster color broke and spilled and spread over the floorboards and merged into a muddy gray, and all six tracked it into the house. In summery weather, the boys rode in the box of the truck and at first they liked it so much they whistled and shouted, they stood and made wings. or held their arms like Superman, and he had to keep knocking on the rear window and signaling them to sit. But when they went anywhere lately the boys huddled down with their backs against the cab, silent and withdrawn, and he could see, as they climbed out over the tail gate at their destination, her gestures and her averted eyes when she was suffering the silent humiliation she suffered most of her term on earth.

He would have taken his own life just to end the torment, to be at peace, as he'd once told Jerome and Charles (and maybe be with her; who could say?), if it wasn't for the five here at the table. And when they were bad or unhappy, he felt there was no use. The boys used up any money he left with them buying candy, and ate breakfast food for most of their meals. None of them ever mentioned their mother.

He looked across at Charles, who sat with his elbows on the tabletop and his eyes lowered, forking food into his mouth as fast as he could. His big skull had a bluish tint to it. A few days ago, for some unaccountable reason, he'd taken out the electric razor and shaved off all his hair.

"Well, what kind of trouble did you cause today?" he asked, and his words made him feel weary and resentful. He was being unjust. He couldn't help it. Charles was always the guilty one, it seemed, and more so since he'd been spending his vacations with Lionell; he might be from another family. He had a bad temper, a savage energy, and was unpredictable. Alpha tended to favor him, yet he was the only one she lost her temper with; one day she caught him striking matches along the foundation of a

house and came up behind him and grabbed his arm,
grabbed up a bundle of the matches, struck them, and
held them under his hand until he understood what it was
like to be burned. He couldn't stand to lose. If a game or
argument didn't go in his favor, he started a fight, and
when he was left alone with the little ones he sometimes
set up strict rules. such as no singing or talking, no TV,
no dinner, or made them march in unison around the
room, and if they violated a rule, or disobeyed him, he
hit them or shoved them into a closet and held them in
darkness until the pickup pulled into the drive again.

Charles gave an impatient scowl, and said, "What did
I do? Nothing." His eyes looked larger now that he had
no hair, and his long eyelashes, catching the light of the
bare bulb overhead, sparkled as he blinked several times.
He was also a practiced liar.

"Nothing? Then what's the matter? Why do you act so
guilty? Why are you all so quiet?"

"We're eating," Charles said.

Jerome sat next to Charles, and Martin said in a restrained and altered tone, as though to an arbiter, "Jerome, what is this?"

Jerome was twelve but knew all of the children's needs,
anticipated their whims, and was guileless and gentle,
and thus cared for them better than most adults. He looked
out of his intelligent eyes, his lips sober, and then shook
his intelligence and made himself a blank.

"Jerome," Martin said, placing both fists, broad as
saucers, on the tabletop. "I asked you a question. What's
going on here?"

"I don't know."

"You don't know?"

"I don't think I really saw it."

"Saw what?"

"Anything that happened."

"Then something *did* happen."

"I don't know."

"You just said it did!"

"I didn't see it happen."

"Ach!"

It was futile. The girls, at the side of the table to his
left, their wide eyes fastened on him, were cringing at the
tone of his voice. It angered him to keep at it this way,

to give it such importance, but he couldn't help himself, and his interrogations and reprimands had a purpose; if he could prove that whatever they'd done had made them so unhappy he could see it, how could they want to put themselves through such unhappiness again? He seldom punished them physically, as she sometimes had; he believed it was unnecessary and wrong, and besides, it frightened him to see an adult's strength (his face disfigured with anger) thrown against a momentarily parentless child. He was especially afraid of his own strength. He stared at the open lime burns on his knuckles, clenching and unclenching his fists, angered even more by his indecisiveness, and then reached for his fork.

He stopped.

Tim, who was across from the girls, alone at that side of the table, was looking with fear at him, then at his brothers and then at his food, which he'd hardly touched.

Tim, who was changed so by her death, had become his favorite. He was no longer serene and good-natured. He fought so ferociously with Jerome and Charles he sometimes hurt himself, or them, and lately he'd been bringing home his own friends—the most tattered, backward, underfed outcasts in his class. When Martin tried to talk to him, he pinched his eyes shut and bared his teeth in a false smile, as though to keep from being reached, or assumed a stunned, dumb look, answered in grunts and winks, and went clumping around like Donny Ennis. He spoke a made-up language Martin couldn't understand, and somehow had acquired a foul tongue; once when he was fixing a trike, he whispered, "You old cunthole." "Hey!" Martin cried. "Where'd you hear *that?*" Tim paled, crossed one eye, bucked his teeth, and said, "I don't know, kind sire, but once I did I surely latched on to it." Some nights he sleepwalked through the house carrying a blanket, calling her by name, and if his wanderings and his voice didn't wake Martin, so he could take him into bed with him, he walked through the entire house, went out the door into the back yard, to the incinerator where she'd planted hollyhocks, and lay down there and slept until morning, or until he was found.

Now his eyes, light green, large and seductive, were traveling around the table with a harried look, as if to find a point to cling to.

With his lime-burned hand, Martin reached out and touched his shoulder. "You didn't do anything, did you, Tim?" he asked, and gave him a shake, and Tim, shrugging off his hand, turned around and took hold of the back of the chair and broke into coughing sobs.

"Jerome! What's this about? Answer me!"

"I don't know how to," Jerome said, and looked aside at Charles, who was still eating as fast as he could.

"Did he hurt Tim?" Martin demanded. "Is Charles the cause of this?"

Jerome lowered his eyes.

"Tim, you can tell me," Martin said. "You don't have to be afraid."

"I'm done," Charles said, and scraped back his chair. "I'm going out."

"You sit right where you are till I'm through with you!"

Charles sat, piled more food on his plate, and started eating again.

"And if we have to sit here all night until I find out what's been going on, we will!"

Tim shifted his weight, his eyes made an anxious circuit of the table, and then, shrinking back in his chair, he cried, "He kicked Arvin!"

"Who?"

"Chuck!"

"Kicked him?"

"Then Arvin went home. He was crying!" Arvin Becker, a frail boy who'd just moved up from Cairo, was Tim's most recent and most enduring friend.

"What is this? Jerome!"

Jerome kept his eyes down, picking at his food, and then murmured, "We were having a track meet over at school and Arvin was on Chuck's side. Tim and I were on the other. Arvin got tired toward the end and didn't want to run, so maybe Chuck did something. I don't know. I didn't see it. I was running, too."

Jerome, who was acting half his age, had said all he was going to, so Martin moved his eyes to Charles. "Is this true?"

"No."

"Don't lie to me!"

"Arvin just started crying and wanted to go home, that's all. He's a baby-face, for ga—goodness' sake."

"Quit eating and look at me when I speak to you! Now nobody starts crying for no reason—I know that, and you know it, too."

"I told him to play right. He wasn't playing right."

"Right? What's *right?*"

Apparently sensing he'd exposed an aspect of himself that had caused trouble in the past, Charles seemed breathless and back in the race again. "We were way ahead in points, and then Arvin faked like he was tired. He wouldn't do anything any more. Then when we were running the mile, he just walked along. He could have got second or third, at least, and we score 5, 3, 1. He didn't care whether we got those last few points. We needed them."

"You mean you hurt him because you were worried about losing?"

"Who says I hurt him?"

"Tim said you kicked him."

"If I had to run every race, he could run at least one. He was just in field events."

"How could you do such a thing?"

"What?"

"Whatever you did."

"Well, what would you do if you were all tired out, and came around the track about the third time, and there was your teammate, walking along like a crippled-up old poopel-de-doo?"

"Watch that tongue."

"Like an old lady."

"So you kicked him."

"I brushed against him. Maybe I nicked him with my foot."

"Can't you leave other people alone? Don't you realize he's one of the few friends Tim's got? Let him walk or crawl or sit on his can or do what he wants, damn it!" Silverware jumped as Martin hit the tabletop. "What's the matter with you? What makes you think you're a judge of others?"

"I know I was running and he wasn't."

"He's not you. He's—"

"He was on my side."

"Will you listen to me!"

Martin started to rise and his belt buckle caught on the edge of the table, upsetting his coffee and a carton of milk. Charles pushed off and tipped his chair over backward, and the slap that was intended for him carried past and struck Susan. She went off her stool as neatly as a bundle and dropped to the floor, and when she realized where she was, she started wailing, and then Marie joined in.

"Now, look! Look what you've made me do," Martin said, and started around the table with the galling details —Susan on the floor, the puddle of coffee and milk beside her, Tim with his hands over his face—streaming along the edge of his vision, sharpening his outrage. Charles was on his hands and knees, scrambling around among the chairs and table legs, trying to make it to a safe spot. Martin got behind him and kicked hard and struck bone and Charles's limbs went flying out as he hit on his stomach, and Martin had a flash of himself slipping on a scaffold and landing hard on his tailbone, and felt pain. He yanked Charles to his feet. "Now get to your room," he said. "Get up there before something worse happens, you hear?"

Charles gave him a furious going over with his eyes before he ran up the stairs. And then Martin realized what he'd done and started trembling. He sent Tim and Jerome outside, took the girls, one in each arm, and carried them to their bedroom and tried to comfort them. Their eyes were wide with terror and Susan wouldn't allow him to touch her. When they were calmed down, he undressed them and put them to bed, hardly aware of what he was doing. The presence in the upstairs room demanded all his attention.

He went into the kitchen and sat at the table. He ached from balancing on a scaffold the whole day, carrying his hawk of heavy plaster, and reaching overhead to skim finish coat on the ceiling. He felt too old to go on with the work. No, there was bookwork to finish, orders to call in, material to line up, his lunch to pack.

He wanted to go upstairs but wasn't sure it was the right thing to do. He didn't want his thoughts to focus; he was afraid of what he'd done. He started eating, but the food was chilly and he had no appetite for it.

He cleared the table, carried the dishes to the sink, shook detergent over them, adjusted the temperature of the water, and let it run as he took a rag from the S-trap under the sink and wiped off the table. Then he got down on his kness, and as he was mopping up the milk and coffee, his vision narrowed, the patch of linoleum he was staring at darkened, became the colored world he was caught in, and he felt faint. He stood up and leaned against the table. An even, abrasive sound was traveling through his consciousness as though it meant to erode it. He hurried over to the sink and shut the water off. The sound stayed.

He dipped a plate in and out of the water, rinsing off the grease, and his sight fastened on the soapy rainbow sliding along the plate's rim. He let it slip beneath the suds and had an image of her turning from the sink, inclining her head to one side and shoving the hair from her cheek with the back of her hand, her face flushed, her eyes moving anxiously around the room, but with an abstract look, as if there was no name for what she was searching for.

He went up the stairs. Charles was lying face down on Jerome's unmade bed, his back heaving, his exclamations and sobs muted by a pillow he held clasped over his head. Martin eased himself onto the edge of the bed, seeing with surprise the dormer he'd added. When had he been organized enough to do that? There was a leak in the flashing or the new asphalt shingles, at the point where the dormer joined the roof, and the aqua plaster below was stained beige and ashen, a crack in it fuming white with lime and calcium deposits.

He tried to pull the pillow away. "Listen. Listen, now. I've tried—"

Charles grabbed at the bedclothes and tucked them in around his face.

"How many times have I told you—" He couldn't stand being sanctimonious. He looked away and saw the bed with Charles's body stretched out on it and part of his own shoulder enclosed in a mirror, and it was as if he were seeing through to the past. The scene, scaled down, dimmer than in hospital light, was a scene he'd lived through before, with her, and he couldn't again; those close to you seemed solid and understandable, while their real selves were off at a distance, a part of the world, and then their individual door in the world opened on them, it closed, and they were gone and weren't seen again.

And now another was opening for this boy, and he sat
with his shoulder caught in a mirror, as helpless as with
her. Then he felt a door opening for him, too. He looked
around for something of this moment to carry with him.
The room seemed filled with a gray rain. Wadded socks
lay on the floor, gathering tufts of dust, there were glinting
tubes of a dismantled radio in the corner, a model flint-
lock made of plastic, a Boy Scout neckerchief with slide,
and the rest of the room was covered with dirty clothes of
the same color. Rain.

"If your mother—" He stopped. The words drew him
down deeper. He took Charles's shoulder and tried to lift
him, but he struggled free and dropped onto the mattress.

"Don't," Martin whispered. "Don't carry on so. Please.
Sit up."

"I'm sorry!"

"I know. Now don't."

"I can't stop!"

"Try to look at it from my—"

"My head hurts! It feels like something's coming out of
it!"

He ran his hand over Charles's skull, and the stiff stubble scratching across his palm—what led Charles to do
this? what did this hark back to?—made him feel even
more helpless and afraid.

"Don't now," he said, and felt the words encircle him.
Father, mother, nurse, teacher, arbiter, guardian, judge—
all the roles were too much. He no longer had the power
to reach through to the children as their father, the man
who loved them above others, and this inability, more
than anything he might do, was the fault breaking in him.

He heard a drumlike thumping and thought his heartbeat had filled him, but the sound was outside, and he
believed it was his last summons, a last lack in himself
he'd have to face up to, and then saw Charles's hand
tapping over the bed in a widening arc, trying to find him.
It touched his knee, backed away, and came down, damp
and hot with perspiration, on his thigh. He took the hand
in his and saw how much it was like hers, and then the
room brightened, and a rearrangement took place in it.

"I'm sorry," Charles said in a muffled voice.

"I am, too. Can you forgive me?"

"Yes!"

"Did I hurt you?"

"Yes!"

"Do you want to come downstairs?"

"No!"

"Do you feel any better now?"

"Yes."

"Jerome and Tim are outdoors. The girls are in bed. I'm sorry they had to see it."

"I didn't mean to. He wasn't playing right."

"I know," Martin said, and lifted him and turned him so they were sitting next to one another. "Let's go downstairs and do the dishes. Then we'll both feel better." He put his arm around Charles's waist and Charles's head fell against his ribs so hard it hurt him. "Will you come downstairs and help me do the dishes?"

31

SNAKE TRAILS

The lot off the Neumillers' rear property line was a meadow of vetch and long-standing alfalfa that nobody mowed. Tim and Charles are crawling through it on their forearms, their elbows damp and smelling of chlorophyll and mint as the grasses shake sharp blossoms and saber tips in front of their eyes, and over the summer from a maze of trails that traverse the entire three-acre lot— snake trails, Tim calls them. They're speeding along on elbows and knees, keeping flat but moving in a fast scramble from one patioramus (Tim again), down a double path that splits around another patioramus—a circular area of packed-down grass with trails radiating off of it in several directions, many of them cul-de-sacs to confuse —and they're evading the girls again!

Headquarters is a pair of four-by-eight concrete slabs, one on top of the other, the upper slab propped open with a rock like one half of a book, moss and leaf stems and damp-stained, hoarded cigarette butts lying on the pebbly texture of the open wedge, and their rallying call is a whippoorwill whistle. They've worked out maneuvers that keep the girls from catching them for weeks, or even seeing them, once they get below the grass, and yet the girls always come looking for them. They're tired of the game now and lie on their backs in a secluded patioramus, sweat drying along their hairlines and stiffening the country smell of meadow air, and watch clouds tow the meadow and the two of them above the surface of the curving earth, and Tim wonders if he'll die on his back, and Charles says, "Uh-oh, here come the girls again." They do a stomach flop, and their eyes, only inches apart

and with no black and green lines of grass stems inter-
vening, betray a communication from the quarter-horses
below their belts, and then glaze, and then Tim cranes his
head and squeezes out a popeyed maniacal look of ab-
ject, utter concupiscence, and says, "Do you want to
tweakle and futz around with their little whistle-holes?"

"Sure."

They stand, bright air around their shoulders and the
sky above, free again, and see the girls a few feet away,
holding hands and looking in opposite directions, neither
of them right. Susan rises on her toes above the level of
the grass and squints her eyes, mouth open wide; then her
caplike coif of brown-blond hair sways and slaps her
face as she shakes her head in startled disbelief.

"There they are!" she cries.

"Sure. We're waiting. What do you think?"

Marie's head is just above the August-browning grass
and she turns to them, her large eyes crisscrossed by
crossed green spears.

"Hey, come on," Charles says. "We'll show you how
our trails work."

"Yeah, I bet," Marie says, and her voice comes from
a greater distance than where she stands.

"Sure," Susan says, and purses her lips, eyes pinched
tight, and shakes her hair into whipping strings. "Then
after that you'll try and make us take our pants down!
Then you'll try and do stuff to our *bottoms* again!"

"Oh, come on," Marie says, in a voice breathy but with
a spangled and chiming tone tracing lines of irregular
music over the air. She parts and steps over higher grass
and lies and goes crawling after Charles, who wonders
whether Susan's following Tim, and has an image of her
with her dress off a shoulder, while he leads Marie into a
patioramus at the center of the meadow, and then slips
into a screened-in hiding place just to the left of it.
Marie crawls in beside him, her skin scarlet, her eyes so
liquid they look trembling, and lays her head on his chest.
Spangled dots in a current flow.

She won't look at him and clings to his chest so hard it
would hurt if her hands weren't tremblingly weak and her
nails chewed below rounded fingertips. Chips of shell in
flesh. He turns her and lifts a swath of hair away and
kisses her damp and feathery sideburn. She tosses her

face to his and kisses his lips and jerks on his neck. He rubs a leg below the knee. She falls back and floats her skirt over her chest and stares with widening eyes and tight lips as she tugs white underwear down shining thighs.

He kisses her hip.

"Oh!" she cries.

He rises, shoulders and knees shuddering and weightless (a rush of sound going in and out his ears like an opening sea), and lowers his face, cheeks burning holes in it, lips a trembling mass, to her stomach, at its base, on the raised curve above the downed wedge with its crease.

"That feels good."

He lifts his lips loose. "What?"

"It feels nice to me."

The whippoorwill whistle tears triangular patches of amber out of the air. He jerks up, then ducks. "Stay here. Pull those up," he says, and goes flat-stomached and thumping to the pair of parted slabs. Tim is waiting with a wild look. He flutters his fluffy eyelashes and says in a mincing voice, *"Did* you?"

"Did I what?"

"Tweakle and futz?"

"Oh, I don't know. I kissed her on the stomach once."

"I might have did a maybe a *whee!* Whistle, whistle, *woof*, chuckle, whistle, wheet-a-wheet!"

Tim shows fangs, rolls striations of shadow over his face, his eyes turning as green-colored and electric as the shoots between them, and says, "Well, fond Chugeloon, now that that's that, how about the old switcheroo?"

"What do you mean?"

"Ah oh, *ho!*"

"You mean *that?*" Charles says.

"You want to give it a try?"

"Well."

"Tiny is in patioramus number five!" Tim cries.

"Patioramus number nine!" Charles cries.

They scramble past one another laughing, and their laughter echoes up as up a well to Tim and Charles over all their years, for now they're crawling in ragged circles around the concrete slabs, still laughing, and then they rise, free for good for now, and call out to the girls, who are off with a flutter of birds, and all four run as if with their lives in their hands toward the house, where none of this has happened.

Or has it? Or not happened? Or rather really happened in out-pressed lines outside their own world in other ways, such as a tiger lily in Turkey along a rock wall, perhaps, or droplets of rain raining on a rainy day over the day-old hills of new Duluth?

*

That same fall, on September –, 195–, wearing a gray shirt and gray pants (the same gray twills he wore as a plasterer) and a geometrically patterned green and beige necktie preserved from the forties, their father walked up the steps of the Pettibone Junior High School —neither happy nor humiliated but knowing that now he could at least be at home most of the time when the children were—where he'd been hired as an instructor in P.E. and mathematics, to begin anew his career as a teacher.

And also that same fall, Lionell and his mother decided that their father and husband, old Ed Jones, couldn't withstand another Minnesota winter, though he seldom complained, and a neighbor of theirs, Scottie Schaack, a thirtyish Serb or Croat or Hungarian with a dark hue about him that seemed to have shaped his face, long, felinelike, the temples dipped and triangular, unsmiling from his meltingly brown wildwood-tangled eyes, who two years before had left for California, wrote to them to say that he was settled and well, in Washington State now, and that opportunities were so much better for everybody on the West Coast.

Lionell and his mother sold the farm, auctioned off the equipment and livestock, and on the day their check cleared the bank, left for Los Angeles with only the old man and their clothes packed into a new Ford sedan they'd bought with part of the down payment.

Ed Jones enacted a seizure so well when he saw the Rocky Mountains it nearly gave him one.

"Take it easy, Dad. You've seen hills before."

"These aren't hills, Lionell, and you know it. These are mountains, boy. I've seen them in the East and once is enough. These are outcroppings of the goddamned innards of the earth, by God, and I'm not going over them! You can let me out right here!"

And then the gently rolling breadth of them at first, the long and local lateral up-and-down glides, and then at their bases blasted rock, cubes and chunks at the bottom of a reddish-brown, steep corrugated slide, where the road curves out to the left around a bronze rock pylon, and over its edge of ticking, white posts with swooping cables between, the first town can be glimpsed from above, the air, and from here until the California desert on the other side Ed Jones won't lift or let anybody lift the pulled-down hat covering his eyes, and when his wife at last convinces him that the mountainy part of the trip is indeed done, after riding long stretches of desert without a curve or a sound, in a well-lit gasoline station, she also reaches to give him an encouraging squeeze, and then jerks back her hand.

"Why, Ed!" she cries. "You've wet your pants, you fool."

"Well, ogha yah?" The muffling hat comes off. "I've got some news for you, milady. I've also gone and *shit* the dirty lousy old horny motherhumpers *too!*"

32

❧

DON'T YOU WISH YOU WERE DEAD

Earl Stuttlemeyer wasn't well liked by anyone. Martin could see that in class. He'd moved into Pettibone from an outlying farm during the spring and wore bib overalls, flannel shirts, and high hook-and-eye shoes, dress that had been acceptable enough while he lived on the farm and was bused in to school, but was now looked upon as the dress of a hick. He had an oval face longer than most adults, parted lips that were fleshy behind, slaty-blue eyes beneath eyebrows so blond they were invisible, and a big gap between his front teeth, both of which were broken off—more than enough to make him an object of derision among his classmates, seventh-graders, who were at one of the most sensitive and snobbish of ages, but he was also uncircumcised and had picked up the nickname of "Needledick, the canary raper." He attacked anybody he suspected of calling him that, and parents complained to the principal that their children were being injured by him at school. Then he swung on an eighth-grade bully who'd been taunting him for weeks and knocked him unconscious. He was suspended from school for three days.

He lived at the edge of town, where there weren't many children his age, and when his widowed grandaunt told him she had too many cats, and wondered if Earl and some of his friends wouldn't get rid of a few, he came and knocked on the Neumillers' front door.

It opened partway and Charles appeared, shadowy and detached behind the screen; he'd finished seventh grade with Earl but wouldn't be twelve until the fall, and was the only one of Earl's acquaintances neutral enough to be called a friend. He was as short as Earl and poor at marbles.

"Stuttlemeyer," Charles said.

"Chuck."

Their mutual reserve and suspicion stood around them like the still Illinois air.

"What are you doing?" Earl asked.

"Making a model airplane."

"Oh, heck."

"Do you want to see it?"

"Sure. Well, ah—"

In the boxy room off the entrance, a single bed stood against the wall, and a rickety card table beside it was covered with balsa shavings, tissue paper, straight pins, glue, and the skeleton of a fuselage.

"What's that stink?" Earl said.

"Banana dope. You paint it on the paper that you first glue over the ribs—like on this fuselage—and it pulls the tissue up tight. Then you keep putting it on until the paper is solid like a drum, and then you assemble the plane, put on the landing gear and struts, and then it's ready to fly."

"How do you fly it?"

"When it's finished, I'd like to buy a motor—maybe free flight." Charles held up a picture, an artist's rendition of the finished plane, and studied it. "Isn't it nice?"

"Uh-huh."

Earl was stunned by the room. A wall of built-in bookshelves was filled with old books laid every which way, and a desk below that opened down was covered with piles of magazines. There were bookshelves along the top of another wall, and glassed-in bookshelves sat just inside the door, reflecting books. The bed was unmade and dozens of snapshots, as though undergoing arrangement, were spread across the twisted sheets. The door of the closet was open and he could see, piled along its bottom, dirty clothes, crushed boxes, work shoes caked with plaster, plaster on the floor, coat hangers, and a pillow spilling feathers. At his house, even in the country, they all made their beds the minute they woke, the floors were waxed and shining, there was a cabinet or a niche for everything loose, and even a special hassock on which you placed the evening paper. A few years back, he'd signed a sympathy card to Charles along with the rest of his class, and had noticed from then on that everybody kept off to the edges of Charles as if he had some sort of disease, but it hadn't ever occurred to Earl that he didn't actually have a mother.

"Is this where you sleep?"

"Not in the summer," Charles said. "It's too hot. It's Dad's room. He hardly ever uses it."

"My aunt, Emma Dawson on the other side of town, wants to get rid of some cats in that barn behind her place."

"What do you mean?"

"She wants me to kill them."

"Oh?"

"Whatever way I want to do it, she said. Do you want to help?"

"Wow! I'm supposed to stay and watch the girls."

"What girls?"

"Over on the other side." Charles went to the doorway and called, "Tim! Hey, Tim!"

There was a response from so far away it seemed it came from another house.

"You mean she really wants you to do this?"

"That's what she said, and my aunt don't lie."

"Did you ever kill one?"

"Sure I choked one to death on the farm once. And then another time I held a bag of them in the water tank till they were drowned." Earl grinned, and then covered his teeth, and he and Charles began to laugh and cough and throw punches at one another's shoulders.

"What is it now?" a plaintive voice said, and Tim came into the room, shirtless, his face and shoulders freckles, wearing blue jeans too big at the waist and rolled high on his shins. "I suppose you want— *Oooo!*" he cried. "A guestus! You have a *guest*us here!" He pulled back, held up his hands, and shook them so quakingly his fingers made noises knocking together.

"Cut it out," Charles said. Tim was usually bashful and spoke in a deferential voice even among the family, with eyes lowered, as though he couldn't bear either smiles or shame, but when Charles had company, he'd speak in altered voices, make exaggerated faces, make up words, do flips that landed him on the floor on the flat of his back—anything to draw attention to himself. He bowed now to Earl and said, with crossed eyes, "I'm Tinvalin."

"That's his new name," Charles said.

"No, ho," Tim said. "I'm Toonvaloon and I'm of a Toonavaloony!" The tip of his tongue appeared and his head jerked like an epileptic's; there were flying flecks of spit."

"Knock it off!"

"Nat-ture-elly, Chelly."

"Earl and I are going out. You have to watch the girls."

"Dad told you to."

"And now I'm telling you."

"You're not my boss."

"I am when Dad's gone."

"That's not what he says."

"Well, *I'm* saying it."

"Oh, yeah?" Tim began shadowboxing with dodging crosses, brushing his nose with his thumb, and saying, "Snift-snift! Snort-snort, snift!"

"Just watch the girls, marmalade face."

"Ahh-yahtatta," Tim said, in imitation of a Chinese. He bucked his teeth, folded his arms, and his face turned Oriental, and then he bowed to them both and went into a clattering dance step.

"If anything happens to my plane—"

"Oh, dear, precious plane, dearie me. *Precious!* Ooo, Allah, Allah, oh, Great God Brown!"

"I have to put on my shoes," Charles said.

Earl followed him through a living room in worse disorder than the other, across gray linoleum with a dull cast to it, and into a kitchen where breakfast-food boxes and dirty dishes sat on a splashed and littered table. Tim rumped into a chair at the table's end, facing them, and cried, "Breakfast food, breakfast food, how I dearly love dear breakfast food!" He stuck a soggy mass in his mouth and swallowed it down. "Three meals a day! Three times a meal! Breakfast food! It'll make you fart and whistle and clap and get *chicken pox*." He picked with his forefingers over his cheeks and forehead, and cried, "Watch the spray!"

Charles and Earl went around the corner and down the steps to the basement, which was damp and chilly and smelled of stale engine oil. Charles pulled a light chain.

The concrete floor was painted gray and a shuffleboard court was marked out in red lines. A high double bed with an aluminum-painted frame sat next to a furnace, and there was a three-hundred-gallon oil tank, white, with rust spots showing through, in the corner beyond the bed; the cement-block walls, once painted light blue, were stained yellow and dark green from seepage, and there were fuzzy looping borders of browns and darker colors surrounding the stains. Two mattresses, placed side by side, lay on the floor. Charles sat on one and began pulling his shoes on over bare feet.

"Is this where you sleep?" Earl asked.

"Yes."

"On those?"

"Oh, no," Charles said. "Over on the bed. These are for our tag-team matches."

"Tag-team matches?"

"Don't you have a television?"

"No," Earl said, and looked ashamed.

"It's wrestling. In a tag team, you each have a partner, and if you're getting trounced and need help, you tag your partner's hand and he comes in the ring and takes over for you. We have them Thursday nights after Boy Scouts. Would you like to try sometime?"

"I'm a mean mother."

They both laughed in the cool and liquid-feeling atmosphere of the basement.

"I'm pretty good, too," Charles said. "Tim and I beat the Wilson brothers last week. He's my partner when Jerome isn't around."

"Tim wrestles the Wilsons?"

"He's really tough for his size. He's even beat me up. When he gets mad, he goes crazy and you can't hold him off." Charles stood up and started climbing the stairs.

"Hey, wait," Earl said. "What's this for?"

Charles stepped back down to the dark doorway where Earl was standing, near the foot of the stairs, and turned on a switch. Four oil-stained steps led to a long room with black walls, a black floor, and a ceiling of oil-stained joists less than five feet high.

"Holy balls," Earl said. "What kind of room is *that?*"

"This place was a gas station once. The part above here was a double garage before it was remodeled, and this was the grease pit. That old grease won't come off. We've even tried muriatic acid."

"It's got a barn gutter right up the middle!"

"That's what they drained the grease into, I guess. There's a big sump hole down at the other end that stinks like shit."

"You'd have to be a midget or something to fit in the place!"

"We didn't use it till last year. Then we made it into a shooting gallery. It's perfect."

At the far end of the confinement, a cardboard backstop reached from ceiling to floor; three wires were strung across standards in front of the backstop, and rows of paper targets, held in the jaws of clothespins, were spaced along each wire. Higher up, a round fruitcake container, with blue-and-black target circles painted on its bottom, and a scattering of dents in it, hung from a wire attached to one of the big, oil-blackened beams.

"What do you shoot with?" Earl asked.

"A BB pistol."

"I've got a .22."

"We could use it on those cats."

"My dad won't ever let me shoot it in town. What about your pistol?"

"It's broke. Tim got mad and threw it on the floor. We're going to have it fixed. Soon, too."

"Boy," Earl said. "You couldn't get me into that scrunched-down place for twenty bucks."

"We shoot from here."

"How do you know if you hit anything?"

"Well, once in a while we do have to go in for a target check. Tim does that."

"I bet he has to wipe his feet off like a bastard afterwards, huh?"

Charles turned off the lights. He let Earl go up the steps ahead, toward the back door with its rectangle of light, and as they stepped into the kitchen Earl stopped with such suddenness Charles bumped into him. In the middle of the floor, close to the sink, Tim lay on his back, his chin high, his mouth opened wide, and the whites of his eyes rolled up; his chest and the gray tile around him were spattered with blood, which was also leaking from his lips. The handle of a butcher knife showed above his rib cage.

"Oh, for God's sake," Charles said. It was about the tenth time Tim had tried this piece of business, which was invented by Charles to frighten the girls; the butcher knife was gripped between arm and rib cage, the "blood" was ketchup. Charles prodded Tim with his toe. "Come on, get up." What if Tim ever did try something like this?

Tim raised his head. "I can't. I'm dying. I have maybe ten seconds left." He dropped his head with a clunk. "Five, four——"

"Get up, goddamnit!"

He jumped to his feet and tossed the knife into the sink. "Thank you for them swear words, Prince Valiance," he said in a falsetto. "You've just saved my life, kind sire. How can I thank the big horseshit hero, wa! wa!"

"Go see what the girls are doing before I clobber you one."

"Clabber-ass," Tim said. He began to shadowbox around, saying his snifts, and went to the door to the other side of the house and started knocking it back and forth between his fists. "The Toonvaloon rat-a-tat-tat bone-cracker, folks. Practicing up. Going to use it on the he-man, the big scary one. Wow!"

Charles walked over and slapped the back of his head. "I told you to get in there. Now go!"

He and Earl went through the living room as Tim shuffled along behind, making his sounds, and just as Charles reached for the knob he felt a slap, halfhearted yet imperative, swipe his hair. He swung around and Tim was dancing in front of him, revolving his fists, so furious his eyes were sunken and close to tears. "Come on," he cried in his voice of challenge. "Come on, you chicken-shit! *Fight!*"

Charles went out the door.

*

The old barn was overrun with cats. There must have been fifty. Charles and Earl made a cursory inspection and then went to the back of the house and Mrs. Dawson, a plump, nervous-voiced woman with black hair wound in such tight curls they seemed ironed in place,

gave them a bowl of scraps, and said, "I haven't put anything out for them for a week or more, so they ought to
go for this like it was gold cream. It'll give you a chance
to grab some. I hate to see it come to this, but they
been killing robins and getting into people's garbage and
causing so much general complaint there's nought I can
do. When I farm them out, they're back the next day,
and when other folks throw out the cats *they* don't want,
they congregate here, and they've been keeping the neighborhood up at night, what with their caterwauling and
making new kitties. If my John was still here, things would
never have come to this pass, may the Lord bless him
where he lies."

They were halfway to the barn when she cried out,
"Now don't kill them all! Especially that white one! I need
me some mousers!"

A rock held a Dutch door at one side of the barn ajar.
They rolled it out of the way and latched the door from
the inside. Until they became accustomed to the dark, the
holes in the roof and walls surrounded them like distant
constellations, and Charles felt as he had once in a plane-
tarium in artificial night—that the earth had shrunk to
the size of a room and he was standing at the North Pole,
fur-warmed and gigantic, and could reach out and ex-
tinguish with a fingertip, one by one, each star. The pin-
points swayed along with his vision as he looked around.
The building must have been a barn for a driving team
at one time; there were closed stalls along the right side,
and the other half was open, with double doors at each
end, as if for parking a carriage; a platform loft above
the stalls, and an alley in front for throwing down hay.
There were also two open stalls filled with shadowy equipment. In a low window, Earl discovered a broken pane,
an "escape exit," and they covered it with a splitting piece
of Masonite.

Earl handed the bowl of scraps to Charles, and cats began running the lengths of themselves along his legs, purr-
ing and miaowing, and pawing at his pants. *Which* white
one, he wondered, and held the bowl higher. Earl stepped
into one of the open stalls and laid out a hand scythe, a
baseball bat, several cylindrical sash weights, twine, a
hammer, and a fishing knife that was badly rusted and
had old scales glittering along its red-brown blade. He cut

a couple of lengths of baling twine, about nine feet each, made noose snares of them, and laid them aside.

He took a gunny sack and went into the open stalls, then the closed ones, looking in the feedboxes and mangers, and whenever he came across a litter of kittens dropped them into the sack. Mother cats followed him, rising on haunches and walking on hind legs to reach the sack, and showed pin-sparkling teeth as they craned up and cried out at him. He tied the top of the sack with twine and started for the door.

"Hey!" Charles cried. "Where the hell do you think you're going?"

"There's an old rain barrel out here behind the barn. I'm going to put the sack in there and then put this on top of them." He turned his ass toward Charles; a sash weight tugged down a rear pocket.

"There're about a dozen cats following you!" Charles cried, and was astonished by his voice; he sounded afraid.

Earl reached in a shirt pocket and lifted a baby kitten out by the scruff of its neck. "They'll follow me back," he said, and smiled, then rolled his eyes.

More cats, twenty or more, had discovered Charles and were swirling and straining against him, switching him with their tails, leaning on his pants with forepaws, punching their claws through, and pressing against him with such strength and persistence he was afraid that if he moved he'd be thrown off balance and step on one. Or fall. He hated cats and the idea that there were creatures so sneaky and feminine. He heard a shrieking like a nail being pulled, and looked up; cats had gathered along the edge of the loft and were staring down at him with extended necks, heads swaying from side to side, as if readying to spring. Earl came into the barn with the kitten between his thumb and forefinger and most of the mother cats following, and shut the door.

"The barrel's empty. I'll just leave those outside till we're done in here." He placed the kitten in a feedbox, petted it, and said, "O.K. Put down the food."

"You put it down," Charles said, and tossed the bowl to him. The swirl of cats followed its flight and by the time Earl got it to the ground were gathered around it like spokes around a hub, and then the cats in the loft began leaping to the floor, one by one, like precision divers, their colors flashing into blurs, and bounded toward the bowl, forcing their way into the mass of milling cats already there. There was a chorus of growls from the center of it.

"O.K.," Earl said. "Where's the biggest, ugliest mother of them all?"

"Right there." Charles pointed out a tiger-striped tom, sitting back like an overlord while it cleaned its mouth with a gray tongue. It had a flattened head, a spray of needlelike vibrissae around its brindled face, and a badly scarred nose. One of its gold eyes, clouded a pearl color from an injury or a disease, was turned over one shoulder toward them.

"Oh, boy," Earl said. "He must be the granddaddy of them all. Look at those nuts on him. Should we castrate him first?"

"No."

"We better use the twines, then. He's going to be a doozy."

Earl looped the nooses together and, when the tom was boxing at a smaller cat, slipped both nooses over its neck, stepped back, and jerked hard. "O.K., you big sonofabitch," he said. "Here's your last time."

The tom backed away, shaking its head as if to say, No, no, you've made a terrible mistake.

Earl reeled it in close, then swung it overhead, nearly as high as the loft, and brought it down on the floor of the stall with a wallop. Then he grabbed the scythe and chopped it across the neck, and it laid back its ears and made gasping sounds as it spat at him.

"Jesus Christ," he said. "Get it with something, Chuck!"

"What?"

"Anything you got!"

Charles grabbed a sash weight, threw it, and missed, and Earl swung again with the scythe and caught the cat on the tail, and it let out a cry of anger and challenge that sent the rest of the cats bolting toward cover. One of them leaped against the piece of Masonite, knocking it loose, and a stream of cats of calico, tortoise shell, many-colored spots, gray, black, white, went pouring out the open window. Earl handed the twines to Charles, was hit in the head by a leaping cat, knocked another down in mid-flight, running a gauntlet of them, and got the Masonite back.

The tom, its back arched and its hackles up, was dancing backward on stiff legs, fighting the leash of twine, and Charles let him have some leeway. "There's got to be a better way of doing this," he said. "We ought to have your rifle."

"Not in town."

"What about stringing him up?"

"We could try." Earl took the twines from him. "Go on up in the hayloft and I'll hand you up these ends."

Charles climbed a ladder of horizontal boards, his heart beating so hard at the base of his throat it was knocking his breath out. Cats in the loft scattered from him. He walked over above Earl, and saw that some spikes had been hammered halfway into the facer board of the loft, perhaps for hanging harness, and lay on his stomach and reached for the twines, but the cat was yowling and leaping from left to right at the end of its tether, and winning the tug of war.

"You bastard," Earl said, and gave a jerk, and the cat came toward him as though it meant business. Earl got the twines to Charles and he pulled them in, feeling a sudden, tremendous, struggling weight at their ends, lifted high, got them next to a spike, and made several turns around it, the cat five feet off the floor, kicking its hind legs, springing them as though to leap through air, and batting at the taut hanging twine with its forepaws. Its head was back, its scarred and battered nose turned up, and its undamaged eye, undimmed by all that had happened, in clear focus, fixed on Charles. He stepped back out of sight. "How long?" he asked, and felt that bats were flapping close around him in the shadowy darkness of the gable near the loft.

"That one I choked took quite a while."

Charles came down and stood beside Earl. The cat kicked and pawed at the twine, twisting itself in circles, making moist guttural noises, and after a prolonged minute of this, the two of them growing more uneasy, there was still no sign it was giving in.

"I guess it doesn't work like with people," Earl said, and picked up a three-tined pitchfork. "Let's try this." Charles went up to the loft and lowered the cat, while

Earl maneuvered a tine on either side of its neck, and then drove the fork into the ground, so it was held as in a stanchion.

"Bring the equipment," Earl said.

Charles moved the weights and killing tools closer, and Earl picked up the baseball bat and whacked the cat's spine. Charles got a hammer and hit it over the head. It fell to its side, pawing, and Earl picked up the fishing knife and stabbed its back but the knife point skidded over its skin without even penetrating it. Earl stuck the knife in the cat's ear. "Hit it!"

"*What?*" Charles said.

"Hit the end of this damn knife here! Hurry!"

"You!"

"I can't! I've got to hold him fast! You got the hammer, hey!"

Charles hit the knife a blow, driving it into the cat's skull, and it released such a piercing cry of pain that Earl jumped back and the pitchfork jerked loose. The cat, with the knife protruding from its ear, came streaking past Charles. He stepped on the trailing twines and the cat went up high, its hindquarters reversing with its head, and hit on its stomach. The knife dislodged. Earl ran over with a sash weight and swung it from overhead against the cat's side, where it made a dull pop. The cat stood, tottered, took off in the opposite direction, and did another flip around as the twine, still under Charles's shoe, drew tight. Earl picked up the pitchfork and stabbed. Its center tine pierced the cat's abdomen and it began to bark like a dog and claw at the fork as though it could climb it.

"Jesus God!" Earl cried. "It's got nine lives!"

"Don't be a dumb-ass!"

"Well, if it still isn't dead, then what?"

"We haven't got it in a vital spot."

"Which one?"

Charles came over with the hammer and hit the cat twice at the base of the skull. Its good eye clouded and closed, its tongue appeared, bloodied and chewed up, and blood ran from its ears and from between its bared and discolored teeth. It lay still at last, larger dead than alive. Earl carried it to a stall, his face altered and set, and dropped it into a five-gallon bucket. "O.K.," he said. "Where's the next?"

"That's it."

"What do you mean?"

"I'm quitting."

"Oh, yeah?"

They studied one another in the gray-graven darkness of the barn, wide-eyed and hesitant.

"Maybe I'll drown those few," Earl said. His fleshy lips were trembling.

"Go ahead."

"You won't tell anybody if I do or don't, huh?"

"Don't worry," Charles said, and stepped outside. In the low afternoon light the lawn under the trees was alive with movement. Somehow the kittens had escaped from the sack and were crawling and tottering through the thick grass toward the doorway where he stood.

Cats poured out of the barn behind him.

*

At home, Tim was in the living room, in a black suit jacket of their father's that came to his knees and a gray wig from an old Halloween costume; he'd found something black, cigar ash, most likely, and rubbed it over his cheeks to represent stubble. He did a skitterish dance up to Charles and said, "Where's Earl?"

"I don't know."

"Killing cats?"

"Where did you hear that?"

"I heard. Did you chicken out?"

"Eat it."

"Arms for the poor," Tim said, flapping a sleeve of the coat. "Arms for the poor." He seemed reluctant to go into the act he'd prepared, for he'd certainly prepared one to go with this costume, and his voice was empty of its usual recklessness and spirit. There were glittering fans of perspiration over the freckles that flared up from his nose.

"What's wrong?" Charles asked.

"Nodding."

"Where are the girls?"

"Over on the other side."

"Why aren't you?"

"I saw you coming back. Where's Earl?"

"Why all this worry about Earl?"

Charles turned to the doorway of their father's room and saw, on the card table there, the cause of Tim's agitation; the tissue for his plane was cut into shreds the size of confetti and the shreds were piled into a neat cone.

"I did it," Tim said.

"*You?* What the hell for!"

"I don't know."

"Do you know this?" Charles said, and punched his chest so hard it resounded.

"Don't," Tim said.

Charles shoved against his shoulders and he went stumbling backward, his face giving off fear and disbelief, and struck the wall with such force his wig flew off, and then fell, quick as a handclap, flat on his ass.

"You thought if Earl was with me, you wouldn't get it, didn't you, damn you!" Charles cried, and slapped the back of his head and sent tears splattering over a jacket sleeve.

"Why'd you do it?"

"I don't know! I started cutting and couldn't stop!"

"How can you be so stupid? You ought to be sent away to the State Institution, for God's sake."

"*No!*"

Charles grabbed a sleeve of the jacket and jerked, rolling him on his back, pulled the sleeve loose, rolled him again, and pulled off the coat. "And on top of it all, you've probably gone and ruined Dad's jacket. How can you be so stupid on top of being stupid!" Knowing he'd struck the sensitive spot.

He dropped the jacket on the couch, and said, "Now quit crying, or you'll get something worse." And heard his mother echo in his voice. He went to the other side of the house, where the girls were sitting at a children's card table on small folding chairs, coloring fashion illustrations from a newspaper ad. Marie, her brunette hair stringy and oil-darkened, seldom washed or set, looked up at him; she had the placid face and nearly circular eyes of the Krulls, but her eyes were even larger, more owl-like. "I'm going to tell Dad you and Tim been fighting again," she said.

"We haven't."

"Sue and I heard."

"I just gave him heck. He ruined my airplane."

"Dee, de, *dee,* de," Susan sang, smiling and swinging a crayon like a metronome in front of her eyes. "Eee, eee, dee, de. You said *I'd* break it, smart one." She gave a toothy grin and stuck the crayon like a hatpin through her hair.

"Did he watch you two?"

"He was with us till you came," Marie said. "He told us why it was more fun to color these than color books."

"How come?"

"Because nobody else ever colors them."

"Everybody knows that," Charles said.

"Did you see his funny clothes?" Susan asked.

"Yes."

"Doesn't he look dumb?" She giggled.

"I guess."

"Dee, de, dee, dum. Like that," she said, and pulled the crayon out and pointed to her coloring. The model's face was a blackened craze.

Charles left the room. He couldn't find Tim anywhere and was about to go outside when he heard sounds from the upstairs. He went up the steps. Their father had put down flooring behind the bedroom with the dormer, up to the front of the house, to make another room, and had fitted a double window in the gable there, but the place stood as it did on the day when he'd hammered home the last flooring nail. Along the stairwell was a wall that was merely studs covered with tar-impregnated paper, or less in spots. Charles went to the door in it and listened there, and then opened the door onto blackness. There weren't any windows beyond the wall, not even a ventilator to let in light, and it was a three-foot drop to the bare joists below; the ceiling of the other side was that much lower, and a floor hadn't been put down yet.

"Tim. Are you in there?"

"Yes! No!"

"Come on out."

"No!"

An extension cord with a bulb screwed into its socket was draped over the doorknob. Charles turned it on and in its dim light could see a row of planks that led to a layer of grain doors that had been placed over the joists to form a platform; unpacked boxes from North Dakota, old suitcases, a grain separator, a broken carom board, and broken furniture were piled on this platform, and Tim lay there on his stomach with his hands over his head. Charles lowered himself onto the planks and walked out to him. "Come on," he said.

"I want to stay in here!"

"Cut it out."

"This is the place I belong!"

Charles tried to lift him up, but he struggled and cried out so, he let him drop.

"It's just that, well, dammit, when I came home and— Anyway, now somebody will have to go somewhere and get me some more of that paper."

"I know! What's the matter with me? Why can't I ever do anything *right?*" Tim rolled his face back and forth on the grain doors.

"Don't, please. You'll hurt yourself."

"I don't care!"

"I shouldn't have got so mad."

"It wouldn't be so bad if—" Tim gasped for air. "If I wasn't so *stupid!*"

"I just said that. You aren't. I was just—'"

"I don't even feel you want me around any more! It's worse than when you hit me!" Tim's fists kicked up spurts of dust as he struck them down.

Charles sat and tried to turn him so they were sitting next to one another, but Tim's head dropped and lay in his lap like a stone. "I like you, Tim," he said. "Especially when you're just yourself. You're my best friend then."

Tim drew up and sat back on his heels. "Really?" His face and stomach were caked with blackened dust from the grain doors, and the dust was streaked and maplike from mucus and tears.

"Yes," Charles said.

Tim put his head on Charles's thigh, and with the touch of it, it seemed to Charles they were sitting in a newly framed house, with only bare rafters above them, laddery beams open to the light. He looked up. Shingle nails showed through the roofing boards and there were gray cobwebs woven like cloth in the spaces between.

"I feel so awful," Tim said.

"I'm sorry I—"

"Not because of you. I feel awful all the time. I'm a sonofabitch. I don't have a mom."

"What do you mean?"

"I never saw her, or if I really did, I don't remember her much."

"Oh, sure."

"No!"

"Sure you do."

"Why can't you ever *believe* me?"

"Oh, you're all right," Charles said, and remembered coming home one day the spring after she died, when the streets were underwater, and finding Tim marching around in the living room as if with a squad of troops, his teeth bared in fury and his eyes crossed, singing in time to his step a song he'd composed: "Oh, you cross-eyed baby, with the hole in your head! Oh, you cross-eyed baby, don't you wish you were dead!" From that day, the song had become his theme; he sang it when he was angry at the girls or frustrated or hyperactive, or too happy to express himself, and Charles had heard him singing it in bed at night when he couldn't sleep. Charles tried to imagine what their mother, who wouldn't have inflicted this unreasoning hurt on Tim, might say to him if she were trying to comfort him and thought of waking one night to total darkness, in the house kept calm and ordered by her, and hearing Tim, who couldn't have been more than three, screaming in his crib across the room, and then her footsteps and voice coming in:

"Little one, little one, what is it?"

"It's a tiger! He's trying to eat me up!"

"There, there, you've just had a bad dream."

"No, no, it's a *real* tiger, I know it's real. When he opens his mouth, it looks like a butterfly!"

And Charles had seen, like a projection upon the blackness, the red-orange and rose and pink and bits of black and white of a tiger's opened mouth, with the feathery edge of a butterfly's wing around it, and felt as he had in the darkened barn when he and Earl, in spite of the wounds they'd inflicted, couldn't make the cat relinquish its hold on life, and wanted to say to Tim, It's all right, I know, I love you, I'll take care of you, or better, or worse, or more, or—

"Hey! What are you two doing in there?" Martin cried.

Charles stared up into the surrounding dark and at the glow of the bulb by the open door. There was nobody there. He'd imagined his father. Then he saw the three of them blazing noisily along an open causeway across naked, wide-open water in Lionell's white-painted, polka-dotted car, the stuttering and flashing white and yellow phosphorescent lines going by on either side, and then a curve with the railing gone and a fountaining gorge emptying around them as they were slowed, stopped, and then drawn straight down, the opened windows letting the car fill with the sucking rush of the sea.

"Tim," he said, his voice coming up from him in a whisper. "Come on, Tim, let's get out of here. I've had enough of this. Let's go."

33

۶§§৯

RED WING

"How many more miles?" Susan asks.

"How should I know?" Martin answers.

"Well, if you don't, who *does?*" She's seven, sitting in the favored seat beside him, and now she turns her square-cut, mature-looking face to her reflection in the side window and sticks out her tongue, still angry that they didn't stop at Santa Claus Land in Anoka. The tongue in the window waggles back. Marie and Charles, in the back seat with blankets and rugs and a big box, look at one another and then intertwine fingers and hold hands; it's hot August and they're returning to Illinois after a long stay in Hyatt, where none of them enjoyed themselves, although none of them talked about it or wondered why, and they'll stop at the farm in Wisconsin to pick up Tim, who's been spending the year with their Great-aunt Sue and Great-uncle Einard, the childless couple Elling used to live with. For several miles there's no sound but the muted hum of the mechanism powering their movement through sapce in the terrestrial and road-restricted car.

And then Susan says again, "How many more miles?"

"I'd judge something over twenty-five to Sue and Einard's," he says. "And then about four hundred to home."

She says, "Then we'll have to stop some place where I can poop or tinkle, because I need some ice cream."

"Need?" he says.

"I have to poop."

"Can't you wait till we get over this?"

They're crossing the bridge from the reddish-brown and silvery-green loaflike bluff at Red Wing, Minnesota —where they saw on a tree-lined street with a broad divider of grass a bandstand and a brick post office, a truckload of turkeys rolling by, and the shoe factory; red wings on buildings everywhere—over the Mississippi to the lower, level land of Wisconsin beyond. Marie drops to the floor between seats, terrified of water, of crossing over it, of bridges, ferries, trestles, and viaducts, and stares at Charles with her tremulous blue and nearly circular eyes, dark now with a question almost of *Who are you?* He stretches out on the seat, searching for approbation, and then puts his hand under her shirt and feels the humidity and heat of her skin, undoes the copper buttons at the side of her jeans and as she arches to slide them and the underwear beneath down below her thighs, her face rose and crimson, her features filled with her singularly lonely fear. He lies above her, takes out his peanut, as Susan calls it, and lets her touch it as he runs his hand over the damp parting of her sparse and silken hair.

"What the Sam Hill's going on back there?" Martin cries, and Marie's shoulders strike against Charles as she struggles to pull herself up.

"I'm trying to sleep," Charles says. "She won't let me."

"Where are we now?" Marie asks, popping upright in the seat.

"About the same four hundred miles from the same old place," Susan says. "Let's stop."

"If I saw a place along here that sold ice cream, believe me, I would," he says above the car noise.

Charles flips up his shirt and does quick double strokes close to his belt and then rises, his face struck in half by August sunlight, and whispers, "Marie. Hey, Marie, have you ever seen this?" and touches his fingers to a pearl-colored pool of his newly leased life-force, and runs the tips of his fingers down the curve of her wrist.

And remains stilled, his face cleft by the sunlight, and wonders over the events that have left him without a mother, doing what he has in this car, rocking and swaying along different planes, with its central bulge like a dividing line between the real and the unreal of the unsorted and transitory but never outlined adolescent world, where in confusion the sexes began to take on their own or other sides, or neither, as with Marie, who is herself alone.

Four

34

❧

BURNING THE COUCH

They're burning the couch. Blue flames scumble low over the cotton wadding and yellowish columns of smoke ascend from the cushions and climb above their heads into the misty-blue, cerulescent sky of June, which the sun, a silver disc, clings to and hovers behind. Tim, tall and skinny, nearly six feet at the age of sixteen, does a happy tap dance over the packed dirt of the back yard, strutting with sudden dips around a pile of cement blocks, bricks, a broken hod, his hands in his pockets and his lips pursed as though whistling, jumps into a mixing vat encrusted with finish coat, kicks around in it and knocks plaster loose, and then does a down-on-one-knee finale, gives his head a shake, and says, "Hotcha!"

Charles, a collegian now, tries the Indian dance the costumed chieftain does between halves of football games at school, but his feet are stuck in self-consciousness. His elbows knock against things the Indian wouldn't do. He flips his long hair back from his eyes.

Tim punches his shoulder. He swings and hits Tim's fist. Tim's harder to hit, now that he's so tall, and what can an older brother, caught like this, do? "Bo hittio pitcha to me now!" Tim says, and Charles runs at him as he takes off for the house; he disappears around the corner, and then, too fast for feet, backs around the other end of the house doing a leg-stretching cakewalk with his hands pumping as though over a scrubboard and his feet popping in loose flaps. "I'm a-workin' off the flab and asshole, folks!" he cries. His teeth are clenched and his eyes crossed. "I'm a-dancin' my way from here to heben and back! Feets, do that thing! I'm idio may-tut!" He

393

does a shuffling stomp that kicks up cinders and dust and then drops into the splits and saves his jewels with an outspread hand. He bounces his weight and then springs up and strolls over, himself again, his long thin fingers in the tops of his pockets, and stares at the couch, and says, "You know, dancing's hard."

"You have to know how to do it."

Tim does a mincing toe-rise with his hands on his chest. "Oh, do we, sweet one," he says. "Do tell me now."

"Eat it."

"Whip it out, Charoontarus."

Charles stares at the couch. Ever since they reached the age of reason they've wanted to burn this, he thinks, this thing that is (was, it's going) the ugliest piece of furniture in the house, a distinction, since most of the pieces, without a woman to watch over them, have been abused so badly over the years they're beginning to resemble castoff wreckage; this maroon-brown monstrosity that dates from their parents' marriage and followed them from Hyatt to here, where it took up residence, as there, in the heart of the living room.

Its wooden arms are loose and can be lifted up like alligator (or "eggilator," as Tim says) jaws, its seat cover is worn through to cotton wadding, which in spots is worn through to the springs—half of which have snapped these past years and have to be covered with rugs to keep them from flesh—and the mechanism that once enabled it to convert into a double bed has collapsed, so it has to be shoved against a wall and its front legs shimmed to keep it from sliding out with a crash and leaving you supine when you sit in it.

They were embarrassed to bring friends into the house, because of it sitting there, and on the occasions when somebody had to confront it directly, they'd work up a patter:

Have a seat if you like to be goosed.

Our grandma made those rugs—aren't they pretty? I don't know what that is underneath of them.

Once I got the right combination of springs and had to be picked off the ceiling.

It has to be assembled before you sit in it. Pick your style.

Don't let it know you're scared.

At breakfast this morning, their father and Jerome, back at carpentry for the summer, started off for work, and then their father, who'd begun dating a widow, reappeared in the kitchen in a rush, as though he'd just noticed the thing, wrote out a check for three hundred dollars, and said, "For God's sake, go get some new furniture."

They whistled and applauded as they used to at the movies when the hero appeared ("Wait! What about the old stuff?" "It doesn't make a bit of difference to me; you can burn it, for all I care." *He* said it) and then borrowed a pickup from their Uncle Fred and parked in the alley behind a furniture store in Havana and picked out, first, a couch, of course, a sturdy Early American couch.

Two maple end tables, a swivel chair of white Naugahyde, a three-foot lamp with a linen shade and an oatmeal-colored base (a reminder, to Charles, of Grandma Jones), and ran out of money. They were loading it all into the pickup, laughing at the looks of the salesmen and themselves—as they later laughed waddling toward the incinerator with the swaying weight of the old couch between them—when a stranger pulled up in the alley beside them, and said, "Say, it looks like somebody's getting married, ha?"

Ha!

It was gasoline they got it going with, and now Tim, who's disappeared for a moment, returns from the house on a run with a large can of lighter fluid and touches up some spots that seem reluctant to burn.

Charles checks the sky again—for a while it looked like rain, and they haven't unloaded the new furniture yet—and sees Bill Ebbinger, their gray neighbor across the alley, leaning on his lath fence with fixed eyes; being seen, Bill Ebbinger, a watchmaker who's now the town constable, walks over with his frail and liver-spotted hands curled at his sides.

"What are you doing?"

"Burning our couch."

"Does your dad know it?"

"Sure."

Will he ask them to put it out?

"I noticed the smoke."

"Oh."

"So did the wife. Sure makes a lot of smoke. Terrific heat, too, just terrific standing here close by it."

Soon, Bill Ebbinger walks off without finding out for his wife *why* they're burning it. Crazy Neumiller kids.

The worst thing, Tim thinks, is that it will be preserved forever; its smoke will reach the atmosphere, fall as rain, feed plant life, and those plants won't be normal.

The worst thing, Charles thinks, is that it's preserved forever in photographs:

Jerome as an infant in a knitted bonnet, propped against its back.

A grinning father in forties dress with his arm around their mother.

Susan as an infant, Tim and Marie on either side of her, a doily on the couch's back, presaging the layers of throw rugs to come.

A picture by a man who came to the house the summer after their mother died, when the five were home alone, and said he'd been sent to do their portrait (a lie; but they were so conscious of how her death had changed them, made them different from their friends, they thought it only natural), and had them line up in graduated order on the couch, covered now with the rugs, and then adjusted his camera, hid under its executioner's hood, and caught everybody leaning back too far—had the shims slipped?—fluffed skirts, bloomers, and the pulled-up pants legs and shinbones of the boys; hunched uneasy shoulders. A row of eyes like holes in air.

Charles punches Tim. Tim hits him. They treadle around the couch in an amateur boxing match. He hits hair. I trammel nobody. Who hits he. I hark three. They do a tango. He grabs my bush. "Is this a lady here, or who's knocking?"

"Pardon me all the way to hell and back. Goodness gophers!"

Hold:

Jerome in his mortarboard with its valedictorian's tassel —a close-up, somehow distorted, so that the couch seems to have its arm around him.

Tippy, their since departed dog, lying in front of a leg with a wedge under it.

A color shot of Marie and Susan displaying new dresses

from Grandma Jones; Christmas wrappings strewn over the room, opened boxes and other tinselly clutter, and way in the background, right at the focal point, where some rugs have slipped down, a white area of wadding stares between them like a cyclops.

And these after Jerome and Charles started using the family camera and purposely tried to keep the couch out of the frame!

Now I can bring Budke here, Charles thinks. He's dated her since high school and she's never been inside the house, although she's been at the front door a few times; one Halloween she and Charles were paired up for a treasure hunt and needed a 1941 penny to complete their list and win, so he sped toward home with her in the car, telling about the pennies he'd collected in jars and tins from the time he lived in that other state, North Dakota, and when she started to get out as though she meant to enter the place, he said, "No, now, wait a minute. That's right. I lost those about a month ago." And drove her off.

A hole appears below a cushion and tines and fangs of flame spout out from it and mingle yellow-orange with the flames of blue. "Oh, Oh, Oh, Oh, *Oh*, Charoontarus!" Tim says, and feeds the hole more fluid as flames hop up the needle-sized stream toward the can where— Couldn't it explode?

Charles studies Tim's maturing face, where the frizzy beginnings of a pink-blond beard sparkle from the fire or sunlight, and suffers a sudden shock, skip-beat, and parting of his being: who *is* Tim? He can see him as a seven-year-old, small for his age, pale freckles over his face and arms, sitting in overalls on the swing beneath the tree at the side of the house, a bare foot trailing in the oval of dirt below, his head bowed, because he's been told by Jerome or Charles to get the hell out of the way of their football game. Or walking across the yard, his hands in his pockets, toward the girls' playhouse, the box of a milk truck removed from its frame and painted chocolate, where he'll lock himself up for the rest of the afternoon, because he's been kicked in the pants for pestering them.

He disappears then. He spends the summer with Sue and Einard, and when their father goes to fetch him for school, he grabs the door, the car bumper, his uncle's legs, and is so desperate their father lets him stay. Einard pays him for helping with the chores and he accumulates an account of four hundred dollars, a fortune to Charles and Jerome, and raises garden products and calves he exhibits at fairs; a photograph arrives with him beside a Holstein steer, smiling and holding a ribbon up. Martin often says in quiet moments, or in the midst of a television program or a meal, "Goodness, how I miss Tim!"

When he returns home (a form of bartering is entered on by Martin and Sue and Einard, whereby Tim will spend one year at home for so many on the farm), his freckles are so enlarged and dark from working outdoors they nearly cover the milk-colored skin of his face: "Freck-butt! Freck-butt!" he says through clenched teeth. He's wiry, charged with excess energy, with eyes that have a look, shy yet violent, that's in the eyes of Yeats, and if angered becomes ashen and compact, a pure source of power, and attacks Jerome and Charles with flying fists, baseball bats, brick-bats, table chairs, and flings Marie and Susan around like rag dolls when they enrage him.

"It's the bone-cracker, folks! It's the dangerous beast without a peer or peter! Watch out for your whistle-holes!"

"Tinvalin" connotes his diminutive size, his high voice, the sheath of protectiveness he keeps around him, and his razor's edge of violence; a neighbor, a plump, gossipy woman with pink glasses perched on a pointed nose and buck teeth, who calls them "You poor kids with no mother," *he* calls "Whit-tea-*whee*ow, Alabozhurs," a name that calls her up like an incantation, and lets you know she's hypocritically Christian and unctuous, and has the name of Lucille. You have to *hear* him do it, of course. He calls Forest Creek "Four-assed dick."

Their father has never had any sort of patience with fooling or impropriety, and since their mother's death has handled all five in a manner that's almost formal, as though he's fashioned his only refuge; his dark and Indianlike looks have deepened and now he's even more silent, and then Tim—is it out of gall at having a life separate from the family's, or insanity?—starts calling him "Heap Big M." And gets away with it! makes their father blush, even, like a farm boy accepting a flower, or the boy he must have once been.

Tim goes to Wisconsin again, and when he materializes next, at age twelve, he's hardly grown but gained fifty pounds, and his face is so fat his cheeks look inflated; his walk is waddling and burdened, his eyes dull, his hands stumpy and covered with warts, and he chews his nails until the ends of his fingers are ragged and bloody. "Tonofabelly," he calls himself, or "Big-prowed sowgut," and at Christmas sings to the tune of "Jolly Old St. Nicholas," " 'Christmas Eve is coming soon, I can tell you that, but please-please don't tell anyone ah that I am too fat!' Merry Chrinchus, everybun!"

And he plays the piano. It's been discovered by a piano teacher from St. Paul that he can master the rudiments of a Chopin mazurka in a week, and he's her prize pupil; but he never plays at home, and when the family asks him to, slips on a string tie, white gloves of Marie's, and crosses his eyes as he sends his hands in a tuneless dance over the keys and then, reaching down, plays the metal pedals at his feet—"The gloves help!" he cries—and then gives a smile all teeth, and says, "Hi, there, sweet ones. Slobberace at the keys." And then falls on the floor and plays dead.

Martin lets him return to Wisconsin for good, and when Charles is a freshman in college, he receives a birthday letter from Tim at a time when he's worrying about his next rent payment, his next meal, even, and finds a twenty-dollar bill enclosed; fumbling through Tim's scratchy, self-effacing script that takes three readings to translate, he learns that Tim is doing well in high school, has grown to five feet ten, is running over the hills and through the woods of the farm to train for the track team in Pettibone next year (further bartering has provided that he shall spend his last year of high school at home, and *then* be free to do what he wants), that he's going to submit more poems for publication in the school paper (Charles didn't know he wrote) and perhaps send a few that have already been printed in it to a national magazine, now that they've seen the air, and that their Great-uncle Einard is growing old and rheumatic and has turned part of the farm over to Tim, so he might have to take it on when he's through with high school, and run it while he attends college part-time; he's going to major in biology. He might buy a new car. One sentence near the end stands out as if in italics: "In your nineteenth year, may God grant you the happiness you have given so unselfishly to me and your friends."

Happiness? All Charles can remember is torment. And *what* friends?

He saw Tim in his latest incarnation at a track meet over the spring break; he was tall and spindly-legged, and in his track briefs looked made of bone. He started out the mile with twenty other runners and on the last lap began passing the entire field as if they were traveling backward, and came sprinting down the final stretch with nobody else in sight and snapped the string, throwing his sweat-cold arms around Charles (who's hardly prepared for this), to break the county record.

Charles looks at Tim, who's near the couch with a leg forward and head bowed, chin on his chest, as though deep in some unreachable thought.

Who *is* he?

What's he thinking, Tim wonders. I sure can feel some thoughts. He's probably wishing now we'd never burned it. He's always liked to save things. Maybe we should have kept it in the basement or the attic, or our room upstairs, as a reminder of the camping trips to the State Forest when I got scared, riding our bikes out to Kyle Lake all that summer, seven miles each way, and going swimming and fishing together and having a few smokes; the time I was sunburned so badly I couldn't sleep, and he sat up with me; how it took two of us to maneuver that big mower mounted on bicycle tires, one pushing, one pulling with a rope, when we mowed the cemetery nobody else ever mowed where Mom is buried; his "pigeon parlor" as he called it—wire cages of pigeons he'd caught in the attic of the old Opera House and kept in that milk truck of the girls'—and how scared of him I was when I let the pigeons go, but he just cursed me out and then watched them circle above us, dark and then light as they swung out around, dark and light, and then were gone.

Charles studies the flames, the glowing network of springs rising from the tatters and ash, and feels remorse and guilt start to well in him, when Tim gives him a shove, and says, "Better stand back," and sprays on so much lighter fluid there's the *whoosh* of a smoke pot in a vanishing act.

Better stand back. The words charge the air between them and make Charles realize that there might be times when he'll need to be protected and that Tim, for all his early frailties, might be a person powerful enough to do it. My brother, Charles thinks, and feels himself shift into another realm, unself-conscious and wholly wordly, where all he has to do is cry "Hey-hey!" and prod the couch to get it burning better, brightly ablaze in the breeze rising out of this afternoon.

"Hey-hey!" Tim answers, and grabs a length of two-by-four and whacks the couch's back and watches a cloud of sparks climb the sky and disappear, and thinks, Some day I might write about this and see these sparks rise again, and wonders, If I do do that, will I feel as I do now that my mother was here?

"They're burning the couch," would be a good way to begin it, perhaps, and then end with her voice in a low-pitched wail of—

They're burning the couch.

Tunes of Tinvalin was printed on the tab of the file folder and typed across the first sheet of paper inside. There were about fifty pages altogether.

ALONG THE ROAD

The little black bird
With tennis-string claws
Perched on the old gray dog.

Slowly the bird
Stepped up and down
The back of the dog,

And then the bird
Stopped at the place
Where the tire had run,

And ate his dinner.

And on the following page:

Ceaselessly it searches the man's heart
Simply for pleasures of the flesh.
But he trembles at the notion
That it searches for a greater food.

He need not worry,
For the maggot has no eyes.

And on the next:

FOR A SOMEBODY

> *love's*
>> *a yes for*
>> *a thing with*
>> *a nobody*
> *but Love's*
>> *a thing with*
>> *a yes for*
>> *a somebody*
> *so Life's*
>> *a thing for*
>> *a sum of*
>> *a body nowhere*

Hmmm, e. e. cummings, Charles thought, and looked up; Tim was across the bedroom, upright in an old kitchen chair, cracking his knuckles, clearing his throat, and growing more nervous with each page Charles turned. Charles was worried that he'd been wrong to ask to read these. Tim had shown them to their father earlier, wondering if perhaps the local printer, who printed the weekly newspaper and pamphlets and auction posters, couldn't print a hundred copies of his collection; he'd pay the cost. Tim kept the poems in a big envelope, which was hidden away in the old suitcase he used each time he went back to Wisconsin. Their father took the envelope to the other side of the house and brought it back after midnight, and said, "I like a lot of them, practically all of them, but I think you should wait until you're twenty-one to publish." The way Tim took the poems and then left the room was the real reason Charles had asked to see them.

THE FLEDGING

> *I fled it.*
> *Feathers around bone*
> *and a body so tiny it must*
> *have been just air when it hit.*
> *Had it tried its first flight yet?*
> *Had other feathers around bone*

crowded or denied it?
Did its mother slap her wing—a cruel crone?
It lay on leaves where ants would lace around it
with ribbons and streamers of gold and red
and bright birthday bows that led
over a sand pyramid down to the
hole where they'd tie it for good.
No matter where I travel or roam,
to the Far East or farther West,
it stays: for I am it,
the fledgling fallen from its nest.

Charles looked up. Tim had stopped his gestures of nervousness and was staring at him in wide-eyed silence as he breathed through his mouth.

"Have you read much Hart, er—Stephen Crane?" Charles asked.

"Oh, sure," Tim said. "Some. What do you think of it?"

"Are these sort of representative?" Charles asked, and flinched at his College English question.

"What do you mean?"

"Do you always write about death?"

"Death?" Tim asked, breathless. He studied Charles with troubled eyes. "Do I?" he said.

"So far."

"Aren't they just symbolic?"

"Everything's symbolic," Charles said, and flinched again.

36

MARIE'S SINGING

Now all of the family was home for Christmas at last. Marie came in the kitchen door after a spate of last-minute shopping with Elaine, giddy with Elaine's giddiness and good cheer, and there were Jerome and Charles, the missing two, at the kitchen table, playing pinochle with Tim and her dad. They hadn't been here since Thanksgiving vacation and she was so happy to see them she almost sang out "Joy to the World!" as she'd been singing all the way home in the car, in "that clangoring alto," as Elaine called it, and then asked her to mellow it so she could see to drive.

"Mrs. Claus returneth," Tim said, and Marie wondered, since her hands were full of packages, how Tim pictured the word: Claws?

Charles looked up from his cards and said, "Hey-hey, Marie," and Jerome said, "How have you been?"

"Fine," she said, smiling and studying them with affection for their brotherly bonds. They were wearing the sweaters she'd sent for their birthdays—they were that thoughtful—and Jerome had on a handsome pair of horn-rimmed glasses, new to her, that made his hollow-cheeked face look fuller and more direct in its lines.

She was relieved that neither got up from the table to greet her or give her a kiss; those moments were so difficult for her to find her way through, and she felt awkward enough as it was. They looked much older than she'd remembered, older than their ages, it seemed, and both were so intelligent and had learned so much at school and otherwise, she was convinced she'd never catch up, and didn't care. She blushed, embarrassed, yet comforted by the feelings they stirred alive in her, and put the packages down on the counter.

"Oh!" she said. She'd tracked in snow and it was melting around her shoes, tattered water around a mouse. She took a sponge from the drainboard of the sink and blotted at the water. The house had to be perfect for Christmas, correctly arranged and immaculate, so the spirit of the season could move unhindered through all of the rooms; she'd spent two weeks cleaning and decorating the place, and now, as usual, was the first to track it up.

"Have you joined the Thespian Club yet?" Charles asked her.

He'd been the president when he was a senior and won the highest award, an Omar, and acted at the university now; his hair was long again, halfway down his neck, and she remembered hearing he was in another play, one by Shakespeare, something with "night" in the title. She'd always wanted to go to the university with her dad to watch him perform, but she assumed she wouldn't understand the play and then wouldn't know what to say to him afterward, and he was so sensitive she was afraid that no matter what she said it might affect their relationship from then on.

"Oh, no," she said. "I'm just a sophomore."

"So? I joined when I was a sophomore."

"But you're so good. I can't act."

"Sure you can."

"I'd feel too dumb standing up in front of all those people."

"Get into makeup or props."

"Maybe next year."

Her dad, who'd been staring at Charles, said, "Will it be necessary for her to grow her hair as long as yours in order to act?"

"Oh, for God's sake," Charles said.

"I used to act in school, too, you know, but that doesn't mean I ran around looking like a bum. I'll give you five dollars right now if you'll run uptown the first thing in the morning and have that stuff cut off."

"It's supposed to be long."

"Wear a wig!"

"Oh, God!" Charles said, and turned the coloring fury of his face on his cards.

She put the sponge in the sink and saw that Tim and her dad, who were paired off against Charles and Jerome, were passing the signals Tim had devised over the fall. She hoped Jerome and Charles had their own set of signals, as they used to, and used them.

Tim crossed his eyes and said through clenched teeth, "Rack 'em up! Rip 'em off! Whip 'em out!"—he plucked a card from the fan in his hand and lifted it high—"Ah, ha! Ah, ya-ta-ta! *Winny*-beat! Whoo, whoooooooo!" His eyes uncrossed. "Feast on this, fond bluver Jerbloom," he said, and flipped the card, an ace, down on the table. "Shazam! The amazing Kutabux does another card-flappling trick!"

Jerome, whose play was next, kept staring at his cards and said in his dispassionate, gravelly drawl, "You're a hebephrenic schizophrenic, Tim."

"Oooo!" Tim said. "Large dictionarized words stream from such a werrietegetable languageopod so highly educated, I see, a pump whistle-*wheet!*"

"Come on, come on," her dad said. "Either play cards or act the fool, one of the two, or let's quit right now."

"I choose the former of those, kind sire," Tim said, and tossed down another ace.

"Ha," her dad said. "That helps."

"You betchum, Big M."

"Play!"

At her dad's elbow was a beanbag ashtray, filled with cigarette butts, orange peels, peanut shells, and the butts and chewed bits of his cigars. She'd have to remember to empty it before it gave off that awful odor of old cigars she'd grown up with most of her life; and she'd have to remember, too, to set out more ashtrays for Jerome and Charles, who smoked in the house now, instead of going out for a walk.

Jerome closed one eye, drew back from his cards like a farmer, and said in a farmer's voice, "Looks like you two are gonna git trounced agin!" And then threw down a trump!

Marie laughed. He never acted in such a slapstick manner unless he was embarrassed. He must be happy to see her. She smiled and the edges of her vision turned rivery-hued and tunnel-like from levitating tears. She picked up the packages, wavering shapes far away from her, and went into the living room, dimly lit and smelling of pine pitch and the countryside from the ceiling-high tree. The television was going, coloring the walls and half the ceiling gray-violet, and above the back of the easy chair she could see a half-moon of big hair curlers, and then, without moving the curlers or taking her eyes from the television, Susan said, in her matter-of-fact voice, "What'd you get me, Mare?"

Sue was as intelligent as the boys—a straight-A student who never had to study—and she'd helped their father grade school papers from the time she was eight. She hadn't ever taken a course in algebra but could solve Marie's nightly problems with hardly a thought (how could anybody add x's and abc's? they were *letters*, deviltry!) and she sometimes felt she'd been born into the family to remind the others to be grateful.

"You'll have to wait till Christmas to find out," she said.

"*You* never wait."

"I know."

"You see everything everybody's got a week before they get it."

"I know," Marie said.

She couldn't bear the uncertainty. She always rewrapped the packages as carefully as she could, adding touches of her own—a larger bow, an arrangement of tape, or a design cut from colored foil or an old Christmas card. Unless they were gifts for her dad. His she had to rewrap exactly as she'd found them, or he'd realize they'd been opened, and he couldn't stand it if anybody knew what he was getting before he did. She arranged the gifts she'd brought in (she'd re-do them later), along with the others under the tree, to balance the colors and best display those most artistically wrapped, and then reached to the stand at the center of the tree and put her finger into it; she'd filled it with water in the morning and added a spoonful of molasses for food, and the level was still high.

She realized she was singing "O Little Town of Bethlehem" under her breath and stopped. It irritated Tim and Charles that she was always singing and humming songs—Tim, especially, and when they were younger he'd named her Hum-Hound. Lately, whenever a song unconsciously rose from her, she'd feel jolted by a punch to her shoulder.

"Hum-Hound! Hum-Hound!" Tim would be saying with eyes so angry his pupils appeared blank. "Goddamn-ass Hum-Hound!"

She rearranged a few of the foil icicles hanging on branches in front of her eyes. She'd used eleven packages to cover the tree. Instead of draping handfuls of icicles here and there, or tossing them at the tree, as the boys always did, and letting them hang where they would, she'd suspended each one separately, as she'd seen somebody else (a friend's mother?) do, and now the tree looked like a fall of silver water from a tip pointing toward infinity. The colored lights were reflected off the icicles, as well as the ornaments—she moved a blue globe with a gold sunburst in its center to another spot—when they were hung right.

A detail was missing. She stepped back and saw that the star at the tip of the tree was lit, casting a red streak across the newly white-painted ceiling. She'd arranged cotton snow around the stand before putting down the packages, the manger scene was set up, and this year she'd repaired a shepherd that hadn't been used as long as she could remember, and had included him among the visitors at the stable, as it must once have been. All the rooms but hers and Susan's were clean, woodwork washed, windows shined, dusting done; and the floors were waxed until the Christmas-tree lights reflected at her feet in the sheen of this one were like a magnified swath of the winter sky's tapestry.

A miniature sleigh of red enamel, filled with candy and nuts, sat in a circle of pine branches on the coffee table, and she could see the wreath on the front door through the venetian blinds. An angel knelt among holly on the television set. There was a candelabra behind her, and candles of red and green and white were standing in pairs on the coffee table, the end tables, the gate-leg table, and the smoking stand.

Candles were so much more appropriate for a celebration than electric lights. With candles burning, there was room for darkness, for the emotions that arose only in subdued light, and the flames swayed as though to music that was perpetually joyful and serene. On Christmas Eve, with all of these lit, they'd be surrounded by a host of separate harmonies united in a dance, and the moving shadows would make it seem even the past had joined them.

She went into the kitchen and four pairs of eyes fixed on her.

"Oh," she said. "Do you want coffee?"

They turned back to their cards and "Sure, sure, sure, sure" went around the table in different tones as though they were bidding. She filled the percolator at the tap and took down the coffee can. In this house, the smell of coffee was a common perfume; any of the four could empty a pot in a couple of hours, and there were times when Jerome and Charles took their mugs upstairs and had coffee and cigarettes just before bed. What did they talk about?

She realized that her dad's voice was pitched as it was only when he spoke to her—higher, imperative, and for some reason always impatient.

"I said, 'Don't you think it's about time you took off your coat?' Can't you hear?"

"Oh, I forgot."

She folded it and placed it over the back of a chair and went to the refrigerator door. She'd also forgotten the platter of cold cuts she'd prepared. They ate hearty meals of several helpings and ate whenever they had the inclination in between, but were always hungry. None of them ever put on weight, though. Why? She picked at her food, hardly more, but was always heavier than she felt she should be; not overweight, really, but never as slim as she'd like, either.

She lifted the waxed paper from the platter, where wedges of cheese and slices of ham, corned beef, and liverwurst were rayed around a central arrangement of olives. Charles and Tim loved green olives. She popped one into her mouth. She put the platter on the table and her dad glanced up at her in an imperious, annoyed way. Was he losing at cards? He couldn't stand to lose. He'd say, "Oh, well, it's just another game," and go into the living room and slump in his chair, brooding, pulling and punishing the hair at the back of his head, and then he'd be at the kitchen table again, riffling the edge of the card deck and saying, "Well, is there anybody in this house brave enough to take a chance?"

He wasn't as restless and displeased with himself since he'd gone back to teaching, and in six years had worked his way up from coach and P.E. instructor in the junior high to the principal of the high school. This seemed to give him deep satisfaction. And since the beginning of the summer he'd been seeing Laura, a youthful-looking, high-spirited widow who lived in Chicago, and had become much happier, more open and demonstrative, than Marie had ever seen him. Though he couldn't carry a tune, he'd come into the kitchen where she was busy with dishes, throw his arms out wide, and sing in the voice of that old movie star, Eddie Nelson, or whoever, "Oh, Marie! *Ah*, Marie . . ."

He'd been driving to Chicago every weekend since the fall, and planned to spend part of the holidays there. Now he slammed down a trump to take a trick, spread his hand out on the table, and said, "I've got the rest," and then tossed the cards to Jerome.

Then turned his annoyed look full on her. "I suppose you spent too much money again today."

"I think the checking account might be overdrawn."

"Over*drawn?*"

"Maybe."

"Maybe? Can't you subtract yet?"

"Well, you know . . ." Her wiggly figures never came out right.

"That money was supposed to last you till the middle of January!"

"I know."

"What do you expect to buy groceries with?"

She blushed and lowered her eyes. "I saw some things I had to get."

"Some 'things.' *What* things?"

"You'll see."

"Ach!"

He turned back to the table, gathering up the cards dealt gingerly by Jerome, and heaved a sigh. Laura was an executive's secretary and a private bookkeeper, and a devout Catholic, too; she planned every move she made months in advance and carried out her plans to the letter, and since their dad had seen how well she managed, he'd become more intolerant than ever with Marie, and her way with money. She knew it wasn't sensible to spend so much at Christmas, when they didn't have that much to begin with, but couldn't help herself, and, anyway, she knew his anger would go when he saw his gift from her.

She'd bought him a maple bedroom valet, with a seat where he could sit as he dressed, a drawer beneath that filled with shoe-care equipment (she'd also got a shoehorn with a handle of deer antler or bone), and a shelf beneath that for shoes; maple shoe trees came with it, and its back was a hanger for suits. He'd become more careful about his dress and appearance, and was always going into the bathroom to brush his teeth or gargle with something; he combed his hair in a new way, to conceal his bald spot; his shoes weren't dull and scuffed, as they used to be; his suits were neatly pressed; and she no longer had to tell him when a tie and sport jacket clashed.

"The coffee will be done in a while," she said. "Is there anything else I can get?"

"You can get me back the money you just spent," he said.

Jerome looked at her and, hardly moving his lips, smiled a faint smile. He was so relaxed and easygoing about the household and family, and college too, she was sure, that she envied him. She smiled back and he twisted up his lips as though he'd tasted lemon, and then turned to his cards.

She picked up her coat and went through the back entry, at the head of the basement stairs, into the other side of the house to the bedroom she shared with Susan.

It was absolutely quiet on this side of the house. Every time she walked through the door, she felt she'd stepped into a private hiding place, a sanctum of her creation that nobody dared disturb. She couldn't hear the television or the sound of voices, and all the clothes seemed to hold silence. They were everywhere. The doors of the closet were thrown back and it bulged with clothes; clean clothes and dirty clothes were piled on the dressers, on the chairs and the beds, which were unmade, and all over the floor; undergarments hung from dresser knobs. Her dad had complained about the condition of the room, especially in the past months, and last week walked in when she was half naked, and shouted, "Gol-*dammit,* get this crap cleaned up before I throw it out the door!" She saw his reddened face in the mirror and herself holding a shirt over her front, and was as startled as she would have been if he'd actually started throwing; it was the first time he'd used profanity around her, which made her feel more naked than she was, and his face was puffed up, plump, crimson, with a force more than anger at her.

She tried to clean it then, and made an effort every day since, but it seemed impossible, and, anyway, she was comfortable here. Besides the clothes and the quiet, the room was always well heated, not like some parts of the house—was overwarm, really—and now was filled with a shuddering glow from a candle burning on the vanity.

The candle was supposed to last for the two weeks of Christmas, but she doubted that it would, unless it could slow itself down; it was already a day and a half ahead. Everything she got for herself was imperfect in some way, it seemed, or destined to break down, like the alarm clock beside the candle, useless, out of alarms, ticks, and the circle of time's company. The vanity was once her mother's and now looked new, thanks to Jerome and Charles, who sanded and stained and refinished it for her over the summer. It was now the same shade as the maple valet. She sat on the vanity bench and put the tip of her index finger into the pool of wax at the top of the candle, and its flame leaped higher. She stared at the finger, turning it to allow the wax to harden, and then held it apart from her others as she pushed back her hair.

Her face bothered her, and always had. Elaine and older women said she was "adorable" or "pretty as a picture," but she thought she looked awful: "Scary-Mare," Tim used to call her, and that seemed more accurate. Her hairline was uneven, her upper lip looked swollen, her nose too small, though not as small as Susan's, and her eyes too big. It was mostly the eyes, moon eyes, as she thought of them, large and circular, like half dollars, larger even than her father's, which were enormous behind his glasses. Her upper lip made a little peak over the lower one. Was that cute, she wondered?

She looked at the photograph she'd placed, years ago, under the molding at the bottom of the vanity mirror, and saw her face around it; it was of her mother, standing in front of a snow-capped lilac, dressed in a dark suit that made her look stocky and short, her hands hidden inside a muff. She was smiling out at anybody who wanted to look back into the moment she stood in. When was it taken? And where in North Dakota? Her dad and the boys were always talking about North Dakota, about the big house they had and the happy times there, but all she could remember was freezing her face so badly once she couldn't open her mouth to bawl out how frozen she was.

This was her favorite photograph of her mother, and she'd taken it from one of the albums and put it here to have it close, so she could remember how her mother looked. She was five when she died—"passed away," they said to her, gone. When she'd put the picture here, she used to stare at it and whisper, as if praying, "Oh, Mom, come back, come back," until she moved herself to tears. But after a while it was too difficult to keep doing, and that made her feel ashamed, unworthy of being her mother's daughter.

Elaine and Rose Marie would say, "Your mother was a wonderful woman—it's a shame you couldn't have known her better," and that made her feel worse; she couldn't remember her mother or say what she was like, even if her saying of it would have the power to bring her back again. Tim had difficulty remembering her, too, although with him it sometimes seemed purposeful, and when they were children they used to try to re-create the feelings they could recall from when she was alive. Tim would lie on his back and pretend to be ill with rheumatic fever, and she'd come into the room and minister to him as she felt their mother might. Or Tim would cover her and pat her back and sing a lullaby their mother sang, about waking from sleep and riding a silvery pony. He couldn't remember all the verses and made some up about them.

Once when she was upset, he took her into the closet off the living room—they were home alone—and was holding her and trying to touch her bottom, or comfort her, and then began to talk; all she could make out were his eyes and the shining wand of the vacuum cleaner, as he went on about a picnic, a blanket with pink stripes in it, pebbles around its edge, putting the pebbles in their mouths, their mother walking up and the two of them being locked inside a hot, stuffy car in punishment, and suddenly it seemed the cleaner wand brightened and the closet filled with cotton. Tim knocked open the door and ran outside, and never mentioned their mother again.

Marie looked at the photograph. Was that you, she

thought. Was it you who did that? Could you have? The picture seemed to be smiling wider. In the next instant there'd be a rustle as a hand reached to her, and her mother would say, "Oh, Marie, of course not!" But how could she know for sure? She couldn't even recall the tone of her voice. It was as if her childhood had passed in darkness; there were no details. Every week she paged through the family albums, all three of them, hoping to find some clue to her makeup and emotional texture at that time. The photographs were like scraps of sewing material for a large and elaborate project—a series of patchwork quilts, perhaps—but somewhere in one of the moves, or in the changes that had taken place in all of them, the pattern to the project had been lost. The photographs held a store of hope for her, though; she could look into a pair of eyes and wonder, What are you thinking? Are you happy, are you sad? How is the day around you, and what happened next? And sometime in the future, if she kept at it, perhaps she could assemble the pieces into—

Whatever it was they were intended to be.

She picked the wax off her fingertips, putting it back around the wick, and went into the kitchen. Her dad and the boys had taken down mugs and poured their own coffee. The kitchen was smoke-filled now. At her dad's elbow was a loaf of bread, the ketchup, and a jar of mustard with a table knife sticking out of its mouth, all of which she'd neglected to put on the table.

"Would you like some rye bread?" she asked. "I got some today."

"No, this is fine."

"Do you want anything else?"

"Not right now."

"Who's winning?"

"Whom do you presume, Mistress Aberdeen-Anguish?" Tim said, and the corners of her dad's lips compressed with a smile. So they were winning after all.

"I'll make some popcorn later," she said.

"Great," Jerome said. "That sounds good."

Charles still looked angry at their father.

She went into the living room and found Susan on her knees under the tree, shaking a package close to her ear while she kept her eyes on the television. "Oh, God,"

Susan said. "You would walk in just now." She tossed the package under the tree and went back to her chair and slumped down in it, and Marie sat on the couch, behind her, and stared at the television screen. She'd developed a habit of watching it out of the corners of her eyes—"Sidewatcher," Tim called her—because she'd watched so much television when she was a child she'd become skeptical of it; none of the programs were very plausible and she couldn't look at them for long without wondering how people in California or New York could appear inside their living room, engaged in performances she could watch the second they were going on without being able to have any sort of effect on them, except on or off, and this made her lose the thread of what they were up to.

She glanced around, checking for the detail she was sure she'd overlooked. The gate-leg table was exactly right with the new furniture the boys had bought. A few months ago her dad had described it, and asked if she'd seen it anywhere. "It was built by a neighbor of ours in Courtenay, a carpenter more than eighty years old, for your mother and me when we were married, so it means a lot to me," he said. She found it on the grain doors in the storeroom upstairs, underneath a mattress covered with a tarp, and cleaned it and rubbed it with oil until her reflection appeared over its grain, and then brought it down last week, along with the decorations, and set it up in the living room as a surprise. "Well," her dad said when he saw it, "I feel as if a part of me has returned at last."

"Ach!" Susan said to the television. "Baloney on you!"

She stomped through the living room, through the kitchen, and then Marie heard the door to their bedroom bang. The program must have been a love story; Sue was in tears. It seemed one of the two always was, and their tears had become so commonplace that Tim and her dad ignored them, and she and Susan didn't pay much attention to one another's, either. Susan would say, "Oh, for God's sake, Marie, are you crying again?" and then in a while Susan would be in tears.

She stared at the shimmer of the table. She liked the design cut with a coping saw from its side supports, like two hourglasses set end to end, and the gold grain that

lifted away from the darker wood in another dimension,
and then she remembered looking at the table like this
another time. It was a Christmas from her past. One of
the leaves was raised, and a tiny Christmas tree, sprayed
with silver paint, was sitting on its top. There were strings
of cranberries and popcorn hung on it. Had she helped
thread the strings? She couldn't remember lights, none at
all, and the tree was too small for icicles. Were they poor
then? Was that in this house?

She turned to the kitchen and through the doorway saw
Tim and Charles and Jerome, but not her dad; all three
were talking with expressions that meant their voices had
risen, and were slamming down cards, but her mind
was so crowded she couldn't hear a sound. The kitchen
was brightly lit and from the living room they seemed to
be inside a yellow cube, closed off from the rest of the
house and her, and she was seeing them for the first
time, as an outsider: they were brothers, it was Christmas,
their mother was missing, and would always be.

And then she had an image of her mother whipping
batter in a bowl held tight against her side, bending to
the oven, carrying a cookie sheet to the kitchen table,
where rows of holiday pastries were spread out on cooling racks, slapping her dad's behind with a spatula when
he tried to snitch one, and then her laughter at his
startled expression. The house was filled with the sweetness of baking for days, and all the while her mother
worked she sang Christmas carols and hymns.

There was a cry of triumph from Tim, and then Jerome shoved away from the table and came and slumped
at the other end of the couch. He'd brought along an ashtray from the kitchen (she'd have to remember to put out
more ashtrays, please!) and he set it on the couch between
them, and then lifted his chin to blow out smoke, the
cords of his neck thick with tension.

"Are you done playing cards already?"

"They're playing three-handed."

"Oh."

"It's harder to cheat that way."

So he'd known about Tim and her dad all along. She
smiled. The light from the television set gave the side of
his face a gray, statuelike cast, and she felt sorry for his
bad feature, his big lips; they were thick, not mobile or

expressive, and it sometimes seemed to her he talked so little because he was self-conscious of how they moved.

"The house looks really nice," he said.

"Oh, thank you."

"I remember how it used to look two or three years ago."

"I know. I'm sorry."

"It wasn't your fault. Nobody picked up after themselves."

"I was the worst."

"Mmmm." His mind had jumped beyond the conversation and he was considering something else.

"You boys are neat now."

"Sometimes. Out of necessity."

"What do you mean?"

"To find things."

"Oh."

"How long has Dad been this way?" he asked.

"How?"

"Angry at you."

"All the time!"

"More, lately?"

"Yes, I guess."

He put his cigarette to his lips several times and his exhaled smoke rolled in overlapping clouds toward the Christmas tree.

"Are you excited about the holidays?" she asked.

"Sort of."

"I am," she said.

"You don't seem in a celebrating mood tonight."

"Oh—" She stared down and evened her skirt against her knee with her thumbs. "I've just been thinking, is all."

"What about?"

"Oh, I don't know. A lot of things." She kept straightening her skirt as if its straightness could bring clarity to this moment that included them all; she was too uncomfortable to mention their mother in front of Jerome.

"About Mom?"

She looked up. The Christmas-tree lights were reflected in galactic dots on his glasses and she couldn't see his eyes.

"Yes," she said.

"What about?"

"Just her. She made times like this so perfect, it seems.

Even if I knew exactly how Dad and you boys wanted Christmas, I'd still ruin it."

"That's how you feel?"

"I can't do anything right."

"Everything you've done around here looks great to me."

"You're just saying that to be nice."

"Nnnnn." There was a long silence, more clouds of smoke, and then he said, "She made mistakes all the time." And after a moment added, "Mom."

"That's not so."

"Sure it is."

"It's not!"

"She made more mistakes than you."

"You're just saying that!"

"Huh-uh. She had more opportunity to make them."

"What do you mean?"

"Older. Five kids."

No matter how much she kept brushing her cheeks, left and right, with the backs of her fingers, she couldn't keep them free of tears.

"When do you think it'll happen?" he asked.

"What?"

"Dad get married."

"This summer!" she said.

"Really? That soon?"

"He's practically said so to Susan and me a couple of times."

"That's what I was thinking."

"Why?"

"Nobody seems too happy around here."

"*He* does."

"I'm sure he's worried about a lot of things—especially how we'll all take it."

"No, he isn't."

"Sure, Marie. Also, it's his second wife. Maybe he's worried things won't work out as well, or else the same. Oh, God."

"Why does he have to get married at all? After so many years? Why can't we stay the way we are? We get along just fine!"

"He's probably been thinking about the rest of his life,

and I doubt that he wants to live it alone. He's still young by his standards."

"*Young?* What about us?"

"I'm sure he's considered our feelings a lot."

"Not Susan's and mine."

"Especially you two's."

"But he never talks to us."

"He will."

She wanted to close her eyes and rest her head on him. "I was just starting to find out who I was in this family!"

"You'll keep on finding out."

"I won't have a chance! There'll be too many others to think about!"

"Just Laura. She's nice."

"She has three kids."

"Her sons are married."

"But her daughter will be here. She's younger than Susan!"

"Mmmm," Jerome said. "Maybe you just don't want to give up the house."

"I don't! I'd never feel right about it! I don't want her to take it away from Mom!"

"She's been gone a long time now, Marie."

"I know she has, I know that! But I'm still here, aren't I? Can't you see that? Can't anybody see that I am?"

37

ৡৡৡ

REQUIEM AND FALL

The dream is very much in season. He's running through
a forest where leaves of every color shower down on him
from an infinite height. There's a fire in the forest, but he
isn't running from it; somebody's at his back, reaching for
him, calling his name. The notes of the name come to
him down through corridors of green. Then the trees thin
and sink and begin to be underbrush, or else the act of
running has rendered him gigantic; he's running through
leafage the height of his knees, treetops or weeds. They
slap at his pants legs and then thin out and are gone altogether and in the silence that comes, with his legs and
arms still working at running, he falls through open sky.
A hand catches him by the shoulder, and the face of Jerome, huge and pale, hangs above him in the mist, wondering with a susurrus of wind in its whisper, "Are you
awake?"

Do dreams speak outside themselves?

"Please. My landlord's nephew got me out of bed with
a note to call Operator Three in Peoria."

He knows Jerome will mention these details (isn't it
the third time he has?), and as Jerome goes through them
now his voice takes on the pattering staccato sound of
water falling from a fountain onto the children's pool in
Pekin where Jerome and he sit as boys in water to their
waists, sullen and unbrotherlike on this overcast August
afternoon. Is it the day Charles falls and cuts his forehead?

"They tried to get you at first. They didn't know your
phone is disconnected."

Jerome's gone home and worked on a carpentry crew

421

for the summer and Charles has stayed in town and helped a widow get her three apartment buildings in shape—repairing wobbly furniture, weaving patches onto rusted window screens, rehanging doors, fumigating for roaches and silverfish, quieting sibilant water closets, patching plaster and scraping and painting and shifting carpets to relocate cigarette burns under a dresser or bed—jobs that the widow's husband, a carpenter, used to do; and has moved into the manager's quarters, three white-painted rooms, in the smallest of the buildings, and is paid by the hour, "Keep your own time," when he works. Fixing himself up in a job that will pay his room and board, he told his father ("What about when you get caught up on the work?"). Fixing that university regulation about no women in your room, he told everybody else. And now Jerome (this Jerome I must tangle with, he thinks) was living in a large apartment with two other seniors and had money to last the semester, if not the year, while Charles, who's worked less and less, hasn't saved a cent; and indeed, just last week, was wondering whether to borrow from Jerome to pay his two-month overdue telephone bill (exposure of his situation; shame), when a gray-clad telephone man with a belt of utensils around him—where was *he?*—appeared at the apartment and unwired the hookup of his phone, and then carried the instrument out the door.

"I know, I know it's disconnected," Charles cries into the wind. *I know!*

"The Peoria operator connected me with Dad."

The idea of the phone company involving their father in this sends up orange coronas that pulse and explode under his closed eyes; then he sees a white screen with a cluster of leaf shadows against it, coal-black fleurs-de-lis that tremble and bend in one direction from the force of the current of the wind in Jerome's voice, as he says, "Grandpa Neumiller died this morning. They think it was a heart attack. Grandma heard him get out of bed and thought he was going off to work. He fell, and when she called he didn't answer."

Charles sits, or sends out the impulses that should result in sitting, and wants to say that this is no joke, but instead, to judge whether it's happening, looks at his hand. It gives off green.

"Dad says Grandma is in real bad shape."

The corner of the bed, a quadrant of Charles's world, falls away with Jerome as he sits in a shaft of sunlight coming through the drawn shade. His face is stained golden. His lips are blue. Green-tinted leaf shadows sway over the gold, and Charles watches the transubstantiation of this figment of a face once his brother's, as it disappears behind the shifting net of green, becomes a grove of distant trees, a shower of parti-colored leaves, droplets of spray holding the last of the sun on a summer—

"The doctor's given her a sedative," Jerome says, and some of his features reappear.

Jerome?

"But it hasn't helped, I guess. Dad says she's too weak to walk, but keeps getting out of bed and going through the house looking for Grandpa, calling his name."

There's silence, and then a wind sends leaves clattering along the concrete walk outside, and the panes of his window hum in and out of harmony with the force of the wind, which elevates him into a higher region where two characters, somehow familiar, act out a story he once knew but now remembers only details of:

The one seated on the bed, the older of the two, will rise up. He does. The two are brothers. The older one leads an exemplary life, or so the other thinks, and the other has observed him since he was a child in order to try to learn the right way to act; the older is taciturn, and seldom allows emotion to show on his face, but the other has discovered that if he watches his—*Jerome*—watches Jerome's eyes, he can sense Jerome's feelings and sometimes anticipate his thoughts. Now, before Jerome rose from the bed, he said something that altered their tie as brothers, and perhaps their lives, and must have been extraordinary and difficult for him to say; there are rainbow-tinted prisms giving off scattered paths of light from his eyes. He brings his sleeve over them, puts his glasses on, and goes to the door.

"They'll be here at five, at my place, to pick us up. The oldest grandsons are going to be pallbearers."

Pallbearers?

Jerome shoves his sleeves into his jacket. "I haven't decided if I'll go to any classes yet." His elbows or wings make ready for flight. "Probably."

"Jill and I were going to a movie this weekend," the other says, searching for the detail to tie him to himself. Dried strawberry runners glittering with gold straw, a Husky-looking dog panting happily behind a fence of wire mesh, its master down on one knee on the other side. Was that right? "What day's today?"

"Friday. The funeral is Monday."

"Did you say they were coming to pick us up?"

"At five. I have to go." Jerome glides over the legs of a body on the living-room floor, and is gone. Leaves of tan and amber, lilac, and bronze shower down on the body, or somebody running, a hand at his shoulder, *Charles!*

He looks over his shoulder to the other room. There was a body on the floor.

"Ah!" he cried, and recoiled from his voice. *It was no dream, I lay broad—* He was seized with shivers that came in irregular broken rushes, as he went to his closet, thinking. *He* doesn't believe it. If he really did, would he walk over here and put on his robe?

He pressed his palms on the dresser top and waited for the first note of grief (which he couldn't explain or know when to expect, and which, in an instant his mind replayed, was related to a butcher knife being whetted on the edge of an earthenware crock, the way it sang, the way the singing made his chest ache) to sound, and the self-absorption formed a film over his eyes and transformed the objects on his dresser—the copper-colored ashtray, the round alarm clock, the gold-framed picture of Jill, the full pack of Lucky Strikes—into talismanic entities suffused with an inner organic yellowishness that shone around their edges, and made them seem to have been arranged by hands other than his to match this moment in time. Jerome?

The way I'm seeing things, he thought, and shook his head, and peeled the line of red cellophane from the cigarettes. He'd been up, after a long argument with Jill, until four in the morning, trying to write a poem for her, and had thrown away everything but "Believe the nude aggressiveness of worms, girl, and settle your hair, gold, over the grove of radiance . . ."

He sat on the edge of the bed and saw his grandfather in a series of snapshots that a twelve-year-old, himself, had taken and arranged in an album; walking down the rode in front of Vince's house, squinting into a transit, standing beside a pair of acetylene tanks with his hands on his hips, staring down; getting into an old Kaiser he drove then; standing at the bottom of a cracked swimming pool, pointing away; looking up from his reclining chair in the living room as he reached across for a cigarette, his face bleached and startled by the flash—never at rest. And then Charles saw him in the same chair, in natural light, gripping its armrests and staring fixed ahead.

Even when the television was on, he'd sit that way, looking away from it, or you'd come into the room and find him there alone and be surprised at how quiet the house was. There were times when he didn't seem to notice you, or merely said hello and then went back to his thought, but when he did talk, it was about you and your concerns, and confirmed what you already felt— that he was thinking about others than himself; in particular, you. The rest of the world was going by in a rush and he was waiting for you to come to him, a monument at rest, and nothing you said could take him by surprise; in his silence he'd encountered more possibilities than you could think about, or imagine, or ever came up. It took just a sentence or two from him to help you see light. Imperturbable. An unshakable head of a tribe. The Chieftain, an old friend, J. D. Prell, always called him.

Charles could see the corncribs, machine sheds, silos, and barns built or repaired by his grandfather—with his sons and sons-in-law and, lately, his grandsons, working as his crew—from the area around Pekin and Spring Lake, all the way down to Springfield and Jacksonville, and from the other side of the Illinois River to Sand Prairie Outlook, and beyond; two stone churches in Havana, the community swimming pool, the investor's mansion and the roadside restaurant-bar, the Second National Bank, the hunting lodge and lookout tower at Chautauqua, service stations along the state highways, motels, the post office in Forest Creek, the Neumiller subdivision in Pettibone, and most of the new houses in Green Valley, Easton, San Jose, Kilbourne, Hartsburg-Emden—

How could they be there and he be gone?

Charles looked up and a white bedroom, empty, dropped around him. There were cigarettes in his lap.

The wind outside, which his thought had dimmed, rose to its real volume and made him shiver again with its strength and the intonations of winter in it. He went to the dresser and lit a cigarette and realized, with the match hitting the ashtray, as if he'd just learned to feel and think, how unnatural it was to have that white thing hanging from his lips. *Dark gloom of a cigarette on—* He jerked his head to one side. His stream of smoke was spreading out flat against the wall and rolling in a widening circular cloud over a calendar above the dresser.

C. J. C. NEUMILLER & SONS, INC.
GENERAL CONTRACTORS, FOREST CREEK, ILL.

was printed on the lower half of the calendar, above the month of October. Soon it would be his birthday. His grandmother gave him the calendar at Christmas, and said, "This is a reminder to come home and see your Grandpa and me more often. Or at least write. And those red dates, those are Sundays. Go to church." He'd been to see them only once since then—had he written?—and when he was away from home he never went to church. *The room grew shadowy with his guilt.*

He crushed out the cigarette and went through the door and stood over the body of Stanely Sucherman, or Speed, as Stanley was called, and demanded to be; his dark spirally hair grew low on his forehead and out from his temples close to his eyebrows, and seemed to be taking advantage of his sleep to invade his pale face. Pale? Speed had a high complexion and his face was usually rose-colored, especially in sleep; an eyelid twitched; he tried to cover a bare shoulder with the quilt. Should Charles wake him? Speed's acquaintances and friends usually sensed that he'd carry their uncertainties and griefs more conscientiously than they, so they unburdened themselves on him and he became so weighted down with worries, none of them his, that he hardly got anything done. He'd registered late and still hadn't found a place to live. Last year he and Charles had done sketches and improvisational comedy in an acting class, and then persuaded the poker-faced owner of a campus coffee house to let them perform in his place.

SPEED & CHARLES
your local home-town campus fags
bits, blackouts, buffoonery, b'zazz
At the Hog's Jowl
Every Thursday night from 8 till you say Auntie, fool.

Charles shoved on Speed's shoulder with his bare foot and was surprised at how Speed, who was as hard to wake as he was, threw off the quilt and backpedaled several steps, making binoculars of the fists he was twisting over his eyes. Speed said, "Hey! It's the long-haired, bare-chested, red-bathrobed Neumiller!"

"Come off it, you—"

"You don't believe me?" Speed said, and offered the binoculars. "Take a look."

"How come you're sleeping on the floor?"

"I love floors!" Speed blinked several times, as he did when he was lying or surprised, and ran the heels of his hands down his wrinkled black denims.

"I thought you were on the couch last night."

"I was, but I love floors. I do! Besides, some good wrist action sent me flying. Whee!"

"If you're going to sleep here, you might as well use the couch."

"Right," Speed said, and picked up the quilt, made by Charles's grandmother, and went to the couch and sat with a plonk.

"What are you doing?"

"I thought I'd catch some more Z's. Unless— Were you expecting Jill?"

"Don't you have any classes?"

"I've missed so many now, I say—" Speed did a flat-handed salute from his chest and his wet lower lip rolled out. "That's what I say."

"I won't be going to any classes, either."

"Good." Speed fell on his back and pulled the quilt up to his throat.

Charles was hurt, or worse, and expected Speed to sense something wrong and interrogate him, as he did in an improvisation, until their minds met and moved along the same lines to a shared revelation; if Charles announced this on his own, it would have the authority of fact, and he wasn't ready to admit or cope with his grandfather's death. He said in a solemn voice, "The way it looks, I won't be going to any classes for a long time."

Speed reached to the coffee table, picked up a roll of Tums by the flag of its torn wrapper, and popped a few in his mouth. "Do you have a cigarette?" he asked.

Charles took the pack from his bathrobe pocket and gave it a toss that Speed caught in one hand.

"Hey, you're really in a great mood when you have to get up before eight," Speed said. "We should do this more often."

The backs of Charles's knees were touching the cushion of the easy chair, so he sat and put his elbow on its wide arm and held his head in his hand, ashamed of involving his grandfather in the sort of pettiness his grandfather walked away from.

"Chuck, I might as well admit it right off. I didn't know what to say or anything, and anyway, I thought you'd like to be alone. I heard Jerome wake you and tell you about your granddad. I figured I'd slip out when you went to the john. I was hoping there wouldn't be another closet scene."

They both laughed. When Jill returned to school this year, she told Charles she wanted to go out more, not just on the fraternity dates she was compelled to go on (she belonged to a socially oriented sorority), but with "other guys," and on the night of her announcement, Speed came into the apartment and found Charles in the bottom of the closet, knocking his head against the wall and slashing around with coat hangers, and crying, "I'm gonna commit suicide! I'm gonna commit suicide!"

"I know how you must feel," Speed said. "My granddad passed on, too, last winter, and I'm still not over it. It's really awful. Really."

Charles was trying to figure out Speed's reasons for pretending to be asleep, and for sustaining the pretext so long.

"If we've got any dough, it's because of him," Speed said. "Our hardware store is really his. He had the worst Yiddish accent you've ever heard, but he called his customers 'Jew bastards! Cockamorons!' I get my sense of humor from him. All he liked to do was fish and pinch pretty tushies. Sound like a coon? I loved him."

Charles's grandfather was standing over him and

Charles was on his back. What was that from? He was ill
in bed a summer and alone at home during the day. There
was a window beside his bed, in his parents' old bedroom,
and a bookshelf ran along the ceiling above the window.
His father told him his grandfather was bothered by a recurring dream about him; the bookshelf was coming loose
and the heavy books falling down on him, and injury was
added to his illness. His grandfather visited him every
afternoon but never mentioned the dream, and then one
day, waking from sleep, Charles discovered a gray mirage
high above him on a chair, stretched across the bed, testing the bookshelf. *Go back to sleep,* his grandfather said.
Everything's all right.

"He was half my size but had a nose twice as big,"
Speed said. "I come into a place from outside, and an
hour later I'm smelling grass, ho ho. Hey, what the hell,
why don't you just *tell* me about your granddad?"

It was as if the floor went, and as Charles fell past
layers of scenes, faces, tones of voice, a landscape of past
love, the descent left him speechless. Then he said, "In our
church we only sang during Lent, at Benediction, and you
could hear him above everybody else. He sang when he
worked, too. Bass. He had a beautiful voice."

Facts. There was nothing in them of who his grandfather was, or what he felt for him. "Once or twice, when
he finished a job under contract, he wouldn't take a check
for the full amount. His bid was the lowest, but he didn't
think he should make such a profit."

"Sounds like a lousy businessman."

"He did all right."

"I mean, you know, ho ho." Speed was blushing and so
nervous he could hardly sit. "Do you want to drop this?"

"Yes."

"I was thinking last night when you were up— Hey,
what were you doing?"

"Nothing."

"A paper? A poem to Jill?"

"You bastard, you looked in my wastebasket!"

"No, honest. I figured she was due for one after the
closet scene. I think you're too good to her."

"Bull."

"Bull, yourself, you old farmer. You should give her
hell, you should shake her up, and then squeeze her

till her eyes pop. And you want to know something else?"

"What?"

"She ain't worth you."

Charles tried to suppress the laugh but it came out in seizures of pain. Then he said, "Grandpa didn't want to retire a few years ago, but my uncles said he could draw his retirement pay, or whatever, and keep on working as a foreman. So they'd have him sweep up the shop, or sharpen saw blades, or run out to the lumberyard for materials. Lackey jobs. He had to lock up his hand tools because they took them out on jobs and lost them or left them out in the rain. He drove a truck called the Green Hornet, which was a joke of theirs, too. It was an old Dodge panel truck painted with red and green house paint, and once belonged to a guy named Jack Paul."

"Hey, maybe we can use that in a bit."

"Jack Paul lived in it—"

"We'll use it!"

"He had a stove inside, and a bed, and drove around the county and slept wherever he happened to be, usually out in the State Forest. The only time you saw him was when he was getting groceries or the mail. He had a big house in town, where a daughter of his lived, and nobody was sure if he lived in the truck because he wanted to, or if something was the matter with him."

"I'll take a guess."

"He died and his daughter had his belongings auctioned off. Grandpa bought the truck. There were other cars and trucks and station wagons the business owned that he could have used, but the last few years all he'd drive was the Green Hornet. It was named for its speed, which was about thirty-five at tops. Of course, he took the *stove* and things out. One day I used it to pick up some materials and it broke down on me. I was ready to push it into the ditch and walk to the closest phone, when a car pulled up. It was Grandpa. He said, 'You're having troubles, huh?' And I said, 'Yeah, how'd you know?' He said, 'I sensed it.' "

"Did he know this Jack Paul very well?"

"Fairly well, I guess."

"You *know* he knew his truck."

"He had tools along in his car and got it running again."

"Too much!"

Charles is riding toward the Kitteridge Farms in a truck and the sun is falling over him in flashes through the branches above the country lane. He's ten. He has on a cloth painter's cap that his grandfather has doubled over at the headband and stapled to fit him, and he pushes it onto the back of his head, copying his grandfather's way of wearing a cap, and turns to his grandfather to see how he looks. There's a small hill ahead and the truck slows and sways in the loose sand. His grandfather reaches for the floor shift, and then says, *Do you want to help me shift gears?* Charles puts his hand under his grandfather's hand. The strength of his hand.

Charles rearranged his weight in the chair and his eyes picked out a straw-colored bar of sunlight on the black-enameled coffee table. "The last time I was home, at my grandparents', that is, he and I were in the living room, just sitting there, when he said, 'I hear you're making quite a name for yourself.' I didn't know what he meant and was embarrassed. 'I mean in the theater,' he said. And then I was really embarrassed, because I'd never told him about being in it. I guess I thought he wouldn't think too highly of it, or something. 'Your dad's shown me some of your notices,' he said. 'I'm glad you've finally found something you like to do and are doing well at it. I'm proud of you.' It's the only time he's been that open with me."

Charles went into the bathroom and closed the door. When he was younger, and got into trouble, his grand-mother would take him aside and say, "Your mother and dad gave you your grandpa's name, and as long as I'm around and have a say, you'll live up to it!" And when she wasn't angry, she'd say to him in a melancholy voice, "You know, you look just like your grandpa when he was a boy."

He stepped in front of the sink, but all he could see in the mirror was a pair of eyes, and they looked anonymous. He couldn't remember his grandfather's face; lips, half a jawline, a high cheekbone, a blue eye, a crew cut thick as a brush and blue-silver—but when he tried to arrange them into a single face, they disappeared. He felt his grandfather leaving him, and his chest constricted with the loss.

He turned on the shower and let it run.

His grandfather would come to the house in the late

summer afternoons, knowing Charles liked to sleep in, and say, "Well, Chuck, do you want to go to work today?" And they'd go together to the construction sites, where his grandfather supervised; everybody knew him and called him C.J.C., and Charles imagined himself having an extra initial, too. And in later years his grandfather had Charles help on the small projects he'd taken up to keep busy— building a playhouse for Jay's daughters, adding a patio onto the Forest Creek house, making cedar chests for granddaughters; and Charles realized, now, that his grandfather must have sensed, even early on, that his problems were unique and was watching out for him.

The constriction tightened, rose, and closed around his throat, and then Speed knocked on the door, and said, "Are you all right in there?"

"Yes."

He took off his robe and got into the shower, whirring spray.

His grandfather had to lift him up so he could reach the register in the foyer to sign his name. And then he took one of his grandfather's hands, Jerome the other, and they went into a long, dimly lit room with a semicircle of faces at one end of it. People seated on metal folding chairs. More chairs propped against the wall. He led them over the carpet to the other end, where hidden lights, flooding an alcove banked with flowers, were so brilliant it seemed the flowers were giving off radiance. Charles's father was kneeling at a *prie-dieu* in the alcove. Charles felt more pressure on his hand. Surrounded by the flowers and parallel to the *prie-dieu*, and only a few feet from it, was a casket. Their grandfather helped them kneel on either side of their father, who touched their shoulders, and then covered his face.

Her dark head was sunk into a pillow of white silk. Charles followed the curve of her throat to her chin, then looked away. Her right hand, resting near her heart, was turned up. The arm was bare. Her white fingers held a white rosary. His eyes went to her neck, her cheek, her cheekbone, the familiar line of her nose, this corner of her lips set tight, sending a deep crease down her chin, her mouth. And then her forehead, the globe of her eye, closed now. Then the whispering and mourning behind him, and a wet mildewed smell mingled with another smell almost like incense, and the odor of too many roses, so cloying it seemed his nose was bleeding the sweet smell. His father had said, "Now, your mother might look different to you. She's been very ill," and he wanted to say, *"Ill, Dad? Ill? Isn't she dead?"*

He could smell the flowers now. He got out of the shower, half dried himself, and went into the other room and sat in the chair. Speed ate the last of the Tums, put the crumpled wrapper on the coffee table, then dropped it into an ashtray.

"Hey, I hope you don't think I was futzing around with how you feel?"

"No."

"There's nothing worse than the jag-off who thinks everything'll be better if you just laugh, ho ho, when all you want to do is be by yourself."

"No." Charles saw Jerome's face above him, and went to his bedroom door. "I better get ready for class."

"You said you weren't going."

"Oh. Well, I guess I will. He'd want me to. Grandpa." Charles stepped into the bedroom, then said, "I mean, he probably would. I didn't mean it that way."

"I know." Speed's voice sounded querulous and indistinct and like the voice of somebody else. Jerome? Charles sat on the bed and looked at the calendar; on its upper half, above the spiral hinge, was a color photograph of the Grand Canyon, and next to the photo he noticed some delicate lines of script, partly obscured by a streak of reflected sunlight, and went to the dresser and read:

> *The SWALLOWS are making*
> *them ready to fly,*
> *wheeling it out on a*
> *windy sky:*
> *goodbye, summer,*
> *goodbye, goodbye . . .*

—George Melville

Moby Dick. He'd been through this moment the same way once before. He saw the copper ashtray and alarm clock and shook his head as though to shake free the dream. He went to the door and Speed wasn't there. The quilt was gone. There was a concussive sucking thud, and then a high whine, and when he realized that Speed *was* there, in the bathroom, he started trembling; what was it he'd done, he thought, as he threw himself across the bed, or hadn't done?

Jill was taking the history of philosophy from a graduate student so brilliant and amusing, she said, that if Speed and Charles came to the class they wouldn't be able to keep up with him. It was a dare, as she'd meant it, and they promised to take her up on it. Since he woke, and even before then, he'd been at the mercy of circumstances beyond his control, and when he came across this offhand promise everything in his mind was displaced by it. He went to the bathroom, knocked on a door that pulled open, and Speed said, "You look like hell."

"I'll see you in Tergulio's class."

Speed's face was glistening and dripping water. He brought a towel to it. "You don't plan to go now? I mean, you know——"

"I told Jill we'd be there."

"Shake her up."

"I have to see her anyway, to tell her."

"I'll tell her. Stay here. You look awful, really."

"I'll see you there at ten," Charles said. He picked up three books that were handy and went through the kitchen, narrow as a corridor, and up the steps and out into fall air. He turned and came back and went to the refrigerator and took out a juice can with triangular holes punched in its top, and as he drank it down (chilly grapefruit with a mouth-shocking taste of metal) Speed stepped into the room, the towel still in his hands, and studied him with what seemed censure. Charles left the apartment and went for a full block before he felt free of Speed's eyes.

The red brick sidewalk blurred, floated up toward him, and then fell away, greatly widened. His gait and carriage changed. He was walking up the drive to his grandfather's house. It was hot, and at this time of evening, when the sound of summer insects started rising from the grass, his grandfather would set the sprinkler out on the terraced lawn, and then he and Charles would go down toward the road, his grandfather's hand swinging at the level of his eyes, and on the way they'd stop to look at the roses on the trellis and to check the level of water in the concrete pond where the big goldfish were, and his grandfather would examine the stake and the binding around the willow he'd planted, and then they'd go over the grass, across the crushed-rock drive to another part of the lawn, shaded by box elders, and here it was Charles's job to test the swings, swing in them all, and then test the seesaw to see if it squeaked, and then they'd go over to the merry-go-round, and his grandfather would stare at it, his fists on his hips, while Charles waited for him to say what he said each time, "This, too, I suppose." Then he'd sit Charles on the merry-go-round and turn it until Charles came around to him, and then turn it once more, to make sure, and then he'd say it needed oil, and they'd go toward the back of the house, checking flower beds along the way, and into the small workshop (cool and damp and smelling of sawdust and burlap), and after they'd straightened up and put the tools in their proper places, his grandfather took the oilcan and they went outside, where it was darker and the sound of insects had grown more shrill, and after the merry-go-round was oiled, his grandfather sat him on it again and pushed against the small of his back to get it going, and then his grandfather appeared and then passed, and reappeared and passed again, faster now, the grass turning to a blur, as Charles closed his eyes and felt himself lift away out into the darkness over this yard that was a playground and garden guarded by a force as true as the center post of the spinning wheel he was on.

Bright sunlight on blacktop made Charles blink. He was in the middle of a street five blocks from his apartment, and most of them in the wrong direction.

He went into a cafeteria across from the quad and got a cup of coffee and sat in a booth. He opened a book. Nearly every evening his grandfather sat out in a chair on the highest terrace of the lawn, looking over the willow and the trellis, past the road and railroad tracks and a vacant lot, to the building that held the office and shop of the business he turned over to his sons, and then he'd glance away and shift his weight and recross his legs and remove his cap and pass his hand over his hair, and then pull the cap lower and look off in another direction, but soon his body gravitated back and he was staring at the building again. And then the cycle of restlessness started over and went on into the night. Charles saw himself drawing up a lawn chair in the darkness and sitting next to his grandfather. The side of his grandfather's face glowed orange as he smoked. His cap was of red leather. Charles would sit here until his grandfather explained exactly what was bothering him and what he was looking for at this hour.

Charles saw that it was almost ten. The place was filling up. The page of the book in front of him was still saying, in its first line, "This condition of the psyche has been proved irreducible, although . . ." He closed it up. There was an empty mug of coffee at his elbow he couldn't remember drinking or touching before this. Whatever he came near this morning was altered, it seemed, or else gone.

On the sidewalk he looked for Jill. There'd always been an air of impromptu and surprise about their encounters; last year, at a dress rehearsal of *Twelfth Night,* he was squinting into the mirror above his makeup table, trying to line an eye, when a form moved from the edge of his mirror to its center and stopped there; his eyes adjusted and he saw a blond girl. "I'm on the makeup crew," she said. "You need my help."

She affected him so much it would have been a risk of his manhood to tell her, so he didn't; he loved her from a distance, telepathically. She walked with smart satisfied strides, as though she was being well taken care of by somebody else, and seemed as distant as he, except in repose; then, with her pillowy lips parted, she looked like a young girl surprised she'd been overtaken by maturity, and saddened by it, in spite of the beauty it brought. She hadn't mastered the expressions that come naturally to most women and her face had the fixed and astonished prettiness of a manikin's. Just when he began to believe he was making headway with his telephathy, she'd laugh at Sir Toby Belch belching to ready himself for an entrance, or line another actor's eyes and lean into him with her knees and ruin everything. But he didn't give up, and on the night of the final performance she came up to him, kissed him on the mouth, and said, "You're my Feste. I love you." Which he didn't hear at first because the texture, the pressure, the softness of her lips had over-powered the rest of his senses.

He sat on the wide windowsill across from Tergulio's room. A radiator under him was clanking and sending up a smell of metallic paint, and burned the backs of his calves when they touched.

"Jill!" he cried. He hadn't seen her, really, among the other students in the hall, but his eye had caught a red skirt and black sweater she wore in combination so much she called it her national costume.

"Oh, good, love," she said, and came over, looking dazed without her glasses. "I was afraid you weren't going to be here."

He took her by the elbows and tried to begin. Her eyebrows went high, questioning him, it seemed, but then he saw that her eyes were widened and opaque with an intimate sadness. Did she already know? Could she sense it from seeing him? "Oh, Jill, I—"

"I know. I feel the same way. It's the fall." She leaned her head on his chest and worked the zipper of his jacket. "You know that paper I did on Blake? The one I worked on for two weeks and thought was so good? I just got it back and he gave me a D on it. I went up after class, and the old fogy *bastard* said, 'It's been copied from somewhere, and the only reason I didn't flunk you on it is I haven't found out where yet.'" She turned her face to him and tears rose above the rims of her eyes. "You know I didn't copy a word! Every one of those ideas is mine!"

Who should he begin with and where? He slid off the sill and took her in his arms, and saw Speed at the end of the hall making signs that he wanted to retreat.

"No, no," Charles said. "Come on."

"What?" Jill asked.

"It's Speed."

Jill turned to him and said, "Oh, great! Now things'll get moving!"

Speed looked at her in bewilderment, then at Charles, then at her.

"I mean in Tergulio's class," she said. She put her hand to his cheek and patted it with her lips pursed. "Aw, poor fella. Tergulio's class, remember? You and Chuckie. Raise hell. Remember?"

Speed's lips went white and she said, "There's the bell. Come on!"

She ran into the room and Charles leaned to Speed and whispered, "I couldn't tell her." Speed blushed.

The class met around two long conference tables pushed end to end and Speed and Charles went to the back of the room, where a smaller table stood in one corner, and sat on its top. Tergulio came in late, looking harried and preoccupied, pulled some mimeographed sheets from his portfolio, passed them around, and told one student to begain reading, and the possibility of class discussion, an open field for repartee, evasion of the subject, and whatever else was on the interlopers' minds, was destroyed. The student began, in a voice that was high and strident, "No positive quality possessed by a false idea is removed by the presence of what is true, in virtue of its being true. For instance, when we look at the sun . . ."

Charles wrote on a scrap of paper, "This isn't history, it's hell." Speed opened his notebook, took out a pencil, and then handed the notebook to Charles, who saw, in wobbly block letters: "THIS KID'S VOICE IS SO HIGH I CAN'T HEAR IT." Charles turned to the wall and a spasm of laughter came so fast it blew streamers of snot over his lips onto his chin. He got out his handkerchief, used it, and had almost recovered when Speed, imitating the reader, cleared his throat in a stringy falsetto. Charles put his head against the wall, held Speed in front of him as a shield, and his laughter rose into swells, the swells into waves—his diaphragm heaving with pain, his brain dark numb jelly jarred by his laugh—and the waves wouldn't let up, until the high voice of the reader became a part of him and his laugh, a part of the pattern his spread hand made against the rough courduroy of Speed's jacket, and then part of his fingernails, and he realized his cheeks were wet with tears, and thought he saw tears down the wall, too.

He scribbled a note—"Please tell Jill. See you after class in the Y"—tore it out and gave it to Speed, and, ignoring the eyes of Jill and Tergulio, left the room. As he went down the stairs, he felt as he'd felt going up or down stairs after an argument with Jill, which was often; that the stairs under him were leading into a recess of sullen, self-habitation, where he'd remain sometimes for days, distant and disaffected and speechless and in pain, playing the martyr to a *mons*.

*

His reflection grazed the dusty glass at the top half of the door, cupped its hands, and vanished as he stared into Jerome's apartment; the arm of a rocker, a bullfight poster, a corner of the black-and-white fiber floor mat, and the study desks and comfortable chairs and couches of a full-sized, expensive basement apartment. Charles knocked again and again nobody answered. One of the three roommates was usually home. He tried the knob and the door swung in, which surprised him; all of them were careful about that. The room and the furniture, and the study desks with their arrangements of books on them, seemed too stilled and personal to intrude upon. He was on his way out when he saw Jerome in the door of his bedroom. His eyes were red-rimmed and contrite. Charles's own behavior since he woke went through his mind, and he stepped past Jerome and into the kitchen and stared out a window along the low ceiling and saw the underside of the lowest branches of an oak, and beyond the oak a section of red brick wall, leaves against brick, bronze against red, and then the colors trembled, and then mingled and went out of focus as his eyes filmed and formed beads radiating lines that shot through the colors and sent them awry. He'd come to Jerome for guidance, and it was that simple; he was to submit, to grieve.

"Did you go to any classes?" Jerome asked.

He nodded.

"I went to my nine o'clock Psych, but didn't feel up to anything after that, so I came back and lay down. I guess I fell asleep. It's almost one-thirty."

The brick wall and the oak leaves jumped into focus; his misreading of a half-asleep look as grief made him feel an important faculty in him was giving out. "Was it a heart attack?" he asked, and his voice sounded too loud for the size of the room.

"That's what they think. There'll be an autopsy."

"What for?"

"It was so unexpected, I suppose they want to make sure."

"Of what?"

"He died of."

"That's awful!"

"It's a formality, I think. I don't know, it might even be a law."

"I don't care!" Charles cried, and the substance went from his legs and left him standing on numb shadows of them. He took a floating step and sank into a chair. A round plaster-of-Paris ashtray sat on the black Formica tabletop.

"Would you like something to eat?" Jerome asked.

"No." He was nauseous.

"A cup of coffee?"

"I guess. Please."

The ashtray became a foreshortened silo on a heat-shimmering plain and heightened his nausea, so he set it on the floor behind him. His hands. Springing from green cuffs, too large and too white, fringed at the wrists and little-finger sides with black hair, they lay on the table like the ashtray. Objects. He moved them to his lap.

"Are you packed?" Jerome asked.

"No."

"I was going to before I fell asleep."

"I don't want to go home. All those people. The funeral."

"I know," Jerome said, and his voice reverberated in a way that said to Charles, *The dead will not come back to us. Don't exhibit them, mourn over them, weep over them, pray over them, lower them into a grave before our eyes. Let their living actions, held in the minds of the living, remain pure. Brought up against that effigy in the coffin, in no way a part of the person we knew, the mind balks, memory comes to a standstill, and they're killed for good.*

"Here," Jerome said. "It's hot. Watch out."

They sat in silence for five minutes before Charles was aware they weren't speaking. Their pasts were nearly identical and, as long as they didn't limit them with language, remained intact, and many of the years of them were interwound with the influence of their grandfather. The stillness of the Forest Creek living room settled around them. Charles was so accustomed to Jerome's manner, it hadn't occurred to him it was an inheritance from their grandfather. His monumental silence. Jerome's hand lay beside his cup, delicate and relaxed, the hand of their mother, and Charles wanted to take it in his.

Jerome looked up. His eyes seemed to say, *I know you're troubled, but you're difficult to help.*

"I imagine Dad will need a lot of help from us," Jerome said. "He sounded upsetting over the phone."

"Upsetting?"

"The way he talked. It was mostly about Grandma, and I'm not sure he knew how he sounded."

"What do you mean?"

"Pretty hysterical."

"Well, will we be able to do anything about it?"

"I hope."

"I better go."

"They'll be here at five."

"Who?"

"Dad didn't know. Maybe just him. I hope he doesn't drive alone."

"That bad?"

"I don't know."

"I'll be here at five."

Jerome enveloped him in a skyey-blue stare that said, *I wish there was more I could do.*

"Goodbye."

"Goodbye."

He looked for Jill again on the street. The air hurt his eyes. He'd left his jacket on and now his body warmth kept draining from him until he felt he'd turned blue. The wind came up and sent a scattering of leaves past his cheek. He blinked and flinched. His lower lip pulled down and started trembling, and then his neck muscles twitched, and he began to shake with chills. His legs didn't feel they were working, but a big low-branched black walnut tree, tilting up the sidewalk it grew beside, advanced on him. If he hit it with his fist, hit it hard, then everything would come to a stop. He leaned against it but his hand wouldn't clench. He felt somebody's eyes on him. In a house close to the walk, the curtain of a window was parted and an elderly woman was staring out at him. He studied her as if to know the reason for this.

Then a handful of objects struck the sidewalk close to the tree, went scattering in a widening circle, and turned into a flock of sparrows. Their tail feathers flicked and emphasized their cries, the excoriation of them in the cold air, as they hopped over the walk and pecked at purplish-brown stains on it, their claws traveling across an inscription in the cement:

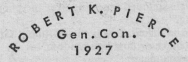

ROBERT K. PIERCE
Gen. Con.
1927

Then he smelled smoke. Burning leaves. A fire. What was that from?

A gray knit glove lay on the lawn next to him, its leather-covered palm turned upward, and beside it was a piece of flat bone the glove seemed to have moved; a ways away, pressed into the grass, was a yellow indentation the shape of the bone. The curtain was lowered and the woman gone.

He took off on a run, stopped outside his apartment long enough to catch his breath, and went down the stairs to the door of his bedroom. Jill was there, with her back to him, putting folded clothes into a suitcase on the bed. He saw her loose hair swinging beside her cheeks, her shoulder blades working in her back, and realized once again, as when he first saw her, how young-girlish and vulnerable she was, and thought, *Mist fell across his eyes through the morning.*

She snapped the locks on the suitcase and set it on the floor, and then sensed him and turned, her eyes wide, and ran to him and held him close. "I was so worried! I'm so sorry! Where *were* you?"

"Walking."

Over her shoulder the gold-framed picture of her smiled out at him.

"*Herman* Melville," he said.

"What?"

"Nothing."

He worked free from her and went to the closet and pushed through coat hangers until he came to a black suit with gray stripes in it. He took it out. "I'll have to wear this one. It's the only black I've got."

"I've never seen it on you. I like it."

"It's my high-school graduation suit, for God's sake."

"I still like it."

"It's the wrong weight for the weather, the pants are baggy, there's a cigarette burn in one knee, and it looks like shit!"

"Don't."

He threw it on the floor.

"Charles!"

He leaned his forehead on the wall and had a vision of himself fumbling around for the suit on the floor of the closet in absolute darkness, lighting matches, clothes hangers clashing, butcher knives and razors, the hour zero, his heartbeat and breathing sounding in his ears, rumors from a drawer, and then he heard in the distance, as if from the high loft at the rear of the church in Hyatt, a voice chanting *Requiem aeternam dona ei, Domine.* it was his grandfather's voice.

"Oh, God!" he cried.

Jill's arms came around him from behind and her breasts widened over his back. "I'm so sorry," she said. "I know how much he meant to you."

"It didn't seem real. Nothing has. I've been waiting for something to happen and it's already happened. He's dead."

"Don't. There's nothing you can do."

"No, he's gone now."

"Oh, no, he's been with you all day. I've felt him."

He turned and saw crystalline tracks dried on her cheeks, and the grief that seemed to be resting outside him, in her and this room and its objects, and in the rooms and apartments and houses beyond, closed around him with such force he felt smothered. She helped him to the bed, sat on its edge, and held his head against her breasts, but he felt stranded in her arms, contained yet abraded, at a distance from the comfort she was trying to give. He took her hair in his hands and kissed her forehead, her face, her lips, her throat, and when that only made him feel more estranged and contained, and more helpless to do anything about it, he swung her legs around and lowered her onto the yielding bed, into the center of grief, and was buried there for as long as they were able.

38

HOME

Jerome pulled the car onto the concrete drive, switched off the headlights and ignition as he coasted to the front door, and then let out the clutch and pushed against the seat, exhausted by the day and the effect of driving on his nerves, and realized that his father, who was in the rear, was shaking the back of the seat in his impatience to get out, and his shaking of its mechanism, the scratch of his fingernails against the fabric, his heavy breathing, were magnified in the silence of the engine and its focusing power, and then there was a pop of a lock on the passenger side as Charles pulled his door handle, and their father went out in such a rush that Charles was jackknifed forward. Martin took a step toward the house, and then turned and leaned his face into the chalky illumination from the car's interior light.

"Do you need any help with your things?"

"We've each got a suitcase is all." Didn't he remember?

"I'll tell Laura you're here."

The aluminum storm door rattled its familiar pattern and he was gone. Jerome was worried about him. He'd arrived at the apartment two hours late, diffident but with the combative grief he'd relinquished after nearly ten years back in his manner again, as he came through the door and said, "It's so sudden and awful, I still don't believe it," the only mention he made of the death. Then he slumped in a chair as if listening to a melody that rose from the center of his state and was as yet wordless, an unlit cigar in his mouth, occasionally pulling himself forward as if to speak, but never did; and then was pacing through all the rooms, anxious to get everybody into the car and leave, and at that point Tommy, their cousin, who'd driven him to the campus, came clattering down the metal-edged stairs, grinning and blushing in his shy manner, sat on a couch and stared around, and said, "Boy, is this some digs." Where'd he get such a word?

Jerome jerked out the keys and went around to the trunk in air redolent of leaf decay and recent rain, his breath blue-gray against its blackness. Nostrillials. Hot bronchials plus holes in the good bold nose. Hello, Tim. Home. Are you up and part of the help we might need these next hours, or days here? A slam echoed off the house and then at his back he felt scatterings of his father's combativeness and an anxious distress.

"I'm glad Tommy was along," Charles said.

"Yes, that was a good idea."

"If he hadn't been, if we wouldn't have had to drop him off at home, we'd probably be at Grandma's right now, and I don't know if I could take that. I mean—"

"I know." Charles was petrified of death and of the emotional demands it imposed.

They went through the garage carrying their suitcases and as Jerome took hold of the kitchen doorknob he found his hand around a beveled novelty that wouldn't turn. He rapped on the door with a raised knuckle and realized that it, too, was a recent addition, and had the ringing sound of a solid core.

"What is it?" Charles asked.

"It's locked."

"*What?* This door is never—'"

"Shhh. I think somebody's coming."

The garage lights went on overhead, rendering them miniature and felonlike in the windows along the back wall, a catch snapped, and the door swung in. "Laura keeps this locked now," their father said. "She'll be right out." He went to the door to the other side of the house and closed it behind him.

Jerome set his suitcase down, surrounded by satiny levels of dark-toned birch. A peninsular counter, with a soffit and cabinets above it, separated this end of the formerly long room from the dining area, and there were other new cabinets lining the walls, built-in, bronze-colored appliances, a new sink, and a new window above it. He'd forgotten about the remodeling. Their father had also enlarged a bedroom on the other side of the house, now the master bedroom, and added a laundry room there, and a sewing room-office. He and Laura were married in August.

"Where is everybody?" Charles asked. He most particularly meant Laura from his tone. He hadn't been home over the summer, as Jerome had, except for the wedding, and found it difficult to accept her as his stepmother. He hardly knew who she was. Her fine features and flawless skin made her seem in her thirties, although she was almost their father's age, and she had a sense of humor that was cosmopolitan and raw; she told Jerome that Pettibone was French for "inadequate tool." She hated the place. She enjoyed going out for drinks and dancing with younger couples, smoked like tar being burned, read popular novels and non-fiction (there was always a book within reach of her bed), and it was a revelation for Jerome to see their father, usually so solemn, teasing and cajoling and telling off-color jokes *sotto voce*, reading instead of watching the tube, getting tipsy on nightcaps, and behaving, in general, as he must have when he was a young man courting their mother, during that other half of his life.

Laura came through the door in a housecoat and slippers. She was tall, taller in high heels than their father, and carried herself as if proud of her height. She came straight to Jerome, took his hand in hers, and said, "I'm so sorry. I know how much you boys were attached to your granddad and he was such a good man. He made me feel a daughter right off. I don't know if it's any consolation to you, I'm not sure how you believe now, but I'm sure his soul is in heaven." She reached over and took Charles's hand. "I'm sorry," she said. "I feel so bad."

She went to the cupboard beside the sink, took out mugs, and plugged in a percolator that was standing ready, her hands trembling as at death's propinquity. Charles brushed past and Jerome saw he was carrying both their suitcases, heading upstairs. That upset? Or so inconsiderate he should be cuffed, the— Laura chose to ignore his exit and Jerome decided that, for now, hers was the best tack, and went to the table and sat down, and felt alone in the room.

"How does your dad seem to you?" she asked.

"It's hard to tell."

"He didn't say much?"

"No."

"To me either. I'm worried sick," she said, and hid herself in the work area of the room. On the door to the other side, a C. J. C. Neumiller & Sons calendar, graced by a view of one wall of the Grand Canyon configured by crossing birds, hung from a safety pin. The family referred to the firm as "the corporation," and it was incorporated, true, but humble-sized, with only the immediate family holding shares of stock, and when his grandfather retired, he merely stepped down from the presidency while retaining his shares, the controlling ones, and Fred, the oldest son still in the business, took over. Fred was his father's opposite (nemesis?), an extrovert who considered politicians and bankers his best friends, and he immediately enlarged the shop, bought new equipment, a couple of trucks, a new station wagon, and then there was a tightening down on money and nobody could get a loan to build; it took prestidigitation and plain luck to keep the family members, much less the crews, in regular work, and when they weren't, everybody blamed Fred, when, for God's sake, it was a circumstance the larger world had brought about. In that instance, anyway.

"How's school now?" Laura asked.

"Oh, all right, I guess." She wanted to talk and if it were any time but now he'd tell her about the trouble he was having there, not academically, really, and not socially, either, except he hardly ever went out with women; he simply didn't know what to do with his screwed-up life. He'd enrolled in pre-med, planning to specialize in pediatrics, or general practice, perhaps, but then got drawn to psychology and stayed this last year to take his Bachelor's in that, in case he decided on psychiatry, which was another field he was considering. Shrink himself. He wouldn't get his degree until the spring but had already been offered, on the basis of an experiment he'd run for a British behavioral psychologist ("Footpound Heart-Ohms," as he transliterated the man's compound name), a substantial fellowship for graduate school. Maybe he should get a Ph.D. and do research, or teach, as—

He'd lit a cigarette and its smoke stung his eyes. He rubbed them and discovered his lids were stiff with the oil of fatigue. Where was his father? Laura put an ashtray on the table and returned to the work area just as the percolator began to rumble and give out a sound as of someone thumping on the countertop. Charles's footsteps could be heard overhead.

"How's Ginny?" he asked.

"As well as can be expected, I guess." Laura shrugged. "You know her."

She was the only child of Laura's he did know. He'd met her sons, who were about his and Charles's age, only a few times, and they'd seemed aloof and protective of her in the manner of a possessive husband. Ginny was ten and nearly as tall as Laura, but skeletally thin and self-conscious of her height, and stood with stooped shoulders, her weight slumped on one hip, her head bowed; she wore eyeglasses, her teeth were being corrected with braces, and she had, it was discovered over the summer, eleven separate allergies.

"It's been hard for her," Laura said.

"You mean here?"

Laura glanced at him and looked away. Her highly arched eyebrows, plucked in pencil-like lines above turquoise eyes, arched higher, and a cautiousness tightened around her mouth. "No, mostly at school. She doesn't like any of her teachers or classes, and not many of the kids, either, I'm afraid."

"How are her grades?"

"Mostly A's. I think she feels they're way behind her down here."

"I imagine she misses Chicago!"

"Oh, yes. She's never been away from the city much since she was a baby, you know. We never seemed to get away much."

"Mmmm." Do *you* miss it, he wanted to ask, and she averted her eyes again.

His father came in and sat down. He'd removed his jacket and tie and as he settled himself at the table released a half sigh, half groan of relief—Laura gave him an anxious glance—and then clasped his hands and squeezed until his fingers were mottled blue-crimson. "If he could have kept his mind off that corporation, he might have lived."

"Yes," Jerome said.

"The latest is they're facing bankruptcy."

"It's that bad?"

"Yes, and it was one of the last things Dad learned before—" He couldn't go on.

Laura brought over bowls of chips and packaged snacks and put them on the table.

During high school and into college, Jerome had worked as bookkeeper for the firm, and he'd seen the downhill trend into red begin; lumber bills remained unpaid, the new equipment was under liens, and there were rumors that Fred, always a drinker, was drinking heavier than usual. Complaints came in about promises broken, appointments missed, buildings falling behind schedule, and his grandfather took them personally, since the business was in his name, and once cornered Fred in the shop, and said, "There's a right way and a wrong way to run this business, and you know it. If you can't do it the right way, then just don't. And I don't mean workmanship. I mean the way you treat people. In case you've forgotten the—" But by that time Fred had walked out on him and then got into a truck and drove off.

"When Dad was about to retire, I went to him and I said, 'Dad, for God's sake, for the family's sake, for your own sake, for your peace of mind, why don't you fold this corporation up, let it go, just dissolve the damn thing! Lord knows it's caused you enough headache and grief as it is. Here's your chance to be rid of that. Sign it away! You've got enough to live on. Relax! If there's anything you want or need, let your sons take care of you for a change. And he said, 'No, what's always kept me going was the idea that I was building up this business for you boys.'

" 'Fine,' I said. 'But what if they don't want it?' *I* don't want it, I told him. I never did, and I'll never have anything to do with it. The only reason I ever did carpenter work—or plastering, either, as far as that goes—was there didn't seem any hope for a while and it was a good way to wear myself out so I could sleep nights.

" 'And look at Jay,' I said. (Your Uncle Jay was the first to really work with your grandpa, but that was so long ago you wouldn't remember.) 'You waited for Jay to get out of the service and pick up with you where he'd left off, you could hardly *bear* waiting, and then when the war was over and he came back and saw an opportunity to make money elsewhere, in plastering, off he went into that. A few years later Vince joined up with him. *I* always wanted to teach. Emil went into government service practically right out of high school, and Davey went off to college and then more school. Who's left?' " He ticked off on his fingers. " 'Fred and Tom. That's it. Two.'

" 'I've always considered my sons-in-law part of the family,' he said.

" 'Fine,' I said. 'Scott and Kev. Four. However you want to count. That's four out of how many, Dad? And how do you know that those four are perfectly satisfied with what they're doing?'

" 'I don't,' he said. 'And I'm glad most of you found out so soon what you wanted to do. But I built up this business for one reason, you boys, and as long as even just one of you's interested in it, I'll keep it going.'

" 'But Dad, Dad, maybe the other boys want to get off on their own, too,' I said. 'Lord knows they're old enough. Maybe they're just staying on to please you. I know Scott wants to get off on his own. He can hardly wait! He's been doing jobs on the side and over the weekends for years now. Maybe Fred and Tom want to, too. Maybe they look at Jay and think, By God, I could be like him. For goodness' sake, Dad, look at Jay yourself. Compared to you, he's a wealthy man, gol-dammit!' "

He struck the tabletop and the bowls bounced.

Laura set steaming mugs in front of them, and then put a hand on his sleeve and whispered, "Please. You mustn't get so upset. I'll leave you two alone now. I know you want to talk." She massaged the muscles of his shoulders, and said in a changed voice, "What time would you like breakfast—" and stopped short, it seemed, of a term of endearment.

"Seven. Fred and I have to go early to see about arrangements."

"Seven, then. Don't overtire yourself. Your mother will need you tomorrow." She kissed his forehead, and his lips quivered and compressed. She looked at Jerome, then away, unease in her eyes, and said, "Good night. If you boys need me, I'm here."

She closed the door to the other side of the house behind her.

The upstairs steps started to creak with the weight of

someone descending them, and Tim came into the kitchen in undershorts, skinnier than ever, half asleep, his eyes dazed and melting, and grabbed Jerome's hand and shook it hard. A mature yet impulsive gesture, and so unexpected Jerome knew he was afraid.

"Where's Chuck?" their father asked.

"He's in—" Tim's voice hit its adolescent register and cracked. "In bed. I don't think he's feeling too well."

Their father glanced toward the door to the other side, and said, "That's where you better get yourself, too, and right this minute, unless you put on some decent clothes."

"Oh," Tim said, and stared down at himself. "Oh, yeah."

He turned away like a somnambulist and went up the stairs.

"He hasn't been doing as well in school," their father said. "He's in a fog most of the time."

Jerome remembered Tim mentioning months ago that Einard might have some surgery done, of a corrective sort, Jerome inferred, since Tim said Einard was doing it mostly to oblige a doctor. Jerome hadn't asked any particulars. Why? A Freudian slit in which fissure? Fear? Einard was the same age as their grandfather. Damn. He got up, astir with restlessness, went to the percolator and poured a splash of coffee in his mug, then filled his father's, which was empty, and sat again.

"How are—"

Tim walked in in a pair of blue jeans, pulled up a chair across from Jerome, crossed his arms over his bare chest, and began nodding off.

"How's Unc?" Jerome asked; Tim's name for Einard.

Tim's eyebrows raised so much he should have been wide-eyed, but his lids stayed at half-mast. "Oh, fine," he said. "Just fine."

"That operation of his turned out all right?"

"Oh, sure."

"What was it for?"

Tim shrugged.

"Abdominal hernia," their father said.

"Where'd you get that?" Tim asked.

"From one of the relations. Olivia, I think." This was Sue and Grandma Jones's oldest sister.

"How come you didn't tell me about it?"

"If you'd write to them more often, the way I keep telling you to, you might have heard it from the source."

"Was it serious?" Jerome asked.

"It could have been, from what I understand of it. The way she sounded, they got it just in time."

They all leaned back from the conversation, as if a corpus of their creation was burning on the table, or about to be burned.

"Will Emil be here?" Jerome asked.

"Of course," their father said. "He's flying out."

Everybody withdrew even more.

Emil was Jerome's boyhood hero, a resident of New York, the most adventurous city, and an agent for the FBI. He'd wanted to enlist in the Army, as Fred and Jay had, but a doctor discovered the scars left by the lid of the gasoline barrel, and X rays revealed a three-inch gap in his tibia bridged by a piece of bone the size of a pencil, and he was rejected; the same with the Navy and the Air Force. He decided to join the FBI, and there was a family story that he'd slept on a park bench in Washington, D.C., until he was accepted; then worked as a file clerk while he went to Washington and Lee, then was made a special agent and assigned to Manhattan, and it was known, in a general way (he couldn't really talk about it, but Fred kept pumping him), that he'd worked on the Brink's and Hiss cases, and was once pinned down by gunfire in a Louisiana swamp for five days. When Jerome was in the seventh grade, he went with his father to visit Emil and his family and went walking a ways from the home on Long Island they'd just moved to, out to the beach, and had his first glimpse of the ocean, that watery plain that washed on foreign shores, and though it was March, he took off his shoes and went wading in it, he was so excited (and so he could say he'd been in the Atlantic Ocean), and gathered a shoe box of shells. Emil took them to Times Square and Rockefeller Center, the U.N., the Fulton Fish Market, and Chinatown, and what Jerome remembered most was how alert and at home Emil was in the crowds—Jerome kept craning up at skyscrapers and bumping into people, even when he took pains not to —and how Emil kept glancing at his wristwatch, and every hour excused himself and stepped into a building or phone booth. "What's all that espionage about?" Jerome's father finally asked. "Since I'm sort of wandering loose, I have to call in on a regular basis," he said. They later learned he hadn't been out of the office for months, because he was carrying information on an underworld figure that only he could testify about. Then why in the world had he taken them on a tour, Martin wondered. "You're protective coloration. Also, I was going stir-crazy in—"

"Tim!" their father shouted so loud that chairs scraped. "Get to bed!"

Tim's arms were crossed as before, and he blinked rheumy, bloodshot eyes. "What?"

"If you're going to just sit there and sleep, get to bed!"

"Oh. O.K."

He was drifting toward the stairway when Jerome said, "I'll see you in the morning."

"Uh-huh."

The sound of his feet, bare, padded, went up the stairs, and their father called, "If I thought you'd hear it, I'd say good night."

"G'night," Tim's retreating voice said, and then his footsteps were silent.

A cameo of Jerome's face, resting on the onyx surface of his coffee, grew larger and larger as he raised his mug until all that was visible was the bold nose and two glassed-in eyes the size and cast of grapeshot. Sheee-*it*, as Fred would say. He couldn't taste anything but heat. Why did he associate coffee with funerals and death, and why drink so much of it if he did? Tasting the edge? Pouring through to his past?

"I hardly know what to do with myself," his father said.

"Do they know what it was for sure?"

"His heart stopped is all I've heard." His voice was drawn inward and so small it seemed Susan's.

"Had you seen him much lately?"

"Much? Every day! He and I were trying to decide what to do about this bankruptcy business. In fact, I talked to him the same night—*Last* night," he said, and paled.

"How did he seem?"

"In low spirits, but perfectly healthy as far as I could see. There was a rumor going around that Fred had lost a check from a job—for nine hundred dollars, supposedly —in a poker game."

"Really?"

"Oh, well, you know how these stories get around. I'm sure there isn't any truth in it, but I suppose Dad heard it, on top of the bankruptcy news. He seemed very depressed."

If there was an irreconcilable deficit in the books, Fred would sometimes take the money to cover it, fifty dollars and above, out of his billfold, bite into his cigar so it stood up at an angle, and say, "Easy come, easy go, bookkeeper boy."

"You don't think it's true, then, about the nine hundred?"

"Oh, no. No, Fred might have a lot of faults, but not that kind. No, he probably got a few beers in him and made up the story himself. You know how he likes to be the center of attention. Oh, hell, everybody does." He gave Jerome a wavering look. "Is it possible Grandpa was alive this morning?"

"He wasn't complaining about anything, or seeing a doctor?"

"No. No, he stopped going to his regular doctor last spring."

"Lauflin?"

"That airplane-flying fellow toward Easton he's been going to the last ten years."

"Why? Lauflin's good."

"Dad said he gave him too many pills." His eyes had been lusterless and introspective, but now a swell of feeling surfaced in them. "My Lord, he was taking fifteen different pills a day—he had a special cabinet in the kitchen he kept them in—and none of them did any good for what was really bothering him, that terrible cough that used to double him up and what he referred to as his stomach trouble. Whatever that was. It was finally decided it wasn't an ulcer. Anyhow, one day he took the conglomeration of pillboxes out of the cupboard, took them out to the incinerator, and burned them. Ha! 'I never felt right about having those in the house,' he said. 'I was always afraid a grandkid might get into them.' He stopped seeing Lauflin and started going to a chiropractor instead."

"A *chiro*practor?"

"Yes, some fellow over at San Jose, about seventy or so —a guy who doesn't look well enough to pop a paper bag, much less crack somebody's back. He wears an old hat and a long overcoat whether it's April or August, and either must be a crackpot or just doesn't care."

"Did he do Grandpa any good?"

"Oh, Dad said he felt pretty good after each treatment, which is more than the pills did. Personally, I think he just liked to talk with the old guy." Now shrinking to Susan's voice again.

"Did Grandpa ever see Luis and Martita?"

"Oh, sure. They were the ones who satisfied him it wasn't an ulcer."

Luis and Martita were a man-and-wife medical team who'd come from Cuba during the Castro insurgency. They were members of the Pettibone parish, and were frowned upon by some parishioners; Martita prayed aloud in a rumbling Latin fervor, crossed herself with her rosary, and kissed its crucifix with a smack you could hear through the church. Some of their children and their relatives had to be left behind in Cuba, and every year, as their practice expanded, another member or two of the family would appear in town. They knew about Jerome's ambitions and called him "Doc" in a bantering but fraternal way, and insisted that he call them Martita and Luis.

"Dr. Martita's been the soul of goodness to your grandma today. She's done everything medically she can, and then she sat down and talked with her for two hours. But then Mom came apart again. I don't know how she'll make it through this. I've never known her to be irrational, and she's not the sort to get irrational no matter what the cause, but she's irrational now. All those sedatives and none have helped. She's still irrational. I have to get her to bed."

He shoved back his chair and left the room.

Jerome drew off his glasses and put his arms on the table and laid his head down on them; it was heavy, off-balance, his sinuses as impacted and raw as when he swam for hours in a chlorinated pool, and he wondered what conversations, if any, were taking place in the homes of his aunts and uncles at this hour. It was a quarter to twelve. He held his hand at arm's length and studied it, first the palm, then the back, and understood that he'd arrived in the world when he had to replace his dead uncle. What depths of futurity did his mother have in her? Was she free now?

He put the mugs in the sink, unplugged the percolator, switched off the lights, and started up the stairs. He stopped at the head of them. In a niche above the landing lit by the light in his room, was the hope chest his grandfather had built for her when the engagement was announced; built in the furnace room of a grade school where he worked as a janitor, Jerome's father had told him, and sometimes slept overnight during the worst of the North Dakota winters in order to keep the furnace stoked with lignite, and was at a loss what to do with himself when he wasn't lugging or shoveling the punklike coal (he'd once in one night burned sixty-seven wheelbarrows of it), and so this chest.

It wasn't cedar or cedar-lined, but plywood stained a cedar color, its outer edges trimmed with brass studs, and the conditions it had risen out of were too far removed in years and experience to affect his judgment of it. It was a durable piece of careful craftsmanship. It had survived the years and all of the moves without a scratch. He could remember his mother using twine to tie a rug around it when they moved from Hyatt. She was the outcast of the family, or so it seemed now, because of her persistent refusal, at first, to convert to the Church, and her outspokenness, too, perhaps, but she and his grandfather were good friends. He once walked into the kitchen in Forest Creek, where they were sitting at the breakfast counter, and saw them laughing in a way he'd never seen either of them laugh before, and realized they were sharing a moment they couldn't share with anybody else, even their own marriage partners, and nearly let the pebbles he had in his hand to show her scatter over the floor. Forgave them. Her especially, and himself. And then had to walk with his head bowed out the back door.

Her laughter. He'd just heard it out of that moment from the past again. He hadn't been able to hear her laughter for years. He touched the chest. A well-worked satiny texture. He could see the reflection of his hand. Inside was needlework she'd done over the years, plus a few articles of each of the five's baby clothes, and mementos of her engagement and marriage; he'd opened it once, and parted some stacks to see deeper into it, and that was enough. He had no desire to handle or examine any of it or look again, ever.

He crossed the landing, went down the old catwalk, and looked into the other room, where Tim and Charles lay on twin beds, the bulks of their covered bodies outlined and leaden-looking in the moonlight. He and Charles lathed and plastered the room a summer ago, paneled the long wall along the stairwell, built in cabinets and desks, put down tile, and then looked at one another in wonder: Why hadn't they done this before? He stepped into his room, shut off the light, and sat on the edge of the bed, feverish, at the threshold of physical illness or depression, and massaged the muscles of his neck; then lay back.

An oblong of moonlight rested on the ceiling above him, defined by the walls of the dormer, so translucent against the plaster it was like an opening into a room a story above. Stairs that let down in a ladder of light. When he was a child and couldn't sleep, he'd lie on his bed in the house in Hyatt, and think, Beyond the bedroom wall is Mom and Dad's bedroom, and all of the other rooms around it, and then the yard around that, and beyond the yard is the town and the countryside with its farms and all the other towns of Stusrud County and then the rest of the counties filling in the state, and beyond North Dakota are the rest of the states and Canada (vague, reassuring shape), and then the oceans beyond North and South America, the globe, until he felt close to a vast source of power, God or the sun, and fell asleep against it. Grandiosity. What an onomatopoetic word.

He turned on his face and felt the coolness of his grandparents' basement, the basement that had once held so many lives, flow up around him. At the far end was the room that had been a bedroom for a while, then for years was his grandfather's office, and now held the loom his grandmother used to make rugs of discarded clothes. The rest was open play area, with the baby swing there, the Ping-Pong table for internecine tournaments, or to spread buffets on when the family gathered, in the center; the rocking horse here, still redly at it in his adolescent mind, beside the cot where he'd had his first cop of tit after a sweaty game of Ping-Pong. A tall cabinet that held toys and games for children of every age, a refrigerator, a washer-dryer, a laundry sink of slate, and, in the far corner, a shower that was merely a raised quadrant of cement with a plastic curtain around it. She bathed there. Alpha among the Indians.

The house above, whose layout and rooms and stairwells and airiness formed a physical part of his past, was started soon after the war, when materials were difficult to get and mostly second-rate, and from the day it was finished had a lived-in, slightly ramshackle feel to it; floors creaked and didn't seem quite true, window frames parted from the siding, which was fir and shed paint like snakeskin, a motley of different tiles was used on the basement stairs and entry landing (the carpenter's children sometimes went without rooves), and then he felt himself (a plumber's son?) travel up the fizzing nozzle of the shower to the tub on the second story, where a loose faucet was always falling off with a clong. Twist-lock electrical outlets that only an adult could operate, without anybody saying, "No, no, don't!"

Up three steps from the entry was the kitchen, whose vintage cabinets of marine plywood had been replaced by his grandfather with cabinets of oak, as he sang "Roll out the barrel" all one afternoon while Jerome helped. The pill cabinet his father had mentioned, where his grandfather kept his cigarettes until he was told by Lauflin to quit smoking (and then didn't really quit, but switched to tipped cigars), was above a broom closet here, too high for him and Charles to reach when they were younger, so they boosted one another up to the cartons of Spuds, later Salems—like finding treasure, at that age, to see a carton of cigarettes in one place—both trying to stifle their laughter, and stole a pack each time they came to the house. Once their grandfather walked in on them with Charles high in the air, and stepped back, and said, "If you want a cigarette, ask for one. You'll ruin your health smoking, as I have, but if you're going to, I'd rather you did it in front of me instead of behind my back."

They couldn't have been more than twelve or thirteen and no mention was made of their stealing. How prepared he seemed for situations that came up. Was he for death? His breath resounded in his lungs as loudly as a rale at times, or he'd suddenly start coughing—his fist to his mouth and his face turning blue—so hard you had to look away and hold your breath for his sake. Surely he had emphysema.

The dining room, then, with big windows looking onto the terraced lawn, and, to the left, opening onto the living room, a ten-foot arch; on recessed shelves on both sides of it were the salt-and-pepper shakers his grandmother collected; and the wall above the dining table was one long mirror lined with glass shelves that held more of them, over seven hundred pairs, at his grandmother's last count, doubled in the mirror—windmills, gas pumps, skunks, flower buds, statuettes of nuns and gnomes, a Billy on a pot, a baseball and glove, a hammer and anvil (anything, really, that came in pairs), and these could be taken down by the grandchildren, over thirty of them, and used as toys.

From the day their mother died until Jerome and Charles went off to college, their family sat at this table every Sunday for dinner. Their grandmother called them "my second family" and prepared meals for them as large as for her first; a main course of roast or turkey with stuffing, creamed mashed potatoes, homemade bread or rolls, vegetables, a salad or two, a fruit bowl, and a dessert that was usually fresh-baked—an extravagance of food, and perhaps one of the few balanced meals they had all week. There were so many side dishes, and so many servings in each, they stayed on for the afternoon, watching television with flushed faces, satiated and drowsy, or went wandering as though underwater through this house so different from theirs, and yet partly theirs, with its order and cleanliness, well-heated rooms, aubusson-colored carpet on the floors and flight of stairs to the second story, plus so many pieces of plush furniture there was an enveloping seat for everyone, and then had supper from the leftovers from dinner, often with uncles and aunts and cousins who'd dropped in, and still there were leftovers. The house seemed a source of bounty that could never give out.

And then he saw, to the left, the door to the bedroom where, just this morning, his grandfather fell dead. He could visualize his grandmother waking with the religious statues and framed absolutions for the family signed by secretaries of two Popes, gifts from Davey, in the room around her, and making up the double bed, and the image of her doing this kept going on and on into the future until he wished his mind would give out.

She was formidable to him years before, fleet and graceful, small, but such a bulwark of authority it seemed she was carrying within her a part of the country of Germany and a great deal of the Catholic Church. She'd mellowed, though, put on weight, and was so at ease with herself and others that if he was asked what she was like now, he'd say, "Gentle and serene." She still had strength, but kept within the boundaries of her solid self, and was gay and girlish about it, as if she hadn't been able to express herself until the last of her children was raised. She and his mother would get along now.

In the days that came she'd have to decide whether to begin a new life or not. And it would be difficult with none of the children growing up and at home. Maybe Marie or Susan could live with her for a year or more, which might also ease the situation at home here, if there was one, as it seemed. Marie would be best. She was more emotional than Susan, and though you could be stalwart and intellectual about death, it helped to be able to empty yourself of it in the most primitive ways. That was why their father had been able to endure all he had, but today he'd begin to show emotion and then retreat from it, as if Laura might find it unmanly in him, and hadn't even been able to speak until he got home. Then the explosion.

Jerome sat, crossed an ankle over his knee, and reached for his shoe; his father used to claim he lay in suspense below waiting for the second one to drop. Fred must feel awful. When he took over the business, it was assumed by everybody, especially Tom, that Tom would have some say in how it was run, since he was the only other son still in it, but Fred handled him no better or worse than any of the foremen—not so much highhanded as unaware Tom was being hurt, because he enjoyed giving orders, manipulating figures and people so much, he assumed everybody shared in the enjoyment. Tom was boyish and nursed his grudges. He and Fred got into shouting arguments over petty details and Tom would throw down his hammer and walk off the job. But then he'd return, shamefaced, knowing his father was being hurt.

Jerome heard Tom's and a lot of the others' grievances in the office where he kept books and made out the payroll, a job that kept him home over the summer when the rest of the family was on vacation. He didn't care. He lived in his grandparents' basement. He sometimes felt the office had a shingle on it. Tom thought he should be allowed to operate with as much autonomy as Scott, Elaine's husband; but Scott operated that way because he never listened to Fred, considering him a philanderer of the business world and a bag of wind, and Tom, who was dutiful and knew his brother's worth, did.

Fred was an intuitive estimator who could look at a set of plans and say within a few hundred dollars what the finished building would cost, and then a day's work on a calculator would prove him right. He could walk through a remodeling job and within minutes hand in a bid on it. His manner won over stuffy and timid prospects, and when he was in the mood and not drinking, he could build period furniture from scratch, from slabs of hardwood, with a craftsmanship that awed even his father. "The Old Master," he'd say of himself with a smile, and bite into his cigar. "How do you get such a finish?" people would ask. "Why, it's hand-rubbed!" He'd stroke the oil glands alongside his nose and hold up a fingertip. "With this."

Tom was a former track star, tall and massively built, and so powerful Jerome had seen him pick up and throw a few yards a three-hundred-pound table planer that broke down and angered him. He and Fred had become so distant their only means of communication was notes on a chalkboard in the shop. If Tom had been able to tell Fred what was bothering him, then their relationship surely would have changed, for Fred was, above all, down to earth and reasonable, and couldn't bear anything he didn't understand or couldn't tinker with until he got it going good.

"She's a broom binder," Tom would say about any job that looked particularly difficult to him. "She's a *barn* burner," Fred would respond, and suddenly they'd be laughing so hard they were embarrassed, and those two phrases, which must have come from somewhere in their childhood and never failed to amuse them, were about their only way of relating as brothers. Unless one of them could fart, and Jerome had seen them walking around a construction site straining and red-faced, trying to rip one off. "A katooshmaker, Lord Windowsmear!"

Fred lived down the street and across the railroad tracks from his parents (the tracks ran through the center of Forest Creek and gave the houses there regular shakings), and after he took control of the business you could hear, more and more, outside the grandparents' house, arguments coming from Fred's. His wife, Gayle, was a tall and handsome woman, nervy and authoritative—"Fred runs the corporation the way he'd like to Gayle," a wag once said—and had a tendency toward theatrics. One day she came in in a fury to see Jerome's grandfather, and versions of the conversation had been replayed so much in the family it had become tenuous domestic history; Jerome's grandmother and Davey were within hearing distance. Jerome was on the cot in the basement.

Gayle began by saying she was concerned about Fred's drinking, and then started to complain about it and berate Fred's manliness.

"I don't know why you've come to me," Jerome's grandfather said.

"You mean you're not concerned about his drinking?"

"Of course. But it's not my place to interfere in his life. Or in yours, either, and if you were my own daughter I'd tell you the same."

"Well, what do you expect *me* to do about it?"

"Work this out with him, between the two of you, as man and wife."

"I've been thinking of a divorce," she said.

Jerome tried to imagine his grandfather's face, and could guess how a Catholic divorce would be looked upon in Forest Creek—a laughing matter, at the least.

"If you've gone so far as to think of that, you've made a breach between the two of you that's going to be hard to mend. And you've made me a party to it. No matter what I say, you'll do what you're inclined to, but since you've made me a party to it, I'll tell you what I think you should do. Get a divorce. You're unhappy, and I can't think of anything worse than living with a man who made me unhappy."

Jerome removed his shoe, then the other, and stood and undressed, hanging his clothes over the chair at his desk in darkness, then set his glasses on the desktop and got under the covers. He was supposed to take after Jay in temperament, not in any physical sense, certainly;

Jay was over six feet, long-boned and good-looking, like Tim, and carried himself with an athletic grace that made it seem he was perpetually walking over a well-sodded fairway toward the next green. He loved golf and hunting upland game. He'd been a photographer during the war, stationed in England, and flew in bombers' underbellies to record the effectiveness of their raids; he'd photographed the fire-bombing of Dresden. He brought home a piece of shrapnel the size of a plate that imbedded itself in a wall a few inches from his head during a V-2 shelling of London. The world's wars.

Jerome heard, years later, that Jay had wanted to marry an older Englishwoman, but hadn't, and when he came home was drinking and behaving so unlike himself that the priest from Havana, Father Hart-Donovan, began following him around bars and drinking at his side. He married, eventually, a girl who was the assistant postmistress in Pettibone, and was, still, the most attractive and well turned of any of Jerome's aunts. She and Jay lived next to his grandparents, beyond the playground, in a house that had begun as a model-looking place for a pair of newlyweds, and had been added on to in a rambling manner with the birth of their children and with Jay's ascendance in the business world over the years, until it covered the end of the block. Jay had four daughters, the only Neumiller without a son, and hadn't drunk since the shivaree for his marriage.

He'd developed a method of plaster-finishing he called peacock-tailing, in which the swirled circles in the sand finish of a ceiling lined up in straight rows no matter which angle they were looked at, and now had a half dozen crews scattered over this area of the state. He'd loaned Jerome five hundred dollars when he started college, and said he'd help pay his way through medical school. If indeed Jerome was taciturn, as everybody implied, then he wouldn't know what name to give Jay's manner. He'd go to see him about a small loan, or merely to talk, hoping to get a feel of how Jay managed so well in the world, and there'd be five- and ten-minute silences as Jay doodled on a pad, or simply stared at Jerome, his fingers steepled under his lips, and finally he'd come out with a line that seemed non-sequitur or purposely cryptic, such as, "Did you see 'The Old Man and the Sea' in *Life?*" which took Jerome three years to understand, and then there'd be ten more minutes of silence.

He was on the road most of the time making estimates, so Vince had become his head foreman. Vince lived on the other side of Forest Creek, in a modern ranch-style house, and was the most private and misunderstood of the Neumillers, perhaps; he had the fewest children, a son and daughter, and everybody who worked with him said he was difficult to get along with, although Jerome never found him to be. Perhaps his work didn't agree with him. He'd tried a variety of other occupations—farming, speculating in oil, working toward a pilot's license, mining (near Zap, North Dakota), TV repair, raising chinchillas —and seemed to abandon all at the moment they were about to turn his way. He'd been troubled by ulcers since he was twenty-one and finally, last fall, underwent semi-experimental surgery in which a length of duodenum and one-third of his stomach were removed; his hair grayed after the operation and furrows deepened in his face. He'd always resembled his father more than any of the sons, but now looked like his father's brother, an older one. He stayed home and read novels and biographies until he dropped off, and exuded a sorrow and listlessness Jerome saw as belonging to an imprisoned artist.

Rose Marie and her husband, Kev, had always lived in Pettibone, "to be away from the family," as Rose Marie archly put it; Pettibone was five miles from Forest Creek. "But then *Kev's* family lives here," she said. "You can't win."

Elaine and Scott lived in the country beyond Forest Creek.

Tom had sold his house in Forest Creek a year ago (nobody knew why) and was now living on the outskirts of Pettibone.

Davey was in Chillicothe, teaching high-school Latin.

Charles cried out from the other room.

Jerome sat up. What tangle of dreams was he fighting his way through? When Jerome was running the experiment for the psychologist, he'd asked Charles to be a subject, since subjects received a ten-dollar fee and he knew Charles could use the money, although it was against his better judgment; good results depended on the neutrality of the tester. He was taking Charles through the first series of tests, holding up picture cards two feet from his face, a tactic meant to intimidate, and when he came to the photograph of a bushy *mons Veneris,* which had been preceded by a mushroom, Charles slapped the table and started laughing so hard Jerome broke up. Charles was abandoned from then on, lost in some sort of inner contact, as he pressed buttons to match flashing patterns of lights on the wall, and then back to more picture cards, and later, when he was done and had left, Jerome sat in the darkened room with the test lights blinking around him, and saw that according to the scale set up by the psychologist, Charles was a borderline psychotic. Anybody with his results was supposed to be given the MMPI. But Jerome wasn't sure he hadn't affected his responses, and as he sat in the room and stared at a wall and then at the mathematically correlated graphs, at the uneven reaction times, the unfurling reels of Charles's breathing and heartbeat, he felt unequal to being a scientist. "Tester botched," he wrote in the logbook after Charles's name, and tore up his results and buried them in a wastebasket.

He turned and lay on his back and put his feet against the wall, flexing and unflexing his toes. G.P.? Pedia— The texture of the plaster, the darkness and the oblong above him made him want to masturbate. He rolled on his side and punched the pillow into a mound. He'd been having trouble sleeping at night, although he could sleep perfectly well during the day. Psychiatrist, pediatrician, Ph.D.? He'd have to make a decision in a few weeks. It depended upon the kind of life he wanted to live, because once the decision was made, that life would take over. He tried to travel outward to the source of power, as he had in Hyatt, but the shape of Illinois, like a half-formed arrowhead, deflected him, and then he saw his profile against the pillow as though on a fluoroscope, with the whorls of his brain gleaming gray-green and neonlike inside the delicate cage of his skull.

He got out of bed, turned on the light, took a psychology text from among the books and clothes in his suitcase, and began to read its wobbly lines one after the other until the print and then his mind came to a close.

*

He rose to the smell of coffee, the oblong above him now sunlight. He'd been dreaming of a day in the fifth grade, a spring afternoon with fall light falling through the high windows, when everybody sat at his desk carving a bust of Abraham Lincoln out of a bar of Ivory soap. The teacher was Mrs. Strawrick. "Quite a name, huh?" she said the first day, introducing herself, and then explained what it meant. She was a stocky woman amused by some unrevealed aspect of herself, and had a noisy laugh that other teachers complained about. She was in her forties and pregnant for the first time that year, due at nearly the same date as his mother, and when she was nearing term she introduced her replacement, her cousin, who was built exactly like her but on a smaller scale, and was named Rakestraw. "She rakes the straw for the *rick!*" Mrs. Strawrick said, and the two women stood at the front of the room shaking with laughter in an identical way, and he relaxed at his desk, realizing there were more inexplicable interrelationships than would ever be revealed to any one person in a lifetime. When Mrs. Strawrick returned to school after her delivery, after his mother had died, she took him aside and said, "I've been thinking of you all this time at home and felt so miserable for you. Then I remembered that maple-leaf cup shelf you made for her at Christmastime, and the industry you worked at it with, cutting it out so well, and then sanding and finishing it just right, and I thought, Surely that gave her a great deal of pleasure in the last days of her life."

He sat up, as feverish as last night, and was sure he was coming down with the flu. He dressed and went downstairs. Susan and Marie were at one side of the kitchen table with their backs to him, Laura and Ginny at the other, and Ginny looked up and smiled, showing the braces on her teeth, and then appeared stricken, as if she'd committed a blunder she couldn't make her way out of, and bowed her head. Marie got up, her features awry and disfigured, and he took her in his arms, and then Susan put her head on his other shoulder and he could feel the heat from their sobs through his shirt. "There, there," he said, and had no idea what else to say.

Over their shoulders Laura sat with eyes downcast, turning and turning her coffee mug on the table, as if the complexities of their ties, when this many were home together, left no room for her, and now she must feel a captive, or worse. He got the girls to their chairs and made them sit; soon, though, Marie got up and ran to the other side of the house, and then Susan got up and followed. He poured himself some coffee with shaking hands, full of fear or hate, and sat at the table.

"They're really very terribly upset," Laura said at last.

"I'm sure you'll be able to find some way to help them," he said. "I don't think I can."

Laura and Ginny looked up, and again, though more circumspectly now, Ginny smiled and beamed all of her daughterly youthfulness out at him.

*

His father came into the room upstairs, in a dark suit and tie, and Jerome closed his book and pushed it to the side of the desk as his father sat on the bed. "The arrangements are all made," he murmured. The strain of the last two days had stretched the skin over the bones of his face like a mask, and Jerome realized how much he'd aged; his hair, once a thatch of glossy curls, was straight and dry-looking, so thin you could see through it in places, and had receded above his broad forehead; his hooded lids were more fatty and drooped at their corners, altering the circular, ingenuous look of his eyes.

He gave Jerome a quick questioning glance, then looked down again. "I have a chore. Fred and some of the others think I should write up something for the paper, a sort of memorial to Dad along with a general note of gratitude to the communities, for the sympathy they've shown, and maybe a few anecdotes to remember him by."

"You're probably the only one who could do it."

"I hardly know where to begin. He led such a full life. I could go back to when we lived on the farm, or even farther than that. Did you know, for instance, that he once attended a seminary?"

"No."

"An abbey around Bismarck. His dad wanted him to become a priest. Grandpa never talked about it, and I'm sure it's because he would have liked to be a priest, but felt it was his duty to stay on the farm and help out his father."

Jerome was doubly amazed. Davey, who was valedictorian of his high-school class when he was sixteen, very close to his parents and pampered, perhaps, since he was so much younger than the others, only three years older than Jerome, had studied to be a priest himself for seven years and then, a few months before his ordination, appeared at home without the rabat and white collar he'd worn since he entered the seminary, and said to Jerome, "I'm not sure why I quit. I guess I didn't have the moral makeup to be a priest." Jerome hadn't ever seen his grandfather so openly brokenhearted and morose.

"I like the story about the Golden Guernsey," he said, and saw his father walking over the plain again to bring the cows in at twilight, in the spring, when he could see the windmills, and getting angry and throwing a rock into the herd and hitting the Guernsey, who fell as if shot —"It probably couldn't happen three times in this world" —and then sitting on a stone beside her and seeing his father come over the fields, expecting a beating to remember the rest of his life, and hearing instead, "Come home and eat now. You've suffered enough."

"I don't think I could write it down," his father said.

This sounded so final, Jerome felt it was what his father should try. "It shows how easily he forgave. And how he understood that children tend to torture themselves more than their parents would."

"Yes." He seemed to test this in his own mind. "You know, I never once saw him in tears, although he was very sensitive, as you know, and certainly had much to grieve about. He lost two children, infants, and you know how much he loved kids—" The intake of breath was so sudden it was as if his father had drawn the last phrase back inside him. Was he trying to emulate *his* father? "He lost his mother when she wasn't so old, and when his dad died, he built the coffin for him and buried him with his own hands." Martin glanced out the sunglazed dormer and blanched, as if that window had once been a doorway through to an end he'd endured. "The death of your mother affected him more than anybody realized then."

Jerome was downstairs on the couch beside his grandmother, trying to learn to crochet, so he'd have a skill to show his mother when she returned from the hospital, and then the telephone rang, and his grandfather, who was in the kitchen, answered: "Yes, this is Mr. Neumiller. *What?* No, no, no, you've made a mistake. This is C. J. C. Neumiller. You don't want me, you want my son Mar— I tell you you don't want to talk to me!" And slammed the receiver down. It was the hospital, calling to say she'd died, and his grandfather wouldn't hear of it.

"I sometimes think he held everything inside so much it might partly explain why he suffered from"—his father lifted his fingers and made quotes—" 'stomach trouble' so much of his life."

Jerome lit a cigarette, backing his eyes from the match heat, and leaned his elbows on his knees, feeling they'd come close.

"After the Depression, and all those years of scrimping, when he finally got into the position of making money himself, his first thoughts were for the family and others. When he saw the plans for the gymnasium here in town, he said, 'Why, this is just a glorified quonset hut.' Which it is. He said it was an eyesore and shouldn't be built, and drew up a set of plans of his own—a beautiful place—and submitted it to the school board. They said it was too expensive. He sat down and showed them with figures how he could build it for only a few thousand more than the tin shed they were considering, and then the community could have a place to be proud of. They wouldn't listen, of course. Grief all along, those people. They got an outfit from somewhere else to put up their quonset, and then there was some kind of strike—union labor, of course—and in the end it cost them more than the building he proposed."

"I didn't know that."

"I've kept my mouth shut about this sort of thing because he did, and I figured that's what he expected from the rest of us."

So combative again and final. Somebody started up the stairs, paused a moment, and then went back down again. His father shifted his weight, and Jerome could see the bulge of his balls at the top of his trouser leg.

"I don't believe anybody knows the complete story behind the swimming pool. For a while the Men's Club bused the local kids to Delavan once a week to go swimming."

"I rode those buses a lot."

"Well, he wanted a place his grandkids and the rest of the kids around could enjoy on their own. So he persuaded the Men's Club to fix up that pool at the edge of town that hadn't been used since the thirties, and was cracked up and going to general waste. He oversaw the construction of it, gratis, and when the club ran out of money, helped them set up a corporation and sell shares of stock. He bought quite a number of shares himself. They still didn't have enough. So he took out a lifetime membership in the club, which cost a few hundred dollars, and persuaded Fred and Jay to do the same. That summer the pool was finished."

"You have to write that down."

"Oh—" His father lifted his hand, saw it was trembling, and let it fall. "Oh, I guess there are better instances of his generosity than that. When we moved here, I had a terrible time finding a home for us. Your mother wasn't feeling well even then, and Dad knew how important it was for her to have a place of her own. This house came up for sale and he said it was structurally sound and could always be fixed up, and told me to take it. I said I didn't have enough to make the down payment. I was short over two thousand. He loaned it to me. It wasn't until last year that I got caught up enough to pay him back. He never once mentioned the money. When I took him the check, he said, 'What's all this for?' I said I'd added some interest for all those years, ten of them. '*Interest?*' he said, and stared at the check, and then folded it up, then *tore* it up, and shoved it in his pocket, and I asked him what the—what the *hell* he thought he was doing, and he said, 'I owe you this, and much more, for all the hours you put in as a young man! working for me! on the farm!' "

Martin shoved up his glasses and gripped the bridge of his nose, and tears ran over the backs of his fingers and dropped in spots over his shirt front. Jerome blinked at the bed, a spangled square with the blur of his father's body against it, and then was out in the back yard, kicking at cinders and weeds as if for something he'd lost, in order to leave his father to himself.

*

There were so many cars around his grandparents' house, Jerome had to park a block down from it, on the side of the street where the railway embankment rose, behind a pickup of Jay's whose tailgate, employing the name of the vehicle's manufacturer, read:

YOU CAN

A' Ford

NEUMILLER QUALITY
LATHING, PATCHING, PLASTERING,
FINISH WORK

He and Charles and Tim and their father got out (the girls had come down with Laura in her car), and went past Jay's, with the green wire fence around it where a hunting dog had once run, and then along the back of the shrubbery-bordered shrine to the Blessed Virgin, built by Davey out of fieldstones from the countryside one summer when he was a young seminarian and wore cutoffs and leather sandals, and seemed to brood too much. The front door of their grandparents' house opened and a tall woman in a pumpkin-colored coat came down the brick-walled walk that descended the three terraces of the lawn.

"I'll be right in," Jerome said as the others headed toward the back of the house. "I think this is Martita. I want to say hello."

He waited on the crushed-rock drive beside a red convertible with the top down. Martita was big-boned and bosomy, but her waist, cinched by her trench-coat belt, was the waist of a young woman, and she came over the lawn with a delicacy and grace he'd always admired, and stared at him with deep-set eyes, which made him recognize again how brown eyes were better for expressing emotional concern than gray or green or blue, and then her lower lip pushed out and gleamed behind its line of lipstick. "My thoughts been with you, Doc."

"Thank you."

"He was a man I sometimes want to hug, if I could. He helped us when other people thought, Do them two understand beans, how they talk. Old man Neumiller, they figure, he sees what's up." She began to wink and her black eyelashes caught.

"Do you know what it was?"

She hefted her heavy shoulders and stared at her feet, small for her size and shod in shoes that showed pastel-painted toes, and then shifted them over the crushed rock in a sudden dance that expressed the mystery of their affinity, and let it rest there. "Could be embolism, infarct, bad tight arteries, his age, and then we seen lots of fluids in his lungs that could put pressure on and inter-fierce with his, you know, the thumpa, thumpa of it. But me, I just figure his heart's broke. 'Why meddle?' says Luis, so we sewn him back up. Does the school still agree on you?"

"Pretty much."

"All the A's still?"

"A couple of B's."

"No worse, now. Do you know your Auntie Rose Marie is P.G. again?"

"Really?"

"Just barely so yet. I tell her not to, but she did."

"How does Grandma seem to you?"

She drew a hand out of her coat and tossed up a syringe, caught it, and put it in her pocket again. "I just shoot her up some more Seconal now. She listened to me once, but no more. It's too deep in her yet. Two days or so, I'll knock again and see does she open inside. Do you still pray, Doc?"

He shrugged and stared down.

"Ah, Doc, you could for her. What you got to loose? And poor Grandpa, his soul, too, huh? I got an idea what purgatory and hell is like."

He looked up and found her brown eyes even on him.

"You'll learn, too, Doc. I gotta go now."

She slid into her convertible and spun away, her head lifted back as though peering over the windshield top, and went across the embankment of the tracks with a dipping leap, on her way to traveling everywhere, as she did even when it wasn't necessary, at speeds up to a hundred, and then telling him to pray. Only the pious could use piety as a tool or club with impunity, or not use it; his grandfather's choice. He went around the back and stopped after he'd passed the garage, sure that he'd seen, at the other end of it, at the front of the car, somebody duck into shadow. Was he going off his gourd now? He stepped into the garage and saw Tommy crouched in the corner below the car hood. Tommy straightened and said, "Oh, it's you. Hi."

"How are you today?"

"Pretty good." Tommy smiled, sending deep dimples into his full cheeks, blushed dark, and then held up a hand, five inches across its back, and revolved it so Jerome could see the cigarette cupped inside. He smiled again. "Had to have a fag."

"Oh."

"Mom'd kill me if she knew about it, jeez."

He was as massive as his namesake, Tom, who was called "Big Tom" to distinguish the two, and had had these same muscle-bunched shoulders, the heavy beard and matted hair over his chest from the time he was sixteen, and yet Elaine, a wisp of a tiny woman, still punished him physically, and he submitted with a strained smile.

"How's your mom?"

"Not so good." Tommy's eye widened. "Me and Dad and Carl don't know what to do. Hoooo, boy!" Carl was Tommy's middle brother.

"What about Laurie?" This was the youngest brother.

"He's been as bad as Mom. *Helk!*" His cry was a whispered hurt.

"Is your dad here?"

"He and Kev and Tom decided to work. I think Fred is, too."

Shoes crunched over the crushed rock at the front of the garage and they held themselves motionless as a woman's voice said, "It seems just weeks ago we were here last," and then the back door closed with the uneven and screechy settling of the worn plunger within its cylindrical sleeve. Tommy stared with wide eyes.

The garage was attached to the house by a glassed-in breeze-way used as a greenhouse, and they'd heard from there a muted wail, some women's voices calling out together, and now a louder, stronger voice, still a woman's, saying, "No, no, no, no, *no!*" It was a version of their grandmother's voice that came belling through the house as though from underwater.

"Boy," Tommy said, "they're sure whooping it up in there."

Boy, is this some digs, Jerome heard again, and remembered this garage filled with their furniture when they moved, and that Tommy's father had been on a destroyer during the war and brought back souvenirs that filled a cabinet in their old country home, and then Jerome had a picture of that place, where the three boys had lived all their lives, large and intact, and then saw the charred remains of it, as it was a summer ago when it burned to the ground before the volunteer fire department got itself assembled, and remembered Tommy walking over the smoking remains that filled the basement, carrying a bucket that contained a mass of melted-together silver dollars—all he'd been able to salvage. A new house was built over the basement of the old one.

"I have to go inside," Jerome said. He felt a victim of years of uncontrollable events.

"You're going to want to leave the second you get in there."

"Probably."

The kitchen was empty. Coffee was going on the stove. Ahead, in the dining room, among a crowd that included Vince and Adele and their son Luke, who had Vince's ambery-brown eyes and straightforward amplification of inner strength, were Charles and Tim and others, and then Jerome saw Emil, and was surprised at how much he resembled Martin; Emil taller and thinner, with Jay's grace, but with Martin's hair of younger years, curly still; his fatty, hooded lids, and the same mole beside his nose. Then Emil saw Jerome, excused himself, and came over and guided him back into the kitchen.

"How are you?" he asked, and his eyes, direct and appraising, went from Jerome's eyes to his mouth to his eyes again, considering and probing, as if to find the answer before Jerome spoke.

"Oh." Jerome shrugged and looked down, unable to bear the intensity of the examination.

"It was terribly sudden," Emil said.

"Yes."

"But I had a feeling it would come."

"Oh?" He looked up and Emil's eyes said to him, *I'm troubled, too, but we seem to understand one another. Let's be reasonable, all right?*

"When I drove away from here the last time, after I'd shaken Dad's hand, I thought, 'I'll never see him again.' I've never had such a thought without its coming true. So in a way I was prepared when the call came, or as much as one can be. We flew in this morning. Kath was just saying how it seemed only weeks that we'd been here."

"Your family came?"

"Just Kathy and Greg and me." Greg was his oldest. "We just got in now. Jay just drove us in."

There was a protuberance above his heart where he carried his pistol.

"How is Jer—er, *Jay* taking it?" Jerome said.

"Terribly. He shouldn't drive. I thought my younger kids wouldn't understand all of this, so I left them home with Kath's mother."

"I can see that."

"It'll be hardest on your dad, of course."

"You've talked to him?"

"Not yet. But that I knew before I got here. He looks upset."

"Yes."

"Elaine, too. With Elaine it's compounded by nerves. Have you talked with your dad?"

"Some. He seems to be working it out in his own way."

"He's probably as upset about Mother at the moment. He was always closest to her of any of us, closer even than Davey, I'd guess. Martin was close to Dad, of course, but he's always been closer to Mother."

This had never occurred to Jerome in such bare terms.

"Dad told me once that he had to stop and consider before he talked to you and your brothers, so he didn't call you Fred or Jay or Vince or my name or any of the others. Did he ever call you by any of our names?"

"Not me."

"Not even in the last year?"

"No."

"Good. Do you think there was much pain involved?"

"I just talked to the doctor, and it wouldn't seem so."

"I hope not. Why suffer at the end when that's all your life has been?" He put a hand on Jerome's shoulder. "It's good to see you. I guess we better go in."

The living room was filled with people not really speaking but sending up a murmur of sound. Elaine came up to him, biting her lower lip, her unguarded eyes enlarged by gray glasses, and her close-cropped hair, as gray as his grandmother's, scratched his neck as she took him in her arms and said, "Oh, Jerome, what are we going to *do?*"

Rose Marie, the aunt Martita mentioned, usually flighty and exuberant, with the looks of a college girl although she'd had eleven children in nearly as many years ("And I won't quit till I have twelve," she said once. "What the hell"), was in a chair with a handkerchief in one hand, her head bowed, a wisp of dark hair clinging to her wet cheek.

Fred's wife, Gayle, was dressed in a stylish black suit and stood with her back against a wall, her jaw clenched, her hands so restless the silver bracelets on her wrists clashed and sent riverlike reflections over the ceiling. Laura and Ginny and Susan and Marie were on a couch with an afghan over it, and next to them was Davey's new wife, Rose, huge with her first pregnancy. Carl, who had fleshy and fuller cheeks than Tommy, and was built as big as him, sat bunched on another couch between Paul, Rose Marie's oldest son, and Fred Jr., all three of whom were freshmen in high school. Younger cousins, from eleven to one and a half, stood around the edges of the room and along the stairwell to the second story, wide-eyed and constrained, as if afraid of what their parents would do next.

Neighbors and friends were moving in and out, carrying pies and pastries and casseroles, and setting them down on the dining-room table, and then going up to Jerome's grandmother to say a few words. She was at the opposite end of the room, on the piano bench, and wouldn't look up at them. Davey stood next to her, his back against the piano, his hands clasped below his belt, staring at the floor, and his profile, at a level with the service and graduation pictures on the piano top, sent a joylessness back through the years-old smiles.

Martin was on the bench beside his mother, holding her hand as he spoke close to her ear. Her glasses were removed and her face, swollen and discolored, looked naked, as at birth. She kept shaking her head and pushing at Martin, whose lips were brown in his bloodless face, and then he looked in appeal around the room with blind eyes, causing Marie, on the couch, to double over, and Ginny to cry, "Oh, *Dad!*" Their grandmother began rocking on the bench and Jerome heard, as if from the fret-

work of strings behind rather than a human source, the
water-blocked wail he'd heard in the garage, which grew
in volume and other-worldliness until Elaine cried
"Mother!" and the other women wailed and joined in.
Holy Lord.

He started toward the bench, but his grandmother lifted
her altered face and cried. "Leave me alone! Let me *go!"*
She pushed at Martin as if to push him aside, and said,
"No, no, no, no, *no!"* and then stood and her knees
started buckling beneath her. Martin and Davey caught
her and helped her back to the bench.

"Let me go *see* him!"

"Mother, Mother, please," Martin said. "He's close."

"If I can't see him, I want to see Martin."

"Mother, please."

She struck her fists on her thighs like a child, and then
began beating on Martin's chest and cried, "I want to see
Martin!"

"Mother, it's me. I'm here."

"I want to *see* him."

Jerome sank in a vacant chair, felt eyes on him, and
realized how many people were on their feet, and was on
his in a second; it was the reclining rocker known by
family members, even the youngest grandchild—uh-
oh, God!—as Grandpa's Chair. He'd seen his grandfather
rise from it during a televised boxing match, shifting and
feinting for the fighter he favored until he found himself,
unfulfilled and abashed, within inches of the screen, gray-
silver light filming his forearms, a ghost of a shadow over
him, and then the finishing dot receding like a face into
infinity. And this was home to him?

*

Jerome lay in bed, the blue oblong above him, and punished and rearranged his pillow, trying to find its position
for the night, and wondered if he should get up and read
for an hour, or promise himself to, and so fall asleep.

"Jerome?"

His father's voice came from the stairwell.

"Yes."

"Would you come downstairs?"

What could it be at this hour? He found his glasses,

pulled on his pants, and was at the bottom of the stairs before he realized there was a sensation in his legs as of sand quavering and circulating and recirculating somewhere below his knees, and nearly fell. His father was at the kitchen table, in a bathrobe, and on the tabletop was an empty mug and a sheaf of papers covered in a large, primary hand.

"I couldn't sleep," his father said.

"Me either."

"I figured as much. I got some things about Grandpa written down."

"Good."

"Well, I'm not sure if they are or not. I just put down what came to mind, and thought you might suggest what to use. Here." He shoved the sheaf of papers in front of Jerome. "I'll go over to the other side."

Jerome picked up the top sheet, blue-lined with a red margin down it, school paper, and for a while merely stared at his father's writing, so regular and well formed, with every letter slanting at the same angle, it seemed out of a penmanship manual from an earlier time. All those years of teaching, of writing on blackboards and erasing it, hadn't affected the care he took to write well.

The top of the page was titled "Recollections and sayings and reactions of my father, C. J. C. Neumiller," and Jerome saw that his father's hand had faltered writing the name.

I can't recall his ever suggesting a vocation for any of us kids when we were young, but I do recall his saying, "I don't care what you become in life, so long as you're honest and do your best at it." About school marks, he often said, "I'm interested in only one grade on your report card—deportment. If that's good, then the rest of it likely will be too."

Jerome's father had then drawn three stars.

I remember a letter I received from him while I was in college, and a statement he made in it. It was in the spring, the spring of '37, I believe, and there were severe floods in most of the country then. As I recall it, he said, "It seems to me that man spends

most of this time trying to improve on God's workmanship, building levees, dams, etc., and then all at
once God reminds him who drew the plans."

* * *

He was deeply religious but never discussed his
religion with anyone. He said, "A man's religion and
family life are private affairs. Everybody knows his
politics."

* * *

He was deeply devoted to the praying of the Rosary
and many times while driving from job to job
would have one in his hand on the steering wheel.
You can be sure he was praying it.

* * *

He was a man who definitely lived in the present
at all times. It fascinated him that most of what we
think of as modern conveniences—the automobile, the
airplane, the telephone, electric lights and appliances, radio and TV—were largely developed in his
time. He often said, "Some people talk about the
good old days. They can have them."

* * *

He understood young people, their problems, hopes,
and desires. Many times when I was young and he
was counseling me, he came so close to what I was
thinking I felt he was reading my thoughts. I suppose
that was why I was so impressed by what he said and
always listened when he spoke. (Maybe it was also
impressive because he never spoke unless he had
something to say.)

* * *

After the birth of his seventh child, he said, "I used
to give out cigars, but I've reached the point now

where the other fellow ought to give me one."

* * *

Jerome hadn't realized he had a sense of humor about his family's size.

Of his children, he often said, "Some people have money; I have nine children. I'm rich."

* * *

He loved the farm and he also liked carpenter work. Of the farm, he said, "This is the best place on earth to raise a family." A favorite expression of his concerning carpentry was, "There are tricks to every trade, but carpentry is all tricks." He also said, "You aren't a real carpenter until you can cover your mistakes with trim."

* * *

You have to go back now 30 or 40 years, to harvest time when the threshing was being done. Farmers would haul their grain into the elevators in horse-drawn wagons. Some of the wagons were of wood and some were heavy galvanized tin. You can imagine the noise that came over the prairie when these returned over the rough roads empty. They were especially noisy in the evening time. Although he was charitable, if someone came to the house and talked a great deal of nonsense, he'd be prompted to say when they left, "An empty wagon makes the most noise."

* * *

There was a long paragraph about the swimming pool, but it was so played down, as though not to offend, that its point was lost, and, anyway, a slash had been drawn through it. He went over and found the percolator empty, and began pacing to let his father know he was finished. Martin was in the doorway. "Well?" he said.

"I like it all."

His father came to the table and tapped the papers to-gether. "All? This isn't even a fraction of it. As I was put-ting this bit down, just trying to get organized, so many other scenes and events came to me, I realized I could write a book about that man." He stared beyond Jerome as if studying the imagined book, its heft and shape and size and color, with all the stories he'd told over the years compressed within its covers, its weight in the world, and where it would fit on the shelf above his desk, and then said, "And someday, I might. Now, though, I don't know if I'll be able to use any of this."

"What do you mean? What's the problem?"

"Oh, I don't know. It's all so personal. 'I'm not sure what Dad would think of it. He was a very sensitive man, as you know."

Jerome closed his mouth on what felt like an incoherent howl.

*

In the morning, at seven-thirty, he went to Mass with his father and Laura while the rest of the family slept in. The church was a mission, and Masses were said at seven-thirty one week and ten the next, alternately (on the early weeks many parishioners went to a Mass in Havana or Pekin, rather than get up so early), and was at the north edge of town, along the highway, across from a place called Mark's Superette, and resembled a wayside chapel, or modest-sized granary, except for its double entry doors of oak and a wooden cross in the gable Tom had in-stalled. The yard around it was enclosed by a wall of stone-faced cement blocks a few feet high, with a flat fin-ished cap crowning it, where everybody sat and gossiped after church, and in the lot to the right, bordered by an identical wall, was Mrs. Strawrick's house. It looked deserted now.

Into the vestibule, not much larger than a closet, where the holy water lay frozen all winter in a metal font at-tached to the inner doors with a wood screw. Three or four dozen people in the pews, many of them relatives; Jay and his wife and daughters, Fred and Fred Jr., Vince with his family, Tom and two of his boys, Elaine with

Tommy and Carl. Jerome had forgotten the knee
weren't padded. He stood for the opening of the Mass
realized, as if he'd risen up into it, that he had a he
ache.

He knelt. Drowsy and enervated from his late-ni
hours, he let the Mass enwrap him in its chrysalis of
miliarity, and felt his fever increase and genitals lift v
a gentle erection; the libidinous taint of these early-morn
Masses, the mingling of waking dreams with the antiqua
Latin, the somnambulistic movements of kneeling
sitting and standing, known by rote, the hand bells ring
at the altar like a distant recollection borne on the wind
the faith of childhood, candle flames dimming his c
science, a feeling of catharsis for the unkindnesses of
previous week, and a marshaling of faith to move v
more kindness, if he could, down the corridor of the n
Oh, chapel of light, the stuttering rays down my eye,
lid opening on a red-filmed scene, the slow process
there, then the light rising up, rays of it, along the
movable stare, the mask of it, immaculate eye, master o
Sexual love as kneeling at a shelter, her rose ass sp
nectar for a good kissing job.

He started from half sleep. At many of these e
Masses there weren't any altar boys, and his grandfat
would go to the communion rail and give the Latin
sponses, retained from boyhood, to the priest; the c
Sunday nights of Lent when the church wasn't hea
Stations of the Cross and then Benediction, the air suffu
with incense, myrrh, purplish smells, Jerome or Cha
swinging the thurible on its chains, hearing the congre
tion that never sang the rest of the year self-consciou
start the songs of Benediction, and then hearing his gra
father, whose quartet was reputed to have such g
harmony they made dishes vibrate on shelves, suddenly
lease his voice as if it were a bird he was releasing,
letting it soar over the others and lift them up with
making it seem a single voice was singing in many to
until the small building reverberated and began to det
itself from its foundation and glide through the last of
spring snows toward summer—or so it felt; Jerome's c
intimation of heaven—especially on the final hymn, "H
God, We Praise Thy Name," when it became clear

his grandfather's only means of expressing emotion was in song.

Everybody stood for the gospel, and then sat again for the sermon, if there was to be one; the priest was Father Hart-Donovan, a white-haired, ruddy outdoorsman, whose specialty was a fifteen-minute Mass. He drove a fast car that a gray Weimaraner always rode in, along with shotguns and shells, and if it was hunting season, he'd step up to the communion rail and say, "Because of our tardiness today, we will dispense with the sermon." A stock phrase, unlike his usual straightforward talk, and then he'd swing back to the altar and rattle through the Latin so rapidly you weren't ever sure whether he said it all or not. He'd gone pheasant hunting to Dakota a few times with Jay and Fred, and they claimed that once they got beyond the border of the state he put his rabat and collar at the bottom of a suitcase filled with clothes from a company called L. L. Bean, and said, "From now on, I'm Tim O'Brian to you guys, and if either of you calls me Father, or lets on I'm a priest, I'll quit hearing your confessions." And yet all he did, they said, was hunt so hard he wore them out, and was once delighted for days when the daughter of the rural couple they boarded with walked onto the porch one night and saw him with his back to her, and said, "Oh, excuse me, Mr. O'Brian," realizing he was taking an outdoors leak.

Today, though it must have been hunting season, he gave a sermon on daily devotion, which he said was not the sort of devotion that reminded him of a horse wearing blinders, but open-minded and questioning, so that one could see new meaning in the Scriptures, in the many mysteries of the Church that nobody seemed to find mysterious any more, now that there'd been some progress in how we lived, and in the everyday changes that took place in nature. Then each day you'd grow, he said, not only as a person, which would also happen, but closer to the Center of Peace of the Universe. He tipped his black-rimmed glasses upward as if to indicate.

Jerome's headache was gone. Father fiddled with the tacks that held the linen to the communion rail, a habit of his, and said, "As you know, we've lost C.J.C. He was a good man, a kind man, and thought so much about his faith you'd think he'd wear it thin, yet became more devout. He was an inspiration to us all with his daily devotion and who he was. Think what a blow it must be to the family to lose him. Offer some prayers this week to them, especially his widow, Marie. There'll be a Requiem for him tomorrow at ten, and the Rosary will be prayed tonight in the funeral home. Now let's say five Our Fathers and ten Hail Marys for the repose of his soul."

*

Jerome walked with Charles through ankle-deep leaves under the overarching elms around the old Opera House, dreading Crowley's, the wide-porched, well-kept, white-frame funeral parlor, and grateful that he'd been in it only once, to view his mother, when they passed an outdoor fireplace of brick that had a cornerstone with names and dates scratched into it, and felt a tug of undertow at his memory.

"That's sure lasted," he said.

"Uh-huh." Charles's hands were in his pockets and he seemed to be looking in every direction except where he intended to go.

They'd helped build the fireplace when they were eleven and twelve, along with Rose Marie's husband, Kev, a brick mason who was the Scoutmaster then, as part of their requirement for the masonry merit badge. Boy Scouts. He'd been in the funeral home another time. Kev wasn't a Catholic and had asked him to ask Mr. Crowley, who was, if the Scouts could have a can of mortician's wax to simulate injuries for a first-aid demonstration at a camporee in Peoria; Charles knew theatrical makeup from their father, and formed lumps and bruises colored with blue and green eye shadow, fashioned cuts and gashes with the wax, and then filled them with artificial blood, a general effect that was so gruesome visitors to their booth thought they'd brought in accident victims from the street, and Charles, who was figuring out how to fake a compound fracture with chicken bones, had to temper his realism.

They went along the Methodist church, with its stone buttresses and tall steeple, where a dozen Legionnaires had once gathered, backed by a second squadron around the Opera House, all armed with shotguns, and had noisily tried to rid the town of its overpopulation of pigeons. Shot rained down a whole day. Was the fall of the least pigeon known? If anybody didn't think so, they should be shat on. The wide porch on the corner of the block was brightly lit, and they started passing parked cars, then went up the steps and across the porch into the anteroom. The air was musty and smelled of some sort of cheese. From the long inner room, carpeted and hung with heavy drapes, he could hear the constrained and broken intakes of breath that couldn't be called sobs, and the mingled exclamations, as if a partly conscious crowd were trapped and in pain, which he'd heard only in this place, and thought that if only the living suffered, as far as was known, then why wasn't there a more humane and private way of alleviating the pain of death than funeral homes?

Charles left his side and an elderly woman in a long black dress, with gray and frizzily thinning hair, came out of the inner room on a cane, her head nodding with the effects of advanced age, and studied him from behind glasses with magnified gray eyes he'd seen before. He went to her and took her free hand, frail as ashes, and said, "Aren't you my Aunt Augustina?"

"Yes, I am," she said. "You must be one of Martin's boys."

"I'm Jerome."

"I think I've seen you twice, though I can't recall the times exactly now, but you surely do resemble your dad. He and your ma always seemed in such a rush when they visited us. Then you went to Illinois, then Clarence went, and the farm got such a shambles. Isn't this a shock about your grandpa, poor man? None of us up north could believe the news. He was through only last summer and all of us were saying how hale and healthy he looked then. I came down with your grandma's brother and sister, and was surprised at the drive. It's so long! We hardly had a chance to talk with Marie, we got in so late. Father Krull wanted so badly to come, too, but he's in a rest home now and feeling poorly, the dear soul. I don't believe I'll be able to go back in that room again. He looks too life-like to me. I keep expecting him to sit up and say, 'What's all this fuss about?' Why, I remember the day when—" Her eyes misted and her head began to wag once more. "Oh, but that's another story," she said, and patted his sleeve. "You go on in and see your grandpa, now."

At the far end of the inner room, in an alcove banked on three sides with flowers, against a raised and beige-lined casket lid, he thought he saw the profile of his grandfather, but looked away and saw him next to Adele, moving from one floral bouquet to the next, examining the cards on them, and then whispering to Adele what seemed words of comfort. Vince. Without his father alive, Vince seemed him.

Martin came in, his walk as burdened as if he'd aged ten years, and sat beside his mother and took her hand. Laura and Ginny followed and sat close. Susan and Marie came in clinging to one another, their heads inclined as if leaning into a terrible wind. Fred stepped out a door down a hall from the alcove with the funeral director, Mr. Crowley, a poker crony, carrying folding chairs, and helped Crowley and his assistant set them in rows, and then went into the anteroom, where businessmen and suppliers were standing around, picked up an unlit cigar, gripped it in his teeth, and began greeting people and resuming conversations as if he knew where each had left off.

Tom was in a chair in the corner farthest from the alcove, by himself, staring down, his big work-stained hands gripped between his thighs. Scott stood in another corner with his arms crossed and heavy eyebrows raised high. Emil was at the front of the room talking to Jay, whose face was gray-green and who leaned against the wall as if propped there, the mainstay, monetarily at least, of the family now. Davey came in without his glasses, an arm around Rosa's waist. Emil would talk to Jay and then break off and go to the casket and clasp his hands and stare at his father as if to recognize a familiar aspect there, and then unclasp them and put them on the casket's edge, his hip against it, angling his head to see his father more full in the face, and then return to Jay, but soon he'd be at the casket again, clasping, reclasping, repeating the same movements in a pattern as formal as a dance.

Rose Marie sat beside somebody Jerome didn't recognize, Kev. Kev didn't come to church and it was the first time Jerome had seen him out of his work clothes. His thick hair was slicked back and bore an indentation from his baseball cap. He sat with his elbows on his knees, in brown pants and a jacket with padded shoulders, murmuring as though to console Rose Marie, and looked more inconsolable than most of the sons.

Jerome went up to the casket so he could leave. He wouldn't look at his grandfather's face; even from a distance it appeared healthy in an artificial way, his hair lilac-colored under the hidden lights; with Jerome's mother the mortician had worked from an old photograph and her hair was waved in the style of the thirties, intolerable to look at, she'd been so vain about her hair and being in style. His grandfather's right hand rested over his abdomen. The fingers and back of it were scarred from accidents with tools, blue-ivory nicks. The upper joint of his little finger was gone. The tip of his index finger wasn't there. An angular piece was sliced away from the top of his thumb, and Jerome saw him and his grandfather in the shop that afternoon, planing down a cabinet door, when blood, thrown from the planer blade, flew over the ceiling and walls—more startling because there was no cry of pain—and spattered their clothes and faces and pooled on the planer table and soaked into the cabinet door, and then his grandfather held up the thumb and pinched its base, wrapped a handkerchief around it, and got into his panel truck and drove off to Martita.

A hand took hold of Jerome and an arm encircled him. "Áre you all right?" It was Emil. "I say, are you all right?"

"Yup," Jerome said, and heard the word in a watery ré-echo in his mind as though four different voices, none of them his own, had spoken.

"You don't look well," Emil said. "Here."

He was led somewhere and seated, and his hearing, which was blocked with a sound like the sea, cleared, and then the veil over his vision cleared, and he went back and sat beside Tom.

Father Hart-Donovan went to the *prie-dieu* at the head of the casket and everybody except the businessmen and Jerome's grandmother and father, who sat with his arm around her, knelt on the carpeted floor and prayed the Rosary. When it was over, people went to the alcove and began filing past the casket, and going out.

"I want to *see* him!" his grandmother said. "I want to say— I want to *see* him."

Martin and Davey took her under her arms and helped

her to her feet. Her knees gave out again. They got better holds, her gray coat bunching and rising above her dress, and she went forward a few steps, supported by them, as a foot lifted and dragged, and when they got close to the casket, said, "I can't, oh, no," and covered her mouth. They turned, their faces ashen, and began to walk her back, but she cried, "No, no, *no!*" and shoved them away with such force her hat flew off, and then turned and threw herself over her husband's chest. People in the crowd cried out. Martin and Davey tried to free her, but she wouldn't let go. Father Hart-Donovan came up and talked close to her ear, and she began to sink where she stood. He took hold of her, and then Martin got on the other side, and they brought her back to her chair again.

Tom and Tommy and Charles and Tim and Kev got up and walked out, and Jerome saw Emil start toward his mother, as he himself went down the hall where he'd first seen Fred, hoping Fred could bring some detachment to the air. He opened the door where the funeral director and Fred had come out with the chairs, and was in a white room with glass-covered cases that held surgical-looking equipment and tools. A white porcelain table tilted up toward him at an angle. There was the perforated plate of a drain at the lower end of it.

*

He stared up at the oblong, too hot with the covers and yet chilled without them, physically ill, and then heard movement in the other bedroom and the sound of bare feet, and Charles, silvery and mirage-looking in the moonlight, came through the door. He searched over the desk and then part of his face was bronzed by a match; he got the cigarette going and sat.

"Could I have one of those?" Jerome asked.

Charles jumped in the chair. "Oh, you're awake. I ran out. I'm sorry. Did I wake you?"

"No."

"Oh, good." He lit a cigarette from the one he had going and passed it on. "How are you feeling?"

"Fair." With the cold he had, cigarettes tasted like the black papery crust around burned marshmallows.

"I'm never going to a funeral again," Charles said.

"I know."

"God!"

Their orange-and-red cigarette ends flared and faded and glided from place to place as if in calligraphic communication with one another.

"I'm going to quit school," Charles said.

"Oh?"

"I'm going out to California or New York."

"Why?"

"Act. See Lionell. Be a bum. What's the difference. There's no use hanging around here. This isn't home any more. It doesn't even feel like the same house."

"Mmmb," Jerome said. Charles had a tendency toward theatrics and was usually too hard on others and, sometimes, himself.

"I don't even feel Dad wants me around any more. It's worse than catching hell. Shit! School's a bore anyway. It's just that Jill— A couple of weeks ago I got a letter from Laura wondering why my checking account in town was overdrawn ten dollars. 'Because I wrote a check,' I felt like writing back. Dad always used to cover those piddly amounts. Oh, hell," he said, and crushed out his cigarette and handed the ashtray to Jerome. "I'm going to sleep."

"Me, too," he said, and rolled over and reached to put the ashtray on the floor, but was hardly aware of it touching down. He'd had an image of Kev again in the funeral home. Kev had been through the worst of the Pacific campaign—Iwo Jima, Tarawa, Okinawa—with the Marines, and had come back so shell-shocked and mentally displaced it was difficult for him to cope with everyday instances without seeing life and death in them. He read Zane Greys and other Westerns over and over, and then, with the advent of TV, had release at the turn of a knob. Their grandfather hired him, out of compassion, at first, and Kev discovered he liked masonry; a few years later he married Rose Marie. Their grandfather once said he thought it was time for Kev to become foreman of a crew, and Kev said, "Thank you, but no. I'll stick right here with masonry, if you don't mind. I'm perfectly satisfied with it." Prepared for the occasion. He was devoted to his family and had evolved into one of the few truly serene men Jerome knew. The only war story he'd heard from Kev was waking in a foxhole to shots, and then a Japanese officer falling into the foxhole on top of him, dead, but the officer also must have shot; Kev's buddy was dead, too.

Tom once went rabbit hunting with a carpenter he was friends with, Ed Jorgensen, and as they were climbing a fence Jorgensen's .22 went off and hit Tom in the calf and the slug passed between both bones without touching them. Jorgensen kept saying, "He went up in the air higher than the fence we just climbed." Which reminded Jerome that Tom had also been a hurdler in high school, besides putting the shot and throwing the disc. The javelin was outlawed while Tom was in school, because a by-stander had been pierced by one. He lived.

Once when Emil was in Forest Creek (he came home a week or so each year), he took Jerome and Charles, boys then, out to the creek the town was named for, pale brown water over low sand bars, and let them pull the trigger of his .38, trained at a floating bottle. Davey made a home movie of the event: The noiseless pistol kicks back in Jerome's and Emil's hands. The camera looks at the bottle. There's a spout of water beside it. Another one. Then the bottle sends a fan-shaped spray of fractured shards across the creek, and rolls and begins to sink as the camera returns to the two of them with big grins. There's a disconcerting blur in the foreground, and then the lens pulls back and focuses, and the blur becomes the silver-colored hair of Grandpa Neumiller. He turns, makes a sign of apology, and steps out of the frame.

Footsteps that sounded tentative and unfamiliar, and yet padded with a sureness out of the past—Jerome saw a sudden specter of Donny Ennis—came over the other room toward him, and then a figure stepped through the door. Charles. He held himself in a different way and his body gave off emanations of uncontrolled emotional surges that were fuguelike but somehow contained. He was sleep-walking. It was the first Jerome had known him to do it. He sat on the bed and his head sank low and bobbed, and he said, "Yeah. Uh-huh. Orange grapefruits. Burn or burden the ring." It was the voice he used when he did Shakespeare. He lay and turned and crawled up the bed, and Jerome, on his side, his hand still on the floor, swung his ass toward him, a position he'd felt complications about, and kicked back his leg, and Charles wrapped both of his around it and dropped an arm across him. He could feel against his thigh Charles's erection grow and throb with his blood beat. Charles sighed. It was how they'd slept together in the double bed— In *this* bed when it was in their room in the house in Hyatt.

Jerome feel asleep. He dreamed about a Japanese woman whose arched body traveled in a second in and out of seven different planes around his enwrapped and heated core as it strode underwater and struck and rocked down narrowing hard-ribbed shore, and he felt from below his scrotum to the end of his expanded glans, a straight line, like a string tripped, strum and sob and open with affection on the bud, the flower, the ring of flesh, and the open door.

*

Martin and Fred stayed at the funeral home and sat up with their father's body through the night.

*

He woke to an empty bed with a fever, grayness in the room, a fullness in his head, and his joints stiff and aching—all the symptoms of the flu. But from where did the gray rain come? His teeth chattered as he got into his suit and tie, and after his first cup of coffee downstairs he was still being racked by disconnected, unpredictable chills he couldn't shake off. He shivered on the way to the funeral home, shivered through a service in a chapel there, conducted for the immediate family, and then aunts and uncles went up to the casket, one by one, for the last time. Martin and Davey tried to help their mother to her feet, but she jerked her elbows around as if irritated by their continual attentions and went to the casket, alone, a handkerchief in one hand, and put her palms to her husband's cheeks and kissed his lips. As she turned away, she kept patting one cheek, as if he were a child of hers asleep, and then covered her face.

The casket lid was closed. The funeral director fastened it down with metal cranks. The grandsons who were pallbearers stayed in the room, as they'd been told to by

Crowley, who had chronic laryngitis and a habit of looking up from the tops of his eyes, and usually wore a gray homburg. He said in a whisper, "The oldest boys, Jerome and Chuck, will be here at the head, where the cross is, and then we'll sort of go down in age but keep the heights balanced. You tall guys, don't lift too high now. The head's the heaviest and the shorter guys are there . . ." Emil's son, Greg, would walk at the head of the casket, and Paul at its foot; Kev was home with the younger children and Paul was wearing the jacket with the padded shoulders his father had worn the night before, and looked as inconsolable as Kev.

Crowley whispered, "At the church we'll have a dolly there at the doors, because the aisle's too narrow for carrying down, and you just put the casket on that. Try to follow Jerome and step off with him, now. He'll also be driving his dad's car, and it'll be the first behind me." He put his homburg, black today, on his bald head. "Now we'll get this into the hearse, and I'll explain some more."

The casket was of walnut, lovely wood. There were tubular rails along each side for carrying. "When I say lift," Crowley whispered, "all of you lift up at the same time. Now *lift*." It was heavier than Jerome supposed; the weight of it pulled his left shoulder low. Then Tommy shifted his stance and Jerome was holding nothing. They carried it out a pair of back doors, down a ramp, and slid it forward over the rollers in the floor of the hearse. Corwley locked it in place. Jerome got behind the wheel of his father's car, Tommy got in next to him, his face contradictory and tense, and Jerome began shivering again as the other pallbearers piled in and the family formed behind.

The cortege pulled out. It wound through the streets of Pettibone and onto the highway, toward the church, which was apparently filled; people were standing in the walled yard around it, and others were gathered along the sidewalk in front. Out, and moving under the directions of Crowley, Jerome and the rest slid the casket from the hearse, went up an embankment to the sidewalk, went up the sidewalk to the church, up the steps to its doors, and placed the casket on the dolly. A few years ago his grandfather had persuaded Father to have an organ installed, an electric one, and a rear pew was removed to accom-

modate it; the nuns who came each week to teach catechism were gathered on chairs around it, ready to sing.
Jerome looked at the filled church, at the businessmen
and neighbors and friends, and then his eyes filmed and
he had an image of milk spilling down a wooden stairs.

The pallbearers went to a front pew roped by a purple
tie, and the Requiem began. The sound of the nuns' voices
and the organ filled the church with a feminine appeal
that seemed to emphasize it was fall. Father came to the
communion rail. "I hardly know where to begin," he said.
"I find it difficult to even speak. I've known C.J.C. for
twenty years now, and he was one of my best friends."
Jerome didn't hear another word; it was so personal, he
knew if he listened he would, like Fred, be blowing his
nose with vehemence, and, like Fred, would have to get
up and leave the church. And then Tom got up and left,
too.

At the end of the Requiem, Jerome and the others followed the casket to the doors. Fred and Tom were standing
in a corner of the yard, their backs to them, and Fred had
a hand on Tom's shoulder. The grandsons lifted the casket
and carried it down to the sidewalk. The slow and uneven
step and scrape of their feet on the cement. The casket
swaying with their steps. Flesh without which they would
not be. A turn, another sidewalk, the irregular step and
rattle of their feet over the leaves. Cars sighing past on
the highway beside them.

The casket rumbled over the rollers and was locked in
place. Jerome got into the following car, Charles and
Tommy and Luke and Carl and Fred Jr. and Tim got in,
and there was a wait as the other cars filled. Then the
hearse began to move toward the corner, past a large hall
where the Stars of the East used to meet, by a house,
then another, the last on this edge of town, and then it
moved faster and Jerome followed, past a vacant lot, the
swimming pool, then started the climb to the Catholic
cemetery, a weedy, untended cemetery on a sandhill,
with a wrought-iron fence, pushed down in spots by van-
dals, around it on three sides; through the gate, broken
off its hinges and perpetually open, and up to the top of
the hill. The hearse stopped. There was a dark mass of
movement on the hilltop. A hundred or more people were
gathered around a canvas shelter where a hump of dirt,

covered with a carpet of artificial grass, lay like a huge log.

The grandsons stood at the rear of the hearse and waited for the funeral party. It couldn't have been more than fifty degrees (Jerome's shoulders kept twitching with chills), but he saw big beads of sweat form on Tommy's forehead and run down his wrists below his sleeves. Crowley whispered, Jerome and Charles took hold of the head, Luke and Tommy took hold, then Carl and Fred Jr., and when the casket was clear of the hearse Tommy's hand slipped off the tubular rail. He stepped away, horrified that it had, and the entire weight of the corner bore down on Jerome. He skipped back to brace himself and there was a shock as he stopped the others. Across from him, Charles was flashing white and gray. Jerome took hold with both hands and could see his face, his glasses, reflected in the casket, and decided to become a priest. A *priest?* What kind of slip was that? No, a doctor, a doctor for life!

Crowley pulled a handkerchief from his breast pocket and handed it to Tommy, and he gripped the carrying rail with it. They moved next to the grave and placed the casket on the velvet-curtained platform. Jerome stepped back to make room for his father and grandmother and uncles and aunts, who were taking seats on the folding chairs under the shelter, and saw, on a flat-bed truck a few feet away, a headstone of granite with *Neumiller* across it, and at its bottom, on the right side, his grandfather's name and the dates of his birth and death, and, on the other side, his grandmother's name, with the date of her birth and a blank square. Beside him was the grave of his mother. Beside it was an oval marker over the grave of the daughter she'd lost in childbirth. The ground that covered them was covered with oak leaves. Oh, Lord, give me a chance, he thought.

Standing close were Augustina, his grandmother's brother and sister, J. D. Prell, Alex Craig, the Cunliffes and the Shaws, and, farther back, Mrs. Strawrick, who shook her head when he caught her eye, appalled by death. Luis and Martita came up and stood on either side of him. In another part of the crowd, higher up, were a dozen of his father's former students, one of them in an Air Force uniform. From the height of the hill he could see the empty swimming pool, and remembered that in his grandfather's last years, when there was little for him to do, he'd come to the pool to check the buildings and equipment, or back-flush the filters, and once heard him say, "When I die, I want to be buried on the hill there, facing the pool, so I can watch my grandchildren."

Father read the graveside rites and then raised a round-headed aspergillum and gave it a shake, and droplets of water scattered over the casket and drew up into mounded beads on the waxed wood. Father rested a hand at the casket's head and turned his eyes up as with a private thought, and the crowd began to disperse and move down the hill.

Gayle was beside Fred, a hand of his in hers, her black-hatted head on his shoulder. Martin sat with a handkerchief in a clenched fist. Laura leaned and whispered to him. He nodded and rose as if from sleep, turned to his mother, and then his knees gave out as hers had. Jerome started for him, but Laura was there. He leaned on her and took hold of a chair until his strength returned, and then got his mother to her feet. He put an arm around her and gripped her free elbow, and they started down the hill with heavy strides, their heads bowed close, and Jerome realized that one of the reasons they'd moved to Illinois was so his father could be close to his mother, and if this hadn't been so, if they'd been different people, or if there'd been a difference in their relationship, then perhaps his father might not have been able to exist after their mother died, and what would they have done without a father?

Jerome got into the car, where Charles and the cousins were waiting, and drove out of the cemetery toward town. Tommy turned to Carl and said, "Is Mom back there?" Carl craned to see out the rear window and said, "No," while the car swayed them all in time to the end of this. Tommy punched the cigarette lighter and pulled out a mashed pack of Lucky Strikes. He shook out two, lit them both, and handed one to Jerome. "Here," he said, "I thought you could use one of these. Jeez, it's really something to think he's dead and going inside that ground there, isn't it?"

*

On the way to Forest Creek on Wednesday, on the way back to school, Jerome tried to think of what to say to help console his grandmother, and saw, halfway there, a black man, the first he'd seen in the county, working on a power-line crew; the man kept his head down Uncle Tom-ishly, but Jerome could feel his eyes feed on him. Good.

They went into the house without knocking and found their grandmother in the dining room, at the table where she'd laid out so many meals for them, staring out the picture window toward the shop. The room was overlaid with a light that made the walls seem insubstantial. At the sight of him and Charles, her lips compressed, tears started dropping off her jaw, and she shook her head as if in apology. Jerome kissed her cheek and she held him from the chair. "I know," he said. "I'll miss you. I'll write. Dad has some good new for you. Marie will be staying here." He chafed her hand between his. "Grandpa was always very strong, and what he'd probably want now is for us to try and be half as strong. It's a way of showing we believed in him."

His words sounded rehearsed in his ears, but she pulled herself from the chair and clung to him for so long he was sure she'd never let go, and he felt how stout and healthy her body was, and must always have been.

*

Two weeks later, at school, he got a letter from his father, thanking him for being so helpful at such a difficult time. He mentioned that Lionell had called from California, sounding drunken and emotional, and wondered why he hadn't been notified in time to attend the funeral, which he surely would have done. "I called your Grandma Jones the same morning I called you at school," he wrote, "and assumed she told him." He also enclosed a clipping from the Pettibone *Courier-Express*.

CARD OF THANKS

As a teacher, much of my life has been taken up with giving assignments to others, and now the family has given me one—that of saying thank you to a community for the many favors that were extended to help console us during our loss and your loss of C.J.C. We are all grateful, but we know, too, that if Dad could have had a last wish it would have been that there be little time spent in grieving and mourning his passing. We all have work to do—our daily work and the more important work of being kind and helpful to one another. No man was more successful in that sense than he. After another thank you from all of us, then, let's be about my father's business.

Tearfully submitted,
Martin C. Neumiller

Jerome put the letter and clipping down on his desk and stared at the wall for an hour. That night he dreamed about a hawk, a hawk high above the crossroads of Hyatt, and saw from its height how it was to watch a dozen shadowed figures of children scatter from the playground of the parochial school and go running down the darkening streets in different directions toward the smells of supper rising in as many individual ways as there were lit and ordered homes anchored along the blocks below, while ahead of him, over the fading squares of fields and summer fallow, lay the dark mass of Hawk's Nest, his unoccupied and rooted throne. Home again with a settling of wings in a cottonwood in the night air. Home again. *Home.*

39

TO GRANDMA JONES

[Portions of this letter, as indicated by ellipses, have been deleted due to the personal nature of the material.—ED.]

606 Race
Urbana, Ill.
April 26, 1963

Dear Grandma.
This must be about the dozenth time. I've tried to write in many different ways and moods, as you probably know, but no words came. I've been trying since last November, when Lionell called and said Grandpa was dead. I was so shocked that none of what I said or wanted to say got through to you. I still don't think he's dead. I see him somewhere in a childlike part of me, and although I know that in the terms of the world he's gone, he's still not for me. He never really will be either, unless I come to California, which I'd like to do at this point in my life, and see that he isn't there with you and Lionell, or if I ever went to Minnesota to the farm and didn't see him there. Walk out the door. And then Lionell was also saying that you were very sick too and so I've been trying to write ever since.
Part of what happened was when I heard about Grandpa, I'd just received a part in a play, a major one where the acting is all-important, and that was Richard II. I've been trying to compliment myself on the role to compensate for how I feel, but I can't. All I can say is it's of the most direct and honest

things I've been through. My director was excellent and drove me up to the stars, so all I had to do was keep a straight face and once in a while smile at him. As the lady in the costume room keeps saying, "You've got a life. Live it awhile, kid." .

That's one production. Then this spring I was asked by the same director and had the very good fortune to be Estragon in Waiting for Godot. Do you know it? Well, Gogo, or Estragon, is this tramp who— Oh, well, your guess is as good as mine. He talks a lot. Sound familiar? But he has to keep the audience up, or interest in the play a Gogo going, and just being smart isn't enough. So here I am, from a king to a bum, huh? What do you say? Or as the king I recently played put it, "Thus play I in one person many people, and none contented." I'm still up on it.

Because I haven't seen you or written for so long, I feel like a lump of avocado pit we put in a jar in grade school once, and then watched it grow, which it did, just barely, but did! I wish I could say now that I have a lot of blossoms all in a row for you. That sounds like the sort of stuff I'm trying to read!

I've been thinking of you so much, I've even written a poem.

> *Thank you, thank you,*
> *Dearest Grandmother, and*
> *Thank you over again.*
> *You've loved and honored*
> *Me all of these years,*
> *Just by being the person you've been.*

Remember all the good times we had together on the farm? I'd walk to the old sunken foundation where the ice blocks were kept under sawdust, and say to Lionell, "Summer is here." It's a way of life I still have left because of you. I remember, too, how we did the dishes and went picking berries together, and how you once leaned against a counter where I was standing and it seemed your weight held up the house. I think you were doing a crossword puzzle.

Well, I know you were because its squares are still a part of me. Forgive me for everything, Grandma, dear . . .

. . . and remember thinking how you were in a way really my mother. I mean, my mother since she's been gone. And you seemed to understand that and, what's more, intended it to be . . . and in another way were more than my mother because you and I always agreed—didn't we?—and I used to argue with her about the ways of life. But you were never angry with me in any sort of way and not ever a fuss, because it seems that even you knew that you meant more than my mother to me. And our relationship has been intact for a much longer time. When I disagreed with her in the way that I did, for instance, it was only her way of telling me she would die soon, I realize now. So I've seen that, too. And I've known you, from the best I can tell, from the day I was three and her only until I was nine, and that's all she knew me. But you've been in touch from the time I was eight or less. So see how much I owe you? You've kept me alive. That's why I had to write this, even if it is hurried, and get it off right away. I'm not even going to look at it again, although I see my handwriting looks funny on some pages. Here. This is for you.

> *Helen, thy beauty is to me*
> *Like those Nicean barks of yore,*
> *That gently, o'er a perfumed sea,*
> *The weary, wayworn wanderer bore*
> *To his own native shore.*

> *All of my love forever,*
> *Charles*

[This letter was returned to Charles by Olivia, his grandmother's oldest sister, who said in her letter to him that his grandmother had died of abdominal cancer two days before Charles's letter arrived, and commiserated with him for the way circumstances had come together; and then said that she would be more than willing to take over—

if he was agreeable, of course—the job of being his
mother from now on. A radiantly speckled maple leaf
lying in blue shadow on the sunshaft-lit seat of a worn and
well-used old captain's chair.—ED.]

Five

࿐

40

FIVE AT THE TABLE

"What's the time?"

"What's the difference?"

"Who wants to know?"

"Where's it at, Captain Marvel?"

"Eat it up," said Neil.

There were five of them at the table. Jackie, the girl with the small hands, sat next to Vi, and Neil and Charles were across from the girls; Happy, who never smiled and had a pseudonym, was at the end of the table, near the steps, fiddling with a light meter from his camera case. They'd been coming into this coffee-house for the last couple of days, though they seldom bought so much as a cup of cappuccino, and the proprietor of the place, Chip, dark and burly, with a Manhattan sense of humor, was more than indulgent to them, and managed to persuade them to sit at a window table as bait. "Smile. Look stoned. Those people from Des Moines and Peoria expect to see freaks like you in a Village coffeehouse." But this afternoon, after a rooftop soiree where the five had poked down a joint apiece, except for Hap, they were so obviously high and unable to contain it that Chip, looking forbidding and concerned, told them to sit in the back room (did he actually care about them?) until they cooled off. It was down three steps from the main part of the restaurant and dimly lit, with a low tin ceiling and three windows along the top of its left wall; a drifter who sometimes waited tables was sleeping across some chairs in a corner, and somebody else was at the rear, in shadow, tuning up a twelve-string guitar; otherwise, they had the room to themselves.

"God," Vi said. "Even tones sound off."

"What's the time?" Jackie asked again.

Her hands had always seemed small to Charles, but now, with his senses bending under the deliquescent effects of Red—or was it Gold?—high-class hemp, they looked unnaturally so, miniature and grotesque, a pair of sudden deformities she was exhibiting on the tabletop—why? —and when they were on the roof (they tried the entries of walk-ups and, when they found one that opened, went up five flights, and then up the sixth and onto the roof to smoke; a cop would have to come through the raised doorway they sat behind to catch them at this level, and by that time they could throw everything overboard) —when they were smoking on the roof, Neil, handing the weed to Charles, whispered, "Dig Jackie's teeny hands. Freaky."

They were prancing around her face, turning on their wrists, performing near her mouth, posing on her chin, and now an index finger tapped her front teeth below her lip that curved up in such a fleshily wrinkled way that whenever Charles could forget about her hands and focus there he felt the buzzing strum of a beginning erection come on.

"Freaky."

Neil was a danger to Charles in reverse. He was eighteen, from Florida, and was now in the Army at Fort Dix —" 'Military Reservation' is right," he said, tugging a skimpy juvenile mustache the Army allowed him to grow, dark-brown, though he had carroty-red hair. He got a pass each weekend ("My master sergeant's gay") and appeared in the Village in a multicolored Mexican pullover with a brown karate belt around it ("I earned that"), a leather headband, a gold ring in his right ear, and went to the weekend acting classes at the David Neuman Modern Acting Studio. Charles, a summer student there, met him through Neuman, in a way; when students disagreed with Neuman, a cruel and demanding Malvolio with streaks of Richard III in him, he sent them onstage and had them perform an improvisation while he, a flawless mimic, mocked every unmotivated move they made, for the entertainment of the rest of the class, all of whom had to laugh or face being the next ones up, and Neil and Charles were appearing onstage so often, sometimes together, it was only natural for Neil to sell Charles a bag of grass so heavily cut with oregano all it gave him was a headache. He'd been promising to make it up to him ever since, as a friend.

"The hands, the hands," Neil said now, and nudged him, and Charles, who'd just received the rapidly approaching roach from Vi, drew on it, his lips hissing as he carbureted in the way that was right for him, and then, stepping down on it with his diaphragm, turned and saw that Jackie's wide brown eyes, moist and dilated the more she smoked, were fixed on him with unconstrained fluidity; smoke was escaping from her lips and slithering through her stare, a waste.

Only sixteen, he thought, and wondered how often she'd smoked this much.

She came up and stood inches away, her upper lip curving up into the architecture of his high, and whispered, "Jesus, was that beautiful."

"What's that?" The words came out in two squeaks from his constricted throat.

"The way you knocked down that toke." Her eyes defocused and then held him with their force again. "It's the most beautiful thing I've seen in my life!"

Neil, next to a ventilator, turned and lay face down and slapped the roof, and cried, "Love at first sight! Love at first sight!" The sunlight gilding his red-gold hair as he rolled.

On their way back, at a metal grate set into the sidewalk, Charles jittered over to Jackie and said, "You see those little bars? Those are little steps. They all go uphill." And then started climbing them. She followed, grabbing on to his belt, and they went straining, leaning forward, holding the side of the building for leverage and balance, going uphill for so long the others got dazed and went on ahead, and when they reached the peak, the summit of the end, the sidewalk, it was only natural for him to take her in his arms (enormous breasts encased in cloth taut as upholstery) and kiss those lips he admired. A policeman rapped on his back with a bat. "Hey," he said. "You two kids been using dope?"

"Yup," Charles said.

"You're high?"

"High as a kite." Kites? The officer looked surprised

under his visor. Was that a flash of a smile from him? He wasn't much older than Charles and had motives in his eyes that were uncommonly well mixed.

"Go on, get out of here. You kind of kids make me sick."

Did he smile again?

"But, sir, we're really high-flying. Honest. Don't you want to arrest us?" Because Neil had told him you couldn't be arrested if you were high but not in possession. Was that true? Jackie, pale amber under her tan, took his arm and led him off, and said, "Don't do that again. It takes some balls, I know, but don't ever do that around me again, you hear?"

"What's the time?" she asked now.

"Come off it."

"Who cares?"

"Plenty of time for you, baby," Neil said.

"Why do—" Charles was interrupted by a delayed laugh.

Jackie came to the Village nearly every day in faded Levi's and a boat-neck top, and every day around six had to have somebody ride home with her on the subway because she was afraid of "perverts" and "the colored," as she called them, and yesterday was Charles's first turn at the task and after an hour-long lurching and clackety ride ("When these get going fast like this with that big zip, I get my gun," Jackie whispered, out of breath, in his ear) that left him in a vague and shattered limbo, the squealing of steel still running ribbons around where his ears should have been, he found himself among high rises with well-kept gardens and parks surrounding them—the Bronx?—and as he joined Jackie in the elevator of one of the most ostentatious of the crenelated banks of flower-bordered buildings, he saw that a single button, *Penthouse,* was lit; her father was a producer, her mother a movie actress, she scatted to him on the way up, *ooo,* and neither of them ever got back to this blankety place until after eight—and then the doors clattered back, she gave him a kiss on the cheek, ran over carpetry that covered her tennies to a copper-painted door, and started digging through her purse, a teenager afraid of her parents and the potential she felt in men, and then the corridor in which she was exposing this protected part of herself for his eyes only was encroached upon by shuddering torms, the black-joined elevator doors, and he fell back toward earth again, a blind light hurtling along the world.

He blinked and his head jerked—Jackie was across the table from him—and suddenly he had to have some sort of solidity. He leaned against the wall somewhere behind, but his center of equipoise stayed where his head had been, and the three shafts of rectangular sunlight, slanting in from the high windows down to the floor, were so substantial in the dim room they were buttresses supporting the wall he touched. How? New ingenuities? His fanny felt hot.

Neil had his elbow on the tabletop, forearm up, in arm-wrestling position, and with nobody opposing him was grunting and straining and trying to make a press—his face was crimson, beads of sweat arrayed over his forehead—and Charles realized he was taking on the world.

"I gotta know the time," Jackie said. "If they ever found out I've been down here, they'd break my back. Ma used to live in the Village, you know. Besides, it feels so strange—being so early, I mean. I mean, being early in the day. Isn't it? I can't explain. I never get stoned before three o'clock."

Neil tried so hard not to laugh that a spray of mist, triangular-shaped, radiated around his lips and began to disperse, fine streamers trailing down from it, into a slow and dim-silver fade through the shaft of sunlight Charles was staring at while *he* tried to control himself. He couldn't look at Jackie or Neil, who were laughing the strained and tattered laughter of those so stoned they can't be sure they're attracting all the attention they think they are, if they are, because he was giddy, giggling, higher than he'd been in his life, which made their laughter like rising water beneath his giddiness, lifting it from below his tightening beltline until he saw he was sliding up the shaft of sunlight, *up* it not down, defying the laws of nature and going in shaking leaps up the buttresses and through the window into the green world.

"Hey," Hap said. "Did you all see that broad?"

The other four turned passive and solemn and their heads, in unison, swiveled toward the doorway behind him.

"No, no," Hap said. "Not here, not now. Jeez, you guys must all be stoned." His close-cropped hair began so far back from his forehead he looked perpetually startled, and with alternate thumbs he kept clearing his eyebrows of sweat, and then flicking them clean, fine spray flying in the light again. "No, I mean that broad I was talking to outside, the blonde, the bombshell, the *big* one. She must have been six feet three. And did you see those knockers on her? Whoh! She was some kind of high-class dish."

"That's a hell of a way to talk about a woman," Vi said, her voice throaty and green-blue with accusing shame.

"Zooks!" Neil said, and hooked his thumbs together and began waving his outstretched hands until they seemed wings, and then were. "Up, Bird of Paradise, seeker after truth, big fella." The wings beat more boldly and began to lift his arms. "Hey, up there! High! High!" He was drawn out of his seat and the wing tips started stuttering slappingly against the tin ceiling. "Eee! Eee! Eee! Motor scooter roto-rooter! *Wheels!* Vine and roses. Jigalong, please. Tote dat barge, lif dat— Hear dem gulls creak! D and D! OD! Take my hand now," he said, and as Charles reached out and Neil sank down it seemed everybody remembered being stoned again, except for Hap, of course, who stared at them with his startled look ("He'll want testimonials later," Neil said), encased in a pair of Tyrolean lederhosen with brightly embroidered braces that formed an H over his T-shirt, so you'd know him whether you were too inwardly spaced to see or hadn't met him in your life or seen him when you did. He was older, thirty or so, and could usually be found near the Square in his shorts and knitted knee socks with a gadget bag and two or three cameras dangling, professional tools; he sold dope and used the equipment for making deliveries (*acid* in a camera?), as if involved in some kind of Eastern European Communistic espionage.

"You can let go of my hand now," Neil said.

Had Charles ever had hold of it?

"I said that's a hell of a way to talk about a woman," Vi said again.

"What do you know?" Hap said.

"I know you bass-ackwards, buddy boy."

"Bull!" Hap was always stopping young, long-legged, big-breasted girls in the street, his face running and glistening with the perspiration that beleaguered him, and saying, after some everyday talk, "Hey, you want to pose for a couple nudies? I got dope." It was enlightening to hear about the kind and number of comers he had, and Vi was one, and an ex-one at that. She sang ballads and blues in a voice that brushed down close to a baritone, a bassoon moving in and out of textured melodies, in a beat-up basement coffeehouse that seemed to keep changing hands every week and acquiring with each change a new name and a different shade of paint around its presently zebra-striped doorway, where burnt and unpalatable espresso, awful coffee, was served for a dollar a cup and a hat was hourly passed for the poor performers. She'd been sleeping there, too, recently, and was beginning to look worn and middle-aged, though she was only twenty or so; black hair oily and thin, pinched into a frizzy bun, violet stains of fatigue beneath her eyes; and she'd begun wearing matronly skirts and homemade blouses of calico, as though preparing to die a pioneer in New York.

"Oh, jeez," she said. "This grass of yours is fallin' apart inside a me, Hap."

"That's you, not the stuff. It's first-class, ask your friends."

"Hey," Jackie said, and leaned toward Charles, pressing her breasts into the tabletop until their tips were flattened into two round areas the size of saucers ("Dig it," Neil whispered), which made her hands, lying in front of them, shrink even more. "Hey, have you ever been to the Top of the Six's?"

"The only place I've ever been," Charles said, "is right here."

Her hands began leaping in the air as if being manipulated by strings, and Charles, in this sentient state supplied by the herb of the earth, realized that somebody must have told her once that she had attractive hands. The purposeful and malign cruelty to children of family friends afraid to confront adults. "It's really neat," she said. "I go there with my folks. They say, 'Where do you want to go this weekend, Jack?' And I say, 'The Top of the Six's,' and we go there and get our table by the window and look out at the park while we eat, at all the lights and taxis moving around down there, and I order butterfly steak. It's beautiful, thin as paper, and evaporates up your nose. And I have wine. They let me have all the wine I want from their bottle and it really sends me up, looking down on the park like that. I want to go there with you and sit at our table and look right at you while we eat. Would you like that?"

"Yes," Charles said.

"Would you like to do it with me?"

"I certainly would."

"Do you have a suit?"

"I used to."

"I'll have to have you wear one there."

"I'll wear one for you."

"I'll pay!"

"Neil," Vi said. "Will you watch me if I get really sick?"

"Right," he said. "I feel it, too."

"Will you watch out for me?"

"Right, baby."

"Because I'm goin' over that line, Neil. I'm headed for it right now."

"I gotcha," he said, his flexed toes beating in a frantic rhythm that made the table wobble, and then leaned to Charles and funneled into his ear in a baby voice, "She's on coke. Been on it a year. Baa-aaa-aaad shit." His leg kept beating and the table swayed up and around as though asserting its existence among them now, more rectangular than square, oblong, with a red-colored carved wooden top.

"Do you know how to handle headwaiters?" Jackie asked.

"I guess," Charles said.

"Because Ma called the one at the Top of the Six's a finicky old bitch."

"I gotcha," Charles said. Did she mean this?

Hap pointed a camera around, and said, "Boy, is this shadow nice."

"You're tellin' *me,* Hap?" Neil cried. "Hooo-*wheee!* Just watch it you don't get my head guillotined in that mother, you hear?"

"I used to have such pep," Vi said. "I ain't got no more pep. Shit."

The table seemed to tilt up toward Charles and he saw both of Neil's legs going at it underneath now, and then Neil began pressing his fingertips on the tabletop in patterns, as if chording on a piano. He leaned his ear close to his hands to listen for a time. His eyes closed. Ah. His face was boyish, and with his thin mustache, which he darkened with mascara (he often slept over), he reminded Charles of photographs of World War I R.A.F. aces—the same feverish bravado in his eyes, with the unnamable tentativeness behind, and when he laughed they went out of focus and looked homicidal and crazed.

Vi studied him, her hazy stare glazed but direct and considering, and said, "You know what coke does to your insides? It eats 'em up. I can feel every frigging cell in my goddamn bod."

"That's it!" Neil said.

"Every one has a set of teeth along the side, real sharp, and they're eating up the side that's left. Cannibals. Imagine that. Look at me and think of that. All those things like alligator teeth in there. *Here.*"

"A crocodile. He's the color of your eyes. He's in your belly," Neil said. *"Grarf!"*

"Ah!" Vi cried, and covered her face.

"Why don't you lay off?" Hap asked.

"Lay off who?" Neil said.

"No, no. Why doesn't she lay off that crap?"

"What we're into here is shock therapy," Neil said. "You dig it, Hap?"

"Bull."

"You want a charge?"

"Why don't you lay off that stuff?" Hap said to her.

Vi moved her eyes to him and they turned as cold as the reptiles around at the edge of hallucination. "Sit on your thumb, you bugger," she said, and poked out her tongue.

"Hey, Hap, why don't you come on up?" Neil said. "Use some of that classy stuff you got. Don't bother to run up on a roof. Eat an ounce here like wheat germ. A bowl, waiter! Or pop one of your"—he picked up a camera of Hap's and looked at its lens—"pop one of your handy Nikon tabs."

"Hands off, asswipe," Hap said, and grabbed it from him.

"Hey, hey, I'ze jes funnin' ya, Hap. A hee hee." A wave of violence radiated from Neil and surges of it kept coming in broadening bands that grew denser in hue. In spite of his boyish face and mustache, he was rough, trim and compact, with concave cheeks granular from acne, a

thick scar through his right eyebrow, and fight scars around
his mouth. One front tooth was broken off ("Karate," he
said), and he bit his upper lip to keep it hidden when he
laughed hard. "Really, Hap," he said. "Or a bit of that
wee Hershey bar you wrap up in tinfoil for my brain?
What is it you call that stuff? Home fries? Are you a
closet dope-freak in disguise?"

Hap cleared the sweat from his eyebrows. "Hell, I ain't
going to mess my life up with that crap. I got enough
problems the way it is. I'd end up in Bellevue, that's what
I'd do. Besides, my old man would kill me if he found
out. He's in— Well, he's got an important job."

"Hap's got a contact! Listen at him *rag!* Doesn't ole
Pops ever wonder where you get all your classy clothes?"

"Lay off, you fruit," Hap said. "I'll burn you so bad
you'll go blind."

Neil's body started jiving in spasms as he tried to contain or create a laugh. "Scary!" he said. "Hoo, boy, I'm
scared shitless. Hey, I'm from Hollywood, Florida, right,
Hap? Right." He spread apart the thumb and forefinger
of each hand and unfurled a marquee. "Hollywood,
Florida, movie capital of the world! Stars! Glamour!
Flashy cars! Go go go go go-go girls! *Dog races.* No, no,
I can't," he said. "Buck up, boy. Aha, thought you had
me, huh? Mother. My mother, God bless her, a lovely
lady—my mother, a big woman, could be a sumo wrestler
—*my mother* works in the mail room of a freight shipping
depot. Hobnobs with the truck drivers. Vroom! Vroom!
Diesel coming through! Daddy's at the courthouse, typing
up county records, tickety tackety tappety rippety. Daddy's
the *fastest typist they have.* And when he comes home,
how does he relax? Right, gets those aching pinkies in
there and tickles the old Mozart and George Gersh. In
my virgin days, I used to think, hey, Dads, ole poopsie,
you got a prob, huh? Because he was always having young
guys over on weekends—greasers in tight pants who ran
around saying, *Wheeee!* He played the piano for them in
a special suit, slippery gold, and one day walked up to me
in those same threads, carrying his electric drill, and said,
'Put 'em up. I'll *grill* ya.' Honk! Honk! Quackers coming
through! You wanna go for an elevator ride? Ka-boom.
Fooled ya, huh? And then when I was eleven I woke up
in the middle of the night, and there was ole Dads beside

the bed with a jug in his hand, looking like he was about to job me. I lived on the beaches for two weeks. Lots of fags. Some lonesome runaway mood music should come in here. Vi? Boo-hoo! 'Why'd you miss so much school?' teach wanted to know. 'Oh, well, Daddy, he—' *hee*—!"

Neil struggled with a cough that came so hard a spray of tears frazzled his face. "Inhale! Exhale! In— There's a skeeter on my peter playing Ping-Pong with my ding-dong! There's another on my brother playing Ping-Pong —with *his* ding-dong! Ahee dem dab, Zulu warrior, zee dem dab Zulu chief! chief! chief! It's like a feather up your ass, or else a flashlight, huh? Ringaling! Operatoree? Slending me a slingslong? *Goo*. Chatsup. Here, cheek a-cheek a-cheek! Yalp! Erb! Brrr-rat-a-tat-tat. Ooo! A-rat-a-tat-tat! Ugh! Buicks with BARs hidden in those old porthole vents, you say, Dick Tracy? Good gad! Dig that *jaw!* Glug! Is that wicked missile headed toward my eye, Mr. Prophet? I—ee ah oh uh I—" He signaled that he couldn't go on and laid his head on the table, on his crossed arms, and his multicolored shirt arched and leaped in a series of seizures intermingled with no-longer, understandable sounds.

"Oh, jeez, Neil," Vi said. "I didn't—"

"Beautiful," Jackie whispered in a new voice, the one that would be hers as a woman, next year.

The man at the rear of the room, who had on a black cowboy hat with the brim pulled low over one eye, moved his chair into a shaft of sunlight, settled the twelve-string in his lap, and started to play, simply and politely at first, and then, as he began to approve of his tuning, went into a growing volume and inventiveness that made the air darken and turn baroque with his stilled and frangible framelike stanzas formed out of the rush of individually illuminated time.

"Oh, jeez," Vi said, and a widening iridescence appeared in the violet depressions of her eyes. "Oh, shit, can that man play some bad-ass blues!"

She put her elbows on the table and covered her face.

Charles leaned against the wall, dizzy, displaced, his eyes flipping as they did past subway posts, and had to concentrate to hold himself within one aspect; he fixed on the chin showing beneath the brim of the black hat, then on the hand fretting the strings, the fingers spreading, barring, standing high, stretching and returning to former chords, moving autonomously, of their own passion, over the strings, while the music, a phenomenon rising from a realm unrelated to the man or his hands, came from the opening in the guitar and across the length of the room, where empty chairs were standing, in widening waves of sound that were silver-colored and struck the front of Charles with the familiarity of his name. He felt his chest part, his ribs lift, and a cavern expand to admit the sound, exposing a region where his heart glowed orange and rode along the current of tones, gliding down smaller steps, leaping to a higher level, sweeping along to a crest that left him breathless, and then dropping into the deep driving plaint of the blues refrain until death drew so near it became a part of the liquid blackness enveloping his heart.

A slow learner? Slow burner? Sad-assed Catholic from the Badlands? No, ho, he wasn't *from* there. Who cares? He'd wake in his rented room at seven or earlier, hours before he wanted to, and find himself thinking of his father, and the day ahead would appear as barren a vista as the plain, so he'd fall back into bed and sleep until noon. And when he woke, he'd be filled with dream fragments of home and how his father changed after his mother died; never spoke unless he had to and then in the most minimal phrases; couldn't look you in the eye; lost thirty pounds; was so restless it was torture for him to sit, and yet sat in front of the television for entire evenings, looking chained to his chair, and the most implausible sort of melodrama had the power to move him so much he had to leave the room. "Oh, if your mother were here," he'd say in a general manner, to the air, and then his eyes would mist and he'd glide off into a wordless reminiscence. Or he'd say, "Oh, I suppose much of my ambition was for her."

He said to Father Schimmelpfennig in a letter that he was ill for company, and a few months later three students he'd taught in Hyatt and who'd graduated since appeared at the house; Jay gave them jobs, and beds were moved into the garage—into the basement in the winter—and they roomed and boarded for occasional groceries, for free, really. His father returned to teaching that fall, but wasn't meticulous about his appearance, as he'd once been, and wore work clothes to school, or mismatched jackets and slacks and no tie, his collar open and a stenciled T-shirt showing beneath, and—

And now Charles realized there was a period in his life he'd closed off until now. His father took a leave of absence from the high school in Pettibone and went back to Hyatt to teach for a year. Red Wing. The girls and Charles went with him (Tim was in Wisconsin, Jerome at the house with the students) and found their father was a hero, a legend in Hyatt, because one year when he'd taught there his basketball team had gone to the state tournament (there were only nine males in the school at the time) and they'd taken third place. The school board wanted him to coach again, of course, but he told them he'd rather let that final record, nearly perfect, stand. The girls stayed with a couple who had children of all ages, and now lived in the old Halvorson place, and he and Charles lived in the Sanderson house, whose back yard bordered on the Black Forest. Charles had changed, his friends had changed, he hadn't thought he'd ever see them again and now didn't know whether he wanted to, and he stayed home often from school, too lethargic and burdened to move. He began to play the baritone. In the fall his father took him to New Rockford on weekends and they had dinner and went to a movie or bowling together, but with the first bad blizzard the car wouldn't start and it sat along the road outside their house until the blinding, drifting snow covered its roof.

There was one bedroom, with one bed, a double bed, and he and his father slept in it together, his father gripping a rosary. A single heater for heat, a cookstove in the kitchen, where his father made their meals— And now Charles realized the hour he was waking in New York was the hour when he and his father had breakfast together. The marshy area of the Black Forest behind the house, a wood lot near the overgrown trellis there; his father splitting kindling, his forearms and back muscles bulging beneath his shirt, striking the splitting wedge so hard it shot through the chunk of cottonwood and stood upright in the chopping block. His father at the cookstove, staring ahead, his eyes omniscient, rolling a walnut between his palms and then the sound of a gunshot as it cracks in his hands. Had he come here to end his love? The silent meals in the tiny kitchen. The vacant, gray-hued, protracted days when Charles is at home, out of school, sitting in bed and playing his baritone to the empty rooms. The dampness of the bedclothes, the dampness of the furniture and rugs, and the corrosive feeling of dampness that rose through the floors of the old house. Wandering from room to room as though on an endless search for a missing essential. Wearing pajamas for the first time since childhood because he slept with his father—flannel pajamas that made him feel like a baby and that he left on all day. His wandering form reflected in the golden bell of the baritone. The unformed pastiness of his face in the mirror. The glory and terror, after years of youthful tingling and mere spasms, of erupting with semen—what to do with the stuff? Fantasies, a hope of promise that came from a feeling he and his mother shared here; melodies unremembered even now all along the flat and the vast grass plains of those low northlands.

And then at school, the altered faces from childhood, as though his friends wore masks, somehow distorted, that made the past seem a charade, and the embarrassment of having his father for a teacher—that new, unalterable relationship. Staring at the floor when his father read poetry aloud at a lectern or, even worse, pacing. Rattling off answers to him with irritation. Averting his eyes when he passed him in the halls. And then at a basketball game his father didn't attend, getting together with the Rimskys and Buddy Schonbeck and Ribs and giving their pooled money to a senior, an epileptic with a deeply seamed face who was able to pass for thirty. He bought them a fifth of whiskey and a half gallon of sweet wine and they drank it off quickly, in an unlocked car during the half, and then went back into the warm gymnasium. Ribs kept nodding off and finally passed out and vomited over the bleachers and had to be carried from the building. It was discovered that he was drunk, not ill, or ill from drunkenness, and the next day the county sheriff arrived at the high school and everybody involved in the drinking (Ribs gave names in his straightforward way) was summoned into the superintendent's office; Charles's father was the superintendent. The sheriff called them dopes and knuckleheads and said he could throw them all in jail, while Charles stared at the floor, feeling his father's eyes on him, and then heard the sheriff say he'd put them on a year's probation if they had a long talk with the superintendent and their parents and minister. The four Catholics went to see Father Schimmelpfennig, who was waiting for them in the confessional, and when it came Charles's turn, he drew aside the purple velvet curtain and knelt in darkness, praying for anonymity, and then the slide at his face shot back and Father said, "Charles, Charles, Charles, I don't believe you'll ever know how much you've hurt your father. It's even hard for me to forgive you."

Now in New York, with the numberless faces going past so relentlessly it could unhinge you if you tried to take in even a part of the press of them, he'd see a feature—a forehead, an eye, a mouth—that reminded him of his father, and there'd be a catch in his stride and he'd slow, feeling his father had seen him but continued on, and sometimes he'd even stop in the street and turn to see.

"What's the *time?*"

"Seven-thirty," Charles said, and felt his chest constrict and the guitar music swell as though implanted there.

"Seven-*thirty?*" Jackie's hands fluttered down and the color left her lips. "Oh, Jesus." She grabbed her purse and went up the three steps in one leap.

"Is it?" Vi asked.

"Hell, it's lucky if it's five," Hap said.

Jackie came back down the steps in a stiff walk, her face less attractive and her eyes blank, and stood at the table and stared at Charles. "You bastard," she said. "You just wrecked my high. You wrecked my high and my head and my whole goddamn *day!* You dirty lying bastard! What the fuck are you trying to *do?*" She turned and leaped up the stairs again.

"No Top of the Sex's for you, poopsie," Neil said, and wriggled his fingers in front of Charles's face.

"Why'd you do that?" Vi said. "She can't help the way she is. She's just a kid. She's hot for you."

"I didn't mean to," Charles said. He was afraid. The four of them had set this up to trap him, victimize him in some way, and were closing in for the kill. He felt his high shift, assume an anchorlike shape between his lungs, and believed it was leaving, so he could defend himself, but it returned with a more powerful surge and locked inside with wires and claws he couldn't escape.

"Oh, God," Vi said. "I didn't mean it that way. I'm sorry. I didn't mean to— Oh, shit, isn't this a lovely day?"

"Where did she go?" Charles asked.

"You're asking *me?*"

Charles slid out from the table, incredulous that his body could move so dreamily (but where was *he?*), and went up the steps; the brightness of the big-windowed room back-reeled within him—there was his face, misshapen, sliding along the shining espresso urns—and the colorfully clad people at his periphery were like hooks that could remove his vision, cut eyeballs on ice. A hand gripped his shoulder hard.

"Chuckie," Neil said. "Friend. I'm supposed to meet a broad later, she said, but if she doesn't show, could I flop at your place?"

The fringe was shaking. Charles was unsure of what he'd asked.

"Hey, hey, poopsie, don't worry, no sex. I'm wearin' the rag." He laughed, biting his lip, and his eyes went out of line. "*May* I stay at your place? Fuel's running low."

Charles saw that for all his debonair worldliness he could be easily hurt. "Sure," he said.

"It'll probably be late if she doesn't show and I can't hook up with anybody else, don't you see." He wrinkled his nose in a rabbity way.

"That's all right."

"Thanks, toots." Neil grabbed his hand and slapped something wrapped in tinfoil into it. "For the time you got burned. I got burned as bad." He punched Charles's shoulder and Charles felt himself shift into a different setting, while his body and face kept riding over a way of time like the roller coaster of the coffee urns.

"Later," Neil said.

"Hey." Charles pushed through to the air outside, hot and damp, tropical to him, and infused with a smell as of toads and snakes and boils. The buildings across the street, painted varying garish shades, reminded him of some moment from his past—the primary-colored cardboard houses he used to set in streets beneath the Christmas tree, or a glance into a book with gaudy, oversimplified pictures of Hometown, Everywhere—but in his state he couldn't place the image or instant it fit. Where, Charles?

He went down MacDougal, away from the Square toward Bleecker, crossed Bleecker, and turned east on it; the face of every passer-by knew he'd hurt Jackie and had to find her, and some smiled at him. His ass felt bigger than it was, which was too big to begin with, and wiggled funny when he walked, as if a wobbly fud were attached, and he felt himself giving off such an obvious aura that everybody on the street, everybody looking down from their apartment windows, could spot him as a mark and move in. A crowd of students was coming his way laughing. He stopped at a storefront and looked in a window until they'd passed. The store was being made into yet another coffeehouse; burlap and construction materials lay on the floor, along with round-topped tables turned upside down. There were wooden platforms at several levels, and around the edges of the platforms, running from the floor to eight feet into the air, were lengths of colored pipe—orange, red, blue, white—that had been fitted together randomly, in patterns that were right-angled hard bends, and that shone neonlike in light of all the days he'd stood in dream, and then he saw himself huffing and puffing on a toilet stool as he slid the needle in and then the black and molecular rush as blindness came and his mind went out.

He adjusted and saw the reflection of a man's face beside his—a distinguished, fine-lipped face, with the querulous and insinuating look of a detective. Tinfoil in his pocket. The face, which was also looking in the window, turned to study him several times, and then moved up.

"Could you give me a quarter or fifty cents?" A harp rasp.

Charles turned to a man of about fifty-five, with sandy-colored hair combed back from his domed forehead, a day's growth of copper-colored stubble, and a belligerent but apologetic seediness in his turquoise eyes.

"I haven't got fifty cents."

"Are we still on speaking terms?" His hoarse voice was a concerned uncle's at bay. "Huh? Have you been coming here a lot?"

"I don't know you."

"No, you probably don't. No, I've lived in this neighborhood longer than you've been alive, sir, and you probably don't even remember me. I saw—" His direct gaze veiled, as though he'd lost the connections inside his thought. "Is this place expensive?"

"I don't know. It's not open yet."

"There you go again. I can see that. I've lived in this neighborhood all my life and I ain't ever seen it. Teddy Cummins and I were altar boys over at St. Anthony's for old Father McKeough—that's how far back I go. Do you serve there now?"

"I'm not from here."

"Sure, sonny. Don't you remember?"

Was this one of the alkies Charles gave money to? He often gave them the last quarter he was carrying, out of compassion, he imagined.

"I saw you just the other day," the man said. "You're a painter. You were carrying one of those—" He outlined several shapes with boxy hands and from his gestures it was clear that he wasn't drunk (although Charles could smell booze on him), but he also wasn't drawing anything definite. "What do you call those?"

"An easel?"

"No, no, no. It's all covered up with something. Real big. You know. You were carrying the whole big deal."

"A canvas?"

"No, no, no. You painters have a name for it."

"I'm not a painter and I wasn't ever carrying anything like that around here, as far as I know."

"Then it was one of your friends. They all look like you, those guys. How's your daddy?"

"What?"

"You're daddy. I haven't seen him for a while, either. How is the old guy?"

"I don't know."

"You don't know! Doesn't he live right over there on Sullivan Street?"

"No. Illinois."

"Well, naturally. But I like to come back once in a while and look the old place over and he should, too. Tell him. I've got to get on down to the Bowery now." He stared up the street and his eyes, overhung by golden eyebrows that glinted in the light, filled with a tentative homeward look that was familiar to Charles; he wasn't sure he didn't know this man, although he was positive he'd never met him before, and then the wires and claws closed in a clasp again.

"The Bowery! Shit! That place stinks! I only— Well, when the old man needs a drink . . . You don't remember your daddy, huh? Well, damn you, you should! Wasn't he there when you wanted the guy?"

"I guess."

"You're damn right he was! You were little then. Sure. Now I remember. And then the next thing I knew you were carrying that what-you-may-call-it around. What's that painter's thing you had, did you say?"

"I didn't."

"Then it was three years ago I saw you with that and I haven't seen you since, have I, Michael?"

"I think you—"

"You're right, it wasn't just the other day, it was three years ago I saw you with that. Now I remember, son, or—"

He stared beyond Charles, uncertain of where they stood, and then his eyes altered, as though he'd seen through to a moment too transfiguring to comprehend, and Charles saw himself in the man's tapered slacks and highly polished shoes, in his well-kept shirt with creases from the laundry cardboard still showing in it, vomit on the collar, and then the man turned and walked away from him and went around the corner, heading south, and Charles took the tinfoil from his pocket and dropped it to the street. But what about Neil? And what if he was there tonight? Charles picked up the packet and took it to his rented room and carefully doled it out to himself over a long while.

41

❧

THE VILLAGE POET

Nine at night in January, that month of introspection and
regret, with snow descending slowly between buildings
from the overdark sky, past lighted windows and patches
of brick, to the shoes he watched as he walked. Trench-
coat night. Would all of the facets of him ever be fulfilled,
without this feeling of one or another leading him astray?
Dear Lord, I— His *I* interfered and didn't know what to
ask or why, or how to talk. Where were the words of the
one inside him since birth? Loss of the lost. He went into
a Ukrainian restaurant on Avenue A, his regular eating
place, and the humid air and the smells of cooked cab-
bage and fatty food made him want to resign from the
race. He hadn't eaten for two days, but what was the real
cause?

A crowd of elderly men in clothes that looked outdated
and European were seated around a U-shaped counter
whose pink Formica surface had white whorls worn in it;
their overcoats were unbuttoned and their hats lay on the
countertop. There were glasses of tea beside their plates.
They could have been on a bus tour from another country,
for their similar Slavic look, but the compact way they
sat, the way they ate with unfazed concentration, put them
on home ground. Three or four winos were scattered
among them, more mummified and misplaced than ever in
this atmosphere, gaunt and unshaven, wearing thrift-shop
jackets over fouled shirts and warming themselves with
coffee that the waiters, old Ukrainians who spoke little
English and affected a façade of belligerence (had they
fled during the Revolution and for a time had to live off

others, Charles wondered), always served to winos, often with a bowl of barley soup, for free.

He sat at a vacant stool, placing a collection of poetry on the counter in front of him, and a gray-haired man with a military bearing a couple of stools down, who, like Charles and the winos, looked out of place here, glanced up from a notebook he was writing in, saw the collection of poems, saw Charles, and then slammed his notebook shut.

At the other end of the counter, the open part of the U, the door into the kitchen swung open and the red face of a waiter appeared through a font of steam. "Kostyk!" he called, and a man across from Charles looked up.

"Varenyky," Kostyk said in an ecclesiastical bass, and made a gesture to pour something over it.

The waiter disappeared into the kitchen with a shout. Another waiter, a wiry, bald-headed fellow with long ear lobes, stood at the shining urns in the center of the counter, talking to a customer while he drew a glass of coffee, and then a third came up to the stainless-steel condiment stand next to the urns, placed a stack of plates on its top, hurried to the cash register at the head of the counter, slammed down keys that popped "95" up in a window, and let the drawer strike his stomach and rebound. They were always busy in here, always in a rush, and their even-tempered nature as they went about their work made Charles want to climb the counter, tie a white towel around his waist, and go at it for free.

Through the glass doors of the condiment stand he could see recessed trays of cole slaw, sliced cucumbers, pickled beets, sour cream, and rice pudding with raisins in it, but no hunger stirred in him. Somebody had written on the misted glass of the window oppostite with a fingertip, but the message was dripping now, a hieroglyph, and it seemed relevant to him that he couldn't read it.

He'd meant to be an actor, and on the day he arrived in the city, before even beginning to look for a place to live, had stuffed his luggage into a locker in Grand Central and gone to a matinee of Burton's *Hamlet*. Burton seemed unfocused, stone-faced, visionary and abstracted, and, indeed, perhaps part of his mind kept going to the crowd that lined the street outside the theater, hoping to get a glimpse of his recent wife, Elizabeth (or so a mounted policeman told Charles), when she came to fetch him at the stage door in her limousine. The supporting cast wasn't much better than most of the actors Charles had worked with in college. Horatio and Claudius and the Queen were excellent in themselves. But every time Polonius appeared onstage, Charles groaned in his seat; this Polonius moved in a hokey shuffle, a sham-darky breaking in a new pair of slippers, and gave off a boredom that bored, reading his succulent and pompous, mellifluous lines as if chatting with a crony on the street corner. Charles left the theater with a headache, and still carried the impression that Laurence Olivier was somewhere in the cast that afternoon that went into night.

He bought copies of *Backstage* and began to go to try-outs, open tryouts, as they were called, or cattle calls, which were shamelessly political and were conducted in storerooms and lofts so shabby he was embarrassed for the people in charge (for Broadway tryouts one had to have an agent, and it was impossible to get an agent unless one had been in a Broadway play), and besides, he felt that if he was as good an actor as he believed himself to be, then he'd be discovered somehow, without having to endure such unpleasantness. So he stopped attending tryouts and sat in his room and read plays and re-rehearsed all the roles he'd ever done, ignoring neighbors' knocks on the walls (Caliban got pretty noisy), and when his money started running out, he felt neither over-anxiousness nor panic; he expected to be doing a lead on Broadway soon.

Everything else he'd expected to discover in the city— knowledge his small-town background hadn't been able to supply, ceaseless excitement, sympathetic souls of his own temperament, wild sex—he hadn't discovered, and he was beginning to suspect this was due to some flaw in him, perhaps because his father, when he'd heard he was dropping out of college with only one semester to go, had said there must be something "damn wrong" with him; either that or what he heard a stranger on a bus say in conversation—"In New York, you know, if you don't have the cash, you're out of it"—was the truth. Or the truth, if there was such a rare and radiant, luxurious surety, lay lost somewhere between.

One Sunday he was walking through the Wall Street

district, awed by the buildings lined along streets so narrow they could have been Hyatt's, and so deserted it seemed an air-raid alarm had been sounded, when a matronly woman came around a corner, breathless, and asked where she could find the entrance to the BMT. "I'm sorry, ma'am," he said, in his flat Midwestern accent. "I couldn't say. In fact, I'm sort of lost myself. I—" She laid her hand on his sleeve and said, "Honey, you don't have to say to me. I know just how you feel. I'm from Brooklyn, too." And once on Park, feeling the resilience of his twenty-three years releasing him from the fact that it was fall and he had no job or acting roles yet, he began to trot along and then broke into a full-fledged sprint, and suddenly people began flattening themselves against buildings and diving into doorways, as though he were an armed robber or assassin on the loose. He didn't run in the streets any more after that.

He hadn't seen Neil or Vi since that surrealistic summer day, and the one time he'd seen Jackie, near Times Square, she'd looked frightened and pursued and kept glancing over her shoulder, her hands performing in the air between them, and said she'd heard that Neil had smashed up an IBM machine and been kicked out of the Army as psycho for that. He saw Hap nearly every day and occasionally bought a nickel bag from him, but decided he'd better give up on dope for a while; once when he was high he spent three hours rearranging his room and fell asleep, and when he woke and saw his arrangement staring back at him, he knew he'd gone mad, at the least.

The taciturn, self-conscious Charles Neumiller he hated ("cursed with the Germanic knack of being stiff, humorless, and on a constant search for the formula or platitude to classify everything," as he expressed it to himself in a German accent; possessed of a "grotesque sense of decorum," as a friend put it) should have become, through the influence of the city, an easy-going and urbane, if not debonair, extroverted ladies' man and sought-out conversationalist. But he still had his same flaws and fears, his likes and dislikes, his weekend drunks, his dissatisfaction; and his reserve and aloofness grew each day: the press of anonymous people, the millions of them, made him feel that if he extended himself beyond who he was, he would, like a droplet falling in a sea, be annihilated. So he had

no friends or lovers, and was on speaking terms with only
a few people at the office where he worked. He was a
delivery boy.

The one time he'd been laid, by an innocent-looking,
seventeen-year-old from Queens, he'd picked up crabs and
a bad case of clap that went to acute prostatitis, and had
to endure a two-week series of shots, in case he'd picked
up anything worse, and the antibiotic, Bicillin, was so
thick it rode inside the muscle of his buttock like a wadded
cloth, putting pressure on his hip socket—so painful that
after one of the shots, on a day when he hadn't eaten
again, he started to faint in the subway, and might have,
if the woman beside him hadn't taken his arm, and said,
"Are you all right, son?"

"No," he said. "Yes," he said, and then got off at the
next stop and went to the roof of the RCA building
(why, he didn't know) and stared over its edge for an
hour. The height put him out of focus for the rest of the
week, and when he went into a small park that same day,
near the mayor's mansion, he discovered that the silky
tails of the squirrels there were transparent, and could be
seen through to trees, ground, grass, and sky—a miracle
performed out of the impermanent air, it seemed, and he
knew he was close to a source that would help him in the
kind of life he'd choose to lead.

He saw the girl from Queens a few days later, and
told her what he had, which must be what she had, because— And she said, "Oh, yeah? Hmmm, I thought it
felt sort of funny down there. We can't ball then, huh?"

His neighbors began to respond to Caliban with a melting pot of language as colorful as Shakespeare's; why had
he chosen this profession anyhow, and hadn't he chosen
it to begin with because he felt it would please his mother
if she were still living, or alive in some form? Perhaps he
should have been a lawyer—act every day for high
fees; or a salesman (insurance?)—use his acting experience to bring in commissions; or a musician—he
could improvise songs on the baritone as soon as he
learned to regulate his embouchure, and played the right
tones not from sheet music, which he couldn't read, but
by gauging the distance from one note to another on the
staff; or a painter—the summer he graduated from high
school he painted, in the space of two weeks, five large

canvases, and felt sexual pleasure in the simple act of rubbing his brush in paint and then over the canvas (Masonite, actually, reversed for its rough texture) and an unearthly exuberance in watching colors bloom beyond mere color, ping and swoon, and take on the shape of his imaginings, and when he'd brought a painting to college and hung it in his dormitory cubicle, a senior in art wanted to know where he'd bought it (he'd constructed a fancy frame for it) and how much it had cost. Or a writer.

Why not? He'd always read poetry and novels and biographies, and had even written a few poems on his own; Tim wrote, their father was always writing, or talking about writing, and writing didn't require any special training or superfluous trappings, or the approval of other people, or their presence, and it was an occupation he could work at every day instead of sitting around his room reciting other people's lines. He got out a letter tablet and pencil and lay on his stomach on the bed. But what about? He thought of a few of Tim's pieces he'd seen, about his mother and North Dakota, of the serenity of his early life and the upheaval after, and of a notion he'd been carrying from his first year in college, and wrote:

A psychologist or poet I suppose would find deep meaning in the fact that I'm writing this down exactly a week after it began, at exactly the same hour. But that's foolishness. Since Edward is away at Fr. Garhopher's playing pinochle, it is only convenience.

I've evaded it long enough and if I keep up at this rate I will evade it forever. That would be wrong.

Last Friday Denny and Ronnie were playing with the Dibson boys in our back yard. I heard an argument and went to the kitchen window. They were contesting the death of Jimmy Dibson. He's the one with the strangely big head. Although I've asked them to please keep away from games of violence, in particular the one they call War, it keeps creeping into their play like water into a sponge. I'm afraid for these boys. They have war in their hearts. The threat of total destruction—the atomic bomb—was forced into their lives. They were born under it. Theirs will be a strange generation, cold and distant, without

*deep feelings, incapable of any strong action other
than violence and what is torn loose from them by
hysteria. And how can we expect more? What raises
such a threat to them can't be separated from their
lives, and for them each person will carry within him
the possibility of destruction. Afraid for their
emotions, their deepest thoughts, their inner beings,
they will remain detached and on the defensive.*

*It's impossible to expect them to separate this threat
from people. The ability to do so is a fault in itself,
as strange and unnatural as those huge white tongues
of fungus that stick out of the trunk of a tall healthy
tree. I think of how I was affected as a child when
I stood in a patch of sunlight in the forest gathering
blueberries or blackberries and turned up to see one
above me, gray and glowing in the shadow of the
leaves, clamped onto the bark.*

They were playing War.

The words had appeared on the page as if falling straight
from his mind. He hadn't done any crossing out, even,
until toward the end. It was a journal his mother was
keeping. But what next? The incident she mentioned in
her first paragraph, the one from a week ago, and the one
he was leading up to, was his father announcing that the
family might move to Illinois; this seemed the turning
point of their closed world. He'd got off the track in that
paragraph about the bomb, which was his notion from
college, but that particular section was so good it had to
stay, right? Then again, did it really sound like his
mother? Would she have thought that? Was this the way
she'd keep a journal? Would she keep one? Or did that
make any difference? He read the page again and with
those thoughts behind his eyes it didn't seem as firm as
before. And his mother had never spent any of her childhood near a forest. Oh, well, nobody else knew that. And
he liked the part about the fungus, which had taken some
work. Then he noticed that the fungus was white the first
time and gray the next. Well the shadow. But could a
journal in which a forest was mentioned be set in North
Dakota? Perhaps it might be better to compose a journal
from a more personal point of view. This time the writing
came harder—it was difficult to even move the pencil—

and he kept crossing out false starts, transposing words, substituting others, putting back the old ones, consulting his paperback dictionary, blacking out entire phrases to hide them, and then whole sentences (conscious all the while of how the sun lay warm on his forearm), and finally, after more than an hour's work, ended with:

> To begin: My name is Karl Vogelwede. I've not yet acted a scene, not to mention a role, successfully; that is, utterly for myself. Even alone I've never acted as I'd prefer to; even then I feel the influence of an audience and go against my better judgment to please. This same absurd self-awareness stultified my religious inclinations as a child. Because of the manner in which I was brought up, in the Roman Catholic faith—the nuns always telling us God observed and looked over everything we did—because of this I felt the presence of a deity persistently, and, feeling it, merely said prayers which I presumed would placate it. I never prayed what I sincerely felt. (Or was it that I was so conscious of Self it was impossible to reach God, if there is one?)

He felt like getting drunk. This was sheer, sheer revelation on every sort of level and plane. He could understand now how his father must have felt during all those years, trying to make sense on paper of the experiences and memories he carried, made more dense and complex with the pressure of time. He washed, put on clean pants, a suit jacket, and was nearly out the door when he came back to the bed, picked up the tablet, and looked at the paragraph again. He read it three times, feeling a fever start in his cheeks, and then took a pencil, crossed it out with a big slash, and wrote below, "What you need is instant fame." And then he went out and got drunk, so drunk he had to continue sipping beer for two days, tapering off slowly to ease the tension and pain, and hadn't tried writing since.

The waiter, broad and red-faced, his straight black hair going gray, his sleeves rolled up to expose muscular arms—a peasant transplanted—came waddling up and put a glass of water down in front of him. "Wot?" he asked.

"The meat loaf," Charles said. "And some coffee." How come they never served him his coffee in a glass? Should he ask them?

He opened the book of poetry. When depression came, settling down on him like the soot that settled over the snow of the city, smothering his senses, all he could do was read, in order to forget where he was. He was tired of the politics of the theater, of working as a delivery boy, walking world-renowned streets on an empty stomach, of living from hand to mouth and more often than not, or so it seemed lately, biting the hand, his hand, that fed him. He saw the plain, where the sky touched the flat land in every direction, blue against green, and the unopened openness of it now seemed a fabrication of his marginalia-oriented and not always perfect memory, and he missed the Midwest, where there were wide lawns, trellises, ditches, rows of hedge, and brick walks lined with elms whose leafy branches canopied the street and spoke in the air above him, making him feel surrounded by a secret, or the source and center of some secret that arrived in a whirlwind of leaves and left as a sign to him one gray glove. Now, when he stepped out of his room, he felt he'd stepped into a bigger room filled with elbows. There was no grass. There were walls on every side. There was a floor made up of asphalt, slate, and sometimes sheets of steel; in front of a few banks it was marble. The smog-darkened sky often made the tall buildings look decapitated, and he came to understand, in a literal sense, "low ceiling."

And when he sought refuge in a park, threading his way through a stream of taxicabs and bicycles, and hacks sometimes, and cars, and stepped into the landscaped area squeezed between walls of brick like an afterthought, he saw externals that resembled trees and grass, but they looked so out of place, yet grew with such deep-green unhealthy profusion in the surroundings, it was as if he'd stepped from a bad dream onto the stage setting for a catastrophe that would be filmed for its apocalyptic content, and then the film destroyed. Even the pigeons there carried, as he saw it, the municipal taint; many were molting, exposing pink heads and pink backs to the bad air, making him imagine they carried all kinds of diseases, and he fed them only out of pity for the poverty of himself.

At home they'd be making preparations for Christmas, going shopping alone and together, setting up and trimming the tree, a task Susan helped with now; stringing up lights in the gables, wreaths in the windows, bells on the doors and mistletoe's pointed leaves and pearly berries above them. Poison. The girls would find the gifts their father had hidden away (he never put them out, knowing they'd open them), and Marie would spend days in the kitchen baking pastries and pies and cakes. The nimbus of serenity around Jerome at this time. Tim's tuneful seasonal turnings on the old upright piano.

No, Laura and Ginny were with them, and there'd be a difference in the way they celebrated now. This was the first Christmas he wouldn't be home, and it was Marie he'd miss; he'd learned that he missed different ones during different seasons, as though each had shaped a particular part of the cycle of his life, and helped form of it a year; in the fall Jerome, in the summertime Tim, Susan in the spring, and Marie in the winter and cold. Marie's presence, merely her presence, made the holidays more festive for him. He hadn't even sent her a gift. A few months ago he'd received a letter from Vince, Vince of all the relations, and in it was a twenty-dollar bill, and at the end of the letter, this: "How I hope you make a go of it at acting, Charles, so dear to me."

His food came and he put aside the book, only partly conscious of the poem he'd been reading, and wondered where he'd turn when he lost the ability to submerge himself in words. Somebody was tapping on his forearm. The man two stools down with the notebook nodded at the collection of poetry. "That's yours?" he asked.

"Yes."

"Have you read his other books?"

"Some."

"Are you interested in poetry?"

"Yes, I guess."

"Ah," the man said, and studied him with eyes that were ice-blue and had the possessed look of a ship captain's, somebody who'd stared in the same way over stretches of sea, intrepid, a look that impaled Charles's reason. The man was about fifty, with blue-gray hair trimmed in a neat crew cut, and a New Englandish, aristocratic face, tanned and weathered and imprinted with fine wrinkles around the eyes, as though to draw attention there. "Are you from New York?" he asked.

"No."

"I thought not. No, it's not in your face. And, anyway, nobody who lives in New York is from New York."

"Oh?"

"Perhaps I shouldn't have put it that way. I'm not demented, by the by, let's begin with that premise. What I should have said is that nobody who knows New York as one knows a woman was born here. Oh, natives have a good idea of its manholes and gridwork—Manhattan is such a small area, actually—and they have their emotional landmarks and sentimental tidbits, all the familiar sites they return to and feel unthreatened in, but only an outsider can feel and say what the city really is. 'Mannahatta, of tall masts, possessed by some strange fire!' Whitman. Was he born here?" he asked himself in sudden consternation. "I wonder. He lied so much.

"Anyway, natives are like fish. A fish is born in water, water is its life, its medium, its 'milieu,' I'd say, if the word weren't so abused, and they go swimming through the city without seeing it, without any feeling for what they see, unless it's a mugging, and should they stray into an unfamiliar neighborhood, you'd think they were at the Antipodes! But," he said, and held up a forefinger, "but let a land animal step into it"—this finger he now stuck into his coffee—"'and he'll say, 'Aha! This is wet, this is water, indeed!' Really, *really*. How long have you been here?"

"Six months."

"Aha, just as I thought! A neophyte." He dried the finger on a napkin. "What do you do?"

"Oh, I deliver—"

"Ah! Which calls to mind a concrete example of this generalizing I've been at. The other day a delivery boy came to the place where I work— Did I say boy? He's a man of sixty-some years. An old man, then, came up to me, looking happy for the first time in ages, and said this was his last day. He was retiring. I began a conversation, surprised to be losing touch with this familiar, alcohol-ravaged face, and learned that he lived in Brooklyn— Do I sound like a schoolmarm to you?"

"No."

"I've been told that I do, perhaps because I overarticulate, can wax pedantic, and find myself entwined in sentences that could have come from a Restoration comedy. But these are only conversational quirks. Poetry is my medium, though I do like to talk."

"Oh."

"During the day I lead a life that's acceptable in the eyes of most of society—I work as a doorman—but at night, yes, I crawl out of that façade, turn clinically bonkers, and strive to write. I'm working on a poetic account of New York. I have been for several years." The brilliance of his eyes, enhanced by silver lashes, grew as he fixed on Charles. "You have inclinations to write, no?"

"No."

"You're sure?"

"Yes."

"That's peculiar. Your book there and then the face— it's in your eyes and lips—both bespeak a poet to me. But back to the Delivery Old Man. I learned from him, since I carry on a kind of underground research, that he was born in Brooklyn, married late, and had no children, and that the firm he worked for—some insurance outfit— carried on all of its business in lower Manhattan. 'I have no gripes!' he said to me. Perhaps he was a church-goer or loved dogs, but here is the point: I asked him about a glass-eyed building I'd seen going up in the East Sixties, and wondered how he, native as he was, felt about such blatant, commercial desecration. He shrugged his shoulders and confessed he couldn't say, because he'd never been above Forty-second Street in his life. I asked him how he accomplished this, why he'd *do* it, or not, and he said, 'It's the same thing up there, isn't it?'

"Imagine the stultified curiosity, the insular bliss! No desire but to exist, unmolested, within the same piddly-poop world from day to day!" He leaned closer, apparently bothered by the stool between them, and whispered, "And there you have the character of three-quarters of your native New Yorkers." The part of him he'd mentioned as emerging when he wrote appeared in his eyes in a series of flittering surges. "Pardon me if I sound harsh, but this is my opinion. Do you *mind* if I have an opinion?"

"Of course not."

"And I believe in man!" he cried, and struck the counter

so close to his water glass that ice jiggled and sloshed in it. Was he juiced? "For instance." He laid his hand on Charles's coatsleeve. "Look at these men around us. They're perhaps not natives— Of course not." He blinked as if he'd just noticed them. "They're foreigners. And what do these fellows so regular in appearance feel of the city? Where are their roots? This restaurant here? A street-corner bar? What do they have but their rowdies and their railroad flats, which most likely smell of borscht, have a smelly cat in them, piles of St. Cyrillic newspapers, some few— Don't you *see?*"

Charles felt uneasy inside the man's stare and the intimacy he'd been assumed into, and felt that the talk was turning on him; when he came to New York, he vowed not to fall into a pattern, as others in the city seemed to him to do, but had, gradually, giving up the vow as his money diminished and hope for a change in himself gave out, and finally set up a pattern of his own, which made him feel settled in the city and somewhat different from everybody else. "So who's at home here?"

"Ah!" the man cried, and from the way his finger went up, it seemed about to go into the coffee again. "There you have one of the facets of the character of the *true* New York!" He smiled with his lips so compressed they turned white, while his eyes wandered and widened until he had the look of a child on a potty-chair, nostrils wide.

"I'm from Oregon, a solitary dissatisfied with pat answers to the truth, myself, the city, the whole kit and caboodle, plus booze!" He put his fingers over the note-book. "Even with my poetry. Yes, yes, there are some jottings in here, but I couldn't permit you to see them, and you know perfectly well why not."

"Why?"

"That face of someone who'd be interested in poetry, and might even write it, a face I might—'"

"You said that."

"You could steal some of my lines!"

"What?"

"Who knows what sort would filch poetry, or why? For fame, money, to make a woman, or just to go whole-hog apeshit for a while. I've been writing since I was your age and haven't ever trusted my poetry with editors, agents, publishers, other poets—no one, you hear! Even at my place of employment— Do you know the Delacroix?"

"No."

"It used to be fancy, but it's not any more, with the spirit of the neighborhood deteriorating, and the building, too, going to pot. I work as a doorman, as I said, to keep myself in scratch that I might poetize nightly, and I carry out my duties with as much dignity as I can summon. But can I be expected to repair clanging radiators and patch cracked shower walls, reweave carpets, banish decades-old stinks in the goddamn cans— Do I have to be expected to do that, too?"

"Certainly not," Charles said, afraid of the fierceness that had come over the man.

"Well, I should hope not, and I hope everybody is happy with my predicament, life and morals on the fly, too." The white-lipped smile disfigured his face again. "I must confess, however, to doing one shameful thing there. Would you like to hear it?"

Charles wasn't sure.

"I often jot down lines while on the job. Ha, you thought it was worse, didn't you! Today, for instance, I wrote something down. Would you like to hear it?"

"I thought you said—"

"Oh, I could *read* something. Reading is different from showing; that's giving it away, this is giving *to*. How about it?"

"Sure."

He scooted over onto the stool next to Charles, laid the notebook down on the counter, ran his hand over its worn, bespattered cover, and began leafing through pages smudged, dog-eared, stained with coffee, ink, wine (blood?), and other substances. He bent over a page and sighed, and Charles looked across his crew cut and saw that the page was covered from top to bottom and edge to edge with a multitude of entries, some in pencil, in ball-point, in ink of several different colors; and all the entries marked with stars, asterisks, and personal symbols— horses, half-moons, diamonds, a sketch of a nose, a door-knob, a shoe. But what largely held Charles's attention, and also sent an uneasy feeling cross-circuiting over him, was that every entry bore the mannerisms of a single hand, yet every one was in a different size and variety of handwriting, as though it changed each hour.

"Ah. Here. This is the one I wrote this afternoon. I have trouble keeping them straight sometimes." He cleared his throat and then checked to make sure nobody but Charles was within hearing distance, and read, *"A shimmy-ass woman shivered my mind, crowned my passage pace after pace this demi-vierge Wednesday. O, jeweled woman—women!—passing under lamplight through blue snow, I with my eye canonize you, a blue eye, a golden-eye, an eye in a prow of jewels, big boobs."*

He sat with his eyes on the notebook. He'd read at a slow rate, pursing his lips around the words as though forming sculptures of their sound, prolonging vowels and ticking at consonants the way classical actors do, and his musical voice reminded Charles of a recording (of Borodin?) that he'd heard one summer night, a minor melody that seemed to rise from the stretches of a desert, strings conferring, woodwinds mourning even on the higher notes, a French horn unfurling it all like a simple *chansonette,* while finger cymbals clashed in the background, their thin sound ringing through the meek theme (as when the poet said *women!*) like stars piercing the night sky. He couldn't separate the words from the voice he'd heard.

The poet lifted his eyes, the possessed look gone from them, troubled and vulnerable, and somehow ashamed, and now that he was so close Charles could see broken blood vessels, coiled like spirochetes, in his corneas, wedge-shaped pink areas where his lids didn't shield his eyes, and a milky liquid lying along his reddened lower lids. Would Tim end up like this?

"Did you like it?" he asked.

"Yes."

"It's sort of a joke, I suppose, but did you hear the words and how they make fables of sound alone, the way the preternatural can seem real, and how, in certain spots, it gives way to a common phrase so you can *see* what you feel?"

"I guess."

"You have the face of someone who would," he said, and once more made a close study of Charles's face. "I felt the words go along a straight line, through a common channel, and into your mind. They've been communicated!

Here, let's try another. Ah, but I don't know if I should read this openly, with so many ears about. I trust you but not these other creeps. Do you have a place we could go?"

"Not really."

"Oh, I see. I understand. Well, then, I'll read another one in this rathole." He started pulling through the pages, and said, "By the way, I'm not a faggot."

"It's not that, it's—"

"That fellow, for instance," he said, pointing his chin toward Charles's book. "Roethke. Wasn't he a fruit?"

"What do you mean?"

"Always whining on about his daddy and those flowers of his."

"So what?"

"Didn't he kill himself trying to prove his masculinity?"

"Not that I know of," Charles said, and remembered reading that Roethke had died in a swimming pool.

"Not that I hold that against him. His pure lines aren't in any way touched by the uncomfortableness of that. I just wanted you to know that what I think of as his particular problem doesn't happen to be mine."

"It wasn't a problem. It was his experience."

"Sure, sure, I've heard that one before. Well, here. Now here is a ditty I feel is important, not just a daily jotting off on a dime. This is part of the long intermeshed account of the city. I'm planning to have it published soon, but refuse to let it go. It's not perfect. The feel has to be of a finely wrought jewel, how they stand alone, inviolate, and sparkle. I'm constantly cutting, inserting, adding on other facets, and then trimming away until it's down to a small shape with sharp edges. Do you know how a poem should feel if you held it between your fingers—like this —do you know, guy?"

"I guess."

"Like a jewel. Otherwise it's corrupt. It's not poetry but crap. Mishmash! A real poem can't follow the configuration of days, can it? No, it has to take its shape *out* of them, unattachable to time, with its own attractive shape, which is the shape of poetry over life. For instance, a real diamond, a jewel, instead of a ball park; or those swimming pools people have—I understand all the rich have them in their back yards or on their rooftops now, damn their hides—one of those pools in a poem would be an aquamarine, oblong and cool, a construct of syllables the senses could bathe in and come out refreshed. Do you see?"

"I'm not sure I'm awake yet."

"Well, here, let me cheer you up! I'll— Are you sure you don't understand?"

"I guess so."

"I don't know whether you do or not, or whether you say that to humor me, but let's forge on. I've been working on this for nine years now, and you perhaps can't relate it to the auxiliary parts—this is one of the final sections; the others are in nineteen other notebooks (no, I'm *not* the guy *The New Yorker* wrote about)—but still it should be able to stand as it is, on its own lapidarylike feet."

He elevated his hand as if in blessing, looked confused, let it drop, and paged backward, then stopped and fished a tangled hair out of the spiral binder and turned on.

Charles had a vision of a book: it would be a journal written by his mother, beginning the day Jerome was born, and would move through her years in Hyatt in an earth-colored, unbroken line, and then begin to explore her past, tentatively at first, as though stalactites were forming below the line, and suddenly drop and move back toward her birth, while the narrative grew thinner and thinner, until, at the journal's end, you'd feel left on paper-thin footing, looking down a sheer cliff. That would be her death. Then a series of multicolored pieces about North Dakota and Illinois, like large rocks in a stratum at the edge of her journal, each piece complete in itself, whole and unshakable, bearing no outward relationship to any other piece, implying that it's impossible to relate experience or contiguous periods of time in terms of continuity in our time (each moment, each year sealed off because it's escaped destruction and has to buttress the chaos battering at it), so that an incident from childhood might have more temporal value than ten years of adulthood, and this particular incident—set off and explored to its limits (this harked back to her journal)—would be more mature than the man carrying it; or it might be seen as outside him, a luminous omnipresence, a portion of his past that lay ahead and was a goal to be achieved if he was to grow— This wasn't entirely clear yet. But the pieces themselves, the rocks of the stratum, would lie

where they were, so you'd bump your head or wedge the
lines apart if they weren't entered on their own terms,
and then as more were added (but not so the book was
like shaking a puzzle box), pressure would be put on
earlier ones, and then at a certain point the first piece
would shift. Then, as another was added, several would
shift at the same time; and then a continual rearrangement,
a giving way begins (somewhere in here would go all the
trouble he'd had with women), and suddenly there's a
feeling of an earthquake, and an abyss opens in the book.
On this side of it, Charles's journal, the actor's journal,
Karl's journal, begins in New York, where the desolation,
the bleakness and anonymity are identical to that of the
plain, but more pernicious: man's constructed the city and
chosen to live in it; the plain is a natural phenomenon he
can always leave; swarms of people shoulder past more
swarms in the city without touching another life; people
move over unpopulated spaces of the plain to have a
specific effect on a particular person—so the city makes
him more conscious than ever of the plain. In his journal
the actor discovers attributes that belong to his mother instead of him, and so, fearfully at first, begins to explore
his past as his mother has, hoping to follow it backward
to hers, and sees everywhere in the city parallels to an
earlier life (these winos would be in it; like the Plains
Indians, caricatures of their former selves from the time
their homes, their spiritual roots, had been usurped;
more committed to illusions than others to reality, and
determined to sustain the illusions by continuing to drink
—fire-water, the Indian's name for it; how could the two
elements mix?—and remaining rootless), and after a
month's work it occurs to him that he's constructing, as
the city's been constructed, his own reality, artificial or
not, and making room for himself to operate within it
(his generation *acting* what hers actually felt?), whereas
his past lies outside him in a state as natural as the plain,
and he begins to long for an early love affair (here he'd
use Jill), but realizes that the affair began as early as
memory, or more. And then he sees his mother signaling
to him from the other side of the book and they reach for
one another across the abyss. (And now it had a title,
The End of Flesh, which would tie these two themes together.) The edge of her journal is, like the border of

North Dakota and he wants to return there, not just metaphorically, and is planning a trip when one afternoon in the New York Public Library he finds in a history volume (like the one his father found; that would have to be in earlier) a paragraph about his great-great-grandfather, on his mother's side, who disappeared from the plain without a trace during a buffalo hunt. He's electrified. He then begins to act out his prose instead of writing it (he'll say that without the voice, without the limbs and their movement through space, his spirit—his flesh?—turns stale) and then the prose begins to act on him; it hangs from him like ropes and chains and unopened padlocks and replicas of all his joyful days gone hard as brass. And then it works inward. He can't eat and it's hard for him to breathe. He puts pieces of it down on pages, finally, like scattering paper over paper in straight lines, and finds himself becoming unburdened, fragile and airlike, and then glances at his hand and sees that he can read his manuscript beneath it; his hand is transparent. This doesn't bother him, he's expected it, he makes a note of it and goes on writing, and at the end of the book his completed journal is discovered by a cleaning lady in an empty room with a mound of hair piled over its top. Maybe then an introduction by somebody who's known him (an editor? his brother?), telling how his family has insituted a search for him that's lasted several years, with Emil involved in it, but found no trace? Or a final paragraph of the actor knocking on the lines of his prose from behind to get out? Or *into* the world of his family? No, he'd remain motionless, flat on the page, like the plain. The plain, the plain, and each page a reminder of the cycle of the book, of course!

And then he remembered those puerile, unpolished, ramble-tongue and tongue-tied paragraphs, those scribblings, in his room, which he'd torn from the letter tablet and hidden in his paperback dictionary, and knew he could never write a book such as this, not in a lifetime or by himself, not without outside help, and never would.

"I seem to have lost you in my process of thumbing here," the poet said.

"No, no. Go on."

"You suddenly don't look so well."

"No, no, go ahead."

"Woman trouble?"

"Always."

"Common at your age. Don't fret about it. She'll come around. When I was in Oregon, just beginning to discover what would be my lifework, like you, I too had troubles, I must admit, with my wife of those days. I'd go off to work and imagine a truckload of spades piling into our bedroom, where she waited, and giving her exactly what she'd always really wanted in every way you can think of. The tragedy of it was it never failed to get me up, as they say now. That's no way to live, is it, boy? There were also other mismatchings, of course; I was too unsettled to be married, I was tippling too much, and the one woman I respected, other than my wife, slapped a paternity suit on me, and if a friend hadn't been having her at the same time, unbeknownst to me, and had the balls to come forward, she well might have won. I had a daughter I didn't want to leave, but had to, eventually, since women are always given custody in such cases, it seems. We were divorced when my daughter was three." He placed his fingertip on a line written across a page in a staggering hand. "This that I'm about to read, then, should be ready-made for miscreants such as we." And in his musical voice, read:

"*Wind riven, a vision of day ringing*
Within the confines of myself,
Where whores and hawkers cry
While folding blue pigeons rise,
White, in the wind, their undersides
Wine and emblems over my morning lament,
Configured windows through which I see
Features of you. Wings flap closed.
Hear the . . ."

He thumbed back a few pages and found some lines scrawled in red ink over a paragraph of minute penciling.

"*O hear the cry of the old sea*
Salt from out beyond Phoenix . . ."

Here he did some fast flipping in another direction and his squiggles of lines were like those characters you make into a movie inside a book by thumbing the edge of its pages in a quicksilvery screen of speed.

> *"As you called me, while I watch their flight,*
> *My eyes satiny coloraturas singing a blues song*
> *To the tune we strummed on one another that night.*

"You hear that? Nice.

> *"This page against myself turns outward now, like you,*
> *In praise of thighs white as white last century,*
> *Winglike, hard, dew, which shed jeweled tears*
> *Down their inward breadth, my selfless bone, the bed*
> *Of ourselves. Lights seem stoved. Do you mourn . . ."*

He started reading an address, said "Shit!" and went back to the beginning of the book and, as if by divination, found:

> *". . . mourn*
> *The mercury tubes that money the night over with green*
> *Beneath our balcony, my Juliet?*

"That was her real name, by the way." He shook his head and smiled. " 'Money the night over with green.' Sheer, sheer—well, just damn good. But let me go on to another part. This seems slow." He paged forward a ways, looked disturbed, and then turned back. "Ah. Here.

> *"Now faces shift across my inner eye*
> *And deaden this present—*

"No, no, wait. Here. Look! You see this? This is an insertion."

Charles glanced at the word, in big block letters, on which his blue-rimmed fingertip was resting: SHIMMER-ING***

"My shimmering eye," he said. *"Shimmering.* Here, let me do that section through, without interruption, so you can get a better feel of it." Preparing to juggle the pages like a conjurer, which he did, he read:

> *"Now faces shift across my shimmering eye*

And deaden this present distrust of you,
Lowering it through the grate of the past
To the firebox of a clattery red stairway.
Limbs flash on the landing there, a pubic patch,
The retreat of flesh, and eyes follow my eyes
Down into mine, my mine of me, and say, Stay.
But the orange chair, the open book, this one,
The torn woodcut of a naked woman signed Mary F,
The dying fern, aurelia, all of these menorrhagias
Left here in neglect, urge me to rise and climb
Up out of this foyer crowded with movables,
And none of them mine, parts of the city now,
Entangled in time immemorial as you,
As we turn again, two to two, winds ringing,
And part from our kiss.

"You hear how that comes in?"

> *"Now to align this night*
With Bethesda's long parlor cars of black remorse,
The—"

Another harried flipping.

"The soda for Mrs. Federman—

"No, no, wait. Here.

"In the ice of, in . . .

"Ach!" He seemed confused. One of his eyes was watering, and white spittle had formed in the corners of his mouth. He paused at a page covered with a rainbow collage of inks, and shook his head. "I'm afraid this isn't going to work. It's all in sections, you see, some polished, some fragmented, some needing to be discarded—and all different facets of the whole. Some, however, are parts of other poems, like the first snippet I read, and some of it, as you can see, is junk. Also, I'm getting the pieces mixed. But most of the parts fit now, and the rest will fit somewhere else, or so I'm hoping, when an end is found. What I should do, I guess, is read a piece complete in itself. Shit!

"I've worked hard to learn the sullen craft, and who knows? I thought I might hit it off somehow the way Pound did in that piece that goes 'Bitter breast-cares have I abided,/ Known on my keel many a care's hold.' " He sighed. "I've picked up my learning harum-scarum in libraries, bookstores, the street, and put a lot of time in in the worst sort of flophouse rooms, whine, whine. I've even been influenced by Ginsberg and, what's more, will admit it. Do you know why?"

Charles shrugged.

"You certainly rely a great deal on body English, don't you? All right, I'll tell you why: because I keep an open mind." He winked at Charles in a purposeful way. "You should, too," he said, and his silvery lashes clung. "The old *sea* salt! Well! This piece complete in itself! I keep re-refining all my earlier things, hoping to fit them into *this* book, and since I don't have a copy of what I'm thinking of here, I'll have to try my battered memory." He put fingers over his eyelids, and said in his reading voice, but with a new soft, slow, still edge, heart cams turning on a central shaft:

> " *'Watch the wind, Melinda, watch the wind!'*—
> *Shaking the earth's surface, sea, leaves, and air,*
> *The wind's going everywhere except where it's been*—
>
> *I call across the lawn as though you'd just sinned.*
> *The grass stems you tossed high are in our hostess's*
> *   dark hair.*

"I suppose your generation would take those stems as other than from a lawn, but so be it.

> " *'Watch the wind, Melinda, watch the wind!'*
> *'O the fairest elements are weather and a child's*
> *   whims,'*
> *Our hostess's eyes say, as more stems fly beyond her*
> *   and her bright stare.*
>
> *The wind's going everywhere except where it's been.*

> "*Be still, be you, Melinda, I want to say, then nothing*
> *You do is unmannerly or on a whim. And look at her*
> *   hair!*

'Watch the wind, Melinda, watch the wind,'

Returns to me in our hostess's voice, and her words be-
*   gin*
A villanelle that none of us knew was there.
The wind's going everywhere except where it's been

And chills me, a father who'd make your round world
*   square,*
When at your age, four, I too was free, fair-haired and
*   fair,*
So watch the wind, Melinda, watch the wind;
The wind's going everywhere except where it's been.

"I'm not sure I've rhymed that quatrain right, but I believe variants exist. I should stop at the library and check on that. Is 'hostess' too impersonal for you?"

Charles shrugged.

"The only other appellation I could think of was 'pretty lady,' and that seemed too butchified and general a term, though I like the sound of it. Pretty lady. Actually, she's a beautiful woman who has a husband who's her match. They lived almost smack on Cannon Beach, where Haystack Rock stands like the point of a fallen star. Oregon. They always had faith in me, in spite of my incorrigibleness then, and, what's more, were always kind to my daughter and wife. Thank you to them, then. I wrote this after a picnic in their back yard. "What's that?" my daughter asked about the caviar, and the host said 'Fish eggs.' Unflappable head on straight. A good heart. A year after the picnic I left for New York and haven't seen Melinda since.

"I never thought I'd be able to leave her, but when I was about to—she was five—we went for a walk along that same Cannon Beach. I sat against a rock, looking over the ocean, wondering where to begin and whose sake this was for, and lit up a cigarette and looked over at her and saw she'd pulled up a wild rose from somewhere and was puffing on it. I realized my *cellular* influence on her in that instant and vowed never to smoke again. I haven't quite kept up, but do well now. Anyway, I carried that image for thirty years, intending to work it into my larger poem as a sort of cautionary tale, but touching, too, dealing as it did with that day, my daughter, and her influence on *me*. And then one night a few years ago I was sitting in a White Rose bar, or a reasonable facsimile of one, tanked up on cheap stuff and full of their free sour food and feeling sorry for myself, when up on the television screen, on came a vignette about a boy walking in the woods with his dad. No dialogue. Nature sounds. Every sorry, sad-eyed SOB in that bar stopped and looked up. The father sat against a tree and lit a cigarette and the boy picked up a stick and stuck it in his mouth, and I thought, 'Holy Jesus! There's my moment! They've stolen it! All they did was substitute the stick for a rose and a boy for my girl!' How does that grab you?"

"Pretty weird."

"You better by damn bet you it was weird, my boy. And the gist of it was to get you to quit smoking. How life had come down on its knees for TV! Some vacuum-brained advertising huckster had sucked in the current of my thought and done *that* to it. It makes you wish you could work in a lead-lined room! But you can't keep yourself from thinking when you walk the streets, or I can't, and then the bastards'll steal from you left and right! They'll suck it out up from you through the TV! They'll take it out the air conditioners! What can a man do?"

"I have no idea."

"Hum," the poet said. "You can hum popular songs. They interfere with the brain currents and also set up activity with whoever else is humming what you are. Also, keep inserting and revising; it mixes them up. But I've told you too much already. I have to go." He slammed his notebook shut and stared at the counter a moment. "Then again, how would you like me to read something else?"

"Sure."

"Well, I hope your memory is less than photographic. This is a facet I wrote when I was wobbling toward madness, and I've been reluctant to look back on it." He opened to a middle page. The faggot prude.

> *"For the wind brings scents of the city tonight,*
> *Accents of sea, leaves, appeasement, and traffic oil—*
> *A wind splintering the intricate jewels of children's*
> *eyes."*

His body tensed, the air around him became charged

with imbalance, and Charles grew afraid for them both; he
closed the notebook, put a hand over his eyes, took out a
pencil, turned the book over, and opened its back cover.
The last page was blank. He looked at Charles and there
was a communion as their separate selves intermingled,
and then, dropping the tone he used when he recited, he
said, "True. But what can blow the wind away?

"Ah!" he cried, causing several customers to look up.
"Ah!" he cried again, and two of the winos, attuned to
impending catastrophe, the authority of the sober world,
police, possible implication, more unpleasantness and remorse, got up and left the restaurant as inconspicuously
as they could.

"There!" the poet said. "See that? What do you think
of *that?*"

Charles started to say he thought it was a nice line.

"But don't you see, don't you feel? Here, here, let me
do that again." He went backward in the book. "Now
listen.

> *"For the wind brings scents of the city tonight,*
>   *Accents of sea, leaves, appeasement, and traffic oil—*
>   *A wind splintering the intricate jewels of children's*
>   *eyes.*
>   *But as their irises rearrange in brighter shades . . .*

"Or something of the sort.

>   *". . . they say,*
> *'Father of Light! What can blow the wind away?'*

"Don't you see? That's it! That's the final facet, the
climax of my piece. That's the end!"

On the last page he scribbled down the lines, then buttoned up his pea coat, tossed some change onto the counter, and with the stalking stride of a small man hurried
out the steamed-up door. The regular customers were
staring at Charles, or rather at the stool beside him where
the aura of the poet still lingered, some with amusement,
some with vexation and disapproval, others with disgust,
a scattering of response so individual it was as if they'd
heard and understood exactly the last stanza the poet

read, and were waiting for the air to settle and resume itself.

Charles's food had gone cold, but he ate with an appetite for once. He'd go to Rockefeller Plaza and watch the ice skaters there, skirts twirling above white thighs, he'd promenade with the shoppers down Fifth and Park and Fifty-seventh Street, he'd make a visit to St. Pat's and pray at the statue of Jude again, he'd find where the carousel was in Central Park, he'd walk Brooklyn Bridge, he'd go into Chinatown and see if they celebrated Christmas there, and he'd buy gifts for his father and Marie and the rest and send them off airmail, with letters, too.

The door swung in, admitting a chill, and the poet, with a blue stocking cap pulled down around his ears, was coming around the counter with a changed countenance. Charles remembered what he'd said about not letting anybody see his poems, and felt afraid again. The poet stopped next to him, looking anxious and constrained, and finally said, "You must forgive me. In my excitement I forgot you." He took the notebook from under his arm and got out his pencil. "What is your name, please?" His tone was formal and cold.

"Charles."

"Charles what?"

"Klein."

"Spelled the same as the store?"

"Yes," Charles said.

"The address is irrelevant." The poet put away the pencil and notebook. "You, young man, whether you know it or not, are a true listener, and that's a rare gift. I was led on, I was inspired, and from that came the line that caused these facets to fuse into a single jewel. I'm going to recopy this book and the others I have at home in their proper order, in a good hand, and deliver them to a reputable publisher. The volume they'll make up, which will be out next year sometime, will be entitled *What Can Blow the Wind Away?* I sense in you an interest beyond mere curiosity, and you seem forthright and patient, a rarity among the New Yorkers I've met, perhaps a poet in your own right, in spirit if not in practice." He reached up and fumbled with his collar as if to cover his throat, and said, "When my book appears, it will be dedicated to you."

He was almost outside before Charles recovered and started rising and said, "Wait," which came out in a cry of pain because his thighs, caught under the counter, reseated him with a shock. He spun his stool around and ran outdoors, and saw the poet stepping over a mound of snow a plow had piled along the curb.

"Wait," Charles said, and came up behind him and took his arm, and then the restaurant door creaked open and a voice called, "Hey, boy, you going to pay?," as the snow under him collapsed and his foot plunged into the icy underground current of the gutter, swaying him like undertow, and he grabbed tighter to the poet for balance and felt, through coat and sweater and clothes, the bone of his arm, fleshless and frail, thin as bird bone.

The poet turned on him with wide eyes.

Charles undid his foot with a sucking sound, his soaked ankle aching in the cold air, and stepped back onto the sidewalk, thigh and chest muscles trembling, and called to the waiter, "I'll be right in, sir!" Dark building with its entrance at an angle to the curb. The sway the water gave him. To the poet, he said, "I'm sorry. Really. Could we meet some other time? I'm really confused."

The poet looked distant and wary, encroached upon, on the defensive. "Well, I don't know. Why do you ask?"

"You could read more of your poems."

"I feel uneasy reading in public."

"You could come up to my room if you like. It's pretty ugly, but it's private."

"I thought you said you didn't have a place."

"I'm ashamed of it."

"Do you have a tape recorder or any other such device there?"

"No."

"Because I wouldn't read in the presence of one."

"Could we meet tomorrow, then, about the same time, say, in the restaurant here, and then go up?"

"I don't know. I'm going to be busy trying to get my notebooks into the proper sequence now. I can't promise you." He sighed and lowered his eyes; lashes clung. "I'm already afraid some of the facets will clash, or that the ending won't be satisfactory still. I've had these inspirations before, not quite as strong as tonight, never this near the end of it, but I've had them, and they sometimes fail. We'll see."

On Charles's hand, like a clue that had been pressed there, was the sensation of his arm, how frail it was and yet was flesh, and now as the man stood drawn into himself against the cold, dwarfed by the wide white streets, the tall buildings, the night sky fuming with gray flakes, his pea-coat collar turned up high around his head, he looked less formidable, small and ordinary, a little ludicrous, even, with his reddened ears protruding from the stocking cap like a child's or half-witted old man's, and Charles understood that this was how other people saw the poet, and realized, now that the shock of the dedication was past, how alone one would have to be to make an offering of that sort to a stranger.

The poet sighed again—two lengthy blue plumes—and looked up; his eyes and nose were watering and a gust of wind sent moisture skidding along the wrinkles under his eyes. "For instance, I see that snow, a natural element, entering with ease man's province, lamplight, and I wonder if my poems, my hard-worked jewels, will ever make a picture like that, a glittering triangle, in some man's mind."

"I like them."

"I believe that, I believe you do, yes. Thus the dedication."

"I'm sorry. I lied."

"Lied?"

"I was— Anyway, my name is Neumiller, not Klein."

The poet's lips parted, a trail of vapor coiled in front of his face, and he said "Neumiller" in a voice that chilled Charles more than the icy underground water.

"Come inside and I'll get us some coffee or something, and try to explain."

"Neumiller, huh?"

"Or we can go up to my place, which is right across the street, there. It's not pretty, as I—"

"Goodbye."

"At least wait here till I pay my check."

"No, buddy."

"Tomorrow?"

"No, you won't be seeing me again, Mr. Neumiller, or Klein, or whoever the hell you are."

"Why not?"

He stalked to the center of the street and stopped in mid-stride as if his strength had left him, and then turned and cried, "You know perfectly *well*—" His voice went up the scale out of reach and cracked with a sound so shrill and unmusical it was as if the sky overarching this part of the city had been shattered and the snowflakes were broken fragments of it floating down around them both. "Because you're going to steal some of my lines!"

Charles wanted to say no, no, he wouldn't steal any of his lines, or if he did, he'd steal only one. "What can blow the wind away," but he wouldn't steal that one, either, really, and then a bus came whining down the street and swung out around the poet where he stood, unyielding, impervious, and when all was quiet again except for the ticking of snow somewhere on tin, he said, "I can also see that you're cheap and sneaky and avaricious, too. I was led on by you, all right! You're going to steal some of my lines or my ideas, or both, you young shit, you impostor, you sonofabitch, and I'm not going to get a single solitary penny for one measly fucking phrase of it, you know that, don't you, *damn you!*"

He turned and walked away through the heavier-falling icy lines and separate faces of flakes of snow, across the street and off through Tompkins Square, and his footsteps soon started filling with blowing, earthbound snow, steps that traveled over the white-woven winter landscape as if in a race.

42

A VISITATION

From the time he was first able to remember, all the way back to when words weren't words but colors and images of states of mind, what he remembered most of all was the quality of the stories his mother told at night. He'd lie on his back, looking at the circle of light cast on the ceiling by the lamp, and she'd sit beside the lamp, her face in shadow, her folded hands in her lap, and tell him about a time before he was born. Her stories were as simple and pure as the circle on the ceiling, and seemed to become a part of the light itself, distinct from him and even from her, so that when he turned on his side or on his stomach as she spoke, or when he turned to look at her, at her lips forming the words of the story, widening into a smile when there was a scene that pleased her, pursing in anger or indignation, relaxing at the corners when she was recalling sadness, even then the location of the story didn't change. Its source, its substance, its beginning and end was the circle of light.

She seemed a medium through which a spirit was passing, and that spirit gathered itself on the ceiling above her, a life in itself, a form he could absorb or look at impassively but whose substance he couldn't ignore; and when she left the room and shut off the light, its presence remained, a circle and breadth that widened above him where he lay. He'd breathe shallowly, feeling it as a heaviness of a mood or emotion more than any moment she'd extracted from time, and then, just as he was dropping off to sleep, he'd feel it descend and pass into him. Here it became a part of his dreams.

The mixture of colors, fragmented pictures doing double

stitches to become whole again, a phrase rising up from the center of a landscape, days unmistakable as mint, springs and fountains feeding every area of mindless thought, her voice; stories about the farms they lived on when she was a child, stories that her grandfather, a homesteader in the state, used to tell her—of grass fires, miles wide, coming toward him over the plain, of being snowed in for two weeks in a one-room shack while accumulating drifts rose toward the top of his stovepipe, of men wandering a mile from their homesteads and becoming lost, because the plain, with its russet covering of grass, was like a desert, the same in every direction. With a shading of amusement in her voice, she said that her grandfather always ended his stories of those days with the phrase, "Ya, sure, that was before we had windmills or trees."

And there were the stories about her and her closest brothers, Conrad and Elling, with seldom a mention of Jerome. Elling was the prankster who searched out a wren's nest and a magpie's nest and switched the two sets of eggs; who put a baby mouse in his father's riding boot, and might have got away with it if he hadn't bragged about it to Conrad; their father flung the boot across the room and broke out the glass door of the china cabinet, and for this, and for beating up Conrad, Elling had to live a week in the barn. He was changed, it was said, by the experience. He discovered some arrowheads while breaking up a new piece of land with the horse plow, and had intelligence enough to stop and dig deeper, discovering the site of a Mandan Indian village, which was sold to the Historical Society of North Dakota, and was now a well-known landmark. He came back from a summer with Sue and Einard and started telling his father how to run the farm, and was so condescending about it that old Jones finally cracked him with a cane so hard across his ass the cane broke in half. "I win!" Elling cried. He was expelled from Concordia College during his first year for touching up the bust of some college founder with red barn paint and for other antics that remained obscure, and then, after such an unpromising start, suprised everybody by leaving the farm and becoming, through hard work and years on the road, the Midwest distributor of Hart Parr tractors and farm machinery.

Conrad was accident-prone. He fell off the Shetland pony, Jake, so tame he was practically a house pet, and broke his collarbone, fell through a hole in the hayloft and broke three ribs, fell off a corral and broke the leg he'd broken falling off Jake another time; was chased around the yard by a turkey gobbler and, while glancing at it in horror over his shoulder, ran into a haystack and broke open his head. He seldom got angry, but when he did he picked up a length of pipe, a branch, a pitchfork—whatever was at hand—and chased Elling up to the porch and into the house. He once said to his mother in a calm voice, "I'm going to kill Elling today." He wanted a dog from the time he could speak, and on his fifth birthday his father gave him a water spaniel a few weeks old, and said, "If I ever see that thing in the house, I'll take down the gun and shoot it, I swear." Conrad named it Curly and carried it in his arms all morning and afternoon, and wouldn't even come in for lunch, but later, when he went in for a drink, took his father's warning to heart and left the dog outside, on the porch, in the safest place he could find, a basket of dirty clothes from the weekly washing his mother was busy at. Before he'd finished his drink, the dog crawled out of the basket and jumped from the wash bench onto a copper boiler below, tipping up its lid, and went sliding into the scalding water. Jones heard its agony and ran onto the porch and saw Conrad trying to lift it out of the boiler with his bare hands (nobody could), and when in the end Jones had to shoot the dog after all, he'd never believe Conrad hadn't put it in the boiler on purpose, because a few weeks before, he'd caught him trying to drown some baby ducks in the horse tank.

Each of her stories about Conrad ended with, "Your Uncle Conrad, I want you to know, has been terribly misunderstood all his life." And there was a shading in her voice that implied, "I, too, have been misunderstood, and when you grow up you can expect the same."

And there were stories whose details he couldn't remember but whose moods he retained; the next day, or weeks later, as he was sitting in the alcove of the bay window, playing with the toys he'd gathered there, one would rise in him and he'd pause with abstracted eyes, testing the quality of what he felt, trying to decide if it was a detail from a story of hers or an incident from his actual life, and one afternoon as he was sitting like this, looking past a windmill built out of Tinkertoy parts, conscious only of a hot brocade (the effect of sunlight coming through the lace curtains of the bay window) spread over his cheek and ear, he heard, from the far end of the front hall, the sound of his mother's voice pitched in surprise, the sound of other voices, and then a racket of laughter.

He stood and the windmill tipped and hit the hardwood floor. He looked down and saw that one of the blades of its fan, a piece of violet paperboard, had come loose. The door to the hall swung open and his mother walked into the room with a broad, heavyset man, a stranger, following in her wake, bringing with him a chilly draft and a fragrance of spring from the outdoors. The stranger smiled, and said, "And this must be Jerry. It's hard to believe he's already so big." The man came to the bay window, the floor trembling under his heavy strides, and held out some pamphlets. "Here," he said, "I brought you these. Go ahead, don't be bashful, take them!"

"Jerome!" his mother said. "What's the matter with you? Don't you know who this is?"

Jerome remembered a similar man with a smell of cold air clinging to him, a stranger who came to the house and gave him a package of Sen-Sen and then tickled him until he turned blue, couldn't catch his breath, and had to have a pan of water thrown in his face. Was this the man? He looked to his mother for confirmation.

"Shame on you," she said. "That's *Elling*."

Jerome's eyes grew; could the Elling of his mother's stories be standing before him, so old and so fat?

"Here," Elling said, and held out the pamphlets again. Jerome took them and Elling removed his hat, placed his hands on his knees, and bent over until his face was only inches from Jerome's. "What's the matter?" he asked. His blond hair, cut close to his skull, sparkled in the sunlight, and his long ears glowed orange, making him look luminous, which made him seem even more unreal. "You're not scared of your uncle? You're not an old fraidycat, are you? You're not afraid I'll tickle you until we have to douse you with water again, huh?"

"He's probably just bashful," a deep voice said, and Jerome looked up. Another man came through the door and stood behind his mother. This one was so tall that his face, which was tanned mahogany up to the hatline (the rest of his forehead was pure white), and his broad shoulders, too, encased in a black overcoat, showed above her crown.

She said, "Well, if you don't remember Elling, who's been here before, you won't remember him."

"How do you do," the man said in his deep bass voice. "I'm Conrad."

Jerome looked at the pamphlets in his hand. On the cover of the top one was a colored picture of a tractor with a man at the controls and some printing under its wheels. Somehow the picture related the phantoms that made up the circle of light on the ceiling, the Elling and Conrad of his mother's stories, to the Elling and Conrad here in the flesh. If they were here. He glanced up and found them smiling at him in uneasiness. He was in the same room with characters out of the past. Strangers. Ghosts.

"If he's just going to stand there and gape, come on and sit down," she said. "Take off your coats."

They put their overcoats on opposite arms of the couch and sat on either side of her, facing Jerome.

"I've got some stuff for the other boys," Elling said.

"They're taking their naps."

"Oh." He looked disappointed.

"I was just talking about you last night," she said.

"The hell," Elling said.

"I was telling the boys about the time you went over to the Ricordati place to bring back those sheep that got out—"

"And traded a lamb for old man Ricordati's .22?" Elling asked. "That time?"

"Yes."

"Dad waled the daylights out of me. I was sure he wouldn't miss the lamb, but I'll be damned if I knew how to account for the .22. You told them that?"

She nodded in an energetic way, a smile on her face, and Elling turned to Jerome and whispered, "Don't believe a word of it. I wasn't ever that dumb."

The adults laughed with an intimacy that excluded Jerome and yet relieved him, too; he was freed from their conversation to do as he pleased. He sat on the floor and began paging through a pamphlet.

"Wheeel, what brought us here today?" Elling said. "To tell you the truth, you might say an accident. Or the concatenations of circumstance." He looked aside at them, but they continued to study him with unchanged expressions of affection and interest; they expected to be dazzled by him.

"I had to make the drive over from Fargo to Valley, anyway, to see my district representative there, and then over to Jimtown and on up to Carrington, and since I'm breaking in my new car and wanted to get some extra miles on it, what I did was first I swung out to home to say hello to the folks, and here was Brother in from Wadena. When he saw the Pontiac and heard I was tired of driving it—why, you can't take it above forty and, God, that gets on my nerves—he offered to chauffeur me the rest of the trip. And since—"

"You're driving his new car?" she asked.

The grin Conrad gave in reply—with his teeth and the whites of his eyes in shining contrast to the tan so deep it made his features indistinct—confirmed or implied there was nothing he'd heard of or seen that would be able to get between him and his pleasure as long as he was back behind that wheel pretty soon.

"Well, you be careful with it, you hear?"

His grin grew wider with every reference to him, as though he'd never been paid this much attention before.

"And since he's been wanting to get into Jimtown from the day he got home, or so he tells me, this was convenient for the both of us. Wheeel, we were driving along, happy as can be, into Jimtown and on up toward Carrington, until we got around Melville, I think it was, when he mentioned he hadn't ever seen Timmy, or your new house here, and wondered if we couldn't make a little side trip and drop in on you, so I said, 'Sure! What the hell! Why not?' "

"I don't understand why you haven't done it sooner. It's been two years."

"Oh, it can't be that long."

"Jerome will soon be six. He was four the last time you were here."

"That was two years ago?"

"Two years this June."

"Ah, damn, two years is a *long time*. It's a good thing Brother was with me this trip, is all I can say, or I probably wouldn't be here now!"

"It's obvious that he cares about others and you don't."

"Oh, now, Alpha, you—"

There was a distant rumbling sound, as of someone moving furniture in an upstairs room, which was so faint and short-lived that by the time they'd listened to make sure they'd heard right, or misheard, the sound had stopped. "Was that Martin?" Elling asked.

"No, he's at school."

"Jerry!" Elling said. "Jerry, you want to ride my pony?" He lifted his hat and patted his knee where he expected Jerome to sit.

"He responds best to Jerome," she said.

Elling paled at the name. "Hey, there, then, *will* you ride my pony? 'Pony boy, pony boy, won't you be my pony boy,' " he sang, jogging his knee in time to the beat. " '*Don't* say no, here we go—' "

Jerome picked up another pamphlet and a look of perplexity darkened Elling's face. "Can he read?" he asked.

"Well, somewhat, although I'm not trying to force it. He won't start school till this fall."

"How are the pictures?" Elling asked.

Jerome looked up and smiled, honored that he was being spoken to as an adult, but since he didn't know how to respond to the honor, equally embarrassed.

"Can't you talk?" she said. "Do you like them or not?"

"Yes."

"We got a word out of him!" Elling cried. "That's a start! When strangers come to our place, my kids hide in the john!"

"Well, you're not strangers," she said. "And if he doesn't know how to behave around his uncles, he can sit there like a dunce."

"I know how he feels," Conrad said. "I was the same way once."

"Oh!" she said. "Do you remember the time you saw those nuns? Mama had taken you into town, into the department store, and was looking through the linens and white things. You didn't know it, but the reason she had you along was to buy you a jacket for your birthday. Two nuns came into the store. You'd never seen a nun in your life, and when you turned around and saw them there, right behind you, you pointed at them and yelled, 'The black ones! The black ones!' Mama was so mortified it's hard to say how much, and I think that's had an effect on my religious life ever since."

She and Elling laughed and Conrad's forehead turned rose-red; then he lowered his eyes. "I didn't know I was supposed to get a jacket," he murmured.

"Talk about being scared!" Elling said. "Remember when we were on the old McGough place, near Dazey, and the folks went out to supper somewhere and left the three of us home alone? We were wondering what we could do without getting into a lot of trouble, as usual, when one of you—why, I think it was you, Alpha—you brought me this book and asked me to read a piece in it, and we all sat down on the couch, like this, except you two were on the either side of me, and I tied into it.

"What kind of a guy wrote that story is what I'd like to know! Houff! Peeeow! It was about this man that stabbed his sister, tied her in chains, and as if that wasn't enough, stuffed her into this moldy tomb in the basement. And then this friend of his comes to visit the guy, and the sister revives or rises from the dead, or wasn't stabbed right to begin with—Christ, who knows!—and she decides to get even, so, sure enough, while they're upstairs talking, up she gets out of the coffin, blood all over her and everything, up the stairs she comes, and walks into the room where they are. Well, just as I got to that part, there was this big boom on the front porch. I was afraid to breathe. Much as I wanted to close that damn book, I couldn't. There was all kinds of scratching and pattering out there, too—*chains, chains,* is what I thought, but it was probably just a chicken—and I swear I even heard the front door open and close. But we sat stockstill—we couldn't move—and I thought, Any second now, we're going to have a corpse coming in that door."

"We sat that way for an hour!" she said. "We were in the same spot when the folks got back! They figured we must have done something awful, we were so quiet, but we never told them, did we? I think we were too ashamed to admit how scared we'd been."

"Ashamed?" Elling said. "My Christ, I was in my teens!"

"I was eight, then," Conrad said. "I remember well."

"There was an old man who lived across the road from us at that farm," she said. "In the little shack beside the granaries. Do you remember him? He had a long white mustache and used to pour his coffee out in a saucer to cool it. What was his real name? Who was he? We called him 'Uncle,' but I know he wasn't our uncle. Was he really related?"

"I think it was Mama's uncle," Elling said. "He spoke some foreign tongue. Finnish, I think. I don't know what happened to him or why we never heard about it. One day he was just gone. Wasn't somebody else living there with him?"

"Some woman," she said. "But I can't remember her name. I don't think they were married, either."

"That doesn't sound like Ma's uncle to me," Elling said. "And it's probably the reason he had to move, too."

"Do you remember when Daddy got into a barroom brawl?"

"Which time?"

"Oh, the worst, I guess."

"Somebody hit him over the head with a bottle of gin. A full one. You could smell him a mile off."

"Do you remember the sheep dog, the collie who ate cigarette butts?"

"Duke," Conrad said.

"Do you remember—"

"Whoa!" Elling said, and held up his hand. "Right here's where we stop. I've got a speech I've been wanting to make for years, and now, by jing, I'm going to make it. This reliving the past happens all the time, even when I'm away from you two—especially when I'm alone— and it's not a mentally healthy way to be. Every time it happens, it's like I'm stepping out of what I don't want to be into who I really am. And that's bad. It's not who I am, actually. I'm *me*. That person's gone. I have to stop myself and say, 'No, no, no, that's all over! Here's where you are now. You have a wife and kids. You have an important job to do.' That's what I say and sometimes it helps, but it doesn't change things much. Old man McGough still means more to me than any millionaire client, and I could damn near tell you how many times the team of bays broke wind on a given workaday: 'A fartin' horse never tires, a fartin' man's the man to hire.' Dad's line. The smallest detail from then is clearer in my mind than what I did last year, or yesterday, or the day before that, and the older I grow and the farther I get from those days, the clearer and more important the details seem. Will the present ever be like that? I don't know. I hate to think that the best times have to be dead and gone before you can appreciate them, and that's why I don't like to remember the past or even talk about it much.

"You mustn't misunderstand me, though. I don't believe in going backwards. A person's got to do what he's got to do and he's got to grow up! But it does seem a shame that the— By God, it *is* a shame, a crying shame, and a crime, and it's not right! That's the way I feel about it, and that's the way everybody else does, too!" He listened for a moment to their silence, and then said, "Isn't it?"

"Well, if—" she began.

"Oh, yes," Conrad said. "Those days are best. I keep going over them and over them again and again, over them and over them, just like they were the only part of my life I really lived. And, you know, it doesn't make any difference how many times I go over them. They never grow tiresome and I never run out of things to think about. Oh, I couldn't begin to tell you the half of it, you two. The hay fields, the grain fields, the way the sun was then, the way the people were, how we were different, too. There've been so many times I've—"

His eyes hazed and he lowered his head. There was a shifting moment between them, and then Elling said, "Why, look! Before we started getting farmed out, if we were ever separated for as much as a day, we started a small rebellion, and, why, now look, now we've been apart for two years, for two whole years, and none of us has even noticed it!"

"Maybe you didn't," she said. "But I did. I've missed you both. I've missed you and I miss the folks."

"Oh, sure you have," Elling said, "I know you have. But it's a different *kind* of missing. We don't throw tantrums like we used to, or drop everything and run off to make sure one or the other is where we think he is, doing what he might be doing. We don't even write. We get by.

We get by somehow and, hell, that's the worst part of it, that we get by."

"Yes," Conrad said, his bass voice blending with the rumbling sound that had begun again. "Yes, and every year it gets worse."

The bay window had been darkening and now it started to rain. She looked at Jerome with a frown, as if he were responsible, and Conrad and Elling glanced at one another and then turned to him, too. He went to the curtain and looked and listened to the rain falling onto the roof, the sidewalk, the lawn, and the leaves of the lilac trees, and then, without a warning flash of light, the first eruption of thunder came and made the panes of the window vibrate beside his face. He lowered the curtain, went to his windmill, and sat down beside it.

"He might be afraid of his uncles," Elling said, "but not of the elements. That's good."

"I was thinking I heard some thunder before," Conrad said. "Well, it's good for the crops."

"But not the roads," she said. "Can't you stay the night?"

"Oh, no," Elling said. "Hell, no. Conrad's got to be back for *chores*. No, just the roads down around Spiritwood are bad. After that, we'll be fine. Modern blacktop now."

"Was there a thunderstorm predicted?" she asked.

"This isn't a thunderstorm," Elling said. "This is a cloudburst."

"Maybe," Conrad said. "But it's not going to let up just yet."

"How do you know?"

"I can feel it in my bad knee, the one I broke when— well, you know."

"I thought that meant trouble."

"Sometimes it means a good hard rain, or has lately."

They looked at one another in a nervous way, and then turned to Jerome, and for the first time since they'd been together, a silence, which contained in it only the sound of rain and the sound of water running off the eaves, filled the room and spread through the house. A sleepy voice started saying "Mom, Mom," from behind the door of the bedroom.

"Tim," she said.

"Good," Conrad said. "I'll get to see him."

"Mom?"

"And now there's Charles. They'll both soon be with us, you can bet on that."

Jerome was trying to reinsert the trapezoid-shaped violet blade back into the slit at the end of the stick. The piece of thin paperboard had been used a lot and its edges were frayed; he wiggled it at the top of the stick; it wouldn't go in. He examined the end of the stick, and then placed it against an incisor and pushed up on it, gently at first, trying to flare the slit, and the buzzing warmth at the roof of his mouth reminded him of attempting that another time, splitting the stick, and running its pointed end into the roof of his mouth. He rubbed his tongue along the ridged skin of his palate, which was itching now, pulled out the stick, and looked at the violet blade. He put it between his lips, compressed them, drew it out, put it there and drew it out again, copying what his mother did with thread before she speared the eye of a needle, and then aligned the dampened edge of the blade with the slit in the stick, stopped, and looked up.

All three of them were staring at him. They shifted their weight on the couch and looked at him uneasily, as if to say, Go on with it. Please. If you get that together, we'll be back on the right track. Go ahead.

Then the three of them locked into place, making it seem he was staring at a photograph that had been snapped of them at that moment, and began receding into the depths of his mind, growing smaller and more faint and retreating as though they were spirits he'd taken by surprise (as indeed they were; that same afternoon, brochures and pamphlets for Hart Parr farm machinery were scattered in the wet grass from an unmarked railroad crossing a hundred yards down the tracks to where the train, dragging with it a Pontiac that held the remnants of two dead men, finally came to a stop; and five years later his mother died after having her stillborn child), until the three of them disappeared altogether, and Jerome, encumbered with the full weight of his twenty-seven years, now an interne, finds himself sitting under lamplight in the sleeping room that will be his home for the next year, thinking, Where did all of that laughter out of the past just now come from? and glimpses Tim and Charles revolving at the edges of a whirlpool of water or air as they echo one another's laughter, in the way that his uncles and mother entered the room laughing, and sees that he's staring at a pamphlet in his lap opened to the first page:

Emergency Room Procedures
Garfield Park Hospital
Chicago, Illinois

43

THE MANY-COLORED UPRIGHT PIANO

Here I am at this old upright piano, banging away just like a breeze and thinking sin. Laura. Bring that phrase back around so it's known it was meant to go off-key and begin again. *Laura.* It's down to a game between her and the two of us still stuck here at home, not counting Ginny, of course, who is hers and will always be hers from this side of the fence; it's not Ginny I hate, I hope, but *her,* as Marie and I have come to call the "her" who's now family magistrate without our ayes or a feel of the place. She'll come up with a fake-pleasant smile and say, Susan, Susan, I want to talk with you and Marie and Ginny in my office awhile, and the talk among her dress patterns and sewing machine and sawed-off, console piano will be about general neatness around the house, or hosing down the kitchen the second after a snack, or getting clothes and cots right off to a closet so people won't know we're such awful slobs (not her words; she's so sweet), and all this is directed at Ginny, or at times Marie, so you know that she knows that *I* know it's intended for me. She won't even give me the thinnest glance, the chicken, the wicked pretender, and I've learned that whenever she says "Girls," it's me she means, *It's Me.*

Money, money, money's another theme. I could always go up to Dads and ask for cash and the most I'd have to put up with was a one-sided, my-sided argument about the amount, but once he married her and I went to hit him up for some, he said he didn't have any money to give any more; *she* was handling that now. He was on an allowance, for God's sake, a kid again! What she's done to the man in him! What's he carrying in his pockets?

Are they sewn shut? Do you think I'd plead with her for more than a minute about a buck? I feel from her that money's made of shame. And Dads, my long-time god, sits in the big chair with nothing in his pants and no you-know-whats, groveling to please her and leave the rest of us in the dust, and keeps pestering Marie and me to call that floating figment of family fate "Mom" and making the contents of my stomach climb up. I can't even remember calling my own mom "Mom" or whatever I called her while she was here.

I could swallow most of the crap, I guess, in the general way I usually swallow crap, but the worst of it is that lately she's been whining about wanting to move. Back to Chicago, no less. And drag all of us along, as if Pettibone, where this patched-together and reasonably peaceful house and all of my friends are, isn't good enough for somebody who teaches music, or did for three years in the Windy City, as Dads has to call the place, trying to ease the feeling that those of us trapped and in collusion here have for it, perhaps ("Well, I'd never think of living in the city itself," Laura said once, "In one of the suburbs, of course," while I thought as far as *I* was concerned, if you're going to live there, then why not in the center of it, huh?); who can teach music, then, and articulate a lot of the feeling she has for it on the keyboard, and can rattle away at typing faster than a bat out of hell, playing another type of tune on those clattery keys, and knows shorthand and can go shopping like an adding machine, and drinks gin in the summer and whiskey the rest of the year —click, click, the ice in the glass, ho hum. There's nothing in the world that bores me more than people who drink, and I've said so two or three times when I was sure she could hear.

I've mentioned to him how much against the move-to-Chicago project I am, but he doesn't hear, either, or if he does, doesn't care, now that he's become dedicated to pleasing nobody but her. How I hate her! How Marie does, too, at times, although she's too honest to keep it inside her or let it glow too long. She's a cheerleader this year, at last, after practicing those leaps and splits and arm pumps and mind-buckling chants from the day she was four, and has a boyfriend who takes her out parking in his car, and will have to give that up if we go, at the

least, and says she won't, but who's to say? In my case,
I've felt cooped and dammed up in dear old Pettibone
from the day I could see, and expect to go off to the
university and break a goal or two, instead of getting married to a farmer the day I graduate, as half of the girls
around here seem to. I'm going somewhere even if it's
from here to hell and back, by jeez!

I don't compare Laura to my mother and find her lack-
ing in every respect to this glorious woman who once
walked the globe, as the boys portray Alpha N. I can't
remember her, not a hair of her, though I wouldn't admit
it to anybody in the family, in or out of it, and I've heard
enough about her to see her however I please, and not
always in a saintly light. An aunt or else a woman friend
of hers once told me she died while she was in the
middle of toilet training me (now, who has a memory
like that?), and I do recall a lot of noise from some
woman or other over what looked at the time like peanut butter in a cup.

What I mostly remember from then is Grandma and
Grandpa N and the *slam! slam!* of the loom as Grandma
banged away at making a rug, and the balls of material
made by cutting up worn-out clothes and sewing the strips
together—huge balls I got to roll over the loom-room floor
—and Grandpa N so stern and solemn, locking me in the
closet one day because of a dirty word, and me feeling
around in the dark through all of those clothes and shoes
and coming across— My scream must have been telling,
because there was light in an instant and old Gramps was
at the door saying, "What is it in there?" in a shaky way,
while I checked it out and saw it was a pink piggy
bank the size of a baby pig, was what it was in there, and
I wanted to say, I'll never forget or forgive you for this,
you old fart, you.

The reason I've been hating her so much is her gall in
bringing *up* this move, knowing that Dad's so entangled in
her he'll commit any sort of crime against us to please her,
and because just yesterday she said, as if it were settled,
"Well, that old piano will have to stay here, of course."
This piano I'm playing now! This lovely old upright that's
been in the house since I can remember, and came all the
way from Hyatt, this piano that Marie and I learned to
play on—and I worked at it, too; there were days when

I sat on this bench so much I could taste it—that Tim would sometimes play when he was home from Wisconsin, and make it appear it was the source of all the mystery in him, or that music was, as he squeezed out with equal ease Chopin and "Dizzy Fingers" and phrases as green and thundery-reeling as the hills around Sue and Einard's place; pastures appeared from the heart of it (was it improvised?), while blue strings wound like a river through them, water he'd walked beside, and I could smell the attacks of his fingers, and perfume, and then he'd stump over the keys with his elbows and clown.

And Jerome and Charles played duets on this when they were in the second grade, or younger yet, and now sometimes as a joke would sit together on the bench, big butts bumping, and play in a toe-stubbing tempo tunes such as "Swinging Along," and it was one of the few times you could see in their faces that they'd been kids once and grown up together, since both of them, here in the present, were so *da-dum* solemn. Surely it was a tie for them to a life that was past, and their music stirred up currents from then whether you liked it or not. And when the guys from North Dakota, the boys from the basketball team, were living in the house here, they'd gather at this old upright over the weekends, and one would chord away while another played the cornet, the third the drums, *rumpa tat tum*, and their music, though not the best I've heard, always made me sigh for an element that must have been carried through them from Hyatt to here and was missing in old Pettibone. Being in Pettibone is a bore, true, Laura, to me, too, I admit it, but who are you to say this paino is or isn't going, or is staying here, while your little pipsqueak of a machine will damn well follow us wherever we move? Or where you choose for us to?

When there's so much of our past in this piece I'm pounding on or off on, huh? It's a bit out of tune and not in such beeoooteefull shape now, as Dads would say, and I've heard from him why it is that it happens to look the way it does; when I was a baby, or not even born yet, he got a can of stripper and stripped its dark-cherry color away, and then tried to stain it blond. But the stripper didn't work well, or else the blond wasn't dark enough, and the half-peeled finish kept peeking through in spots; then he ran out of stain and used two different colors on one of the ends, trying to match up with the original blond, but neither color did. Those two colors are with us yet. The cover for the keys and some of the underparts, like those columns on either side, were never stripped or stained at all, so the original finish is also here to see.

But hear these chords, these suspensions, resolutions, and more chords, *Laura*. I can see you in your swivel chair, your book in your lap, scowling at this. You do know your music and must feel the hate in this. Soon you'll come over with your martyred look and ask me to stop. I will. I feel sorry for you for the latest you've gone through. Jerome is the only one who's been kind to you and Jerome is never here any more, lately, I say, as I send out more rays of—

Let's switch to the she of you for a more comfortable tune: Last summer she had to quit smoking because it bothered her so much in "this humid downstate air," and then went to a doctor who found one of those lumps that every woman must fear from the time she develops, as *I* have, and had to go into the hospital and have a breast removed, her left. Then had to be driven to Peoria for some sort of treatments under a machine, but never talked about it to us. For two months her arm was in a sling and then was so painful to move, she had to support it with her other hand. Now she was cured, the doctors said, and wore something to make her look whole, but for months after it happened, and now, still, I feel I'll never want to have sex. Not that that's the cause, of course (Marie and I decided right away that both of them were too old), but that's how I feel.

Males! I've helped Dad grade papers from the time I was eight, picking up math and parts of speech from him, and enjoyed the help I was able to give over those years when he was alone, but lately he's been handing me *all* his papers to grade, while he goes off with you. Did you know that? And there are the games Tim and Charles used to play when we were too young to understand what they were doing. I know Ginny's brothers were never as involved in that as those two. Somewhere in one of the albums is a pair of pictures taken by Charles the day he got out the makeup kit and created two different faces of

me. Look them up. In one I'm wearing an Angora tam
and have mascara-ringed eyes, rouged cheeks, a rosebud
mouth, and look like my conception (formed in later
years, of course) of a French whore. In the other, there
are wrinkles and lines in my face, bags under my eyes,
some of my teeth blacked out and others made to look
like fangs, and I've got on a frizzy wig that Tim used to
wear, plus a cone-shaped hat for the occasion: a witch.
Oh, boyohboyoh*boy!* Which of the two of us is his idea of
the real me, or women in general, I wonder, huh? Because another time, later, Laura, when Marie was budding
and I was just beginning to start, he came up with his
lieutenant, Tim, who had a tape measure, and said, Ah,
maybe we should marry—uh, measure your, ah, you-
know-whats.

What do you mean? Why? What?

For brassieres.

Glong! Coming out with a tape measure yet! Just so
they could get their fingers on us and then with all the
measuring and adjusting and rearranging and remeasuring
they had to do, I felt my fur tighten and fringes tingle
along the edge as— Oh, *damn them!*

Let's be friends. I'll make this move in a mouselike way,
assuming that's what you want, just to get out of this
place and see where my mind can begin, if you'll stop
looking so martyred and meet Dad each day with your
usual smile. And bring this piano along. Are you listening
to me? One last phrase. It's the piece I heard you im-
provising the afternoon you thought you were alone in the
house and drew me walking to you to see who it was who
played, and though I can't do it with your grace or skill,
or experience, or technique, here:

She watched him empty all of himself into her and be-
come molecular and indistinct, mingling with her feelings
for him and all the hard fantasies she'd ever had of men,
boards and stones under her back, rocks in her pillar, and
then he was a speck afloat on the sea of her breaking
around an endless peninsula, and the faster and erratic
sounds sent her revolving farther and farther over unex-
plored and then uncharted shores, until she cried out and
kicked the bed and the wall and then him again with the
end of it, and floated back down to herself through herself,

*through layers of many-hued and anomalous shapes, like
late water lilies in the bay of a lake, and kissed his face.*
So then who am I? And who am I to talk?
Plump tiddle lump pump, *whang! whang!*

44

꧁꧂

THE END

Charles was the first of the children to marry and put out the lines to link his generation of the family to families other than his. He began to find regular employment as the voice-over for television commercials, and moved from the Lower East Side to the East Fifties, where he met Katherine. She'd graduated from Columbia but had become disenchanted with the confines of academic life, and was now one of the numberless apparitionlike beauties who can be seen covering the midtown streets of Manhattan with a portfolio in tow, looking for work as a model; she'd been a dancing-singing extra in a series of commercials for a soft drink that all but promised eternal youth, and was featured below the knees in a photo campaign for a foot deodorant called *Ahhh!* A dream job. Until she married Charles, she'd been largely supported by her father, an industrial contractor from Cicero, a widower who had no sons and wasn't able to stay in school beyond the eighth grade, and was indignant at the use she was making of her college education. He refused to attend her wedding ("The guy makes money talking on TV?") and said, "I won't have anything more to do with you, Kath, and there won't be any more dough." But about once a month he'd call at four or five in the morning, drunk and maudlin, and talk to her as if she were still seven. She miscarried in the first year of their marriage and there was an aura about her and Charles, an introspective sadness and an attention to the smallest moods in one another, that made you feel they'd never have any children; they couldn't be near one another without touching or holding hands; they had a dog, Lady.

Tim was married a year and a half later, in September, and Charles couldn't attend the wedding because he was deep in the miasma of analysis. Tim had met his wife, Cheri, in the registrar's office of the university he attended, where she worked as a secretary, and they were secretly engaged until Tim received his B.A. Cheri had a straightforward look, impish and flirting, that seemed to apprasie the world outside with the healthy appetite some people have for food. After she and Tim had been dating awhile, he learned that she was a Catholic, which he was trying to be, and that she'd been raised on a farm only twenty-five miles from Sue and Einard's, where Tim still lived; and although Tim and she hadn't met before, they discovered, as they sifted through their pasts, that they'd been to many of the same dances and social gatherings of the small-town rural area—River Falls, Bay City, Hager, and Red Wing—when they were younger. Tim was hired that summer as an instructor in high-school biology in northwestern Wisconsin, and within a year Cheri gave birth to a daughter, Martin's first grandchild. She was given Alpha as her middle name.

Jerome was doing an additional internship in general practice at Cook County Hospital, in order to broaden his spectrum of experience, and on the weekends and when he wasn't on duty, he went to a Panther storefront clinic in a South Side neighborhood and worked there, donating his time and any medications he could shake free from the hospital; at the end of a long letter to Tim, he wrote, "I'm trying, as I think you can see, to be a Savior." He'd once sat up for three days with a woman dying of uremia.

Marie was majoring in Special Education for the mentally retarded, handicapped, and clinically insane. She'd become the most handsome of the children, with a high noble forehead somewhat like their father's, large eyes with many-hued depths of sympathy in them, and a mouth that looked swollen and bruised in a way that she, being airy and innocent-minded, probably wouldn't think of as sexual. Susan, who was the brightest and certainly the most carefree of the children, or so she seemed to the rest, quit college at the end of her first year, as Martin had unhappily predicted ("Because she's so headstrong and has her own ideas, like her mother"), and married the boy she'd been dating there. They moved to a Chicago suburb, where he started as the produce manager of a supermarket, and then was moving up to managing the store when he won a lottery that guaranteed him a sizable income for the next ten years, and now was trying to decide what to do while still keeping on at his job. Susan was the bookkeeper for a physician and worked six days a week.

Ginny was now taller than Laura, well over six feet, and was still as thin as before, but her braces had been removed and with them a degree of awkwardness went, and her face cleared and took on an inquisitive, ascetic look. She wanted to become a model and Katherine was her heroine. Ginny wrote her long, affectionate letters, asking about the clothes she should wear to complement her height, what hairdo would go best with her shape of face, and was it difficult to become a model? Charles and Katherine invited her to New York over a spring vacation and took her for walks down Park and Madison and Fifth, around the fountain and into the Plaza for lunch, and on the long hack ride through Central Park; and one night Charles took her to the Rainbow Room, paid a waiter for a table next to the orchestra, and he and Ginny danced close to the microphone where Duke Ellington stood and cheered them on. She was doing a younger, Chicagoish version of the dance he was doing, and he realized he must look like a dirty little old gangster out with his daughter. He'd been drinking too much lately and drank too much again that night, and when they got back to the apartment gave Ginny a smeary kiss, sat her on the couch and let his head fall in her lap, and said, "Agh, Ginny, babe, how I'd love to eat you up."

Martin had been attending night school at Bradley University, and one time when Tim came home, his father led him over to the other side of the house and pointed out a Master's Degree that hung, framed, on the wall. He said he was looking for another job; he couldn't advance any further in Pettibone, now that he was superintendent, and the duties of an administrator in a small-town high-school district bored him. And Laura had never liked living downstate; the heat and humidity affected her so much she had to lie in her bedroom on the worst of the summer days with the shades drawn and the air conditioner going, in order to breathe. She missed the department stores of

Chicago, the restaurants there, her beauty parlor, the theater, the museums, the municipal pace, the nightlife, and her friends. She and Martin were sometimes reduced to going to drive-in movies, where there were always a few of his students who honked and waved at them and gave the O.K. sign. Laura became so despondent the doctors believed she was beginning her change of life, and then the tumor was discovered and her breast excised.

Martin was offered a job in Eglington, a medium-sized town in northern Illinois, near the Wisconsin border, in an area of hills and unclouded lakes, only fifty miles from Chicago; he'd work as a guidance counselor, the kind of job he'd always wanted, where he'd be involved in one-to-one relationships with a large number of students, and might have a hand in helping them decide their future lives. He found a house on a double lot landscaped with evergreens, elms and oaks, and a weeping willow fifty feet tall. It was a one-story ranch-style house, nearly as wide as it was long, with stout walls of poured concrete, rambling and big, pink, really two houses in one; it had been a neighborhood clinic and had a full basement where the doctor and his family had lived, while the upstairs, which had since been remodeled, had held the emergency, X-ray, and examining rooms. The living room itself, formerly the waiting room, was over thirty-five feet long, and had a fireplace in it. The house was large enough to accommodate all the children, both Laura's and his, if all of them wanted to gather at one time.

It was decided. They sold the house in Pettibone and moved into the new one, and Martin later said to Jerome, "You know, I just learned that Laura never liked that place of ours. It wasn't her house and she never felt comfortable in it, and to tell you the truth, *I* was glad to get out. There were too many ghosts in the walls."

Before the school year officially began, Laura became ill and had to undergo another painful series of radiation treatments, and once done with them couldn't stand the smell of cigarette smoke, and then the smell of coffee. She seemed otherwise recovered, however, and when Charles and Katherine visited at Christmas, the first Katherine met Laura, she looked healthier than Charles had seen her, and was in high spirits the whole time; teasing Martin until he blushed, cajoled him into serving and having some Christmas cheer, persuaded Katherine to go bowling with her, although Katherine disliked, to say the least, the sport (but won); and when she wasn't busy in the kitchen, was at her typewriter, typing reports for Martin. She'd made all her Christmas gifts by hand that year, and gave Katherine and Charles a knitted afghan.

At the beginning of the next summer she became ill again and was sent to Madison and went through another series of radiation treatments and received, in addition, injections of a new drug being tested experimentally in the treatment of cancer. The injections left her so ill they had to be discontinued. Sometime later, in New York, Charles woke to the phone at four in the morning, got out of bed groaning about Katherine's drunken, déclassé father, and discovered Jerome on the line; he said that Laura had just undergone another operation. "When Dad told me about it, I got in touch with the specialist who's been working with her, and made sure it was the kind of operation I thought it was. I don't want to sound like the Grim Reaper, but from what little I know about medicine, I think it's safe to say that this operation is usually only done as a last resort, to try and prolong the patient's life a bit more."

"How long?"

"A few months."

"Does Dad realize this?"

"I told him."

"What did he say?"

"He seemed to know as much. He asked me to call you."

*

Charles opened his eyes. The ceiling was the wrong color, the walls too far away, and the bed more giving than it should be. He'd been to the Gypsy Tea Kettle on Forty-second Street a few days ago, and the black-haired, handsome woman had sat across from him and flipped over a card, and said, "Oh. A dark woman will be troubling you soon. You know her. She's troubled you before. It has to do with distance, traveling maybe, and there might be death involved," and Charles had immediately assumed that the fortuneteller was referring to his mother.

Why do I always think of *me,* he thought, and lifted up on an elbow and looked out the window. It was late September. The foliage of an oak outside shuddered gold-crimson, and the white bench beneath the oak, where he'd once seen Laura sit and read, and the stone birdbath beside the bench, were littered with fallen leaves. The grass of the lawn was bright green. Two postcards of pastoral scenes were inserted in the sash of the window before him, and on the walls were a bronze crucifix, two portraits of children Laura had drawn, and a reproduction of Dali's "St. John of the Cross." Laura was dead. This was her bedroom.

He turned to Katherine. She lay on her left side, her shoulders bare, her curly hair streaming over her pillow and the bedclothes; the curve of her cheek and her straight forehead, the scattering of faint freckles over her shoulder blades, a pale vein beside her spine that made her seem more vulnerable than she was, her breath indenting a bulge in the sheet. No, he couldn't touch her now. An oblong of reflected sunlight, rippling like water from the agitated leaves outdoors, strummed on the ceiling above him; the cortege, the casket resting over the grave, the handshakes, the veiled faces and tears, and then the smell of his father's cigar as they rode back in the rented limousine, Laura laid to rest in a Chicago cemetery, in a family plot next to her first husband, the funeral banquet over, and now this: "What did you think of it?"

"What?" Charles asked.

"The funeral."

Charles glanced at his father, surprised at the question, and wondered for the third or fourth time in the past couple of days, Who is this man? He sat back in a corner of the limousine, looking out the window, his cigar ash only inches from the glass, a black hat pushed back beyond his broad forehead, exposing a wide irregular widow's peak and coils of gray in his hair. "What do you mean?" Charles asked.

"How did you think it was handled?"

There were two limousines for Laura's immediate family, besides the hearse burdened with her and her flowers, a police escort that led the cortege from Eglington to the cemetery in Chicago, over a hundred people who sat down to a three-course meal in a suburban restaurant afterward, where Charles met Laura's relatives from Chicago, Minneapolis–St. Paul, and the West Coast, plus an airlines pilot with a cabin in the Canadian north, who said to Charles, "I see we're friends," Laura's mother, as youthful and handsome as Laura, but with silver hair, was, in spite of her wordly mien, the trial-crossed mother of a dead oldest child. Many of Charles's relatives from Pettibone and Forest Creek were there and seemed surprised to see him, and did his father now want his opinion, or the opinion of somebody from a city in the East? Wouldn't the chauffeur, who was also the head of the funeral home, overhear?

"I thought it went fine," he said.

"The church service, too?"

It was in a big brick church in Eglington, Charles's first encounter with the new Mass, where the priest stood behind the altar, facing the congregation, and spoke English instead of the familiar Latin; no silver-sounding altar bells sanctifying the air at the consecration; none of the pomp and circumstance and costuming that in the past had seemed arbirtary, and sometimes out of line. The plainsong of the Requiem, sung by a children's choir, was effective no matter the language it was sung in. "I thought it went well, yes."

"I didn't like the eulogy," his father said, and glanced at him. The priest had had a look that could be called illuminated or cruel, and spoke in a dry and detached way of Laura and her faith, of her suffering and serenity even to the end; and all the while he went on, a black speck, a fly, kept circling and hovering near his head and he kept slapping at it, always missing, and Charles remembered a poem about a fly being present and buzzing when somebody died.

"Did you see the way that fly kept pestering him?" his father said. "I think Laura would have liked that. She couldn't stand that priest."

"Oh, really?"

"She hated the guy's guts. Ach! I wondered if he felt the same way, possibly, and it showed. Ptou!" He fumbled with and spat at a brown bit of cigar leaf on his lower lip. "Oh," he cried then. "Oh, how my bad knee hurts and aches on me when I'm in a car like this and can't drive!"

Who was this? When Charles got into Eglington, by

commuter from Chicago, and found that his father was at the funeral home, he went directly there from the house and his father met him at the door and backed him into the foyer, shaking his hand so hard it hurt, and said, "Goodness, I'm so glad you could come. I wasn't sure you'd make it."

"Well, of course," Charles said, seeing the gleam and ingenuousness of his eyes, and wanted to say there was no question about his being here when Laura had died.,

"And you brought Katherine! How good of you!" His father took her up in a big hug, and Charles was sure that it was the first time he'd done this; and then later, as they stepped into the viewing room, Katherine whispered, "Oh, how beautiful she is!" and his father nodded in agreement, and then a tear tipped and slid down over the fatty circle beneath one eye. Charles couldn't have considered the possibility of beauty in such a setting, given his nature, his silence and solemnity in the presence of death, and would never have imagined his father agreeing with such a statement, and yet Katherine was right; Laura's face was a manifestation of peace, serene and composed, her skin so translucent it was as if life had left her flesh with her visible accord.

Charles went to Ginny, who was in a chair at the front of the room, near the casket, her head bowed, and touched her shoulder and said, "Do you feel bad?" And was startled at his words. And then today, at the cemetery, he'd gone up to one of his step-brothers, who was standing beside a large gravestone off from the family group, as if to hide himself, and started to say, since his mother had died, "I'm sorry, I believe I know how you feel," but no sounds came from his mouth. He tried again; his voice wouldn't work, his professional instrument gone, as if divisive parts of him were impaneled against its autonomy. The step-brother put a hand on *his* shoulder and said, "I understand. It's hard to know what to say at times like this."

Charles didn't want to sleep in this bedroom, which hadn't been used during the weeks Laura was in the hospital, but felt occupied, and was cold, colder than any other part of the house, unnaturally cold, he thought, but his father said, "Oh, no, no! No, you have the room. I've been sleeping down in the basement for—I've been

sleeping down there since the beginning of summer. You've
got Katherine with you. *You* have it." And looked so plead-
ing and constrained Charles couldn't refuse.

He heard a noise from the kitchen now and got out of
bed, naked, and on a vanity next to him, on a tray whose
bottom was a mirror that doubled each object and made it
seem suspended in space, were bottles of perfume, a compact, lipstick, a comb, cologne and body lotion, a snapshot
of Susan; next to the tray, a hinged frame with pictures
of Ginny at two ages, a statuette of a Balinese dancer,
red, a hand mirror; a book, *Ship of Fools,* with a marker
in it, a turquoise kerchief of linen-looking cloth, a piece
of brown wrapping paper, a radio, a stack of library books
with clear plastic covers. A three-tiered bookshelf beside
the bed lined with recent books.

On a desk across the room, on a green blotter, were
orders for magazine subscriptions, food coupons, Laura's
reading glasses in a turquoise case embroidered with floral
work, a box of caramels, clippings of recipes, bottles of
pills and capsules, pencils and ballpoints, Get Well cards,
stationery, a box of comical cocktail napkins, a catalogue
for religious articles, and, now that the room had been
invaded, Katherine's barrette. A blue night light, a flat
glowing disc, clung to a receptacle on the wall above the
desk. The objects gathered around to give the days color
and variety and reason and shape were unanimous reminders of her mortality now, but the network of nuances
linking them, the personal hand that had arranged them,
was still intact, and rendered them an eloquence he tried
to comprehend.

"Oh," Katherine said from behind in her low-throated,
morning voice. "You're already up. You're up before me.
Does this feel like home to you?"

*

In a new jacket and shirt, he went down the carpeted hall
from the bedroom out to the kitchen, and at the sound of
his feet on tile Marie turned from the sink, her eyes
dimmed with some inner perplexity. "Good morning," she
said, and studied his face as if to fathom his waking mood.
"Did you sleep well?"

"Is Dad up?"

"He hasn't slept for a week. I've been trying not to make noise. Have I much?"

"Hardly at all."

"There's coffee if you want."

"Please. Yes."

She poured him a cup and he sat at the table, facing her and a large window above the sink, and as she put the coffeepot back and started putting away dishes, passing in and out of sunlight, her shoulder-length hair changed from black to reddish-black to black again, and she moved from task to task in a way that reminded him of his mother or his grandmother on a sunlit day such as this. He couldn't remember which of the two, his past was so dense with them. Marie was less self-effacing than before, but was still dedicated to their father with an unwavering awe that had begun in childhood, and was going to stay home from college for a semester, perhaps a year, in order to help him adjust to living alone. Susan and Tim and Jerome had gone back to their jobs, and he and Katherine had reservations to fly out of O'Hare in the early evening.

There were footsteps on the basement stairs, and Marie looked toward the hall door, looked at Charles, and then turned back to the sink, as if to forestall this; their father came into the room, his face haggard, dark pouches of fatigue beneath his eyes, and sat at the end of the table. Charles said good morning and his father nodded at him and looked away. Marie brought over a cup of coffee, and said, "How are you feeling?"

"Better. I slept."

He sipped at the coffee while his left hand, resting on the table close to Charles, remained clenched in such a tight fist it seemed he was about to swing; as soon as he relaxed it, his hand trembled where it lay. "What bothers me most now is Ginny," he said. "I'd always expected she'd live here. I woke up thinking of her."

Ginny had decided to live with her older brother, Don, who was thirty, married and childless, and owned the house in Chicago where their mother once lived; her younger brother had just returned from the Air Force. Charles had met the step-brothers only twice, but when he saw them at the funeral home with Ginny, when all of them went up to the casket for the last time, he could tell from the way they moved with harmony in a group of three, stepped and touched and held and moved around one another, that they were brothers and sister so close they should remain together in a family as long as they could.

His father said, "I suppose some provisions should have been made for her earlier, but Laura and I never talked about that. Maybe this is what Laura wanted. But Ginny lost her father when she was practically a baby, and she needs an older man."

"Doesn't she want to live with Don?"

"Oh, she wants both, I guess, and is torn. She and I got close this year. She came and asked what I thought she should do, because Don and his wife were begging her to come with them, so I said, 'Do whatever you feel is best.' Maybe I shouldn't have. She's so impressionable."

"This way, she can decide for herself what she wants."

"Yes. I told her no matter what happened, no matter how long from now it might be, this house was always open to her."

"I'm sure that's the kind of support she needs."

"I guess. I also suggested she might want to live with her grandmother—Laura's mother—in Chicago."

"Wherever she decides, then, you'll know that's where she wants to be."

"That's what's most important, I guess."

"I'm sure she'll want to visit a lot."

"Oh, I *know* she'll want to visit! That's not the point. The point is— Well, it's selfish of me, I know, but I want her here with me all the time."

"Good morning!"

Katherine stood in the doorway in a flowered skirt and billowy-sleeved Cossack blouse of white silk that revealed her torso and brassiere, her hair falling from her tipped head over her shoulders as if for some vast mirror she arranged herself in, her carriage jaunty, her body fashioned from hard knocks into this present graceful one, her face and eyes aglow with such an earthly grace of good morning that Marie and Martin both had to smile at her.

*

In front of Charles was a list that began "meat loaf and brownies—Mr. Butson, Penny Link—ham." He was at the kitchen table, using the telephone book and one of his father's old Christmas-card lists to look up addresses, and Marie was across from him, writing out cards of gratitude; Katherine was putting together a lunch from the food that had been brought to the house—the dishes marked with white tape to identify their owners—and Martin was pacing from room to room with a restlessness that upset Charles and augured worse to come, he feared. His father would come to the door and say to Marie, "You did remember the Novotnys?"

"Yes."

"They let us borrow their car."

"I know," she said. "I drove it home."

"Oh, of course." And then a few minutes later he'd say, "You said you got the Novotnys, didn't you?"

Besides the list in front of Charles, there were three other pages of names, some of them, from Pettibone and North Dakota, familiar to him (for these he used the Christmas-card list), but the majority from Eglington, and Charles wondered how his father and Laura had come to know so many people in a year's time; he and Katherine had lived in Manhattan for nearly three years and Charles didn't have more than a half-dozen acquaintances, none of whom he'd expect at his funeral. In what ways had his brothers and sisters branched out into their particular worlds over the years they'd been apart?

On the morning of the funeral, all of them had gathered again at this table (for the first time in how long?) to have breakfast together, or at least coffee, in the case of those going to communion, since liquids were permissable now in the newer, lax rulings of the Church; grace was said, and Charles, who hadn't believed in much of the Church since he left for college, but usually went to Mass when he came home, to please his father, fell into the sign of the cross and the saying of the grace as if he'd been doing it every day, but he noticed that Jerome, across from him, sat with his clasped hands on the tabletop and stared around at them as if observing a pagan rite. What was on his mind then? His eyes were so considering and serene, and for some reason reminded Charles of their mother, and of a recent dream he'd had of her, the first he could remember in almost twenty years, since the one of blue china ("Amazing," his analyst said, when he heard this); she appeared with tatters of a sheet or grave cerements clinging to her, her hair in a dark tangle, a brown scarf about her mottled head, and stepped into this kitchen where they sat, in a smiling and mischievous mood, and kissed Martin and made him blush because he had another wife, and then disappeared.

Charles's father came into the kitchen again, and said to him, "Have I ever shown you around town?"

"No, we were just here that first Christmas, and then a few hours last summer when—"

"Oh, of course," his father said, and left the room.

Charles and Katherine had stopped on their way farther west on a vacation, and Charles's father had looked preoccupied and besieged and said that Laura was resting in her bedroom; the three of them were talking at one end of the long living room when Laura appeared at the other, in a housecoat and slippers, looking pale and diminished, at the borderline of an irreversible decision about to be made. She and Charles started toward one another and then both hesitated at the same time, as if to say, I'm afraid of it, too, meaning death, and then Charles went to her and took her in his arms.

Martin came into the kitchen again with his hands in his pockets, jingling change, and said, "Have you seen my garden at Mrs. Clinton's?"

"No," Charles said, "I—"

"We'll have to go there, too, sometime. You'd like to meet her. She knows Orson Welles from way back when he was a boy and went to a boarding school here in town. It's since been closed down, but she has some wonderful stories about his early years."

"He went to school here?"

"This is no small place."

Could it be a school such as the school in *Citizen Kane?* Welles was one of Charles's heroes, as his father knew, not only because of his mastery as an actor and director, but because of his voice, the envy of anybody who had to use his voice as a professional.

"We could go see her any time," his father said, and left the room. Marie looked up and she and Charles exchanged a searching, brother-to-sister look, and then Marie's eyes shrank and took on a darker shade, and she shook her head and turned back to whatever she was writing. Charles saw that Katherine, at the sink, was studying them; she knew about their childhood. He began paging through the directory and his father came through the hall door. "Chuck."

"Yes."

"Come here."

Charles followed him down to the basement, into the small, central, windowless room he used as an office, across the hall from a bathroom with a shower built of glass blocks; here were the bookshelves that once sat in the upstairs room of the old Halvorson house, with dark-colored novels, their dust jackets removed, arranged behind the glass panels in neat rows. A five-foot-high filing cabinet of oak stood beside the desk; a walk-in closet was lined with shelves that held condensed and book-club editions of books, and his father's collection of *Reader's Digests* dating back to 1931. His father opened a drawer in the desk, took out a metal box, set it on top of the desk, and opened it; inside were stacks of ten- and twenty-dollar bills bound with crisscrossed rubber bands of different colors.

"I've been doing handyman work and odd jobs around town, and I've kept all the money I've made from them in here, in cash, and it's a good thing I did. I offered it to Laura and she said, 'No, no, Martin, that's yours.' Our bank accounts were in both our names, of course, so they've been frozen and will stay that way awhile, because of the legal tie-ups. If I hadn't had this put away, I would have had to borrow to get through this time. I might have had to borrow from you." He gave Charles a direct look. "Could I have?"

"Of course."

His father took something from the bottom of the box and put it in Charles's hands: paper, with faint lines over it, as though somebody had attempted a drawing, a few half-formed letters, and some words and phrases Charles couldn't make out. Then he realized he could read:

yes, better
is it on?
nose—sometimes an itch
now my face
ice

He looked up and found his father staring beyond him. "Laura wrote it in her last hours, in the hospital when—" He threw up his hands. "She couldn't really talk, it was so hard for her to breathe, and she wrote down what she wanted. I'd like you to have it."

"What?"

"I want you to have it."

"But I—" Again his voice wouldn't work.

"Yes. I'm giving all the drawings she did in her last year, those drawings of hers of children, to Ginny and her boys. I want you to have this."

"But." Now Charles could make out, all around the edges of the paper, "t.y.,ty.,ty.," and realized it was an abbreviation for thank you, and saw Laura as if shown her feminine center and source of strength.

"She died a beautiful death. There was no pain at the end and never any struggle. Her breathing just got slower and slower and then all at once stopped, and she closed her eyes. That was her death. I was with her." He walked out of the room.

Charles sat at the desk and stared at the scrap of paper, trying to find further meaning or more of Laura in it, but nothing else would appear. He closed the box and set it aside, next to the shell of the painted turtle his father had filled with cement and used as a paperweight. The desk was of oak and had sat under the stairway to the second story of the Halvorson place, and it was at this desk that his father graded papers or worked on his life-insurance files; the large roll-top desk in his office upstairs was reserved for work on his book. Charles had last heard him mention the book two years ago; they were talking on the phone, long distance, when Charles said that he'd started seeing an analyst, because there were some portions of his past that seemed impossible for him to cope with alone (neglecting to reveal that when he read even a newspaper, every word in his periphery with "ide" or "ui" in it, jolted him with the possibility of suicide), and his father said, "Oh, I know what you mean about the past. I've been trying to work on my book again and I get all my notes and letters and materials up and out and organize them, and then get out my paper and sharpen my pencils and sit down at the desk, all ready to write, and then everything that's happened simply over-

whelms me. I can't write a word. So much has gone over
the bridge since then, there's no language that can hold it,
at least not for me."

And now there was more.

Charles went upstairs and put the piece of paper in his
portfolio on the bedroom chair, took some stationery out,
and went back to the basement and sat at the desk.
"Dear Bill," he wrote. Bill was his agent in New York, a
retreating, paternal man in his fifties, originally from
Minnesota, one of the few people Charles liked to drink
with, because Bill could handle his liquor even less well
than Charles, who was tipsy after two drinks, and when
Bill became drunk he wasn't mean or aggressive, as some
drunks are, but lyrical about the north country that he
and Charles both loved. Since they'd met—and their
meetings were never wholly on a business basis—they'd
been promising one another to go on a fishing trip to the
Boundary Waters, Quetico–Superior canoe area of upper
Minnesota and lower Ontario, near Rainy Lake.

Dear Bill,

*I know I said I'd be back in two days, but my
father has been acting so unlike himself that I'm afraid
for him, and feel I have to stay on longer, at least a
week, perhaps two. I realize you have some work
lined up, but I don't think any of it is really that
pressing. All I can think of is Taft-Reardon. I have
to do those two 10-sec radio spots, to go with that
60-sec TV blurb-up I did for them last winter. The
10-sec things don't have to be synced, so I could just
as well do them here. I know what the Taft-R——
booth and equipment are like, and know I can make
as high a quality tape on my own recorder, which I
have here. But don't tell them that. Just say I have
my own recording facilities, won't be in the city for
two weeks, and if it's all right with them, could I
please do the tapes here, and would they airmail me
the copy so I can at least rehearse.*

*If anything else comes through, say I won't be
available for at least two weeks.*

*I've forgotten what it's like to see so many trees in
one place at one time and they're all in color now. If
we ever make that fishing trip, we'll have to stop here*

*so you and Dad can reminisce. He'd like somebody
like you to talk to.*

*Love from Katherine and me,
Charles*

He set the letter aside. He'd always told Bill he could
do his work from anywhere in the world, and this would
be his chance to test that; New York wasn't rewarding to
him any more, and he'd ceased to need the population
and the pace of the city as goads. He hoped to collect
enough residuals this year to make the down payment on
a farm in Canada, or Maine, or upstate New York, or
even Wisconsin or Minnesota, closer to home, where his
heart made a more regular noise. He could see a big,
white, many-porched farmhouse, with a gambrel roof,
perhaps, plus plenty of dormers, and a ways from the
house, in a broken-down horse barn, he'd build an inner
shell that would leave the barn looking as it had, but inside would install a pair of recording studios outfitted with
the best electronic equipment he could afford. There was
a certain amount of greed and pride and envy and avarice
and sloth and ambition and gluttony and other of the
basic sins in him that he'd learned by now to watch out
for; he and Katherine had been buying antiques and going
to auctions in the countryside within a few-hundred-miles
radius of New York, and their apartment was filled with
pieces of furniture he hadn't refinished yet.

It seemed that the generation selling out at auctions or
selling to dealers, those in their late sixties or so, was the
last generation to care about the continuity of possessions;
their families, their sons and daughters and grandchildren,
seemed to want to get rid of the old pieces for the money
they were worth now and get something new; have no
family hanging heavy about them. Wood and fabric and
leather and other natural materials absorbed the sorrows and joys of those who lived and moved among them
or carried or wore them. Only a finish could be sanded
away. A chair might reveal its entire history if touched
and handled and listened to with enough patience, as an
area of the earth could, or a body held against yours. And
yet possessiveness and pride, along with their counter-
balancing force, fear, were the real barriers to feeling. If
you played with too many objects and appliances, you

could come to think of the universe as a toy. In a perfect world you'd have whatever you wanted and live with it without harming others or yourself. Charles knocked on the desktop with his knuckles. The spirit wasn't any more vaporous than oak or a skein of yarn or a bowl of colored agates. Links lost within the chain.

He pushed back and turned in the chair, and sunlight, coming through the open bathroom across the hall, spread over his legs and across the forearms of his jacket. He revolved his wrist, and his wedding ring sent a shaft of gold up through his right eye. He rubbed a knot of sensation under his chin that the light aroused. He missed his mother more than he'd ever be able to tell Katherine. Unless, to Katherine, the missing in him somehow so obviously showed, it had drawn her to him. He hoped not. He hoped they had a child soon and hoped it was a daughter. It seemed to him that a girl would be easier to love. It was a natural relationship for a man and wouldn't involve so much internal parental intervention. A boy, on the other hand, would make him feel he had to be a formed and formal entity, a father, and he didn't feel ready to be a father to any sort of son just yet. Maybe later, when they had their farm and could live the life they wanted in relative seclusion. He sighed. That might be years. He'd have to learn more and work hard in order to sustain such a place, meanwhile trusting that the right place would happen soon, and if it didn't, then maybe it wouldn't have happened for him no matter what and might not have been right for him if it had. Or for Katherine. He felt flexible enough now, at last, he was sure, to go at least halfway with her.

Still, he hoped it was a daughter. A girl wouldn't vindicate his mother's death, as he'd once thought; nothing would, in the way that his business and financial success, his period of analysis and reclaimed integration, the various stages and characters he'd passed through, his variety of experience in this multifaceted world of multiplying possibility (he was aware as he sat here of the curve of the earth and its tilt and spin), his marriage to Katherine and Katherine's radiance of character and sympathetic strength —in the way that none of this displaced her death: she was safe now, anyway, he felt, wherever she was, even as dust in the ground, and if she existed anywhere else in another state, then perhaps she looked down on him in smiling empathy. It was all he asked, and could do with less as long as Katherine was with him. Her love redoubled his and sheathed her in a luminous generosity he could only marvel at and never match. A girl might open up more of her to him, if he were able to watch a daughter of hers grow into the world and see how she made a place for herself. He hoped it was a girl and hoped she'd be saved these roller-coaster rhythms of his time and age.

He touched his ring and prayed.

He put the letter in an envelope and sealed it to take upstairs, and saw that his father had gone through his billfold; there was a pile of credit cards at the back of the desk, the combination to a safe, a key, a bank card with his and Laura's signatures on it, photos of Ginny and Susan, and of Laura with two of her sisters, some stamps glued together, and a piece of folded paper that had taken brown stains along its edges from the billfold. He unfolded the paper and saw:

A DESERTED BARN

I am a deserted barn,
                     my cattle robbed from me,
   My horses gone,
Light leaking in my sides, sun piercing my tin roof
   Where it's torn,
   I am a deserted barn.

   Dung's still in my gutter;
It shrinks each year as side planks shrink,
Letting in more of the elements,
                   and flies.

Worried by termites, dung beetles,
   Maggots and rats,
   Visited by pigeons and owls and bats and hawks,
Unable to say who or what shall enter,
                   or what shall not,
   I am a deserted barn.

I stand near Devil's Lake,
A gray shape at the edge of a recent slough;
   Starlings come to my peak,

Dirty, and perch there;
                              swallows light on bent
   Lightning rods whose blue
   Globes have gone to
A tenant's son and his .22.

   My door is torn.
It sags from rusted rails it once rolled upon,
   Waiting for a wind to lift it loose;
Then a bigger wind will take out
   My back wall.

   But winter is what I fear,
                              when swallows and hawks
Abandon me, when insects and rodents retreat,
   When starlings, like the last of bad thoughts, go off,
   And nothing is left to fill me
Except reflections—
                      reflections, at noon,
   From the cold cloak of snow and
Reflections, at night, from the reflected light of the
   moon.

                    Happy Birthday to You, Dad!
                    All My Love, Tinvalin!

Charles refolded the poem and put it back. It loosened
the roots of so many fears in him—or, Scares the shit out
of me, as he thought—that he had to leave the basement
and go upstairs. He addressed the sealed envelope and put
it with the notes of gratitude to be mailed. Katherine wasn't
in the kitchen and he couldn't see or sense her anywhere
close. She was the most difficult woman to keep track of,
or so it seemed at times, and then she'd appear as if from
the edge of dream into the center or his consciousness and
add order and dimension each moment she was there.

He sat down across from Marie, gathered up the two
lists, and opened the telephone book again.

meat loaf and brownies—Mr. Butson
Penny Link—ham
flowers—senior class
telegram—sympathy, Wm. Hollingsworth
Mr. & Mrs. Bob Novotny—pie, flowers, transportation

The list began in his father's hand—

"Pardon?" Charles said. Marie had asked him a question and was now studying him with troubled eyes.

"Remember all that stuff we used to do when we were kids?"

"What stuff?"

"Oh, you know." She wrinkled her nose.

"Sort of," he said, and it was Jerome's voice that came from his chest. The meter of Marie's speech always made him feel she was talking in a telegraphic language; their childhood sex.

"Wasn't it awful?" she said.

"Oh, I don't know. I read or heard somewhere that it happens in about sixty or seventy percent of families where the boys and girls are anywhere close in age." He'd heard this from his analyst. "I think it's something you grow out of."

"Wasn't it a sin?"

"We were just kids." Or *you* were, Marie.

"Somebody told me it was a sin once."

"Who?"

"The oldest Mitchell girl, when we were back in Hyatt that time."

"When I was in high school?"

"Yes."

"You mean, *Alix Mitchell?*" His voice went high.

"Yes."

"I used to date her!"

"I know."

"Why did you tell her anything like that? No wonder she acted the way she did! She was jealous!"

There was a murmur of laughter from Marie, and Charles remembered standing on the high curb of the curving slab of cement around the house, the slab supervised and troweled by his grandfather, while the Mitchell girl, who lived in the house now and was a year older than he was, stood below him on the ground so he could reach to kiss her lips; he didn't grow above five feet until he was sixteen, and then just six inches above; Grandpa Jones.

Mr. & Mrs. Bob Novotny—pie, flowers, transportation

The list began in his father's hand, regular and neat, and after the first five entries became so ragged it was almost unreadable, and then Marie's hand took over, and the sight of this and of the next names on the list, Phil and Lou Rynerson, shadowy figures out of the past, along with Marie's fears and the lines of Tim's poem still echoing in his mind, formed burning lines behind each eye, and then the print in the telephone book stirred and slid to one side.

Katherine came up from behind and ran a hand up his neck under his hair, and said, "Why don't we stay on a bit longer? At least a week, say. I'd love to see more of the fall here. Wouldn't you?"

*

When Charles woke the next day, close to noon, he saw out the bedroom window that his father was in the yard raking leaves. It was colder and the branches of the trees seemed more bare than the day before. After lunch, his father told him to get ready to see the town. "It's chilly," he said. "And we'll probably be outside a lot." Charles put on a jacket and went out into the long pine-paneled porch off the kitchen, to the glass of the storm door. The fifty-foot willow at the edge of the lawn was still bright green, the streamers of leaves cascading down from it swaying in the wind like a woman's hair, and beyond was a panoply of pure yellow-gold—beech and maple leaves lit by the sun, a trembling insubstantiality to each leaf. How young I feel, he thought, and rubbed an itch on his nose that seemed to originate inside the thought.

His father appeared, and they went out the door and were halfway to the car when he said, "Oh. That's right. Just a minute. I was—" He went into the house and came back with the stack of library books, four of them, from Laura's bedroom, and shifted them from hand to hand as if to give them to Charles, and finally said, "I have to return these. Laura checked them out before she left for the hospital." And then did give them to Charles.

They got into the car, his father at the wheel, and backed away from the house and coasted down the street, "That's Bob Novotny's," his father said. "He's the jeweler. This is Mrs. Gould's. Her son draws Dick Tracy, you know. He has a beautiful house in the country, just outside town. Maybe we'll drive by later. I did some repair work for his mother and then I worked on his grounds one afternoon, trying to get them in shape for the summer. He has a gardener, but it's too much for just one man to handle."

He turned and drove down a tree-lined street covered with leaves, and there was the noisy swirl and crush of them under the car. "This is Al Green's place. A nice house, don't you think? He's in the real-estate business. This is Ben Lenehan's office. He's our insurance man." They stopped at a red light suspended among half-leaved branches against the sky. "We'll drive around the square next. I think you'd like to see it."

Charles was a bit surprised that his father was being so talkative, but perhaps it was what he needed, and Charles decided to encourage it, and then forgot the decision the second it was made, he liked so much to hear his father talk; as a child and adolescent, and especially in high school, he'd been embarrassed by the way his father pronounced certain words—prairie as pray-ree, foyer as foi-yay, area as *a*-reea—but he'd learned in his work that if he could recall how his father pronounced a word, he was almost invariably right.

The square was the center of the town, a tree-shaded park with walks crossing it and a stone statue of a Union soldier, his musket at parade rest, above a fountain, plus a band pavilion set a little farther back. One-way traffic traveled over the brick-paved street past walls of four- and five-story brick buildings with long rows of arched windows with limestone sills, all of which gave the impression of being within an ordered, walled fortress that guarded its residents and outlyers well. "Most of the good shops in the area are right here around the square or just off it. It makes shopping so easy that way. There's the post office over there. This is the old Opera House where Orson Welles used to act. He did his first roles right there. He directed some of the plays he was in, too, or so Mrs. Clinton's told me." They turned off the square and went a few blocks down another street to a wood-frame house with a high foundation of fieldstone. "This is her place," he said, and shut off the car. "The Benedictine sisters live in this big warehouse-looking thing right next to her.

I put up their storm windows for them this fall. Fifty windows! Then I painted their kitchen, too." He got out and Charles opened his door and stepped onto a cushiony layer of colored leaves.

"Yes," his father said. "I should rake this soon. I do that, too. She's getting up in her seventies and is bothered by emphysema."

"How come you know so many people?"

"What?"

"How did you get to know so many people in town?"

"Oh, Laura got around a lot. She belonged to clubs and sewing and card groups, and the Church, of course. And then I did some painting and plumbing and repair work for the Links, our neighbors just across the way, and the next thing I knew, *dozens* of people wanted me to work for them. It seems there's nobody around who can do general repairs and carpenter work any more, or nobody who wants to. I had all the jobs I could handle after school and on weekends and during the summer, and I could have had twice as much. I didn't care about the money, though it's good to have now, of course; it was mostly a way of keeping myself busy when Laura got so ill. I knew her time was up. I guess I knew it for a year and I think Laura's mother did, too. There were strange unpredictable ups and downs, but after that second operation she was never herself, never, and if I wouldn't have had something to do—with my hands, I mean—I would have lost my mind entirely."

They went up the drive to the back door and his father knocked on it, waited a few minutes, then knocked again. "She's probably lying down," he said. "She needs to rest a lot. We'll try later. I want you to see the garden anyway. I haven't been over for almost two weeks, because of— It used to be a lovely garden, I understand —well, you'll see—but Mrs. Clinton's husband passed away several years ago and she wasn't able to keep up with it herself."

He stopped behind the house, on a raised, domelike grassy area with a formal rock garden around it, and put a hand on a wooden lawn chair beneath a rosebud tree. "Mrs. Clinton said her husband would sit here for whole evenings and look over the garden and smoke his pipe. This chair was in her garage, all rotted and falling apart, and I fixed it for her and painted it the color she said it used to be, this green."

The yard beyond was enclosed on three sides by a line of brush and trees, and down from the rock garden were formal beds of flowers, many of them dying on their stems now, and beyond the flower beds a kitchen garden about sixty feet long, with its rows evenly spaced and in neat lines. There were more flowers to the right of it and beside them a hand cultivator turned upside down. His father said, "When I first came here, this was so overgrown with brush and weeds you couldn't walk through it. I told Mrs. Clinton I'd clean it out for her and keep her flower beds in shape—she makes arrangements of dried flowers—if I could have half the garden. She said I could have it all. Her flowers mean that much to her. It took me a month and a half just to get down to ground I could till, and I got the garden in late. I still have to clean off the rest of the right side there. That used to be a strawberry patch."

He went down a deep-worn path into the garden. "Oh, yes, look at these weeds. I'll have to get them out now, before they take over again." He bent to a row of onions and began pulling up weeds. Charles straddled a row of carrot tops next to them, and his father said, "Why don't you just pull up those few carrots that are left? And a few of these onions, too. We'll take them home to Katherine."

Charles pulled up the carrots and knocked the moist soil off them, pulled up some onions, shaking minuscule clods from their clinging hair roots, and then snapped off a large rhubarb leaf, elephant ears as he and Jerome used to call them, and laid the vegetables over it. His father was tearing up larger weeds from the strawberry patch. Charles started weeding the edge of the garden and heard somebody calling, "Young man, yoo hoo! Oh, young ma-an!"

In the next yard, through the crosshatch of branches and limbs, he saw a nun standing beside a clothesline post, a rope in one hand. "Young ma-an, could you help me with this, please?" She did mean him. He pushed his way through the brush and went toward her with his head bowed; for ten years he hadn't been able to look a nun or a priest in the eye, feeling as he'd felt when he was a child and had sinned—that they could see into the depths of him and recognize a doomed Catholic, hamstrung by degradation and condemned to hell. Even the detached and placid nuns who sat in Grand Central with collection plates in their laps made him glance away, when their gazes met, as if to avoid the evil eye.

"This has come loose," she said, holding out the rope. "I can't reach, but I hope you can, and would you tie it back up for me, please?"

"Sure."

He reached up, strung the rope through a metal eye, and tied it tight. "That's two half-hitches," he said. "It'll hold."

"Oh, thank you, thank you so much."

She was shorter than Susan and had a hearty, big-toothed smile, and her eyes, deep brown, were fixed on him with such an unvarying look of gratitude he couldn't turn away. She was younger than he was.

"Are you Mr. Neumiller's son?"

"Yes."

"The resemblance is so striking, as I'm sure you've been told. We're praying for your mother's soul this week, and I'm going to add some prayers of my own while I hang out the clothes."

"That's very kind of you."

"I'll say a prayer for you."

"Thank you," he said, and wondered if this was what church-going people called a blessing, in or out of disguise. He went to the garden and weeded again, for an hour or so, watching his shadow grow longer in front of him, and thought of jolting down a furrow on a tractor with Lionell, and of how farming was so much a private part of the past in him, and then his father came up, and said "I guess we'd better be going now. I have other things I have to do." His face had color in it for the first time since Charles had been home, and he seemed refreshed. Charles grabbed up the leaf of vegetables and followed him to the door. He knocked again and while waiting turned to Charles with the first direct look since he'd shown him the money in the basement. "Why do you dress up so?" he asked.

Charles fingered the lapel of his jacket. "Oh, I don't know. Habit, I guess."

"You mean you have to dress up like that every day?"

"Just about."

"What for? Nobody sees you when all you do is talk into a microphone."

"The people who hire me do."

"Huh! It sounds just about as bad as teaching school!" He tried the door, again, rattling it open and shut a few times, and then shook his head. "I guess she's out at her son's. He lives a few miles toward the next town. That's too bad. I really wanted you to meet her, and her you."

"Could we stop another day?"

"How many days are you staying?"

"Oh, about a week, I suppose."

"Good, then. That's what we'll do."

At the car Charles put the vegetables on the floor in the back, and then got in and the library books slid over the seat toward him. His father put his hand on the stack of them and said, "I better do this. The library is only a couple of houses down and closes soon, I think."

The Midwestern predilection for driving a block and a half when it would be simpler and faster, not to say healthier and less expensive, to walk, which Charles was as guilty of as the next one. It was a new library, a long, low building of buff-colored brick with plate-glass windows in redwood frames across its front; one gable touched the ground. They went through the plate-glass doors into a sunny open area with metal bookshelves along the walls and a rank of metal shelves to the left. Long reading tables, set far apart and gilded by the late-afternoon sun, were like slabs of bronze to read from. His father went up to a counter and put the books down and a petite woman with silvery hair and the complexion and figure of a twenty-year-old, holding her lip-sticked mouth firm, came out of a glass-windowed office to the counter across from him. "Oh, Mr. Neumiller, it's you." She had a French accent and stared out of gray eyes with a wide-encompassing sympathy that also contained an appeal, a plea, almost.

"These are the books Laura had out."

"Oh, Mr. Neumiller, I'm so sorry about her. Please accept my deepest sympathy."

Martin nodded.

"She was the best reader in town, my most regular customer, and it brightened my day just to see her walk through the door, she was so beautiful."

He nodded, and then shook his head with such sudden fierceness tears flew all over the books and spattered the counter on either side of them. He swung away, his face a child's, and went for the door and Charles had to take several quick breaths, as though he'd accepted a blow to the stomach, before he could move; his legs were so numb he wasn't conscious of his feet striking down, and it was as if the building were traveling, at the speed it chose, backward around him. He stopped at the swishing door. His father was in the passenger seat, staring sightlessly out the side window, so Charles got in behind the wheel, as if asked, smelling an odor of disruption and fear, and was about to say he'd seen enough of the town, when his father said, "Go over to the corner here and take a left."

He drove out of town with his father directing him, past a country club and golf course with hilly greens so bright this late in the year they looked made of emerald, and seemed a timeless, unpopulated paradise in the midst of the fall world. The countryside became more rolling and deciduous, and then Charles was directed down a graveled drive bordered by an orchard, which curved around to a colonial-style house, a newly built one, with a pair of cars in the double garage and a yellow convertible at the entrance. "This is Clarence Woodruff's," his father said. "He's starting a new, sort of exclusive subdivision out here. I've worked for him in his house and on the grounds, and he mentioned a while ago that he had a little job for me to do. I'm not quite sure what yet. An hour's work, he said."

Charles followed him through the garage, where a glazed black Lincoln reflected the varied size of the two of them, and at the back door his father pressed a button that rang a pair of chimes inside, and then a tall man, with a ruddily tanned face and a white crew cut, opened the door, a mixture of perplexity and astonishment in his slaty eyes. "Martin," he said.

"I've come about that job you mentioned."

"Well, you didn't have to come so *soon*. I mean—"

"It's best if I keep busy."

"Well, sure. Whatever you say, Martin." The man began shaking his arms and legs, held at stiffened length

while he balanced on one foot, as if something unbend-
able in him had given way and his limbs were rubbery
hoses or rugs he was shaking clean. "It's not really that
much. I could've done it myself, I suppose. Come on in.
We're getting a draft or a chill tonight. We got so goddamn many gadgets to keep adjusted you'd think we lived
in the zoo. Come on. I'll show you here."

They followed him through a kitchen that looked like
the one in Pettibone after it had been remodeled, with
dark-stained cabinets of birch and a peninsular luncheon
counter, a rule of order reigning over it, and into a small
bedroom. "It's this friggity-shit old carpet," he said, and
kicked at it with his toe. "She says it's worn out, the wife,
that is, and wants to put in one of those Persian things."

"So you want it taken up?" Martin asked, and Charles
heard a new note in his voice, and saw how weary he was.

"Yes."

"We'll have to get that quarter round off first. I'll go
get some tools."

Charles and the man started maneuvering around in
the doorway to let him out. "Oh," he said. "Oh, I'm sorry.
This is my son Charles. Charles, this is—"

"Clarence Woodruff!" The man smiled and took
Charles's hand, and said, "Say, you don't happen to be the
boy of his who does that Rollie McPherson sonofagun, do
you?"

"Yes," Charles said. Rollie McPherson was a cartoon
character in a commercial for McPherson's beer; Charles
was his voice.

"Well, I'll be damned! I've told your dad he's one of
my favorite characters on TV, and I mean it, too! Could
you do me a sample of him?" He gave Charles's hand a
quick shake.

In a rumbling bass that was a cross between Charles's
conception of Falstaff and Mr. Magoo, Charles said,
" 'These *love*-el-ly tankards are loaded with thee ah lus-
cious ha-ah-*oney* of the earth!' "

"Well, I'll be go-to-hell," the man said. "It *is* you."

"Yes," Charles's father said. "It's amazing what he can
do with that voice."

My God, Charles thought, he believes in what I do.

"While I get the tools, Chuck, you could start moving
some of the furniture to one side, I guess."

"Just handle that biggest dresser like it was eggs," the man said. "It's one of the wife's heirlooms. I can't even keep my socks in it. She'd go on the warpath if it got scratched or nicked up."

Charles moved the smaller pieces, and when his father returned with the tools, they moved the big dresser together, then the bed. They pried the quarter round away from the baseboard and used screwdrivers along the edge of the carpet to pop loose the tacks, which they put into a big coppery ashtray that had been beside the bed, and then into a can, because, as Charles's father said, "I save everything like that." They loosened one half of the carpet and folded it back, then folded back the pad, exposing a hardwood floor that had the honeycombed pattern of the pad imprinted on it in accumulated grit. Martin asked for a vacuum cleaner and swept up the dirt and sand, while the man said, "It's a good thing the wife's out mayor campaigning with a floozie friend, or she'd be mortified to death. You'd think she never cleaned in here, when all she does is sweep and scrub and bitch about dirt." He asked them if they wanted a drink.

"I don't drink," Martin said. "But my son here might like something."

"No, thank you," Charles said. And then, "Oh, well, if you have a beer, a beer might be nice."

"A McPherson's?"

"Why not?"

"You can tell your bosses when you see them that I buy their beer because of you." The man winked and came back with a pewter mug. Charles took a long draught and found it was largely foam, and then was disoriented to see the room appear in a curve through the glass bottom of the mug, as if he were drinking the room up, too. He set the mug aside and as he moved around, popping up tacks, took sips from it with his eyes closed. When the carpet was completely loose, they carried it and the pad out to the garage, and Martin vacuumed the rest of the floor. They moved the furniture back, and as they were leaving, after the man had thanked Martin and reminded him to turn in his time, Martin asked whether he minded if they gathered some of his apples.

"Oh, no, no," the man said. "Heck, no. Take all you want."

"I'll take out my pay in them," Martin said.

"No, no, now you turn in your time, too, Martin, you hear?"

They put the tool chest in the trunk of the car and Charles's father took out a cardboard box he'd brought. They walked up the crest of a low hill to the orchard; the hill was steeper on the opposite side and the beige and raspberry-colored trees, heaped near its base where it fell away to a plain, were like a heavy brocade. Fallen apples lay in the grass at their feet and the fall sun, low and bronze in a lime-colored sky, was reflected on the rounded side of each one. Nature's wholeness in infinity. Charles and his father filled the box in no time flat, and the ridged pile of apples seemed to glow from the returned strength of being clustered close in numbers at their end. "Let me get another box," his father said. "I want to get some of the rest of these."

"Are you sure you want so many?"

"What do you mean?"

"Isn't this enough?"

"They're all windfall. If I didn't take them, they'd go bad and be lost. I doubt if he even has any of these picked. Land is a new business now."

They filled the second box and put both of them in the trunk, and then his father lifted his left hand and looked at the inside of his wrist, where he wore his watch, his fingers clenched into his palm, and said, "It feels like a storm to me."

They got in, with him behind the wheel, and drove off. The sun was beginning to set and the wind rose, blowing leaves from the tree-lined road against the windshield in gusts, and it became so cold Charles closed his wind-wing.

"*That* feels like winter," his father said.

With the wing closed, Charles could feel the compact quality of the car around them as it moved itself and their bodies through the tinted underworld of the changing countryside, and saw a girl on a horse come galloping toward them down in the ditch at his side of the road, laughing, laughing and lashing her black horse with a little stick she held, her hair streaming backward over her shoulders, and as they passed she smiled and cried out and waved her stick at Charles and he turned and saw a

Siamese cat with a sphinxlike face riding on the back of
the saddle behind her buttocks, active over its leather
curve, and then the cat's teeth bared in a wide-mouthed
miaow or yawn, and the entourage of them gradually grew
smaller as they galloped toward the sun.

"Is she a student of yours?" Charles asked.

"Not that I know of."

"She's certainly friendly."

"That she is, yes."

When they brought the apples into the house, Marie
said, "Oh, there are so *many,*" and Katherine said, "We'll
have to do something about them." She mentioned a fall
she'd spent on an aunt's farm farther north, and soon the
house was filled with a smell of cinnamon and sugar and
cooking apples as she and Marie prepared a large caldron
of applesauce to can. Through a picture window in the
living room, Charles could see that the length of the street
was lined with burning leaves. Legs and rakes moved in
front of and among the orange-red mounds. It was the
time of evening when everybody wants to wander in their
own thoughts for a while, one part of the world preparing
the food, the other anticipating its daily gift of kingdom
come.

His father started a fire in the fireplace and stared at it,
distant and subdued, as if the day for him were already
complete, and then ate dinner in silence, staring ahead
with the same look, his left hand lying beside his plate
in a fist again. He excused himself and went down to the
basement to bed. Marie and Katherine got the applesauce
into jars, and then Marie finished off the notes of gratitude.
Charles clicked on the television in the living room.

"Are you coming to bed?" Katherine asked.

"Soon."

He found half a bottle of cooking wine in the cupboard
and sat down in a swivel rocker in front of the television
set, taking occasional sips of the salty-tasting stuff, and
watched the usual evening fare and then a late show about
a newspaper reporter in New York; since he'd just come
from there, all of the sets seemed inconsistent and made
of cardboard, and then another movie went through his
mind like the twinning of a paradox, and it was 3 A.M.
His retinas and the back of his brain felt scorched from so
much television, which he never watched in New York,

not even to hear himself, and shouldn't have watched in total darkness, and he got into bed feeling led astray and badly abused. His head ached. He thought he heard rain falling with force in waves that seemed arranged in patterns over different areas of the flat roof.

Katherine turned and kissed his shoulder.

"Oh," he said. "I woke you up."

"Not really. I've been waiting."

"I'm sorry."

"I'm horny," she said.

"Oh."

"It's been days—*weeks*, it seems."

"I know." He put a hand over her breasts and felt her nipples already erect.

"It's running down my leg," she said, and then jounced the bed and wiggled herself until he was on top of her. She was moving with so much abandon by the time he entered, he lost a moment, and then almost himself, and then seemed to swell to twice his size. She clenched and became relaxed and erratic in a way that traveled over his length. She began again. He was striking glistening ramparts. He held back until her body softened in the familiar way, and felt his sperm had sprung from his arches and emptied his tendons all the way to the center of his crotch; his legs were numb and immobile. He rested on her breasts and then lifted up on an elbow. She was asleep.

He looked toward the window. If it was raining before, it had stopped; there was a moon. In its pale light the bench below the oak glowed as though phosphorescent, as bright as the blue disc of the night light against the wall, the round pool of luminescence like an opening onto another world. He started and grabbed at the covers. Had she knocked? He could feel somebody waiting there. He got out of bed, his pubic hair damp and matted, feeling wet to his knees, on the threshold of fever or another bout of mental illness, pulled on his underpants, and opened the door. The hall was empty. There was a light burning in the kitchen at its end. Had he left it on?

The kitchen was empty, the living room was empty, and he turned off the lights as he passed through them, came back to the bedroom, closed the door, and got into bed. He sat up.

The presence was inside the room.

Had he been thinking of his mother toward sleep? Sometimes when he thought of her or tried to reconstruct a scene from the past that contained her, he was able to sense her close. He could feel the presence across the room, in front of the window, too tall and slow-moving to be his mother; it was Laura's height, and passed in front of the window as though pacing, and he remembered sitting outside on the bench once, reading, as Laura used to, and looking up to see her staring out this window and beginning to pace the moment he saw her, as if in a cell, and then, jarred loose by the confusion in his mind, a fragment of a movie he'd seen in a Lamaze class, when Katherine was pregnant, returned, and he saw the woman on a table with a sheet covering her, her legs up, her buttocks showing and bloodied, a mucus-wrapped head emerging from her engorged and slick vagina, opened like a wide-open mouth. And then, from beyond the walls and floor of the bedroom, he heard his father cry out.

He got out of bed, off-balance, jerking up his legs as if to pull them out of entanglements he couldn't see, his calves so heavy it was as if sand were circulating inside them, put on his bathrobe, went out the door and switched on the hall light, and then, feeling harried by an outside force, turned on all the lights in the kitchen, and in the living room turned on the lamp next to the rocker and sat across from it, just to see. Footsteps were climbing the basement stairs. They padded around the kitchen and then his father appeared in the door. "Chuck," he said. "You're up."

"I couldn't sleep."

"Neither could I." His father sat in the rocker and swiveled a few times and then stopped with his profile to Charles.

"Is i— i— i— Is i— i— i—" Charles was stuttering so badly he had to cough into his hand; the back of it was covered with a slick platelike area redder than the rest of his skin, which didn't itch or cause any pain, but when he saw it in unguarded moments, as now, as a dermatologist might, it made him wonder about the complexity of his insides. "Is there any booze in this house?" he asked. "Other than that cooking wine that was in the cupboard?"

"I think Laura kept some liquor in that pantry off the kitchen."

Charles went to the pantry, which had stepped shelves that followed the stairwell to the basement below, and found a bottle of Canadian whiskey. "There's some hard stuff here," he called out, and his voice went high. "Do you want some?" In a whisper, he added, "It's a hundred proof."

"Yes. I'll take a little, I guess."

Charles filled two tumblers half full and ran some water into them. He gave a glass to his father and sat across from him and watched as he poured the whiskey down, the whole glass of it at once, as if it were milk. "Phew!" he cried. "I don't know how you can stand to drink that stuff!"

"Most people don't drink it that way. You're supposed to savor it."

"I figure the sooner I get it over with, the better. And the way it goes through me, it'd make just as much sense to pour it directly in the toilet bowl."

Charles couldn't even smile at this. "The strangest thing just happened," he said. "I don't know if I dozed off, or what, but when I woke, it felt like Laura was in the room."

His father moved his shoulders as though to make himself more comfortable and furrows of folds formed in the robe over the mound of his stomach. "Sometimes I feel she's right next to me," he said. "I've felt that with your mother, too."

He reached to the end table where the lamp stood, tipping the rocker forward, and took a half-smoked cigar from the ashtray and got it going until arches of flame stood up from it, his profile glowing with the light, and stared at the empty television set. Charles took another sip of the whiskey and felt that the cooled-down fireplace next to him, where only grainy ashes lay, was a cave leading off the house and out of this moment, a way to go.

"I was thinking of Ginny again," his father said.

"Yes, it's sad about her."

"It is."

The smoke from his motionless cigar rose in a gray line that turned silver-tinged in the light and then was gray again above.

"I suppose I should get to bed," his father said.

"Me, too."

His father laid the burning cigar down in the ashtray and stared ahead, his eyes clear and considering, as if staring the unwanted (to Charles) presence in the face, and seemed absorbed in listening; and Charles studied him and the rising smoke, like a line linking them to a simpler time, he remembered all the other nights in his life when he'd sat up with him, listening to his stories, in the other side of the house in Pettibone, in hotel and motel rooms while they were on vacation, in the little Sanderson house where he and his father lived that year they went back—

"Pardon?" Charles said. He'd dropped into half sleep and now realized his father had spoken.

"My life is like a book," Martin said. He held his hands together at the heels like an opened book. "There is one chapter, there is one story after another. When I met Laura, I told her about your mother and I said that that half of my book was already done. Some parts of it were sad, others were beautiful, I told her, but I didn't regret any of it, and I told her that, too. I spent some good years working on it, as I felt and like to think now. I told her how there might be moments when I wanted to look back at an earlier, happier time, and she understood; she felt the same way about her first husband. If there was a chapter I didn't like, then why look back on it, I thought. Why torture myself over something that's over and done with? It's a simple philosophy, but it's worked for me.

"But *now*," he said, and raised and lowered his hands as though weighing the book. "Now Laura's gone, your mother's gone, Marie will be going back to school soon, and I won't have Ginny here the way I wanted. Susan and you boys already have lives of your own. All I have to look forward to is retirement. Then I can get a few acres with a house, or a small farm maybe, maybe even in North Dakota. Then again, maybe I wouldn't like it there any more—who can say? All those empty spaces with nothing but a pair of railroad tracks stretched out as straight as a string. None of my friends where they used to live and the country itself changed so, with so many trees and new sloughs and small lakes, you'd hardly recognize the place. Water-fowl everywhere. I stopped in Mahomet a few years ago to look at my old elementary school, and the whole section of town where it used to stand was underwater.

"Not that all the changes everywhere are for the worse, of course. Your mother would be overjoyed that she could sing in the church now. How she wanted to test her voice along with the Mass! How she loved to sing! I remember how your Granddad Neumiller kept going back north every summer toward the end of his life and staying longer each time, but I don't know if he was ever really serious about wanting to live there again, in that cold storage box way at the—

"I've got my retirement to look forward to and the grandchildren you kids will have. I want to watch them grow up. That's enough. The rest of it, all that's happened in the past, all those early years up until now, all of that's done. I have no desire to look back on it again. Maybe a chapter will be added someday that will change all of this. Or maybe it's better to leave it as it stands and let it go from me, as it feels it wants to. And so," he said, and placed his open hands together flat, "I close the book."

Charles felt blankness and dislocation and saw, at the end of the upstairs hall in the Halvorson house in Hyatt, the swirls of coppery brown and rose and bronze and gold and the ordered pigeonholes on the roll-top desk, huge and immovable, imprisoned in its room, and found himself enwrapped in his father's watery-blue and wavering stare, and then his father lifted his hands to apply quotes, and said, "Tomorrow I'll probably wake and say, 'To Be Continued for Life.' The birds are already singing now. Listen to how many of them there are out there. Oh, let's both of us get back to our beds and try to sleep for a while. We all need some sleep around here. Sleep well. And thank you for being here with me. Sleep well, sleep well."